The
Blades
of War

The Eres Chronicles Book II

by MB Mooney

www.mbmooney.com

This book is dedicated to the missionaries and martyrs of the faith who have inspired me. Whether those I know personally or have read in amazing books, the world is not worthy of you.

And to the select but vocal fans of The Living Stone who continually and consistently asked me when the sequel would arrive. Here it is.

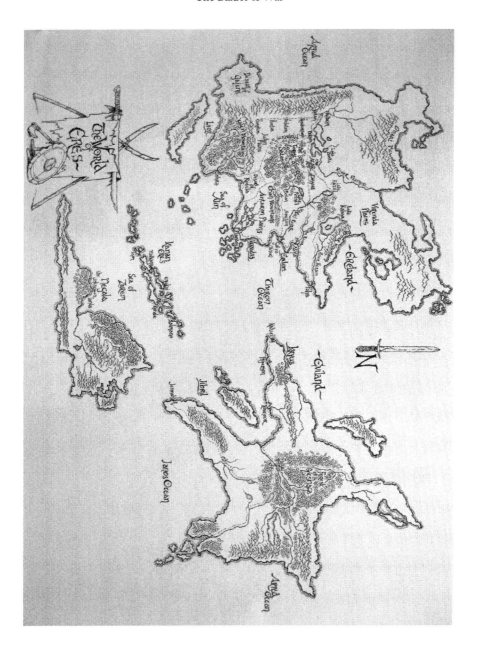

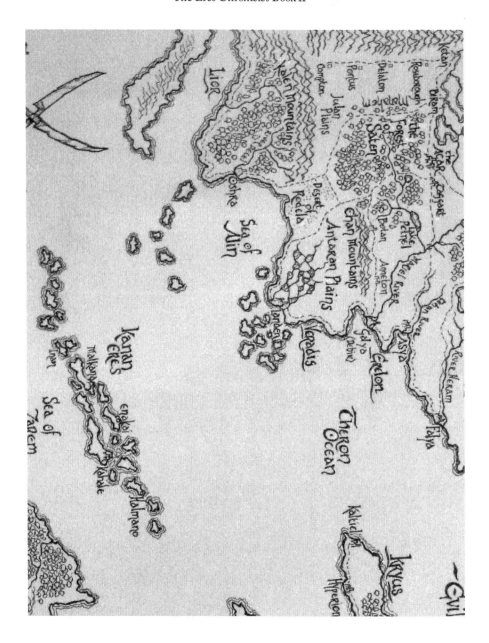

Prologue

The Burning Man

Spring brought new life to the land of men. Buds of yellow and crimson grew in the branches of the dragontrees of Asya. But Freyd Fa'Yador knew today would be a day of death.

A single man stood condemned by the Empire upon the stone platform that faced the main Square of the city of Asya. And while the norm was for the First Captain of the guard to stand before the men, women, and children of Asya and read the charges and light the kindling that would burn the criminal to death, the Steward of Asya himself stood next to the man sentenced to a horrifying death.

Nialus, the Steward of the city of Asya, faced the people of Asya with pride and satisfaction. Thin and graceful with long dark hair and bright blue eyes, he wore a long, fine, white silk robe with a red sash and belt around his waist that carried a bejeweled sword.

Arrayed across the stone platform and evenly divided on either side of the condemned man, two hundred Kryan archers stood motionless, arrows notched and held at ready as they looked over the crowd. At the base of the platform and along the whole wall before the Steward's palace was a full legion of militan, 5,000 elves with shields, spears, and gladi at their hips. Cityguard were interspersed at the main streets that led into the Square, more than a thousand of them.

The Square was full of the citizens of Asya, their attendance required to see what happened to those that were the "enemies of the Empire." In the middle of the Square, the center of the crowd, a massive golden statue stood. The image of Tanicus towered over the people, his hand outstretched to the west.

Freyd stood near the back of the crowd. He was able to contain his nervousness and anxiety, clasping his hands before him to keep them from shaking. The hood of his cloak was pulled as far down over his head as possible and still maintain sight of the man on the platform. Freyd was ready to flee at any moment.

The condemned man on the stage was his friend and the father of the girl Freyd's son had married. His name was Jyson Re'Wyl.

Next to Freyd stood Jyson's wife, Rose, also covered in a long green cloak with the hood set forward enough to hide her face and see the killing of her husband.

Freyd had tried to convince the woman to stay home, to run. He possessed connections and money enough to send her anywhere she wished. Freyd didn't know if he could protect her here in the city. They hunted her, too. She was stashed in one of his safe houses on the northwestern part of the city, near the docks, but Kryus recently shipped two extra legions into Asya to crush any thought of rebellion.

Stories and gossip, whispers of events far to the west, had found their way into Asya. Humanity had risen up and taken the city of Ketan – a city now free of elven control – after battling a horde of creatures from the Underland. Some said the demics were dead men come to life, others that they were five mitres tall with six arms. But the walls of Ketan held and the men fought like heroes of old. Freyd heard the men of Manahem fought this evil for two ninedays, almost starving to death. Still others said that it was the whole of the autumn.

The most amazing stories came of the man who led them to freedom. The *Brendel*.

Tales claimed he was not a man but a god, and that he never tired, never suffered a wound. Some claimed he singlehandedly held back the legions of evil creatures that assailed the city of Ketan with his bare hands, his fists like large hammers.

Others said he did not use his fists but had a sword. A unique sword, and it was that sword that gave him power.

The stories of revolution in Ketan motivated the Kryan Empire to root out any who believed that men should be free, any who possessed faith in El. In Asya, that led Kryan agents to Jyson and Rose. The militan caught Jyson, but Rose escaped due to her husband's sacrifice. She had come to Freyd for help, but despite Freyd's pleas for her to leave the city, Rose insisted on coming to the Square to see her husband burned at the stake.

Glancing up at the bright sun and the clear azure sky, Freyd thought, *it is quite a beautiful day.*

Two elves of the Cityguard flanked Jyson. He stood tall, but looked like crit. A long gray canvas shirt was his only clothing, tied at the waist with a tattered rope, it hung to his knees but was stained with blood and the gods only knew what else. His hair had been shaved down and the white beard ripped from his face, existing now only in patches. Bruises and lacerations covered his malformed face, the right eye swollen shut and lips cracked, dry and bleeding. Several teeth were missing. His hands were bound before him.

Behind Jyson was a tall, blackened pole of treated wood. At the bottom of the stake, the elves piled kindling and surrounded the wood with gray brick.

Through what few channels remained to Freyd, he had heard that they tortured Jyson for days, a ninedays or more, to get him to give up other rebels, other believers in El, namely his wife. He refused to speak at all, so they decided to make a more public example of him.

Now Steward Nialus stepped forward. Every movement announced his authority. Freyd wondered if they trained such elves to appear that way. The crowd fell silent. "This man, Jyson Re'Wyl, is an enemy of the Empire," Nialus announced.

The Steward's voice carried through the Square, bouncing off of the white stone around him. Murmurs of anger invaded upon the silence.

Nialus continued. "His Emperor, the great High Evilord Tanicus the Compassionate, the Righteous and Powerful, has done nothing but provide for the men and women of Ereland, given you his protection and his provision." Nialus glanced at Jyson with a look of disgust. Jyson continued to gaze out over the crowd. "In return for that protection and provision, this man has spread deception about our great and mighty Emperor and the Kryan Empire, all in the name of his rebellious faith in an imaginary god."

The Steward raised a parchment before him and began to read. "Jyson Re'Wyl is found guilty of the following charges by the only recognized authority in this land, the Emperor Tanicus and the Kryan Empire: insurrection, rebellion, and propagation of myths." Nialus lowered the paper and wheeled on Jyson. "Jyson Re'Wyl, you have been found an enemy of the Empire. The punishment for this is death by burning at the stake." The Steward lowered the parchment. "Let justice be done." The Steward nodded to the Cityguard next to the man.

They didn't need any further instruction. One guard cut Jyson's bonds while the other drug him back to the stake. His only clothing was ripped from his body. Jyson did not resist. He stepped backwards onto the kindling and held his head high as his hands were wrapped around the stake behind him and gathered on the other side. A guard pulled out a long metal spike and a hammer. He gathered Jyson's hands and used the hammer to put the spike through both hands and into the wood.

Jyson writhed and cried out.

Next to Freyd, Rose groaned and bent at the waist. "Jyson," she whispered like a prayer.

Freyd almost panicked, but didn't, putting his left arm around her, pulling her close, shushing her, scanning to see if anyone heard her. No one seemed to notice. The man on the platform transfixed them.

"We can leave," he muttered. "Let's go. You don't have to watch this."

The woman set her jaw, raised her eyes, and shook her head. *Shog me a goat*, Freyd thought.

The Steward produced a torch and one of the guard lit it with a flint, and Nialus lifted the torch high for all to see.

"This is what happens when you rebel against your Emperor, the Great Liberator!" the Steward cried and leaned down to light the kindling.

"Great and mighty El," Rose breathed. "Help him."

The kindling caught fire and spread. Jyson didn't look down at the flames that gathered at his bare feet. The flames began to reach his skin. He gritted his teeth and looked over the swarm of humanity. Standing as tall as he was able, which pulled against the spike in his hands, he lifted his face to the sky, and he cried out.

"Yosu!"

With all the countless executions he had witnessed, this had never happened. Other condemned men and women screamed, begged for their life, cursed the gods. But Freyd watched his friend, Jyson, stand against the pain, against the injustice, and cry out Yosu's name.

Freyd watched as the crowd became anxious, nervous. People regarded each other, some with faces of anger and others with terror. Men and women began to mutter to each other, phrases and tones of temper.

Jyson took a deep breath and cried out the name again as fire engulfed his legs to the knees. "Yosu!"

Freyd glanced from the crowd to the Steward, who became enraged and spoke to the Cityguard, giving some instruction Freyd could not hear over the growing noise of the crowd. One guard stepped closer to Jyson, and as the flames were up to his waist, the guard reached out and struck him across the cheek with the butt of his spear. Freyd heard the guard say, "Shut up!"

Jyson collapsed and his head whipped to the side, dazed by the blow. The guard stepped back, but within a moment, after Jyson collected himself, he stood to his full height again.

Taking in the people of Asya, Jyson sneered, but it was almost a smile. He straightened, and he opened his mouth to speak.

As if on cue, the crowd fell silent.

"The *Brendel* is coming," he said, and then he repeated it louder. "The *Brendel* is coming!"

The crowd reacted. For some, hands and voices were raised in fury against the elves of Kryus. Others screamed at the protestors, cursing and trying to silence them.

The Kryan archers faced the crowd and considered the Steward with nervous eyes, unsure at the chaos that began to erupt below them. The militan on the ground below the platform raised their shields and spears just a little higher.

I knew this was a mistake, Freyd thought, scanning around him for the quickest exit. *Maybe back through to the street behind or to the left.*

Rose was speaking next to him. He leaned in close. She pushed back her hood and he could see her mouth the words. Tears streamed down her cheeks.

"*Brendel*," she said. Over and over. "*Brendel*."

The chant grew in volume and intensity. *Brendel*. Over and over.

But the entire crowd did not join. Many men and women among the throng pushed and shouted curses at those that carried the chant, trying to silence them. It was soon to be a full-fledged riot. Freyd could see it evolve, and it scared the living crit out of him.

The Steward leered at the mass of people around him, the archers, then Jyson. The flames had reached Jyson's chest and his neck, blistering skin and flesh, and he shuddered with agony. But even through the pain, unimaginable to Freyd, he was mouthing the same words, as if he led those who chanted.

Brendel. Brendel. Brendel.

Drawing his sword and filled with a rage of his own, the Steward had enough. He pushed one of the guard out of the way and swung his bejeweled sword in a long arc and cut through Jyson's neck in one full swipe, blood spouting a mitre high and the man's head falling forward and rolling down through the flames and off the platform onto the militan below.

Many cheered at his death, raising fists.

Those who had chanted along with Jyson screamed in outrage, throwing things at the platform, at the Steward, yelling the word even louder.

Brendel! Brendel! Brendel!

The crowd pressed forward and against each other. The mass of humanity became a roiling storm about to break, pushing against the militan with faces of wrath and bile. And fear.

Fights broke out among the swarm of activity in the Square, and the chant for the *Brendel* faltered as men began to oppose one another, shoving, striking, choking their neighbors.

The Steward froze for a moment, his eyes bulging in horror.

Freyd held tight to Rose, and he shouted in her ear. "Let's go," he said. "Now!" She was not a frail woman, but he was not a mouse of a man; so he was able to pull her, almost pick her up and physically carry her, out of the crowd and into an alley hoping that no Cityguard saw them. With one arm Freyd gripped her shoulders, and he led her back into the alley.

Even from the alley, Freyd could see the Steward recover from his fear, his horror morph into anger, a scowl on his face as he shouted at the archers. From this distance, Freyd didn't hear what was said, but the intent was clear. The archers rotated and began to fire into the crowd. People began to fall, screaming, dying. He saw an old woman with a bloody arrow through her neck, a boy with two arrows in his chest.

Some in the crowd began to run, howling in fear. Others became more enraged and attacked the militan.

This was no Cityguard standing before them. This was a Kryan Legion, militan of the greatest army on Eres, the most feared force in the world. They knew how to react swiftly and decisively, and so they did.

Shields linked together to form a wall of protection, and spears found their way through that wall to stab and run people through. The Legion moved forward as one, trampling and killing as they advanced.

What remained of the *Brendel* chant came to an end. The Square was filled instead with one constant roar of shouting and the screams of the dying. Freyd saw a spear with a child hanging from it run another man through, their open-mouth screams indistinguishable from the deafening noise of the riot. Men, women, children, all were equal before the advancing Legion. Freyd tried to look the other way. He couldn't.

"Oh, El, no," Rose said, and thankfully did, because it roused him from his shock at the sight of death before him.

"Shog me," Freyd said, and he grabbed Rose's hand and ran.

She ran with him. Together they weaved through the alley to come upon a side street that allowed them to move west. Freyd made them pause for a moment to peek back up the street toward the Square. A few people ran through the streets, in no discernible direction. The guard and the militan were all focused on the Square, and so Freyd bolted away from the slaughter with Rose holding his hand and at his heels.

The noise died away as they made their way through the city, empty because of the assembly at the Square today, eerily quiet now. He had trouble catching his breath but he didn't stop.

Within a half hour, they made it to the safe house where Rose stayed, an apartment in a poor tenement near the warehouses and the docks.

Closing the door behind them, he turned to Rose. Her hair was a mess of blond and gray; she was flushed and heaving for breath.

"Pack," he said. "We're leaving the city. Right now while we can. You have to get out of here."

She faced him more fully. "No, Freyd, I am not leaving."

"What?" he exclaimed. "Didn't you see what just happened? This city is a breakin' war zone!"

"Which is why I will stay," she said.

He caught his breath, and blinked a few times, measuring her. She was serious.

"Crit on a frog, woman," he said. "You're shoggin' insane."

Rose walked over to the small table, the only furniture in the room besides an old black chair and a pallet on the floor. She reached into her bag and pulled out a parchment. Moving back to Freyd, she handed it to him.

He hesitated, but he took it from her. "What is this?"

"Read it," she said. "Please."

He heaved a deep sigh. *Breakin' crazy*, he thought. But he lifted the parchment to his face and began to read aloud. Due to the fact he was not a great reader and the fear coursing through him, he stuttered and stammered through the words.

"He will be born in the land of men but travel far away. His return will be a sign that man will rise and claim their freedom from the chains of others and the bondage they place upon themselves."

Freyd met Rose's stare.

"Continue," she said, calm and quiet.

"He will be the rebirth of the Sohan-el. The sword that gives him life will take his life. He will be inflicted with deep wounds, and those scars will follow him all his days. He is not a man, but a sword, and El will wield him as a sword, a blade to cut out the heart of those who enslave and oppress."

Rose spoke as if every word were one closer to sobbing. "Now do you understand?"

"Not in the shoggin' least!" he said. "What the break does this mean?"

She reached out and took the parchment from him.

"It means it is happening. After centuries of being enslaved to our own stupidity and the will of an evil tyrant, El has brought the man that will lead us to freedom. The world will burn and be reborn."

"This *Brendel* character."

"Yes."

Freyd put his hands on hips. "That man that came through a few months ago, the one that took Aden and freed the Prophet, he's the one you're talking about."

"Caleb, yes."

"But he's just a man," Freyd said. "He was impressive for a crazy person, I'll grant, but Rose …" He stepped forward, closer to her, and he took her hands, trying to reason with her. "Rose, he cannot win. In the end, he's just a man. He can't win. Not against the Empire."

"He may be only a man, but El is with him. That makes him something more, far more. And he doesn't have to win," she said. "It isn't about winning. It is bigger than that."

"I don't understand," he said.

Rose smiled at him. She reached up and stroked the side of his face. "I know. You've always been such a good friend to us, so kind." She took his hand again and gripped it. "But the time has come, and you must choose for yourself. Do you believe? Will you stand and fight? Or will you run? There is no middle ground left. You must choose."

"Choose what?" he said. "We need to go. Please, Rose. This place … men are fighting and killing each other. The Legions here will slaughter us." He exhaled, his heart heavy. "There's nothing to fight for. Nothing to save."

"There's always something to save. With El, there is always hope. Don't you see? That is why I must stay. People will need reason and truth, a way to learn how to fight for love instead of the anger and hate you saw today. I cannot leave them there."

Freyd ran a hand through his thinning hair. "Why does it have to be you?"

One of her brows rose as she regarded him. "Who else is there?"

His mouth opened, but he didn't have an answer.

"I will teach and gather and lead them to a better way than you saw today," she continued. "They will need hope more than ever. And in time, he will come."

"He? Caleb? This *Brendel*?"

"Yes. He will come," she said. Her face altered from a visage of peace and calm to a deep frown. "*And he will kill all who oppress.*"

A chill went up his spine.

"But how do you know?" he begged her. "How can you know?"

"Two reasons," she said. "First, because I hear the voice of El."

Insanity, he thought. "And the second?"

She cocked her head at him. "Because he's the *Brendel*. He is the Sword of El. That is why he was made."

The brothers Yon and Mychal were working their fields the day Yosu walked by and called them by name.

It was the heat of the day, and the brothers were very tired.

"Come with me," Yosu said.

"We have heard of you," Yon the elder said. "Your teaching, miracles, and a sword that was never forged."

"I am more than those things," Yosu said.

"Then who are you?" Mychal the younger asked.

"I send the tempest, but I am the calm. I decide justice, but I am mercy. I fight wars, but I am peace. I judge the sin, but I am the righteous."

Yon and Mychal looked at one another. "We do not understand."

Yosu beheld the sky. "Do you see the sun?"

"Yes."

"It is the sun that gives life, bears down with its heat and light. But the people of this world are lost, gazing down at their shadows. Will you help me point to the First Light that gives life?"

"But what can we do?" Mychal asked. "We are simple farmers."

"Follow me and I will make you warriors and leaders of a kingdom you cannot see with your eyes but you will feel with your heart, and teach you a freedom no one can take away."

"If we go with you, when will we return?" Yon said.

"There is no end to what I begin, and where I am going, there is no return," Yosu said.

They left with Yosu that day.

- From the Ydu, the 5th scroll, translated into common tongue by the Prophet

The Blades of War will descend upon the land, and sorrow and death. But there will be hope, a light in the darkness.

- From the Fyrwrit, 2nd Letter of Gabryel to the founders of the river-town of Asya, translated into Common Tongue by the Prophet

CHAPTER 1

TO THE HARVEST

She stood in a vast field, the golden wheat rising to her waist. The field stretched farther than she could see. It reminded her of home, of Delaton and Compton, of the plains of Manahem that seemed bigger than the sky at times.

Eshlyn smiled, extended her palms and brushed the top of the plants as she stepped forward, walking to the east. Her husband would be pleased with the crop this year, and she was proud of her work that led to such bounty. She thought of the warmth of her husband's touch and embrace, how her new baby was safe at home in the wooden crib next to the bed. Her heart was full and content.

"It is ready for harvest," a voice said.

Eshlyn peered up from the wheat to the east. She recognized the voice, but it was not the voice of her husband. A man stood far away. Holding a hand over her eyes, she squinted against the brightness of the sun high overhead. The man had long gray hair and wore a long red tunic. She could see a forest behind him.

A dark cloud appeared and covered the sun, covering the land with shadow.

Another step towards the man and she could see him better now. The man swiveled to the side as if to enter the forest. He wore a crown like a king and a belt with an empty scabbard at his side. She did not know the man, but felt as if she should.

"Yes," she said. "The field is ready for harvest."

Even at this distance, she could see the king frown.

"No, Eshlyn," he said. "Not the field."

She could see now what blocked out the sun. It was not a dark cloud but black smoke, billowing up from the forest behind the man in the crown.

"If not the field," she said. "Then what?"

Flames licked the sky now, trees like torches. The fire inched closer to the king.

"Eres," he said. "The world is ready for the harvest."

Her heart constricted in fear. The sky darkened with smoke. Ogling the flames nearing the king, she waved at him to move away from it.

He held out his hand. "Come," he beckoned her.

She swallowed. "Where?"

But she knew the answer, a deeper part of her knew but couldn't – or wouldn't – say the words.

The forest was a blaze now behind him. The king glanced at the burning trees then back at her. "To the harvest," he said.

She hesitated, stopping in mid-stride. Leave her husband? Her baby?

The king entered the burning forest.

"Come," she heard him say one more time. "Come to the harvest."

Eshlyn awoke in her bedroom in Ketan, Javyn slept next to her in a smaller trundle in the corner. She sat up, sweating, and she wiped tears from her cheek. The morning sun peeked through the canvas curtains over the window.

And glimpsing down, she was gripping Kenric's unforged sword. She rubbed the marriage bracelet on her wrist and pulled the sword to her chest. She cried for her dead husband, as she had a thousand times, but now quiet and familiar. But she wept for something different, as well, something she felt and had dreaded now for the long winter.

Everything was about to change.

———

It was two hours before dawn when Iletus was awakened by faint skittering noises in the brush fifteen mitres to the south of his camp.

The fire burned low, orange embers still warm enough to keep him comfortable, although, in the break of spring, the air on the plains of Manahem carried a slight chill. His elven eyes opened, the sky dark, but he could see well enough with the three moons in an arcing pattern to the north.

Iletus was a half-day ride from Ketan and two days out of Biram, and he had camped around dusk of the day before, not wanting to come upon that city while it was dark. There were stories about the city now controlled by men. An elf like himself might not be welcome during the day; he could be seen as a threat in the middle of the night if he came upon those gates while the moons were high in the evening sky.

He listened intently to those noises fifteen mitres away. They were not the noises of any animal he knew, as much as he was in a foreign land. And they were not human. They were something else.

Iletus rose to a crouch without a sound. Dressed only in underbreeches, he silently slid toward the wagon and patted the horse when passing. Whatever was out there was hunting. He could feel it. An elf and a horse would make a good meal. Underneath the small wagon, a hidden compartment held a sword. It came free easily, and as he pulled the blade from the sheath a ringing sound disturbed the quiet. Iletus remained crouched, facing the brush to the south. His long, straight red hair fell to the side of his face while bright green eyes scanned a copse of trees in the distance.

The sword was one of the finest in the world. He had bought it the only other time he traveled this particular road, two hundred and fifty years ago, and paid a hefty sum for it. The hilt was gilded and wrapped in crizzard leather, the best grip made. The blade was thin and had a slight curve, only one edge to it, sharp enough to castrate a gnat but strong enough to withstand any other blade. The sword of a Bladeguard.

There was another blade stronger, however. The unforged blade was a thing of myth and legend now, but he had encountered one long ago. Perhaps he would see one again, soon.

Iletus held the sword up in front of him and skulked, in a constant low crouch, to a position between the horse and the foliage nearby.

They all attacked at once, screeching and growling, perhaps ten of them. Monsters, yes, but sad ones at that. The creatures were shorter than dwarves, and emaciated, with red skin and black eyes and teeth and horns and talons on their long arms and shorter legs. The only coordination to their attack was that it was all at once.

He leapt to meet them.

The sword caught the moonlight upon the silver blade as he sliced through two at once, cleaving them both in half. Iletus spun, his hair fanning out around him. He kicked one away with his left leg, grabbed another by the neck with his left hand as he cut down two more with the sword. Upon completing his spin, he snapped the neck of the imp in his grip and stabbed one on his left before ducking two that came at him from the other side. Pivoting again, his right leg swept around and upended three of them. Iletus jumped high over another and came down upon two more, decapitating one and slicing through the torso of another.

Three of the remaining six – he had been wrong, the count was originally twelve – ran from him and towards the horse, which began to rear up and try to pull away. Fastened to a tree, the horse panicked against it.

Iletus bounded back to the horse and slew the three of them with two quick strokes, cutting them down from behind. He swiveled on a heel to face the three that were left. The monsters came quickly and hoped to reach him in a vulnerable position. They failed.

Quiet surrounded him, as it always did after a battle. For a moment he stood, his legs spread far apart, the blade raised high. Only the sound of his own breathing whispered into the night. He had not broken a sweat.

He ripped a loincloth from one of the dead bodies and wiped the black blood off of his blade.

So, he thought. *Those are demics.*

Iletus surveyed the west, to Ketan. He was awake now. The horse was awake. He might as well continue his journey to Ketan and the revolution that waited there.

Taking a deep breath, he sheathed the sword again, placed it back in its hiding place, and got dressed. The horse was hitched to the wagon within minutes of covering the fire with dirt and gathering his things back in the jockeybox of the wagon. He put up the hood of his red silken cloak against the cool morning wind.

Dawn met him an hour and a half later, announcing itself with a bright orange horizon behind. After another three hours of travel, he perceived the imposing spectacle of the city of Ketan and the mountains of Gatehm beyond.

Iletus remembered it from more than two centuries before, but the city appeared different to him now -- not different due to a lack of memory, but due to recent events. The walls of the city were massive. Behind those walls, though, men were now free. Or so they thought.

The gates were open, but ten men in breastplates stood there with spears in their hands. Iletus neared the gates, and the men came to attention. One man, with dark hair and a scar across his left arm, walked forward to meet the elf. He smiled.

Iletus pushed back the hood of his cloak.

The men lowered their spears to point at him and blocked the gate. The man in front pulled a gladus from his waist and retreated a step.

"What is your business here, elf?" the man said.

The elf bowed from the wagon. "My name is Iletus. What is your name?"

The man did not answer at first, casting a glance back at his friends before meeting the elf's gaze again. "My name is Crawn," he said. "And you haven't answered my question."

Iletus nodded. "You are correct. I have not. I gave you my name because I thought you might recognize it. I have come to see Caleb, the man you call the *Brendel*."

Crawn scoffed. "You breakin' maddy, eh? You think we're just gonna let an elf go see the *Brendel*?"

"Probably not. But, if I may suggest, you could tell him that I am here. I am sure he would appreciate your diligence in this matter."

"How do you know?" Crawn asked.

"Because I helped train him."

—•—

Step. Thrust. Block. Stab. Turn. Step. Strike. Parry.

Aden repeated the forms as Caleb called them out to the group of men and women gathered in the old ballroom in the palace of Ketan, a large room emptied of all but weapons and other warrior paraphernalia so that Caleb could train the rebirth of the *Sohan-el*.

Twenty-one men and women stood in a disciplined line, also obeying the forms as Caleb spoke them, all as one. They did this every morning after prayer and a reading from the scriptures, and had for the last four months through the winter. Some days were more strenuous than others, but they always trained.

Looking down the line, every face now belonged to people Aden considered close friends, if not family. Athelwulf, with thick black hair and dark brown skin, was to his right in the line while he towered over the shorter Aden. Just after the Battle of Ketan, Esai had gone to the Ghosts of Saten, and Athelwulf returned with Esai and little more than a thousand men and women from the forest trailing behind.

Esai was here, too, on the other side of Athelwulf, shorter with close-cropped hair, wide features, and near black skin. He had traded his signature two-sword style for the singular beautiful blade in his hand.

To Aden's left was Eshlyn, who somehow ran the whole city and took care of her son in the day that remained after training with them through lunch. She was as beautiful as ever with long dark hair and light skin, if not more so with her divided skirts and her dead husband's sword in her hand. She had proven herself strong and athletic, capable of handling the training.

Beyond Eshlyn was Xander, her brother. The whole group marveled at his growth and skill. He was quickly becoming one of the more accomplished swordsmen in the group, and all with one arm – his *left* arm, at that, losing the right one in the Battle of Ketan. The sweat was pronounced on his face, fixed in concentration.

On the other side of Esai was Carys, Caleb's sister. She still wore the leathers and green cloth of the Ghosts of Saten. Her shoulder-length blond hair was pulled back behind her and exposed her child-like features.

The other fifteen were people of the Saten chosen by Caleb and Athelwulf, people who were both talented fighters and leaders, men and women who believed in El and inspired others.

All twenty-one, twenty-two including Caleb, carried unforged swords. The *Sohan-el* were reborn.

Eshlyn carried her deceased husband's sword, passed down from the last King of Manahem, Judai. Caleb and Aden had been the first in more than three centuries to climb Mount Elarus and face the Living Stone to receive theirs. Carys, Athelwulf, and Esai had gone to the Living Stone at the beginning of autumn, as soon as Carys had healed enough from her battle wounds.

The others had gone just as the first thaw of winter came two ninedays ago. A larger group had left Ketan and made the trek, twenty-eight in total, but not everyone had endured the trip or proved brave enough to face the dark cloud that surrounded the top of Mount Elarus. Five yielded to the hardship and abandoned the climb up the side of the mountain. Six others reached the roiling and violent dark barrier and shrank back due to fear.

Aden could understand. He had been barely able to do it himself.

Seventeen of the original group had returned, found worthy by the Stone and given a sword. Each person remained quiet about what they had experienced and had learned from El. No one had to tell them to keep it to themselves; it wasn't an instruction from Caleb. Each knew deep within that what El spoke to them in the black tempest was private and for his or her soul alone. And the encounter with the Stone itself was such a mystery, it was simply something one must experience. They returned as Caleb and Aden had: sober, both at peace and disturbed in a way they would not try to explain.

But that shared experience connected these men and women deeper than friendship. Aden would say deeper than family, but he knew nothing of that to compare. Even so, Aden knew it was good and right.

A ninedays ago, Caleb found an artisan in Ketan that he felt could give a proper tattoo, and soon all of them had a tree growing out of a stone on the inside of their right forearm, the mark of a *Sohan-el* – Aden's arm was still sore.

All but Eshlyn, that is. She declined, feeling that since she hadn't made the trek to the Stone herself, she shouldn't have one, but she would take the training. Caleb respected her decision. He deferred to her often.

At times, Caleb seemed more at peace, more calm, which only added to how intimidating he was to most people. But beneath the calm, what seemed like serenity, Aden could still sense a passion deep within the man, a mixture of anger and resolve waiting to be unleashed.

Caleb's gaze moved over each person.

"The Vow," he said.

The ancient *Sohan-el* took a Vow before journeying to the Living Stone. But since most here had received their unforged sword and tattoo before being fully trained, Caleb had modified the Vow for them to say every day during their training.

Each knew it by heart.

"*Before the Light of El, the hand of Yosu, and the witness of the Living, I dedicate my soul, my heart, and my life to defend the innocent, free the oppressed, and spread light in dark places.*"

"Very good," Caleb said, and every person stood straight, their swords at their side. "But remember, those are only words, and they mean nothing unless you live them. Live them now, while we are at peace and safe, and you will live them when the time comes to fight. You have not become

Sohan-el to achieve a position or to rule it over others. You have a purpose. To serve. To give your life for the good of others. To fight so others can live. Just as Yosu taught." Caleb allowed the words to hang in the air for a moment. "Let's do some sparring before the mid-day." He paired them up, Aden with Lyam, a young man only a few years older than Aden, but taller. Lyam had been born and raised in the forest of Saten, and his smile was genuine.

Aden shook hands with Lyam, and they embraced. Then they stood two sword lengths apart, and bowed low to one another. The group had sparred with wooden swords for the first few months, but now that they all possessed unforged swords, Caleb told them it was time to train with their own weapons, as they would in a fight or a battle. It was more dangerous, but Aden and the rest of the group had learned exponentially more over the past two ninedays.

Training with the unforged sword was odd. Aden possessed limited experience with a regular gladus, the Kryan short sword, but the unforged sword was vastly different. Yes, it was a greater quality blade, longer, stronger, all those things. But it also seemed to be … *alive* was the only way Aden could describe it. It moved with Aden, sometimes against him, guiding him at times, other times resisting him depending upon the situation. He caught thoughts that were not his own. And the more he learned of forms from Caleb, the more the sword would bring to his mind, as if they were connected somehow.

They had been sparring for only a half hour or so when Tamya burst in. Everyone stopped and turned towards the door of the ballroom for two reasons. First, if there was an interruption during their training, then something serious was happening. Second, at Tamya's heel was her pet bloodwolf, Hema.

Aden remembered well when Caleb had rescued Tamya from execution in Biram those months ago. She stayed with Athelwulf and the Ghosts of Saten as Caleb and the others continued their journey to Ketan and the Living Stone.

While with Athelwulf in the Forest, she found a bloodwolf pup near death and nursed it to health. The frightening creature never left her side as she came to Ketan with Athelwulf to join the revolution.

Tamya's hate of the elves ran deep due to the deaths of her husband and child, both killed for her husband's belief in El. And even though Aden had become one of her only friends here in Ketan, Tamya always held something back, isolated herself as much as the community would allow. Her presence in Ketan was clear – she wanted to kill elves.

The bloodwolf made everyone nervous – except Caleb; nothing seemed to make Caleb nervous.

"Cal," Tamya shouted into the training room, and her voice echoed in the large space. She was one of the few that felt comfortable enough to use his nickname. Caleb didn't seem to mind. Aden guessed that fighting bloodwolves with the *Brendel* in the Saten gave her that right. Hema, the bloodwolf, sat on his haunches when she stopped. "Zalman needs you at the palace entrance. Says it's urgent."

Caleb rubbed his chin. Zalman – a large man who was now the Captain of the Guard – rarely thought anything was urgent. "I'll be right there."

Tamya sniffed and left the room, Hema at her heels.

Addressing the group, Caleb said, "Aden, Eshlyn, with me. The rest of you, continue. Ath, take over. I'll send word back if I need you."

And then he put his sword in his scabbard and began to march to the door, trusting they would follow. Aden joined the others as they sheathed their swords and fell into step behind Caleb.

Exiting the palace, Aden let the others walk ahead and fell back to keep pace with Tamya and Hema. He stole a glance at Tamya. She wore a simple green tunic and tan leather breeches with the leather moccasins, the simple clothes of the forest people. Two swords hung at her hips, made for her by Bweth the weaponsmaster. Her hair was cut short, exposing the elven ears that belied her half-elf status, but that, combined with her chocolate skin, only made her more alluring and exotic to Aden.

"What is going on?" Aden murmured.

She shrugged. "No one tell me," she said.

They strode out through the main yard and then through the tall trees rimming the field. As they continued beyond to the arch that opened through the smaller wall around the palace, Aden frowned.

Standing at the arch were ten men, all with gladi drawn, and Zalman, who towered over an elf that waited before them. The elf had long red hair, piercing green eyes and a red cloak over his shoulders. He wore a simple white tunic with black breeches and black leather boots.

Tamya drew her two swords, longer and thinner than gladi but still short swords, beautiful weapons, as were everything that Bweth made. Hema spread his forelegs, bared his teeth, and growled loudly. Aden tensed at the growl, and his hand went to his own sword.

Caleb flashed a warning at Tamya with his eyes. She knelt and put an arm around the bloodwolf and muttered calming words to him, even though her own face was a snarl.

Aden stopped beside Caleb, who faced the elf. Eshlyn stood on Caleb's other side.

Caleb and the elf stared at each other for a long moment.

"Caleb," Zalman said. "This elf say he know you."

No one moved, watching as the two of them stared at each other. Finally, Caleb said, "Well, break me," and stepped forward in a rush and embraced the elf. "Ah, my friend. It is good to see you."

The elf returned the embrace. "You have done well, I see," he muttered in Caleb's ear.

The rest of the group relaxed visibly. Except for Tamya, who sheathed her swords, but she kept a hand gripping the red fur of the wolf at her side, both of them sneering at the elf.

Caleb and the elf separated, smiling at the other.

"What are you doing here?" Caleb said, in a tone both warm and sad.

"Much has happened, boy," Iletus said, his face crestfallen. "We must talk, you and me."

"Yes, of course," Caleb said.

Iletus paused before continuing. "But first, I have something for you. A great treasure." Iletus spoke to Zalman and the other guards around him. "Bring my wagon here, please."

A man led a horse pulling a small wagon – a merchant wagon, it seemed to Aden – up to the archway. Three trunks were tucked in the back of the wagon. Iletus leapt into the wagon with a grace and ability that caused Aden's brows to rise. Caleb followed him. Iletus opened one of the trunks, and Caleb looked to Iletus and then back to the trunk with a blank face.

"Aden," Caleb said. "Come here."

Aden started at his name being called, but he ambled forward and hopped up on the wagon with them – notably not with the quickness and grace of Iletus. Staring down in the trunk, Aden said, "Well, crit on a frog."

Books. They were filled with books.

Iletus smiled at him. "Upon leaving Kaltiel and the Citadel, I stopped in Hyperion, and the library there. I … borrowed these from the underground vaults."

"They are the books of men," Caleb said, and Aden caught a hint of awe in his voice. "Histories, journals, commentaries on the Ydu and Fyrwrit, books thought lost to time."

"But they kept them?" Aden asked.

"In an Empire built on the control of knowledge," Iletus said, "the hubris of that control necessitated that they keep a copy of such things, even if they found them dangerous, and hide them."

"It has been my experience that things in secret vaults have a way of making their way out," Caleb said.

"I believe history would agree with you," Iletus said. "For good or ill."

"Aden," Caleb said, "would you see that these books get to the new library? Iletus and I must talk."

Aden studied the interior of the trunk again, filled with books. "Yeah, sure."

A treasure indeed.

———

Caleb watched his old friend step into the largest office in the nearby administration quarters, the room where Caleb now had regular meetings with the leadership of the city. Big and spacious, the room had a long wooden table in the center with comfortable chairs. Motioning to the end of the table, Caleb invited Iletus to sit.

Iletus appeared just the same, his straight red hair that hung to his waist, the long nose and bright eyes. He was one of the most dangerous people on Eres, and he had run from Kryus all the way to Ketan. Caleb dreaded hearing what news Iletus possessed. If it meant the Bladeguard's flight from the Citadel and Kryus, then it was bad indeed.

Caleb knew this day would come. After sending Macarus and the other elves away following the Battle of Ketan, he knew it was only a matter of time before Tanicus responded and Galen's part in the rebellion made known. The army now in Ketan was Caleb's preparation for it. Sooner or later, what had begun here in ketan would have to move beyond the walls of the city.

A young woman entered with a tray of dark, strong tea and thick brown bread, placed it at the end of the table and left. He sat across from Iletus at the table.

"So," Caleb said. "Tell me."

Iletus leaned back in his chair, a mug of tea in his hand. "First, I would like to hear how it is going here. I've heard rumors and read the report from that First Captain ..."

"Macarus," Caleb said.

"Yes," Iletus said. "Macarus. So I know the basics. There was a battle here with some creatures from the Underland, nasty little things."

"Demics."

Iletus sipped his tea. "I ran into a few while camping just outside of the city."

"Not a total surprise. Most drowned after we flooded the area from the dam, but the water didn't kill them all. Some are still around. We run into them from time to time, but they're not usually a problem. I take it you handled them without incident."

Iletus waved a hand in the air. "Easily. So you took over the city and after the battle, it is now completely under your control."

"Not all *my* control. We have a council of elders, some that you met today, a council of leadership, and a head elder. A woman, Eshlyn, and the former Second Assistant to the Steward, Chamren, they really run the city. We got through the winter only because of their amazing administrative gifts."

"I see you have your own army, or at least a Citywatch," Iletus said.

"After the battle, we did form a type of security force, both to keep peace here in the city and guard the wall. There hasn't been any trouble. Most who were uncomfortable with being free from elven control left and went somewhere else, most likely Biram or beyond, and mostly for more Sorcos."

Caleb leaned forward. "I've been raising an army. We have some people from the forest of Saten, trained fighters, and I've been instructing a force of volunteers in the afternoon. They are coming together."

"How many do you have?"

"Total? Six thousand."

"Against the Kryan Legions?" Iletus asked, setting his mug on the table.

"It is only a beginning." Caleb rubbed his beard. "And I've been training *Sohan-el*, real ones."

"So it is true." Iletus' eyes narrowed at Caleb. "Do you have an unforged sword?"

Caleb pulled the sword from his waist and laid the blade upon the table.

Iletus could only stare for several moments, his face catching the light from the blade.

"In a way, it is a simple sword," Iletus said. "I can … feel its power."

"It is all true," Caleb said. "The Living Stone, the unforged sword came right from the Stone and into my hands."

Iletus shook his head in awe. "And there are more of them? More besides this one?"

"I am training twenty-one *Sohan-el*, all with unforged swords and tattoos."

Iletus frowned. "I believe tradition was that a person train for years before receiving a tattoo or traveling to the Stone."

"That is true," Caleb said. "And I thought the same thing. But Aden changed my mind."

"Who?"

"You met him earlier," Caleb said. "Aden, a young man who helped me free the Prophet and joined me on my journey here."

"And what did he say that made you change your mind?"

Caleb chuckled. "It wasn't what he said, it was what he did, who he is. Going to the Stone, Aden taught me something: the Stone doesn't test skill. It tests the heart. And Aden has the heart of a *Sohan-el* if not the skill. I can teach skill. I cannot teach that heart. Aden went with me up the mountain, and the Stone gave him a sword same as me."

"Interesting," Iletus said, transfixed by the sword. "May I?" he asked.

"Of course," Caleb said, and he leaned back and away.

The elf grabbed the sword by the hilt and lifted it. He gasped. "It is so light, but it feels so strong. I can almost hear … a voice. Like a whisper when I hold it, but I can't make out the words."

"That is how it is, always. And it seems that for those who truly believe in El, they can hear the sword speak to them."

"Does it speak to you?"

"Sometimes."

"Incredible," Iletus said. His stare on the blade, he handed the sword back to Caleb, and Caleb placed it back within its sheath. "You've done well, boy. Very well. But what do you know of the rest of the world? What do you know of the other cities of men?"

"Almost nothing," Caleb admitted. "We've been here for the winter and very isolated, which has kept us relatively safe, for now, but also insulated against any news of the outside. What is happening?"

Iletus took a deep breath and exhaled through his nostrils. "The story of what transpired here has spread, boy, spread over the world. How could it not? It is quite the story. A demon horde against an ancient city, humanity able to beat them back, and then expelling the elves from Ketan. You declared yourself free, declared it to the Emperor of the most powerful Empire in the world. They speak the name of the *Brendel* in reverent tones in the back rooms of taverns but curse your name in the great elven halls of power.

"Tanicus has sent more legions into Asya, Galya, Oshra, and Landen, even little Falya is not immune. And the Bladeguard are more active than ever. Together with the militan in the cities, they are rooting out all resistance, in some cases killing indiscriminately to instill fear."

Caleb groaned.

"Tens of thousands, maybe hundreds of thousands have died. And the humans of those cities are rioting, unorganized, easily divided and beaten. They only know rumors and false tales of what has happened here, and as glorious as I believe it is, they are limited by their ignorance and fear and hate. Men are killing one another as much as trying to fight against the elves."

Caleb said, "Break me."

"You started something, boy, and like a match put to kindling covered in oil, it has burned quick and full. You began it, but you cannot contain it. The world is burning."

"El help me," Caleb whispered, like a prayer. He meant it like a prayer.

He felt Iletus' hand on his shoulder. "He has helped you. The Imperial Senate is in an uproar. With recent conflicts with Faltiel and Jibril, Kryus is spread too thin and it is costing a fortune. The Empire is being plunged further into debt to the dwarves, and there are rumblings against Tanicus at home, for the first time. Some who have been silent in their opposition to the current regime are beginning to make small movements against the Emperor. Two Senators have been murdered within the last month."

Caleb grit his teeth. The plan had been for Caleb and his Uncle Reyan to build the revolution, over time, exposing themselves and the resistance when they were ready. But El had other plans. The demic attack had forced his hand, to take control and lead humanity, and Caleb watched men rise and build something amazing in this city over the past few months. He couldn't change it now, and he wouldn't if he could. But the world was burning just the same.

"What of Galen? You haven't told me of him."

But he knew. Even before Iletus spoke, he knew. Back in Anneton, after rescuing Tamya from the Steward there, he knew his master Galen would be compromised. Now, after taking control of a city of men with the very Letter of Regency Galen got for him, the wrath of the Emperor would be fierce. Caleb wondered, *Is he dead? Did they capture him?*

Iletus hesitated before speaking. "As rumors began to be confirmed, and the reports came in, Galen told me that I must come to you and help you. He sent me away before ..."

"Before ...?"

The elf drew in a deep and heavy sigh. "They have him, my boy. Tanicus has him and knows everything."

Chapter 2

The Worldbreaker

Galen, the Blademaster of the Citadel, the Hero of the Kryan Ascendancy, the best swordmaster alive, was dragged into the High Evilord's throneroom. Exhausted and in pain, he wore tattered clothes; his long white hair was tangled and matted. Bruises and lacerations covered his body from the constant beatings over the past two days.

Two Sunguard, the Emperor's personal guard dressed in shining golden armor, each had an arm, and they pulled Galen through the open double doors, also made of gold, and over the marble floor mined from the mountains of the dwarven Kingdom of Valahal. The floor was smooth and cool against his legs. The guard lifted him and set him down ten mitres from the throne itself, empty for now.

Rising to his feet, Galen scanned the room, his wrists twisting slowly against the ropes that bound his hands behind him. Six other Sunguard stood guard in the room, each dressed in a flowing white robe and a golden breastplate. Their faces were covered by a golden helmet, except for their bright eyes. Galen noted the golden swords each Sunguard wore at their hip.

Teetering, Galen squinted as he heard movement behind the throne.

The throne itself was made of Jennahan glass with veins of gold and silver running through the back, arms and legs. The window to Galen's right let in an abundant amount of sunlight, and the throne caught and threw the light across the room, as if the throne itself were a lamp. The back of the throne reached four mitres tall in spires like the towers of a palace.

From the left of the throne, the Emperor of Kryus, Tanicus the High Evilord, appeared. He was, Galen had to admit, the most beautiful creature he had ever seen.

While average height for an elf, nothing else about him was average. His blond, silken hair was held away from his forehead with gold and silver combs. His oval face framed his full lips, large sapphire eyes, and thin nose. Every aspect of the elf's face and figure was balanced and symmetrical, as if an ancient artist from Hyperion had sculpted and modeled the Emperor.

Tanicus rounded the side of the throne. His long, white robe with billowing sleeves glistened in its finery. A crown of gold holly leaves rimmed his head. He gazed down at Galen. Then the Emperor sat upon his throne.

Galen swayed in his weakness.

"I am disappointed in you, Galen," Tanicus said in a soft voice.

"I can imagine," Galen answered.

"You came to me with this grand idea of training a human, a man, as a Bladeguard. This man would be able to infiltrate the most secret corners of resistance in Eleron. He would bring us the head of the Prophet and all who tried to spread that idiotic ideology about a single god who created our beautiful world. That's what you told me."

"Yes," Galen said.

"But you lied to me."

Galen did not answer.

"And if that wasn't enough, you put a Letter of Regency before me, telling me it was for a new Bladeguard, but it was for this man, Caleb, was it not?"

"It was for him."

"But you knew I would never have given such a Letter to any human, Bladeguard or no, did you not?"

"I suspected."

"So you deceived me then, as well, no?"

"Yes."

"The great Galen. My champion. The hero of Kryus. You, who led my Bladeguard in battle against Elowen and defeated her; you, who I trusted with my most delicate and confidential missions, who I made the Blademaster of the Citadel where the greatest warriors of my Empire are trained."

The Emperor's piercing blue eyes bore into him. Galen did not flinch.

"It is the way of betrayal, my friend. I read once that betrayals can only come from friends, those we trust. Enemies cannot betray us, can they? We expect their sword to reach for our heart. But we do not think that a friend, an ally, will place a dagger at our back."

"Do you have friends, Tanicus?"

Tanicus raised a brow at him.

"I admit that I betrayed your trust, as my conscience dictated that I must," Galen said. "But did you truly think we were friends?" Galen chuckled, mirthless. "Do you think these elves around you and under you are your friends? You rule by fear and violence and control. Do you truly believe that wins you friends?"

Tanicus grinned. "You are a swords-elf even standing there, beaten and exposed, naked and known as the traitor you are before me. You have courage."

"No. It took me decades to finally move against you. I was afraid like so many others, afraid to speak out or fight back, even after all I saw and learned as I read those ancient scriptures, but in the end, it was a boy, an angry and reckless young boy who taught me to fully confront the fear and do what is right. I was a coward for so long. But no longer."

"But why, Galen? Why have you betrayed me?"

"Why?" Galen inhaled, his heart full of grief at a being with so much power and yet no understanding. "You rule as a tyrant, spreading your power as far as you can, even to the ends of Eres. You've taken the wealth of a whole race of people, humanity, but Kryus is still deep in debt. You grow your armies while the people you are supposed to protect starve and waste away. And to think, I helped you attain that power you abuse." Galen paused. "There is a better way."

"Do you not do the same with the sword?" Tanicus said. "When you face another in battle, do you show compassion on him and allow him to be your equal? That is a sure way to lose that battle. You take every advantage you can and you crush your opponent."

"That is a way to *fight*," Galen said. "But not to rule. You act the compassionate Lord, but you use the illusion of provision to place people under your heel. And those that will not bow? You destroy them with your mighty armies and Bladeguard like me. I could no longer be a part of such evil."

Tanicus sat motionless for a moment. Then he laughed. "Evil? You think there is good and evil in the world? Then you are the one deceived. There is power and need, a great need for progress and protection from the chaos that threatens all of Eres. To define with terms like good or evil is infantile."

"There is good in this world. I've seen it. And I realized that I was part of killing the good for too long. No longer."

"Your solution, therefore, was to train a *human* and try to use him against me? He started this rebellion using my power, my name. You think this threatens me?"

"Yes. I think it terrifies you."

"Me? I am the most powerful being in the world!"

"Perhaps, but you will not live forever. You will die, and all that you built around you will crumble because you won't be at its center, manipulating and holding it together."

Galen was weak from agony. But even half dead, Galen was still dangerous. He made movements that appeared to be slight adjustments while on his knees, winces that belied his pain, but in truth, he was working against the bonds that held his wrists.

"And who will kill me?" Tanicus beamed in mocking delight. "This Caleb you sent back to his homeland? He cannot win. Soon he will be burning at the stake, you can be sure."

"If you met him for yourself, you would know you have reason for your fear. Caleb is a man like I have not seen since King Judai, and maybe even greater. A man of faith, the greatest blademaster since … well, me. He is an artist with a blade; a weapon. Those scriptures that you tried to destroy, they contain prophecies, powerful ones, and he is a man of prophecy."

The High Evilord scoffed. "Do you hear yourself, Galen? You are an educated elf. You know these things are myths and falsehoods designed to do the very things with which you accuse me, to control and oppress. Scriptures? Prophecy? Faith? These are weak things, hallucinations of those who need to believe in a phantom rather than the real, waking world."

Another twist of his arm, miniscule and hardly worth noticing. In his periphery, Galen regarded the stoic stances of the Sunguard around the room. They did not suspect a thing. Were they so prideful? Pride was the greatest weakness.

"I used to believe as you do, Tanicus. But I have a feeling you will soon see that faith and prophecy are more powerful and tangible than you can understand. You will see that faith and prophecy have power to set people free and empower the weak."

Tanicus frowned, hesitating, troubled. "I cannot believe my ears. I thought that I was dealing with some conspiracy, that at the root of your betrayal, I would find someone else vying for power, perhaps even you as the ringleader. But what I find is empty ideas of faith and freedom. Tell me true, Galen." The Emperor leaned forward. "Are you a believer?"

Galen paused. He suppressed a grunt as he pulled against the bonds. They were loose. So close now. "Yes, I am."

"By the nine gods," Tanicus said. "Do you know what is happening to these men you say are going to be free?"

"You are slaughtering them."

"Like the animals they are. And they are animals, you know. They are like little beasts, having sex and procreating without restraint, killing one another even now. They will war with one another as quickly as they oppose us. But you remember that from the past. You are far older than I. I protect them, provide for them, and they revolt against me. I hold back the chaos that would destroy them. I kill a few to save the whole.

"You say what I do is evil. Where is your god now, Galen? You believe. Then tell me, where is he? Why does he not stop me from slaughtering his people?"

"I don't know. But I do know that the story is not yet over. There is a free city of men now, and that happened in a matter of days. Do you not think that El has more planned and is ready to move in his time? The story of El will go beyond you and your time of tyranny and evil."

His arms were one more twist away from being free. Did they truly think that Galen, the Blademaster of the Citadel, the Hero of Kryus, the elf that trained more than two hundred Bladeguard over the centuries, had been defeated and captured against his will?

The memory of his battle with the last elven *Sohan-el*, Elowen, haunted him, and facing the Emperor one last time, it was as fresh as the day it happened – Galen with his two best students at his side, Iletus and Julius, was sent by the new High Evilord, Tanicus, to kill her.

Elowen had led a small but vocal opposition to Tanicus' policies in the land of men. As a loyal servant of the nation of Kryus, Galen obeyed his Evilord and confronted Elowen at the Debir, the ancient temple of El near Galya. They caught her alone in the middle of the night.

Even against three blademasters, Elowen and her unforged sword were almost a match for them. Almost. There was blood and fire after a long battle, and Galen still possessed the scars from the injuries he sustained. But in the end they defeated her and burned down the Dror – the holy place – on top of her body.

Galen had been instrumental in finishing off the last of the *Sohan-el*. Long ago, he felt pride at the achievement. Now, after centuries, all he felt was shame and guilt. His only recourse for redemption was to help bring the *Sohan-el* back to Eres and end the reign of Tanicus, to undo what he had done. His work with Caleb was finished.

And now that he stood before the Emperor in the throne room, Galen's work could be complete and he could die at peace.

"You are a fool for bringing me into your sanctum," Galen said. "*Pride destroys the proud as sure as fire consumes the finest palace.*" He quoted from the Fyrwrit.

His hands were now free.

Galen crouched lower and reached over to his left and grabbed the sword of the Sunguard there in one motion, pulling the golden sword free. He rose, spinning and slicing through the small space between the bottom of the golden helmet and the armor along the shoulders, cutting through the neck from the guard on his right. Completing the turn, he stabbed the Sunguard on his left through the opening for the eyes of the helmet.

It all happened within a second.

As the turn brought him to face the Emperor again, Galen launched the sword like a spear at Tanicus' heart. Galen knew that his aim was true. This was why he allowed himself to be taken, after all. He trusted no one else with this task.

The sword flew five mitres. Tanicus calmly watched the weapon hurl towards him and held up his right hand. The sword came to a dead stop a mitre away from the Emperor's heart, hanging in the air. Tanicus smirked as he motioned with a flick of his wrist, and the sword melted, suspended and smoking. The beautiful sword became a hunk of metal and then clattered to the marble steps below the Emperor. Galen could feel the heat from the disfigured blade.

Tanicus stood, raising both hands now, and Galen was caught in an unseen grip and lifted off his feet. He couldn't move. The air felt suddenly stale and cold.

The Emperor of Kryus used magic, manipulating the natural world with a mystical power, an ancient discipline made illegal long ago due to its inherent danger.

"You … you are a Worldbreaker!" he whispered, all he could manage. The other Sunguard in the room had not moved. They knew.

"You are not the only one who can keep a secret," the Emperor said as he stepped down from the dais and glided within a pace of Galen. "As we speak, the wheels are in motion to kill your *Brendel*. He will beg for death before it is over. As will you."

Tanicus, the High Evilord of Kryus, showed his teeth in a half snarl, half smile. Galen felt as if an invisible hand reached into his chest and began to squeeze his heart.

Galen screamed in pain.

"But even though you will beg for it, I will not give you death. I will show you what power is," Tanicus said. "I have plans for the Blademaster of the Citadel. And by the time I am done with you, I will be the only god you believe in."

———

General Pyram was not normally a nervous elf. He was today.

No one could tell. His face expressed the same angry scowl that the Kryan Legion in Taggart always associated with him as he sat at the simple desk in his office.

Pyram was tall for an elf, with broad shoulders and thick arms. His graying, receding hairline belied what most suspected: a human somewhere in his ancestry, one of the main reasons he would never be promoted higher than General. It was an accomplishment, in fact, to get this far. He began as a militan five hundred years ago and through his continued victories against overwhelming odds and the favor of the nine gods, he climbed through the ranks.

The scar across the right side of his face was the reward for a particular charge in a battle against the elven nation of Jibril, uphill against a thousand Jibrilan troops with only two hundred in his own force. At the end of the day, he had taken that hill. They slaughtered every Jibrilan elf. Only ten of his original two hundred survived, but they won. The ugly scar on his cheek was deep and forced down that side of his mouth.

Other officers would comment – only once – how he never laughed, never smiled, how his face never varied from that constant, furious frown, even when complimenting a militan. The other officers would ask him: as a commander of a Kryan Legion in the quiet and remote outpost of Taggart, during a time of peace, could he not relax?

To General Pyram, that was precisely the point. When one relaxes, one loses.

A veteran of several campaigns, including the War of Liberation that the Emperor brought upon the nations of men, Pyram knew that no people, no matter how stupid or ignorant or beaten, was ever in complete subjection. Only fools believed such things. Resistance, retaliation, revenge and rebellion were a day away. So he stayed prepared.

The biggest confirmation of his diligence was the revolution that had begun at Ketan.

And it was a revolution. The Kryan government would spin and minimize it, like they always did, until they crushed the rebellion, and then the Emperor would take credit for destroying the threat to the Empire. Tanicus would be a hero again.

But men had taken control of a city last autumn and declared their own freedom from the rule of elves. He heard tell of this *Brendel*, like he was a monster, a conqueror, and a saint. Rumors. Pyram had interviewed three humans, men who had left the city to keep their supply of Sorcos, that drug that helped keep the population compliant. As loyal as they claimed to be to the Kryan Empire and the Emperor, they spoke of this *Brendel* in hushed tones, like he was unbeatable, and their testimony about a battle with these horrid creatures was consistent.

But no man was unbeatable.

Tanicus would deal with the rebellion and call on Pyram to be involved in the first strike against the city of Ketan, the people of Manahem, and this man, the *Brendel*. Tanicus was not known for his soft response. It would be harsh and brutal.

The knock came at the door.

The Bladeguard, thought Pyram.

They arrived a half-hour ago, around mid-day. He had been informed that the Bladeguard possessed the correct Letters of Regency and the tattoos. Two of them. He had never heard of two Bladeguard being sent to such a remote location. It underscored the importance of this revolution to the Emperor.

He stood behind his desk, his hand on the sword at his side.

"Come." Pyram said.

The door opened, and his assistant, Andos, a short and thin elf, bowed as he entered, moving fast. Andos was nervous. And who wouldn't be? Two Bladeguard walked in behind him.

The first was older with short dark hair and strong features. The second had long brown hair and a long oval face with a narrow mouth. They both wore long white robes with swords at their side. And they both had a tattoo of a stone with a tree growing from it on the inside of their right arm.

Andos bowed again, without a word, closing the door behind him as he left the room.

"Welcome, gentlelves," Pyram said. "I am General Pyram, commander of Taggart and the Legion here."

The older elf spoke first. "My name is Cyprian." He nodded to the younger. "This is Saben." Cyprian sauntered up to the desk and produced a parchment, laying it upon the surface. "This is a Letter of Regency."

Pyram didn't glance down at it. Andos had checked the Letters. Why show them again? "Are you taking control of this outpost?"

"Not yet," Cyprian said. "But we reserve the option. We come with orders from the Emperor."

"And they are?"

Cyprian clasped his hands before him. "Crush this *Brendel* and burn Manahem to the ground."

"Do you bring more troops?" Pyram asked.

Cyprian raised a brow. "Do you need them?"

"I would rather have them and not need them, than to lack them when necessary."

"Another Legion will be on its way here soon," Cyprian said. "There are … issues in Asya. We will use what we have for now."

"I understand," Pyram said. "And what is the strategy?"

Cyprian inclined his head to Saben. Saben, still standing by the door, opened it. Three more elves entered the room. They were all the same size and wore long dark gray robes that melted in the shadows with large hoods pulled down so their faces couldn't be seen.

Wraithguard. Three of them. Pyram's heart began to pound in his chest. He was surprised Andos wasn't critting in his pants. Maybe he did after he left the room.

The Wraith were the Emperor's chosen assassins, a living death sentence. Pyram had never seen one in action, but the legends were that all who did were dead. How much of that was Imperial propaganda and how much was truth remained unclear. Standing in the same room with them now, their very presence – motionless and silent – made him believe the latter.

Saben closed the door behind them after the Wraiths entered the room. They stood in a line to Pyram's right, looking down at the floor.

"*Three* Wraith?" Pyram asked. "For one man?"

"He is trained as a Bladeguard, by our most formidable master, Galen," Cyprian said. "You do not know this human."

"I do not, that is true," he said.

"We do," Saben said, stepping forward and rubbing the tattoo on his arm. "Trained with him."

"They leave tonight," Cyprian said.

"And then?" Pyram muttered, now inspecting the Letter of Regency on his desk.

"Get your troops ready to move, General," Cyprian said. "We march upon Ketan."

Pyram contemplated the Wraith. *Sending three Wraith and marching upon the city?* "This man must be dangerous, indeed."

Cyprian met Pyram's eyes. "One way or another, General, we will end this revolution and burn Ketan to the ground."

Chapter 3

The Call

Still wearing the divided skirts and the blouse from the morning training, Eshlyn made her way to the meeting with the other leaders of the city that evening, the sky growing dim and orange in the west.

Her husband's unforged sword also hung at her hip. Eshlyn rubbed the golden marriage bracelet as she walked through the arch and across the field to the administration quarters. Along with her son Javyn, the sword and the bracelet were constant reminders of Kenric, who had died almost six months ago. These reminders were beginning to cause her confusion because of her growing attraction to Caleb De'Ador, the *Brendel*.

Why deny it? She hadn't told anyone, but she knew what it felt like to be drawn to a man, to find him attractive, both his physical appearance and his character. And they spent so much time together. Not only the *Sohan-el* training but in council meetings and making decisions for the administration of the city when he almost always deferred to her. She looked forward to talking with him about these matters, as perfunctory as they ended up being at times, hearing his thoughts and his respect of her opinions.

Everything had happened in a chaotic rush in the month after Kenric's death. Traveling with her son in her arms up the Manahem road to warn her people of impending doom, and then the horrific Battle of Ketan with the Demics. And even though dead, Kenric had been with her in her dreams, somehow communicating with her through the unforged sword. Eshlyn hadn't begun to mourn until after the battle.

She grieved alone, in quiet moments in the middle of the night after Javyn was asleep and the world finally allowed her to deal with those deep emotions. Kenric was the love of her life, an intense but healthy love that taught her as much about herself as she learned of him. Although she didn't think it possible, the grieving began to subside and she was healing. But without him, what was she? Who was she?

Lady Eshlyn, at least that's what they called her. As the Head Elder of the city of Ketan, she was somehow able to unify citizens from other towns and Ketan and see them through the winter. Chamren, Athelwulf, and her father, Eliot, were invaluable in that effort, as well.

She was also a mother to her son, but she never seemed to have enough time for him. Javyn was toddling now and becoming more mischievous. His curious mind wanted to experience everything. Morgan, Eshlyn's mother, took care of him throughout the day. Eshlyn trusted her mother, an amazing woman, but she wanted to be more involved with her son.

A widow, a leader, a mother. She was all of these things but felt a failure at each.

She experienced an odd betrayal when she thought fondly of Caleb, as if she shouldn't feel such things for another man. She still loved Kenric. In her soul, she knew Kenric would never fault her for moving on without him, just as she would never have burdened him with similar thoughts if she were gone, but emotions did not bow easily to reason and truth.

She rubbed again the precious bracelet on her wrist as she entered the room, Chamren at her heels. They knew Caleb had met with the elf earlier in the day, and there was news from the outside. By afternoon the whole city was in a buzz with rumors, desperate for information after their winter isolation. Was the Kryan Army on their way here? Would there be another battle?

Eshlyn felt a stirring within her when she heard about the mysterious elf that came to visit Caleb. It was an odd mix of fear and expectation. The peaceful winter would soon be at an end.

They knew it wouldn't last, but it had been such a glorious time. Citizens pulled together and united to protect the city from the demic horde and carried that unity into creating an environment within Ketan of peace and growth. People learned new trades, skills, or stepped into roles of leadership. She saw the physician's assistants under the elven rule become noted doctors and healers. The palace was transformed into a hospital and the old Kryan temple into a library and school. Crime was rare or nonexistent. The people had jobs to do and a purpose, and with each success, more were willing to contribute.

The citizens of Ketan were rediscovering old and ancient beliefs, beliefs that once helped shape humanity into a force for good in the world. Drew, a friend of the Prophet from Biram, and others were copying the Prophet's translations of the Ydu and Fyrwrit at amazing speed. People discussed these new ideas, enlightened again to a faith that could help them become people worthy of freedom. Eshlyn found herself enraptured with the ideas of El and Yosu, caught up in the stories and teachings with wonder and awe like a child. She was not alone.

And many considered her their leader. In the midst of this human renaissance, she and Caleb were the guiding forces. The *Brendel* and Lady Eshlyn. The stubborn girl from Delaton who wanted to buck tradition and start her own business was now the head elder of a city of men. It overwhelmed her at times.

But over all of this joy and rediscovery, a dread hung over the citizens. The Empire would not sit quiet long. And between the *Sohan-el* and the army, Caleb was anticipating those inevitable events. The city prepared for war while they enjoyed peace.

As she entered the room, she saw that the rest of the elders and leaders were already gathered. Around the table sat Caleb, Aden, Carys, Athelwulf, Chamren, and Zalman. The group greeted her as she closed the door behind her and sat at the table.

Caleb began the meeting by relating what Iletus had told him. Tanicus had sent more militan to the major cities to quell the riots and violence. Thousands of humans were dying, and many fought each other instead of the Empire.

The room fell quiet. While not surprising to any, it was sobering.

"What can we do?" Aden asked after a few moments.

Caleb leaned back in his chair, and it creaked as he knuckled his moustache. "We all knew this was coming," Caleb said. "It is time."

"Time for what?" Aden asked.

"For the men and women of Eres to join the revolution," Caleb said. "All of them."

"To the real?" Carys asked, skepticism in her tone.

"Yes," Caleb continued. "Ketan was unique, even before the battle with the demics. Manahem didn't have the level of Kryan domination and control that other places in Ereland do. South of Ketan, people were self-sufficient and enjoyed almost complete self-rule. Here in Ketan, where you had an elven Steward, the First Captain was a reasonable elf who actually cared and many of the regulations didn't apply here." He pointed at Chamren. "You even had a human as one of the assistants to the Steward.

"There was a common enemy to fight, a real threat to survival, that necessitated unity and rising up to do for yourself even more than before, a reason to break rules that might have been ingrained, but a good reason.

"And there was capable leadership. Not only me, but also some of the men and women in this room. We were able to guide this city into something good and healthy.

"These cities may not possess these advantages. They are being blamed for our actions by the Empire and their response is unorganized hate and anger, even against one another."

"Okay," Carys said. "So what do we do? How do we get them to join us?"

Caleb sighed. "They don't really know what happened here. They didn't have this experience. All they have are rumors and half-truths."

Eshlyn recalled a vision of a burning forest, and a king beckoning her to follow him into the flames. Her heart sank.

"We can't bring them here," Eshlyn said. "You're talking about going to them."

Caleb hesitated before answering. "Yes."

"You have a plan, don't you?" Chamren said, his weak chin rising.

"He's always got a shoggin' plan," Zalman mumbled. "They just don't always work."

"I've been thinking about this all afternoon, and praying, seeking some sort of wisdom in all this," Caleb started to explain, sitting up straight as he talked. "We've been safe here. Macarus gave us time. The winter gave us time. Break it, the slow moving bureaucracy of the Empire gave us time. Our actions here have had repercussions across the world."

"We're not responsible for how others react," Eshlyn said. "That is maddy. We are responsible for our own actions, to the real, just as the Empire is, and all the humans in all these places."

"Maybe," Caleb said. "Maybe we can't be held responsible for what anyone else does, but the question remains, what do we do? Knowing what we know now, having the information available to us and the resources to help, shouldn't we do something? Who else can? And if we don't, who will?"

"*Peace will reign when truth is revealed, when those in darkness see the light,*" Aden quoted from the Fyrwrit, although Eshlyn didn't remember the exact reference. She recognized it, and the words pulled at her soul.

Caleb paused, his chest heaving with a deep breath. Eshlyn could have said the next words for him.

"Yes. So we'll be sending two groups out. One to Oshra in Lior. The other to Landen in Veradis."

"Not Asya?" Aden said.

"Not yet. Once we move the army from here, Asya will be our target, I think, as the primary seat of Kryan power on the continent. We must concentrate on the other two capitals in Ereland."

Carys scanned the room. "Which of us are you sending? That's what this is about."

Caleb said, "To Oshra, I think we should send Athelwulf, Esai, and Eshlyn."

Her heart constricted when she heard her name. She blinked but said nothing. Chamren glanced at her with worry.

"And Landen?" Zalman asked, but Eshlyn could see he already knew.

"You and Aden to Landen," Caleb confirmed. "And we'll need to have someone who has contacts with the criminal authority in the city."

"You're thinking of sending Shan?" Zalman said, his voice rising. "The one that tried to burn the Steward at the stake after the Battle of Ketan?"

"I think we've come to an understanding since then," Caleb argued.

"I don't trust him," Eshlyn said. The Rat, they called him, and she thought it an appropriate moniker.

"While the crinklehouse is closed down, he still manages and sells the women in secret," Chamren added.

Eshlyn saw Carys glare over at Zalman.

"I know," Caleb said. "And I don't really trust him, either."

"Then why haven't we shut him down, kicked him out of the city?" Athelwulf asked.

"We've done what we can," Caleb said. "He must see the rest of the path for himself."

"Why send him, then," Chamren asked. "If you don't fully trust him?"

"Landen has the most extensive criminal element in all of Ereland," Caleb answered. "It is an ancient society, called the Dygol. They have lords, rules and a whole underground society that Kryus allowed to remain. In part, it was because they could manipulate that society."

"Shan is connected with the Dygol, related to one of the Dygol lords," Zalman said, but he was frowning, troubled.

"We need him," Caleb said. "His connection with the underground element could make the difference. Plus, Aden and Zalman will deal with him."

"Do we need this Dygol at all?" Athelwulf asked. "Are there other contacts from the Prophet that we might be able to use?"

"Yes, and Aden will talk to them, as well," Caleb said. "But without the cooperation from the Dygol, it will be difficult."

Eshlyn cleared her throat. "So, why Aden and me?" she asked. "We have no connection to those places."

"Aden knew the Prophet; Reyan gave him those scriptures. He was a part of the whole journey from Asya to Ketan. He can articulate what has been happening here as well as anyone. And you," Caleb said to her, "were the one that led people to safety and away from the demics. Your testimony is important, and you were instrumental in making Ketan a free city of men. I can't think of any two better people to send."

It made sense to her mind, but her heart sank. He was right, she knew in that instant. Who better to go? She had been the one to warn Manahem about the demics, and she knew how to take an unorganized city and give it purpose, make it efficient. She lowered her eyes to her hands in her lap. She didn't want to go, didn't want to leave Javyn, her family, her friends. Caleb.

Come to the harvest …

"Why aren't you going?" Chamren said. "You could take the army and deal with these threats."

"Both cities are too far," Caleb said. "A smaller group would make better time." He grimaced. "The men of Oshra and Landen have known force and control. If we give them the same, even with good intentions and the truth, we've only made them dependent upon us instead of the elves." Caleb grew thoughtful. "No. They must organize, rise, and unite for themselves, or we've taught them nothing. The men and women of Oshra and Landen must join the revolution, not be rescued by it, or all we will have done is trade them one master for another.

"And we cannot fight Kryus by ourselves. Others will have to join the fight.

"In order for humanity to be free and united, all of us, local cities and communities must stand strong and independent and work with one another against the Empire."

"But what can we do?" Athelwulf asked. "Just three people? You mentioned all the advantages that we had here. What can three people do in these cities filled with thousands of men and elves?"

"When I came to Ketan, I knew the situation here was desperate, hopeless," Caleb said. "I had a small group of people I trusted with me. I had no idea that people like Eshlyn, Chamren, Eliot, and even Macarus were to be part of the picture.

"I suspect there are men and women in these cities, as well, able and called to lead. They just need someone to help them see how it can be done. El provided here in Ketan, and as hopeless as it may seem, I have faith El will do the same in Oshra and Landen."

"And if he doesn't?"

"Get out of there and return. You'll be needed here."

"What about running the city while I'm gone?" Eshlyn said. "I've been elected by the people here."

"It won't be the same, I agree," Caleb said. "But Chamren can handle it, and your father has been working with you the whole time. The people trust him. I think they'll choose him to take your place."

She couldn't fault her father's leadership; he was a good man and a strong leader. Caleb seemed to have this all worked out.

"I'm not going," Aden said.

Everyone turned to the young man.

"What?" Caleb said, as if he didn't hear it the first time.

But he did. Aden repeated it anyway. "I'm not going. I'm staying here."

"Break me, Aden, what are you talking about?" Caleb asked.

Aden scowled back at him. "I don't think I'm supposed to go. Send someone else. I'm supposed to be here."

"Why?" Caleb said, leaning forward in his chair and putting his hands on the table. "Why do you want to stay?"

"I didn't say I want to stay," Aden corrected.

"Okay, then, why don't you want to go?" Caleb said, his voice low.

"I didn't say that, either," Aden said.

"Break it all, man," Caleb said. "Can you give me any reason for refusing what I ask of you?"

"Not really," Aden said. "Don't know myself for sure; it just don't feel right that I go. And for that, I'm sorry."

"But if not you, who can I send?"

Aden shrugged his shoulders.

"I'll go," Carys said, her voice loud and firm.

Caleb spun on her with a hard look.

Carys sat up straight. Eshlyn had grown close to Carys over the past few months, training with Caleb's younger sister and working with her in different aspects for the new army. Eshlyn knew the stubborn visage on Carys' face. Caleb might be a great swordsman, but this was not a battle he could win.

"I knew the Prophet, too, if you remember," Carys said. "And I've been here, involved in the whole thing. And I've been to Landen before, met whatever contacts Uncle Reyan had there. I can tell them, convince them. Send me. I think I'm supposed to go."

"No."

His sister set her jaw. *Stubbornness runs in the family*, Eshlyn thought. "Why not?" Carys asked.

The room was quiet and awkward. Caleb pursed his lips.

"And don't say 'cause it's too dangerous, Cubby. It's not too dangerous for Eshlyn or Aden."

He glared at his sister. Eshlyn knew he hated when she called him Cubby. He clenched his fists.

Eshlyn reached down and grabbed the hilt of her husband's sword. And even though she didn't want to, she knew in that instant that she was meant to go to Oshra. She couldn't deny the message of the dream or the feeling in her gruts that confirmed it.

Her heart was pained with the thought of leaving Javyn. She couldn't take him this time. He would be safer here, with her mother and behind the walls of this city. But she knew, as difficult and dangerous as it would be, Caleb was right and true. People were lost and dying, but there was hope for them, if they could only see it. She remembered how desperate she was for safety and hope not long ago, carrying her child across the plains to Ketan.

Here in Ketan, Eshlyn found more than safety, she discovered a purpose. Children like Javyn were dying in Oshra families desperate for the hope she had found. She had to go. *I will defend the innocent, free the oppressed, and spread light in dark places.*

But Caleb was wrong about his sister. Carys was also supposed to go instead of Aden.

Eshlyn looked up at Caleb, and swallowed hard. "I'll go," she said.

Caleb seemed to relax.

"But on one condition," Eshlyn said.

Caleb's brow furrowed. "What ..."

"Carys goes and Aden stays here."

Carys beamed at Eshlyn.

"Now we're making deals?" Caleb asked. "What the shog ..."

Eshlyn spoke to Athelwulf. "Will you go with me, to Oshra?"

Athelwulf's face was troubled, but he nodded at her. "Yes. I will go."

"Good," Eshlyn said. "Thank you. Chamren, do you think you and my father can handle things here without me?"

Chamren's gaze went back and forth from Caleb to Eshlyn, but he said, "I would rather have you here, but yes, we can manage."

"That is easy," Eshlyn said. "Zalman, are there men who could take over the Citywatch?"

"Easy enough," Zalman said. "I have some good men. Perhaps Malen."

"Good choice," Eshlyn said. Malen had come with Esai and Athelwulf from the Ghosts of Saten. She turned to Caleb. "And I believe Esai and Shan will go as you request. This is the right thing. You've thought this through, and I believe it is from El. Not the easy thing, maybe the hardest thing, but the right thing. We want men to be free to follow their conscience, correct?"

Caleb's steel gray eyes burrowed into her. He also didn't like the ideas of freedom being thrown back into his face.

But she did it anyway.

"I know you do. And you are right to do so. We've just heard Aden say his conscience is to stay. And Carys that she should go. I believe that we should listen to these two people who have already sacrificed so much. We all respect your leadership in this and respect your opinion. What do you say?"

The room was quiet for a long stretch of time.

Caleb rubbed his chin and sat back. "Very well," he said.

"Good, then it is settled. When are we leaving?"

It took a moment, but he answered. "I was thinking tomorrow morning. We don't have much time to waste on this. People in those cities are dying."

Again, Eshlyn's heart felt tight at the thought of leaving her son – and Caleb, break it all – but she ignored it. She thought of the sweeping flames through the forest in the dream, the growing smoke that blackened the sky. "I agree. If we are to do this, it is for them, and there is not time to waste."

"Yes," Caleb said.

"Then we are all in agreement?" Eshlyn asked as she scanned the room, and she stood.

The rest of the group also rose and began to shuffle out the door. Eshlyn stood to say goodbye to Athelwulf before he left. He discussed the provisions they would need with Chamren as they made their exit.

Aden touched Eshlyn's shoulder as he left and grinned at her as if to thank her.

Carys turned to face her brother.

Eshlyn was about to leave the siblings alone, but she heard Caleb say, "You can stay." His voice was soft. She closed the door to leave the three of them in the room.

"Don't be piffed," Carys said. "Please. I have to do this."

"I just don't understand. You *hate* Zalman," Caleb said. "You do nothing but complain about him to me and how he uses the crinkles. You really want to spend that much time with him? To work with him?"

"Is it about what we want?" Carys clicked her tongue. "He is a big gedder," she said, and Eshlyn stifled a chuckle at the term. A *gedder* was a slang term for the Gedai, the legendary race of giants north of the elven land of Faltiel. They were supposed to be twice as tall as a human. And brainless. "But I can handle him."

"Zalman is right," Caleb said. "Shan is someone you'll have to watch. But we need him."

"Then I'll handle him, too," Carys said.

Caleb snorted. "Maybe I'm being overprotective, but Car, you have to understand, if I lose you …"

Carys grinned at him. "You'll what? Quit?"

"Honestly, I really don't know what I'd do."

Eshlyn watched as Caleb's countenance fell, a rare moment of transparency few ever saw.

Carys stood and moved around the table to her brother. She leaned over and kissed him, tenderly on the cheek and the forehead. Eshlyn could see the tears in her eyes. "I do understand. And I love you, too."

He grabbed her hands, and he pulled her down to him, burying his face in her neck. Carys pulled away, smiling at him, tears on her cheek, and then she moved to leave. As she passed Eshlyn, they embraced, like sisters. And then Carys left the room.

Eshlyn was alone with Caleb now, and silence hung for a few moments.

Caleb didn't look at her when he spoke. "They have my master, Galen," he said.

"Who? Kryus?"

"That is one of the reasons Iletus is here. To help us, yes, but also because he's a criminal in his own country. He escaped, but Galen did not. How they caught him, I'd love to hear, but if he's alive, he's suffering at the hands of the Emperor."

"I'm sorry," she said. There was a weight on his shoulders now; it was visible to her. She wondered if others ever saw it, or if he allowed them.

"I feel responsible, which is maddy, of course," he said. "He sent me on this path as much as I chose it. He knew the risks, and if anyone can take care of himself, it is Galen. But I wish it were different. I wish there was something I could do to help him."

Caleb was quiet for a long moment, and she watched him. He would always do the right thing. Still, he listened to those who challenged him, even changed if he thought it right, whether those were from a boy like Aden or a woman from a country town. Eshlyn knew enough men in her young life to realize Caleb was rare. Yes, stubborn, overprotective, reckless, and self-critical, which was a bad combination to the real, but no matter what it cost him, he would do what was right.

She understood. It was the same for her.

"I know it is hard to let Carys go," she said.

"Why does she want to leave?" he asked.

"I suspect she feels it is the right thing, like she said, like El would have her go," Eshlyn said. "But you must also know, Caleb, that she spent time among the Ghosts in the Saten for years, and she was known as simply Carys. She grew into her own woman there, learning to lead and fight. She wasn't Caleb's little sister there.

"Carys loves you, but here?" Eshlyn shuffled closer to the table, standing before him. "Here, she is the *Brendel*'s little sister. You are an imposing presence, and you cast an enormous shadow. As the *Brendel*? You are a symbol of something greater. Perhaps she wants to get out from that shadow and be her own woman."

"You're right," he said. He regarded her for a moment. What did he see in her? "And I also wanted to let you know that I understand what it is that I'm asking of you, the sacrifice. I realize leaving your son here and traveling for an undetermined period of time is huge. And I'm sorry that I ask it of you."

Ah, so he isn't ignorant of what he asks, she thought.

"You like asking the impossible of me," Eshlyn said. "I'm almost getting used to it."

"You're one of the few capable of the impossible," Caleb said. He stood and faced her. "I hope the people of Oshra understand our sacrifice in doing without you."

"So you're not trying to get rid of me?" She wanted it to sound like a joke, to lighten the mood.

Caleb smiled, a sad and kind expression. "Not at all," he said. "I'd have you with me at all times, if possible."

She cocked her head at him.

"Well, I'm sure you need to go home and see your son before he goes to bed, spend what time you can with him before tomorrow." Caleb began to escort her to the door.

"Yes," she agreed as she allowed him to open the door for her.

"Good night, Eshlyn," Caleb said as she left.

"Good night," she answered before the long hike home to prepare to leave on the journey to Oshra.

50

CHAPTER 4

LIGHT TO DARK PLACES

"Hey, there, Zal," a voice called from behind him. "Haven't see you in a while."

It was early morning, and Zalman had gathered his things and proceeded to the gate to meet with the other five people that were leaving the city of Ketan today.

Recognizing the voice, he turned to see Kyrna, one of the ladies of the evening that used to work at Lady Ursla's Crinkle Inn. When Zalman worked for Shan, the Rat, Kyrna had been his favorite.

The last few months had changed him, slowly. He didn't believe in all that El crit, no, not that, but Caleb was a good leader and gave men purpose and reason to live. The city had transformed. It was good.

Goodness, however, only made him more skeptical. His experience had been that every good thing was a façade. So while a part of him was inspired, a large remnant of his soul waited for it all to be exposed as full of crit. People used one another for game or sport, and one way or another, he would see it with the men and women here in Ketan, as well. It was only a matter of time.

"Been busy," he said, and he continued to stride towards the gate, his battleaxes at his hips and a large pack over his shoulder. She followed.

"Yeah," she said. "I'm impressed. One o' my clients now the First Captain o' the Watch."

He wanted to argue, but was she wrong? It felt strange. "Well, someone else is taking over, a good man by the name of Malen, since I'm leaving."

"I know," she said. "I heard. Why are *you* goin'?"

He hesitated. He didn't know how to explain it without sounding stupid. To go spread hope? Sounded so trite. "Some people need our help."

"You going to help, and you're taking Shan with you?" She laughed.

It annoyed him that he agreed with her.

"Well, I hear that you leavin' and I thought for the sure you woulda come to us last night. You know, as a goodbye. Been a couple months since you warmed my bed."

More like her purse, he thought. There had been fewer clients over winter. "Sorry. Like I said. Been busy. Busy last night packing and things, getting ready. And I needed my sleep before the journey."

Kyrna placed a hand on a hip and huffed at him. "You never needed sleep before!"

He paused. To his right, he could see Caleb and Carys approaching them. Carys saw Kyrna and glared at him.

Back when the latest group went to the Living Stone, two ninedays ago, he almost went with them. He wanted to see for himself. But recognizing the look in Carys' eye now, how she despised him, he was glad he didn't. No way could he have deserved an unforged sword.

"I gotta go," he said to Kyrna. "But you be safe, you hear?"

She frowned, obviously being dismissed, but she slinked away.

He continued to walk, and Caleb and Carys were soon by his side.

"Morn," he said.

"Morn," Caleb said.

Carys said nothing.

As they neared the gate, Caleb touched Zalman's arm and said, "Speak with me for a moment."

Carys gave her brother a quizzical squint.

"Just for a moment," Caleb said to her. "Be right there."

Zalman faced Caleb as Carys departed.

"Two things," Caleb said, his voice low but dangerous, and he leaned in close. He held up one finger. "First, you do not touch my sister."

"Caleb, I ..."

"You understand me?"

Zalman nodded.

Caleb continued, now holding up two fingers. "Second. You watch out for her. I am making you personally responsible for her safety. She returns without a scratch."

"You know that's maddy," Zalman began.

Caleb cut him off and lowered his hand. "Don't care. You are a good man, and I like and trust you, but I need to be clear on this. You make sure you don't touch her and that she returns to me without a scratch, or I will kill you."

Zalman started to laugh, but one look in Caleb's cold gray eyes convinced him the man wasn't trying to be funny. Zalman was afraid of no man, but at that moment, he wasn't so sure he shouldn't be afraid of this one.

"We have an understanding?" Caleb asked.

"Understood," Zalman said.

"Good," Caleb said, and he strode off to the gate. "Let's go."

Zalman followed him to the gate.

A large group waited for them. They passed through the gate, but Zalman hung back as the rest of the crowd gathered. He searched but couldn't see Shan, but then he felt a presence behind him.

"Off for a little trip, are we?" Shan said.

Zalman rotated to his left to see the man standing there.

Just over fifty years old with short gray hair and a slight belly on him, Shan had a full, gray handlebar mustache that flapped when he spoke and spread when he smiled. The man's head was covered with a wide-brimmed hat, black and made of sturdy material. Wearing a white shirt with a leather jacket and pants, his black boots went up to his knees, and he wore a short sword on each hip. They had been made for him in Landen, and he managed to keep them hidden while in Ketan. But now that the elves were gone, he wore them proudly, claiming to have slain over sixty demics on the wall during the battle.

Zalman had stood not far away from the man during the battle. It had not been near that many.

Shan had been known as the Rat, the most powerful man among the criminals in Ketan before the battle months ago, always escaping the First Captain, Macarus. During that time, Zalman worked for Shan, the Rat, as muscle.

After the Battle for Ketan, Shan tried to execute the elven Steward of Ketan along with a couple other officials, and Caleb had stopped him. While the Rat claimed to have reformed, changed since then, Zalman wasn't so sure. The Rat had always been about profit and being in the right position to make coin, and Zalman couldn't say anything the man had done over the past few months disproved that.

But people could say the same about Zalman. Couldn't they afford the Rat the same opportunity? Ketan was a second chance for many.

"It's been a long time since I've been back to Landen," Shan said. "Are you excited about seeing your homeland?"

"Not sure I have a homeland," Zalman said. "Left when I was a boy. Ketan, over the last couple months, been more a home to me than anything."

"Well, I will be glad to see my family," Shan said. "I haven't spoken with them in a long time."

Zalman peered at him. "Didn't you say there was some trouble between you and your family?"

"Did I?"

"Yeah," Zalman said.

"Perhaps I did," Shan said. "But when my family learns I've been working with the infamous *Brendel*, surely they'll welcome me back with open arms."

"Never had a family I could say that about. You sure yours will help us?"

Shan lifted a pack across his shoulder, settled it there, and adjusted his hat against the sun in the east. "I know my family," he muttered. "And they will do what profits them best. We shall just have to help them see the profit in it, no?"

———

Eshlyn stood with her parents and her brother. She held her son in her arms. He was getting big, almost too big to carry, but she wanted to smell his hair, feel his arms around her shoulder, his legs around her waist, one last time.

No one knew how long they would be gone. It would take a few ninedays just to journey there and back, and there would be so much to do while gone. No telling what they would find and what it would take to try and make any sort of change. While the goal was clear, it was a blind trip, and it scared her, despite the fact she knew she should go.

Javyn could be running around and too big to carry when she returned. It broke her heart.

Xander stepped closer to her. "I'll miss you, Esh," he said.

She smiled. "I'm proud of you, little bro," she said. "You've grown so much, become a man. Ken would have been so proud."

He blushed. "Thanks," he said and embraced her.

Eshlyn's parents, Eliot and Morgan, also moved near and hugged her, her father still limping on his wooden leg. After moments of declaring their love and hope that she be safe, Eshlyn drew away from everyone and spoke to her son. He studied her with an odd expression. He understood something was happening. How to explain it?

"Ma has to go now, baby," she said. "I want you to stay with Gran here and be a good boy."

He was so innocent and young. How could she leave him? She drew him close, her stomach tightening against a sob. When it came down to it, she didn't know if she could.

The image of the burning forest came to her mind. Thousands were dying all over the world. How many of them mothers with sons or daughters? How many of them despairing for the safety her own son enjoyed?

Every one, each in their own way.

… *spread light in dark places.*

Come to the harvest …

"Mama?" her son cried.

Desperate, she clutched him until he whined from the pressure. She whispered in his ear. "I love you more than anything. Remember that."

Handing her son over to her mother, she grabbed her pack and went to her horse.

It was the most difficult thing she had ever done.

———

Caleb said his goodbyes to Esai and Athelwulf, then Zalman and Shan, giving them final encouragement and instruction.

Eshlyn stood by her horse. Caleb stepped over to her and saw she had been crying. She noticed his approach and wiped her cheeks, forcing a smile and glancing over at her parents as they carried her son away.

He stood within a pace of her.

The morning sun was yellow and warm, and it fell across her face. He wanted to say things that gave her strength, gave her hope, but the vision of her in the early spring dawn, her cheeks flushed from the slight chill, left him speechless.

"I guess it is goodbye," she said, a whisper.

He extended his hand, and she took it. On an impulse, he pulled her to him and pressed her into his arms. She gasped in surprise.

It was uncomfortable, and he was a little unsure of how long to hold her. But he retreated from her. She had a problem meeting his eyes.

"Sorry," he said. "I'm going to miss you."

She stammered before saying, "Watch out for Xander. He's still young."

"I will," he said.

Eshlyn mounted her horse, Blackie, and she peered down at him.

"Make sure you come back to us," Caleb said to her. "We need you."

She nodded to him as she rode to join the others.

His sister eyed him as she tightened the strap on the saddle of her horse.

"What?" he said, walking over to her.

"You're like a teenager at a belltime dance with her sometimes."

He knew who Carys meant. Eshlyn. "No, I'm not," he protested.

Carys chuckled at him. "You can fight Bladeguard and Demilords without a thought, but speaking to that woman without getting your tongue in knots is something you've yet to conquer."

"Why are you busting my gruts?" he said. "We're supposed to be saying tearful goodbyes."

"You're right," she said. "You're not still angry at me, are you?"

"I will be out of my mind in fury if you don't come back." It sounded like a joke, but he meant it.

She chuckled again and then embraced him.

Caleb was struck in that moment with the memory of her in his arms, hiding in a cave from the Cityguard. He had held her tight, ready to kill or die to protect her, as they heard the distant screams and cries of their mother.

"I'm serious," he whispered into her ear while his arms embraced her now. "You come back to me. That's an order."

"I'll see what I can do about that." He released her and kissed her cheek. "I love you," she said.

"I love you," he said. "Be safe."

She was soon in the saddle of her horse, her pack sitting behind her. She joined the others, and six horses made their way off to the south.

He wondered, as he watched them leave, if he would see any of them again.

CHAPTER 5

TO AWAKEN LOVE WITHIN

General Pyram fixed his frown on his assistant, Andos, that morning, as the elf approached. Andos, as usual, bore it with grace, a bow and a salute – his right fist across his chest.

"I have a message from the Bladeguard, Sir," Andos said.

Andos was a good elf, a great assistant. Pyram had officers, but they were career-minded military elves, people who would argue or agree with him because they wanted his job one day – sooner than later, he supposed. So his officers, while technically obedient, were also searching for any opportunity to catch him in a bad decision. Andos was not a career elf. He knew his strengths, which were administration and service. While serving with Pyram, however, he had also developed a clever mind for strategy. Pyram would trust his assistant to lead before any of his other officers.

Pyram stood in the northern yard and watched the archers practice. He heard the thumping of arrows against wooden targets shot from their short bows. They were average archers. This remote of an outpost didn't tend to get the best recruits, even though Pyram asked for that very thing, knowing that one day they might regret listening to him. That day might be coming very soon.

"And what is their message?" Pyram muttered.

"They want me to inform you that since we received word reinforcements are on their way, the Legion will be moving out in the morning."

"How many troops will they be taking?"

"I believe their intention is to take them all, the whole Legion."

Pyram's frown lessened, his version of a grin. These Bladeguard must believe that since he was the general in charge of the most remote outpost of the Kryan military, that he must be a fool. Pyram was not a fool.

"Tell them 'no.'"

"Anything else, Sir? Or just 'no.'"

"Just that one word will suffice. Thank you."

Andos bowed and saluted again before he rushed off.

Pyram took his flask from his belt and took a swig. Good Kryan liquor. The strongest they made. He bared his teeth as he swallowed it down, feeling the warmth in his belly, the tingling down his throat, and he exhaled.

Dawn had been hours ago, but the sun was low enough to be in his eyes when he faced the east, the wind crisp across his face. The winter had been cold, but not too harsh. He had done much of his fighting in Landen all those years ago, and he fell in love with the balmy weather there, never too cold. He welcomed warmer weather.

Within five minutes, Andos returned with both Bladeguard on his heels. They both scowled as they ambled up to him. Andos hung back and allowed them to face Pyram apart from him. The General took one more swig and placed the flask back in his belt.

He aimed his frown at Cyprian and Saben.

"Gentlelves," he said, his voice low. "A fine morning."

Cyprian began. "Your assistant gave us your response." It was like an accusation.

"That is good," Pyram said. "Since I told him to."

"*No?*" Cyprian asked. "That was your response?"

"Even better that he got it correct," Pyram said.

"Would you care to tell us what the message means?" Cyprian said.

"It is a denial of your request to take my Legion west," Pyram noted. "I thought that would be clear."

Cyprian raised a brow. "It was not a request. This Legion will be leaving in the morning."

"Interesting," Pyram said. "But since these are my elves, I say we go nowhere tomorrow."

Cyprian shared a glance with Saben. "These are the Emperor's elves."

"And is he here? No. This is how the chain of command works. I obey the Emperor, but the militan under my command? They obey me. Without question. Otherwise we would not function as a military unit. Hence, until Tanicus comes to take my place or removes me from my position, they are mine. And I will do with them what I see fit."

Saben decided to speak. "We are the voice of the Emperor."

"You are?" Pyram wondered. "I have met the Emperor, and you sound nothing like him."

"We carry his authority," Saben said.

"Your role in a military campaign is simple and clear," Pyram said. "Support, counsel, and intelligence. If 'his authority' refers to those Letters of Regency, then you must adhere to a procedure to take my position, namely claiming that I have been remiss in some way to my duty and getting another local officer to concur. Now, I do believe you would have no trouble finding an officer that would give such testimony out of fear of you, if not some other more selfish reason; then you would be able to remove me. And the Legion would then be yours to do as you please. Until then, gentlelves, this Legion is mine to command."

"You *want* us to remove you?" Cyprian asked.

"I sincerely wish you would," Pyram said. "I have a fine estate north of Hyperion, surrounded by rolling hills and a fine sprawling house that I haven't seen in a decade or more. I could retire there. I miss that place. You are free to claim Directive XVII and go through the process if you wish." Then the General took a step towards the Bladeguard, glowered at them, and placed his hand on the hilt of his sword. "But do not threaten me with a shogging piece of paper. And do not send me a breakin' message again telling me what you will do with my elves. Come to me and make a request, and I will make a decision. I am here for the glory of the Empire, and have the scars to prove it. Trust that I will do what I feel is best for the Emperor and Kryus." He stood straight again and examined the archers mostly hitting their targets beyond him in the yard. "I know these elves, sirs. I mean no disrespect. But I know their training and their capabilities and I have fought and commanded in dozens of battles. I trust my own counsel more than yours, I guarantee you, no matter what your piece of paper says. If you have a request, I will listen."

It was quiet for a whole minute. He didn't look at them, and he didn't speak. They would be the ones to break the silence, and he was unsure of what they would do. They could remove him right there, and he was certain that they would not let him go to his home near Hyperion if they did.

But he would not allow some breakin' Bladeguard to disrespect him in the very outpost that he called his home for five decades and had commanded well. Not without a fight. He had bled buckets for this Empire. He deserved more than that.

"General Pyram," Cyprian began. "We request the use of your Legion on the Emperor's errand in the west."

"And what do you intend to do with my troops? The *Brendel* is safe behind some rather infamous walls. Is your strategy to lay siege to Ketan?"

"If we must," Cyprian said. "But our tactic is to bring death and pain upon the human citizens of Biram."

Pyram disguised his disgust. "To what purpose?"

"It will draw him out," Saben said. "Make him vulnerable."

"How do you know he will leave the safety of Ketan?" Pyram asked.

"We trained with him," Cyprian said. "We know his weakness. He is reckless and overconfident, rushing to protect others. When he hears of the suffering in Biram, he will run from those walls to meet us."

Pyram rubbed his chin and considered their strategy. He was not certain the plan would work; was this *Brendel* as bosaur-headed as they believed? But what could he truly say? He couldn't stop them if he wanted to. The Emperor sent his Bladeguard and the Empire made way for them.

"You may take three fourths of my Legion," Pyram said. "I will stay here with a minimal force to protect this outpost if a human army somehow gets around you through the forest. A thousand elves should be enough to hold

Taggart until the reinforcements arrive, and little more than four thousand militan should give you plenty to harrow the countryside until I can send those reinforcements to you. Will that satisfy?"

Cyprian and Saben both appeared angry. "That will do for now," Cyprian said.

"Good," Pyram said. "I thank you for your patience. Now, if you will excuse us, Andos and I must make preparations and choose how to best divide the Legion and fortify this outpost. You will have four thousand elves to take with you in the morning."

"Thank you," Cyprian said, and he saluted.

The General watched the two Bladeguard stride away. Then he exhaled.

Andos slid next to the General. "Well done, sir," he said. "But I fear you may have made an enemy."

"Did I ever tell you of the time I led a platoon of militan into the cave dwelling of a dwarven stronghold? How we fought for three ninedays, drank dirty spring water and hunted grider to survive?"

"Yessir," Andos said. "Many times."

"It is not Bladeguard that scare me the most," Pyram said. "Point of fact, it is not the power of the Emperor that most makes me afraid." He sniffed. "Although if you ever tell anyone that, I will empty your breakin' gruts on the ground and make you eat them."

"Yessir."

"You know what scares me the most?"

"No, sir."

"Stupidity. Stupidity will kill you faster than anything in the whole of Eres. It ends Empires, Andos, whole Empires. And you can find stupidity everywhere: politics, the military, religion, even education. Especially education. It is everywhere. That is one enemy I feel I will always fight and never eradicate."

———

It took the travelers two days to get to Roseborough from Ketan. They passed through the big town in silence, sobered by the destruction and the quiet. While not many died here – thankfully the mayor had seen reason in time to evacuate the citizens before the demics arrived – Carys observed the bones of animals, and she was faced with the reality that rebuilding Roseborough, and also the other towns to the south, would be a difficult task. Carys watched as Eshlyn gazed further to the south as they turned east to cross the plains.

Athelwulf led the way across the plains, with Carys and Esai helping him guide the group to the edge of the forest. Athelwulf and Esai had led a thousand Ghosts this way not four months before, avoiding the road that would take them by Taggart and the elven outpost there.

Following two days of traveling over the Julai Plains, Athelwulf led them into the Forest of Saten. There was no road; they had to weave through the big trees and the thick brush, so they camped only a few hours into the forest where they found a clearing.

Carys knew they weren't too far from their old Ghost Camp. She knew the forest well, and she remembered her times with Athelwulf fondly.

Traveling to the Stone together the previous fall had further strengthened their bond. Even though she did not admit it to anyone, Ath had known she was still in pain on the journey. He knew her too well, had been responsible for her training. Reaching the mountain, he helped her as he could, as did Esai.

After facing down demics and coming close to her own death, she didn't think a cloud would have scared her as much as it did. But it wasn't the black tempest that had frightened her but what lurked inside, a presence she knew but had never experienced so intimately. There was love there, she had felt it, but a furious and wild love more untamable than the roiling storm that had stood in her way.

She had stepped forward anyway. And within the cloud and smoke, she spoke to El, knew his power, his mind, his heart. And the love. The amount of love terrified her. It was too much. There was wrath within El, too, righteous anger at all that oppressed and abused what he had created and designed, but she had expected that. It almost made sense. But the love? How could anyone expect that? It was a love more intense than the anger, and she knew it was not the wrath that would change Eres but the love.

Without eyes or body in that place, she had wept from her soul for joy and sorrow. In fact, in that moment, they were the same.

Touching the Living Stone after that, the blade piercing her heart, she had known the desire and the power of El to redeem every human, elf, and dwarf in Eres. Break it, El desired the redemption of all creation.

Armed with that experience, she knew she had to go and spread that truth. No matter what it cost.

Now in the forest of Saten, a place she thought of as home, they traveled the rest of the day and set up camp quickly that evening, with Eshlyn and Carys on one side of the fire and the four men on the other. Eating through their provisions, they talked, but Carys noticed that Zalman and Shan sat away from the rest of the group, taking their meals by themselves and never joining the conversation.

The next morning, Athelwulf had the group up and moving just after dawn since their trek through the forest would be slow until they got to the road.

After an hour of riding, Ath held up his fist, and the whole group pulled their horses to a stop and froze. Soon Carys could hear the noise, as well.

"Someone is in the forest," Athelwulf whispered, difficult to hear among the wind whistling through the trees.

Carys straightened in her saddle, and her gaze inspected the forest to the south. Yes, feet running, but quiet. The rest of the group scanned the dark shadows of the forest around them. They hadn't developed the ability to hear and discern the sounds of the forest as Carys had, to distinguish the rustling of leaves from the fall of footsteps. This person nearing them was good, though, she admitted. He or she was a Ghost of Saten.

Athelwulf obviously came to the same conclusion, and faster than she, more than likely. He said, his voice loud and booming, "We are friends! I am Athelwulf, once leader of the Hollow Camp. Carys and Esai are also with me. Come and speak with us."

Like Ath had called a spirit from the forest, a young man emerged from fifteen mitres ahead of them. Carys heard Eshlyn gasp behind her and Zalman grunt.

Esai chuckled. "Ah, so it is Pyter," he said. "Good to see you, my friend."

Pyter had long dark hair, bushy and down his back, dressed in greens and deer leather like other Ghosts, and he carried a bow at his side and a gladi at his belt. "Well met, Esai!" he said. And then bowed to Athelwulf. "The great captain of the Hollow Camp. It is an honor to be with you again."

"It has been a while," Athelwulf said. "But well met. What are you doing this far from your camp?"

"I have been sent to give you a message from Mother Natali," Pyter said.

Carys contained her surprise. Mother Natali was the caretaker of the Father Tree and a leader of sorts among the Ghosts. Her role was undefined: part priestess and guide, all the captains listened to her and sought her wisdom. And they obeyed her every instruction when it came to the Father Tree.

Athelwulf sat calm on his horse. "What is her message?" he asked.

"Mother requests your presence at the junction of the Saten road," Pyter said. "She has made camp there and says she would like to speak with you."

"I will gladly speak with her," Athelwulf said. "We will go there at once. Will you ride with us or do you have other business?"

"I must get back to my camp to the south," Pyter said. "But I pray El will show his goodness on your journey, great Athelwulf."

"Thank you, Pyter," Athelwulf said.

Pyter raised his left hand and cried out, "Well met, Esai!"

"Well met!" Esai called as Pyter disappeared once again into the forest.

Athelwulf swiveled in his saddle and addressed the group. "Come, let us go," he said.

"Wait a minute," Shan said. Riding his horse from the back of the line, he passed the others to pull within a few paces of Athelwulf. "This woman beckons, and so we just go? We've got a long way yet. Can we take time for this little detour?"

Carys glared at him. "Mother Natali is a wise woman. She can only help us."

"By detaining us?" Shan asked. "Back me up here, Zal."

Zalman only shook his head.

Shan looked back to Athelwulf, and Ath's face was blank and calm. "I also do not wish to have any unnecessary delays," Ath said. "But Mother requests our presence, and she does not do so lightly. If she knows we are in the forest, she likely knows our quest. Carys is correct. She can only help us."

His jaw dropping, Shan took stock of the group. "Did you hear what he just said? How did she know we were in the forest?" He chuckled. "Some sort of fairy forest magic?"

Esai's horse was beside Carys as she bared her teeth at him. "Watch your mouth," Carys said. "Don't mock her. She sees things. El shows her things."

Shan raised his hands in surrender. "I mean no disrespect," he said. "Landen and Oshra are both far, and we still have the desert to pass. Our supplies will only last so long."

"Lady Eshlyn," Athelwulf said. "What say you?"

"If El wishes us to know something, even through this woman," Eshlyn said. "Then he will also provide what we need. We should go see her if she can help."

Esai reached out to lay a hand upon Carys' arm, to calm her. It didn't. "You do not understand," he said, speaking to Shan. "And that is because you do not know. Mother would not detain us unnecessarily, and the Ghosts will see that we are more than well supplied for our trip. When the Mother camps beyond the Father Tree, she brings quite the congregation with her, and men and women come to give her honor."

Shan's frown only grew as Esai talked.

"Carys?" Athelwulf said.

"You know my mind," she answered.

"Then it is settled. We will go to see the Mother," Athelwulf said. "El will show his goodness. Any who do not wish to join us, you may ride on without us, but I suggest that we stay together as much as we can."

Shan adjusted his wide-brimmed hat and said, "Very well, then. We shall see this mother of yours."

Carys took a deep breath as Athelwulf rode off with Shan, Eshlyn, and Zalman following. Before moving forward, she turned to Esai, who still sat nearby, and she muttered, "Is it wrong to want to kick him in the gruts?"

Esai chuckled. "Come. El will show his goodness."

She growled. "He'd better."

It was late afternoon as they neared the junction where Mother Natali camped, the sun lowering in the sky while the shadows within the forest lengthened.

Zalman realized Esai had not been exaggerating about the congregation. The camp was twenty tents or more spread out along the road and among the trees, tall tents that were dark brown and blended in with the surrounding forest. The largest tent sat straight ahead, and Zalman was sure that the Mother would be in that tent.

He was not wrong. As they approached, an old woman exited the tent, flanked by two younger women who seemed to be attendants. Athelwulf stopped his horse two mitres away from the woman, who stood straight.

"Hello, Mother," he said.

Mother Natali was short, perhaps shorter than an elf woman, with white, wrinkled and leathery skin. Her hair was thick and bushy in a mixture of white and gray. She wore a green woolen dress that hung to her ankles. But as Zalman grew closer, the most striking feature was her eyes. They were bright green and shone among the shadows of the forest.

"Athelwulf, my son," Mother said. "Welcome to my camp."

He bowed to her from his horse. "You are most kind." He dismounted, and the rest of the group followed suit. Soon the horses were led away and tied to nearby branches, and the group stood with Athelwulf.

"Carys and Esai I know," Mother said. "But who are the rest?"

Athelwulf pointed at the group as he introduced them. "This is Shan, of Veradis and Landen by birth but most recently from Ketan."

"Welcome to our camp," she told him, but Shan just nodded curtly at her. "Who is the big one?" Mother asked with a grin.

"That is Zalman," Ath said, and Zalman grinned at her. "Once a great Qadi-bol player but now the commander of the Citywatch of Ketan."

Zalman grunted.

"Qadi-bol?" Mother asked. "You mean that fool game with the little balls that costs an ungodly amount of money to run?"

Athelwulf laughed. "Yes, Mother."

"They could feed a whole kingdom with the money from that fool game," she muttered. Mother glanced back at Zalman. "I am glad you are no longer a part of that."

"Me, too," he said.

"It is unfortunate that people associate stupidity with the large, do you agree?" she asked.

"I don't know," he stammered.

"You're not stupid, are you?" she said.

His brow knitted at her.

"Good. Wise enough not to answer. Welcome to the camp."

"Thank you."

"And this," Athelwulf continued, "is Eshlyn, from the south of Manahem but recently voted the head elder of Ketan."

Mother directed her gaze to Eshlyn and held it there for some time. "Lady Eshlyn, I presume," she said at last.

Zalman saw Eshlyn blush. "You know me?"

"I know many things and hear much more than I know," Mother said. "Yes, I have heard of Lady Eshlyn. We will talk later."

Eshlyn smiled but seemed nervous.

Addressing all six of them, Mother Natali said, "Please rest in our camp. We have extra tents for you to sleep in tonight and dinner is being prepared. We shall eat soon." Then she turned to Athelwulf. "Come. Walk with me."

―――――

Athelwulf fell into step beside Mother Natali as she walked into the forest. She was hundreds of years old, and at times she appeared so brittle, but he was amazed at how deftly she maneuvered through the brush with the loose dress billowing about her without disturbing branches or twigs. He knew it to be a figment of his imagination, but it was like the forest made way for her.

"You are traveling to the place of your birth," she said. He noted she did not say "home." This forest would always be his home.

"To Lior, yes, but not the place of my birth," he said. "We travel to Oshra to speak with the men in that city."

"I understand, to Oshra. But also to the place of your birth."

"We had not planned to go to the mountains."

"Have you not learned that El has his own plans?"

He did.

Mother Natali stepped over a log, and he helped her by holding a low branch so she could pass. "Ever since you came to us," she said. "We knew this day would come. It has arrived."

"I haven't spoken to my family in so long," Athelwulf said. "And we did not part well. I shamed them."

Mother stopped and faced him. *She is so small*, he thought, but her very presence both overwhelmed and comforted. Reaching her hands to his face, she cupped it with her palms.

"Love is bigger than shame, my dear," she said. "Always. Has not El taught us this?"

"I know the teaching," he said. "But my father is sure to remember the shame."

As it darkened in the forest with the setting sun, her eyes glowed brighter. "Then you must remind him of the love. It is there within him."

"How can I remind him?"

She released him, and he stood straight again.

"Do you remember when you first came to us?"

"Almost every day."

"There was such sadness and bitterness in you then, such poison. Such shame." She grimaced and then spat as if she could still taste it. "But there was great love there as well. How did I awaken it within you?"

He grinned at her. "With your great love to me."

"That is how."

———

Zalman sat down to a feast.

There was venison and turkey and berries and greens galore; he could not imagine where it all came from or how they carted it here, but he was happy for it after five days of dry rations and water. He and Shan sat apart from the rest.

"At least the food is good," Shan said. "That old woman gives me the creeps."

Zalman chuckled. He understood. When she looked at him, he felt exposed, although he was unsure exactly what he wanted to hide. Even so … "I like her."

Shan paused, staring at Zalman for a moment, chewing on more than the fruit in his mouth. He shook a bone at the larger man. "You used to work for me, you know," Shan said. "I remember that man."

"So do I."

"He was not someone you would shog with," Shan said. "But your appetites were simple. Food, women, ale. Especially women. You were someone I understood. I miss that man, Zal."

Zalman thought for a moment while he gnawed on a leg of turkey. "I'm not sure I do."

"Ever since that battle, you've taken on responsibility, become a man trusted by the *Brendel*." Shan said the name with mocking overemphasis. "It has to be killing you."

"What?"

"Not to be free to do what you want, of course. You're so busy under the thumb of Caleb's moral idea of freedom, his heightened sense of righteousness, that you don't have any fun anymore."

"You were there in the city," he said. "You know what he did and what they've done. And I am free. I can leave any time. I'm … proud to be a part of it. For now."

"Don't tell me you believe all of Caleb's crit," Shan said.

"Ain't all crit," Zalman mumbled. "And I don't know all that I believe, but I know something different is happening. Can't you see it?"

"Yes, yes, I'll admit that we've seen some amazing things. And within such times of change, opportunities arise for those who will take advantage. That is what I see." "You would.""That's right. We all have our gifts, my friend. Instead of the black market, if humanity does remove the elves from power, then I make money as a legitimate businessman. What is wrong with that?"

"You're talking about profit while people are dying in these other cities." Zal grunted. "You know the strength of the Empire and the corruption and the abuse as well as anyone. Don't you want to help Caleb and the others fight for something better?"

"Think about what you're saying. You've been abducted by the cause. What about how you used to live? The ale and women, eh? It was fun, wasn't it?"

"For a time, yeah." Zalman ran a hand over his bald head. "And I'm not a part of their cause. Never been part of any cause."

"Then when we get to Landen, let me show you the town, my friend. Once we make contact with my family, you will have the best crinkles at your fingertips."

Zalman gave a bitter scoff. "That's not why we're going. This is breakin' serious. The Empire don't shog around with this crit. If you aren't careful, you could get us all killed."

Shan adjusted the wide-brimmed hat and knuckled his mustache. "Don't worry about me," he said. "I can take care of myself. If there is a way to help with this rebellion and come out in the coin, I'll find it. Trust me."

Zalman scowled at the man. *That's the thing*, he thought. *I don't trust you at all.*

———

After dinner was over, the Ghosts gathered what was left, preparing to settle for the evening, and Eshlyn stood and stretched. She had sat in the saddle all day and now on the ground eating a lavish meal. Her back ached. She breathed in the cool air of the forest, and it smelled like moss and pine and clay, with a hint of mint. The thick canopy kept her vision from the moons and cast a deep darkness all around, but the small fires throughout the sprawling camp illuminated the area with a dim yellow light.

A young woman wove through the crowd of Ghosts and addressed Eshlyn. "Mother would like to speak with you," the woman said. "If it is a convenient time for you."

Eshlyn swallowed. "Yes, that would be to the fine."

"Good," the young woman said. "Then come with me."

She led Eshlyn back the way she came and to the tall green tent that belonged to Mother Natali. The young woman held the flap open and bowed. Eshlyn entered the tent and the flap closed behind her.

A lamp lit the interior with a low white light. Mother Natali sat cross-legged at the back of the small space, just enough for perhaps four or five people to sleep. Blankets were folded and piled in the corner. A wooden tray sat before the Mother, and on the tray was a clay pot with two clay mugs.

Mother Natali smiled at Eshlyn. She gestured with a bony hand at the bare spot across from her. "Please. Sit."

Eshlyn sat, cross-legged like the Mother.

"Do you like tea?" Mother said as she reached for the handle to the pot. Eshlyn could see steam coming from the pot.

"I do. But I should serve you." She was unsure of the right thing to do. Mother was an elder and a revered woman, and in Manahem, Eshlyn would have been expected to serve. But this was also Mother's home, of a sort.

"You are my guest," Mother Natali said. "I will serve, if you are not opposed."

"I am not."

Mother poured the hot tea into the mugs, a dark but minty smell. Eshlyn waited until Mother lifted her mug, and she did the same, blowing across the hot liquid before taking a sip.

She coughed when she tasted the tea, sweeter than she imagined. It was thick with mint and honey. *So that is where the smell of mint came from,* she thought.

Mother Natali sipped the sweet tea with a satisfied grin upon her face. "Drink it, daughter," Mother said. "We have much bitterness in our lives already, and more to come, I imagine. Take the sweet moments when you have them."

Eshlyn thought of her son, Javyn, and hoped he was safe and happy. But she missed him. She had never been without him for this long. She more than missed him. She ached for him.

"I thought that you and I should talk and visit," Mother said. "Have some tea together."

"I am glad you made time for me."

"Made time?" Mother chuckled. "Lady Eshlyn, you are the reason I asked to see your group before you left."

Eshlyn was sipping her tea, and some went down the back of her throat as she coughed and cleared her throat. "Me?"

"I wonder if you know who you are."

Eshlyn frowned and sipped her tea.

"You feel divided, pulled in every direction," Mother continued. "And even though most see you as confident and wise, you mostly feel unsure."

"Yes. How did you know?"

Mother chuckled. "I am a woman, Lady, and I have lived for a long time. It takes no supernatural revelation to see those things. I have experienced them myself."

Eshlyn sighed. "I am a mother and an elder and a widow, and now," glimpsing down at the sword at her side, "a *Sohan-el* I suppose. All these responsibilities compete for my attention and time, and it is maddening."

"I understand."

"Any advice you can give would be welcome."

"I cannot give you all that you seek," Mother said. "And what I can give will only frustrate you further. But you are strong enough. You are all of them at once. You must be all of them at once."

"But how?" she whispered.

"That is what you must find on this journey. That is your path. I wouldn't tell you if I did not think you could bear to know. You have lost so much, Lady. And you will lose so much more. We all will."

"More? What do you know?"

"That war is coming," Mother said. "It is here. And many will yet die. Great sorrow is ahead. I was here for the last war. I only pray to El that the end of this great sorrow will be joy and freedom."

"Wait. You were here for the last war? The War of Liberation?"

"Yes."

"But that was over three hundred years ago," Eshlyn said.

"That is true."

Eshlyn whispered. "How old are you?"

Mother set down her tea upon the wooden tray. "I was born here in the forest. I was but a girl when Tanicus swept across the land and laid so much of it to ruin, rebuilding it in his own image.

"My grandmother was an elf, and so I have grown old but slower than a human. It is not the blessing you may believe it to be. I have outlived my family, watched as they all died one way or another.

"Now my family is the people of this forest, and helping them survive and thrive has been my path. You must find your own path, as I have."

Mother Natali picked up her tea again and took a sip.

Eshlyn set down her mug and rose to leave.

"Stay a while longer, Lady," Mother said. "And finish your tea. You will leave us soon enough. Remember to savor the sweet moments while you have them."

Eshlyn sat and watched while Mother refilled her cup.

Mother smiled at her before taking another drink. "Or create them if you have to. The fate of the world might depend upon it."

CHAPTER 6

A GOOD HEART

Tamya worked with the Citywatch in the morning but trained with the army in the afternoons.

Every soldier trained in every discipline: the sword, the spear, and the bow, an hour each. Caleb wished every soldier to be competent in every weapon, flexible, the opposite of the specialization and strict structure of the Kryan legions.

Tamya was a platoon captain of Aden's division. This meant she was forced to spend a great deal of time with the young man. Almost every day. It was rare for Caleb to give a day off of training for either the *Sohan-el* or the army. They would have to fight soon, he said, and they needed to be ready.

The day's rounds of group training were over, and she was free to work as she pleased. Tamya found an unoccupied corner of the field and pulled out her swords, perfectly weighted by Bweth for her, and she began to go through the forms Athelwulf and Esai taught her. Aside from Caleb, Esai was the most experienced with the skill of using two swords, and he had trained her. Now that he left, she trained by herself.

Hema – her pet bloodwolf – lay quietly nearby, his snout across his forelegs, bored.

Tamya remembered when she came across the bloodwolf den in the forest, hidden well within the brush. Tamya would not have found it if not for the crying.

Running through the forest with another Ghost as part of her initial instruction under Athelwulf, she had heard the weak whimper off to her right and slowed. The young woman with her didn't hear it, and she huffed at Tamya, impatient. But Tamya ignored the young woman. She stopped and froze, listening. Through the sound of the breeze through the branches overhead, the sound reached her again. It was to her right. She moved toward it.

The young woman with her had followed, just as intrigued. Tamya came upon the copse of trees, pulling back thick brush to expose a small area, a nest of some sort that had been carefully constructed with dead leaves and twigs. Within the center of the small den were six small pups with red fur.

"Oh," the young woman had said. "Bloodwolf pups."

Five were dead, their bodies stiff already. But one still drew breath and made a pitiful little noise. Tamya was amazed she could hear it while running. It sounded so quiet then.

"Must've belonged to one of the bloodwolves you met along the road," the young woman said.

Met along the road? Those beasts almost killed her and the people with her. She owned the scars to prove it. They still ached.

The young woman then pulled out her gladus. "This one is the only one still alive. Might as well put it out of its misery."

Tamya reached out and stayed her hand, glaring at her. "What?"

"It is suffering," the young woman said to her. "It is a mercy to kill it. No other wolf has come to claim it or nurse it to health. And even if one did, this pup would become a fierce beast we might have to fight again sometime. Much easier and simpler to kill it now."

The young woman raised the short sword to end the life of the little pup.

Tamya knew the fear of the bloodwolves, better than most perhaps. The young woman made sense, but Tamya couldn't do it. She could fight and kill a ferocious animal out to have her for lunch, but she couldn't bring herself to end the life of this crying, whimpering pup. She didn't know why.

"Stop," she interjected, and the young woman did, her brows rising at Tamya. "I'll take it. Nurse it to health."

The young woman laughed at her there in the midst of the forest, but she lowered the sword. "You will take one as a pet?"

"Hasn't it been done before?"

The woman chuckled again. "No one would be that maddy to try to have a bloodwolf as a pet. They are wild killers. They hunt us and anything else that moves in the forest."

"This one didn't."

"But it will."

"Perhaps." She reached down and picked up the pup. "But I will take him with me just the same."

The young woman shrugged. "You'll have to talk to Ath about it, but it is your choice."

Tamya had gone back to the camp with the pup in her arms. Athelwulf watched her bring it to him, and he listened to her story without a word.

"You want to keep it," he said.

"Yes."

"How will you nurse it back to health? Do you know how?"

"No," she admitted. "Will you help me?"

He gave her a blank stare for a long minute. "I will let you keep this animal, and I will help you save its life, if possible." Then his dark eyes hardened. "But it is an animal that cannot be tamed, Tamya. You must realize that. A killer will always lurk within him. The first time I believe he is a danger to this camp, I will kill him myself."

She assented. She had not meant to tame it. Just save it.

Over the following ninedays, she used goat's milk and then mushed up venison and turkey to feed the pup. He recovered quickly and followed her everywhere she went. It made the camp nervous, but they learned to ignore it, however some would lay a hand on their gladus when she came near with the animal. When it came time for a name, Athelwulf named him. Hema.

"What does that mean?" she had asked him.

"*Wrath* in the First Tongue," he said.

She let the name stick and brought him with her when Ath and the other Ghosts came to join Caleb.

Now in the yard in Ketan, separate from the rest of the army, it was just Tamya and her bloodwolf. He was not a pet and never would be. Hema was a friend. He watched her lazily as she made her body and mind a weapon with those two thin, short swords, turning and moving through a dance of death with unseen enemies.

With Hema close to her, she felt safe, protected. She understood the irony after her experience with a pack of the beasts in the Saten Forest, and she noticed the fearful and wary looks from others when he was near. They could shog off.

"Esai taught you well," she heard Aden say behind her.

It startled her, but she didn't react. She was motionless for a moment, in a low crouch, her legs far apart, one sword high, the other in a low guard. She stood but didn't answer him.

She did frown over at Hema, though. The wolf would growl when anyone came close to her. Why didn't he growl when Aden was near? The wolf yawned.

Aden walked towards her, wiping his sweaty face with the back of his sleeve. "You know, I'm surprised you didn't want to go with Athelwulf to Oshra," he said. "Weren't you born there?"

She glared at him. He asked too many questions, always fishing for information about her past. He had watched her husband burn at the stake and knew the elves killed her little baby. What more did the shogger need to know?

"Ain't no reason to go back," she said. "Nothing there for me anymore."

The image of a garden in a palace came unbidden to her mind. Blood on everything. She dismissed it as quickly as she could.

"Okay," Aden said. He sniffed the air, cooler now that the sun was setting. "Some of the other platoon captains were going to get together and play a round of Tablets after dinner. You want to come?"

She didn't even bother answering. He always asked, and she always declined. Taking out a smooth stone from the pocket of her breeches, she began to sharpen one of her swords.

"Well, I guess it is good night, then," he said and gave her an awkward wave. "Good night."

She forced a half smile and watched him leave.

Aden was a good man and a fine leader for the division. He didn't have much experience in war or battle, just the recent battle of Ketan, so he brought his platoon captains together as much as he could to get their counsel and advice. He used his lack of knowledge to build a team, and that was admirable. In a battle, they would fight to the death for one another. Tamya liked that. They would kill a lot of elves that way.

But Aden's heart was good. Too good. Too pure. She had known men with good hearts before. They were dangerous.

✦

Carys and the other five travelers left Mother Natali's camp early and traveled south for another two days before they reached the fork in the road at the northern edge of the Desert of Rodria.

Before they left, the Ghosts gave them a host of supplies, and the travelers' saddlebags were bursting from the dried venison and fruits and full water bags, all things they would need as they rode through the dry waste of the desert.

Athelwulf had them camp for the night where the road split, one to the southeast towards Veradis and Landen, one to the southwest to the nation of Lior. They would spend one last night together before they went their separate ways.

As they settled in for the night, Athelwulf went off alone, sitting on a large boulder, viewing the three moons of Eres and smoking his pipe. Carys followed him. She climbed up the stone and sat next to him, enjoying the scent of his tobacco. He smiled down at her, a brotherly welcome.

They sat next to each other for a long time in silence. Athelwulf was as much family to her as Caleb. She leaned into him and rested her head on his shoulder.

"Why are goodbyes so difficult?" she asked.

"Because we were not created for them. We were created to love and love deeply, close to one another. El designed us to live forever with one another."

"How do you know that?"

"Because we desire it," he said. "And because one day, after this life is over, we will have that desire fulfilled in the Everworld. For now, we fight and struggle. But there will be a joy we cannot understand."

"There is joy here, too," Carys said.

"Yes," he said. "And deep love, as well. But since we were designed for that next place, we grieve when we part on this side. It is right that we do. To have sorrow and grieve means we've let our hearts be open to others and received them into ourselves. Like you did to me."

"Me?" she laughed. "It was you that took in that little girl and helped her to live without being so breakin' angry and hurt all the time."

"You were not as far away as you think," he said. "It was an honor to watch you heal and grow into the woman you've become."

She didn't speak because she thought that if she did, she would cry. And she wanted to be strong.

"You must lead those men, Carys," he said with a gesture at Zalman and Shan sitting apart from the camp again.

"They do what I say," she said.

"They submit out of duty, not friendship," he said. "Leadership is more than getting others to obey."

"You want me to be friends with the Rat?" she said, sitting up and blinking at him. "And that womanizing brute?"

"If you want your mission to succeed, then yes. How can you prove to the people of Landen that there is a better way if you must fight with the men you are to lead? That is the way of the elves and the world. Not the way of Yosu and El."

Carys squinted at him. She hated it when the man was right.

"You know the man I am now, but you did not know the man I was twenty years ago."

"Oh?" she said, now curious. "And what type of man were you?"

"Worse than those men, I guarantee you," Ath said. "Much. I was so lost, Carys. So lost." He regarded the dark sky again. The three moons were off to the north. His eyes glistened. Was he crying?

He gazed down at her again. "The Rat is lost in his own greed. But are so many men different? That is what the elves have taught them. It is what he had to learn to survive in a place like Landen and among the Dygol. He must be taught something greater. "Zalman is different. He possesses an honor that he, himself, may not understand. It is why Caleb trusts him even though the man struggles through his own vices. He is not your enemy. He will help you."

There *was* an honor to Zalman she didn't quite understand, an integrity despite the rest of him that so infuriated her.

"I'll do my best," she said.

"Knowing you?" Ath said. "That will be more than enough."

Chapter 7

From Whence Comes the Light

Three figures crouched on the far side of the Rumer River, water rushing by them in a torrent. It was a month past the first thaw of spring, and the snow and ice of the mountains were melting and running down into the river. The Kulbrim Dam helped decrease the strength of the water, but not enough to make swimming the river an easy task.

Across the river from their position was the great city of Ketan.

The night was dark. They had waited until there was an overcast sky, hiding the light of the moons.

One of the figures lifted a short bow and fired an arrow across the rushing water, a light but strong elven cord tied to the fletching. The arrow hit its mark, the post of one of the nearest docks. It was past the middle of the night, and the docks were deserted. The city was asleep, and while the elves were capable of handling any threat, they preferred to enter the city without incident. It would make fulfilling their mission more likely.

They tied the other end of the cord to a tree on their side of the river. First, two of the elves made it across the river with their weapons and cloaks in packs on their back. The third elf, the strongest swimmer, untied the cord from the tree and the other two pulled him across.

Soaked, they scanned the dock to confirm they were alone. The three elves all removed their packs, clothing themselves in shimmering dark gray cloaks that melted in the shadows, and then armed themselves.

The first elf – Synal – was armed with a metal whip and a gladus. The second – Chumas – held two *wacyr*, weapons that had short blades extending from both sides of a black handle. The third – Nyus – was covered with pockets that held throwing daggers. He also carried a gladus on his hip.

There was no leader among them. They had no concern for their own safety or life. They had only one thought: the target. With that singular focus, they were given information, which they each memorized – a map of the city among other things. And they were given three names from the reports by the former Steward and First Captain.

Caleb. Eshlyn. Aden.

A noise from the other end of the dock and the three elves scattered. Chumas leapt upon the nearest boat, to his left. Synal moved to his right and dropped to hang off the dock. Nyus pulled two daggers from his body and ran down the pier towards the noise, his own feet soundless. He melted into the shadow behind a large post just as a man turned the corner.

The man was not dressed as any sort of guard. He wore plain clothes, clutching a thin jacket against the night chill of the early spring.

Even though soaked to the skin, Nyus and the others did not feel the chill. Wraith did not feel such things.

Stumbling down the dock, the man muttered to himself. Nyus listened but didn't catch anything that related to his mission, so he didn't care.

The man neared the elf's position, and when he got within three mitres, Nyus slid from the shadow and threw both daggers. Nyus heard the man gasp as the daggers sunk into his chest, his face twisted in pain and confusion, then he dropped to the wooden deck, dead.

Nyus stood over the man with daggers in both hands again, making sure the man was dead and passing his eyes over the rest of the area. He heard nothing.

The other two Wraith emerged from their hiding places and helped Nyus retrieve his two daggers and throw the dead man into the river. The swift river carried the dead body far into the night.

The three elves moved through the shadows along the docks and approached the city. They found guard at two entrances, both standing alert. The third entrance was a door to the back of a warehouse, locked with no guard. But they could open a locked door. Synal pulled small metal rods from his belt and picked the lock on the heavy, thick iron door. It opened with a creak, and they entered the warehouse, locking the door again behind them.

It was pitch black in the warehouse, and they found their way into the main storage area, climbing through a window and out into the empty street of northern Ketan two hours before dawn.

The Wraith were now in the city.

Half-starved and dehydrated, Galen lay on the stone floor of his small cell, shivering, shaking, and sleeping in fits.

He didn't know how long he had been in the dark place. It was somewhere beneath the palace, a dungeon. He had been in so much pain when they brought him down, and it had been so dark, pitch black. For days there had been no light. Someone would give him a cup of water, but not at any regular interval so he could gauge the time. He felt lost in time and place.

As the master of the Bladeguard, he had trained elves to survive in these circumstances. He clung to his training through the endless hours of darkness, thirst, and hunger. They tried to break him before they interrogated him. But no elf knew better than Galen how to endure torture and questioning. He helped write the book on it.

A noise in the hall, footsteps getting closer, sandals against stone. Galen focused, trying to memorize every detail. A hint of light peeked from under the door to his cell.

The door opened with a loud creak, and the small lamp was blinding. Galen cowered against the back corner of his small cell, throwing an arm across his face.

"I am here to teach you, Galen."

Tanicus. The Emperor who was also a Worldbreaker.

Tebelrivyn, the system of magic that was also called Worldbreaking, manipulated the forces and materials of nature. Only elves were gifted in the discipline and most only possessed one of the powers of manipulation: over the mind, stone, vegetation, water, air, or life. But the magic came with a cost. Manipulating one of the forces weakened the nature of certain natural material. For instance, manipulating the mind of a being also caused memory loss. Creating flame or changing the composition of the air in a room could remove all oxygen from the same area.

The magic, therefore, was powerful, but with a price.

In the beginning, those gifted were also the Nican, the priests of the nine elven gods. The more powerful the sorcerer, the higher rank within the religion.

There were a few, however rare, that possessed all six of the abilities associated with *Tebelrivyn*, the original High Nican. Their power was unlimited, but it drove them mad and destroyed the fabric of Eres. Those were called Worldbreakers.

Hence, after much abuse and several major events of great destruction, the major governments of the world outlawed *Tebelrivyn* – first the lands of men, then dwarves, and last the elves.

And when Galen had confronted Tanicus in the Imperial throne room, the Emperor used two of the abilities, air and life. Legend had it, if an elf possessed more than one, he or she possessed them all.

Tanicus had kept this secret for centuries. He was a Worldbreaker – one of the most powerful beings in the history of Eres.

Galen groaned. It made more sense now, why Tanicus had felt so threatened those centuries before by Elowen and then King Judai, the last *Sohan-el*, and why he sought to kill them and replace the *Sohan-el* with the Bladeguard: legend told that a warrior with an unforged sword was all that could stand against a Worldbreaker.

Tanicus brought a stool with him, a golden stool, and he sat upon it. "Tell me, Galen. What do you know of this imaginary god you believe in?"

Galen did not look up; he couldn't.

"I – I ... what?"

"You told me you believe in this god – this El – correct?"

Trying to control his breathing, Galen shivered, his body weakened and wracked.

"Yes," he answered the Emperor.

"So tell me what you know of him."

Galen tried to focus and choose his words carefully. "He is the one who created the world, the living races, divided the one race into three according to their sin, and he sent Yosu to teach us how to live and become one again."

Tanicus gave a mocking chuckle. "Yes, the Creator. So disappointing that you have believed such a myth after being taught better. But I am here to help. There was no Creation, as you call it. All came from the forces of nature coming together and forming what we see, which is why we worship them. They give us power. They give me power."

Galen shuddered.

"And what evidence do we have that the races were all one?" Tanicus asked.

The Emperor waited for an answer. Galen could not give him one. So much knowledge had been lost.

"Exactly. Laughable. We are as we have always been, and elves the greatest of them all."

"Which justifies why you must rule them?" Galen stated.

"Yes, we must. It is our responsibility. Consider how the powers of nature have gifted us. Who could deny our superiority based on the evidence?"

"El denies it," Galen said.

"Of course he does," Tanicus said. "The god no one sees or hears tells us to disbelieve what we see around us, what we can prove to be true? That only makes him evil, if there is such a thing."

Galen gritted his teeth. "He is not evil. Only good."

"You truly believe that?"

"Yes," Galen said. "And more."

"Oh?"

"Because he is good, he is just. He remembers the innocent and the weak and those who suffer. He remembers the oppressor. And there will be a reckoning."

Tanicus laughed again. "How quaint, your ideas of right and wrong. There is no good or evil, only power. But for the sake of argument, tell me, do you believe what I have done to the men of Ereland is unjust?"

Galen paused but answered. "Yes."

"Then if El is good," Tanicus said. "Why did he not stop me?"

"We were a part of our own downfall, and man is no different," Galen said. "He must participate in his own redemption, see the truth for himself and choose it if he is to be free."

"That makes El an evil god."

"No ..."

"Oh, yes. He is good but he does not stop what you say is evil? Well, evil by your own definition, that is. And he leads you to believe lies? Only an evil god would do such a thing."

"They are not lies ..."

"Let us see if he will stop what I am about to do to you," Tanicus said.

Galen was overwhelmed by sudden torment in every centimitre of his being, as if every part of him were being stretched and pulled apart. Every nerve cried out at his torture, and he could not contain the scream. He possessed no control over himself in that moment. He writhed on the stone floor amidst his own waste.

Tanicus spoke, his voice coming distant to Galen. "I am taking away the life from your body and strengthening my own form with your energy. I am feeding upon your very soul and storing that energy within me. If I complete the process, you will die, just a husk of an elf. Think on it, the greatest swordmaster in the world brought to nothing within a moment."

But the Emperor did not finish the process. Galen felt himself thinning, wasting away, dying. He knew death would come in the next few seconds. Then Tanicus ceased.

Galen did not have the strength to move. Peering down at his arm, it was only skin and bones.

"Do you pray, Galen?"

The Blademaster did not answer. *So much pain.*

Tanicus repeated himself. "Do you pray?"

Galen managed a weak rasp. "Yes."

"Then pray. I want to hear you pray to your god. Ask him to save you."

"No."

"Come now. I can keep you in this state for an indefinite period of time. It will last as long as you disobey."

He did not have the power to resist, and to his shame, he only wished for a relief from the agony. So he obeyed. "Great and mighty El. I ... I ask that you do as you will. Show me your goodness."

"Ask him to save you."

Galen moaned, "And that ... you save me."

Tanicus sat silent in the light of that dim, yet blinding, lamp, and crossed his arms, waiting.

Nothing happened except miserable travail.

"We could wait longer," the Emperor said. "But I have made my point. He cannot save you or help you. But I can."

Then Tanicus stretched out his hand to Galen, and he felt the life enter his body again. Compared to the pain from before, it was ecstasy, like pure pleasure poured into his body and mind. His eyes fluttered. He was alive.

Tanicus stood, gripping the golden stool in one hand and the lamp in the other. "Remember. That was me. I am your god now. You were once my greatest weapon against those that oppose me. You will be again."

And then the Emperor left the cell, closing the door behind him, throwing Galen into darkness.

The Blademaster of the Citadel realized something in that moment. He could not endure this. No training could possibly prepare him or help him now. It was only a matter of time before Tanicus broke him.

Galen wept in complete and utter despair.

Chapter 8

The Wraith

"Leave the city?" Lyam cried. "You've got to be joking. Why?"

"That's what the army is for," Caleb said to the group of men and women before him. "What they are designed for, to engage the Kryan legions outside these walls."

Caleb perused the leadership around the table – the division leaders. Chamren, Iletus, and Eliot Te'Lyn were also in attendance.

It had been a ninedays since Carys, Eshlyn, and the others left for Oshra and Landen.

Eliot had been elected as the next head elder, taking over for his daughter. It had been an easy choice between him and the former mayor of Roseborough, Mr. De'Sy, but there was never a sure bet when it came to voting or politics, unless you somehow fixed the results. Caleb was glad to see Eliot chosen by the people of Ketan.

"I thought we built an army to be better prepared for when the elves came here," Lyam said, and a few muttered agreement.

"Leave and go where?" Aden asked.

"There is a legion a ninedays away or less in Taggart," Caleb said. "We need to get the army out and mobile before we're trapped in the city."

"What do you mean, 'trapped'?" Lyam said. "This is the safest place we can be."

"Kryus won't just sit outside the breakin' walls," Bweth said. "They will bring siege works. They'll have the numbers and try to starve us out."

"We need to have a plan for supplies, then," Chamren said. "We made it through the winter, but we won't have enough to last a siege."

"What about the farmland south of here?" Xander asked. "Plenty there."

"They would be killed by the legions," Bweth answered. "Sure as iron, they would."

Not for the first time, Caleb was impressed by Bweth's knowledge of the Kryan military. He knew she had worked with them as a blacksmith, making weapons, before being assigned here in Ketan to provide blades for the Bladeguard. But with her martial skill and knowledge of Kryan strategy, she knew more than a blacksmith should. He made a mental note to ask her sometime.

"What about the dwarves?" Eliot asked Bweth. "Could we send word to them? Trade or ask for help?"

"If we could sail across the Arpad Ocean, that could work," Bweth answered. "But how?"

"All we have are fishing boats, merchant river ships," Chamren said. "Nothing that could make the trip with any certainty. And the route to the ocean is through the frozen north. Dangerous, especially as the ice melts with spring coming on."

Caleb ran a hand down his face. "The army needs to be mobile. We could get supplies from the Ghosts and maybe some towns along the way. The Kryan legions move slow. Outside the walls, we choose our own battleground."

"This is maddy," Lyam chuckled, mirthless. "We have the strongest walls in Eres. Why not use them? If you take the army, what will we have left? The Watch?"

Hunter, Bweth's husband, entered the room, and he sat next to his wife. He had a patch over one eye with a vicious scar across his cheek, but his other eye softened as he shared a smile with his wife. His dark skinned hand covered her light toned one.

"You're correct," Caleb said. "We can't take the whole army. We need to discuss the men needed on the wall if the Empire does come. The rest can leave with the army." He turned to Chamren. "How could we get more supplies? Plant to the north? Maybe get volunteers to go south? Planting season is on us."

Lyam threw up his hands in exasperation. "Planting? That is suicide if the elves come here as you say."

"It is suicide if we don't," Xander said. "Will the Ghosts be able to supply us from the south or the east if Legions show up at our gates?"

Bweth cleared her throat, opening her mouth to speak but was cut off by Lyam.

"Will dead farmers be able to?" Lyam responded.

"What about up north?" Aden asked. "Those men of the north probably farmed up there, to the sure."

"Yes," Chamren said. "If we could keep the docks open, and we could get volunteers to start farms and settlements north of the Kulbrim Dam, then we could keep a supply to the city."

"But the elves aren't afraid of the water like those demics," Lyam said. "It is the same problem. If Kryus finds out about those settlements, and we're under siege here, then they can destroy them as easily as to the south."

"Gentlemen," Bweth said.

Caleb stifled a yawn. He had not been sleeping well. "True. Which is why the army needs to be out there," he pointed over their heads but glowerd at Lyam, "keeping the Legions on the run and choosing the field of battle. We could disrupt their supply lines, strike at opportune times, hide in the Saten if we need to."

"What will keep them from chasing you *and* sieging this city?" Lyam asked.

"They will be chasing the *Brendel*," Aden said.

"Gentlemen!" Bweth shouted.

The room became quiet.

"Breakin' men," Bweth muttered. "Shoggit if you don't make it difficult to make a crittin' announcement."

Caleb turned to her. "Announcement?"

Bweth peeked at Hunter again. He smiled at her with his black eyes, and she blushed again. Why was she acting like a schoolgirl all of a sudden? They were already married.

"We are pregnant," she said, and Hunter took her hand.

The whole room responded with shouts of congratulations.

"How long have you known?" Eliot asked.

"We are three months along," Bweth said. "We wanted to wait until it was farther along until we told people."

Pregnancies between different races were prone to miscarriage. They were possible but rare. He laughed in delight. "I am happy for you both," Caleb said. "So good to hear a bit of good news. Life in the world. It is a good thing. Congratulations, Hunter." Caleb stood and reached across the table, shaking the man's hand.

Everyone else in the room did the same, shaking hands, patting them on the back. As the room settled and they sat again, Caleb said, "New order of business, I guess. Who will you choose to take over your division?"

"I'm sorry," Bweth said. "Take over my division?"

"Yeah," Caleb said. "Now that you're pregnant, I thought you'd ..." He read the warning on Hunter's face and trailed off.

"I'm not stepping down, if that's what you're implying," Bweth said, frowning. "And why would I?"

"Well, I just thought ..."

"My grandmother bore my father on the slopes of Mount Kodobe during the battle of Kodobe," Bweth said. "They cut the shoggin' cord and then she got back up and killed a few elves before the battle ended. Then she nursed my da for the first time."

Caleb raised his hands in surrender. "I apologize," he said. "I assumed. Won't happen again."

"Thank you," Bweth said and grinned at him.

Caleb said, "I appreciate your input today, all of you. We will have to decide on the best way to take a force out to fight the Empire and still leave a sufficient force to hold out here until help can arrive, as well as supplies during a possible siege. Let's think details and hammer them out tomorrow night."

Eliot smiled and stood. "I agree."

The rest of the group began to break up, talking amongst themselves. Hunter scrunched his shoulders. Caleb chuckled at him. Bweth let him give her a kiss on the cheek before she took her leave. Hunter walked her home.

One after one, they left. Lyam seemed frustrated and quiet. Caleb made a note to speak to him later. The rest of the group was full of joy at the impending birth, speaking of it to each other as they filtered out.

Chamren stayed behind. "You seem tired," he said to Caleb.

"I'll be fine," Caleb said. "I haven't been sleeping well."

"And you've been working harder than ever," Chamren said. "Making sure that the election was handled well and helping Eliot with the transition."

"There is a lot to be done," Caleb said. "And no one here, besides Iletus and Bweth, knows what we're really up against. No matter what we do, we are outmatched. El will have to help us."

Chamren grinned. "As he did before."

"Yes, he did."

"Any reason to believe he will not again?"

Caleb chuckled. "Aren't I the one that's supposed to give these inspiring speeches? I am the *Brendel*, after all."

"You can't do it all," Chamren said. "Go home. It is getting late."

"I just wanted to take these maps back to my office across town, check on things at the coliseum, and then I'll be on my way home," Caleb said and gathered the maps on the table.

Chamren took the maps from him. "You let me do that. I would like to check on things on that side of city anyway, and my home is closer. Get to bed. Get some sleep."

He wanted to argue with Chamren, but the man was correct. He did need the rest. Caleb allowed the man to take the papers and maps. "If you insist," he said.

"I do," Chamren said.

—+—

Tamya waited outside of the administration building where Caleb and the others met. She sat on the steps and stroked Hema's red fur.

The *Sohan-el* and other division captains made their way out of the building, talking. As Aden exited, talking with Hunter, Tamya stood. He passed her, and she walked with him. He raised a brow when he noticed her, but then gestured to Hunter.

"Hunter and Bweth are pregnant," he said with that goofy smile.

"Oh," was all she said. She tried not to think of her baby's head being bashed against a stone.

"Congratulations again," Aden told Hunter.

"Thank you," Hunter said, regarding Tamya and her bloodwolf with a wary look.

Aden told him goodnight and then whirled on Tamya, laying his hand on his sword.

That unforged sword.

"You may not be happy for them," Aden said. "And I can understand. But you could pretend, you know?"

She scowled at him and crossed her arms. "Are you going to lecture me?"

He rolled his eyes. "You were the one waiting here. Did you need something?"

She cleared her throat. "I know Caleb is thinking about getting the army ready to move," she said. "Did they decide anything in there or just more talk?"

"You could ask him," Aden said. "Or anyone. Why me?"

"Because you're my division captain," she said. "Forget it. I'll ask him in the morning." She moved to leave. "Come on, Hema."

"Wait a minute," Aden said, and she hesitated. He sighed. "Walk me home."

"What?"

"I'm tired and I'm going home. If you want me to tell you about the meeting, walk with me. Your place isn't far from there."

His ears were too big for his head, and that nose was too sharp. She glared at him for another moment.

Aden scoffed and tread away.

She glanced down at Hema. The wolf peered up at her with questioning eyes. "You're no help," she told him.

And then she fell into step next to Aden, the wolf padding along behind.

He told her about the meeting as they walked to his house. They strode through the archway to the main thoroughfare, took a right and down another street that led to a row of townhouses.

"I hope our division goes with the force that moves out," she said. *More opportunity to fight and kill elves*, she thought.

"We'll see," Aden said as they neared his home. It had belonged to one of the elven officials, and he complained about it being too big. She was in an apartment four streets down, not far. "I'm sure a part of Caleb's plan will be allowing people to decide."

"Good," she said, stopping as he reached his door.

Aden paused as he placed his hand on the latch. "Good things can happen, you know."

She didn't answer, scratching behind Hema's ear.

"Like Bweth and Hunter," he said. "They got married right after the battle, and now she's pregnant. She's even going to keep her division, pregnant and all."

"So?"

"So, I guess I just like that they found something good in the midst of everything," he said. "They actually have something to fight for instead of against. Isn't that the way it should be?"

Tamya shook her head. *Having something to fight for meant something to lose*, she thought. How could she be happy for them when joy today only caused greater pain tomorrow?

Aden's shoulders slumped. He opened his door and said, "See you." Then he entered his house and closed the door behind him, leaving her alone with Hema.

She stood there a moment, staring at the door, hating her own fear and anger, and the fact that she couldn't say one thing nice to a man and his wife who were expecting to bring a life into the world. All she could think was to warn them ... and to make the elves pay for what they had done to her.

Just then, Hema growled and his hackles rose.

—┼—

As Caleb laid a hand upon his sword, he decided not to go to the coliseum after all. He felt like visiting the Te'Lyn home. Morgan would be there, caring for her grandson.

It had been a few days since he had checked on the boy, Eshlyn's son, and it wasn't so late that Eliot wouldn't be able to talk for a few minutes.

A hundred mitres down the street from the Te'Lyan home, a block down from the apartment building where many of the old citizens of Delaton and Roseborough lived, he saw an outline move, a figure of shadows that wasn't natural in the moonlit night.

It was something alive that wanted to keep to the shadows.

He quickened his pace, jogging in silence. Nothing that tried to keep to the shadows had good intentions.

Drawing his sword, he felt an indignant, protective feeling. This being was lurking its way toward the Te'Lyn home.

Caleb bared his teeth; he was ten mitres away from the figure.

The stalker disappeared down the alley next to the home, and Caleb broke into a sprint.

As he turned the corner and into the alley, he came to an instant halt and had to block several strikes from two *wacyr*; the double blades were dizzying in their speed. The dark cloak around the figure billowed as he spun and kicked. Caleb retreated a step and leaned back, but he came forward with a swipe of the unforged sword, which the stalker deflected.

The shadow was good.

Cursing, Caleb struck high, then low, the stalker taking steps further into the alley but able to keep Caleb's blade from finding any purchase. Caleb feinted low then struck high. As the stalker moved to block, Caleb swept the stalker's knee with his left foot, and he heard a snap as the knee buckled. The stalker made no sound of alarm or pain. His attack continued unabated, even as he stumbled, and Caleb caught a *wacyr* blade upon his left forearm, a deep cut.

Overwhelming the stalker with his strikes, Caleb waited for an opening and then kicked up and caught his opponent under the chin. The head whipped back, and the hood of the cloak dropped, revealing an elf with completely white eyes.

Caleb thrust his sword through the stalker's chest. The elf blew out a breath, in the throes of death, but managed to swipe at Caleb with a *wacyr*. Caleb ducked, the blades missing him by centimitres, and he pushed the elf assassin away from him. Then he pulled the sword free and swung the unforged blade through the assassin at the waist, cutting the elf clean in two.

Caleb looked down at both halves of the corpse and the white eyes.

There were Wraith in the city.

No one was safe.

———

Aden closed the door behind him and took a deep breath, running his hand through his dark bushy hair. He was so drawn to Tamya, but she always evaded him. Aden knew his questioning annoyed her, but she was locked within her anger and bitterness. He wished he could pull her back from that ledge, but that wasn't his job. It couldn't be.

He proceeded through the entryway and down the hallway, rubbing his face with his right hand as his left hand rested on his sword. It was dark in his house. He thought about whether he should light a lamp and read more of the Ydu tonight or just get undressed and sleep.

Aden had already read through the Ydu and the Fyrwrit twice over the winter, and he was on his third time through now. Caleb sometimes gave him a hard time about all the candles he used, reading late into the night, but Aden loved the reading, seeing new things each time through.

He also possessed two of the books from the ones Iletus brought with him, *The Tales of the Sohan-el*, most of them stories from the two or three generations after Yosu's disciples, compiled by Erryn Ka'Chel, an ancient historian, and *Elucidation of the Oracles* by Moss Ja'Dan, written five centuries ago. Both were fascinating reads, the adventures and self-sacrifice of the *Sohan-el* were inspiring, and Moss Ja'Dan possessed great insight on the prophecies of the *Brendel*, the *Arendel*, the *Daegrael*, and the *Isael*.

But he was not living a fantasy or theory of the future: he had seen the *Brendel* and the *Arendel* for himself. The *Daegrael* – the dawnlight of El – and the *Isael* – the fire of El – were mysteries. The book discussed different theories on how they were all connected, the most prevalent being that once the *Brendel* appeared, the other two would follow. Perhaps he would read more of Moss Ja'Dan before settling in for sleep.

As he entered the main room, the sword spoke to him.

Duck.

He ducked.

Something metal struck the wall to his left, and there was a shadow off to his right, moving along the far wall. The sword was in his hands in an instant, and he was fully aware of his surroundings, watching the figure move. Two more flashes of metal hurtled toward him, and he batted them away with his blade. They clattered to the ground, and he thought, *daggers*, as he stole a glance in their direction.

He lowered into a crouch and slid off to his right, keeping as much distance as he could between himself and the person in the room. Two more daggers flew his way, and he battled those away as two more followed. He dodged one and the other clipped his shoulder.

He saw the figure move across the large window while more glints of moonlight gleamed on daggers being thrown at him. He batted three but one stuck in his right shoulder and another in his hip. He stumbled as he struck two more out of the air and dodged another, but the fourth found its way into his right thigh, and he went down.

———

Chamren proceeded across the city, first down the long thoroughfare and then took a right turn down a side street that led him closer to the military complex.

He loved this city. Ketan had been his home since birth. He couldn't imagine living anywhere else, and the way the men and women of Ketan had risen to the call of freedom made him proud. And even more proud that he was able to lead and serve these people.

Chamren carried the lamp into Caleb's office at the military complex. Laying the lamp down on the desk, he arranged the maps as best he could. Yawning, he rubbed the end of his nose. He had a great deal of work to do in the morning. The transition to Eliot from Eshlyn as Head Elder took some adjustment on his part. Eliot was a fine man, but Chamren and Eshlyn had worked so well together. She was gone now.

With one last glimpse at the maps, he thought maybe he had forgotten something, a strange feeling in the back of his mind. But no, he remembered everything.

As he spun around, a strip of sharpened metal links shot out from the shadows in the corner and wrapped tight around his right arm, and as it was pulled, it cut deep into his skin, slicing until it removed his arm at the elbow.

Chamren cried out and fell to his knees. He watched his bloody forearm hit the floor with a sickening splat.

A figure moved to his right, emerging from the shadows. It was a shadow, but no, as his vision focused, he could tell it was a person under some sort of cloak. He peered down at his missing limb. He had the presence of mind to realize he was losing a lot of blood.

The cloaked person approached him, the bloody metal whip trailing behind him. The figure lifted a hand and pushed back the hood of the cloak. It was an elf with pale skin and short, cropped black hair.

But his eyes. His eyes were not natural. They were solid white and resembled death. What was a dead elf doing here in the city?

Chamren blinked slowly. His vision narrowed. He tried to stand, taking hold of the top of the desk, and he pulled himself, stumbling, to his feet.

He tried to speak, but only stammering sounds came out.

He smelled an awful stench; he had crit himself.

The elf's face twisted in disgust.

"You are not the *Brendel*," he said, but the voice was monotone and deep. No emotion. No caring. "You are not Caleb."

Chamren grabbed the stump of his right arm with his left hand, squeezing it, but the blood pumped through his fingers. He cried out with the pain. He wanted to be brave, to fight back, to make his death mean something, but he was losing consciousness. And he was so afraid. *Don't beg*, he thought. *As long as I don't beg, I'll be fine. Maybe if I reason with him.*

"Wait ..." he began, but the elf lifted his arm and flicked his wrist and the metal whip lashed around his neck. Chamren gasped and reached up with the one hand that remained of his body and grabbed the sharp links. The elf pulled hard on the whip.

And that was the last detail Chamren saw.

———

Aden crawled along the floor as the dark figure approached him. Moving caused him pain, but he had to get away from this killer. There was a chair over by the window. If he could get behind the chair and out through the window, he could escape. But he wasn't fooling himself; he couldn't move that fast.

He was near the window, but the figure in the dark cloak stood over him now with a dagger in each hand.

"Aden," the figure said with a voice but unlike any voice Aden had ever heard. There was no life within it. The figure raised the daggers to throw them down. Aden turned to get his sword up across his body.

He heard the growl just before the window imploded with the force of a bloodwolf tearing through wood and glass. The killer in a cloak revolved just enough to bear the full force of the large wolf as it ripped into him with teeth and claws, snarling.

Tamya leapt through the decimated window behind her wolf, her swords out and spinning in her hands. The bloodwolf, enraged, roared and barked as it found purchase on the killer's shoulder. The killer did not shout or cry out in pain, but he was able to roll on the ground and throw the bloodwolf off of him. Hema whimpered as he hit the floor.

But now that the wolf was out of the way, Tamya was free to attack.

Aden wondered if the killer wished for the bloodwolf again.

He faced her from the ground and raised his hands with daggers in them. She cut the hands from his arms, the appendages spinning across the room trailing blood in opposite directions.

Still no sound or noise of pain from the killer.

He tried to rise on his elbows, blood pouring from his wrists, and the hood of his cloak fell away. Aden could see white eyes reflecting the moonlight. Aden shivered.

The bloodwolf was on his feet again, snarling, his hackles up.

Tamya growled, much like the wolf, and she stepped over the killer, raised her swords, and plunged them both into his heart. He twitched and spasmed and then died.

As the killer's body fell to the floor, Hema took a few heaving breaths, and then he laid down.

"Hema!" Tamya cried, jumping over the corpse at her feet and to the wolf. Crawling over to the wolf, Aden could see in the moonlight that he was cut and bleeding from vaulting through the window. The wolf whimpered in pain as Tamya knelt beside him.

"Upstairs," Aden said. "Get blankets."

She hopped up and sprinted up the stairs, returning with blankets. Aden helped her find the deepest cuts and put pressure on the wounds.

Tamya finally scrutinized him. "Oh, crit," she said. "You're hurt."

"I'll be okay," he said. "I think. I'll keep pressure on here. You need to go get help. He needs a physician."

"You need one, too," she scolded.

"Probably," he said, feeling faint. "So hurry, okay?"

CHAPTER 9

GOING TO HUNT

The road ran southwest towards Lior. It skirted the desert rather than cutting through it, which was fortunate. While the road was dry, along the way they passed brush and tall grasses, even some tough vegetation the horses could chew on. The weather warmed significantly as they traveled south, becoming quite hot, and so the group began to sweat during the day. The horses needed more water, and the two days' ride past the Desert of Rodria was difficult on the animals. But thanks to the Ghosts, their rations were just enough.

Eshlyn lived in Manahem her whole life and never made it to the city of Ketan until her son's life was at stake. Her world had been small. She always dreamed of traveling, seeing the big world with Kenric and Javyn. She remembered a night when she and Ken laid in bed together, naked and close, and they spoke of being so successful with the farm that they could spend a season traveling to places like Landen and Asya. They laughed together; it was a silly dream, and they knew it. But it is fun to make wishes and share desires with the one you love.

She had seen the thick and ominous Forest of Saten and talked with an ancient woman. The sunrise across the desert was breathtaking in its vastness and myriad of colors. She thought the sky along the Julan Plains was big; the heavens above the Rodria was like El opening the firmament and smiling at his own handiwork. No roads ran through the Desert of Rodria, a wasteland, but the sky above it was resplendent. Did all such things come together? Death and beauty? She wondered.

After two more days along the desert, the vegetation transformed to green again, growing taller and thicker until they reached the coast of the Sea of Alin. They entered the land of Lior, and she could feel the air become more humid, coinciding with the rise of the Forest of Lior dominating the landscape to the west. The road continued to hug the coast, never closer than two hundred mitres away and always within sight.

The jungle Forest of Lior was thick with black trunks of large trees and branches with enormous dark green leaves of various shapes, bright fruit hanging from those branches in different colors: purple, red, orange, and yellow. It was loud with the noise of life, different animals within the branches of trees or roaming along the floor. It overflowed with life.

The bugs of the jungle were constant companions. Whether crawling or flying or biting or buzzing, the insects seemed to get louder and hungrier at night when she attempted to sleep.

Esai and Athelwulf kept watch overnight, working out a rotation between them. Since she found it difficult to sleep through the barrage of insects, she asked to do her part, but they refused her.

"No offense, Lady Eshlyn," Esai said. "But you don't know what to watch for. There is death in that forest for those who don't know, and even some that do."

Athelwulf simply nodded.

"Then teach me," she said. "We have time, to the sure."

So they did. They taught her of the animals that inhabited the forest, too many to really count, but most, if not all, were deadly. Jungle cats, reptiles, and insects were listed, and to be honest, she didn't catch them all. They even spoke to her of wild bosaur.

"Stay as far away from them as you can," Esai said. "You get one agitated, they will charge and spear you."

"I thought bosaur were docile beasts," she said. "Like a cow."

"They can be, when domesticated," Ath said. "But even the domesticated ones can be vicious. Very dangerous creatures."

But it was the ocean that took her breath away. The smell of the salt water, the sound of the waves – either lapping or crashing – a constant music combined to both keep her enthralled and set her at ease. She slept like never before, sucking in the salty humidity and being rocked to sleep by the Creator's heartbeat.

The first night they camped along the coast, in tall, ample blades of grass, she took the last watch of the night and watched the sunrise over the sea. The waves massaged the shore.

Watching the ocean with the dawn, she thought of her son, leagues away and safe, she hoped. Would she ever see him again? He felt so far away, and she did not know what awaited them in Oshra, besides danger and the violence of the most powerful Empire on Eres. Fear began to grip her heart again.

Savor the sweet moments. Or create them.

As Esai and Ath woke and began striking camp, she said, "I want to jump in the water."

The men shared a glance. "I'm sorry?" Esai said. Ath grinned.

Eshlyn breathed in the warm breeze coming off the water. "Would you lose all respect for me if I ran and dove into those waves?"

Esai and Ath both laughed. Athelwulf was already shedding his tunic, now bare to the waist.

"No, Lady," Athelwulf said. "We will join you." Esai was following Ath's lead, and they removed their moccasins.

She rolled up the legs of her divided skirt, stripped down to her undertunic, and removed her boots. Then she laughed – the first time she laughed in a long time – and raced towards the water. When she reached the beach, she took three long, leaping strides as the water got deeper, and then she dove into the ocean. Esai and Athelwulf were right behind her.

For just a few moments, she could believe she was alone in the world, and it felt to the fine – alone with Esai and Athelwulf, to the sure, but isolated and at peace. The world was falling apart, to be put aright again, if the prophecies were true, but for this short time she could be Eshlyn, smiling.

After swimming for an hour, she emerged from the water. Athelwulf came up to her with a creature in a shell with several arms; he carried it carefully since it had two longer limbs with pinchers.

He smiled at her. "You ever had a seanut?"

"That doesn't look like a nut," she said.

"Just a name." Athelwulf took his hands and grabbed two pieces of the animal's shell, and he pulled the living thing apart. It writhed in pain and death.

Eshlyn gulped, horrified.

Ath smiled, however, kneeling to set one half of the shell on the rocks of the shore, and he reached in with a hand and scooped out the pink paste of its flesh and held it out to her. "You eat it," he said. "It is a delicacy."

She was trying not to be sick. But she could tell that Athelwulf was offering her what was, in his mind, a gift and sharing something of his land and heritage. So she took the pink flesh, put it in her mouth, and forced herself to chew it. It tasted like salty apple and mushed pork. Eshlyn forced a smile.

Riveted by the sea again, and swallowing the seanut down, she felt both great joy and sorrow. Joy in the moment and sorrow at what lay ahead.

"How bad do you think it will be?"

"In Oshra?"

Esai was coming out of the water, breathing hard but beaming.

"Yes," she said. "In Oshra."

"Kryus has a tight hold on that city," Athelwulf said. "Long before the War of Liberation, the elves took advantage of the division between the tribes in Lior." He shook his head, frowning. "The tribes may not even know why they hate the other. But Kryus has them convinced the power and authority of the Empire is the only thing that keeps them from complete self-destruction."

Eshlyn sniffed. "Is that true?"

Athelwulf shrugged and squinted at the sun in the east. "If we are to believe the report from Iletus, not proving them wrong, are they?"

"Doesn't sound like it, to the sure," Eshlyn said. "But that's why we're going, isn't it?"

"It is," Athelwulf said.

They were silent for a moment, watching Esai shake the water from his body and approach them, the red and purple sky behind him.

"It is beautiful here," Eshlyn declared.

"Oh, yes, Lady," Ath said. "Very beautiful. I almost forgot how beautiful."

Esai stood by them now, and he stared down at the rocks below.

"Seanut! Ah, good!" he said, bending down and pressing his face into the meat of the half shell. He ate it with slurping noises.

Among the peaceful waves and idyllic dawn that morning, Eshlyn was sick now, vomiting upon the beach.

—+—

Chamren's coffin was set within the arch that led to the palace estate, a closed coffin due to the mangled body, and the whole city of Ketan passed by and paid their respects. Some laid spring flowers upon the coffin, others stones with short phrases or words upon them. It took the whole morning. A few former citizens of Delaton and Roseborough played somber dirges for hours, several of them they wrote, different men and women switching out and taking the lead vocals. The *Sohan-el* and other leadership of the city stood there the entire time, a few singing along if they knew the words, but mostly silent.

After the last of the citizens said their goodbyes to Chamren, the *Sohan-el* and Eliot, Hunter, and Bweth took him back to the yard by the palace, dug the grave, and laid him within it.

Caleb spoke. "We have lost a great friend and brother today. Even before he learned of El and Yosu, Chamren's heart understood what it meant to be free, to be selfless. Once he heard of El, it was like he had been called home again. Now his home is in the Everworld, and if we are lucky, we will join him there when our time is done here.

"The Empire has struck. More will come. Wraith, legions, they will come. But we will honor Chamren by fighting for what he believed in, the freedom of men."

Caleb thought of the Prophet. *Take care of him, Uncle Reyan.*

Eliot uttered a short prayer, Aden read from the scriptures, and the group began to leave. Caleb stayed, gazing down at the fresh dirt.

Aden stood next to him, leaning on a crutch, and his shoulder was wrapped in bandages under his tunic.

"How's your leg?" Caleb asked.

"Physician say not that bad. Heal in a few days."

Quick healer, Caleb thought. He had heard the young man's injuries were far worse. "The wolf?"

"Lost a lot of blood, but physician stitched him up. He'll recover. Tamya hasn't left his side."

"Good," Caleb said. "That's good."

Iletus had hovered off to the side, and he now approached them, standing on the other side of Caleb.

"He gave his life for me," Caleb said. "He died in my place."

"Would you have given yours for him?"

"Yes." For him, Reyan, and so many others.

"Then it is as it should be," Aden said.

"How did you get so breakin' smart?" Caleb said.

Aden peered at him with tears gleaming in his eyes. "I believe you know better than most," he said.

The image of Reyan, the Prophet, lying dead upon the floor of the inn in Biram came to his thoughts, along with Earon, his cousin the traitor, running from the room.

Caleb cleared his throat. "Three Wraith."

"Three Wraith," Iletus said.

"They were after me, Aden, and Eshlyn," Caleb said.

"Yes," Iletus said. "But they did not know Lady Eshlyn had left. They would have killed her family. You saved their lives."

"And Tamya and Hema saved Aden," Caleb muttered.

"To the sure," Aden said.

"But one remains," Caleb said. He turned to Iletus. "Galen never told me what exactly the Wraith are, always avoided the subject when it came up."

"That's because he didn't know," Iletus said. "No one does. We know they are skilled martial artists, but we don't know how they become what they are. We know what they do. They feel no pain or emotion. Their one focus is whatever mission Tanicus gives them. You must kill them to stop them. They are the perfect assassins."

"Saw all that," Aden said. "What about the white eyes? How do they get those white eyes? And the black writing on their body?"

When examining the bodies, one of the physicians called Caleb and others in to show them blackened scars, like dead festering skin on the bodies of the Wraith. The blackened skin was some sort of script, ancient runes that no one in Ketan could recognize – not Iletus or Caleb or Drew. An old, forgotten language, they assumed.

"Don't know," Iletus said. "But if one yet lives, no one in this city is safe. He might have learned that Eshlyn is gone. The two of you are targets."

"I'm no one's target," Caleb growled. "He is mine. We will set a curfew, tell everyone to be locked safely away. Then you are going to be bait."

"Wha – me?" Aden said. "Crit on a frog. Bait for what?"

"Iletus and I are going to hunt."

—†—

"We have a decision to make," Shan said as they stopped in the early afternoon. The road before them split, one path continuing on along the seacoast and another led to the southeast.

No crit, Carys thought. She leaned forward in the saddle, clenching her teeth so the words wouldn't escape her.

The road along the edge of the Rodria had been dry and hot. Even as a child, traveling with her Uncle Reyan, she never made this journey. The heat sucked the energy right out of her, and there was no way out of the sun, little vegetation for kilomitres. They used their cloaks to give some shade during the day, except for Shan, who was glad for his wide-brimmed hat.

The nights were a partial relief – relief from the heat and sun, but the darkness brought a shocking chill over them. They had to huddle in the evening just to stay warm enough to sleep. She hated that.

Fortunately, that had been for only two days. Now they were in northern Veradis, which was still dry with its flat, tan grasslands, shrubs and trees, but the breeze off the coast gave some comfort and humidity. Carys squinted up at the bright noonday sun bearing down upon them.

Zalman moved his horse next to hers. "The road south goes along the coast; we'll hit some small towns in a day or more and be able to resupply."

"The southeast road is faster." Shan pointed that way with an open hand. "And we could reach a small lake settlement by nightfall."

"The southeast road takes us to the lake and canal system of Veradis," Zalman said. "It is slow travel on horse."

"Unless you rent a flatboat," Shan stated and wiped sweat from his face with the back of his sleeve. "And we could float right into Landen, which would cut our travel time in half and save money with less supplies."

Several smaller lakes dotted the rocky landscape and distinguished the southern half of Veradis from the north. Natural rivers or streams connected some, but the First Men dug canals and established a web of waterways for travel and trade. Carys and her companions could, in fact, travel to Landen by boat if they took that road.

"More checkpoints on the canals," Zalman said. "More trade for them to regulate. Towns along the coast are mostly fishermen, and they trade with the outer isles. We have weapons. We'd move easier along the sea."

"Check points are only a problem if we are transporting goods. I can get us by checkpoints without a problem."

Zalman turned his shaved head back at Carys. "He means give them coin. Guard at the checkpoints take bribes. More expense."

Carys sucked in air through her teeth. "Don't have endless supply of coin, but if we have less supply to buy, it should be enough." Their biggest need was water, after passing the desert. They had food enough for a few more days, which could last them even to Landen if they made good time through the canals.

"More dangerous," Zalman mumbled.

Her gut told her two things – first, they should go the faster way and that meant the canals. Second, she shouldn't trust Shan farther than she could piff, which meant she agreed with both men, in a way. But it was her decision to make, so she groaned and made it.

"We're not here to be safe," Carys said. "We'll go southeast and through the canals."

CHAPTER 10

OSHRA

While his heritage was Liorian, Esai was born in the Forest of Saten. He was raised among the Ghosts in the ancient and secret Drytweld city of Jowel around the *Abaes*, the Father Tree. His parents were from Oshra and moved to the forest when pregnant with their second child. They knew the Saten was a place safe from the elves, and they did not have the money for the Kryan fine for their second child. Not wanting to kill the baby with the infanti, they escaped to the forest. And the forest was what Esai knew. He had visited the capital of Lior twice before, however. And just like the previous two visits, he now approached the city with an ache in his heart. The city of Oshra rose from the jungle with its tall towers and massive buildings. The rainforest parted for the impressive center of the city, but the rest of the metropolis sprawled into the jungle as if one with it. Every structure was made with black Liorian wood. The tall towers of the palace and the Kryan Temple gleamed like ebony, shining smooth. A majority of the city, however, was low and flat, few buildings more than two stories.

Esai knew the deep rhythms of the Saten, and his family was the diverse – but free – people there. It was odd that he felt such a connection to this place. Perhaps it was due to the stories his mother told him or a simple feeling of kinship. Maybe it was the tragic story that surrounded his parents' homeland. Esai listened as Athelwulf explained this to Eshlyn.

"Lior was the first nation of men to fall to Kryus," Athelwulf began. "A century before the War of Liberation, a series of tropical storms ravaged the coast, destroying villages and homes and much of the city of Oshra. Livelihoods were lost, and hundreds of thousands of people were plunged into starvation and homelessness. The King of Oshra was a corrupt man, and the nation was already divided between the three main tribes of Lior. They had been for generations, and he barely had control of the nation before the disaster. Resources became scarce, and war broke out between the tribes, all killing one another. The King was desperate, and he appealed to Kryus for help."

Esai inhaled slowly as he gazed to his left. They had passed several abandoned villages over the past couple days. Only a few were populated anymore; Kryus controlled the fishing industry throughout the Sea of Alin. The select villages that remained possessed permission from the Empire and served as outposts for the corporate fishing vessels.

"What of the other nations of men?" Eshlyn asked. "Manahem, Veradis, Erelon?"

"The King did ask them for help, however half-hearted," Athelwulf responded. "But the friendship among the nations of men was long past. They were more likely to go to war with each other than give aid. And many within those nations believed that Liorians were somewhat less than human, based only on our black skin. This fed their apathy."

"To the real?" Eshlyn said. "Just based on skin? Why?"

"Men believe odd things sometimes," Athelwulf said.

"Do people still think this way?"

"Some in Erelon and Veradis," Athelwulf said. "But now that much of mankind is under Imperial control, they have better things to worry about."

Esai ran into this way of thinking even within the Saten. Periodically, a man from Erelon would join them and see Athelwulf and question Athelwulf's ability to lead, based on his Liorian heritage. This was not a welcome perspective among the Ghosts; Mother Natali had done well in instructing the people there to judge based on character and not outward appearances. She was a half-elf herself.

"To the sure," Eshlyn said. "Misery makes companions."

Athelwulf snorted. "Yes."

"So Kryus gave Lior aid?" Eshlyn asked.

"Tanicus was already trying to gain more control of the trade along the Sea of Alin, especially the resources of Lior like wood from the forest and the gold in the northern mountains. He offered to help, but his price was that Lior must come under absolute Kryan control."

"And the King agreed?"

Esai swung his eyes to the right. The forest was thick and dripped with vegetation, the colors vibrant. He could see a small group of Ushpa, smaller monkeys, racing and playing in the trees. Up ahead, Esai observed the docks of Oshra extending out into the sea.

"He felt he had no choice," Athelwulf said. "Tanicus offered him a stewardship of the nation, so the King signed over the nation of Lior to the Kryan Empire.

"The Emperor then sent his Legions and placed Oshra and the other major cities under martial law. Tanicus manipulated the national divisions, declaring that Kryus alone could keep the peace between the factions. Within a generation, the Steward was an elf and Kryus controlled the mines, the fishing and lumber industries, and the men and women of Lior – once a proud and strong people – became slaves to the Empire."

They were all quiet for a moment, somber. Esai saw smaller houses to his right, simple wooden shacks with people milling about, most of them emaciated, barely dressed, and smelling of Sorcos, even at the outskirts of the city. The people watched them as they passed with empty, half-dead eyes.

Esai, Athelwulf, and Eshlyn had hidden their swords in their packs two days ago, wrapping the blades with canvas and surrounding the weapons with their other supplies and clothes. But Esai wondered if these men, women and children would notice the swords if they were blazing in the open sunlight, as drugged as they were.

For Esai, switching to a single blade from his previous two-sword style had been quite the adjustment, but the unforged sword helped with the transition. A living weapon, the simple, light and strong sword was a joy to learn.

"Is Lior still divided?" Eshlyn asked.

"Yes. The elven Steward is deft at pitting the three main southern tribes against one another," Athelwulf said.

Eshlyn's gaze was also upon the people as they rode.

Esai looked from her to Ath. "There is a fourth tribe."

Eshlyn's brow rose. "A fourth?"

Athelwulf was quiet for a moment. "They live in the Kaleti Mountains to the north, isolated and away from Kryan control, much like the towns of southern Manahem."

Eshlyn sighed. "So to help Lior and Oshra, we must get these tribes that have hated one another for centuries to begin working together."

"That would help," Athelwulf said.

Eshlyn muttered to herself. "Caleb gives me the impossible yet again."

Esai rode his horse closer to Eshlyn. "You are not alone. We are with you. And El."

"Sounds like a supernatural job, to the real," she said. "Who is our contact?"

"The Prophet's primary contact in the city," Esai said. "Ekandayo, the elder of the Zwi tribe."

"What do we know about him?" she asked. "Can we trust him?"

"Met him once," Esai said.

It had been on Esai's second visit to Oshra, and the leader of the Zwi tribe met Esai and another Ghost, Robyn, in a dark corner of the common room at an inn on the outskirts of the city. Ekandayo had not said much, and he was hesitant to help Esai and Robyn at all, for fear of what the other tribes might say; and he was afraid of being betrayed. The Empire had eyes and ears everywhere in Oshra.

Athelwulf said, "The Prophet trusted him."

"From what I understand, the Prophet also trusted his own son," Eshlyn said. "So we will see about this Ekandayo. I pray we can trust him."

The great city of Oshra loomed before them. *Yes*, he thought with a heavy heart. *We will see.*

———

Xander lurked in the alley next to the house where his parents, little Javyn, Aden, Tamya and the bloodwolf were staying.

It was an hour past midnight, and the cloudy sky hid the light of the three moons. Chamren's death had been two nights past, and the city was under a strict curfew, people sleeping in large groups with men of the Citywatch interspersed among them, all veterans of the Battle of Ketan. The only people out on the streets were Iletus and the *Sohan-el*.

Caleb was using Aden and Eshlyn's family as bait, but he moved them to a different place each night to keep it from appearing too obvious. The bloodwolf was among them because he was able to sense the Wraith nearby and could give warning as he did the night of the attack, saving Aden's life in the process. Two more people had disappeared, one from before Chamren's death and the other from yesterday. It was dangerous to be anywhere alone.

As Caleb explained, however, to be a *Sohan-el* is to face danger for the good of others. Xander insisted he be close to his family, to protect them. Caleb was also nearby, since odds were that the Wraith would strike here. The other sixteen *Sohan-el* and Iletus were in other strategic places around the city.

Striding to the front corner of the house, Xander put his hand on his sword and felt the power there, like a whisper or a hum in his heart.

His training was rigorous; no one really knew how much. After losing the lower half of his right arm in the Battle of Ketan, people assumed he would surrender his goal of learning the sword. Many thought he should assist his father and sister somehow, but his father knew Xander's heart. Xander was passionate about training with Caleb, and so Xander had gone to Caleb with his father's blessing.

Caleb had been honest with the young man. "Since you are new to it, there isn't much you have to relearn. But make no mistake, you will have to work twice as hard as the others."

Xander wasn't stupid; he knew that well and expressed that to Caleb. So Caleb agreed to count Xander among the *Sohan-el* disciples that day.

It had been difficult, even more difficult than he imagined. The training was hard enough for those with two hands, but learning to use one hand, his off-hand, required hours of extra work each day. As a *Sohan-el*, he also led a division of the army, so any extra work was done in the evening when others rested or socialized. Several times he was desperate to quit, but Eshlyn and his father continued to encourage him. Xander made it through the winter as a prized pupil.

Only a few ninedays ago, he took the trek to the Living Stone. When others had quit, turned back without facing the rigors of the climb and the fear of the dark storm, he had forced himself forward.

Xander's experience with El had transformed him at his core – feeling the words spoken to him within the center of his being, words of peace and urgency and power all at once. He felt whole in that place; and he would always remember that moment. The sword he received from the Stone was perfect for him: thinner and lighter than the others but just as strong. El and the Stone had tested his heart and found him worthy. He was part of a revolution of freedom and the rebirth of an ancient order of warrior-leaders.

And to think – just six months before, trying to get a pig drunk with his best friend Joob was his most pressing priority.

Here in the darkness of the city, Xander felt a presence behind him, towards the back of the house. There was no noise, but he froze. He drew his sword and turned without a sound. There was a shadow in the corner of his eye, to his right and hugging the side of the house ten mitres away.

Then the bloodwolf howled from inside the house.

The shadow moved, and Xander was fortunate to see an arcing flash of metal hurtle towards his head. Tucking his sword, he dove forward and rolled to the left. He heard steel scraping against the brick, and he stood and lunged with a swipe of the sword.

The Wraith dodged easily and faced him with a long metal whip in each hand.

Well, crit, Xander thought.

Xander retreated, and one whip lashed out at him, missing his stomach by mere centimitres. The other was not far behind, and Xander lifted his sword to block. The steel links wound around the blade. As Xander twisted the sword, the whip slid off the edge, and Xander continued to back down the alley to the street beyond. He felt claustrophobic in the confines of the alley and those metal whips scared the shog out of him.

The Wraith advanced, draped and hooded in a gray cloak, faceless in the shadow of the cowl. Xander jumped back as one whip swung low and then ducked as the next one lashed high with a metallic snap. As the Wraith struck again with a whip, Xander blocked with the sword and cut through the whip. Half of the weapon went flying to his left, and the Wraith hesitated, dropping the broken weapon to the street and pulling a short sword from his hip.

Another swipe came from a whip, and Xander dodged and retreated. The Wraith followed the whip with a stab from the gladus, which Xander was barely able to avoid. The whip swung towards Xander and he parried it with his sword. The whip wound around the blade again, but this time the Wraith flicked his wrist and tugged.

The sword was yanked from Xander's grip. He watched, helpless, as the unforged sword flew mitres away from him.

The Wraith moved forward quickly, lashing with the whip and thrusting with the gladus. Xander retreated, spun, and weaved to escape the furious attack. The metal whip caught him across the shin, cutting the flesh, but not too deep.

Xander realized his mistake in allowing the fight to come to the street. Those whips had an advantage in an open space, keeping an opponent at a distance. Now Xander was without his sword, and the Wraith was pushing him away from his weapon with his attacks.

But the young man had fought before he became a *Sohan-el*. Not anything well-trained or intelligent, but one could not be best friends with Joob the Boob without being able to survive – if not win – a brawl or two.

Waiting for his moment, it came as the Wraith finished both a lash with the whip and a swipe of the sword; Xander launched himself with a yell at the Wraith and tackled the assassin. Xander was on top of the elf, punching the assassin in the face with his left fist and the stump at the end of his right arm. The Wraith dropped both the sword and the whip in the chaos and melee, bringing his hands up to protect his face and ward Xander off.

The Wraith was on his back but managed to strike Xander in the ribs, a precise blow that expelled the breath from the young man. Desperate, Xander reared back and rammed the Wraith in the face with his forehead. He heard a sickening crunch, and as he straightened again, he could see the Wraith's nose pouring blood.

At this point, any normal being would have been down to stay, but the Wraith barely seemed affected. The elf struck Xander twice, once in the neck with the side of one hand and again on the bridge of the nose with the knuckles of the other. Dizzy and still breathless, Xander was easily pushed off of the Wraith onto his back.

His consciousness waning, Xander groaned and writhed on the ground. His vision narrowed, but he could see the Wraith stand and move to pick up his metal whip, the one still intact. The elf stepped back towards Xander, raising the whip above him.

As Xander tried to crawl away, his hand touched steel. Not the steel of the unforged sword, he knew somehow, but the assassin's gladus. He grabbed the hilt. With the strength left within him, he rolled and heaved the gladus at the elf; the fine elven blade sunk deep within the Wraith's chest. The Wraith grunted, took two steps back, and sat on his haunches.

Xander's breaths came short and shallow, thinking he could relax. It was over. He lay prostrate on the ground, but he turned enough to see the Wraith pull the gladus out of his own chest and stand.

The Wraith stumbled towards him, blood pumping from his chest, and Xander could only see him as a shadow, his vision darkening further in the night. He knew he was passing out, but he willed himself to an elbow, trying to stand. *How the shog was that thing still alive?* Xander had to get up. Maybe get to the unforged sword. *Where was it?*

He heard a distant rush of wind, like a faint whisper, and as he looked up, the shadow was now in pieces and falling in slow motion to the street with wet thuds.

Dead? Xander didn't know, but he was wrong before. So he tried to get up again but couldn't.

A hand touched his shoulder.

"He's gone, Xander," a voice said. *Caleb?* "Rest now."

And Xander laid his face on the cold stone of the street and gave way to unconsciousness.

———

Esai and Eshlyn stood before the entrance to *The Dancing Leaves*, a small inn on the outskirts of the city of Oshra. The inn leaned a little to the left and appeared ready to fall at a strong gust of wind, but it was made with Liorian wood, strong and thick. Esai knew it would stand longer than the humans that stood here. Large trees towered over *The Dancing Leaves*, throwing shade over the structure as the sun set to the west.

He looked behind him and saw Athelwulf a hundred paces down the muddy street, kneeling and speaking to a young boy bone thin with a round belly. The child wore only loose brown short breeches, and he nodded at Athelwulf. Ath slipped a copper stone in the boy's hand, and the boy ran off down the street.

Standing, Athelwulf joined them before the entrance. "The elves have their eyes," he said. "And so must we."

Esai led them into the main room of the inn. The room was dim and filled with tables and chairs, although each was a different shape and size. Eshlyn and Athelwulf followed him to the back corner where they sat. The three of them wore long, light cloaks to hide the swords they wore.

A man in a white apron and tunic approached the table within the next few minutes, leery of the strangers. He was barefoot on the dirt floor of the inn.

"Need somethin'?" the man asked.

"Yes," Esai said. "Three ales, please." He placed three copper stones on the table before them.

The man scowled but collected the coppers, wiping them on his dirty apron and walking back to the small kitchen. Esai watched the entrance to the inn while they waited for him to return. A narrow staircase with a crooked banister led upstairs to the rooms for rent. Then he scanned the rest of the patrons.

Fifteen other people were scattered through the room, most of them sitting with another in small groups of two or three, all of them dark-skinned, barefoot and clothed in short, tattered breeches or longer plain tunics. Except for one. A light-skinned man with a dark beard sat in the corner on the opposite side of the room. His long, dirty, unkempt hair hung over his face, and his tunic and breeches were tattered. He was dirty and barefoot.

Esai's attention was diverted from the man, however, as Ekandayo entered the inn.

Ekandayo was a taller man with very dark skin, as dark as Athelwulf and older, with short gray hair and a long, gray beard. He wore a long dress tunic with an intricate pattern of orange and red shapes and stripes, and a small orange cap sat on his head.

Two men entered the room with the chief, their eyes darting around the room for any threats or problems. Ekandayo was calm, his own gaze slowly measuring the room and falling upon Esai and his companions in the corner. His face remained blank, but he turned to whisper something to his men and wound towards them through the tables. The two men, both younger with longer fine tunics of their own in bright colors, stayed at the entrance.

The serving man returned with their ales, and he started when he noticed Ekandayo approaching. "Good chief," the serving man said with a bow. "Need somethin'?"

Ekandayo sat at the remaining place at the table. "One of your ales," he said. He did not place any money on the table, and the serving man did not seem to expect it.

"Yes, good," the serving man said and went back into the kitchen again.

The tribal elder leaned back in his chair and regarded the three of them. Esai heard Eshlyn gulp and saw Athelwulf stroke his long, thick beard.

Ekandayo crossed his legs and placed his hands in his lap. "This place has the strongest ale in the city," he said. "And one of the few places untouched by the violence of recent months."

Esai took a sip of the ale. "It is good," he said. Eshlyn and Athelwulf both took a drink of theirs. Eshlyn stifled a cough.

Ekandayo said to Esai, "You, I know. These I do not."

Esai introduced Eshlyn and Athelwulf to Ekandayo.

"Well met," Ekandayo said. "But it is a dangerous time in Oshra, very dangerous for you to be here and contact me."

"Yes," Eshlyn said. "And we thank you for coming."

"Do not thank me yet."

The serving man reappeared with an ale, bowed, and left. Ekandayo waited until the man was out of earshot before continuing.

"We hear rumors and things here in the city. Events in far places that have nothing to do with Oshra. Yet these events bring more militans to our shores." Ekandayo lowered his voice. "I hear the Prophet is dead."

Eshlyn leaned forward. "Yes, it is true."

"That is bad," Ekandayo said. "He was good man. How did he die?"

"He was killed by a Bladeguard in Biram," Esai said.

"He gave many hope," Ekandayo said. "Even when it is hopeless."

"Yes," Esai said. "He did."

"It is never hopeless," Eshlyn said. "And that is why we are here."

Ekandayo said, "We also hear of this *Brendel,* and a city of men free of the elves."

"Ketan," Eshlyn said. "We have come from there."

"Is it true what they say?" Ekandayo asked. "Is he three mitres tall with fists of steel?"

Eshlyn clenched her stomach but a chuckle still escaped her throat.

"No," Esai said, grinning. "He is a man same as you or me, but he is a great warrior and the rebirth of the ancient *Sohan-el.*"

Ekandayo frowned. "Those old fish tales again. The Prophet spoke of such things."

"They are coming true," Esai said. "The *Brendel* has begun a revolution in Ketan."

"Your revolution in Ketan has caused the deaths of many in Oshra," Ekandayo said. His lip curled. "The Pike has returned."

Esai grimaced, and Athelwulf moaned.

"What is the Pike?" Eshlyn asked.

Ekandayo averted his eyes, and Esai's nostrils flared. "Not a *what* but a *who*," Esai said. "When the Empire first took control of Oshra, there were some that tried to resist. Tanicus sent his most ruthless general, First General Wyus. He earned the name, the Pike."

"He earned that name by beheading thousands and displaying their heads on pikes throughout the city," Athelwulf muttered.

Eshlyn winced at the thought. "You're saying he came with the Kryan legions?"

"Yes," Ekandayo said. "The Emperor insures that we will not rebel. It is effective."

"We are sorry to hear that," Athelwulf said. "But that only means that the people of Oshra need the hope of El even more than we knew."

"What hope can you bring?" Ekandayo asked. "You are three against legions. Mention Ketan and you will see the reaction of those in Oshra. Many curse the *Brendel.* They become more loyal to the Empire and their masters. Others use his name to gather power to themselves."

"And you?" Eshlyn said. "How do you use his name?"

"I don't. As always, I try to survive," the chief said. "The tribes of Oshra visit violence upon one another when the Empire isn't slaughtering us."

The chief leaned upon the table. "I cannot lie. Your *freedom* has caused much suffering here."

"It is not our freedom that has caused this," Esai said. "And you know it. It is the Empire. Are we to allow the fear of what others may do keep us from being free?"

"The Prophet spoke of these things," Ekandayo mumbled. "And he is dead. Life in fear is better than death in freedom."

"Is it?" Eshlyn said. "The Empire kills and rapes you one way or the other. And you kill one another rather than stand up to the ones who enslave you."

"What do you know, woman?" the elder said. "You pink skins come from far lands and tell us how we must live. You know nothing of the evil that awaits us if we fight. You are not much different from the elves."

Eshlyn leaned even further forward, glaring at the man, but Esai placed a hand on her arm. "Are we pink skins, Ekandayo?" Esai said. "Are we the ones cutting down your forest and robbing your mountains of gold? Are we the ones murdering your children and babes in the streets? I am sorry to hear that it has gotten worse, but it is more of what Kryus will do unless this city unites and stands together."

"Unite?" Ekandayo's jaw dropped. "Insanity."

"Are we animals the elves believe us to be? Or are we men?" Esai asked. Why was Athelwulf so quiet? "Insanity is to turn on one another in our time of need. Unity is the only thing that will save this city and your people. The men in Oshra outnumber the elves."

"We need to meet with all the tribes, together," Eshlyn said. "Can you set up a meeting?"

"Of course," Ekandayo said with scorn. "And I can get you all the gold in the Kryan bank while I am at it. The others would kill me as soon as look at me."

Athelwulf spoke at last, his voice deep. "Not if you sent them a branch from the Peace Tree."

The Zwi chief also hesitated before answering. "Those are the old ways of Lior."

Esai had heard mention of the legend of the Peace Tree, an ancient tradition from when the men of Lior were free. When one carried a branch of the Peace Tree to a meeting, they were sworn to meet without violence. "Sometimes it takes old ways to lead us to new ones," he said.

Ekandayo leaned back again and scratched his chin. "Yes. But men have short memories. Few remember those old ways. Fewer will respect them."

"They will remember them," Athelwulf said. "And respect them. And they will take the first steps to becoming men again."

Ekandayo was quiet for a long moment, his arms crossed over his chest.

The pink skin man in the opposite corner ordered another ale. By all the mugs upon the table before him, this was the next of many. As the serving man neared, the light skinned man looked up, and the hair fell away from his face.

Esai's heart pounded within him. Hard to tell with the beard, but the man looked familiar.

"I will send a branch of the Peace Tree to the other two tribes tonight," Ekandayo said. "If they respond, I send you a message here."

"To the fine," Eshlyn said.

Ekandayo took another swig of his ale, and he stood. "I do this for the Prophet," he said. "And his memory. He was brave and good. But do not hope for the answer you desire. I do not know if the men of Oshra can change, nor do I believe they want to."

Athelwulf cleared his throat. "They can change."

Eshlyn stood to face him. "We have seen it."

"We will believe for you. For now," Esai said and stood.

The elder gave Esai a slight bow and left *The Dancing Leaves*, and his two men trailed him.

After he left, Eshlyn sat and heaved a deep breath. "Break it all," she said.

"That was a minor miracle," Athelwulf agreed.

But Esai was still watching the man in the corner. He was sipping his ale, his hair down in front of his face again. That haggard face sparked a memory within Esai.

No, Esai thought. *Could it be?*

"Sounds like we'll need a major miracle to get the three tribes together," Eshlyn said.

He had been so young then, years ago. But the Prophet had come through to speak to the Ghosts, and Esai went with his family to see him. The Prophet had his wife, son, and Carys with him.

Esai began to walk over to the opposite corner of the room.

"Esai?" Athelwulf said.

But he was intent on the man in the corner. He stood before the pink skin man. The man looked up at him.

"Leave me the shog alone," the man said in a hoarse voice. He took another drink, ale spilling onto his beard. He smelled of Sorcos.

"Look at me," Esai said.

The man sneered up at him, and Esai reached down and grabbed the collar of his tunic, lifting him up. The man was taller than Esai but weak from the ale and the drugs. Esai pushed the man's bushy black hair out of his face.

Glazed, drunk, Sorced eyes. Dark and dirty face streaked with sweat. Older, but it was him. The same face. He remembered playing with him and Carys in the forest, years before he saw Carys again when she was with Athelwulf's camp.

And now the man recognized him, as well. His eyes bulged at Esai, and a croak escaped the man's throat.

Both hands on the collar of the man's tunic, Esai growled and dragged the man out of the corner toward the entrance of *The Dancing Leaves*.

"Esai!" Eshlyn said from behind him, but he ignored her.

He hauled the man outside into the night. It was dark now and he towed the man, groaning, into the shadows. Esai was aware of Eshlyn and Athelwulf behind him, saying his name. In the shadows beneath a large tree, Esai pushed the man against the trunk, reached into his cloak and pulled his unforged sword from the scabbard beneath his cloak.

"No," the man moaned.

"Esai!" Eshlyn cried.

He bared his teeth at his two companions. "This is Earon Be'Luthel," he told them. "The son of the Prophet. And the man who killed him."

Esai whirled on Earon. "You killed the *Arendel*, the Prophet of El, the Messenger to Eres of life to come!"

"No!" Earon yelled. "I didn't ... I ..."

Esai lifted the sword, ready to execute the man. The unforged sword was heavy, and he clenched his teeth with the effort.

A strong hand grabbed his wrist. Esai spun on Athelwulf.

Athelwulf held his gaze, calm and firm. "No," he said. "Not like this."

"But he killed his father, the Prophet," Esai said. "He must die."

"Perhaps," Athelwulf said. "But not like this."

CHAPTER 11

IKRAM

"Well, you mangers," Gleb said. "You ever seen a bigga piece of skut come outta yo bund?" The flatboat captain was pointing at the town up ahead. Gleb had dark bronze skin and a single tuft of hair at the top of his head. He had grown it out and braided it, the white hair hanging down over his shoulder and across his bare chest. Gleb smiled and laughed at his own joke, showing his four remaining teeth.

The flatboat carried their packs and horses and didn't have room for much else. It was a series of long, thick logs tied together, gray from use and the sun, and flat planks had been nailed upon the logs. Gleb pushed and guided the flatboat with a long pole and the simple rudder.

Zalman stood and stared down the canal at the town of Ikram. The flatboat captain was right. It wasn't much to look at, but they needed to stop for the night, even if they just camped along the canal just outside of the town. As they neared Ikram, Zalman could see the familiar beige stone of the houses and buildings with flat ceilings framed with wood. He knew this town well – what were the chances they would stop here? But somehow he had known they would.

The air was dry, and the grassland around them was as brown as the stone, blowing in the light breeze.

Shan stood next to him. "Gleb is an idiot, but he's right about that town," he said in Zalman's ear. "A piece of skut for sure."

"It's only for the night," Zalman muttered.

Shan shook his head. "Can't wait to get to Landen." He walked back to his horse to get it ready to step off of the boat at the short dock.

There was the common store and the tavern just beyond it. Most of the men here worked out in the grassland among the vineyards owned by the Empire. A Kryan flatboat came a few times a year to take whatever those vineyards produced. The men picked grapes and drank their lives away down at the tavern.

Zalman could feel her presence on the other side of him. "We need some fresh water," Carys said. "You think we can get some here?"

"Fresh? Maybe. Clean? Not much of this town is clean."

She scoffed. "I can see that from here. But we're only a day or two away from Landen."

"Day and a half," he said.

The sun was setting to their right, and Zalman blinked as he turned in that direction. The evening wind rustled across the grasslands. He bent down and shouldered his pack, heavy with the battleaxes wrapped and hidden within it. They did need water, and perhaps there would be some clean from the well behind the tavern. But he doubted it. The well water was rarely clean. A rain was one of the few times they would have clean water, catching it in wooden barrels from the roofs of buildings.

Gleb ran the flatboat right up to the shortest and lowest of the three piers. They waited until the boat was secure and then led their horses up on the dock and toward the town. Zalman sighed and led his horse in the direction of the tavern.

Zalman glanced behind him. "The store won't have many supplies," he said to Carys. "But you can check. There's a well here behind the tavern. The water won't be clean, but it won't make you sick."

Carys eyed him but said nothing.

Tying the horse to the pole in front of the tavern, Zalman needed to duck to enter the establishment. The tavern was just as dark and dusty as he remembered. The man behind the bar was no different than years before, still an old, tall, leathery man with a long pipe in his mouth and stringy white hair on his head. Dree was his name.

Dree peered up but didn't recognize Zalman, which wasn't surprising. Zalman had been a young, skinny, lanky kid before he left. With hair. "Don't get much strangers here, friend," Dree grumbled, a puff of smoke escaping his thin lips surrounded by a white beard and mustache.

Zalman scanned the room as he leaned against the bar. They were the only people in the tavern. "I have coin and just want an ale," he said.

The man poured him a mug.

Shan and Carys entered the tavern, and Carys grimaced, putting a hand over her nose. "What is that smell?" she whispered to Shan as they joined Zalman at the bar.

"That is the smell of a skut canal town," Shan muttered, pulling on his wide-brimmed hat.

Dree stepped back over and set a mug of ale before Zalman. He nodded at the newcomers. "They gonna want one, too?"

Carys set three copper stones on the bar. "Please."

Dree poured two more mugs. Zalman waited for them and raised his mug to Carys and Shan before drinking. Carys grinned while she did the same, and they drank together.

Shan spun and spit it out upon the clay floor. "Mang me," he said. "That tastes like pure piff."

Zalman watched Carys and was proud of her as she managed to swallow the warm, watery ale. He took another drink. *Tastes like home*, he thought.

She turned to Dree. "We need a place to stay the night," she said.

"Passin' through?" Dree asked.

"Passin' through," she confirmed.

"Won't be many to give a room to strangers," Dree said. "But you can bunk out beneath the tarp behind the tavern. If you got more o' those coppers."

"He'll let us stay on the covered roof of the store for a little extra. It's probably worth it. I'll let you negotiate," Zalman said. "Need to stretch my legs." He drained the rest of his ale, set the mug down on the bar again. "Make sure one of you stays with the horses." He left the tavern.

The horses were all tied there at the post. Zalman could see two men over near the common store, watching him. He took a deep breath and moved to his right and into the row of houses that began thirty mitres beyond the tavern.

Zalman wondered if Ikram had been this small back then. It must have been. How could things seem so small but loom so large in a memory?

The houses along this row were all the same, one-room boxes made out of stone and clay and reeds. A few had porches or sitting areas on the roof or out behind the house. He could see a woman laying out laundry on a line between two of the houses. It made him think of his mother.

The last house on the row. He stood before it as a dry breeze kicked up dust across his leather boots. The house was empty; he could see it had been abandoned years ago. But that wasn't surprising. Both of his parents had been addicted to Sorcos and coughing like they would die any minute when he left. That was a decade ago. Now, the house was barely standing. He could knock it down with his fists and thought about doing it, but instead he moved around to the back of the house. There, twenty mitres away, next to a copse of rust-colored shrubbery, he saw two mounds of dirt marked with piles of rocks.

That was the measure of their life, he thought. *Nameless stones in a forgotten skut town.*

He felt her near him before he saw her, the shoulder-length blond hair tied back with a green ribbon.

"This was your home," Carys said, almost a whisper. "You grew up here."

Staring at the graves, he nodded.

"When did you leave?"

"I was sixteen when I left," he said. "Just old enough to think I knew it all. Better than them, for the sure."

"These are ... your parents?"

Zalman grunted. "My father wasn't ... well, he wasn't what you would call a good man. He barely worked. All he cared about was enough to get more Sorcos and ale. It poisoned him."

"And your ma?"

"She cared, but she was just as strung out as he was."

"So you left."

He didn't answer. It hadn't really been a question.

"Where did you go?"

Away from here, he thought. Nothing else mattered to him then. "Where else? Landen."

I yelled at them and called them names when I left, he wanted to say to her. He had been skinny but tall, and his father was so sick. *It was nothing to push him down and beat him like he beat me when I was younger. But I got too big for him to beat me. And then I was big enough to return the favor.*

"And Qadi-bol?"

"I was starving, and I saw a game one night. Anyone could get a ticket. You could see a game easier than get a job or food." He crossed his arms. "And the way the crowd roared for those men, and they were like heroes there on the green, greener grass than I had ever seen. I decided that's what I wanted to do."

"And so you did."

He had stolen food and money to buy a set of paddles and practiced over his first year in Landen, obsessed with his new purpose. He tried out for a local team. Within another year, at the age of eighteen, he was known as the most violent and brutal player in the local circuit. The Landen city team heard of him and had him try out. He broke two arms in tryouts alone. The owner of the team, an elf all bones and ears, laughed and offered him a place on the team right then.

"I did."

"Not that I ever paid much attention, but I understand you were very popular."

Zalman examined the graves again. He never came back. He had more money than he could ever have used, and maybe he could have saved them. But he didn't even think about them. While he refused Sorcos, he was high on fame and women and adulation.

"Why did you leave it? All that fame. You were a hero. Why give it up?"

Zalman remembered the day he realized that four armed, elven bodyguards followed him everywhere he went. He had to ask permission for anything outside of the game, practice and training. They brought him women and any vice he asked for, but they would not grant him his freedom. He was a human, always less from their perspective. There had been a moment when the crowds were frantic with their cheers, and he had thought to himself, *I was freer back in Ikram, a piece of skut town.*

"Because fame and money, it is only another form of slavery," he said. "And I realized that while I was popular, I was the biggest slave of them all."

"So you ran."

"I ran."

"And they just let you go?"

Fighting through the guards, he had killed three of them with his bare hands in Galya, and their blood poured over the streets of that city known for peace. He hid and ran for days in that city. After leaving Galya, he crossed the countryside to the north and making his way as far from the elves as he could. And that meant Ketan. He needed money for food and women, so he worked for Shan, the Rat.

"No. But they couldn't stop me."

Carys raised a brow at him. "No crit."

"No crit."

"Well, I got the roof of the store," she said. "We're eating at the tavern before we bed down for the night. Is the food going to be as bad as the ale?"

He grinned down at his boots. "Worse."

"Shoggers," she muttered. "You gonna join us soon?"

"Soon," he said.

"To the fine." She started to leave but stopped. "You know, you're a big gedder, for the real. But I'm glad you ran. No one does that, gives that up. Now I think I understand why Caleb trusts you."

He didn't know how to respond at first to the rare compliment. "Thank you."

"Come quick before your food gets cold, hear?"

"Yeah," he said as she left. But what she didn't know was that the food at that tavern would never be warm in the first place.

"What are we going to do with him?" Esai asked. It was clear whom he meant.

Athelwulf watched Earon while they met in the room at the inn. Earon was bound and gagged in the corner, his eyes vacant. Esai stood near the door, leaning against it, and glared at the son of the Prophet.

It had been a tense night. The room they rented at *The Dancing Leaves* was small and cramped for four people. Possessing only one bed, which they gave to Eshlyn, the three men had slept on the floor. There had been arguing in the streets during the night, a fight that moved past them. They didn't get much sleep.

Here in the dawn, Esai was silent and brooding, which Athelwulf could understand.

Athelwulf stretched from sleeping on the hard wood floor. Eshlyn sat on the bed, and Athelwulf stepped to stand near the small open window. The branches of a tree moved and threw shadows across the room from the morning sun.

"We're not going to just kill him," Eshlyn said, but her voice wasn't as firm or confident as usual.

"No," Athelwulf said, clasping his hands behind him. "That is not our place."

Esai grit his teeth. "Then whose place is it?"

"Caleb and Carys," Athelwulf said. "They are his family, and they were there when the Prophet was killed. They know his betrayal more than anyone. They should decide his fate."

"But they're not here," Eshlyn said. "Do you mean to take him with us?"

"Back to Ketan, yes."

"That is too much," Esai protested. "It is dangerous for us here, now. The Pike is in the city. We cannot carry him around, bound and gagged, while we meet with the city leaders."

"I have to agree with Esai," Eshlyn said. "We don't know how bad the city is, to the real, and there's talk of militan all over the streets. Lugging around a tied up human is asking for too much attention."

"We will have to try," Athelwulf said.

"And if we meet with the elders?" Esai asked. "We going to have him tied up in the corner while we try to convince them to unite?"

Athelwulf looked over at Earon. Even from this distance, he could smell the man, the sweat and the drugs in his system. "Yes."

Esai threw up his hands in exasperation. "We kill him. We know what Caleb and Carys told us. How will taking him to Ketan change that? It puts us in danger, more danger than we need. It is justice to kill him for his betrayal, and we can kill him now."

"I don't want to kill him," Eshlyn said. "But we can't take him with us. Maybe we could ask Ekandayo to hold him for us."

Athelwulf thought of his father and an ancient city in the mountains; he could see his father's hate and anger even now in his mind.

"No," Athelwulf said. "I will take responsibility for him. I do not know if we can trust Ekandayo. Earon must face Caleb and Carys, and they must decide his fate. I know this, so I will be responsible for him, no matter what happens."

A knock came at the door. All of three of them had hands on their swords in an instant. Esai stepped as far into the room as he could, and one of Ekandayo's men from the night before stood at the door as Esai opened it.

"I have a message from Ekandayo," the man said with a glance at the bound man in the corner.

Eshlyn stood to join the others. "Please, speak it."

"The others responded to the branch from the Peace Tree," he said. "The meeting is tonight at the southern edge of the city, near the docks. I will come get you this afternoon."

Eshlyn bowed. "Thank you," she said. "And please give our regards to Ekandayo."

He bowed in return and left the small room.

Eshlyn turned to Athelwulf. "You're going to take him down to that meeting with ropes around his wrists and a gag in his mouth?"

Earon's eyes pleaded with them. For what, Athelwulf didn't know. But he could relate to Earon's plight. The young man needed to face Caleb and Carys. They needed it, too. Like he needed to face his father.

"Lady Eshlyn," Athelwulf said. "Trust me. He comes with us."

"I do trust you, Ath," she said. "He's your responsibility."

"Thank you."

"But if he becomes too much trouble," Eshlyn said. "If Esai doesn't kill him, I will."

—┼—

Later that afternoon, the same man came to get Eshlyn and her companions from *The Dancing Leaves* and lead them to the meeting. Eshlyn learned his name. Hyan. They gathered their horses from a nearby stable. Earon rode with Athelwulf, his hands bound before him and a cloth in his mouth. Athelwulf put a cloak over him with the hood down to hide his face. Hyan did not have a horse; he preferred to walk. So they rode at a slow pace through the streets of Oshra.

They had to travel through the middle of the city to get to the warehouse where they would be meeting with the elders of the three tribes. Eshlyn could see starving and dead residents littering the streets. A child no older than Javyn clung naked to his mother, both of them starving in their own filth, their eyes glazed and drugged. But they passed thousands like her – old men and young, women and children. The smell of death and waste was everywhere, and it overpowered her. Her heart broke, and she almost stopped several times to try to help. But what could she do? She had money, but not near enough for them all. People were killing one another while these people needed help?

Tears streaked her cheeks as they neared the Steward's palace. She gawked at the imposing building, far taller than any building in Ketan. The palace was made of black Liorian wood and intricately carved as if by the gods themselves. The main tower of the palace seemed to touch the very clouds.

Next they passed the Kryan Temple, and its spires were beautiful with the shapes of waves or fire carved all along the structure. There were no walls around the city of Oshra; the jungle and the sea were its walls, but high walls rose around the Temple and the palace. Cityguard and militan surrounded both structures, armed with gladi, spears and shields.

Along the top of the walls, bloody and bloated heads had been set upon pikes. There were hundreds of them, young and old, male and female, children, many with faces frozen in grimaces of pain or horror. Ravens and vultures picked the flesh the victims, flies buzzing in clouds around the dead.

Eshlyn and her group rode in stunned silence as they came under the scrutiny from the guard, but they passed without incident.

A platoon of militan marched across a side street behind them, and Eshlyn breathed a little easier when they were gone.

Another half hour and they were among lower buildings again, homes and businesses. Hyan led them to a longer building, not much of a warehouse to Eshlyn's estimation.

Dismounting, Eshlyn strolled into the main door. The sun had sunk under the horizon, and the sky was a bright purple. Esai, Ath and Earon entered behind her. A few lamps around the walls lit the room. Wooden crates lined the walls of the warehouse, but the middle of the room was clear for a group to stand. Athelwulf held a longer rope in his hands that was tied to the bindings at Earon's wrist. He lashed Earon to one of the nearby boxes, like an animal. They were alone until Ekandayo and his two men strode into the warehouse. Ekandayo wore a similar long dress tunic and hat, this time with colors of yellow and red. He carried a mitre long branch of wood with a white blossom at the end.

"Welcome," he said.

"Thank you," Esai said. "You honor us and the memory of the Prophet."

"The elders are afraid," Ekandayo said. "The Pike is gathering the militan."

"Why?" Eshlyn asked

"I do not know," Ekandayo said. "Perhaps they are amassing because they believe there will be another riot or violence between factions."

"Or they are going to incite their own violence and clean the streets themselves," Esai said.

"Maybe the elves know we're in the city," Eshlyn said.

"Also possible," Ekandayo said. "Nevertheless, the other elders have agreed in fear over what Kryus will try to do." He glimpsed at Earon. "Who is that?"

Athelwulf raised a hand. "He is with me. There is no reason for worry."

Ekandayo did not seem convinced. "Why is he gagged?"

"We do not wish to hear what he has to say," Eshlyn said. *And I don't want Esai killing him for what he will say*, Eshlyn wanted to add.

The door opened again, and the three *Sohan-el* put hands in their cloaks and on their swords. Another man walked into the room with two more behind him. The man in front was obviously in charge. Younger and shorter than Ekandayo, he wore a long dress tunic, but the colors were

The Blades of War

darker, black and gray in amazing patterns. The man held a branch with a white blossom in his left hand.

"Ekandayo," the man said.

"Sabriel," Ekandayo replied. "Thank you for coming."

"A branch of the Peace Tree," Sabriel said, standing now ten paces away, holding out the branch with the blossom to them all. "I could not believe it. We have not used this in generations."

"Recent events have been unusual," Ekandayo said. "And so I felt it time to recover the old ways." He laid his branch in the center of the floor.

"We shall see," Sabriel said and dropped his branch to join Ekandayo's

Another group of three entered the warehouse, led this time by a woman. She was tall, taller than Eshlyn, and beautiful. Her long hair hung behind her in braids, and she wore a long skirt in blue and white circular patterns that seemed to whisper when she walked. Above the skirt, her waist was bare and a strip of cloth, matching her skirt, covered her breasts, and a long piece of cloth was draped over her shoulder, also of the same material.

"Jubali," Sabriel spat.

But Jubali did not react, and neither did the men behind her. Carrying her own branch with a white blossom, she strode to join them standing in the center of the warehouse.

"Thank you for coming, Jubali," Ekandayo said.

"The Peace Tree is of the old ways," Jubali said, gazing down at the branch in her hand. "I trust that this meeting will not meet any bloodshed, as was the custom for our ancestors."

"No blood will be spilt by me or those with me," Ekandayo said. "Too much blood over the years. We need no more of it."

Jubali hesitated, pensive, and then placed her branch with the other two.

"That *sounds* good," Sabriel said, stepping forward. "But we shall see. Who are these with you?"

Ekandayo introduced Esai, Eshlyn, and Athelwulf to Jubali of the Xon tribe and Sabriel of the Moffa.

"And why are they here?" Jubali asked.

Eshlyn was reminded of Musters along the Manahem road a few months ago, back before the winter. But those were her people, and she had needed her father's help to move even a fraction of those people to safety. Here she was a "pink skin" with centuries of hate to overcome within days or shorter, and they were going to try to convince them to unite and be free with a bound human behind them. She took a deep breath and stepped forward.

I will defend the innocent, free the oppressed, and spread light in dark places.

"We are the reason Ekandayo called you," Eshlyn said.

They faced her, and Esai stood next to her.

"You may have heard of the revolution that has begun in Ketan," Eshlyn said.

"We have heard rumors of such things," Jubali said. "But surely they are rumors, not to be believed."

"We are here to tell you the truth," Eshlyn said. "There is a revolution in the city of Ketan. Man has risen and they are free. The elves left, and humanity runs the city."

"And Tanicus has not wiped you from Eres?" Sabriel asked.

"No," Esai said.

"You have met him in battle?" Jubali asked.

"No," Eshlyn answered. "But we repelled an attack of demics from the Underland. A man came and taught us to fight, led us to protect ourselves and stand free."

"This *Brendel*," Sabriel said with a grimace.

"Yes," Esai said. "A great warrior."

"And why is this great warrior not here?" Jubali said. "We could use his help."

Sabriel scoffed. "Use his help? The man is a menace, if he even exists at all. You could be lying to us. How could we know?"

Eshlyn clenched her teeth. "He sent us in his stead. Athelwulf and Esai are great warriors, as well. We three are *Sohan-el*, the ancient warrior leaders of El. The old ways are returning, and El is calling men to be what they were created to be."

"But you have not faced Tanicus," Jubali said. "You may have fought some creatures from the Underland, as ridiculous as that is to believe, but Tanicus and his legions are another matter."

"That is what the Empire would have you believe," Esai said. "They are strong, yes, but if humanity were united against the Empire, we could beat them."

"United?" Sabriel sniffed. "More fish stories. Do you know what goes on here?"

"We do," Eshlyn said. "And that is why we came. You must put away your hate and begin to work together. End your division, and you will outnumber the militan. Once you stand up to the elves, they will leave."

"Leave?" Sabriel gaped. "The elves are all that keep us alive."

"There was a time," Eshlyn said. "When the men of Lior ruled themselves and kept the peace and were friends with the other nations of men."

"So long ago it doesn't matter," Sabriel said. "Every man and woman in Oshra has been raised to hate the other tribes."

"Not every man and woman," Ekandayo said. "Some have tried to learn different."

"You are all the people of Lior." Eshlyn's hands moved as she talked, and she glided forward. "You can live united and strong. We have seen it in Ketan."

Jubali lowered her head. "Perhaps in Ketan, but this is not Ketan."

"We need the elves," Sabriel repeated. "The elves feed and clothe us. Without them our people would starve."

And put your heads on spikes," Esai said. "Don't forget that."

"Break you," Sabriel said and spun on Esai. "Yes, they kill, but how would we survive without them? Who would feed us, give us what we need? You?"

"You know that is not the answer," Esai said. "Take back your lives from the Empire and learn to provide for yourself."

Sabriel sneered at him. "In your fantasy land, let's say we do get rid of the Empire. The skut dogs of the Xon would only take their place and kill us at will. Who would protect us from them?"

"This comes from the crab boggers of the Moffa?" Jubali asked.

Eshlyn could see the men in the room grow nervous, angry.

"I am sorry," Ekandayo said to Eshlyn. "I do not know that we can change."

Athelwulf then stepped forward and spoke, pushing back the hood from his face. "You can change."

The room grew quiet at his voice, at the authority within it. He spoke quiet but firm.

"*And they believed in Yosu, and those that were once weak and corrupt became the men they were created to be, and more than men. They became the* Sohan-el."

"Ath?" Eshlyn said. She recognized the quote from the Ydu, the testimony.

"My name was not always Athelwulf," he said. "And I have not always been the man you see before you."

Athelwulf moved to the center of the group, and he scanned their faces. Eshlyn swallowed, transfixed.

"I was born in Lior," he began. "But not in Oshra. I was born far to the north in the Kaleti Mountains."

"The Beorgai tribe," Ekandayo said. "The fourth tribe?"

"The tribe made of outcasts and deserters," Sabriel said.

"No," Ekandayo said. "The Prophet spoke to me of them once. He said they were those of the three tribes that refused to fight one another. They refused to kill other men of Lior and retreated into the mountains."

"Yes," Athelwulf said. "My father is Kiano, the elder of the Beorgai. He raised me to believe in El. But as happens with fathers and sons, I was rebellious and wanted to leave. I did not want to learn to be an elder after him. We had angry words, and I left. I braved the rainforest alone, and I came to Oshra. Over time, I became notorious in the city as a violent man, a criminal."

Jubali squinted. "Wait …"

"I was drunk and high on Sorcos every waking moment. I only cared about the next high, the next naked woman, and I would kill or beat anything to get what I wanted."

"What was your name?" Ekandayo asked, peering at Athelwulf. "Your real name."

"Namir was the name my father gave me."

The people of Lior in the room reacted. Some gasped, others took a step back.

Eshlyn swallowed hard. Had Athelwulf ever been that kind of man? She knew him to be such a strong, kind and compassionate man, to think of him as a killer and thief was difficult to believe.

"I see you heard of me," Ath said.

Sabriel pointed at him. "Murderer."

"Yes. I murdered. I killed. I did unspeakable things. I was addicted to Sorcos, and I became violent when the withdrawal symptoms hit. One night, I was looking for a fix, and the Citywatch tried to restrain me, a squad of them, but I killed them. I killed them all."

"They had swords, gladi, surely," Jubali said.

"Yes," Ath said.

"What weapon did you have?" Sabriel asked.

Athelwulf lifted his hands. "Just these. You do not need a weapon to kill."

"Great and mighty El," Ekandayo said.

"I knew that the elves would not overlook this," Athelwulf said. "They did not care if I killed other humans. Despite their rhetoric, they encouraged it in their own ways. But killing elves was a different story. They would scour the city for me."

Athelwulf let his hands drop again to his side. "I was a coward. I could not stay in the city. I could not go home to my father. I was not worthy. So I went north to the Forest of Saten to hide. And to die."

"But you didn't die," Esai said.

"No. I wandered the forest, and I began to go through withdrawals. One of the Ghosts found me near death and brought me to Mother Natali. She bound me within a tomb, an isolated place, to either beat the addiction or die. I survived. But I was not human. I was broken, full of remorse and guilt. Mother Natali gave me time to heal and taught me the truth of El. She gave me a new name." Athelwulf reached up and touched his heart. "El healed me. It took months, but I was able to stand again. Then I learned to hunt, to fight, and to be one of the Ghosts. Then a leader.

"A month ago, I stood at the top of Mount Elarus," he said. "El spoke so clearly to me; my heart broke once again at his mercy and love and strength. Then I placed my hands upon the Stone. It tested my heart and found me pure. Do you see? The *Ebenelif* tested my heart and found me pure. Me. A murderer. It was a miracle."

Athelwulf surveyed the faces in the room. "*And they believed in Yosu, and those that were once weak and corrupt became the men they were created to be, and more than men. They became the* Sohan-el." He repeated the words with intent and deliberation, his voice quiet and soft, and yet he held more authority than if he had shouted the words.

"You can change," Ath continued. "Miracles can happen. Man once believed in El, but he lost his way. But he can be shown a better way. You can change. It will be hard, I know. But if I can change, anyone can change. Humanity can change."

When Eshlyn was a child, her father told her of an ancient ritual the First Men had performed in Manahem. The elders would gather in Ketan. To show their unity, their brotherhood, they would announce their names, cut their palms and clasp their hands before the congregation of men and women. *All blood is red*, her father had said to her. *No matter what the man or woman is on the outside, all blood is red and gives life.*

Eshlyn felt the tears on her cheeks as she moved to stand before Athelwulf. She understood then why he protected Earon, why he desired to bring Earon back to Caleb and Carys. Eshlyn reached into her cloak and pulled out Kenric's unforged sword.

A chorus of noise and yelling erupted around her. "No bloodshed!" Ekandayo cried.

"This is a tradition from my people," Eshlyn answered. Holding out her own arm, she cut down the inside of her left palm. Blood dripped down her hand and forearm.

Eshlyn faced Athelwulf. "I am Eshlyn of Delaton in Manahem. And I am a woman created to be strong and free. And this man is my brother."

Athelwulf grinned at her, his own eyes brimming with tears. "Lady Eshlyn," he whispered. He pulled his own unforged sword from his hilt and sliced across his own left palm. "My name is Athelwulf of the Ghosts of the Saten, and this pink skin is my sister."

Esai was close to them now. He drew his sword and cut himself. "I am Esai of the Ghosts of Saten, and this is my brother and sister."

Eshlyn grinned at him. She turned to Ekandayo and grabbed his left arm. His men moved forward.

"It is all right," Ekandayo said to them, and they stopped.

Eshlyn cut across his palm.

"My name is Ekandayo of the Zwi tribe of Lior," he said. "And these are my brothers and sisters."

Eshlyn smiled at him and slid over to Jubali. Her eyes were storms of conflict. Eshlyn held out her own bloody hand.

Jubali glanced over at Sabriel and his men, scowls covering their faces. "You do not understand," Jubali said. "The hate and violence between us runs deep, generations and generations back, even before the Empire came."

"The love of El runs deeper still," Athelwulf said.

"This is useless," Sabriel said. "We need the elves. Standing against them only makes it worse. We all know this. It is impossible to change."

"No," Athelwulf said. "With El's help, any man can change."

Sabriel growled at Ath. "This from a murderer? We all heard of Namir, the animal, the hunter of Oshra."

"What better example do you require?" Esai asked.

Sabriel glared at him.

Athelwulf and Esai both took steps toward Sabriel.

"Be our brother," Esai said, pleading with the chief. "Sabriel of the Moffa tribe, be our brother."

The chief of the Moffa set his jaw. "I cannot."

The door to the warehouse opened again. Eshlyn watched a young boy run into the midst of them. He darted for Athelwulf, who frowned and knelt down to catch the running boy.

"Ath," the boy said, breathless.

"Dyam," Athelwulf said. "What is it?"

"They're comin', Ath," Dyam said. "They're comin'."

"Who is coming?" Eshlyn asked.

"Platoons of militans," Dyam said. "Led by the Pike. Comin' this way. And they settin' fire to the city as they come."

Chapter 12

To Heal a Burning City

"How many platoons?" Eshlyn asked, her heart suddenly beating strong in her chest. She walked up to the boy and Athelwulf.

Dyam looked up at her. "Two I seen. Maybe more."

Ekandayo was beside her now. "And you're sure they come here?"

"Right down the main street there," the boy said.

Athelwulf caught the boy's gaze. "How far away?"

Shrugging back, the boy said, "Maybe ten minutes."

Eshlyn heard Jubali's voice. "And they are setting fire to the city?"

"Yeah," he answered.

Ekandayo groaned. "The city is made almost entirely of wood. Fire will sweep this city in a matter of hours."

Athelwulf gazed up at Jubali, Ekandayo, and now Sabriel, who had joined them. "Where is the safest place? From a fire?"

The three elders shared a glance, unsure at first. Finally Jubali spoke. "The docks at the River Decel. There is a long field before the docks, dirt roads leading to them. If the fire gets too close, then the river can be safe. Or across it."

Ekandayo concurred. "The elves have their boats along the sea to the east, none at the docks along the river."

Producing another coin from his belt – a silver moon, Eshlyn saw – Athelwulf put the moon in the boy's hand. "You have done well. This is for you and your brothers to share, understand?"

Dyam looked wide-eyed at the coin in his hand. "Yeah."

"Then go and run as fast as you can to the docks at the river. You know the place?"

"Yeah," the boy said.

"Good," Athelwulf said, and he patted the boy on the shoulder. "Now go."

The boy raced off.

"Betrayed," Sabriel said. "Someone spoke to the elves."

Jubali crossed her arms under her breasts. "Agreed. But who?"

Sabriel pointed at Ekandayo. "This man called the meeting, and knew these people came from the *Brendel*."

Ekandayo sneered back at Sabriel. "And what of you? We know your affinity for the elves. Perhaps you have spies among my men and sold us out."

Athelwulf approached one of Ekandayo's men. "Go to our horses and bring us our bags."

The man hesitated, checking with Ekandayo for confirmation, which Ekandayo gave, and then the man darted out the door.

"I did nothing," Sabriel said, his hands balled into fists. "Why would I sell us out to the elves while standing here?"

"Why would I?" Ekandayo shouted. "I have tried for years to get us to stop fighting one another. Why would I betray the first opportunity we have had to accomplish that?"

"Let us be honest," Jubali said. "None of us here may be working with the elves, but any number of our people could be. We cannot root them all out. Anyone could have told the Empire about this meeting. And they may not even know about these from Ketan."

Sabriel frowned at her and rubbed his beard.

"Unfortunately, that is true," Ekandayo said. "I trust these men with me, but the elves have spies of which we are unaware. It could have been anyone."

"I knew it was mistake to come here," Jubali said. "Do you see what your plotting against the elves has done? What it will do? Only bring more death."

Both Ath and Esai wrapped their bloody palms with a cloth. Athelwulf handed one to Eshlyn, and she tied it across the cut, wincing as she made her hand into a fist.

Ekandayo's man came back with all three large canvas bags from Eshlyn, Athelwulf, and Esai's horses. Athelwulf pulled his away from the man and began to dig in the pack.

Eshlyn sighed. *What will it take for these to see we are not their enemy?* she thought. *Or that they are not enemies of one another?* "We did not set fire to the city. The Empire did that. They seek to bring fear upon you. We will fight to save what we can. But we cannot do it alone. What will you do?"

Athelwulf extracted his short bow from his pack and strung it. Esai was next to him and rummaging through his own pack for his bow.

Eshlyn scrutinized the elders. "You make your choice here and now. You can work together and save this city, or bicker and fight each other while the whole thing burns to the breakin' ground."

The three elders eyed their own men and then one another.

"The docks at the river are a good place," Ekandayo said. "We can get people to safety there, a great number of people away from the fire."

Jubali's nostrils flared. "And we can each get our people to get buckets, or anything that holds water, to the river and set up a chain to fight the fires, at least contain them so they do not spread."

"You forget," Sabriel said with contempt in his voice. "Fifty to a hundred militan are on their way here and will be here soon. Who knows how much more the boy didn't see. How are we going to get past them? We will be dead in the streets."

Athelwulf stepped forward with Esai behind him, each with a short bow in one hand and an unforged sword in the other. The cuts on their hands were wrapped in cloth.

"We will draw them off," Athelwulf said. "I know these streets well. I used to rule them, in my own way. I will again."

Eshlyn had her own sword in her hand. "I'll come with you."

"No," Athelwulf said. "I must ask you to take Earon with you to the river docks. I am sorry I cannot take him with me, but we must be unhindered as we lead the chase through the streets."

"Or we could kill him now," Esai said, but Eshlyn didn't think he sounded as convinced of that action as before.

Eshlyn turned back to Earon, his eyes glazed but aware, full of fear and desperation. Facing Athelwulf again, she said, "I'll take him with me. I understand."

"Thank you," Athelwulf said.

Her brow furrowed at him, however. "If he gives me any trouble, I can't promise I won't kill him anyway."

"I understand. When we have drawn the militan off and away, we will meet you at the docks."

Eshlyn smiled at them. "We'll see you there."

Athelwulf breathed heavy and glanced at Esai. They both raced out of the warehouse on foot.

There was a flash in her memory of Kenric, her husband, running to fight the demics in their hometown while she escaped with their son, Javyn. It froze her for a moment, but only a moment.

Eshlyn spun on the three elders. "They will buy us what time they can. Let's not waste it. You each go to your people and organize them, get them to the river so we can begin working together. We meet at the docks."

"What will you do?" Sabriel asked.

"I will gather and organize at the docks until you get there," Eshlyn said. "It would help if you sent one of your men with me to help, since they are more familiar with your people and confirm we are working together."

They each agreed, and Eshlyn grabbed their packs to take them back outside to the horses. The other men and women followed her outside the door.

And they all stood motionless, viewing the city.

Down the street and to the east, they could already see the flames climbing to the sky, black smoke even darker than the evening sky, billowing a half kilomitre away.

"Break it all," Eshlyn mumbled. "The whole city's like kindling for a hearth."

"Those two men gave their life for us," Jubali whispered from a pace away. She also stared at the flames in the distance. "For the good of the city. Two against legions."

"That is what *Sohan-el* do," Eshlyn said. "But do not worry. I've seen both men fight. I'd be more concerned about those legions."

—

Keeping to the right side of the street, Athelwulf led Esai north. Within a minute, Athelwulf could see the militan marching south towards them. Ducking behind a barrel next to a shack of a butcher shop that was closed for the evening, they crouched low.

Flames and smoke filled the sky a few hundred mitres to the north.

The First Sergeant rode on a black stallion next to four lines of elves, each one in a breastplate and helmet with shield, spear, and gladus. The four militan in front had their shields raised and their spears forward; the elves on the outside of the formation carried their shields to their side to protect the flank. Athelwulf could see torches regularly spaced among them.

Esai stole a view around Athelwulf. "That's two platoons. Fifty elves?"

"Maybe more."

Athelwulf knew the strength of the Kryan military: organization, specialization, structure, and uniformity. They conquered men with these advantages. Chaos and evasion would be their weapons tonight. First, they had to divert them.

"Plan?" Esai asked.

Athelwulf sheathed his sword and pulled an arrow from the handful he had in his quiver. "Make ourselves a target."

Esai mimicked him. They each had twenty-one arrows in their quiver, Ghost-made fine arrows.

"Don't take out the First Sergeant. We want him to give orders to follow. And since these are short bows, we'll have to wait until they are close." He nocked an arrow. "Shoot once and then you follow me to the east."

Esai set his own arrow.

The platoons were fifty mitres away now. Athelwulf emerged from behind the barrel and walked to the middle of the street with Esai following him. He pulled the arrow back.

The First Sergeant noticed the two men aiming arrows at them, and then he called for the formation to halt, raising a gloved hand.

"Wait until they move again," Athelwulf said, only loud enough for Esai to hear.

Both platoons stopped as one, but as they stopped, they closed ranks so their shields were a wall before them.

"Aim for their feet," Athelwulf whispered, but he did not move.

Esai grunted assent. Both men aimed.

The First Sergeant studied them for a moment, a large blue plume on his helmet. He raised his hand and called for a charge.

"Hold," Athelwulf mumbled. "I have the left."

"The right."

Kryan legions were trained to be more than a military unit; they were more like a force of nature. Every militan knew just what to do. They all simultaneously broke into a jog, their short boots a uniform rhythm upon the dirt of the street, the shields and spears firm and unmoving even as they advanced.

When the front ranks were thirty mitres away, Athelwulf said, "Now."

Both men fired at once, adjusting their aim at the last second, firing down and into the legs of the front ranks. Athelwulf's arrow went through a foot, and the elf tumbled in pain with a cry. Esai's shaft stuck into the meat of another's shin; that elf squealed in agony and twisted as he fell.

The elves behind the wounded also fell. Some tried to leap their companions, others trampled the ones on the ground. The charge stalled, and the First Sergeant cursed and inspected the two men that stood up to his platoons. Athelwulf grinned. Could the First Sergeant see him grin? Didn't matter.

Twenty mitres away now, elves falling over one another, desperate to re-form a line, the sergeant yelling.

Athelwulf lowered his bow and pulled his sword. Esai did the same.

The night sky was clear, and there was a growing yellow light from the flames behind the elves as they approached. The unforged swords caught that light and blazed white and yellow in the night.

Neither man spoke for another moment. Athelwulf pivoted and ran to the east down a side street between the shack of a butcher shop and a larger bakery, Esai at his heels.

And Athelwulf prayed that the militan would follow.

—

Eshlyn grabbed Blackie's reins in the street outside the warehouse. "Take the horses," she said to the elders. "Three of you and three horses. They'll help you get to your people faster."

She could hear yelling and noise up ahead on the street to the north.

Ekandayo frowned at her. "What of you?"

Kenric's sword was still in her hand. "I'll be okay on foot," she said. "And your men will be with me. It is more important for you to have the speed."

Jubali took Esai's horse. "Thank you, Eshlyn," she said after she mounted it.

"Just get your people to safety," she said as Ekandayo climbed upon Athelwulf's horse. "And meet me at the docks."

"We will," Ekandayo said. "El be with you."

"And with you," she said as Ekandayo rode off to the east and Jubali to the west.

Sabriel ambled towards her. "You are either brave or suicidal," he said.

"We are followers of El," she said. "It can be difficult to tell the difference."

His face went blank, but he stepped up onto Blackie.

"This is my horse," she said to him. "I expect her back."

Sabriel did not answer; he shook his head and rode off to the north.

More noise from up the street, pounding of feet upon the dirt of the road. Were the flames reaching higher?

Ekandayo's man, Hyan, stepped close to her. "Come," he said. "We must go."

Earon was still bound and gagged behind her, but on his feet. Holding a rope like a leash to his wrists, she was alone with seven men, all of them angry and confused; it didn't take a breakin' prophet or a feeling from Kenric's sword to see that.

She gestured to the west. "Lead on," she said.

—+—

Esai followed Athelwulf through the streets of Oshra, always glancing back to see if the militan were following. With shields and spears and the need to stay in a formation, the militan were not fast as a unit. The two men could easily outrun the elves, so their goal was to draw the soldiers away, not to escape.

After five minutes, and the militan trotting towards them more than fifty mitres away, Athelwulf stopped, focused on the troops behind them.

"That is only one platoon," he said.

Esai could see he was correct. He saw twenty-five elves with a commander on foot. "Where is the other one?" Esai asked.

"We need to find out."

"So now we're going to be hunting militan instead of running from them?"

Athelwulf sheathed his sword and pulled another arrow from his quiver. The platoon was forty mitres away.

"We've been hunting them. They just don't know it yet."

Namir, the hunter of Oshra, Sabriel had said. Only now hunting for a different reason.

Esai watched him pull back the arrow and fire. The shaft twisted in the air as it arced down the street and then fell into the face of the platoon commander, killing the elf instantly. The platoon halted, faces darting to one another and the enemy that just took out their commander.

"I haven't seen shooting like that since Carys," Esai muttered.

"Who do you think taught her?" Athelwulf caught a whiff of smoke in the air. "They will dither for a while. Come."

Athelwulf ran north for two streets and then took a left to go back west. He was doubling back on the other platoon, Esai realized.

The streets of Ketan were evenly spaced and created regular blocks throughout the city, making it easy to navigate. The streets of Oshra, however, had no pattern. Some were straight, others curved back around themselves, and still others made wild corners along a winding course. Only a man with Athelwulf's past could successfully navigate such a labyrinth. It was like knowing the Forest of Saten, an organic presence that took love and time to learn.

They could hear the roaring of flames to the north, close by, and the smoke was beginning to lay upon the city. People were out in the streets, some crying and afraid, others dazed, drugged out on Sorcos. Esai and Ath both yelled at them to get to the river docks as they ran past.

Two streets west, Athelwulf led them south again at a dead sprint. Athelwulf had twenty years on Esai, but Esai was impressed at the man's speed. Within a minute, they could see the other platoon, but this time they approached the elves from behind. The platoon was at the warehouse now, where they met minutes before and adjusting west to follow the others. The buildings on either side of them were on fire, recently put to the torch. The platoon had paused to begin burning the warehouse.

Citizens ran random through the streets, and when they came close to the elven militan, the elves bereft of torches would cut down the men, women, and children as they neared. The militan laughed and encouraged one another to continue the slaughter like it was a game.

Cursing to himself in anger, Esai darted across the street and kept to the shadows to the right – dodging the flames – while Athelwulf did the same on the left. Their swords were sheathed, and arrows were nocked as they crept up behind the militan. Now thirty mitres away, Athelwulf caught his gaze and flashed a finger at him and pointed to the arrow. *One shot*, Esai understood. They didn't have a host of arrows to waste; Ghosts made their own arrows, so being stingy with them was normal.

Taking two steps out into the street, Esai drew back the shaft and aimed at the back of a militan on the right. He knew without looking that Ath did the same on the left. Esai waited for Athelwulf to fire, and then his arrow followed through the air. Both arrows connected – Athelwulf's through the back of the neck of one militan and Esai's dug into the back of another's thigh. The first fell dead, but the second screamed in surprise and pain.

The whole platoon began to change direction, yelling and repositioning their lines to face the men behind them. Thankfully, Esai saw men and women escape.

The First Sergeant of the platoon came around his soldiers on his horse. The Sergeant began to reorganize his troops. In the last few seconds, the fires had engulfed whole buildings, the flames roaring and cracking around them all.

Esai glanced back north, and while much of the city he could see was burning, he believed they could make it through the streets.

As the platoon formed up and began to run in their direction, the First Sergeant charging this time at the front, Athelwulf eyed Esai.

"Try to keep up," he said and took off at a sprint.

+—

Eshlyn, Hyan, and the others reached the docks. It was difficult to discern, but she thought it took them a half hour of running through the winding, narrow streets of Oshra before they made it to the southwest edge of the city.

Jubali had been correct; this was a good place to gather, and others had already comprehended this. Hundreds, perhaps a couple thousand, huddled at the docks. There was a large field – some type of public square or market area – between the docks and the buildings of the city, mostly residences from what Eshlyn could see. She crossed the field at a jog.

As she neared the docks, she noticed boats, vessels for fishing or travel more suited to the river than the sea beyond to the east of the city. She could smell and hear the water of the river. The scent of the river mixed with the hint of the smoke behind her and the sweat and odor of the people ahead of her.

Hyan was next to her as they reached the crowd, who watched her warily.

Eshlyn carried a long sword, after all.

One of Jubali's men, a big tall one with a bald head, carried Earon as they ran. Even if Earon had wanted to cooperate, he was weak and wouldn't be able to run very fast, so this man – Parta was his name – offered to carry the traitor.

A few paces away from the crowd now, Eshlyn stopped and addressed them. "People of Oshra," she said, projecting her voice as well as she could. "We must find buckets, small barrels, anything we can to take water back into the city and fight those fires."

The crowd quieted but did not move. She turned and raised an eyebrow at Hyan.

He grunted and stepped forward. "Please listen to this pink skin," he said, his voice even louder, booming across the people. "The elves have set fire to the city, and we must try to contain the destruction before it consumes all of Oshra."

Murmurs among those huddled against one another. "Why would they set fire to the city?" a woman asked near her.

"I don't know," Eshlyn said. "But that isn't important right now. We have to get a line going to carry water into the city."

"This woman comes from Ketan," Hyan said. "From the *Brendel*."

More talking from the crowd, some shouting. "That man is evil!"

"He eats the souls of the elves!"

"The elves come for *her*!"

Well, that didn't help, Eshlyn thought.

Eshlyn lifted the sword and saw its reflection flash over the people nearby. People gasped, and women clutched their naked children to their thighs. "If you are injured or unable to help," Eshlyn said, and she pointed with the sword to the right, north of the docks. "Please move to the side. Those of you who can help, search the docks and the boats for whatever we can use to carry water."

Feet shuffled, and one or two began to move, but most stood or sat where they were.

Don't they care what happens to their city, their homes? she asked herself. But she saw fear in their eyes. There might be some apathy, as well, as an effect of years of subjugation and Sorcos, but there was still fear.

She raised the sword again. "Listen," she cried. "I know you are afraid. I am, too. We are all afraid. I swear to you that I am here to help, that is all. But if we are to save your city, then we must face this fear together."

A few more moved, some to the right to get out of the way, others to search the docks and the boats for receptacles that could carry water.

Hyan spoke from beside her as she lowered the sword again. "You ask them to go back into a burning city, and they know that the elves are there, waiting for them."

"And now they think that the elves are hunting the people from Ketan, too," Eshlyn said.

"Well, aren't they?"

She glared at him. "We don't know that."

"It is a safe assumption. The elves have their ways of knowing."

"But you didn't have to tell *them* that!" she said.

Hyan shrugged.

"Break it all," she said, taking a step closer to him. "Your elder told you to help me. Is this your idea of help?"

He didn't answer.

"Go with those people trying to find buckets or whatever and form them in a line from the river once they do." She leaned closer. "Please."

Hyan hesitated. Then he nodded and walked through the crowd towards the docks.

Eshlyn turned to the other men nearby. Parta had set Earon back down on his feet by now, and she took the rope tied to the traitor's wrists. "You men go help, too," she said. "Form them in a line to the city so we can transport the water to the flames."

They hesitated, but they complied.

Dragging Earon with her, Eshlyn entered the crowd as well. She began grabbing men and women who appeared healthy and able, lifting them from their feet or pushing them towards the docks, forcing them to help.

She was sent to save this city. Oshra would not burn down to the ground. Not if she could help it.

———

Athelwulf led Esai through a confusing journey of twists through streets and alleys, but the young man was doing well.

"We doubling back again," Esai said as they ran.

Athelwulf slowed. The Kryan military strengths – the organization and specialization – needed singular leadership and absolute obedience to work as efficiently as it did. The remaining platoon that followed them was being directed by a First Sergeant. "We need to take out that Sergeant before we meet them at the docks."

"You know where you're leading them, don't you?"

He did. There was an intersection up ahead, and the elven platoon would pass through there in a few minutes. He knew the perfect vantage point...

As they turned right down another street, a squad of militan stood and blocked the way ten paces away. The eight elves were as surprised as Athelwulf and Esai, shuffling to ready their shields and spears. Athelwulf did not slow as he shouldered the bow and pulled his sword.

Caleb once told Athelwulf that the ancient *Sohan-el* were something to behold. Legends told of them taking on hundreds of enemies alone, impossible stories, but even impossible legends possessed a root of truth, if not more than that. This eight-elf squad of militan faced two warriors of El.

The unforged swords were the perfect weapons; they cut through spears and shields, never slowing as both men furiously attacked. Even the fine elven blades of the gladi were sheared when the militan attempted to block with their weapons. Athelwulf and Esai said nothing and made little sound, their minds engrossed and focused on the battle, but the dirt street was filled with shouts of confusion and fear – and cries and whimpers of death. Ten seconds passed and the two men stood alone, pieces of elven weapons and limbs and blood all around them.

Once the battle was over, Athelwulf felt pain on his left arm. Glimpsing down, he had been cut across his upper arm. It bled but did not appear to be too deep. He hadn't noticed when it happened.

"Are you hurt?" Esai asked, trotting towards him.

"I will be okay," Athelwulf said. "Come, we don't have much time left."

Continuing down the dirt street, Athelwulf stopped at a taller building, an Oshran tenement, smaller than those in Ketan, but similar. He went into the alley where a ladder took them to the roof. They climbed the ladder and stood on the slanted wooden tiles of the roof.

They could take in the city from here, and a quarter of the city was in flames. It caused both of them to stop. Athelwulf viewed the devastation. How long had it been? Little more than a half hour and a quarter of the city consumed in flame.

"Great and mighty El," Esai whispered.

"We must hurry and help them at the docks," Athelwulf said. "We need to contain the fires, and I have not seen any with water."

"There is the platoon," Esai said in a quiet and calm voice, and he pointed to the south.

A hundred mitres away, the First Captain with the large blue plume on his helmet led his platoon through the city. After being led on a chase, the elves seemed tired and unsure, even as they stuck to their rigid formation. Elves sought the shadows around them.

"This is a perfect place for an ambush," Esai said.

Athelwulf remembered this spot well. The whole city, every street, held sharp memories for him. As drugged and drunk as he had been then, he could recall moments now in stark detail. There had been a riot in this intersection, and he and his friends did ambush a few men from a rival gang here. He killed three men that day with his bare hands. *All for money and lust*, he thought.

"Get ready," he said and nocked an arrow.

Esai set his own after pulling the bow from his shoulder.

"We both aim for the First Captain," Athelwulf said.

Esai aimed down the shaft.

Sixty mitres away, Athelwulf said, "You have him?"

"Yes," Esai answered.

"Ready … and fire."

They both fired at once at the First Captain, and both arrows found their mark. The First Captain groaned as one arrow hit him in the left thigh and the other – Athelwulf's – hit him in the throat. He tottered and then fell from his black stallion, the helmet with the blue plume rolling on the ground as he hit and lay writhing.

The platoon reacted. Some scanned the area and one found the shadows on the roof. Yelling and shouting at one another, some tried in vain to save the First Captain.

"Come," Athelwulf said to Esai as he moved back over the roof to the ladder. "Let us get to the docks."

———

By the time Eshlyn saw Jubali arrive at the docks, a line was forming. At one end of the line, there were people plunging buckets and other receptacles into the river. Then the water was passed down and into the city. She had to coerce too many, which she was loathe to do, but it had to be done. Earon was lashed to the mast of a nearby fishing boat.

She pushed a strand of dark hair out of her eyes as she met Jubali. The woman was on Esai's horse, and hundreds of people followed her from the city, many of them carrying a bucket or small pitcher.

"Thank El you are here," Eshlyn said.

Jubali glowered at the crowd, hundreds of men and women standing while few worked. "What is going on? Why are these others not working?"

Eshlyn put her hands on her hips. "We tried to get them to help. I had to force many of these that are helping."

Jubali rode the horse further into the crowd that sat or stood apart from those helping. "For those of the Xon tribe," she called out, and her voice carried an authority that Eshlyn envied. How did she do that? "Unless you have a broken limb, you must help save this city. Get in this line and get water to stop the flames."

The hundreds behind her moved into the line, and more than half of those left in the crowd began to join, as well. Their feet shuffled slowly, but they obeyed.

"Thank you," Eshlyn said.

The woman's face was twisted in anger. "They are afraid, but that can no longer be an excuse."

Eshlyn couldn't argue that point.

Ekandayo arrived next, proceeding from the city to the docks with hundreds in his wake. He rode Athelwulf's horse to join Eshlyn and Jubali. His face was soaked with sweat, and he beckoned to the people behind him. A good many of them carried buckets or bedpans, as well. "Come! As I told you, help carry water back into the city. We must stop the fires."

The men and women with Ekandayo rushed forward, ready to help.

Eshlyn helped Ekandayo form a separate line that would lead further east into the city, which took some time. Standing with Jubali and Ekandayo at the edge of the city, they could tell that the fires were spreading towards the center of Oshra, close to the palace and temple. She hoped they could stop the conflagration before it swallowed the city whole.

"Where is Sabriel?" Eshlyn asked.

"He should have arrived before me," Ekandayo said. "His people are in the north."

"It is concerning that he is not here yet," Jubali said. "Should we send someone for him?"

Eshlyn thought of her horse, Blackie, and Ath and Esai within the burning city. A third of the city had not joined them, but should they take effort away from the people carrying water into the city? It was just beginning to work. She touched the golden marriage bracelet on her right wrist. "No," she said. "Let us wait a while longer. And pray. We should pray."

———

Sabriel rode that pink skin woman's horse and led his people through the burning maze of streets through Oshra. Several times he had to turn the column around and find a different way as burning buildings had fallen across the street and blocked it.

Thousands of people followed him through the streets, the number growing as they wound their way to the west and the south. Doubling back when the way was blocked took precious time they couldn't waste, but the burning of the city determined his choices.

He was young for a chief, only forty-five years old. His father had grown sick, and the Imperial physicians were unable to help him. They had only wanted to give him Sorcos and other drugs to make him comfortable. Sabriel watched, helpless, as his father wasted away and died. That had been five years ago. Even though he was young, he took the responsibility seriously, sometimes too seriously, his wife would tell him.

She looked up at him now, still beautiful after all these years, still beautiful despite the soot and sweat covering her oval face. She walked beside him and helped to organize and guide as they moved to safety.

The fire sweeping through the city was a living thing, riding the wind and jumping and spreading across Sabriel's home, a being with an insatiable appetite for destruction. The people of the Moffa tribe that he guided through the narrow ways had their faces covered with cloth, their shoulders hunched, their heads lowered while they coughed and struggled for breath. Several carried loved ones that had collapsed from the lack of oxygen.

Sabriel, the chief of the Moffa, knew the city well, and his mind worked, mapping out the quickest route to get his people to safety.

The city of Oshra sprawled like branches or tentacles of a living being. This was the place of his birth, the home for the large family of the Moffa, and as he led the procession to safety, he watched his home die.

The elves had set fire to the city. The Empire that claimed to be their protector brought wanton devastation. Rooting out rebellion he could understand. But he could not comprehend random killing of the innocent. The anger within him began to burn and boil like the flames around him, beginning with a spark and becoming its own conflagration within his soul with every setback as he tried to get his people to safety.

But they relied upon the elves for their provision and safety. Was there any truth to what Athelwulf and Eshlyn had said? And that Esai? Were their words really an option for the tribes of Lior?

Up ahead, he saw an open and wide street where the fire had not yet reached, a way that led to the outskirts of the city and to the river. The anger within Sabriel cooled for a moment at the sliver of hope before him. They were almost there. With the flames chewing through the buildings behind them, he hurried his people in that direction.

As he made the turn, however, he pulled up on the horse's reins and cursed. Fifty mitres down the broad street, Sabriel saw over two hundred elven militan in formation across the road, their spears at the ready and their shields linked together like a wall.

The people of the Moffa behind him cried out and halted in their tracks; hundreds milled about him as they pressed forward, running from the fire behind but pausing at the might of the Empire before them.

An elf sat upon a horse to the right, just behind the front line of the militan. He wore the armor and plume of a general, a First General of the Kryan Legion.

General Wyus. The Pike.

Sabriel gave his wife a hard stare and rode forward. He stopped five mitres away from the Kryan militan and addressed the First General, the Pike.

It took an act of will to bow to the Pike, but Sabriel could hear the hum and crackle of the flames and the cries of his people behind him. He chose his words carefully. "Lord General of the Kryan Empire, our protector and provider," he said. "My name is Sabriel Go'Lian of the Moffa tribe of the nation of Lior, the subjects of the Emperor of Tanicus, whom we both serve. We are seeking refuge from the fire at the river. I humbly ask that you allow us to pass."

The Pike narrowed his eyes at Sabriel, and for a moment, Sabriel wasn't sure whether or not the General was going to answer him at all.

"No one leaves," the Pike said. "We have received information that the city is harboring enemies of the Empire in their midst, men from the city of Ketan, rebels from the man they call the *Brendel*."

"We have also heard those rumors," Sabriel said. "But I can assure you, those people are not among us. We are only seeking refuge."

The Pike scanned the throng of Lior. "There are many among you. How can you be so sure?"

Sabriel scoffed and waved behind him at the tired, half-naked and filthy people cowering in fear. "Do these look like revolutionaries to you? We are simply the servants of the Empire seeking to get to safety. Let us pass!"

"Anyone can be a revolutionary," the Pike said.

"Please," Sabriel said. "Look at us. We have no weapons. We are no threat to you or the Empire."

"I have reason to suspect every human in Oshra," the Pike replied.

Sabriel glanced over his shoulder at the encroaching flames. No way back now. The only way was forward.

He growled in frustration. "So thousands of innocents will die?"

"To protect the Empire, yes," the Pike said. "Millions more if necessary." The Pike glared at him. "Or one."

Sabriel was speechless.

The Pike called to the front line of the militan. "First squad, take that man into custody," he said. "For questioning."

Fifteen militan from the front line rushed him. The horse reared, and Sabriel fell with a shout and landed on the hard dirt of the street on his back, the breath knocked from him. He heard his wife scream his name as hands grabbed his arms and lifted him to his feet.

The Pike said one word. "Sergeant." And the Sergeant of the squad pulled his gladus and set the blade against Sabriel's neck, cold steel even in the heat of the flames that continued to surround them.

"People of Oshra, our time is short," the General said. "You will give me the rebels among you or I will take this man's head from his body. You have ten seconds."

The front line of the militan formed up again, linking their shields and lowering their spears. The intention was clear. They were going to sweep over the men, women, and children of the Moffa and kill them all.

Thousands of humans cried out, screamed, shouted, searching in fear for some way out and finding none. Many fell to their knees, helpless and resigned to their death.

"Five seconds," the Pike said. And even though Sabriel could not see his face, he thought he heard a grin in the elf's voice.

"No," Sabriel moaned. "No!"

"Time's up," the Pike said. "Sergeant?"

Sabriel could see the grin this time as the elf drew back his gladus. Hands tightened around him.

Hearing the thud first, Sabriel's mind took a moment to register the arrow that suddenly sunk into the Sergeant's neck. The elf squeaked in pain and fell back, and droplets of blood splattered across Sabriel's face.

There was a curse from another elf near him, and the hands holding Sabriel loosened. Within another split second, two more arrows found their home within a militan around the Moffa chief. Sabriel twisted free and dropped to his knees as another arrow brought down a militan.

The elves were shouting now, their heads swiveling on their shoulders, their shields up.

Sabriel took advantage of the distraction and scurried away and back to his people, past the pink skin woman's horse and over two dead elves.

From behind the militan, more shouts of pain and screams of death as elves fell and died. Arrows from their rear, now, and the militan whirled to adjust as more of them collapsed with arrows through an eye or their neck or sunk deep into their back or chest. The elves stood in a close formation, so it took time for them to react. Sabriel did not know how many died as he crawled back to his people.

His wife grabbed his elbow and pulled Sabriel to his feet, frozen in shock at nearly losing his life.

The Pike shouted orders now and commanded the front line of the militan to attack, to move forward, as he pointed up to Sabriel's left and the second story of the building there. Two more arrows flew from the window, taking one militan on the front line through the ear. The second arrow arced towards the Pike.

The General drew his sword and cut the arrow in half from the air.

A figure appeared in the window, almost four mitres above them. It was Esai with his sword blazing bright in his hand as it reflected the red and yellow light of the flames creeping down the street.

Sabriel watched as Esai sneered at the elves below him and jumped from the building.

With a swing of his sword, Esai batted away a spear aimed at him as he landed atop one of the militan that had been holding Sabriel. The elf broke Esai's fall as his knees rammed the militan's chestplate. They hit the ground together, the militan under Esai, and the *Sohan-el* rolled forward, coming up in a crouch and swinging his sword, cutting through the legs of another militan nearby. The militan fell with a gurgle, and blood sprayed from the stumps of his legs.

More than a dozen dead elves already littered the space between the Kryan division and the Moffa tribe, and as Esai kept moving, he grabbed a shield and a spear from the ground within a heartbeat. With the shield attached to his left forearm, the spear in his left hand, and that beautiful sword in his right, Esai waded into the hundred elves that stood before him.

All Sabriel could do was watch, as if time slowed and the noise was drowned out by his awe. Esai blocked spears with his shield or ducked them, swung his own spear to gain space and distance, and then he attacked with the sword. The sword in his hand cut through the elven shields and armor, ravaging the front line of the Kryan division. One by one he killed them, and in a few seconds, twenty or more elves were dead, and Esai stepped over them to bring down even more.

Not without cost, however. Sabriel could see cuts and gashes along the man's thigh and upper arm and a deep one in his side above his hip, but none of those seemed to affect him. Esai moved with efficiency and speed and precision.

Half of the division was turned away from Esai, concentrating on a threat behind them, and within moments, the wall of Kryan militan broke before Sabriel and the Moffa. Dozens of elves were dead at the rear of the Kryan position, and he could see a taller Liorian man in a green tunic and brown breeches with long matted hair flying about him as he spun and killed with an elven shield in one hand and one of those unforged swords in the other. He took a limb off an elf with a swipe and cut through the gut of another as he reversed his swing.

Namir the Hunter of Oshra. Now Athelwulf the *Sohan-el*.

What better example do you require?

Between the flames behind and around them, the battle joined before them, the broken Kryan formations, the din of shouting and howls of the dying, the whole scene was chaos and confusion.

Sabriel took a step forward, his wife clutching at his arm. He shrugged her off. A few paces away, centimitres away from the fingers of a militan, he noticed a gladus lay in the dust and dirt.

A roar pierced the noise and chaos and Sabriel's gaze rose to see the Pike enter the battle. The Pike charged towards Esai on his large warhorse.

Taking another step forward, Sabriel cried out. "Esai!"

Esai spun in a circle out of the path of the horse and attacked at the same time, stabbing the horse through the side with the spear. The horse shrieked and reared. The Pike cut down with his sword, which Esai blocked with his own. As the warhorse fell to the side, the Pike leapt with almost supernatural grace, flipping backwards to land in a crouch.

While distracted with the Pike's charge, a militan stabbed Esai from behind with a spear, the blade sinking deep into Esai's shoulder. Dropping his spear, Esai spun with a wail and cut the elf's head from his body with the unforged sword. The wood of the spear had snapped during the turn and the blade protruded from Esai's shoulder.

More militan crowded him.

Sabriel strode forward, his eyes drawn to the gladus before him.

The Pike was up, now, and advanced upon Esai with his sword raised. The young man tried to get the shield up in time, but the wound on his left shoulder pained him, and he could only turn the Pike's slash, and the General's blade swiped across his chest, blood spraying in an arc. Esai grunted, his breathing labored now, as he sidestepped another stab from a militan to his left and cut the militan's arm from his body. But the Pike took advantage of another distraction and swung at Esai's head, which the man was able to duck.

Sabriel knelt down and picked up the gladus. He heard his wife say his name again. He looked from the short sword to Esai.

Esai snarled as he somehow transformed his narrow escape into an attack, swiping at the Pike, forcing the General to block and retreat a step. Esai shuffled his feet forward and kept up the attack on the Pike. The man was not as fast as he was a moment ago, carried as he seemed to be by will alone, but he was fast enough to keep the Pike on his heels.

The *Sohan-el* left puddles of blood from numerous wounds in his wake.

Only a few militan were still standing, perhaps 30 or more, and many of those were engaged with Athelwulf five mitres away, but a militan approached Esai from behind with a spear and a gladus, one in each hand.

"No!" Sabriel said, and he sprinted forward with the gladus in his hand.

Esai either did not hear him or was so focused on his own adversary that he could not risk a distraction. He did not react, but the militan did, recoiling at the sight of the Moffa chief racing towards him. The militan could not respond in time, but Sabriel possessed no experience with the sword; his swing missed badly. Their bodies collided, and they fell together.

Sabriel heard the militan inhale shaprly as they tumbled in an awkward embrace, and when Sabriel came up to his hands and knees, the militan stared at him with empty eyes and a gladus sunk to the hilt into his chest. Whose sword was that? Sabriel didn't know.

By the nine gods, he thought.

Noticing movement to his right, he straightened on his knees to see another militan bearing down on him with a gladus. Sabriel's own hands were empty, and he brought them up in front of his face as the militan swung at him.

A spear appeared from over Sabriel's shoulder and impaled the militan where he stood. Sabriel fell back on his haunches and viewed his wife with a horrified look on her face and tears streaming from her face. A hundred more men and women of the Moffa followed behind her, many of them picking up spears, gladi, and shields, pressing forward.

His wife dropped the spear and helped him to his feet, and she fell into his arms as the Moffa passed them, running down what remained of the militan. Holding his wife, he turned in time to see Esai continuing to battle the Pike. They struck and parried, and suddenly, Esai knocked aside the

Pike's sword and gave a final, desperate horizontal swing that took the Pike's head from his body.

The head flew a mitre into the air, blood spurting behind it, and it fell to the ground a second after the General's body collapsed. With his own wounds covering him in blood, Esai stumbled forward, dropping his sword. He reached down and grabbed an elven spear.

Sabriel broke from his wife's embrace, took her hand, and walked towards Esai.

The *Sohan-el* picked up the Pike's head, and with a pained grimace, he lifted the head and shoved the neck onto the butt end of the spear with a sickening, wet sound. Facing the final moments of the battle on the streets of Oshra, the city burning down around him, Esai lifted the head into the air above him. With a bellowing cry, he stabbed the end of the spear into the ground. The spear standing on its own now, Esai's knees gave out and he crumpled.

"Esai!" Sabriel called and reached him in time to catch him and guide him to the ground, his wife kneeling down with him.

Athelwulf stood over them now. "Great and mighty El," he breathed.

Sabriel glowered at his wife. "Get the people to the river," he said. "Please."

His wife frowned at him with resolve and stood. He could hear her shouting at the Moffa people. Thousands ran by him away from the fire and to safety.

Athelwulf knelt next to Esai.

"Will he live?" Sabriel pleaded with the man.

Athelwulf only grit his teeth, tears brimming in his eyes.

"No," Sabriel said, pressing his hand against the gushing gash across Esai's chest, trying to stifle the blood loss.

Esai's eyes opened to slits. "Sabriel," he said.

Sabriel hushed him, but the man kept talking.

"My sword," he said.

Sniffling, Sabriel cast his gaze around and reached back to grab the hilt of the sword, bringing it around to lay it upon Esai's chest.

"Here it is," Sabriel said.

Esai licked his lips, his breathing shallow. "I … climbed a mountain to get that sword," he said.

Sabriel gripped Esai's bloody tunic.

"But before I received the sword, El spoke to me."

More people running by him, his wife calling to them, the heavy footsteps and feet shuffling, the flames on either side of them now.

"I was there, in the blackness. I could not see with my eyes or hear with my ears … but I knew. I was closer to him than anything ever in my life. I was … connected to everything, to life himself. And he spoke to me. To me."

Athelwulf reached out and put a hand upon Esai.

"He showed me a burning city. And he asked me a question. *Will you give your life to heal the burning city?* That is what he asked me. And do you know what I answered?"

Sabriel could only breathe.

"I said, 'yes,' my brother. I told him I would."

Tears streamed into Athelwulf's thick beard, but he made no sound.

"Are you my brother, Sabriel?"

"Yes," he said. "I am your brother. And you are mine."

Esai took his sword and pressed it to Sabriel's chest. "Here, my brother. I have many brothers, all over Eres. Fight with your brothers. Do not hate them. Stand with them. Love them, and no matter what happens, live or die, you will be free."

The chief of the Moffa grabbed the sword as Esai gave it to him.

Esai's eyes closed, gasping for one last breath that he never gained, and fell still.

———

The night began hot, but with the flames and smoke of the burning city, it was now sweltering. Eshlyn had sweat through her blouse, and her hair was soaked as she carried water to fight the flames consuming Oshra.

Over the last hour, the people of Oshra, under leadership from Jubali and Ekandayo, had pulled together and formed three lines that carried water into the city. And the last report was that the fires were not spreading. They might even be fighting them back.

There was also concern that the fire would spread into the surrounding forest, so they began to direct the lines of relief to the edges of the city, especially to the northeast.

Wiping at the beads of sweat on her forehead, she stood straight and took a deep breath, and coughed. The wind was blowing the smoke towards her. She lifted a hand to her mouth as she cleared her throat.

As she arched her back, stretching it, she could see a column of people emerge from the edge of the city. She separated from the line and moved to intersect them, noticing Jubali and Ekandayo doing the same. At the front of the column, she could see the intricate patterns of Sabriel's long dress tunic and his short cap, and he carried someone in his arms – a bloody Esai.

No, no, no, no, she kept thinking.

She broke into a run, whimpering. Behind Sabriel, Athelwulf led her horse, Blackie, and a thousand, or two thousand, people dressed in tatters and covered in sweat and soot.

Reaching them, she could tell that Esai was dead. His skin was ashen, and he wasn't breathing. "Put him down," she said, and Sabriel complied, laying his body on the ground there in the middle of the vast field before the docks. She knelt down next to the body, and Athelwulf joined her. Tears mixed with the sweat on her face.

"Oh, Esai," Eshlyn said.

"The Pike and a division of militan were keeping Sabriel's people from getting to safety," Athelwulf explained. "We attacked to make a way for them. There were so many. He fought well."

The three elders all stood around them.

"I am sorry," Jubali said.

"He gave his life for us," Sabriel said, his voice a broken, quiet sound. "He could have gone to safety. But instead he fought so we could live."

Eshlyn placed her hand upon the top of Esai's head, touching the short curls there. She kissed his forehead and sat up again. "That is what he was taught to do," she said. "Fight for the oppressed and the innocent."

Glancing up, she saw Esai's sword in Sabriel's hand.

"Just as the Prophet taught," Ekandayo said.

"And lived and died for," Athelwulf said. He caught Eshlyn's gaze with his own. "They know we are here."

"What?" she asked.

"The Pike spoke with Sabriel," Athelwulf said. "The elves know we have come from Caleb and Ketan."

"So they burn the whole breakin' city?" Eshlyn asked.

"They do what they feel they must," Athelwulf said. "Burning a city is worth retaining their control."

"Like burning a house to kill a snake," Eshlyn said. "Insanity."

"Yes," Athelwulf said, gazing down at the young man again.

Eshlyn sighed. "I think we have the fire contained," she said. "And now with the help of the Moffa, we can continue to fight it back. In the next few days, Athelwulf and I will continue to meet and help the elders work together. People will need new homes. We'll need to organize ..."

As she looked at Athelwulf, she paused, his face full of conflict.

"What?" she asked him.

"You are free to stay here and help," Athelwulf said. "But tomorrow, I am leaving."

"Break it all, Athelwulf," she said. "We just shoggin' got here!"

"That is true," he said.

Running a hand back through her sweaty hair, she collected herself. He was going to leave this city, now, when they needed him the most. What was his problem? He ...

"Your father," she said. "You're going north to see your family."

"Time is short, Lady Eshlyn," Athelwulf said. "I feel El ... calling me. North. To the mountains. I will take Earon with me."

"Can't you wait a few days," Eshlyn asked. "A ninedays? I'll come with you."

"I do not think I can wait," he said, staring down at Esai's body.

"Go with him, Lady Eshlyn," Sabriel said as he stood above her.

Lifting her chin, she raised a questioning brow at him.

Sabriel gripped Esai's unforged sword before him in both hands.

"We will take care of the people of Oshra, together," Sabriel said. "I thank you, all three of you, for what you've done. I cannot speak for the others, but for my part, and the Moffa, we will act as brothers again."

"As shall we," Ekandayo said. "The men of Lior will stand together, help one another. El will help us. He already has."

Jubali turned her fierce eyes to the Moffa chief. "Sabriel?" she said, as if she did not believe his words.

"Tonight, I saw things I never thought I would see. I saw Namir, the Hunter of Oshra, fight for the lives of others, willing to give his life so others could live. I saw a changed man, Jubali." Sabriel pointed down at Esai. "And this young man, he put the head of the Pike on a breakin' pike."

"He *what*?" Eshlyn said as Jubali grunted in surprise and Ekandayo cursed in shock.

"I saw sacrifice and great courage," Sabriel continued. "I saw something greater than simple survival, and I cannot pretend otherwise. But we must stand together, fight together, if we hope to realize the freedom these men and women spoke of."

Jubali examined the thousands of people, all three tribes of Lior, working together to put out the fires that ruined their city.

Eshlyn regarded the woman. "Jubali? What say you?"

Jubali faced Sabriel. "Years of fighting, violence, revenge between our peoples. You will give it up? Let it go?"

"I will try," he answered. "I can only promise I will try. But I don't think I can go back to that. Not after tonight."

Jubali crossed her arms. "Then the people of the Xon will also try."

Ekandayo placed a hand on Eshlyn's shoulder. "Eshlyn, my sister," he said. "I believe you can go with Athelwulf north to the Beorgai."

Exhaling and leaning back on her haunches, she nodded over at Athelwulf. "Very well," she said. "We leave tomorrow."

"Why does Bana Sahat seek to destroy?" Gabryel asked. "Why did he create the demics and seek to rule Eres?"

"Bana Sahat, or Sahat the Younger, as he was called long ago, was once a great leader among the One Race," Yosu responded. "He followed and worshipped El. But he wanted to be more, and he thought the way to more power was through fear and hate and violence and lust. That is not the way of El. And so his selfishness killed all that was good in his heart, and he began the Great Abomination."

Gabryel asked, "You teach us that El seeks the redemption of Eres, the three races, all of creation. What about Bana Sahat? Can he be redeemed?"

The Master was silent for a long time.

"Anyone can be redeemed," Yosu said. "But great redemption is painful and humbling. And it must be chosen. There is no escape from this. Although the redemption of El is worth any cost, many will not make that choice."

Mychal sat next to the Master. "What of Sahat the Elder? What happened to him?"

Yosu's eyes lowered to the grass at his feet. "That is a story for another day."

- From the Ydu, 5th scroll, translated into Common Tongue by the Prophet.

CHAPTER 13

LANDEN

"Excuse me, sir," the Assistant Steward said as he opened the door to the main office.

Lunas, the Steward of Biram, glanced up from his desk and the papers there that he was perusing. "Yes?" Now that he considered his Assistant, the elf appeared nervous, which was unusual.

"Well, sir … there are … ah, two elves to see you."

Standing, Lunas ran his hands over his white robe and adjusted his red sash and the sword belt at his hip. "Who are these elves?"

"I – I believe they are Bladeguard."

Lunas froze. He should have been prepared for this. With all that had happened in Ketan, he knew the Empire would respond, and now that it was spring, it was time. He knew this. He also feared it. He remembered what those legions did to the land of men centuries ago. The memories had not dimmed.

"Did you see their Letters of Regency?"

The Assistant shook his head, but there was great fear in his eyes.

"Where are they?"

"Waiting for you outside, sir."

"Thank you," Lunas told his Assistant.

"And … uh, sir?"

"Yes?"

The Assistant grimaced. "There are soldiers with them."

Lunas rounded his desk and stood with his Assistant at the doorway. "How many?"

"Almost a full legion."

Lunas silently walked past the elf and down the hall.

Being the Steward of Biram was not the most prized position in the Empire. That fat elf, Desiderus, used to complain every time they met about how horrible it was to be Steward of Ketan. But Ketan was a great city, an ancient city, and while Desiderus' powers were limited there, at least the Steward of Ketan lived in a real palace and sat on a legendary throne. Lunas lived in a house not even big enough to be considered a mansion, much less a palace. And while he had absolute control in Biram, Lunas did not have the diversions available to him here that Desiderus had possessed in Ketan.

But that fat elf was surely dead. It did not matter that his powers were limited; one did not lose a city of the Empire to the dogs of men and live. Not when Tanicus was Emperor. But what did that mean for Lunas?

As Lunas exited the main administration building and viewed the host of militan standing at full attention in the middle of his city in their organized rows, he hesitated and sucked in a deep breath through his nose. Yes, his assistant was correct. Not quite a complete legion. Based on the number of the divisions, a quick count gave him four thousand militan in Biram. He peered down the marble steps to the ground where two elves stood apart from the soldiers.

Bladeguard.

Approaching them, he gave them a salute, a fist across his chest. They did not smile or respond in any way.

"I am Cyprian," one said. "And this is Saben. We are now in control of your city."

"You are invoking Directive XVII?" Lunas asked.

Cyprian handed over a parchment as his answer. Lunas opened the parchment but knew what it would be. A Letter of Regency. Signed and sealed by Tanicus.

"There is no reason for this," Lunas grumbled. "We have this city completely under our control."

"Truly?" Saben spoke, taking the parchment back, folding it and placing it in his belt. Lunas' eyes lingered on the fine sword there. "Have any of your citizens left for Ketan?"

"There have been some," Lunas said. "How can we control every human? But some fleeing the rebellion in Ketan have come here."

"That does not sound like you have things under complete control, Steward," Cyprian said.

His Assistant stood next to him now, facing the Bladeguard. "There have been no riots or uprisings here," the Assistant said.

"And what of the uprising only a few kilomitres away in Ketan?" Cyprian asked, his voice calm. "What did you do about that?"

"What could we do?" Lunas said. "We have a few hundred Cityguard, enough for Biram, but what could we do against the walls of Ketan? We waited for the Empire to send legions, and we are now more than willing to house these soldiers and be a staging area for the siege of Ketan. The elves and humans in Biram will cooperate fully."

"I appreciate that, Steward," Cyprian said. "But we do not need your cooperation."

"I urge you to reconsider," the Assistant said. "The men and elves of Biram know Lunas. They will take direction from him much easier, and this will help keep the peace."

"Keep the peace?" Saben said. "What makes you think we are here to keep the peace?"

"What direction do these humans need?" Cyprian added. "They need little direction to die."

Lunas cocked his head at the Bladeguard. "Die?"

"Yes," Cyprian said. "Die." The Bladeguard addressed the Assistant. "Do you agree and bear witness to the need for Directive XVII?"

The Assistant's brow furled. "I do not. As we have stated, and you can clearly see, Biram needs no crisis management. We are willing to cooperate in any way you require. There is no need to remove the Steward."

"What we require is absolute control of the city and the Cityguard," Saben said. "Now do you bear witness?"

"No," the Assistant said. "I do not."

Lunas was filled with a sense of pride at his Assistant, his friend for decades.

"Unfortunate," Saben said. "But there are other ways."

Before another second passed, Saben's sword was out and plunged through the Assistant's chest. The Assistant grunted, gazing down in surprise at the blade through him and the blood around the wound; then he fell to the ground, and Saben pulled his blade free as the Assistant fell.

Lunas gasped and turned to plead with Cyprian, obviously the elder of the two. He would be more reasonable. But as he faced Cyprian, he felt a great pain in his own chest and found he couldn't breathe except to groan. Glancing down, Cyprian's blade was through his heart. Lunas fixed Cyprian with a questioning stare.

"Like I said," Cyprian said. "You need little direction to die."

And that was the last thing Lunas heard before he knew only darkness.

—+—

Darkness. Galen wondered if darkness was alive. He understood, in his mind, that darkness was only the absence of light. Darkness had no substance in itself. It was only an expression of nothing. But when he existed for long hours alone without any light, darkness took on personality and character. Not that it spoke to him. Not yet, at least. He wasn't that far gone. However, he saw things, felt things in the darkness. Perhaps it possessed substance after all.

Galen was weak and dying. No more food. He received water from time to time, but no food. He was starving to death. His hunger went beyond pain.

He heard the footsteps down the hall, two sets, and he recognized Tanicus as one. Tanicus glided with his usual confidence and purpose. The other with him shuffled along. Even the footsteps sounded afraid.

The door opened, and even though the light was dim, it blinded him. He covered his face and cowered in the corner of his own filth. A human man was thrown against the wall next to Galen, and the man sobbed like a child. As his eyes adjusted, Galen could see the man was older and balding with stringy white hair. The man wore only short underbreeches, and he pressed himself against the wall, trying to get away from Tanicus.

Tanicus himself entered the room and sat on his golden stool and raised his palm. Within his palm, a tongue of white flame hovered, created by the magic of Tebelrivyn. Galen only associated the Emperor now with light and deliverance. He was relieved to see the Emperor, happy for the light.

"Humans make excellent slaves, don't you think?" Tanicus said.

The human in the room whimpered.

Galen couldn't respond. His throat could no longer make a sound. His hunger debilitated him; he was so close to death.

"They breed like rodents," Tanicus continued as if he were part of a real conversation. "You can never truly get rid of them. They are an infestation. Nevertheless, there are always enough of them to use as slaves. As many as I kill, there will always be more."

The Emperor extended the hand that carried the flame into the center of the room. Galen watched as the flame grew and lengthened, reaching towards him, and then the flame spread across his naked skin.

Galen shrieked, a sad sound, much quieter than it should have been compared to the pain that covered every inch of his crackling and blackening skin. He writhed on the floor, and as he thought he would pass out from the pain and exhaustion, Tanicus stopped.

"You have been a difficult one to break," Tanicus said. "But I expected that. This process is usually much shorter. We are making progress, however. It is only a matter of time."

The Emperor extended his hand towards the human. The old man went rigid, crying out, his eyes rolling back. Galen knew the feeling. Tanicus was extracting the life from the man. In a few more moments, the man laid dead, his body dry and dusty skin and bones.

"Remember this," Tanicus said.

Tanicus extended his hand now to Galen. First, his body began to heal, the skin changing from black to a pinkish color, the pain receding, and Galen gasped in pleasure. Beyond the healing, Galen felt life and power fill his limbs, his chest, his being. His hunger and exhaustion abated. Within seconds, he went from barely hanging on to life to feeling centuries younger again.

"You do not need to eat," Tanicus explained. "With the power I can give, nothing can kill you. I can keep you alive forever like this. All it will cost is the lives of more men and women. And there will always be more."

Even though he had energy again, Galen was speechless. He stared at the corpse next to him, glad for the life running through his veins and horrified at the cost.

"Do you realize the gift I offer?" Tanicus said. "We elves live for thousands of years, but we are not immortal, not like the legends say. Eventually, we grow old and die. But with this gift, Galen, I can keep you young and strong forever. With me, you will be unstoppable. Think on that."

Tanicus created a flame in his hand again. The flame was thin but intense, and it stretched out towards Galen's naked, healed skin. Galen began to struggle, but the Emperor held him fast with the power of air tight around him. As Galen lay rigid, the flame burned symbols into his skin, and Galen cried out as he watched the flame move and char his body.

Once it was done, Tanicus stood, the light dim again with the small tongue of white flame in his hand, and took his stool with him. "That, I will not heal," the Emperor said. "I mark you as mine."

He closed the door behind him and left Galen in darkness again.

Galen's friend. Darkness.

He felt utter despair at how he longed for the Emperor to return.

———

The canal broadened as it neared the city of Landen. Set on a long island within the delta where all the canals of Veradis met, Landen was surrounded by water. Seven bridges crossed the channel from the mainland to the city, long brown stone arching pathways with carved pillars of grapes and vines. A high wall protected the city, rising from the water, and there were gates within the wall at the connection of each bridge. Beyond the wall, Carys could see high buildings, rectangular and thick. All of it was made with the same brown stone in shades of tan. Flags of color flew from the highest buildings.

"Ah," she heard Shan say from behind her. "Home."

Zalman grunted.

Three gates led to the city from the water and under the wall. One was expansive and tall for the large merchant and war vessels. The other two were smaller for travelers and fishing boats. Each gate was an archway with an iron grate that would fall down to stop invaders.

The water around the city was filled with boats and ships of all sizes and shapes, many of them fishing boats. Carys could begin to smell the salt water as the canals dumped into the sea. Maneuvering along the canals was simple for Gleb and his flatboat. But here was chaos, and Gleb's leathery face was fixed with a pensive visage as he dodged the vessels around the city. He was better at it than Carys would have wagered, and while there was a close call with a large ship, the flatboat made it through one of the smaller arches.

"The great city of Landen," Shan said, his voice excited. "You will see, Carys. It is a fine city. Makes Ketan look like a village."

After moving through the gate, the water was still and easier to navigate. They made it to a short dock and began to leave Gleb and his flatboat. Carys paid the man, even adding in a few coppers as extra. The man had done a good job. Zalman and Shan took the horses off of the boat, loaded down with their bags.

The docks were ringed with a series of stone steps leading up into the city. Level paths on a slight incline for wagons or horses were spaced among the steps. They led their horses up those inclines and into the city.

The stench hit Carys immediately. She placed a hand over her nose. "Your great city smells like fish and crit," she said.

Shan didn't respond.

Zalman chuckled. "The city has earned that smell."

Waving a hand of dismissal, Shan smirked. "You will see," he said. "There is much more to Landen than the smell at the docks."

There were people everywhere, dressed in longer tunics of plain colors, mostly white or tan with belts at the waist and sandals on their feet, if they wore any shoes at all. Women wore longer robes to their feet, also in plain colors. The streets were narrow and made of stone, covered in filth. They had to push their way through the noisy crowds, and the citizens of Landen cursed at them and made their opinion known. Although once they caught a glimpse of Zalman, they thought better of making any trouble.

Shops and homes and tenements were all made from the same brown, bland stone, cubic and rectangular shapes with narrow windows. Most of the doorways had leather or cloth as an entrance to the building.

The wall kept the breeze from the street, and so it was hot and thick, and every smell was a new stench in Carys' nostrils. She could, however, smell incense every now and then, but not enough to cover the other odors.

They passed more than one brothel, and once a woman approached them, her face painted in bright colors to seem younger than she was.

"Oh, you've already got the two men with you, eh?" the woman winked at Carys.

Carys stumbled. "What?"

The woman paced them and now grinned up at Zalman. "You bring the girl with you, and the three o' you get a discount," she said.

"No thanks," Zalman said and brushed her aside.

Shan chuckled as the woman huffed and marched away to find another potential customer.

"Did she mean a discount on …?" Carys began.

"On shoggin', for sure," Shan said, his eyes twinkling.

Another common sight along the streets through the city was the street performers and freaks dressed in bright and gaudy clothes. Carys saw jugglers, acrobats, and musicians with various levels of skill, but the freaks were tragic, standing there or attempting some silly talent so others could gawk at them, all in the hopes someone would give them coin, even a copper pebble. She saw conjoined girl twins who sang a very sensual song and a man with tumors on his face that made him resemble a bosaur, painted to complete the appearance.

The streets were narrow, so it was difficult to pass by without seeing and touching and smelling everything up close. Carys found it a challenge to keep a blank face, which she achieved. Most of the time.

Cityguard and militan were everywhere in pairs or in squads. A whole platoon passed before them, pushing their way through. The people of Landen cringed when the elves passed. Once a squad of militan grabbed a street performer, a young man singing a quaint and moving love song. He wore a long purple and orange tunic, and he cried out his innocence as the squad pulled him down the street.

Men, women, even children, looked away and did nothing.

Carys and her companions finally made their way to a smaller market area with a broken fountain at its center. She stopped to get some space and air from the people pressing in around her. And to talk.

The two men leaned in close as she talked in a low volume. She was still thinking of that singer taken by the militan. "First order of business," she said. "We will meet with some of the Prophet's contacts, a woman I knew from Asya and her husband."

"I don't think so," Shan said, pulling his wide-brimmed black hat further down over his eyes. "The power of the city is in the Dygol, and my Uncle Lorcan is the Lord of the Northern Dygol. We should meet with him before we do anything else."

"I understand," Carys said. "And we will, don't worry. But I feel we should check in with my friends first, hear their take on what is going on in the city."

"Who are these people?" Zalman asked. "Your friends."

"Her name is Leni, and she was the daughter of Uncle Reyan's primary contacts in Asya, Jyson and Rose. Caleb heard about them when he was in Asya last year, and he told me how to find them."

"And her husband?" Zalman asked.

"His name is Finn Fa'Yador," she answered. "Son of someone important in Asya, too. They moved here a couple years ago."

"I am sure they are fine people," Shan said. "But they will know nothing of the inner workings of the Dygol. My uncle will know far more, if it is information you seek."

Carys inclined her head towards him. "It is more than information I seek. It is the discernment of a friend, a woman I trust."

"It is a waste of time," Shan muttered.

"You have been away for many years," Zalman said to Shan. "What's the rush?"

"No rush. Lorcan will give us fine accommodations and we can begin to speak with him about what is really going on in the city."

"It will not hurt to wait one more day," Zalman muttered. "I agree, Carys. I say we speak with your friend, learn what we can, if anything, and then go meet with Shan's family."

"Thank you," Carys said. "We're here to help this city. We will need to take our time and get a good idea of the situation from all angles before we can know how it is we will help. And this is how I see best to do that. To the fine?"

Shan regarded her and pursed his lips.

"Good," she said. "Now let's go find an inn with a room high above the crittin' stench of these streets."

Chapter 14

A Cry of Death

What he remembered most about that night was Caleb's eyes. More than his father's despair, more than Carys' visage of failure and disappointment, more than even the sword through his father's gut – more than anything, he remembered Caleb's eyes. He recalled those other moments, too, no doubt, all of them pictures burned into his mind and his soul. But what haunted him, what followed him in the dark was Caleb's steel gray glare.

It wasn't human. Earon couldn't imagine anything that cold or dead existed in the world. But it did. Those eyes condemned him and called him names, names that he knew were true: *traitor, murderer*. And no matter how much Sorcos he took or liquor he drank, he saw those eyes and heard those words clear as a whisper in his heart.

He wanted to die, but he wanted another hit of Sorcos more. He was beginning to feel the desperation, the withdrawals. It wasn't bad yet, not near as bad as he knew it could be, but he could taste the disaster that was to come. He knew people died from Sorcos withdrawals, and fear gripped his heart along with the addiction. Not fear of death, but fear of dying without getting more Sorcos.

There was another unfortunate effect of two days without Sorcos or liquor. His mind and his vision cleared. He sat on a dead man's horse and watched as his captors dug deep into the dirt and soil of the rainforest with small hand shovels at the base of a great tree near the Decel River. They needed to get through a thick layer of dead leaves before reaching the soil, and now the hole was long and narrow. A flock of large, colorful birds glided across the rushing water of the river beyond, landing in the branches of the trees across from them.

Looking down at his hands, they were bound, but Athelwulf had removed his gag for good last night, telling him no one could hear him in the forest. No one but wild bosaur or spotted panthers or small carnivorous monkeys.

They finished the grave and sat back, covered in sweat and dirt. After taking a moment to collect themselves, Eshlyn and Athelwulf grabbed Esai's body and lay him within the ground.

Earon had met Esai years before when they were both young and ready to take on the world, or at least the elves. They weren't ever close, but Earon wasn't close to many in those days. His mother, Caleb before he left, and Carys, yes. Intimacy was impossible with anyone else when their time in any one place never lasted more than a few ninedays. So he knew Esai as well as he knew the thousands of others on his travels, drug around by his father.

His father. The Prophet. A man he lived with but never knew or understood.

Athelwulf spoke first, and even though Earon turned his face away to peer into the trees, trying not to hear, he heard the words – words that praised Esai's bravery and integrity, the selflessness at giving his life for El and for the people of Oshra. They were fine enough words. Trite and full of crit, but fine. Words no one would ever try to say about Earon.

Caleb's eyes. *Traitor. Murderer.*

Now Eshlyn was speaking, her voice choking with more words of pride and sorrow for a great man. Words they needed to hear, he was sure, but empty and meaningless. Didn't they all see how meaningless it all was? Better to be numb and wait for the death that came to all. His right hand began to shake, a slight tremor, and he gripped the saddle to stop it.

Athelwulf gave him a knowing look.

He grit his teeth and thoughts of his mother came unbeckoned into his mind. He remembered the loneliness in her stare when no one was watching, the deep sadness that poured from her in those silent moments. If she caught him staring, she would quickly smile and put on a face of strength. Did she long for her husband as much as he longed for a father? A real father? He would never get to ask her now.

Carys' voice, aching. *Oh, Earon …*

Eshlyn finished speaking, wiped her cheeks of tears. She and Athelwulf shared a glance and then used their small shovels to cover the body again.

The sun set in the west, and Earon gazed over to his left to see a dark orange begin to cover the horizon.

Athelwulf said a prayer and sang a song, recycled phrases from the scriptures and from his father's old sermons. Did the clichés really make them feel better? They seemed to. Maybe they had for him, once. But he knew better.

Earon felt a pain in his stomach, an uncomfortable ache more than a pain, but he knew what it was. He had heard the stories.

As he heard footsteps close to him, he saw Athelwulf approach. "We'll camp here tonight," the man said.

"Next to a dead man's grave?" Earon asked.

Athelwulf scanned the area, the clearing where they stood. "As good a place as any."

Earon felt a pain in his abdomen, and he bent a little at the waist, wincing.

"You're feeling it," Athelwulf said, rubbing the dirt from his hands on his pants. It wasn't a question.

Earon frowned at him.

"It begins gradually," Athelwulf said. "First a slight shaking of the hands. Then maybe an ache in the stomach. Soon you will have the chills and shake all over. And the pain? It will spread throughout your whole body. Your heart will race, and you will wish you were dead."

I wish that now, Earon thought. "You trying to scare me?"

"I suspect something far worse scares you," he said.

Traitor. Murderer.

"I am only trying to tell you the truth," Athelwulf muttered. "Prepare you for what is to come."

Earon squinted at the man. "You've been through it."

"Yes."

"Is it as bad as they say?"

"Worse."

Earon swallowed. "Then why go through it?"

"Why? The son of the Prophet asks me why," he mumbled. Athelwulf's chin rose again. "Because addiction is a lie. Your body feels that it needs a thing, Sorcos in this case, but it does not need that thing to survive. It is poison. It is slowly killing you, but your body and mind cry for it. Everything within you screams that you need it or you will die. But it is the thing that will end up killing you, bondage more than those ropes around your wrist and that gag I took from your mouth. And the truth is … you were born to be free."

"Some do die without it," Earon said. "I could die without it."

Athelwulf gathered the supplies for the camp from the back of the horse. "That's the problem. You think you are alive now."

This time it was his father's voice that echoed in his brain.

Oh, Earon, what have you done …

———

Based on a recommendation from Shan, they got two rooms at *The Resting Stone*, an inn closer to the northern side of the city. It was more expensive than Carys wanted to pay, but it was eight stories tall – and the inn had two available rooms on the seventh floor, one for Carys and one for the men.

The eighth floor was the kitchen and the common room that included a seating area on the roof. The evening was warm but a breeze blew across the roof of the inn. Carys sat at a small table with Zalman and Shan, all with cold ales sitting in front of them. The roof was covered with wooden awnings and sheer red and orange cloth.

Carys turned and recognized the woman who stepped onto the roof of *The Resting Stone*. Wearing a longer light blue robe with a leather belt, she had short, auburn hair and bright hazel eyes. A man with dark hair and eyes walked behind her.

Standing, Carys waved at Leni from across the roof. Leni waved back, whispered something to her husband, and walked over to them.

Leni extended a hand as she neared the table, and Zalman and Shan both stood. "When I got your message, I couldn't believe it," Leni said. "Finn almost convinced me not to come."

Leni's husband, Finn, ran a small fishing company on the eastern side of town. He owned two boats and employed a handful of men. Carys had sent a message with one of the servant girls of *The Resting Stone*.

Finn regarded the men, his face going blank when he saw Zalman. "It is a dangerous time in Landen right now," he said.

Carys took Leni's hand. "I'm glad you took the risk. It is good to see you."

"Been a while," Leni said.

"Too long," Carys said. "Let me introduce you. This is Zalman and Shan."

"Well met," Leni said. "I am Leni and this is my husband, Finn."

"Good to meet you," Carys said. "Please, sit."

Finn had to grab a couple chairs from nearby, and all five of them sat close around the small table on the corner of the roof.

They ordered drinks from the waitress, and Leni turned to Carys, her face serious. "Have you heard any word on Asya?"

"You mean your parents," Carys said. Leni's parents, Jyson and Rose, had been one of the Prophet's main contacts in Asya, and his close friends.

Leni nodded.

"I'm sorry," Carys said. "Only that it is bad there. When was the last you heard from them?"

Leni exhaled. "Months ago. And I've been worried. It is worse than you think, at least from what we hear here, what the Empire hasn't been able to censor. So much killing and violence."

"I'm sorry," Carys said. "I'm sure they're okay. They were prepared for such a day."

"Yes, they were," Leni said.

"We'll be praying," Carys said, and she heard the stifled snort from Shan.

"Thank you," Leni said. She smiled now at Carys. "It is good to see you. You look just like you did as a girl. Slightly taller."

"Only slightly. And I was thinking the same about you. You've barely changed."

"Except you have that look in your eye," Leni said.

"What look?"

"That look that says you need something from me."

Carys' brow knitted. "I used to have that look?"

"No. Your uncle did."

Carys' eyes lowered.

"Are the rumors true?" Leni said, her voice low. "Is he really dead?"

Carys' mind went back to that tragic night at *The Crying Eagle*; her heart filled with sadness and anger at once. "Yeah. I was there. Earon betrayed him. A Bladeguard killed him."

Leni leaned back. "A Bladeguard? And you were there? How did you escape?"

Leaning in close, Cayrs said. "Caleb killed him."

"Caleb?" Leni cried, then her gaze flicked around the room as she realized she spoke too loud. Quieter, she said, "I thought he was dead."

"He disappeared, and some assumed he was dead. But no, he is very much alive." Taking a few moments, Carys explained what happened to Caleb: that the elves took him to train as a Bladeguard then infiltrate the Prophet's network. But instead, Caleb had returned to bring back the *Sohan-el* and start a revolution among men.

"So he's the *Brendel*," Leni said.

"Wait, the *Brendel*?" Finn asked. "You know this guy? I thought he was this half-man with wings and long blades as hands."

Zalman grunted, and Shan laughed out loud.

"The *Brendel* is just a man, if it is Caleb," Leni told her husband. "Hard to believe that stubborn and mischievous young man is leading a revolution."

Finn shrugged. "I'm sure every revolutionary was once a little kid who crit his pants," he responded and then faced Carys. "And you came here from him? From Ketan?"

"We did," Zalman said.

"So that is true, as well?" Finn asked. "There really is a free city of men?"

"Yes," Carys said. "The revolution has begun."

"Maybe in Ketan," Finn said. "But here in Landen, everyone is standing as if on an old bridge about to collapse from under them."

There was an awkward hesitation, and then Leni asked, "What do you need of us?"

"This," Carys said, spreading her hands to the table. "To talk with an old friend and to hear what is really going on in the city."

"You want to know what is going on?" Finn asked. "The Empire shook down every citizen in Landen over the last month, taking their time to see who had contraband paraphernalia ..."

"Did they find ...?" Carys began.

Leni shook her head. "I didn't bring any copies of anything with me," she said. "They found nothing."

"But they found some of your uncle's other contacts," Finn said. "And killed most of them."

"Most?" Zalman asked.

"Others just disappeared," Leni said. "More than a few were my friends."

"Which put us under more suspicion than you can imagine," Finn said. "I still think they are watching us." He shot a glare at Leni.

Leni smirked back at him. "Which is one of the reasons why he didn't want to come tonight," she said and turned back to Carys. "We're fine. None the worse."

"I'm glad," Carys said. "What else can you tell me?"

"The Empire moved an extra legion into the city," Finn said. "They are preparing for something. Or want to make sure they are prepared. Your business in Ketan has them more nervous than a guppy at a shark party."

"Have there been riots?" Carys asked. "From the citizens?"

"No," Leni said. "The Dygol have helped to keep some peace, mostly due to their deals with the elves."

"But the northern and southern Dygol are almost at war themselves," Finn said. "It wouldn't take much for those two families to come to violence."

The waitress came with Leni and Finn's drinks.

"Carys said you are a fisherman," Shan said, waiting until the girl left.

"I am a businessman," Finn corrected. "And I run a small fishing business, yes."

Shan tipped his hat. "My apologies. How old are you?"

"Twenty-two."

"Impressive," Shan said. "How did you manage such success at your age?"

"My father gave me some money when I left Asya," Finn said. "Enough to start a business. He wanted me to open a tavern or inn, follow somewhat in his footsteps, but I didn't want to go that route."

"And you went into fishing," Carys said. "A good trade."

"Yes," Shan said. "What Kryan corporation do you work for?"

Kryus controlled the trade along the Sea of Alin and Theron Ocean by way of several elven corporations, and most of the profit went back into the coffers of the Empire.

Finn raised his chin. "In that way, I am my father's son. I am an independent contractor. I work for any that will work with me."

"I am even more impressed," Shan said. "But in order for you to do that, you must be connected with either the northern or southern Dygol. I would guess the northern?"

"Neither," Finn said.

"That's impossible," Shan barked.

"I don't want to owe anyone, so we work together as equals, as friends. And so far, it has been a good relationship with both the Dygol and the corporations."

Shan said, "That is more than dangerous, my friend. You cannot trust that to last. How long have you been in the city?"

"Almost a year," Leni said.

"I guarantee you," Shan said, moving closer. "If you don't get protection from one of the Dygol, you will be out of business in six months. Let me get you a meeting with Lorcan. He will protect you."

"*Lord* Lorcan?" Finn said. "And take half of my profits and put men out of a job?"

"Better than no business at all," Shan said.

"Thank you for wanting to help," Leni said. "But I think we can manage."

Shan glowered at the table and hissed. He upended his drink, finishing it. "I need another drink," he said, stood, and traipsed downstairs.

The people at the table were quiet. Zalman eyed Carys and glimpsed the stairs down to the bar below, conflict on his face.

"It's okay," she said. "Leave him."

Zalman's face turned from her to the stairs and back before rubbing a hand over his bald head, but he stayed.

"We're sorry," Leni said.

"Don't be," Carys said. "This is exactly why I wanted to come to you first, because I knew you wouldn't feel a loyalty to either the elves or the Dygol. And if we are to begin talking with the Dygol, I wanted an honest opinion first."

"You're going to meet with the Dygol?" Finn asked.

"We have to," Carys said. "You said it yourself, this city is one event away from moving to riots or violence. The people of the city need to be unified, work together against the elves. We need people to join the revolution, not just the people in Ketan. And the Dygol are in a prime position to help with that."

"The Dygol aren't about helping anyone," Leni said. "I don't see them signing up for a revolution. They are only in it for money or power."

"That has to change for the people of this city to survive," Carys said.

"From what I've heard of the Dygol," Finn said. "That isn't going to happen."

Carys glanced at Zalman before saying, "We will have to try. That is why we are here."

"I have had some dealings with Lord Thren, in the south," Finn said. "He seems more reasonable than Lorcan. But that's not saying much."

"We're meeting with Lorcan tomorrow," Zalman said.

Leni reached out and touched her arm. "Carys," she said. "You have to be careful with Lorcan. He's the most ruthless man in the city."

Carys thought of the large man sitting next to her. Zalman had money and the adoration of thousands, women at his whim, but he ran from it because he knew he wasn't free. He fled to the one place he thought he could be free. And even though he was a big gedder, he was a man her brother trusted. She was beginning to see the honor in him.

Was it natural for a man to desire freedom? She didn't know. Maybe it wasn't. But she knew that Zalman was an example of someone who might have once seemed hopeless to some. And here he was with her, trying to bring freedom to others.

"We have to start somewhere," Carys said. "Men have to change, even the most ruthless, for us to have any chance to be free. And we will start with Lord Lorcan tomorrow night."

Leni smiled. "Now you sound like him." Carys didn't need to ask whom. "We'll keep an ear out. If we hear anything, we'll let you know."

"Thank you," Carys said.

Finn scratched his chin, peering at Zalman. "Breakit, but you look familiar. Should I know you from somewhere?"

Zalman emptied his own glass. "I need another drink," he said, standing and marching back to the stairs.

Carys chuckled as she watched him leave.

———————

Zalman found his way down to the bar. The room was dim, lit by candles along the wall, and he saw Shan at the bar. In the few moments since Zalman last saw the man, Shan had picked up a couple crinkles, although here in Landen they were called bedcoiners. Both women were dressed in shorter robes just past their hips and low neckline that exposed most of their breasts.

Noticing him approaching, Shan raised a glass of liquor. "Zalman," he said. "Good of you to join us." The bedcoiners possessed glazed eyes, however inviting their smiles were. "These ladies have been kind enough to drink with me. This is Ryquel," a bleached blond, "and this is Tana," a woman with hair too red, colored unnaturally. "We're having a drink before they come back downstairs with me. Come and partake."

Shan's implication was clear – more than a drink.

Zalman leaned against the bar. "Nice to meet you, ladies," Zalman said. "Wait over at the next table, ladies. Shan and I need to have a word."

The bedcoiners leered at Shan, their smiles never changing. Shan grinned at them, touching their arms while he guided them to the table. "Ryquel, Tana," he said. "I will be with you in a moment." The women shuffled and swayed their way to the table. Shan watched them go and then turned back to Zalman. "Like I said. I love Landen."

"What are you up to?" Zalman asked. "Why are you here?"

Shan cocked his head at him. "Well, I was here about to have a lovely evening with those two ladies there."

"For a price."

"There is always a price."

"That is not what I meant."

"Then what did you mean?"

Zalman moved closer to Shan, bowing down so when he whispered, the man could hear him. "Why are you in Landen, here with Carys?"

"Caleb made it clear that I was to use my connections with the Dygol and get her a meeting. You appear upset. Is this about the young idiots upstairs?" Shan sniffed while he sipped his drink, then bared his teeth. "The Dygol are only playing for time. He will come under someone's protection or lose everything. The Dygol will get what they feel is theirs."

"Is that what you are doing, Rat? Are you here to get what you feel is yours?"

Shan's brow furrowed. "What are you saying?"

"Caleb sent Carys here to help the people of this city, to help them unite against the elves."

"I understand that."

"Do you? I think you are here for yourself, to profit from this whole arrangement somehow."

Shan grinned. "What a world some of you live in," he said. "Why can't it be both? Why must I make some self-righteous choice? Not too long ago, you would have been down here getting the bedcoiners on your own, not sending them away. You've let Caleb's idealism addle your fine brain. We can help the people of the town *and* profit from it all at once."

Zalman's nostrils flared as he leaned in even closer. "Listen. This Lord Lorcan of yours has a reputation of being a ruthless man. If she gets hurt because of your manipulations, I will kill you. Are we clear?"

"Ah," Shan said. "There is the Zalman I know and love. Not so righteous after all. Of course Lorcan has that reputation. How would he compete with the southern Dygol? By rolling over every time he was challenged? He has done what he has done to survive. And if Carys can convince him he needs to work with her to survive, he will do so. Otherwise, I promise nothing."

"You cannot promise her safety?"

"My friend, I cannot promise my own. But I did get us a meeting. Now I am going to collect those lovely ladies before they wander off. Will you be coming down to the room with us?"

Zalman scowled at him. "No."

"Suit yourself," Shan said, finishing his drink with one swallow. "Then I wouldn't come to the room for another couple hours. Are we clear?"

Zalman's fists clenched, but he did not speak.

"I shall see you in the morning, then," Shan said. He strolled over to the women, took their hands, and led them downstairs.

Zalman ordered a drink from the tender. He might be here for a while.

—

Van stood at the gate of Ketan, the noon sun bearing down upon him. He was thankful he didn't have to stand in a steel helmet or breastplate. The spring had come quickly, and it was hot. Shifting his weight, he scratched his arse.

Twenty-eight years old and hailing from Delaton, Van knew Eshlyn when she was a little girl. Bratty girl, to the real. Her da was always a good man, and Van had no problem voting for the man to take over as head elder in Ketan. People called her Lady Eshlyn now, which was to the fine with him, but he remembered well how she piffed people off in the town, especially Bain and his family. Which made Van like her all the more, to the real.

Lady Eshlyn left some time ago now, and the city was even more tense after Chamren's death and a curfew, which had been lifted since Caleb told everyone all the Wraith were dead now. How could he know? How could anyone know?

Wraith. In their city. Van wondered sometimes if he had stepped into a dream. He left with Eliot and Eshlyn to come to Ketan, fought demics on the wall, and now served as a part of the Citywatch in a city now ruled by men. Free of the elves. But it was real.

Something on the horizon, to his left, moving along the road from Biram. He stepped out from the gate and into the vast field in front of the wall of Ketan. He squinted in the sun, trying to see what trudged towards them. It could be a demic. He heard some of them survived, but they hated the sunlight, he remembered all too well. It was that size, though, a child maybe, staggering along the road. As it got closer, he could see it was a child in bedclothes, tattered and torn and soiled.

What was a breakin' child doing out here alone?

He moved out along the Manahem road to where the road to Biram intersected it.

"Van?" he heard from behind him.

"You see that?" another asked. "Is that a kid?"

But the voices were further back now. He jogged out to the kid, a boy he could see now. Van held his spear to the side as he ran, and he scanned the tree line to the east and the flat fields to his right as he ran further out from the city.

The boy was ten mitres away now, his lips dried and cracked. Had he walked all the way from Biram? The boy noticed him now, his eyes focusing with effort, and then he stopped. The boy began to weep, and he swayed, exhausted.

Van dropped the spear and let the boy fall into his arms. "I got you," he said.

"My ma, my da," the boy kept saying, but his voice was dry and hoarse.

He yelled over his shoulder. "Water! Get me some water!" He heard commotion behind him as he gave his attention back to the boy. "It will be to the fine. They're bringing water."

Another of the Citywatch, Boe, appeared next to Van and gave him a bucket of clean drinking water. Van dipped his hand into the water, cupping it, at dropped it over the boy's lips. The boy leaned forward for more, and Van gave it to him, handful by handful.

"My da, my ma," he said again.

"What happened, boy?" Boe asked, on his knees now. Other men stood around them.

"They killed 'em," the boy said through his sobs. "They killed my ma and da."

"Who did?" Van asked.

"The elves," the boy said.

The men were silent for a sober moment.

"Why did they kill your ma and da?" Van whispered.

The boy stopped sobbing long enough to say, "Not just my ma and da. They kill my lil' sister. On a spear."

Van pointed to one of the men standing nearby. "Get Caleb," he said, a deep sadness overcoming. "Get Caleb now."

CHAPTER 15

THE HEART OF MAN

"What did the boy say?"

Xander spoke first, addressing Aden and Caleb. Generally, when Caleb called meetings of the *Sohan-el* and the other leaders of Ketan, he would share the purpose or set the agenda, perhaps open the floor with a few short words. Tonight, however, he sat against the wall, his arms crossed over his chest.

The large meeting room was full. Along with the *Sohan-el* who remained in the city, Hunter, Bweth, and Tamya sat in wooden chairs scattered among the council of elders, Eliot and Drew among them. Iletus stood in the corner near Caleb. Hema, the bloodwolf, lay healed and quiet at Tamya's feet.

The Kingstaff of El was propped up against the wall behind Caleb. Even from here, Aden could see the ancient script with the words that said, when translated, *To lead with compassion, justice, and strength.*

Aden waited for a moment, watching Caleb, waiting for him to answer. The man didn't move, so Aden answered Xander. "The boy's name is Weyn. And he says a legion is now in Biram."

"We knew that," Bweth said, shifting in her seat, Hunter next to her holding her hand. The rumors spread fast in Ketan. "But any more details?"

Glancing at Caleb and noticing the man didn't seem to be paying attention to the discussion, Aden sighed and blinked slowly. He had been in the room with Eliot, Morgan, and Caleb when Weyn told his story. Aden didn't care to hear it the first time, much less repeat it. He peered over at Eliot. The head elder of Ketan scratched his beard and didn't speak.

"He's an eleven year old boy that saw his family massacred by elves," Aden began. "It was difficult to get details out of him, but we got basics. The legion arrived a few days ago, led by two elves, both Bladeguard."

"How did he know?" Iletus asked.

"The Bladeguard gathered everyone in the center of town and told them who they were," Aden said. "Announced that the Steward was dead and they were now in charge. They even shared their names. Cyprian and Saben."

Aden remembered their names from Caleb's stories of his Bladeguard training back at the Kryan Citadel. A muscle on Caleb's jaw twitched.

Lyam sat forward. "They killed the Steward?"

"Probably," Iletus said. "Sounds like they used Directive XVII."

"Like you did here," Bweth said to Caleb.

He didn't respond.

"Not know," Aden said. "Boy didn't know. But after their announcement, the legion split into platoons and squads and took over people's houses for their own. So a squad went to Weyn's house at the edge of town. The squad got drunk. And then they took his baby sister and started to ..." Aden paused for a trembling breath. "Well, they started throwing the girl up in the air and trying to catch her. On a spear."

Reactions from around the room: squirming in chairs, gasps.

Caleb flinched.

Bweth leaned forward with a sneer. Aden almost took a step backwards. "How old was the girl?"

"Eight months," Aden said. "Of course, Weyn's parents tried to stop them, but the elves laughed at them and killed them. And continued their game."

"How did the boy escape?" Iletus asked.

"Somehow, in the middle o' the chaos," Aden answered. "He slipped out and ran. He said a few chased him, but since they were drunk, he outran them easy. Knowing the woods around Biram, he lost them. Then he had one thought." Aden turned to Caleb now. "Get to the *Brendel*. Tell the *Brendel*." Aden blew a breath and ran a hand through his hair, facing the others again. "He made his way to the river and followed it here. He didn't trust the road; didn't know if the elves would be there. He hasn't eaten in days, but near the river he had fresh water. Now he's here."

Blank stares around the room as it fell into complete and heavy silence.

"So what do we do?" Xander asked the question on everyone's mind.

Iletus looked at Caleb and then talked to the room. "It is a trap."

"How do you know?" Eliot asked.

"Because it is what I taught them to do," Iletus said. "It is what they were taught to do. Find a weakness. Exploit it. Draw an enemy into an even weaker position. This is calculated."

Hunter frowned, deep in thought, as he leaned forward. "What kind of trap?"

Iletus rubbed his chin. "The Empire sent Cyprian and Saben, the two Bladeguard Caleb has the most history with, the most conflict, and the ones who know him best. They announce their names and then a boy escaped. One boy."

"Wait," Xander said. "Are you saying they let the boy go on purpose?"

"Yes," Bweth agreed and spoke with confidence. And anger. "And that is exactly what happened."

"But we don't know this," Eliot said. "All we have is a scared and traumatized boy."

"Why do we not have a hundred refugees from Biram?" Iletus asked. "Why just this boy?" He stepped closer to Caleb. "Those Bladeguard know Caleb. It is their job to know. Elves killed the boy's parents. And a sister."

"But how do they know about your past?" Lyam asked Caleb. "I thought you kept those secret from the elves when you were training." No movement from Caleb.

"Galen," Aden said to Iletus. "You think they got it out of Galen."

Iletus nodded.

"So they kill this family and let this boy go, all to get Caleb to do what, exactly?" Eliot asked.

"Leave the safety of the walls of Ketan and bring the battle to them in Biram," Aden said.

"Exactly," Iletus confirmed. "They don't want to lay siege to Ketan and the walls here." The elf glanced over at Caleb. "They also know Caleb's penchant to be … stubborn and reckless. Saben and Cyprian know this firsthand. They used his wife, Danelle, to get to him back in the Citadel, and now they are using the small city of Biram to get him to react, to rush into a battle with a legion entrenched in a defensible position. It is a trap."

"But what about the other people in Biram?" Xander sat up and lifted his shoulders. "If Kryus is willing to do this, then don't we need to go help the men there?"

Iletus murmured, "All the people of Biram are likely dead."

"Again, we don't know that," Xander said.

Bweth sniffed. "No evidence, aye, but the elf is probably right. If any lived, we would have more shoggin' refugees here."

"They could be on their way," Eliot suggested.

"Not likely," Iletus said. "And even if there were others alive and in danger, how would stepping into a trap help them?"

"We kill all the elves in Biram," Tamya said, and the bloodwolf at her feet raised his head. She stretched down to scratch behind his ear. "That's how."

Aden saw Caleb's eyes focus for a moment, narrowing at Tamya, and then he gazed off again.

"No," Lyam said. "The elf is right. They're bringing us into a trap, and we can't help anyone if we're all dead. We should do what they're doing; draw them into a battle here, where we have the advantage behind the walls of Ketan. One legion isn't near enough to beat us here."

"We've gone over that," Bweth said. "Reinforcements are on the way for sure. We don't want our whole army caught behind these walls and starved out."

Tamya's teeth clenched. "And a siege, even with one legion, could take too long."

"I understand, but we have what is before us," Eliot said. "And that is this. If we send an army to Biram, we have neither the numbers nor surprise."

"So we stay here," Lyam said. "Make sure we are ready for a battle here."

"How would we know if and when reinforcements do come?" Xander questioned. "With new information, we might need a new decision."

"We could send scouts with ways to signal the city," Lyam said. "A few Ghosts would be quiet and hidden enough to find out what we need far in advance and send a pigeon or another way of communication."

"Lyam," Eliot began, "we will have to rely upon your judgment as to who would be ..."

Caleb stood, his chair scraping against the wooden floor, and the room stopped. He reached behind him and grabbed the Kingstaff, his palm gripping the inscription for *justice*. Breathing through his teeth, he stepped around the table and began to leave the room.

"Caleb," Aden said. "Where you goin'?"

Stopping at the door, he turned to the room. "I have a lot to do. I am going to Biram, and any are welcome to come with me."

"Weren't you listening?" Lyam asked. "It is a trap."

"Then it is working," Caleb muttered.

Iletus moved to the center of the room to address Caleb. "It is what they want you to do. They have a legion prepared and ready."

"No. They *think* they want this," Caleb corrected. "You say they know me, and that is true. But I know them, as well. They underestimate me. And now they are underestimating us and the army we have built here."

"So you're going to lead us all into a Kryan trap?" Lyam asked.

"You don't have to go," Caleb said. "If you want to stay and help the Citywatch protect Ketan, we need men and women to do that, too. But this wouldn't have happened if I was out there with the army, fighting the elves."

Caleb flashed cold and angry eyes at Lyam, and Lyam grunted, turning away.

Caleb turned to Iletus. "My father told me a story once. A farmer was losing his chickens to a wild animal in the middle of the night. This happened for three nights before the farmer decided to do something about it. He thought it was a fox and set out a trap overnight. In the morning, he went out to check the trap, and he found a bear. The bear was wounded by the smaller trap, but all it did was enrage it. The bear killed the farmer."

"Which one are you?" Aden asked. "The bear or the farmer?"

"We'll see."

Tamya stood, as did others. "I'm with you," she said.

Iletus shook his head. "Yes, Cyprian and Saben have underestimated you, but think of Danelle. If you go, even if you win, what will be the cost?"

Caleb grimaced at the elf. "There is a cost to every decision, and now it is no different. We have freedom here, but there is death and suffering in Oshra and Landen and Asya. Biram is lost, maybe dead, while we sit here, while we sat here and dithered. There will be a cost if I stay or if I go. I choose to go, even if it is a trap."

Facing the rest of the room, Caleb said, "It will take a day or two to decide how many and who should go and stay. We will meet again tomorrow night to discuss this. Think and pray on it. El will help us."

Caleb spun on a heel and left the room.

One by one, Aden watched the others leave the room in silence. Tamya grinned at him as she left, a dark look, Hema at her heels. In the end, only Iletus and Aden were left. Iletus stood in the middle of the room, staring at his boots, his hands clasped behind his back.

Moving to stand next to the elf, Aden put a hand on the hilt of his sword. "Is he wrong?" Aden asked. "Should we stay here?"

"What do you think?"

Aden hesitated before speaking. "I've seen the man break his uncle from the Pyts, take out a Bladeguard with a staff, unite a city of men and elves to fight the demics, and kill a Demilord. It is hard to doubt him."

"But you do."

Aden cleared his throat. "Sometimes, yeah."

Iletus fell silent for a few heartbeats. "They beat him for the first three months of training."

"What? Who?"

"There were three other students at the Citadel when Caleb came to train to be a Bladeguard. No one wanted him there, but the other students were furious.

"The selection process to be accepted into Bladeguard training is extensive, and even then, half the students quit, the training is so difficult. Everyone was against Caleb succeeding. What better way for him to fail than for him to quit?

"After those rigorous days of lessons, they would wait until they found him alone … and they beat him. They would do no permanent damage, but enough to cause pain. Imagine your *Sohan-el* training with bruises and lesions all over your body. Every day. Caleb almost quit."

Aden couldn't imagine it. The training was difficult enough as it was. To do so in constant pain and injury? "He didn't quit. What did Caleb do?"

"What could he do? No one cared. Except for Galen. But Galen knew that he couldn't stop it. As the Blademaster, he couldn't appear to show favorites, and he was already under such scrutiny for bringing Caleb there in the first place. And Galen couldn't protect the boy every moment anyway."

"So?" Aden encouraged.

"Galen did the only thing he could. He taught Caleb how to fight, privately, how to protect and defend himself, which put an even greater strain on the boy. But Caleb had purpose then, and he took to it like none I've ever seen. One morning, it was the three elves that attended lessons with cuts and bruises. It stopped after that."

"What are you trying to tell me?"

"While the beatings stopped, that is how Caleb lived for sixteen years, under constant threat and danger, the target of scheme after scheme to see him fail. Sixteen years, Aden. I don't know if anyone can really understand how he kept going. Maybe revenge. A sense of justice."

"His faith in El," Aden said.

"Perhaps. I don't know if going to Biram is right or wrong, but I know that if anyone can win there, it is he. I just don't know what it will cost us."

Aden considered the elf's words. He knew Caleb's commitment to the revolution. Shog a frog, the man believed the whole thing would end with his own death. How much more committed can you get? But was it to a fault?

"There is one thing you forget when you tell me all the amazing things you have seen of Caleb, however," Iletus said.

"What is that?"

"You helped him."

———

"I'll take the first watch," Eshlyn said as they went to bed down for the night. She watched as Athelwulf checked the ropes around Earon's wrists, making sure they were tight enough to hold him but loose enough not to cut off the man's circulation. Earon's wrists were chafing, however, and Eshlyn winced as she saw the dark red marks.

"If you wish," Athelwulf said to her, but his voice belied his concern. "Just remember that the dangers can be worse at night, more difficult to see." He said this every night, repeating the types of animals that would attack even humans in the middle of the night: pythons, panthers, tigers, and even men, men that killed for sport and their own lusts. Animals, as vicious as they could be, killed to survive. Men would kill for no reason.

Although, considering Earon, she thought, some had reason to kill, however right or wrong those reasons might be.

They had traveled for two days now, moving north from the river yesterday. She trusted Athelwulf's navigation, but she felt lost in the middle of the rainforest, even more lost than in the Forest of Saten. The Forest of Lior was a beautiful place to be lost, to the sure. With the canopy far overhead and the striking diversity of colors, both bright and dark, that marked the animals and plants around them, Eshlyn traveled in awe and wonder.

And silence. The men with her were both brooding and quiet, Athelwulf thinking about the looming confrontation with his estranged father and Earon considering … She didn't know exactly what Earon's thoughts were, but his anger and growing pain were clear. Athelwulf tried to speak to him from time to time, but he received little in response. Ath did remark to her that Earon was beginning to go through withdrawals, to prepare her. It would not be a pleasant ride in a day or so.

Leaning up against a tree, she laid Kenric's unforged sword over her lap and settled in.

Before he lay down for the evening, Earon glowered at her.

"You remind me of my mother," he said.

"I do?"

"She was strong and compassionate, gave every centimitre of herself for the good of others. I don't even know if she gave it a thought before making the sacrifice. If another would benefit, she would give it."

"I've heard Caleb speak of her," Eshlyn said. "She sounds like an amazing woman."

"Oh, she was." Earon twisted and bent for a moment in pain. "She also gave her life to another man's cause, and it cost her everything. I wonder if she really ever loved my father, especially towards the end. She gave so much to a man she never saw. He was never around. Even absent, he took it all from her. The cause required it. Life after life martyred. And she was one."

His hands were shaking, and he tried to smile. But it was more like a sneer. "You're like her in that, too. Caleb believes he is a man of prophecy, just like my father did, all for words in an ancient book so full of holes and inconsistencies that it could only appeal to idiots or fools. And if you keep running errands for Caleb, it will take your life, too. Your son will never know his mother. All for a cause destined to fail."

Eshlyn turned her face away from him, feeling the anger welling up within her. She didn't like his words, but she had to admit to herself they touched a raw place within her. Was the traitor right? Why had Caleb sent her away? It did make sense, and she had felt her own conviction to go, but did her attraction to the man have something to do with it?

Caleb was trained as an elven Bladeguard, trained in tactics that would help him know just what to say and do to play such a game. Was he manipulating her? What would the man sacrifice for the redemption of men? She gripped the hilt of Kenric's sword and touched the golden bracelet on her wrist.

She sneered at the man. "You crit on your mother's grave, traitor," she said.

He recoiled, blinking.

"If your mother was anything like me, maybe stronger from what I can tell, then she made those choices in full belief that she was doing the right thing. I married the man I did because I loved him more than air. And I am here for my own reasons. I love my son so much it hurts. Do you love anything that much? I doubt it. I died a little the day I left him to come here."

She paused to take a breath, but he didn't respond. His face was blank.

"But I want my son to live in a different world than exists today. I want him to grow up free, to know what it means to fight for what is right and true, for the innocent and weak, for their freedom as much as his own, if not more. And yes, I will give my life for that. You say she was like me? Then your mother did the same. She gave her life so her son could live free and strong, not under the thumb of tyranny. El help you. You took her sacrifice and betrayed the man she loved, your own father."

The tears welled in his eyes, and he clenched his bound fists.

"I would suggest you consider that before you judge her so. And go to sleep before I lose my temper and take off your breakin' head with my dead husband's sword."

Taking in air through his nose, Earon shuddered as he lay down and faced away from her.

———

Carys followed Shan through the narrow and noisy streets as they neared the great and ancient building on the northern side of Landen. Zalman strode behind her.

The waning sunlight hit the western top floors of the building, twenty stories tall. It was shaped like the others around it, rectangular, made of smooth sepia stone with all right angles and small open windows. The street they proceeded on led straight to the massive wooden double doors. Eight men guarded the door.

She was the only one that brought her weapon. Shan insisted they all leave their weapons back at the inn. He made it clear that they would have a more civil conversation unarmed, but Carys knew she represented her brother and the revolution. The unforged sword was a symbol of that revolution, so she wore it underneath her cloak.

"That is Lord Lorcan's palace," Shan explained as they paraded towards the large building. They had also left their horses back at the inn. "The Dygol have been a part of this great city for thousands of years. The elves could not change that any more than they could change the great walls that protect us. Even when kings ruled this land, they relied upon the lords of the Dygol to manage the city and the trade from around the world. Over the centuries, they were more official than others, but their presence was constant. They toppled and installed kings, started wars and brought peace.

"The elves realized the power and efficiency of using the Dygol to control the city. It was more efficient than attempting to dismantle it."

"But that means the Dygol is deep into the Kryan pockets," Zalman said. "And you expect them to help us?"

"As I said before," Shan answered. "You must make it worth their while."

"We don't have money to bribe them," Carys said.

"Bribe is such an ugly word," Shan said. "Profit is their language. If you were to travel to a faraway country, would you not learn their language to negotiate with them? Is that not, at the very least, polite? That is all I ask of you. As you speak to them, realize they will understand words that promise them greater advantage in the future."

The large double doors were close enough now to see the intricate carvings upon them, dragons of the sea and crashing waves.

"I'll do my best," Carys said. "But I'm not adept at making deals. My talents lie elsewhere."

Shan chuckled. "Yes, running through the forest won't help you here. And putting an arrow through his throat would surely end the discussion."

They stood in front of the guard now, and Shan smiled and gave them a slight bow. "Gentlemen," he said. "I am Shan of the Northern Dygol, cousin to Lord Lorcan. We have come to meet with him and the other elders of the Dygol tonight."

Two of the guard shared a glance, but they pushed open the door for them. A third was sent to inform Lorcan his guests had arrived.

Shan led them through the doors and into a spacious room with high ceilings and stone pillars through the center. Men and women milled about the room, which was furnished with couches and tables and chairs and a large bar to Carys' left. The people were dressed in simple tunics and robes, and they all turned to see the newcomers but quickly lost interest.

But Carys could tell that there were several thugs throughout the room, at least twenty, and their stares, while nonchalant, lingered a second longer. She could see a dagger stuck in a few belts. At the far end of the room, a staircase led up. Next to it, one led down, into basement levels, she assumed.

One man with a wooden leg seemed interested in her in particular. His eyes followed her as she walked through the room, a drink in his hand and speaking with one of the Dygol thugs. She met his gaze, and he started as if waking from a deep memory, looking away.

Carys continued to follow Shan's wide-brimmed black hat through the room. She looked quickly back at Zalman, and he glowered at the room as if waiting for the crowd to attack him. As they neared the staircase, the guard returned and ushered them up to a private audience with Lord Lorcan.

They climbed three stories and meandered down a long hallway to a parlor, opulent and spacious, but far smaller than the room they first went through. Fewer people populated this room, as well. A quick count brought it to ten, all men, and all tall and thick. All except one. He stood at the end of a long bar and wore a long tunic past his knees and a fine leather belt with a long dagger. Jewelry covered him: rings on his fingers, gold and silver bracelets on his arms, and a series of chains around his neck. He had long, full white hair, combed back and down past his shoulders. In middle age, his bearded face appeared mature but not old with tan skin and chiseled features.

Shan bowed when he entered the room. "Cousin Lorcan," he said. "It is good to see you."

A man next to the door escorted Shan to Lorcan as they entered.

Starting as he noticed the man, Shan said. "Hello, Kyson."

Kyson was tall with bronze skin and short blond hair, and he regarded Shan with disdain. The other eight men stood around the room, surrounding them. Carys attempted to appear calm and in control.

"It has been a long time, Shan," Lorcan said, grinning, but the grin didn't touch his eyes.

"Decades, I know," Shan said, now within two paces of Lorcan. "I know I left suddenly." The other man, Kyson, hovered near Carys. She stuck her hand in her cloak to be closer to her sword. Zalman stood on the other side of her.

"I think we all understand why," Lorcan said, and he waved a hand in the air. "Introduce me to you friends." She could hear Shan swallow from a mitre away.

Shan presented both Carys and Zalman.

"Not the Zalman Be'Frial of Qadi-bol fame," Lorcan said.

After Zalman did not answer, Shan said, "The one and same."

Lorcan inclined his head to all three. "Well met," he said. "Welcome to our fair city. How do you like Landen?"

Zalman stayed quiet, but Carys shrugged. "Been here before, long ago. It is a fine enough city. Still smells like crit, though."

Lorcan threw his head back and laughed. "Yes, it does. But we can forgive such faults from time to time, can't we?"

"Of course," Shan said.

"Would any of you like a drink?" Lorcan asked.

Zalman grunted a denial, but Carys said, "Water, please."

"Water?" Lorcan said. "I have the finest wines and liquor in all of Landen. And you ask for water."

"I only ask for what I need," Carys said.

Lorcan's brow rose at that. "Very well. Shan, I remember you drank the Veraden malt, is that correct?"

"Yes," Shan said. "That is correct."

Gesturing near Carys, Lorcan said, "Kyson, if you please."

"Yes, sir," the man said and moved to the bar to fix the drinks. He gave Shan the small glass of malt and handed Carys her glass of water.

"We are all here," Lord Lorcan said. "Now do you wish to tell me why you have returned after so many years?"

Carys stepped forward. This was it, her chance. She convinced her brother to send her instead of Aden to talk to the people of Landen, to help them. Besides the elves, this was one of the two most powerful men in the city.

"We have come to ask for your help," she said. "You may have heard of the revolution taking place in Ketan."

"I have," Lorcan said. "And this man, this *Brendel.*"

"Yes," Carys said. "He is my brother."

"Really? I have heard he was born in the fires of a volcano north of Falya, where the gods forged him as a weapon, his skin tougher than steel. This is your brother?"

She grinned and heard Shan chuckle nervously. "Not exactly. He is a man like any other, only a great warrior and leader. Ketan is free from the rule of elves." Carys opened her cloak to reveal the hilt of the sword; the men in the room tensed, but no one moved. They did, however, focus their attention on the unforged sword. "The ancient *Sohan-el* have been reborn. This is an unforged sword, given to me by the only true god, El, at the top of Mount Elarus. According to prophecy, the *Brendel* and the *Sohan-el* will help humanity break the chains that have been upon them for generations and bring humanity back to El. The revolution, Lord Lorcan, has begun."

"That is quite a story," Lorcan admitted and sipped his own drink from the bar. "But how can *I* help you?"

"The elves do not want humanity to be free," Carys said. "While we live free from the elves in Ketan, they seek to punish the men and women of places like Asya, Oshra, and Landen."

"True," Lorcan said. "It has been more difficult lately."

Carys took another step towards the Dygolor. "Then join the revolution. Help us make this city safe for men, maybe free. If we can unite Landen, if you and the southern Dygol can put aside any differences and work together, you would be a force for good in this city. You could maybe even remove the elves from power altogether."

Lorcan scoffed. "If you want to help this city, why don't you just surrender to the elves?"

"Excuse me?"

"It seems to me, if your revolution is causing problems here," Lorcan continued, "then the solution is the end of your little revolution. Perhaps your surrender would make things better. Not only here, as you say, but in Oshra and Asya and the whole realm."

"We want men free," she said. "El wants them free. Free from the control of the elves and their own lusts. Free everywhere, not only in Ketan."

"Ah, yes, your god again. The elves have gods, too, you know. Nine, I believe, to your one." Lorcan took another sip from his own glass. "And you believe you can set Landen free?"

"Together we can, yes," she said. "You have so much influence here. With the power of El, you could use it for good."

"Use it for good?" Lord Lorcan questioned. "What is it you believe I do?" He scratched his beard. "I keep many of the people of this city from ever having to deal with the elves at all. They deal with me, and I deal with the Steward."

Shan lowered his head, shaking it, his drink half gone in his hand.

"You could do so much more," Carys said. "Please. Think of how much better it could be without the elves."

"Yes, it would be better, to a degree," Lorcan said. "But the elves serve a purpose, do they not? Let's say that I do help you, and I come to some sort of agreement to work with the southern Dygol. What would be in it for me?"

Shoggers, Carys thought. "The good of the city."

"I understand. We let these men and women and the poor all run rampant throughout our narrow stench of a city while we fight the greatest army in the world. Sounds fine. While it would be nice not to kiss the bund of an elven Steward, it seems like an immense risk with no reward. What would be in it for me?"

Carys stammered. "I can't promise you anything. Isn't freedom its own reward?"

Lorcan's laugh dripped with contempt. "Not to a Dygolor, no. If I did do what you ask, then I would require complete control of the city."

Her heart sank. "And the southern Dygol?"

He took another sip of his drink and hissed at the liquor. "They work for me or give me some sort of tribute. We could work that out when the time comes."

Shan moaned and touched his forehead. His eyes closed, and he leaned forward onto the bar.

"I don't know if I have any authority to promise anything like that," Carys said. "Or would want to. We would only be trading one type of slavery for another."

"Then why the break are you here?" Lorcan asked.

"I told you. To ask for your help. To join the revolution."

"You did tell me," Lorcan said, his face falling to a frown. "And I tell you. I have a much better idea." Lord Lorcan raised his hand and twirled a finger.

And Carys felt a cold edge of a blade against her throat, her right hand grabbed from behind and bent behind her. Her glass dropped to the stone floor and shattered.

Shog me, she thought. *How did he breakin' get behind me?*

Zalman stood three paces away. His fists immediately clenched and he moved towards her.

Carys felt the dagger at her throat begin to press into her skin. She gasped and then heard Kyson's voice in her ear. "Stop right there, Qadi-bol champion. I've seen you play. Even you aren't that fast."

The big man froze a heartbeat away, but he bared his teeth and growled. His nostrils flared.

Shan dropped to his knees, holding his stomach, his own glass exploding as it hit the floor. His wide-brimmed hat fell.

"You poisoned him," Carys said.

"Of course I did," Lorcan said, stepping closer to Shan. "Did he ever tell you why he ran from Landen all the way to Ketan? He was skimming money from his father, the Dygolor at the time, my uncle. Shan, his only son, was stealing from his father. And so he ran when his father found out. And who would go to Ketan to find him?" Lorcan bent down to speak to Shan. "Did you feel that now he was dead, you would be forgiven?"

Lorcan drew the dagger from his belt.

Shan produced a choking sound.

Lorcan focused on Carys again. "The Dygol never forgive," he said, reached down, and drew the blade across Shan's throat. Shan's eyes went glassy, but he put a hand to his neck, the blood spraying across the floor through his fingers. Then Shan pitched forward and fell dead.

Two men approached Zalman from behind, clutching at his wrists with ropes in their hands. He snarled at them, punching one in the nose, and the man went flying two mitres back. Twisting around, he pulled the other man in an arc and threw him into the other man.

Carys bared her teeth as the knife drew blood on her neck. She could feel it trickling down her skin. "I would cooperate," Kyson said, almost lifting her off her feet with his other hand. Her arm felt as if it would come out of her socket.

Zalman glowered at Kyson, breathing heavy. He growled again and put his hands behind his back. Two more men neared him, more cautious than the last, but Zalman allowed them to tie his hands behind his back.

"Here is what I was thinking would be best for me," Lord Lorcan said as he stepped over Shan's dead body, his feet crunching on broken glass, and walked to stand before Carys. "I take the sister of the *Brendel* and give her to the Emperor. That should endear me even more to the Steward here in Landen, don't you think?"

"Yes, sir," Kyson said, as if he was the one being spoken to.

"You see," Lorcan continued. "I don't believe you have any ability to give me anything for my trouble. Even if I did help you, how could you guarantee control over the southern Dygol and the whole city? You couldn't. But the elves ..." He raised a ringed finger in the air. "Ah, they could do just that. Right now. And with the sister of the *Brendel* as a hostage, that is further leverage to get him to surrender, which – as stated before – is even better for this great city."

But Car, you don't understand. If I lose you ... I honestly don't know what I would do.

She wanted to weep, but she refused to give the men in the room the satisfaction.

"Don't do this," she said. "Please."

"It is done. Take them downstairs," Lorcan said. "The elves will be here for them in the morning."

Zalman turned his face to Lord Lorcan, and his lip curled. "You say the Dygol never forgive?" Zalman said. "Neither do I."

One of the men behind Zalman – of the four around him now – lifted a club and slammed it across the big man's bald head. Zalman staggered but only went to his knees. Somehow Zalman held onto consciousness; the thug behind him hit him again, harder this time, and he went down for good.

"Idiots," Lorcan muttered. "Now you have to carry him."

CHAPTER 16

FORGIVENESS

Earon swayed in the saddle of a dead man's horse. But wait. Was he the dead man? The only way he knew he wasn't dead was the growing pain within his gut.

They traveled throughout the morning, and he sweat through every stitch of clothes he had. He begged Athelwulf to take off all his clothes; he would ride naked. Athelwulf took off the top tunic, which gave relief for a few moments in the suffocating heat, but then the chills came, violent shaking that almost toppled him from his horse. He begged now for blankets, anything. But Athelwulf refused.

"All the clothes or blankets in the world will not help," Athelwulf had said. "You must endure it. It will get worse before it is over. Much worse."

Worse?

Earon cursed them both, a running stream of filth that they ignored. Then he wept. He would have been ashamed, but he was past that now.

He needed Sorcos. He would die without it.

Would he die with it? Yes, probably. Athelwulf was right. But it didn't matter. He had to have the drug.

How could he get any, out here in the middle of the breakin' jungle? He was sure neither of these shoggers had any. Self-righteous crit suckers. Plenty existed back in Oshra. Yes. He had to go back to Oshra.

"Please," he pleaded with them. "Take me back to the city. I'll do anything you want. I'll go see Caleb and Carys. I'll crawl there if I have to. Just take me back and we can get enough for however long. I won't even try to escape. I promise."

"Won't be in time," Athelwulf said. "We're three days from Oshra, at best. You'll be into the worst of it by then. We're closer to the Beorgai at this point."

"Do they have any there?" Earon asked.

"I doubt it," Athelwulf said. "But even if they do, you're not getting any."

"I thought that you believed in a god of love and compassion," Earon spat. "This is love? Can't you see I'm in some serious breakin' pain here? What kind of god puts you through pain? What kind of sick people watch me go through this and do nothing? I thought I had problems, but you two are hypocrites to the highest degree. Shog the both of you. Shog you to the breakin' Underland. If you cared or believed in El at all, you'd help me."

Neither would answer him. He could see it bothered Eshlyn, though, so he began to speak to her.

"You're a mother," he said. "Please. Think about your son. What if he was here, in pain, in need, begging you to help him? Wouldn't you help him? Crying out to you. Think about it. Answer me!"

She was close enough now, and he leaned towards her. "Shut up," she said and backhanded him across the side of the face.

Earon chuckled. "Heh. Yeah. The good herald of peace and freedom. Beating a bound man."

"That's enough," Athelwulf said, moving his horse between them. He turned to Eshlyn. "Ride behind us the rest of the way. I can handle this."

"I can handle it, too," Eshlyn said to him. "I'm sorry. Won't happen again."

"Do not worry or apologize," Athelwulf said. "It is better if he is alone with me. Trust me."

She frowned at him but let her horse hang back twenty mitres or so.

Earon shook as a wave of pain passed through his brain. He cried out.

"Please," he whispered. "I'm sorry. I won't talk again. Ever. If you'll take me back to the city. Get me some Sorcos."

"I know you feel like you will die without it, but it is the only way you will live. This is best."

Earon cursed at him again, but the man ignored him.

By the afternoon, he stopped cursing. He stopped begging. He fell into a deep despair. His eyes were closed for minutes at a time. The pain continued, and he knew he would die. Could he speed it up somehow?

The vegetation was less thick for a time, he noticed, larger clearings of high grasses that let through the blazing sun. The peaks of the Kaleti Mountains rose in the distance over the tall trees above him.

Athelwulf shushed him. Earon opened his eyes. Had he been making noise? Groaning. Moaning, maybe?

Over to the left, as his blurred vision began to focus, he saw something different in the forest. A herd of bosaur.

They were hulking creatures, their backs higher than a horse's head, their skin leathery and spotted with bright colors. Possessing four thick legs with flat round feet and three white claws, their foreheads were large bony frills with one large protruding horn. They had long snouts with a shorter horn above their large nostrils. Earon watched as they grazed on the long grasses, calm and content, their short, thick tails swaying behind them as they ate. He squinted and counted more than fifty of the large, docile beasts.

Docile. Except when frightened by a loud noise, Earon remembered. At least, that's what his father had told him. Then they could stampede. And a bosaur stampede was a dangerous thing. A deadly thing.

He glanced back at Eshlyn, and she was back twenty mitres or so like before, staring in awe at the bosaur herd. Turning back to Athelwulf, the man was also contemplating the herd, appearing very concerned.

Well, he thought. *If I'm going to die anyway …*

He screamed at the top of his lungs. The bosaur herd lifted their snouts towards him.

Athelwulf twisted in his saddle to face Earon. "No, Earon! Don't!"

Earon continued to scream. The herd of animals began to shuffle and move, bumping into one another.

He heard Athelwulf shout back at Eshlyn. "Lady Eshlyn! Run! Move!"

The herd steered in Earon's direction, and began to bolt. *Oh, crit*, Earon thought. *I forgot. They charge toward the noise.*

I really am going to die.

⊢—

Athelwulf had a decision to make and a split second in which to make it. His eyes darted from Eshlyn and back to the charging herd. She looked his way with fear in her gaze. He did not have time to save her.

El help her, he prayed, and then he grabbed the reins of Earon's horse and spurred his own, also holding onto his own saddle for survival as the horses bolted. Seeing the herd of bosaur coming towards them, they needed little encouragement to begin sprinting through the forest.

He saw Eshlyn go down amidst the stampede.

Athelwulf knew bosaur well; his father's tribe raised and trained them. Bosaur were as fast as a horse, if not faster, so he had to guide them into the thick of the forest to hinder the speed and danger of the charging herd, maybe deter them altogether, like waves crashing upon the rocks.

Racing north, Athelwulf took them to the east and into more dense vegetation, the ample trunks of the black Liorian trees closer to them. He weaved in and out as the herd chased him, and he could hear them smashing through behind him, feet thundering. He stole a glance over his shoulder, and a towering tree was toppled when its trunk was shattered by the bosaur.

Shouting at the horse, spurring the animal on, he swerved again to the north, to the thickest part of the forest ahead. He could see three trees together within thirty mitres, and if he could get them there, they might be shielded from the stampede. So he steered his horse again to the right, holding onto the reins of Earon's horse as tightly as he could. The copse of trees neared, and he pulled them into the midst of them.

He dismounted and pulled both horses on the northern side of the trunk of the largest tree, but there was only room for one horse. He let go of the reins of his own horse, pulling Earon's closer. A second later, the herd passed by, and Athelwulf felt like he was in the center of a storm cloud during a tempest. He could hear Earon screaming in fear. Athelwulf watched, helpless, as his own horse was speared by a bosaur horn, squealing, and drug past them and out of sight.

After the longest minute as the bosaur herd ran further to the north, Athelwulf emerged, leading Earon's horse behind him. Earon sobbed. Athelwulf did not speak.

They were a kilomitre or more from where they began, but it wasn't difficult to trace back to their original position, following the destruction from the bosaur. Walking the horse, however, took an eternity of its own. The sun moved behind the trees to the west by the time he noticed the trampled and mangled corpse of Eshlyn's horse, Blackie, or what was left of it. Two legs were missing, torn from the body, and the head was turned the wrong direction. A trail of blood led further back to where he had seen Eshlyn go down. Earon fell quiet and stopped sobbing.

He imagined the worst, his teeth clenched. But when they reached the start of the stampede, he could see no sign of Eshlyn, which meant one of two options – either she had also been drug by the bosaur, only past where they hid, or she had survived and wandered off. And she would know the way to the mountains was north, but he could not track her in that direction among the demolition of the stampede.

Athelwulf yelled her name as loud as he could several times, but he heard only his own echo. Nothing from Eshlyn. He put his hands on his hips. Either she was lost wandering the forest or dead farther north.

And to the west, he could see dark clouds moving fast towards them. Once the rain hit, she would be near impossible to find, if she was even alive.

He grabbed Earon from the horse and threw him to the ground. The man cried out. Athelwulf gripped him by the neck, and Earon gasped.

"I should kill you now," Athelwulf said. "You just lost Lady Eshlyn."

—+—

Bound at the wrists and ankles with thick rope, Carys faced the reality of her own failure.

She and Zalman lay next to one another in a cell in the basement of Lord Lorcan's palace. The dark room was sparse but for the iron cage in the corner where Lorcan's men placed them and two stools for the thugs to sit while they guarded them.

After convincing her brother to let her come to Landen, she traveled all this way to become a captive pawn against him. Shan's death hung on her conscience; he had miscalculated his influence and his cousin's mercy, but she should have listened to Leni and Finn. They tried to warn her. She hoped they would be safe.

Zalman sat with his back against the side of the iron cage, bound to the bars. Conscious now, he slumped forward. Blood trickled down the back of his head. Silent, he wouldn't look at her. Perhaps he felt like a failure, as well. His job had been to help protect her on this mission.

She wasn't angry with the big gedder, though. It had been her decision to come to the meeting unarmed, against his suggestion. *You can never refight a battle*, Athelwulf used to tell her, and he was right. They had taken a risk, a bold and needed one, and they made mistakes. She didn't blame him. She wished she could talk to him, but what would she say? They were watching, and she felt it prudent to stay quiet.

One of Lorcan's men was going to give a message to the Steward, and the elves would be here in the morning, perhaps sooner. If she was used as a hostage against her brother, she didn't know what he would do; but it wouldn't be pretty. And it wouldn't be good.

They had to find a way out of here.

Two men guarded them, and Kyson was one of them. He held the unforged sword in his hand. The second man was shuffling his Tablets.

"So this is the famed sword of those ancient warriors," Kyson said.

Who was he talking to? The other man didn't seem to be paying attention. And Carys wasn't going to respond.

"The *Brendel*," Kyson continued. "What a name. Some old language no one speaks anymore. What does it even mean?"

The thug grunted.

The blade of El, she wanted to say, but she held her tongue.

Kyson watched Carys now, and she didn't like his leering at her. His stare was dark and full of lust. It made her want to squirm, although she didn't. She wouldn't. But she was even more aware, if possible, of her helpless position. She glanced over at Zalman. He hadn't moved.

"Rebelling against the *elves*," Kyson said. "Such breakin' stupidity. Have you seen their legions?" He was definitely talking to her now. "Do you know how much money the Empire has? They control it all, and you want to take them down? So stupid."

Kyson stood from his stool, the unforged sword in his hand and lust in his eye.

"So tell me how this sword is supposed to be so special," he said. "What does it do?"

It could cut through the iron bars around them like they were dead wood. But she wasn't going to tell him that.

He was at the door of the cage, glancing from the sword to her. "And you really went to a magic mountain that gave you a sword? Like something out of a story. Hard to believe."

Carys did squirm underneath his stare this time, but she acted like she was trying to sit up. Kyson breathed deeply through his nose.

"You're a pretty thing," he said.

Her heart began to race, and she grit her teeth. Zalman's head rose.

"Isn't she a pretty thing?" he asked, his voice louder now

The other guard peeked up from his Tablets and snorted back to his game.

"Leave her alone," Zalman whispered, his voice hoarse with anger or pain.

Kyson chuckled at the large man. "Or what? What will you do if I don't?"

Zalman didn't answer, but his eyes promised murder.

"Hey," Kyson called over his shoulder.

"What?" the guard mumbled.

"Leave us alone for a while, why don't you," Kyson said.

The thug's gaze flicked to Carys for a moment before settling on Kyson. "You gonna play me Tablets later?"

"Yeah, later," Kyson said.

The thug shrugged and collected his Tablets. Standing from the stool, he left the room. The door closed behind him with a hollow sound.

Kyson grinned at Carys and plod back to his stool. He leaned the unforged sword against the wall and returned, pulling his long dagger from his belt, the one that had been against her neck. He spoke to Zalman.

"You realize you're pretty breakin' expendable, right? I mean, since you're from Ketan, the elves'll want to talk to you too, probably. But you're just muscle. She's the leverage against her brother. You're nothin'."

Zalman's eyes never wavered or left Kyson. Carys swallowed hard, her breaths coming short in her chest.

Kyson took the key out of his belt and opened the cage. The narrow door squealed on its hinges. Zalman bared his teeth and pulled against the iron of the cage.

"I could kill you, and no one would be upset. Her, I would catch some heat if I killed. They'll want her alive. But just alive. The elves won't care about ... other things."

Zalman growled at him.

Carys was afraid. She had fought demics from the Underland and traveled the world. She was a *Sohan-el*, breakit, so why was she so afraid? She shifted her bound body until she was sitting up now, her back against the cage, as far away from the door as she could be. But she had a feeling it wouldn't be far enough.

"No," was all she could say, a whisper, a plea, and she hated herself for it. She sneered at him instead, balling her hands into fists.

"Maybe I'll kill you later," Kyson said. "But first maybe you'll just watch."

He raised the dagger and slinked towards her.

Zalman strained against the ropes and the iron bars, his muscles bulging with the effort, the ropes cutting into his skin. But he was a man, and those bars were iron. Even the great Zalman – the man that opened the Kulbrim and killed a thousand demics – wasn't that strong.

Kyson knelt before her, the dagger before him.

She could scream, but who would hear that actually cared? The other man in the room left without a thought.

Kyson drew closer to her, and even though her feet were bound together, she kicked out at him, spitting at him. "Shog you, shogger," she said, over and over. But he was bigger and easily held her legs down with his left hand. His grin at her grew as he leaned in and cut the cords around her ankles.

Carys struck out at him with both fists, hitting him in the nose. He cried out and fell back. Gasping, he touched his upper lip with his left hand, and blood came with it.

He wasn't grinning anymore. She kicked out at him, striking him once, but he rushed her in anger. "You lil' bedcoiner," he grumbled and slapped her across the face. He slapped her again and again, the back of her head banging against the iron bars. She tried to fight, kicking and hitting, but she was getting dizzy as he struck her.

She could hear Zalman roar nearby, and he was loud. Was he far away? She couldn't tell anymore, but she was repeating, "No, no."

He pulled her legs apart and now she was on her back. She couldn't breathe through her nose anymore. Her vision blurred with tears and pain and fought to maintain consciousness. He grabbed at her tunic, her green tunic, comfortable since she wore it so often, like a part of her, and she heard him cut it down the middle, ripping it off of her.

Zalman bellowed in anger. Oddly, she found herself wishing she could comfort him, let him know it was going to be okay. Why?

Kyson ripped the tunic off of her, and she was naked now from the waist up, pulling her arms in to cover her breasts. He struck her again, but why? She wasn't fighting back. It was all noise and chaos: Kyson's breathing, Zalman's bellowing and fighting against the iron, her own heart pounding like a drum in her chest, her writhing body scraping along the stone floor.

Carys heard a new sound, however, in the midst of the noise. Kyson's breathing transformed into a choking sound, a rattle in his chest. She tried to focus her vision. Kyson knelt before her, but his back was arched.

Zalman was silent now, his eyes savage.

A blade grew out of Kyson's chest, and he dropped his dagger to clutch the blade as it was rammed through him. Blood erupted from his mouth, and he peered at her one last time with fear and confusion before he fell over to his right, dead.

As he fell, she could see a man standing over her. He held her bloody unforged sword in his hand. He had a wooden leg. She scrambled backwards to sit up, panting.

"S'okay," the man whispered. "Not gonna hurt you."

She searched his face for a moment. Then she raised her bound hands to him. He extended the sword to her and cut the ropes from her wrists. He turned and cut the ropes from Zalman, as well. Zalman immediately took off his own tunic and covered her with it. His tunic was like a short dress over her, but she pulled it over her nakedness.

Zalman stood, towering over the man with the wooden leg. "Who are you?"

"A friend," the man said and tried to hand the sword to Zalman.

Zalman shook his head. "It's hers. Give it to her."

Carys struggled to her feet, swaying, and Zalman caught her arm to steady her. She coughed and spit on Kyson's dead body. Reaching out, she took the sword. "Thank you," she said.

Wooden-leg said, "We have to go." He picked up the dagger from the ground. He had a club in his belt.

Gathering herself, she tested her body, and while she was a little dizzy, her head was clearing. She probably looked like crit with bruises on her face, but those would heal.

"Can you run?" the man asked.

As fast as a man with a wooden leg, at least, she thought. "Yeah."

Zalman faced her. "Can you fight?"

"Yes," she said without hesitation. She wanted to fight. Maybe she needed to. Her heart raced, and she knew she was in shock. But Zal was right. They had to go. She would do what needed to be done. She gripped the blade in both hands and breathed deep.

Zalman lurched out of the cage and then out of the room, like a jungle animal ready to attack. She stepped over Kyson's dead body to follow with the wooden leg tapping on the stone behind her. The other guard was unconscious in the hall, out from wooden-leg's club, she supposed. As Zalman jogged to the stairs that led up to the main floors, wooden-leg halted them.

"I know a way out the back," he said. "You need to come with me to the docks. I have a boat there."

"Why the docks?" Carys asked.

"Leni and Finn are there waiting for us," he said. "At my boat."

"Leni sent you?" Carys asked.

"Told me to keep an eye on you. Knew I worked here with Lorcan sometimes. Now we gotta go. Out the back, so they not see."

"No," Zalman said. "We're going out the front door."

Wooden-leg gulped.

Carys stared up at Zalman. The man's face was fixed in anger and resolve. He was going out the front door, and she couldn't stop him. Not with a face like that. And she didn't know if she wanted to stop him. Her choice was whether he would go alone. And that wasn't much of a choice.

She turned to wooden-leg. "Are you coming with us?"

"With you?" he responded. "When they see me, I'm dead if I show my face in this town again."

Zalman scowled down at the man. "You really think you're coming back here after this?"

Carys brushed her blond hair out of her face and twirled the unforged sword. Her balance was returning. "Time to decide."

Wooden-leg shrugged. "I was ready to leave this town anyway," he said.

Zalman's only response was to climb the stairs up the three flights that led to the main floor of the palace. They didn't encounter anyone as they ascended, and within seconds, the three of them emerged from the stairwell to the main room on the first floor of the palace. Paintings hung on the wall, she could see the bar to the right and forty or more people milling about among the furniture and the thick pillars through the middle of the room. She figured half of the people were hired thugs.

She raised her sword when she saw Lord Lorcan leaning against the long bar in the middle of the room.

"Stay behind me," Zalman said to her without turning around. "And watch my back."

"Done," she said. "Sorry you don't have your axes."

"Don't want them tonight," he said.

Only a few near them had noticed them, and they froze. One middle-aged woman dropped her drink. Some conversations continued, but the room quieted.

"Lorcan!" Zalman yelled, and the room fell silent.

The Dygolor's brow furrowed, and his head revolved slow towards them. Carys wished she had her bow. He would be dead now.

"Remember," Zalman said. "Neither one of us forgives."

Lorcan recovered, and he scoffed. "You could have escaped, and you came up here? You're outnumbered. You're as good as dead."

Zalman scanned the room. "Anyone who wants to live," he said. "Should leave." He wasn't shouting, but they heard him well enough. "You have ten seconds." Then he started counting.

"One. Two."

The woman that dropped her drink waddled quickly away, and more followed her as she went.

"Three. Four. Five."

The thugs around the room set down their own drinks and pulled a club or dagger from a belt and moved to surround them.

"Six. Seven. Eight."

More people left out the double doors, everyone except the thugs and Lorcan. The eight guard from outside entered the room.

"Nine. Ten."

Carys had seen the man fight on the top of the wall at the Battle of Ketan, but it continued to surprise her how fast a man that big could move. It didn't seem possible, but here it was.

Zalman bounded to his right and picked up a table two mitres in diameter, made out of yellow dragontree wood, and he threw it at a group of five men that approached them. Two of them were able to dodge, and three went down, limbs flailing. Grabbing a man to his left around the neck, he twisted and tossed him to the right into another two. A thug with a club attacked from the left, and Zalman turned his shoulder into the strike, punching with the other hand. The thug's feet flew out from under him, and he fell back, unconscious.

A group of three came from behind her, and she took the arm off of one with the sword. She twirled and sliced through the belly of another. Wooden-leg smashed the third in the face.

She glanced and saw Zalman moving, constantly moving. If any were paces away, he would pick up furniture and throw it at them. He dodged daggers and clubs and used his fists as hammers. He lifted a short couch, the frame of dragontree wood and covered with red cushions, and hurled it five mitres at another pair of thugs. Both went down. Zalman caught the wrist of a thug to his right and broke the arm at the elbow, almost tearing the arm off with his bare hands. The thug screamed, and Zalman knocked him away with a kick to the abdomen.

Zalman was making his way to Lorcan. And by the visage on Lorcan's face, he knew it.

More men from the left, four this time, wary of her sword, but while her face hurt and the long tunic was cumbersome around her, she was trained by Athelwulf and the *Brendel*. They never touched her. Her sword took off a leg at the knee while she kicked out at a second man. She spun and cut another across the chest and arm. Wooden-leg did his part with the fourth, blocking a club with his own and stabbing with the dagger.

In a moment of respite, she saw Lorcan back away and then twirl around to run. He was less than ten mitres away.

"Give me the dagger," she said to wooden-leg and stuck out her right hand. He did as asked, and she grabbed the blade, turned and cast it at the retreating Dygolor. The dagger hurtled through the air and stuck him between the shoulder blades. He cried out and fell.

No more time. Another pair came at her from the right this time. She leapt and took the head off the first and thrust the unforged sword through the chest of the second. Wooden-leg had a club in both hands now and beat a thug in the face with them.

Less than ten men remained, and they were cautious. Zalman attacked with more vigor, like an animal that smelled fear. He backhanded one with a fist across the jaw and snatched another's head, snapping the neck as he twisted it in his grip.

Carys launched herself at two more, and she killed them both even as they retreated. Wooden-leg watched her, his mouth agape.

The last four turned and ran.

But Zalman was upon them, grabbing them and pulling two down, tackling the remaining two. As they went down, she heard Zalman growl and men scream as bones snapped, and they were silent. The two he threw down, Carys rushed and killed as they tried to stand and scurry away.

No one stood against them.

Zalman rose, tossing lifeless bodies off of him, and he stalked over to where Lord Lorcan crawled. The Lord of the Dygol moaned and cried in pain.

After pulling the dagger from his back and tossing it aside, Zalman clutched the collar of Lorcan's tunic, lifted, and pressed him against the bar. The man cried out in pain, his breath coming in heaves.

Zalman grasped Lorcan's head and snapped his neck, letting the corpse fall to the ground. Zalman leaned over and against the bar with both hands.

Carys walked up to him. The man was covered in the blood of others and his own. He had several smaller cuts on his arms and shoulders and a nasty gash across his left arm. She remembered the first time she met him – he had a wound from a demic claw across the meat of his arm, just like that, and she had stitched it up for him.

She touched his arm now. He flinched.

"Come on," she said. "It's over. Time to go."

He wouldn't move. "I'm sorry," he whispered. "I wasn't strong enough …"

"It's okay," she said, moving even closer. "It's not your fault. I'll be okay. El helped us."

She had lied to him; she didn't feel it was okay at all. But they needed to move.

Wooden-leg stood behind her. "We really have to go," he said, viewing the carnage.

Zalman trudged out of the main door. She took a deep breath and followed him out into the street.

Wooden-leg took them through back streets, even narrower than the main streets, so they wound their way southeast to the docks. No one followed them; Wooden-leg insisted they check three times.

Carys was exhausted. She wished they had their horses, thankful that she didn't have to go at a full run to keep up with their rescuer. She swayed and stumbled more than once, however.

They made it to the docks within the hour. Wandering down a specific pier, she saw Leni and Finn waiting at the end of it.

The moons were bright, but Carys was within ten paces before she saw Leni react. "Great and mighty El," Leni breathed, noticing her beaten face and Zalman's injuries. He was still covered with blood. But she approached Carys. "Are you alright?"

"I'm fine," she said, however much she wanted to fall into the woman's arms and weep. She cast her gaze away and saw the yacht tied at the end of the dock. Wooden-leg hopped over the side and into the yacht, his boat. She read the words on the side. The *Happy Lamb*.

Finn hovered nearby, carrying two large bags, hers and Zalman's.

The name was familiar and distracted her. She was so tired, so it took her a minute. *The Happy Lamb*.

"Wait," she cried and pushed away from Leni, facing Wooden-leg. "This is your boat?"

He stopped near the mast. "Yeah,"

Carys narrowed her eyes at him. "Who are you?"

"I told you, a friend."

"No," she said and pointed at him with the unforged sword. "What is your name?"

He sighed. "My name is Chronch."

"*The Happy Lamb*," she said. "You took my brother to Galya and tried to kill him."

"He what?" Finn said.

Zalman stood next to her now.

Chronch lifted both hands in surrender. "Hey, your brother didn't kill me when he had a chance," he said. "Even after I tried to kill him. He shoulda killed me, but he didn't. He showed me a kindness, gave me this boat."

"Why didn't you ever tell us this?" Leni asked.

"What was I supposed t'say?" Chronch asked. "I came to Landen, and I started doin' odd jobs for Lorcan. Then I see Finn in the street, and I used t'work for his daddy..."

"And he started doing jobs for me, too," Finn finished. He turned to Carys and Zalman. "I swear, if I had known..."

"I'm a friend, I tell you true," Chronch said. "Would I have risked m'neck tonight if I not?"

Carys glared at him.

"If I not workin' for both Finn and Lorcan, you still be in that basement," he said. "I feel I owe your brother. Soon as I hear about the *Brendel* and changes in Ketan, I knew it were him. I knew it. So when Finn ask me to look out f'you, I do it. Glad to do it. And then I in Lorcan's palace, and I see them carryin' you downstairs and Shan's dead body out to the back, I know it bad."

"He came right to us," Leni said. "And volunteered to take you out of the city in his boat."

"She tell true," Chronch said. "Please let me help you. I was wrong, I know, to try and kill your brother and the Prophet. But I changed, I swear it. I want to be part of the revolution, the redemption o' men."

Carys raised her gaze to Zalman.

"He proved himself," Zalman said. "And people do change."

"Hold a minute," Carys said to Leni, the earlier statement sticking in her mind. "Leaving the city on his boat? We're not going anywhere."

"You have to," Finn said. "They reported your presence to the elves. You escaped from the palace, but the elves will be combing this city when they find you're not there. It won't be safe for you."

"And you killed Lorcan," Chronch muttered.

Finn dropped the bags. "You killed Lorcan?"

"Well, technically, he did," Carys said, using a thumb to point at Zalman. "What can I say? Don't piff on the gedder."

"I'll try and remember that," Finn said, dropping his hands to his side. "But that just makes it worse. The northern Dygol will be in disarray. Different family members will vie for power. What a breakin' mess."

"Exactly," Carys said. "We have to stay and fix it. Not run."

"How?" Leni said.

"We go to this other Dygolor in the south," Carys said. "Talk to him."

"Think about this," Finn said. "You went to meet with Lorcan and now he's dead."

"And about thirty of his men," Chronch muttered.

Finn shook his head. "We can only hope Kyson isn't the one to take over. That man is even worse than Lorcan."

"We killed him, too," Carys said. She pointed at Chronch. "Actually, he killed Kyson."

"Great," Leni said. "Is there anyone left alive at the palace?"

Zalman rolled his shoulders.

"Like Finn was trying to say, that is worse," Leni said. "Your meeting with the northern Dygol left the lord and thirty of his men dead. You won't get anywhere near Lord Thren. That is, when you're not in hiding from the legions of militan in the city hunting you."

"But if we leave now," Carys said. "Then we failed. We came to help the city, not make it worse. We can't leave like this."

"I'm sorry," Leni said. "But you can't help now. It would take all our resources just to keep you alive, much less try and unite the city."

Zalman grunted and gestured at Finn. "He could talk to that Lord Thren."

Finn scowled at him.

"You said you knew the man, and that he was reasonable," Zalman continued. "And didn't your da work for the underground in Asya?"

"No. I said *more* reasonable," Finn said. "And that not sayin' much."

"So you talk to him and see," Zalman said. He turned to Leni. "Your parents were contacts for the Prophet in Asya, right?"

Leni nodded at him.

"Then the both of you go and talk to this Lord Thren," he said. "Finn's father was some crime boss in Asya, so he can negotiate and say what Lord Thren needs to hear about how to take over the whole Dygol in the city. Leni knows the quotes and scriptures and things like Caleb always talks about. You know, the inspiring crit. The two of you together can do it."

That was the most Carys had ever heard from the man at once. "Sounds like ... a perfect idea," she said.

He didn't look at her.

Finn scratched his chin. "I don't know," he said.

Leni smirked at her husband. "Sounds maddy. But it could work."

Maybe our visit here wasn't a complete failure after all, Carys thought.

"If you will try," Carys said. "We will go with Chronch."

Frowning at her, Finn said, "That's cheap negotiating, but okay. We'll try."

"Good enough for me," she said.

They said their goodbyes, placing their bags and other supplies on the yacht. Zalman and Carys cleaned their wounds as best they could.

She was barely holding it together, and Zalman wouldn't look at her. She couldn't get the images of Kyson, and his words, out of her mind now that the fighting was over. She shook her head several times as she stifled sobs.

Isn't she a pretty thing?

As Chronch took the boat out of the dock and through the stone arch in the city wall, he addressed them.

"Where you goin'? How do I take you back to your brother?"

She stood at the mast. "Don't know. Is there a good way to go back to Ketan?"

"No really," Chronch said. "Not without goin' through places controlled by elves. Asya is real bad right now, what I hear. Maybe Galya? You could make your way across west and through the Saten."

"We could," she said. It would be nice to spend time with the Ghosts.

"Or back to Oshra," Chronch said. "Make your way north."

"Yeah," she said. "Doesn't feel right, though."

Zalman lay at the bow, his axes on his belt. "Do we have to go back to Ketan?"

She scrunched her face at him. "What do you mean?"

"So we can't stay in Landen. Why does that mean we go back to Ketan?"

"It doesn't, but what else is there?" she asked.

"We're on a boat," Zalman said. "You're the *Brendel*'s sister. We could go to other elven nations and ask for their support, or the dwarves."

"Or the Pirates," Chronch said.

She spun on him as he steered at the stern. "The Pirates?"

"Only sayin', they close. Only a few days to the south. And I might be knowin' some friends that work with Lord Aeric."

"How could the Pirates help us?" she asked, but she could feel something was right about this.

"Don't know," Chronch said.

"They're just people with boats used to fighting or avoiding the Kryan Navy," Zalman said.

The most powerful navy in the world, she thought. Caleb was building an army to fight the legions on the ground, but if she could help bring the Pirates into the revolution ...

"Shoggers," she mumbled. "We're going to see the Pirates."

CHAPTER 17

THE MAHAKAR

Rolling hills surrounded Eshlyn, and she walked along a path. The sky was clear again. She did not stand in a field of wheat this time, only the wild grasses along the Julan Plains. Or like them. She proceeded north on the path.

It was not the Manahem road, though. No, she knew that well-worn road like the lines of her own palm. This was a narrow path, only enough room for her to walk.

Far in the distance, a lone door stood at the top of the hill. The path led her to that door. No building or structure attached to it, only a door. Next to the door, a man stood, waiting for her.

It was the same man, a king in a long red tunic and black pants and boots, an empty scabbard at his side. The golden crown made him appear older and more majestic.

She halted on the path. She felt alone.

"Who are you?" she asked.

"This is your choice," he said without answering her question, and she knew he spoke of the door. "Only you can decide."

"What is beyond the door?"

"It is your path." As if that explained everything.

"But I cannot see beyond it." And it was true. Even here on the vast plains, she could not see where the door would take her.

"No," he said, and he sounded sad. "You cannot."

"What will happen to me if I go through that door?" she asked. "To Javyn? To my friends?" She was afraid for them all, for their safety. She did not want any of them hurt or dead.

"Those are the wrong questions."

"Then what is the right one?"

The King cocked his head at her. "Will you be free?"

Eshlyn woke that morning to the sound of rain.

She sat up with a gasp. Disoriented, she wiped the hair out of her face, and then she felt the precipitation, big drops that passed through the leaves of the tree overhead. The wind bent the branches of the tree, and she heard the distant sound of thunder. Soon the rain became a deluge, drenching her. She stood and realized she was lucky to be alive.

The memory of falling from the horse, from Blackie, and the image of her horse – Kenric's horse – impaled by a bosaur horn. She couldn't escape the screaming as the horse died and was drug beyond her. She remembered scrambling, and how she survived, she didn't know. But she somehow made it to the trunk of a nearby tree, covered in dirt and sweat, as the stampede passed her. She climbed up the tree and into the branches.

The tree hadn't been a perfect hiding place, however. While it was a massive tree, she could feel it shudder from the impacts of bosaur herd, and it began to bend over. Just as the last of the herd rumbled by, the tree ripped up from its roots and fell over. Screaming, she had hugged a branch. She thought she was dead, to the sure, as the ground rose up to crush her between the dirt and the tree, but at the last moment, the tree twisted and she jumped to the side.

Scared, she had run through the forest. For how long, she didn't know, but several minutes at least. When she stopped to collect herself, she realized she had been running west away from the stampede.

Athelwulf and Earon had bolted away from the stampede. She remembered that. But what direction had they gone? North? She thought north. Had they survived? She knew they had been on a journey to the mountains, to the north, but Athelwulf was her guide to a very specific and hidden destination within the mountains. She couldn't find it without him, but she couldn't sit and wait for him here. If they were dead, she would sit forever. The Kaleti Mountains towered on the northern horizon.

She was lost. All she possessed were the clothes on her back, tattered and filthy now, and her unforged sword – her pack had been lost with Blackie. But she knew she should go north. She had begun traveling in that direction, black clouds covering the heavens as she traveled.

But after two hours, darkness fell, and she had found a large tree that she sat against and was asleep within moments, weeping for her horse.

Now the morning rain soaked her, but she took off her tunic and used it to collect some of the rainwater and drink it. Her canteen had been on the horse. After a few good draughts, she put her tunic back on and roamed north. Dirty and wet with some scratches and a turned ankle, it wasn't comfortable walking, but she considered herself fortunate it wasn't worse. She should be dead.

The rain continued through the morning, but it subsided by the middle of the day. The sun peeked through the clouds again, and the temperature became sweltering hot and humid. The landscape began to incline, and as she noticed more stones and rocks amidst the vegetation, she was in the foothills of the mountains.

By the late afternoon, when the skies were clear, she began to hear the bellowing roar of some animal. The sound was distant, a little to the left, more to the northwest, but she couldn't see anything through the trees. Stopping to hear more clearly, she wondered if she should see what it was.

Athelwulf had lectured her several times about the dangers of the forest, how the rainforest of Lior was one of the most dangerous places in the world. Perhaps she should travel away from the noise instead of closer to it. Eshlyn pulled the unforged sword from the scabbard.

But the animal sound was pained, maybe angry, and constant. Could be hurt. The sound drew her in a way she couldn't explain.

She crept towards the sound, and as she neared it, she could tell the noise belonged to a large beast of some sort, which was even more reason not to get closer. She was curious, however. Eshlyn approached the source of the bellows as quietly as she could. She was no Ghost like Athelwulf, Carys, or Esai. They could sprint through thick brush in complete silence. Within a few minutes, other sounds accompanied the painful growls – thrashing of leaves and the beating of wings.

And the voices of men.

As she pushed her way through the brush, she saw a clearing up ahead. Past the clearing was a pond fed by a waterfall. Two men were fifteen mitres away in the center of the clearing that was ringed with large trees. And while the scene was beautiful, it was the creature that held her attention.

At the far end of the clearing near the pool, she could see a large white tiger with gray stripes, at least as tall as a horse, and it had massive wings with white feathers.

It was the most magnificent creature she had ever seen.

The tiger was caught in an iron trap, its back left foot snagged by iron teeth pressing into the tiger's flesh. Blood dripped from the tiger's paw. An iron chain anchored the trap to the trunk of a tree. The tiger bellowed in pain and roared at the two men at the center of the clearing as it attempted to fly away, its wings spread and flapping.

They were smaller men, about her height, bone thin and covered in dirt. They wore large loincloths and carried long spears with stone blades tied to the end with vines. She could see their hair was long and matted, one older with gray locks.

With her sword trailing her, Eshlyn stepped carefully through the trees to the edge of the clearing so she could hear the men better as they spoke, but they didn't talk loud enough to be heard over the furious tiger.

The men hefted their spears and hesitated before moving in different directions, the elder to the right and the younger opposite to surround the creature. The younger's legs shook, Eshlyn supposed with fear. They advanced on the tiger, and within a few paces, the tiger swiped at them with its front paws and snapped at them. The iron chain restrained the tiger. The men stabbed from separate angles, and the tiger couldn't protect itself from them both. The younger stabbed the tiger in the shoulder and stepped back quickly as the tiger attacked.

These two men were going to kill this beautiful creature.

Eshlyn stepped from her hiding place among the trees and marched to the middle of the clearing, raising Kenric's sword before her.

"That is enough," she said, projecting her voice.

The tiger noticed her before the men did, and growled at her, glaring with bright yellow eyes. Noticing this, the men backed away from their prey and turned to see her. The younger man sneered at her, but the elder grinned. He sidled towards her, and the younger one took his lead and followed.

"Are you lost, pink skin?" the elder asked.

Standing firm with the sword raised, she said, "No." Which was a lie. She was. "But that is not important now. You need to let that beautiful creature go."

The elder smiled, toothless, and gestured back at the tiger with wings. "This? Yes. Very pretty. But bad animal."

Eshlyn frowned at him. "Bad how?"

"Oh, bad-bad. He attack animals of the forest and men. Been here last day-day."

The younger started at the last part of that statement. And with her hand on the sword, she knew it to be a lie.

She tried not to stare up at the tiger, but it was difficult. It was so captivating.

"Even so," she said. "Today you will let him go."

"Can't do that," the elder said, eyeing her sword. "You know what he is?"

Eshlyn shook her head.

"This is the Mahakar," the elder said. "To some, he not exist. At all. Legend of the forest of Lior."

"But we catch him," the younger said with pride.

"If he is the only of his kind, why would you kill him?" Eshlyn asked.

"I say to you," the elder responded. "He a killer."

"And his hide worth mountain o' coin," the younger added.

Ah, she thought. *So it comes down to money.*

"Coin is no reason to kill an animal," Eshlyn said.

"A mountain o' coin is plenty reason," the younger said. "Think o' the elves. They pay big-big-big for the hide of the Mahakar."

"And he bad-bad killer," the elder repeated. "So it good to kill him for two reasons. Money and safety."

Eshlyn looked at the Mahakar again. His nostrils flared as he snarled at them with long, sharp teeth. Something did not feel right, and she gripped the sword tight.

"Sorry," she said to the men. "Not today."

The elder leered at her. "What you gonna do?" He pointed his spear at her. The younger did the same.

Eshlyn fell into the fighting stance Caleb taught her, a slight crouch, the sword in a low guard. "I do not wish to fight."

"You are free to go," the elder said.

Taking in a deep breath and blowing a strand of dark hair out of her face, she cleared her throat. "So are you. This is your chance. Leave now. I'll set him free."

"With what?" the elder asked. "That a good sword, but those iron chains. Don't think so. We know the catch of the trap."

"Then teach me before you go," she said.

"No," the elder said. "We catch, we keep. Law around here, pink skin. And maybe we catch you, keep you, too." He took another step towards her with a leer.

Eshlyn swallowed but didn't answer.

The two men shared a glance, and then the elder stabbed out at her with his spear.

Her only real experience fighting with a sword was with a few demics during the Battle of Ketan and sparring with the other *Sohan-el*. But when the man thrust his spear at her, Caleb's training took over, her mind went blank, and she reacted. Stepping aside, she evaded the strike and cut his spear in two. She spun and stabbed him through the side. The old man choked and spit up blood and fell over on his face.

The younger watched open-mouthed. "Da!" he cried, and his face transformed from fear to fury. He charged her with a scream. Eshlyn easily dodged him, and as she moved aside, she sliced along his ribcage. The sword cut deep, halfway into his abdomen, spilling blood and gore as he fell.

In a matter of heartbeats, she had killed two men.

She gasped at the sight of the men writhing on the ground and bleeding to death, the smell of blood and crit in her nostrils. In the Battle of Ketan, she had seen gruesome injuries and the shocking blood of violence and the stench of death.

But she had never been the cause. She had never killed a man.

Backing away, she grit her teeth at the nausea that threatened to overwhelm her.

"No," she said, trying to deny it, but there it was. Had he said, "Da," when attacking her? Was this a father and son?

She fell to her knees in the grass and began to weep. She had killed them without a thought, so fast. The desire to protect the Mahakar was right, but did she need to kill them? They had crude weapons, and she had an unforged sword and martial training from a great swordsman.

"I'm so sorry," she said. Eshlyn watched, helpless, while the father and son bled out and breathed their last. It took a while.

Wiping her face, she rose from the ground, and she walked to the Mahakar. He sat up and stared at her, quiet and intense in his yellow-eyed if he were intelligent and taking her measure. As she neared him, he ⨼ his teeth at her. Otherwise, he didn't move. She stopped within five ⨼tres of him and wiped the tears from her face with the back of her sleeve.

"I'm going to free you now," she said. "Hold still, and this will all be over in a minute." The Mahakar closed his mouth, and Eshlyn titled her head at it. "Can you understand me? I hope so. Because I don't want to be your lunch. That would just be the perfect end to this critty day."

With the sword – covered in human blood – held out and away from the animal, she slowly strode around to his left side. The back left foot was injured but not mangled. Approaching the teeth of the trap, she examined the contraption. It seemed like a spring-loaded trap something like her father used for foxes back in Delaton, although this one was much larger. Scratching her cheek, she thought she could break the spring and open the mandibles of the trap with a well-placed strike with the unforged sword, which would cut through even iron with enough force.

On her feet again, she leaned over and spoke again to the animal. "Okay, so don't move. Don't be afraid. I'm just going to try and cut the thing loose." The Mahakar turned to her. Was that a frown? Did the animal understand her?

She raised the sword and brought it down upon the spring mechanism. The trap came apart in pieces with a clang, and the clamps opened and fell from the Mahakar's paw.

The Mahakar spun and faced her, ready to leap, baring his teeth and snarling at her. All she could do was stand there and point the unforged sword at the animal.

The yellow eyes of the animal fixed upon the sword, and the snarl disappeared. Instead, the Mahakar brought his nose forward and smelled the sword. And then he sneezed, and he retreated a step. Was that surprise?

Lifting his great head far above her, the Mahakar filled his lungs with air and gave a deafening roar, and he rose up on his hind legs and beat his wings in the air. Eshlyn fell back on her arse and covered her ears and cringed at the wind and grass swirling from his powerful wings. In another second, the Mahakar was above her, in the air, hovering with a parting glance at her before flying away.

In that parting glance, she felt a message from the creature. Not words, more like an impression, but she could translate it. *Thank you.*

As she watched the Mahakar soar away over the trees, she exhaled. "Great," she said. Alone again. She glimpsed back at the two corpses in the grass. "You're welcome."

—⊢—

Athelwulf led the horse that carried the screaming man through the forest.

Earon was in full Sorcos withdrawal now. If he could have spared the time, Athelwulf would have found a place to tie the man up and wait out a day or two for the withdrawals to pass. Athelwulf was concerned the noise would attract animals or even another bosaur herd. But worse would be other men in the forest. Hermits and criminals would make their way into the forest from Oshra or some of the other villages or cities in Lior. Some were harmless. Others were almost like animals themselves.

He used the first day to search for Eshlyn, but between the rain and the destruction of the bosaur stampede, he could find no tracks that led anywhere. It was a vast forest, however, and he knew that didn't mean she was dead. Without him she would be lost. Being lost in the forest of Lior was a death sentence. He prayed for her, that El would help her survive. If she was alive at all.

The second day, he decided to make his way to the Beorgai. He traveled northeast as they entered the foothills of the mountains. It would be another day, maybe two.

When he wasn't praying for Eshlyn, he was praying that Earon would pass through his ordeal quickly. The constant begging and screaming were exhausting. Although a part of Athelwulf wanted to see the young man suffer after losing Eshlyn, he found a small amount of compassion within himself – hadn't he been willing to do worse in his own addiction all those years ago? So he continued to beg El for Eshlyn's safety.

The coming confrontation with his father was foremost on his mind, however. What would he say? After more than twenty years, what could he say? But he knew he must face him, ask his forgiveness, if it was at all possible. And Athelwulf knew that with El, anything was possible.

The end of the second day, he found a good spot for camp, took Earon from the horse, and tied the man to the trunk of a tree. Earon writhed and screamed, but he was weak and easily managed. Athelwulf tried to give the man some water, as much as he could while he squirmed in his delirium. Getting Earon to eat was useless, so Athelwulf didn't even try. But without water for a few days, he would surely die, so he dumped water into Earon's mouth, getting half of it down his face, neck, and the front of his sweat-stained tunic.

Athelwulf didn't start a fire. He didn't need one. Eating dry rations from his pack, he watched Earon in the middle of his violent withdrawals. Taking a sip from his own canteen, Athelwulf took a cloth and poured some water over it.

Earon mumbled incoherent phrases and words, no language or meaning except in his own mind. He might be hallucinating. As Athelwulf got closer, he could make out a couple words.

"Traitor. Murderer."

Athelwulf was visited by memories of the pain, the torture, the begging for release that had harrowed him all those years ago, all still fresher than

..d have guessed. But mixed in with those memories of distress and
were visions of Mother Natali caring for him after he emerged from
, tomb, speaking words of hope and love, teaching him of what it meant
.o have faith in El. He gave a sad grin as Mother Natali's compassion gave
him strength more than a decade later.

He sat next to Earon and wiped the man's sweaty forehead with the wet
cloth. "This is the worst of it," Athelwulf said while the man yelled and
screamed. Athelwulf remembered Mother Natali coming to him in the
middle of his withdrawal, in a Tomb in the Forest of Saten. He didn't recall
what she said, but her presence helped him somehow.

"You have another day to endure it, and then you'll be through the
worst. Hold on. You can make it."

And then you'll face Caleb and Carys and their justice or mercy, he
thought. *Just as I will face my father in another day, if he'll even see me.*

He spent the next hour speaking to Earon, wiping his brow, and
waiting until the current spell subsided. Then he kept watch the rest of the
night.

—

Caleb sat on his horse at the gates of Ketan and watched the army file out of
the city to make the trek to Biram. The midday sun hung high in the clear
sky.

He wore a breastplate made for him by Bweth. The unforged sword
was in its scabbard, and he carried the Kingstaff across his lap. He felt like a
fool with the breastplate. He refused to wear the helmet. Bweth and Hunter
and their apprentices had made breastplates for the whole army, or
adapted the ones from the Citywatch elves. But if he didn't wear one, then
neither would the rest of the army. Some might, but not all, and he felt they
needed the breastplates, at least. So he wore his.

Aden sat on his horse to Caleb's left. Iletus sat on a horse to his right.

Four thousand men and women walked past him, in fifteen divisions.
Aden was one of the division leaders, but his would bring up the rear
guard. Tamya, with her bloodwolf at her side, would lead them to the gate.
Aden had begun calling the army the *Hamon-el*, an ancient term from the
Ydu, Yosu's army. Caleb let it stick. They would need all the inspiration
they could muster in the coming days.

Each soldier in the *Hamon-el* was armed with a sword, a breastplate,
and a bow. Half had spears and shields. Every man and woman carried his
and her own supplies in a pack. They had been trained to fight as
individuals, in small groups or in a larger force. It was a flexible and deadly
army, he knew.

Lyam, a *Sohan-el*, passed by leading his division, his face crestfallen.

"You could stay," Caleb said to him as he passed.

The young man paused to answer as his division kept marching. "The *Hamon-el* goes to battle," he said. "They are my brothers, my family and friends. This is my place, for good or ill."

"Are you sure?" Caleb asked.

"I am."

"Then you are welcome, of course." Caleb shifted in his saddle. "Did you send the scouts?"

This might be a trap, but he would have all the information he could gather. The Ghosts of Saten knew the region better than anyone, and they moved faster and more silent than the wind. With Athelwulf, Carys, and Esai gone, he relied upon Lyam to pick ten people to scout ahead and report back.

"They left this morning," Lyam said. "We should get reports soon." Even without horses, the Ghosts would move faster than an entire legion.

"Good," Caleb said.

Lyam jogged forward to lead his division again.

The next division to pass was Bweth and Hunter's. He tried to get her to stay in the city and send one of her apprentices. But she would have none of it. The *Hamon-el* would need an armorer and blacksmith on hand, so she was going. She would also be fighting with her division, he reminded her, but she had dismissed that, as well.

Caleb was beginning to realize that he wasn't much of a general or king. That was the thing about telling people they were meant to be free. He couldn't just tell them what to do and expect absolute obedience. He had to lead them and let them make their own decisions. It was the most maddening thing in the world.

Caleb glanced over at Aden, who seemed as uncomfortable in his breastplate as Caleb. Aden's face was pensive. Caleb knew that face.

"What's on your mind," he asked Aden.

"Do you think this is the best choice? Going out to meet a Kryan legion? Into a trap? I'm not saying it is wrong or even feels wrong. But it seems maddy."

Caleb watched as Xander's division passed next.

"Do you know what I wanted to be when I was a kid?" Caleb asked.

Aden shook his head.

"A farmer," Caleb explained. "My da was a farmer, and he was the best man I knew. He was so strong." Caleb scratched his beard. "Naturally, I wanted to be a farmer, have my own land and help things grow. My da was so breakin' good at it. I would help him, even that young. That was what I was going to do for the rest of my life. I thought that would make me happy."

Aden lifted a brow at him. "So?"

‿b was silent for a moment, watching the army he raised and ‿d pass by him. Many of them marching to their death. That was ‿re he led them.

"So my mother was captured, and probably raped, by elven Cityguard because we harbored people that believed in El. And we did help them. And then my father was caught as he tried to rescue her. They were both burned alive. Years later, I was playing Sand-bol and abducted and given a chance to be a Bladeguard."

He remembered Iletus' words about Danelle, and the pain of losing her settled within him. However he tried to distance himself from the grief, it was a wound that stayed fresh, refusing to heal. Was Iletus right? Were Saben and Cyprian manipulating him into making a monumental mistake? Was he risking too much?

Caleb took a deep breath. "Yes, I think this is the best decision, but it is out of a host of options. And I like none of them. There are no guarantees. We can make our plans, but those plans can change in a moment. We have a good, flexible army that was built to cause havoc in the open. It seems best to take advantage of that while we can. But I won't lie to you. We could all die tomorrow."

"How do you decide, then? If there no guarantees?"

It was difficult to sift through the pain of the past, to see beyond his rage and desire for vengeance, but as Caleb laid his hand upon the unforged sword, he felt an assurance at taking the battle to the legion.

Caleb smiled at him. "You remember when I met you and you insisted on coming with me. What did you keep saying to me?"

Aden grinned back. "I'd see it to the end," he said.

"I think you were right," Caleb said. "But it was maddy for you to want to come with me and the Prophet after we just broke out of the Pyts. It was the most dangerous thing you could have done. How did you know?"

"Dunno. Just knew."

"That's how I know it is time to go."

Aden gazed out over the army as it passed. Tamya approached with his division.

"You know I'm still with you," Aden said. "That hasn't changed."

"I know," Caleb said. "And I am glad."

CHAPTER 18

THE BASHAWYN

He prayed for the Light to come. Because when the Light came, he brought Life with him.

A prisoner in darkness, the nameless elf sat in the corner of his cell, gazing with expectation at the door. Bodies of the dead were piled in the opposite corner, five of them, now. Once men, they were instruments in the nameless elf's survival. Given the power and the strength he now possessed, they were worth the cost.

Black scars covered his body, writing he did not comprehend, but the etchings in his skin, however painful, also gave him strength. When the Light spoke, the script on his skin bade him obey. At first he resisted, but no longer.

He had not always been nameless. Long ago, in another life, he had a name. He remembered that much – a name, a life, a home. He even recalled how he had felt his cause and purpose was so important. What they were, he had lost. Lost. But his purpose now was so much greater, so sure.

His purpose was now to serve and obey the Light.

The nameless elf had been foolish to resist. Deceived. Why had he fought so hard? He didn't have the memories and it didn't matter. The Light was his source of Life. He did not eat. The Light gave him all he needed.

Hunger ached in his body. He was starving, he knew. But the Light would come. The Light would not let him die. The Light told him that he was now unstoppable. He would live forever.

While he prayed, his thoughts focused on the Light, he saw the crack underneath the door cast a dim glimmer. The sound of footsteps reached his ears, and it was a beautiful sound because the Light approached – and he carried another man with him.

The nameless elf sat straight against the back wall of the cell. The light grew stronger, brighter. The door opened, and the blinding light entered his cell, a white flame blazing from the palm of the Light. The nameless elf did not cower or close his eyes at the heat and power of the light. No. He let the light burn his eyes, tears streaming down his face at the joy and pain.

The Light threw the moaning man down at his feet.

"Who are you?" the Light asked.

"I am the shadow in the darkness. I am vengeance. I am death."

"And who do you serve?"

, nameless elf bowed with his forehead touching the cold stone of the cell. "I serve the Light and the Light alone."

"Very good," the Light said.

Groans of anguish came from the man between them. He squirmed and went rigid in agony, chocking on his own cries until he fell silent.

And the nameless elf felt his hunger satisfied and strength enter his limbs. He was given Life.

"You are almost ready," the Light said. "My greatest creation yet."

—⬩—

Eshlyn decided to spend the night at the pool near the waterfall. It was a few hours before dark, but she could see bright orange fish in the clear, clean water and decided this was the best place to camp for the evening.

First she stripped herself down and rinsed her clothes in the pool. There was a small tear here or there, but the tunic and divided skirts were intact and useful, just dirty and smeared. She laid the clothes out on a low branch on a tree at the edge of the clearing to dry.

Removing her boots, she waded out into the pool, stark naked, up to her thigh. No one but dead men could watch her now. While she still had the light, she wanted fish for her hunger; it had been a day and half since she last ate. She stood as motionless as possible, and lifted the unforged sword above the water, the blade down. After a few minutes, the fish returned to swim around her. It took her three attempts and a half hour or more, but she finally speared one on the sword. Throwing it on the bank of the pool, she took the time to spear three more. She didn't miss again.

Eshlyn stood at the bank and looked at the dead men at the center of the clearing. She felt as if she should do something, bury them or say some words. But she didn't have her hand shovel and the words failed her. Could she dig with the sword? Eshlyn walked to the edge of the clearing and found a soft spot in the grass between two large roots of a tree. Using the sword, she began to hack at the ground. It came up easily, and so she continued to work at it until she dug a shallow grave she thought would hold both men.

They were thin men but dead weight, so she dragged them over to the grave with some effort. The hand shovel would have helped with the loose dirt, but she could use her hands to cover the graves. It was dark by the time she finished. She stood over the graves of the men she killed. Did they deserve it? Were they good men? How could she know in the mere minutes she knew them? Possibly they were hungry and could use the money from the Mahakar pet.

What had Caleb's vow been? *I will defend the innocent, free the oppressed, and spread light in dark places.* That had been the vow of the *Sohan-el* on the way to the Living Stone. Did it apply to her, a woman

212

trained but with her dead husband's sword? Maybe she wasn't a *Sohan-el* like the others, but the principle was sound. And she believed in it as a guide, to the sure.

Were the men innocent? No, they were going to kill an innocent, beautiful creature. She did not regret protecting the animal. But she did regret killing a father and a son. Naked, she blinked down at the shallow grave.

"I pray to El for forgiveness. No one should ever kill without a thought. I may not be a *Sohan-el*, but I fight for the same god and the freedom of men. And so I make my own vow. I will not kill again unless it is necessary. I will do my best to preserve life, not take it. I am sorry, but that is all I can do. But that is my promise."

The three moons hung in the northern sky, and she bathed in the pool, washing the blood and the dirt and sweat from her body. Getting out of the pool, she stood drying in the breeze. Hungry but without a way to make a fire, she ate one of the fish, picking the meat from the bones and stuffing it raw into her mouth.

She remembered her journey from Campton to Ketan and those long lonely nights. But she had her son, Javyn, with her, and she had known the road to travel. Here her only company was a shallow grave and whatever lurked in the dark forest around her. She didn't even have the horse she loved, Blackie.

Would she see her son ever again? Would she die out here in the vast and dangerous forest? Was it a mistake to come on this quest? She didn't know if Athelwulf or Earon were still alive, and she could keep moving north. But how could she find the Beorgai in the mountains? She could travel south, to the river and make her way back to Oshra. But that was days of traveling alone with only the clothes on her back and a sword.

Dressing, she leaned against the trunk of a tree and laid the unforged sword across her lap. She had never felt so alone, afraid, defeated, and lost in her whole life.

"I don't know what to do," she said.

———

The Happy Lamb sailed south for two days. Carys had never been on a boat that long, and she found it gave her time to think. Too much time. Chronch said they would be in Enakai, the home city of Aeric the Pirate Lord, within the next day.

She found herself jealous for a storm or a battle or something to divert her attention.

Isn't she a pretty thing?

y slept on the deck, and while Zalman said few words to her, he *s* made sure he was between her and Chronch. She wasn't afraid of onch, and she was a little angry that Zalman felt he needed to protect *er*. At the same time, as misguided as it might be, she realized he cared enough to want to protect her.

Did he hear her crying in the middle of the night? If he did, he gave no sign.

Leave us alone for a while, why don't you ...

The evening of the second day, she turned to Zalman, angry. "Why won't you look at me? Or talk to me?"

He sighed and faced her. It was slow, like he had to force himself. "Did we have deep conversations before?"

"No," she said. "But ever since Landen, since we left, you've been ... different."

Zalman gazed out to the ocean again, and it was like being punched in the gruts. For a minute, she did not think he would answer. "I'm sorry," he said. "It's not you. I failed. My one job was to protect you, and I failed."

Carys felt like her heart sunk into her stomach. "So I'm almost ..." But she couldn't finish the thought. "And you're breakin' making it about *you*?"

"I'm sorry," he said. "But you asked."

True, she thought. Didn't make it feel better, though. "But there was nothing you could have done."

"Could have refused to let you go to Lorcan. Could have seen that shogger sneak up behind you. Should have listened to my heart that Shan was full of crit."

She frowned at him. "Those were my decisions, too. Mine. Do you blame me?"

Zalman grimaced. "No."

"Controlling people isn't protecting them, you big gedder," she said. "We all made mistakes, Shan, too. We're in this together, right?"

"You're right. But still ..." Zalman regarded the moons hovering over the waves to the east.

"Wait," she said. "You said, your one job. What did you mean?"

"Nothing," he mumbled.

"Not nothing," Carys said. She narrowed her eyes at him. "What did my brother say to you before we left?"

He lowered his head for a moment before facing her. "He said ... that if you got a scratch, one scratch, he would kill me."

"And you breakin' believed him."

"Have you met your brother?" Zalman ran a hand over his bald head. "Don't wanna find out how serious he was. Either way, that was my one reason for being here." He reached out and pointed at her neck, where Kyson's dagger drew blood. "There's a scratch." He lowered his hand. "More than a scratch."

He didn't mean on her skin.

"Shoggers," she said. Even here, in the middle of the ocean, she couldn't get away from her brother. She loved him and thought the world of him. But even here, she couldn't get away from his protectiveness. Zalman was just another instrument for Caleb.

Why couldn't Zalman see that what she needed right now was a friend? Not another older brother or someone to feel guilty for not protecting her, but a friend who believed in her and realized she had been more terrified in those moments in Lorcan's basement than she could even admit. Glancing at Zalman, he was the only friend she had within a thousand kilomitres. And instead he gave her the same distance she remembered from her Uncle Reyan all those years ago.

"I thought," she began, but she couldn't finish. *I thought we could be friends. I thought maybe I wouldn't have to do this alone.*

His eyes questioned her.

"Never mind," she said and showed him the back of her.

—

The sunlight woke Eshlyn in the morning, and her back ached as she rose from her slumber against the tree. She noticed the day was peaceful and bright. The waterfall at the far end of the pool calmed her. She picked apart another fish for breakfast and drank from the clear pool.

Standing there in the growing sunlight, she considered what to do. Keep moving north and hope for some sign of Athelwulf and Earon or move south back to Oshra? Either way was a risk and a danger, but staying wasn't an option.

She thought about the Mahakar, the desire to see the animal again welling up within her. She had never even heard of the creature, not as a fire tale or even part of Athelwulf's warnings. Was he as rare as the men had claimed? She felt he was pure and wild.

And free. He was free to fly or hunt or rest. She envied that. She never felt that free and unhindered, that wild. Her life had been a constant series of obligations and responsibilities. Her life with Kenric and Javyn brought immense joy, that was true, and she was no slave. She was raised to make choices and be free. But so often she didn't feel free. Not like the Mahakar. Not like that lone and undomesticated beast.

Eshlyn heard the roar high above her before she saw him. She scanned the bright blue cloudless sky. The Mahakar appeared high in the east, and she placed a hand over her eyes to block the glare of the sun as he circled above her, gliding. The Mahakar's wings flapped twice, and he descended, his hind feet lowering and preparing to land. Her heart beat hard within

. she took a deep breath, frozen in awe, watching him land not ten
from her.

The animal watched her, sitting, his long tail lazy as it moved behind
him, the wings folded at his side. She sought his yellow eyes, seeing again
the intelligence and purity within. And the danger, the wildness.

"Did you come because I was thinking about you?" she asked him.

In response, he lay prostrate before her, placing his head on his
forelegs.

She thought, *I should be more afraid.* Her heart raced, but she did not
feel the terror that logic dictated she should feel when faced with such a
large, wild animal.

Approaching him, she extended her hand, and he did not react while
she touched the fur behind his ear. It twitched as she felt the soft coat,
stroking him gently. He lay still while she rubbed her hands across his back.
As she studied his back leg, she could see it was still injured.

"Come with me, okay?" she said. She beckoned him with her hands and
led him to the bank of the pool. She touched his shoulder and encouraged
him to lie back down. He did, parallel to the pool.

She dipped her hands into the pool and washed his foot. The
punctures weren't deep, and she rinsed them out with the water. The
Mahakar made a low growl within his chest. It wasn't a dangerous sound,
perhaps like a purr. She patted his hindquarters and shushed him. After she
was done, she stood, and he curled to lick his injured paw.

He peered at her then, and she felt he was trying to communicate
something to her. Not in words but something. Like an invitation. Yes, an
invitation.

Gasping, she understood and could put it into words. He invited her to
get on his back ... and ride him.

The concept staggered her, the idea of riding this huge creature, of
flying above the trees. Her skin crawled in fear.

But she desperately wanted to do it.

Eshlyn smoothed her divided skirts and tunic – why she didn't know,
they were so tattered – and adjusted her belt and scabbard. Touching the
bracelet at her wrist, she took a deep breath to attempt to still her heart. She
took a step towards the beast, and he uncurled to allow her to approach
him from the side. She was aware of her boots crunching on the grass and
then how they left the ground when she pressed her body into his shoulder,
grabbed handfuls of his fur, and pulled herself onto his back, straddling
him just behind his shoulders, like a horse. Her hands found purchase, and
she made sure the sword was off to the side along her left leg.

Her nostrils flared. "Okay. I'm ready."

He stood and his wings extended, rose, and lowered with a powerful
thrust, and the body of the Mahakar lifted. Eshlyn hung on with her hands

and her legs, clinging for life as the animal left the ground and elevated, taking off above the tree line within seconds.

And then the Mahakar flew, soaring, the wind beating her face and screaming in her ears. Her eyes leaked tears against the current of air. The Mahakar continued to ascend, higher and higher. She stole a glance over the animal's shoulder and surveyed the forest far below. It was beautiful from this height, too, but in a different way. What loomed so large on the ground before was now small. She could see how the forest lived and breathed as one, how it all fit together, and that gave her a feeling of joy and wonder at El's creation and the power and majesty of it. Trees swayed together in the breeze, made way for the small streams and pillars of stone at the foothills of the Kaleti Mountains.

They sailed west, as high as the peaks of the mountains to the north. Her hair snapped against her cheek in the wind.

And in that moment, her lips parted, her teeth bared, and her face broke into a smile, pure and full of joy. And the tears she cried were tears of happiness. Her arms and legs were sore from holding on so tightly, so she relaxed. If she fell, it would be to her death, but the fear only fueled the excitement. She had never felt more alive.

For the first time in a long time, she didn't feel like she had anywhere to be, any responsibility. She was not a *Sohan-el*, or a mother, or a widow, or Lady Eshlyn the head elder of Ketan. Her name or position didn't matter here. She felt free and pure and wild. There was no revolution, no oppression, no war to fight. Only joy. She was nameless. And everything was clear to her. Simple.

The Mahakar spread his wings and glided.

And through her tears, she threw back her head and laughed. It came from deep within her gut, and it was loud. She sat up on the Mahakar's back. She spread out her own arms, continuing to laugh.

After a few minutes, she leaned over and threw her arms around the Mahakar. "Thank you," she whispered. Could he hear her? Feel her somehow? "Thank you."

Below her, she watched the top of the trees pass them, and then the forest stopped. The trees and vegetation just ended.

Instead, she saw leagues and leagues of emptiness, of grass and stumps and devastation. It spread far in the distance to the west. Her mouth hung open, and with her face in his fur, she said, "Will you take me down there?"

They descended, and she held on as the Mahakar hovered for a moment before landing.

She slid off of his back and walked forward a few steps. This was once a beautiful forest like she had been traveling in over the past few days. And men and elves had cut it down to sell the wood. All the ships and furniture and buildings made of Liorian wood – they came from here. All she could

,t and south, was flat grass and mud and stumps of trees. It was a
.and, a wound upon Eres.

She faced him. "You wanted me to see this?"

The animal didn't respond. He was perusing the devastation, as well.

As she scanned the ground around her, she said, "You wanted me to
see this."

And even though it had been a wonderful moment, pure and free and
without a revolution or a cause or a war to fight, she knew that wasn't a
moment meant to last. But it was one to remember – joy in the midst of
tragedies like the one before her.

She drew close to the Mahakar, and he looked down at her. "Thank
you," she said. "So much. But I have more to ask of you, if I can. Do you
know of the people that live in the mountains? They are a tribe, the Beorgai.
I don't know where they are, but can you take me to them?"

The Mahakar lay down as a response. She steeled herself and climbed
up onto his back again.

Within another second, they were in the air, circling around and
swinging to the northeast, flying closer to the mountains. She could see
something within the cliffs. She tried pulling gently on the fur at the
animal's neck, and she was pleased to find that the Mahakar made a slight
alteration to the left, even closer to the peaks.

She saw a series of camps, like prisons, and deep holes dug into the
mountains. Iron wagons filled with rock and gold and silver traveled
between the holes and the camps. Men and women, dark-skinned, naked
and bound with shackles, worked and shuffled about. The sun glistened off
of breastplates and helmets and spears – elven militan or some sort of
guard.

The mines. She had heard about the mines and the human slaves there.
It was like the Underland itself. She could feel the suffering and pain even
from far above. An outrage began to simmer within her, and it grew. The
fury was as pure as the joy had been before. Except, she hadn't lost the joy.
It remained. The anger had been added to it. She knew in that instant, the
Mahakar meant to show her this, too.She patted the Mahakar on the
shoulder. "Take me to the Beorgai," she said.

After another two hours of flight, the peaks of the Kaleti racing by, the
animal slowed and descended. She peered to her right and saw an ancient
stone city hidden among the trees in the mountains. It was perhaps half as
big as Ketan with short stone walls. The buildings within were also made of
gray stone, most small structures, although a few appeared larger. Two
herds of bosaur were in a pen outside the city on the northern side.
Hundreds of terraces were cut into the mountain above the city, and crops
grew there. People milled about between buildings, dressed in brightly
colored robes and dresses, and some sort of common area sat at the center
of the city.

Using her hands, she guided the Mahakar. "Put me down there in that open area," she said.

As the animal plunged for a landing and neared the city, people began to notice them. And they pointed and screamed and yelled. In the thirty seconds that it took to descend and land, a crowd gathered in a ring at the edge of the common area.

She was prepared for the jolt this time as they landed, and she sat up once the Mahakar came to a rest.

As Eshlyn gazed out over the gaping crowd, she watched as they all bent to a knee and bowed to her.

She squeaked in surprise. An old man pushed his way through the crowd. He stood straight and tall. Some kind of leader? After gaining some separation from the crowd, he also went to a knee.

"The *Bashawyn* has come," he said. "El have mercy on us."

"Break it all," Eshlyn muttered.

Chapter 19

Enakai

The morning of the third day out of Landen, *The Happy Lamb* pulled into the city of Enakai among the archipelago called The Pirate Lands.

As they approached the island, Zalman saw the great cliffs. Even from a distance, the ridges were imposing. The nearer they came to the island, the larger they appeared. The whole northern side of the island was a series of tall, sheer peaks that rose hundreds of mitres into the sky, perhaps a thousand. When they pulled into the docks, Zalman craned his neck and couldn't see the top of the white cliff before him, but he could see the caves and stairways that had been cut into the rock.

Enakai was a city cut into the cliff and ridges. It spread upwards the whole distance, as far as he could see. Stairways and ramps made their way from level to level without any pattern; the lowest levels had large open areas and structures. After those levels, several stories were made of smaller residences and shops. Above that, three hundred mitres up the escarpment were homes and edifices.

The elves had no authority here, so Zalman and Carys both wore their weapons in the light of the day. As they pulled into port, Zalman could see others wearing weapons, makeshift or otherwise, few of them elven in make. Most of the men were bare-chested and wore simple short trousers. The women also wore short trousers or skirts and a piece of cloth to cover their breasts. The people were darker skinned than those of Veradis but not as dark as Lior. The natives of Enakai had slanted eyes and round faces. They wore their hair long and thick and black.

Zalman could see other races, however, mixed in among the people of Enakai, from Veradis and Lior and the pink skins of the north.

Dozens of ships of all shapes and types were docked at Enakai. Chronch pointed to the largest one, far to their right. "That is Lord Aeric's ship," he said. "*The Last Serpent.* You're lucky. That means he here. He spends months out at sea."

Lucky? Zalman wondered. *We'll see.*

Gathering their packs, Zalman and Carys followed Chronch to the wooden platforms along the narrow shore before the rocks of the cliff. He stayed as close to Carys as he thought reasonable. She didn't seem to like his hovering, so he tried to keep some distance between them. But he constantly scanned the people passing by or congregating at a boat or a local shop. His hands were always ready to pull the axes from his belt.

ys was upset with him, and he understood. However, she wasn't at his failure in Landen but for the emotional distance as a result of guilt. This confused him. He thought she hated him. He was convinced it. Why did she want his affection now?

Carys was a fine, brave warrior and a noble leader, but he didn't think he could really understand her. She believed things he didn't comprehend. He saw the integrity and strength of her faith, and Caleb's, but it seemed too idealistic and naïve to him. The world was a brutal place, and there were few people he could trust. But he trusted Caleb and – as much as she seemed to hate him – Carys.

Their vision of what man could be was admirable. While the freedom of Ketan had been a fine and honorable thing, it had only been a few months. Men would prove themselves selfish, like Shan and Lorcan and Kyson. A part of him waited for it all to fall apart again, which was why he felt like such a failure in Landen. He knew better. He knew that life on Eres was one of betrayal and tragedy.

He wanted to believe it could be different. Even as recent events in Ketan with Caleb and others proved it might be possible, he just didn't believe it. Not completely. But he would protect and fight for their vision, as naïve as it seemed. It was better than the alternative, to take and consume without any other purpose, any greater cause. He had been that hopeless before. This was different.

She cried in the middle of the night, sobbing but trying to stay quiet. He wanted to say something, but what? How could he comfort her? She didn't want his comfort. He had never felt that angry in his entire life, tied to the bars and helpless while that man tried to rape her. It made him feel insane. He had released his fury and hate on the men in Lorcan's palace, thinking it would satisfy the darkness within him, but when she wept, he could hear the words again. And the anger returned, the fury.

Maybe I'll kill you later. But first maybe you'll just watch.

Chronch led them to a man leaning against a wooden booth, smoking a thin cigarette. "Dock master?" Chronch said.

"Oi," the man said. "What you got?"

"Yacht by name of *Happy Lamb*," Chronch said and pointed down the pier to the boat. "There."

The dock master, a wiry older man with thinning hair, squinted at all three of them as if seeing them for the first time. "And who you be?"

"Visitors from Ketan," Chronch said. "We friends and come to be friends. We follow the ways while we here."

"Finer," the dock master said. "That'll be a coppa a day."

Chronch glanced at Carys. She pulled out three copper stones and handed them over to the dock master.

The man scoffed at the stones in his hand. "Kryan coin?"

"You don't take Kryan?" Carys asked.

The dock master frowned. "Oi, we take it. But that be two a day, then."

Zalman's chest filled and stepped closer to the dock master, towering over him.

"Copper is copper," Carys said. She handed him one more stone. "This should be enough, don't you think?"

The dock master scratched his neck. "Finer. But you know the elves cut their copper with tin, doncha?"

"Maybe," Carys said. "But not enough for two a day."

"Finer," the man said and pocketed the stones in his purse.

"Haps you could help us and earn some extra coin?" Chronch said, ignoring Carys' raised brow at him.

"Haps I could," the dock master said.

"Need to know where we could find Lord Aeric," Chronch said.

"Ah, well, what would a visitor want with the Piralor?"

"Don't the ways see the finery of welcoming a visitor?" Chronch asked.

"That it do," the dock master said. He held out his hand.

Carys put three more coppers into his hand. He continued to hold it open. Chronch leaned over and whispered in her ear; Zalman couldn't hear it, but she groaned and put a bronze star in his hand.

The dock master smirked at the coin. "Kryan coin," he muttered and put it in his purse. "Lord Aeric up at the *Steamy Crag*. Ev'body knows. But he not long for Enakai. Got business out at sea soon."

"Then we should hurry," Carys said. "Thank you."

Chronch led them away.

"Well met to you," the dock master said as they left.

Chronch hobbled to a nearby stairwell and climbed up to the next level, Carys beside him and Zalman striding behind, his stare inspecting their surroundings.

"What are 'the ways'?" Carys asked.

"The ways are the rules here," Chronch said, his voice low. "Rules of honor and fairness. Everyone in the Pirate Lands follows them."

"Bribery part of the ways?" Zalman asked.

Chronch snorted. "Sometimes. When you have a position like that, it part of the ways, yeah."

"Honor among thieves," Carys said.

They climbed level upon level, up past the main residences. A broad walkway open to the air was common and signified a new part of the city. Residences seemed small and, for the most part, simple. Most of the communal life seemed to happen out on the walkways in small groups. Chronch stopped in front of a long, open edifice.

"This be *The Steamy Crag*," Chronch said.

Zalman peeked into the structure – a tavern of some sort with a high ceiling and small wooden tables and chairs. It smelled of watery ale, sweat, and urine. Men and women sat around at tables and the bar to the left.

⸝ Pirate Lord is in here?" Carys asked.

⸝ hen you on a boat with your people for months at a time, you used ⸝in' with them, close," Chronch said. "He has a place up top, but he ⸝nds his time down here during the day."

Carys studied the main room for a moment. She pointed to the back corner. "That him there?"

A tall man in a red shirt and a sword at his hip lounged at a small table. He was a native of Enakai, Zalman could tell, and his thick black hair was past his shoulders.

"That be him," Chronch confirmed.

She hesitated before entering *The Steamy Crag*, and Zalman followed close at her heels. Chronch waited and shambled behind Zalman.

Weaving through the tables in the room, Aeric noticed the three of them as she approached. Four men sat with him. They each wore blades and tensed when they noticed Zalman, who put his hands on the handles of his axes.

"Well," Aeric said, sitting up. "We have visitors."

"You are Lord Aeric, correct?" Carys asked.

"I am," Aeric said. "One and same." He smiled, but Zalman saw his hand move to his sword. "Who might be asking?"

"My name is Carys. This is Zalman and Chronch. Well met."

"Well met to you," Aeric said. "And now we are no longer strangers. Shall we have some ale?" He lifted a clay mug of ale with the hand not on his sword.

"No thank you," Carys said.

"Yay, we will," Chronch said. "One for each of us." She glared back at him, but he muttered. "And *we pay*."

"Yes, we will all take a mug, please," Carys said through a forced smile more like a snarl.

"Katryn!" Aeric called.

A woman from across the room smiled at him. "Oi!" she replied.

"Eight mugs of ale for us and our visitors!" he shouted.

"Oi!" she said and strode behind the bar.

The four men with Aeric relaxed, and the Lord moved his hand away from his sword.

"Eight?" Carys whispered to Chronch.

He shushed her. Zalman was more worried about Chronch's safety at this point.

"Now," Aeric said. "What can I do for you?"

Carys was silent for a moment, and Zalman could tell she was angry. He inclined his head to her for encouragement.

"We are from the city of Ketan," she said.

Aeric's face went blank. "Ketan?"

"Yes. The men of Ketan are now free from the power of the elves. A revolution has begun in the lands of men. We would like to talk with you, meet with you about all that has happened."

The Pirate Lord stared at Carys for a heartbeat; then he smiled. "I should like to hear about this," he said. "We have heard rumors, you understand. But first-hand information is always best." Aeric turned to the man who sat next to him. "Bade. Take them up to my house and give them rooms. See that they have whatever they need." Aeric examined the three of them. "And give them proper clothes." He met Carys' eyes. "You will have dinner with me tonight, and we will talk."

"Sir?" Bade questioned.

"They are ambassadors from another tribe," Aeric explained. "And we must see that they are treated as such. Understand?"

The man sighed but stood. "Finer."

Aeric stood and leaned in close to Carys. He spoke quietly, but Zalman could hear. "Do not worry. You are safe on my word. We cannot speak of these things here. But we shall have the liberty tonight."

Carys' jowls clenched. "Tonight then. At your word."

Chronch glanced at her before facing Aeric again. "Your word honors the ways."

Aeric smiled at them again, but his eyes were sad. "Oi. Thank you. Tonight."

———

Climbing into the mountains, Athelwulf found the hidden city of Da'ar as if more than twenty years had not passed.

After a day of traveling in the foothills, Earon was motionless and silent on the horse, brooding. The worst of the withdrawals were gone. The young man shook from time to time, but Athelwulf could see the relief in Earon's countenance. He remembered well the relief in his own heart when the worst had been over and he survived. Then he was to fight other battles. And so would Earon.

Athelwulf found the path through the trees as it wound back and forth. The path led to a tremendous stone bridge over a tributary of the Decel River, rushing far below. He walked across the bridge with Earon riding the horse. The path continued up into the mountains for another hour, vines hanging above him between the branches of trees, the call of birds familiar in his memory.

As he turned a corner on the dirt path, he saw the city surrounded by a gray wall five mitres tall. A thick wooden gate stood open, and he could see the buildings inside.

. had been built thousands of years ago by the first tribes of men as ₒved into Lior. It was abandoned when the cities of the south grew. ₌s Lior became more divided and controlled by the elves, the leaders of ₌ Beorgai moved north and reclaimed the ancient city where they stayed ₌idden and unmolested by the elves.

Athelwulf stood at the gate for a moment. He couldn't see anyone close to the gate. Where were the people of the city? Hearing some noise further in, he strode forward. He shuffled down the road to the center of town, and could see a crowd of people gathered there. As he neared the crowd, a few noticed him and parted. He took more steps, cautious but curious. No one spoke to him. It was as if they anticipated him. Some sneered at him and others averted their eyes, but they made a path through the crowd.

The crowd ringed the common field at the center of town, and as they parted, Athelwulf could see something in the middle of them. It was a large, winged, white tiger.

Athelwulf froze. He had never believed it was real. The Mahakar.

The animal lay with a bosaur leg in its paws, gnawing on the meat and bone. On the far side of the field, he saw Eshlyn, and she was talking to his father and another woman. Eshlyn noticed him, as well, and ran over to meet him.

Seeing Eshlyn overcame even his shock at the Mahakar. She was alive. "Thank the mighty El," he whispered to himself, thanking the Creator for keeping her safe.

"Athelwulf," she said as she threw herself into an embrace. Athelwulf lifted her in his arms with a laugh. "I thought you were lost to me." Eshlyn looked up at Earon. "Both of you."

Athelwulf smiled at her and pulled away. Then he shot a glare at Earon.

"Eshlyn," Earon began. "Please forgive me. I ... startled the bosaur. You could have died. I'm sorry."

"It was a maddy thing to do, to the real," Eshlyn said. "But it has all worked out, it seems. I forgive you."

Athelwulf's eyes were drawn to the beast not ten paces away. "Lady Eshlyn," he said. "I feared the worst. How did find your way here?"

She pointed at the beast chewing on the bosaur meat. "My new friend here gave me a ride."

"Your new ... wait, the Mahakar let you ride him?" Athelwulf asked.

"Yeah," Eshlyn said. "He's an amazing animal." She hesitated. "He understands me somehow. I asked him to bring me here, and he did."

He met her gaze. "Eshlyn. You rode the Mahakar ... and communicated with him?"

Eshlyn's smile slipped. "That's what I said. Ath, what's the matter?"

He was speechless. He didn't know how to tell her.

His father approached with the woman, who seemed familiar to him. Could it be? "Shecayah?" he asked. His sister?

She stopped a few paces away. "How do you know who I am?" she said.

Athelwulf looked at Eshlyn. "You didn't tell them," he said.

"Sorry. I just arrived an hour or so ago. Kiano was trying to explain some prophecy to me."

Kiano, Athelwulf's father, stood before him now. He had aged over the years, but he was still tall and confident. His hair and beard were gray, and he had grown thin. But Athelwulf could see the father he had cursed and abandoned. "And who is this?" his father asked.

Eshlyn stood aside. Athelwulf handed her the reins of Earon's horse.

"Father," he said. "It is I. Your son. Namir."

"Namir?" Shecayah said, searching his face.

"Yes, sister," Athelwulf said. "It is I."

The transformation on his father's face was like an arrow in the heart. His face twisted into a visage of rage and hate. He took a deep breath and shouted, *"Foredain! Foredain!"*

Men came barreling from beyond the crowd. They carried thick, flat blades that curved around their hands. Kiano grabbed his daughter, Athelwulf's sister, and pulled her back as the men surrounded him. Athelwulf raised his hands in surrender. Eshlyn's eyes went wide, and she dropped the reins of Earon's horse and darted to Athelwulf's side. Her sword was drawn in a split second, and she crouched between Athelwulf and his father.

"Stop," she cried. "Have you gone insane? This is your son."

The men stopped at her behest, but they remained in position, surrounding him and holding their weapons at ready.

The Mahakar rose from his meal, blood and flesh in his long sharp teeth, and he snarled at them. Eshlyn put up a hand to stay the beast. And to Athelwulf's amazement, the animal paused. "You too," she said. "Everyone calm down."

"Bashawyn," Kiano said to her. He called her by the name. "I have no son. This is *Foredain*." He spat the words.

She turned to Athelwulf. "What does that mean?"

"Traitor," Athelwulf answered. "Betrayer. It is one of their names for the Bana Sahat, the Lord of the Underland. It means the enemy, too. Traitors are the enemy of all men."

"All men?" Eshlyn asked him.

"Yes." How to explain? In his culture, any betrayal was the highest form of evil. It is what the Sahat brothers had done thousands and thousands of years ago, bringing the desolation upon Eres.

Eshlyn faced his father again. "What are you going to do to him?"

"What is always done to enemies. We will kill him," his father said. Athelwulf's heart sank.

.nen moved forward with their weapons at the ready.

ɔ," Eshlyn said, and the sword in her hand began to shake. "I'm
. I cannot allow this. This is my friend. He is a good man."

"By our law, he is not a good man," Kiano told her. "By our law, he
.ıust die."

"It is alright, Lady Eshlyn," Athelwulf said. "I knew this was the way."

"You too?" she said. "No martyrs today, okay? Break it all, we're going
to calm down and talk about this."

Athelwulf could see the conflict with his father. If he believed she was
the *Bashawyn* – and it seemed as if she was – then he would heed her. But
he did not like it. "It is law," he said. "He must die for his sin."

Eshlyn glanced at Athelwulf and back to his father. "Your son, Namir,
is dead. He died twenty years ago. Allow me to introduce you to Athelwulf.
He is a captain of the Ghosts of Saten, a believer in El. He has been to the
Living Stone and found worthy of an unforged sword. And he is my friend
and brother. No one is killing him today."

Shecayah touched her father on the arm. "The *Bashawyn* has spoken."

Kiano's sneer stayed fixed upon Athelwulf. "She has spoken."

The men around them lowered their weapons.

"I guess I have," Eshlyn said. "Now where can we talk?"

Kiano didn't answer. Shecayah turned to Eshlyn. "My father's house
has a large room. We can speak there."

"To the fine," Eshlyn said. "That is more like it. Why don't you meet us
there? I've got a couple things I need to do. We'll be right behind you."

Shecayah took her father's hand. "Come, Father. Let's go." He tore his
hate-filled eyes away from Athelwulf and walked away with Shecayah.

After she watched them leave, Eshlyn put her sword back in its
scabbard and whispered to Athelwulf. "What is going on? Why are they
acting like that towards me? They are obeying me."

"You are the *Bashawyn*. They will do what you say."

Eshlyn stifled a curse and pointed to two of the men around them with
weapons. "You two," she said and pointed at Earon. "See this man? Make
sure he doesn't go anywhere." She handed one the reins of Earon's horse.

"Yes, *Bashawyn*," he said.

She shook her head as they led Earon away. "That is odd," she said.

Athelwulf stared as she moved to the Mahakar. The animal lowered its
head, and she reached up and touched him. She whispered something to
him, inaudible to Athelwulf, and the Mahakar rose up on his hind legs,
extended his wings, and launched himself into flight.

She really did speak to the animal.

Athelwulf regarded his childhood home, and he realized everything
was going to change.

Eshlyn looked over at him. "I assume you know where your da's house
is," she said.

"I do," he said.

"Then lead the way," she said.

Athelwulf proceeded to the northeastern part of the city, the crowd and other citizens observing them both with gaping mouths or scowls or ignoring them altogether.

Eshlyn spoke to him as they walked. "What is this *Bashawyn*?"

"The Beorgai was not a tribe in the days when the elves took over Lior. They were the men and women that still believed in and worshipped El. They came from the other three tribes, the ones we met in Oshra. Since they were the last to hold onto faith in El, a few knew of the existence of this city. Da'ar. Here we were hidden and isolated."

"Did the elves never know they were here?"

"Perhaps," Athelwulf admitted. "But the Beorgai kept to themselves and did not bother Kryus' new order. So if they knew, the elves didn't bother with us."

"What does this have to do with the *Bashawyn*?"

"The priest-elder wanted people to be safe, but he uttered a prophecy one night. His oracle was that one day, when the *Brendel* appeared, El would show them a sign that it was time to enter the world again and abandon their isolation. That sign was this: a woman would come to them, riding the ancient and legendary creature, the Mahakar. She would come with a message. She would be the Herald Queen. The *Bashawyn*."

Eshlyn was quiet for a long time.

"I only ask that you be careful," Athelwulf said. "They will take what you say as a message from El. And because you are here, they believe that all they once knew is over."

"Very well," she said.

They reached his father's house. It wasn't much larger than the other homes, but it did have a spacious meeting room for when the elders needed to convene. The house and the grounds around it held thousands of memories for Athelwulf, and they all came rushing back to him at once, a bevy of emotions overwhelming him.

Athelwulf entered the meeting room. Eshlyn followed him. His father and Shecayah both stood at the far end of the room. Athelwulf trudged to the center of the room with an act of will, near the long wooden table. He could go no further.

Shecayah approached him with a grin, but her eyes betrayed her sadness. "My brother," she said.

He grinned back at her. Was the same sadness in his own expression? "You were but a child when I left all those years ago. And look, you have become a beautiful woman."

She chuckled, a light and easy sound, and touched the thick hair of his beard. "You hide a face under all this," she said. Tears escaped onto her cheek. "Oh, Namir."

ached up and took her hand. "Please. Call me Athelwulf. That is
.y name."

ls the name your mother gave you not good enough?" his father said
m mitres away.

Athelwulf didn't realize that all the old feelings, the old rebellion and anger, would be waiting for him in this moment. Biting back a retort, he denied himself the right to lash back at his father. He had cursed him enough.

"Where is my mother?" Athelwulf asked. "Is she here?"

His father crossed his arms and glared at him.

"She died five years ago," Shecayah said.

Athelwulf's stomach tightened. He remembered his mother, a beautiful woman, strong and intelligent, and an image came to him of her teaching him, telling him the stories of their tribe as they sat together under a great tree high in the mountains.

"How ... how did she die?" Athelwulf asked, and his voice faltered.

While his father remained silent, Shecayah took a step toward him. "An illness the doctors could not heal," she said. "An infection in her chest. Her heart gave out."

More pain filled his heart. His mother, gone, and he had not been here to hold her hand as she passed to the Everworld. He would never be able to ask her forgiveness, too, for leaving and causing so much agony.

"I am sorry," Athelwulf said. "I longed to see her, as well."

"Why?" his father said. "Why did you return at all?"

Athelwulf took a deep breath. "I am here to ask your forgiveness, Father." He stepped around his sister, and she turned to stand next to him.

His father snorted with scorn. "Death is what you deserve."

"That is true," Athelwulf said. "I have no reason or excuse. I have shamed you. I cursed you with ancient words that I knew were forbidden. I ran from my responsibilities and duties as your son. I became a thief and worse on the streets of Oshra, a slave addicted to my own lusts. I deserve death and more.

"But I have changed. Due to the love and grace given by the people of the Saten, I am alive and know the love of El. And just as El is merciful and good, I throw myself on your mercy and ask for your forgiveness as El forgives. When we repent to him, does he not forgive? I only ask the same of you."

Athelwulf's father continued to glower at him, and the muscles in his face tightened. "You spoke the *eldaman*," he said.

The *eldaman* was an ancient curse, and the elders said that the Bana Sahat wrote it unto El before the First Men. Translated, it declared a deep desire that the one that bore him would die an eternal death, and all bonds between the father and son were severed.

"Yes. I did. I did it out of anger. I said it because I knew it would hurt you. It was an evil thing."

"You think I can forgive such a thing?"

"I do not know, but I ask it." Athelwulf took a step towards his father. "I wish I could take it back, but I cannot. All I have is my regret. But I love you and want to make it right, if I can. Is there no way to make it right?"

"The law gives a way," his father said. "Your death, but the *Bashawyn* forbids it."

"Is there no other way?" Eshlyn asked.

"Not while we both live," Kiano said.

Athelwulf lowered his head, and a tear fell from his eye. He was a child again in his father's house, desperate for his father's love. But another part of him was grieved at the hardness of his father's heart.

Pulling the unforged sword from his back, he laid it upon the table. It glimmered and shone in the sunlight from the windows. "I have been to Elarus," Athelwulf said. "And I have laid my bare hands upon the Living Stone. I know I have been a shame to you. But I have changed. El found me worthy enough to make me a *Sohan-el*, a warrior leader of El. Me. Can't you?"

His father stared at the sword for a long time, and then he turned away.

Athelwulf's heart broke. Not truly for his own forgiveness; El had forgiven him and changed him long ago. But he mourned the slavery of his father's own heart.

"I am sorry for that," Athelwulf said. He picked up his sword and sheathed it on his back.

"Shecayah will show you to the guest house," his father said. "And out of respect to the *Bashawyn*, I will not require your death today. Some things will change. But you will not set foot in your mother's house again."

Athelwulf bowed to his father. "I will obey."

Shecayah led them from the house and took them down a road to a small house. Before she left, she embraced him. "He did not say I could not come and see you," she said in his ear.

He smiled at her. "I am glad. It will be good to get to know my sister as a woman."

She kissed his cheek and left.

Eshlyn stood with him outside of the house, and as Athelwulf faced her, he could see her anger and bitterness.

"Do not judge him," Athelwulf said.

"But he's your father," she said. "I could never say those things to my son."

"I hope that is true. But you must understand. He is responsible for the safety and rule of this community. He loves these people. They are all his family. He feels he must be hard and strict to keep them safe."

"Are you telling me that his unforgiveness is love?"

"No," Athelwulf said, his voice low. He remembered how his father had raised him, the deep-seeded beliefs of his tribe, his community. Athelwulf once believed them, as well, but Mother Natali had taught him a different way. "But he believes it is love."

He watched as Eshlyn considered his words. "Even so," she said. "You said that prophecy means that everything is about to change."

"Yes."

She met his eyes, and he swore he could see a fire within them.

"Tomorrow, they will see what this change really means. The *Bashawyn* has a message for them."

Chapter 20

The Pirate Lord

A tall mirror stood in the corner of the room, and she stood before it now.

The bruises on her cheeks were gone and the cut along her neck, as well. But while the physical injuries were gone, the memories remained, and staring at herself in the mirror, she began to cry again. Why couldn't she let it go? Nothing had happened, but she couldn't shake the feeling of guilt and shame and helplessness. Uncle Reyan and Athelwulf had not taught her to be a victim, not at all. So why did she feel so powerless? She wiped the tears from her face and undressed, then took the dirty and worn trousers, boots, and tunic and laid them on the bed.

She began to wash with the cloth and the water in the basin. It would feel good to be clean. Even after scrubbing her whole body down, however, something didn't feel clean. So she washed again. And again. Parts of her body were red from the scrubbing, but she couldn't feel clean for some reason.

Isn't she a pretty thing?

The knock came at the door. Answering it, a woman gave her a dress and told her dinner would be in a half hour. Carys looked from the dress to the woman like she was insane, but the woman bowed and left without another word.

Carys laid the dress on the bed of her room, a long bright orange and red dress that would hang loose upon her body. She stared at it for several minutes.

Courage, she told herself. *There is work to do.*

Tying her hair back with a green ribbon, she pulled the dress over her body. She went barefoot down the hall to dinner.

Cut from the white stone, the dining room was long and narrow with a wooden table through the center. Aeric sat at the end and stood when she entered. Zalman and Chronch sat to his left.

The Pirate Lord lifted a clay mug to her. A bottle of wine sat near him. "Carys, thank you for wearing the dress I sent. You are as beautiful as the sunset on the ocean, if not more."

She ignored the image in her mind of a man with a long dagger. Or tried to.

Aeric gestured to the seat to his right. "Please, come join us."

Zalman gave Aeric a frown.

The room smelled of cooked fish, and her stomach rumbled at the odor. Fruits were piled on platters in the middle of the table, and candles gave the room a soft light.

As she padded over to her seat, she noticed both Zalman and Chronch making an effort not to look at her. Aeric pulled the chair out for her while she sat.

"Thank you," she said.

"Of course," Aeric said, and he sat back at the head of the table.

A woman, the same one that brought her dress, brought out plates filled with fish and greens, like seaweed but prepared with sharp spices. Aeric lifted the wine bottle and eyed the mug before her. "May I?"

"Yes, please," she said.

She didn't think it was possible, but Zalman's frown deepened as he took a sip of his own wine.

"Eat, I beg of you," Aeric said. "And tell me of all that happened in Ketan."

As they ate, Carys relayed the events over the past few months: her finding her brother again, the death of the Prophet, their preparation in Ketan and the battle there against the demics. She explained how the elves left and Ketan was now free of their control. She concluded by describing their attempt at meeting with the Dygol in Landen, their capture, escape, and decision to come to see the pirates.

She left out the attempted rape, and she felt the tension in Zalman and Chronch.

"Fascinating," Aeric said. "And you came here. What can I do for you?"

"We need as much help as we can get," Carys said. "Especially from those who have been free from the elves for so long."

Aeric sipped his wine.

"My brother, Caleb, has built an army, but he is already outnumbered in Ereland. And Kryus will be sending more legions and resources to Ereland to crush any revolution. You have ships and experience fighting the elves. You could raid the convoys from Kryus and stop them from ever reaching the land of men."

Leaning back, Aeric finished his wine and set the mug on the table. "Interesting. And what would we gain from this?"

Her stomach tightened, and she grimaced. What was it with men and their need for profit? But she probably wouldn't get anywhere by insulting him. After dealing with the Dygol, she had prepared for this with the Pirates. "You would get to keep the resources you take on your raids. Ships, weapons, whatever. You could use those things or sell them to other elven or dwarven nations."

Aeric grinned at her. "You are even more clever than you are beautiful. That is rare in this world." He sat up. "Before I answer, I must ask. What do you know of our lands?"

"Very little," she said. "They are called the Pirate Lands where we come from, and I know there was once a war between you and the elves that ended in an armistice, I believe. The War of Accession."

"Yes, the War of Accession. Do you know why it was called that?"

"I don't," Carys said.

Aeric poured his mug full again and offered wine to the rest of the table. All but Chronch refused.

"Before I answer you, indulge me, if you will," Aeric said.

"Of course," Carys said.

"We were not pirates hundreds of years ago. We were the Kanan Eres, a loose confederation of city-states here in this group of islands. We traded with the lands of men, elves, and dwarves. Each city-state had its own lord, or king, depending upon the city. When Kryus conquered the lands of men, they sought to dominate the trade along the Theron Ocean and the Sea of Alin. Naturally, we of the Kanan Eres were obstacles in that path.

"So the most powerful navy in Eres brought their ships to war against us. Our only salvation was that the Empire was spread thin keeping the continent of men under control. Otherwise, we would have been destroyed. We nearly were anyway. They called it the War of Accession because they allowed us to remain apart from their control. But they still control the trade with Landen, Oshra, Asya, Galya, and even the major ports across the ocean. We have limited access to the other elven nations. They do not wish to awaken the ire of Tanicus and his legions.

"So what did we have left? Ships built for war and no one to trade with. So we steal to live, to survive. We steal from elven, human, and dwarven nations along the trade routes from Eviland to Ereland. And this is who we have become, the pirates you see before you.

"We were once a proud and thriving culture, a diverse region that traded with the whole of Eres. Our warriors had honor and our leaders strength.

"We are criminals now, not warriors. We are the monsters of the seas, evil spirits that hunt the waters and strike fear into hearts."

Lord Aeric took a sip of his wine and bared his teeth.

"We are who we need to be," he said. "So we do not starve. So our children will survive another day. A greater cause than that is beyond what we are able to do."

"You won't help us?" Carys asked.

"I am sorry," Aeric said. "I do not believe we can."

Carys took a deep breath. She caught the Pirate Lord's eyes.

"I disagree," she said. "You can. And you must."

Aeric lifted a brow at her.

"Where did 'the ways' come from?" she asked.

"An old tradition," Aeric mumbled. "Very old."

"But a tradition of honor," she said. "You say you are monsters and yet you hold onto an old system of honor and hospitality. That does not sound like a monster to me."

"Even monsters must have rules, Carys. We are no different."

"No," she said, thinking of the men in Landen, dismissing another image of Kyson pressing down upon her in the dark. "Believe me. Some monsters don't have rules or honor. You spoke of the people you once were. Men and women of honor and strength, warriors and merchants, traders open to the diversity of the world."

Aeric's eyes narrowed.

"With El," she said. "Nothing is so lost that you cannot find it again. You asked what you could gain if you joined our revolution? Here is my answer: you could become the people of honor you once were. You will not have to steal and kill to eat. You will trade again with the great nations and cities of Eres, freely. What is that worth to you?"

The Pirate Lord was quiet for a long time.

"It is an inspiring thought," he said. "But I do not believe we can be those people again. The past cannot be reclaimed, no matter how much you desire it. What nations would trade with us, now that we are known as thieves? Besides, we would not survive another war. Some seek to expand our activity, which would naturally bring us into more conflict with the Empire, but we barely survived the last war with Kryus when we were strong.

"We are weak, and what little unity we have is tenuous. Even now, my leadership is being challenged by another lord."

Carys paused and laid a finger across her chin. "What does this challenge consist of?" she asked.

"The ways are clear," Aeric said. "A duel on the high seas."

Shoggers, Carys thought and shared a glance with Zalman and Chronch.

"I tell you what I can do," Aeric said.

"What is that?" Carys asked.

"Sail with me," Aeric said. "Come with me to the challenge. It should be quite the show." He smirked at Carys and took a drink of his wine. "At the very least, I would have the company of a clever and beautiful woman for a few more days."

Carys watched Zalman glare at the Pirate Lord.

After what happened in Landen, she was prepared to see this as a victory. No one had died, and they were not in a dungeon – yet. This man seemed more reasonable, however much a flatterer, which she could never trust. He could be a friend, in any event, if he stayed alive long enough.

And if other lords did desire to expand activity and engage Kryus more, she would want to meet them.

She met Zalman's eyes and questioned with her own. He shrugged.

"We will sail with you," Carys said.

"What about my boat?" Chronch said.

"You can stay here, as my guest, and I will bring Carys and Zalman back once the challenge is met," Aeric said. "Or have them brought back if I cannot do it myself."

"Good for me," Chronch agreed.

"Oi," Aeric said. "We leave in the morning."

—

Earon awoke famished.

The pains in his stomach were different. Hunger spoke to him through rumblings in his abdomen. He sat up from the mat on the floor. For the first time in a long time, his hair was brushed, his beard combed through and clean. His hands were unbound and free. His mind was clear.

Traitor. Murderer.

He was in a small room of a house made with stones and mud. The large open windows allowed the mountain breeze to cool the room. He stood and ventured into the next room.

Athelwulf sat at a small table by a wood stove. He chewed on a hunk of bread and fruits were set before him.

"Come," Athelwulf said without glancing up. "Eat." He gestured to a plate across from him of bread and fruit.

Earon stepped to the chair and sat. "Why am I not tied up anymore?"

"You were a slave to the addiction and your own lust," Athelwulf said. "Now you are free. Of the addiction, at least."

"The withdrawals might be gone, but I still want Sorcos. Even though I know it is poison. I don't feel free of it."

Athelwulf took a bite of bread. "Just because you do not feel free doesn't mean that you are not. It will get better over time."

"Will it?"

"Yes."

Earon peered down at the plate and the food. He hadn't eaten in days. He saw Caleb in his mind, even worse now that his thoughts were clear, and he heard his father's voice.

Earon, what have you done ...

"I killed my father," he said, and he choked back a sob.

"I know."

Athelwulf's voice was calm. No judgment. An agreement of the facts.

Athelwulf continued to eat.

"Did you hear me?" Earon asked. "I said I killed my father."

"I heard you."

"I betrayed him. I was so angry. But stupid. Anger makes you stupid."

Athelwulf lifted a wooden cup and took a drink of water.

Earon continued. "I remember when my father first believed he was the *Arendel*, the fulfillment of an ancient prophecy. At first, he would humbly deflect it, but one day he accepted the title. I saw how it fueled him. It became an obsession. Because if he was the *Arendel*, then the *Brendel* was not far behind. I never really believed it, not in all of it, not like he did. I believed the scriptures, just not war, revolution, violence. I didn't think the elves were the embodiment of evil. I thought there had to be another way than war. So we argued. Or we just didn't talk at all."

Athelwulf nodded, listening.

"But while everyone had the Prophet, I never had a father. Caleb, Carys, my mother, they were my world, all I knew. Then Caleb disappeared, and Carys and I clung to each other. How could we do any different? I could tell her anything. And we were united against my father. Now she hates me."

Her voice in his head and the disappointment in her visage, the despair, *Oh, Earon ...*

"Perhaps," Athelwulf said.

Earon wiped his nose with his forearm. "My mother was amazing. She tried to help, you know. When she was captured and killed, what was left of my world fell apart. My father ... he didn't even *try* to save her, to help her – I couldn't forgive him.

"Even Carys couldn't console me. Ironic that the Prophet, known for his eloquence, said nothing. I didn't even try to talk to him. I just left.

"So I made my way alone with nothing but the clothes on my back. I made my way to Galya. I was addicted to Sorcos within the year."

Taking a bite from a red and green fruit, Athelwulf put his elbows on the table.

"And when a Bladeguard found me and took me captive, I thought I was dead. He held me for a few days, but then he explained all the misunderstandings and the truth of what happened to my mother. 'We are not your enemy,' Zarek told me. 'The Empire is not your enemy.' He promised that if I helped him find my father, no harm would come to him.

"He swore. Gave his word. And then he offered me money and Sorcos." He caught Athelwulf's gaze and felt a tear fall from his eye. "So I did. I helped him. I betrayed my own father. And now he's dead. I killed him. I killed my father."

Take me. I'll surrender now if you let the others go. Zarek's blade plunged into his father's chest.

"I understand," Athelwulf said.

"Esai was right, back in Oshra," Earon said. "I deserve to die. Don't I? Don't I deserve to die?"

"Do I deserve to die?" Athelwulf asked.

"What?"

"I am *foredain*, like you. I cursed my father," he said. "Betrayed him in my own way. The law says I must die. Do I deserve it?"

Earon remembered the scene from yesterday, however dull his mind had been - Athelwulf's father demanding his death, Eshlyn and that frightening beast stepping in to stop them.

"I don't know," Earon said.

"I do," Athelwulf said. "I deserve to die. And in a way, I have. Would it be justice for me to die? Yes. But do you know what is a greater justice?"

Earon shook his head.

"Redemption. I saw my own evil and changed, and El gave me his strength to change. And I experienced his mercy and forgiveness. Do you know why I rebelled against my father?"

Athelwulf waited for an answer, so Earon gave him one. "No."

"I was young and did not want the responsibility of leading this community, of keeping it safe. It bore down upon me like a weight I thought I could never lift."

Earon swallowed hard. "I understand," he said.

"But after I changed and overcame my addiction, I became the captain of the Ghosts of Saten. I led them, kept them safe. And now I am a *Sohan-el*, a warrior-leader of El. I became the very thing I thought I could never be."

Athelwulf stood and wiped his hands on a cloth. "That is the justice of El, Earon. Do you deserve to die? Yes. But if you repent and become the man you were created to be, that will satisfy the justice of El more than your death ever could."

Earon lowered his eyes.

"Now eat," Athelwulf said. "Eshlyn is meeting with the elders this morning, and I must be there."

"You're leaving me alone?"

Athelwulf stopped at the door and smirked at him. "You believe you've ever been alone?"

And then he left.

Earon hesitated for a moment, staring at the food. Then he tore into it, groaning in pleasure as he ate.

Eshlyn stood in the center of town, at the field where she landed with the Mahakar the day before. She sent the animal away yesterday, but she knew within her that he would return if she called.

She wanted the meeting in the center of the city so that the citizens could attend. They would need to hear this as well.

The elders were all in attendance, Kiano in the middle of them, frowning at her. Shecayah stood with the elders and her husband, Tobiah. At last, she saw Athelwulf reach the field. He came to stand next to her. He wore his green tunic, leather breeches and moccasins. The sword was in its scabbard on his back.

"Good morning," he said to her.

"Morn," she said. "How is Earon?"

"Better," Athelwulf said. "His greatest battle is before him, but he is ready for it now."

"To the fine," Eshlyn said. "Are you ready?"

"Does it matter?"

She turned to Kiano. "Time to begin," she said.

Kiano stepped forward. He raised his hand and the crowd fell silent. "The *Bashawyn* has come to us," he announced. "Many of you saw her with the Mahakar yesterday. And as the prophecy says, she has come with a message." He lowered his hand and moved aside.

"Thank you," Eshlyn said. She scanned the crowd, faces filled with fear. She remembered Athelwulf's caution, but she also knew the conviction in her heart.

"I have two things to tell you," Eshlyn said. "You have enjoyed generations of peace here, and I can understand how that has been a comfort for you and your families, your children. But revolution has come to the land of men. It is time for you to join the world again, to fight for the freedom and peace of others, to bring them the peace you've enjoyed here for so long.

"Yesterday, I rode the great Mahakar. He took me over the trees and the mountains. It was a joyous time. But he also wanted me to see the suffering of your brothers and sisters in the mines. It is time for us to go and free the slaves in the mines."

Shecayah covered her mouth with her hand, and her husband put his arm around her shoulders. Many shook their heads in disbelief. Murmurs weaved through the people. Kiano did not react.

"But there is a second thing I must tell you," Eshlyn said, projecting her voice. "This is something you must choose. Do not join the revolution because I told you to do it. Do not leave your homes and put your lives at risk because of a prophecy. That would be wrong. No one made me leave my home and family, my son, to come to Lior and spread the hope of El. I chose it because I believe that men should be free. All men.

"So must you. Do you believe that men should be free? Not just the few here in this great city, but all men? Your brothers and sisters are in chains kilomitres away from here in the mountains. Will you take up arms to free them with me? Not because I rode that beautiful animal, but because you believe it is the right thing to do?"

The crowd was silent. Kiano took a step closer to her. "Will you go alone?"

"If I must," she answered.

"Not alone," Shecayah's husband, Tobiah, said. He kissed his wife and stepped forward. "I will go."

Eshlyn watched as another forty men volunteered.

Kiano growled. "You will lead them all to their deaths," he declared.

Eshlyn neared him. "*I will defend the innocent, free the oppressed, and spread light in dark places.*"

The elder flinched. "What is that?"

"The vow of the *Sohan-el*," she said. "They have returned. And I saw those mines, Kiano. That is one of the darkest places I have ever seen. They are like wounds on the soul of Eres. That is where we will go."

Athelwulf cleared his throat. "Father," he said. "I ask your permission to go, as well."

"My permission?" Kiano asked. "It is up to the *Bashawyn*."

"No," Athelwulf said. "I have wronged you, and I will stay and submit to your judgment, if that is your decision. But I wish to go with Lady Eshlyn and fight to free these slaves."

"Wait a minute," Eshlyn said, meeting Athelwulf's eyes. "You can't be serious. You can't actually mean you will submit to …" She couldn't finish the thought.

"I do," Athelwulf answered. "And I must. It is not right to deny justice, to acquit those that have done wrong. I have done wrong and must face my accuser and whatever consequences he deems necessary."

"Ath," she pleaded.

"Trust me in this," Athelwulf said to her. "Please." He then bowed to his father. "Father, what is your wish?"

Kiano was quiet a long time, glaring down at his son. "*Bashawyn*," he said at last. "Is Namir a great warrior?"

"Namir is no more," Eshlyn said. "Namir is dead. Athelwulf is one of the greatest men and warriors I have ever seen."

Kiano's gaze hardened at his son. "Then this Athelwulf, as you call him, will go with you. He will protect the *Bashawyn* and the men of the Beorgai. Then he will face my judgment when he returns."

"Thank you," Athelwulf said as he straightened.

"When do you leave?" Kiano asked Eshlyn.

"Tomorrow," Eshlyn said. "First light."

———

Caleb rode his horse at the front of the column of the *Hamon-el*, the divisions spread out behind him. Biram was close, maybe two hours away at the present pace.

The scouts returned from time to time and reported that no elves were waiting to ambush them along the road. Caleb was not surprised. The legion would prefer to use the buildings and streets of the city to entrench themselves and watch his army break against them like torrential rain upon walls of brick.

Iletus rode next to him. The sun was high in the east, almost midday. Somehow Iletus made the breastplate appear fashionable, and that annoyed him.

Two scouts came running up the road from Biram. Caleb could see the fear on their faces. Caleb held up a hand and the column halted. The scouts, dressed in the tunics and leather breeches of the Ghosts of Saten and carrying a gladus and a short bow, stopped in front of Caleb and Iletus. They were out of breath and leaned over, their chests heaving.

"What is it?" Caleb asked them. "Were there scouts?"

"They dead now," one of them said.

Caleb waited.

They shared a glance. "Biram. It's …" the other began but didn't finish.

"It's what?" Caleb encouraged.

"You have to come see, Caleb," the other said. "I can't … you have to come see."

Caleb shouted behind him. "Bring me Aden."

The call for the young man passed down the column, and within minutes, Aden trotted up on his horse. "What's goin' on?"

"Come with us," Caleb said, and he spurred his horse on to a dead run, Aden and Iletus behind him.

Riding at a sprint along the road, they closed the distance to Biram in a half hour. As he passed around a bend in the road, he could see Biram three hundred mitres away. *Break me*, he thought, and walked his horse closer, to within two hundred mitres.

He pulled up his horse, and the stallion reared before settling.

"Great and mighty El," Caleb said. He heard Aden curse next to him.

The city of Biram was ringed with long, sharpened poles at regular intervals. The citizens of Biram, men and women and children, were impaled naked upon the poles. Several were flayed, their skin removed from their bodies. There were hundreds of them, maybe a thousand, each face contorted in a mask of terror and agony. Dried blood and gore covered the poles. Vultures and ravens picked at the bodies, the flesh. They had removed some meat to the bone. Swarms of flies danced among the remains.

He could smell the stench of crit and death from where he stood. Other men and women were nailed to the buildings that faced the west. They had been dead for days.

He heard Iletus sigh, but he couldn't take his eyes off of the horror before him.

"They're all dead," Aden said. "They killed everyone."

Caleb's shock turned to sadness and rage. He gripped the Kingstaff across his lap.

"This was their strategy. They want you to fight them angry," Iletus said.

He took a deep breath, and the fury within him cooled. He became cold as ice, and his heart was hard as steel. The *Brendel*. The blade of El.

"No," Caleb said, and a part of him wondered at the ice in his voice. "They don't."

Chapter 21

The Battle of Biram

The main road into Biram stretched out before Xander's division as they approached from the east.

Corpses on poles rose to meet them. As they planned their attack earlier, Caleb explained that the elves were attempting to cause fear and anger. *Don't be overcome by emotion,* Caleb said. *Clear your mind and lead others to do the same. There will be time to grieve later. Today we act.*

Xander wanted to follow those directions; he knew Caleb spoke true, but it was difficult with the bodies of mangled and tortured children staring down at him.

He had 250 men with him, also divided into five platoons, each of those into five squads, each with good men to lead them. They were all good men – a mixture of Ghosts from Saten and the people of Manahem, many of whom fought in the Battle of Ketan against the demics.

Peering to the west, a division of the Kryan legion was in position, blocking the main road with shields and spears, several militan deep. He could count four hundred militan. For all practical purposes, it was a wall in their way, but Xander held an unforged sword in his hand.

Caleb had sent twelve of his fifteen divisions into the city at various points. The elves couldn't defend every entry in force, and the overall strategy was to get the army into the city and fight from within. The Kryan forces could defend a position well, but it took time for them to move and adjust. Once Caleb's army was in the city, they could flank platoons and divisions or attack from the rear. Caleb held back the last three divisions with Iletus as reinforcements if one of the divisions needed it.

The major entry points would be key to the legion, so they would concentrate their militan there; someone needed to attack those positions to keep their attention outward and give others opportunity to enter and maneuver easily. The road into Biram from the east was such a point. Xander volunteered his division to take it.

He wore a brown leather tunic, breeches, and boots with a steel breastplate. At the end of the stump of his right arm, Bweth Ironhorn had fashioned a small round shield that attached to the arm and shoulder with straps. Xander held the unforged sword in his left hand.

Viewing the early afternoon sun, it was almost time to attack. He turned behind him and waved his lieutenants into position. The division was spread out along the edges of the road in the trees and brush a hundred and fifty mitres from the legion. The elves knew they were there, but he didn't want to give them a clear target. His fifty best archers with longbows were waiting at the rear. Once inside the city, the longbows wouldn't be much use, so they were to cover the attack then join once the rest of the division was engaged.

It was time. Other divisions would be making their attacks now at more vulnerable points, so they needed to keep this division busy.

The Kryan legion was like a wall. So they fashioned a battering ram. Cutting down a tree – the unforged swords were better than the sharpest axe – Xander had the men lay it on a wagon, one of the few the army had with them towards the back of the column. Taking the wagon through the brush, grass, and trees around Biram had taken them the better part of two hours. The two horses were unhitched, and with the archers to the rear, the makeshift ram now sat at the edge of the road.

He nodded to the first squad, and they began to push the wagon towards the elves. Xander jogged beside the wagon, the wheels squeaking next to him, and within a minute the ram was at running speed.

Xander raised the round shield. The bowmen behind him set their arrows, pulled and held. He lowered his shield; they fired the first volley.

The lieutenants didn't need any further instruction. They knew they would follow him as he attacked. The battering ram would be the tip of the charge that would break through the center of that line. Xander took a deep breath as the arrows arced down the road and fell among the elves.

Two hundred men with long spears followed the wagon in a "V" formation. The elves ahead of them lifted their shields to catch the arrows. Volleys continued to fall among them. There was no need for accuracy. The strategy was to keep the elven heads down while Xander charged. One hundred mitres away now.

A militan fell – an arrow made it through. Long arrows were raining down upon them, and he could hear the curses of the elves now. He sneered as he glanced up at the dead human bodies impaled above him.

Seventy-five mitres away.

A few militan towards the rear stood to fire their shortbows at his division. Several militan went down as another human volley fell among the elves, but a few elven arrows flew in his direction, one at his feet, others into the log next to him. He heard a cry and heard the tumble behind him, but he didn't slow. Xander's archers adjusted their aim and most of the militan archers flailed as arrows punctured their body. The longbows possessed better range.

Twenty-five mitres.

The spears behind him leveled, and Xander shouted; the humans put forth another burst of speed into the ram. Xander could hear the breathing of the men and the clattering of weapons around him, smelled the sweat and dust around him. He bared his teeth as the arrows from his division kept falling.

Five mitres away, Xander brought his sword over his head. He could see the elven line dig in, the elves behind them lean forward to support the front. The log crashed into the line with a thunderous sound, and bodies, shields, and spears went flying backwards and to the side. Other elves were crushed underneath the wheels of the wagon. The log and wagon barely slowed; a gap formed in the line.

As Xander neared the line, he brought his sword down and hacked a spear in two, and bringing the sword back around, he sliced at the shield. The unforged sword cut through the shield and the arm behind it. He heard the elf yell in pain as blood spouted in the air, but he continued to cut into the elves on the front of the line, his round shield batting away several spear blades.

The men behind him crashed into the line a second after him, their spears spreading out and finding seams to stab elves behind them or snapping against elven shields. Several of his men were killed; in his periphery he saw brothers and friends impaled on spears, hacked with swords, screaming as they died. He knew their names but would not stop to grieve them now. Xander heard shouting and screaming, steel against steel, the hacking of flesh as men and elves sought to kill one another. He focused on the snarling faces of the elves before him, and he cut through more shields, killing a militan and further opening a hole in the front line.

More of his men pressed into the center of the line, more of them dying, human blood spraying as they fell to gladi and spears. Other men made their way through, grabbing shields so the men behind them could strike at the elves. Xander felt a strike scrape across his breastplate, and he ducked the following swing and stabbed the elf in the neck. He twisted to block another spear with his round shield and cut the elf's arm from the shoulder.

Xander could see the back of the line, elves dead or wounded with arrows in their flesh. As he watched, another human division attacked from the rear, Pynt's division. He heard Pynt, the *Sohan-el* and former Ghost of Saten, shouting orders. They blitzed the rear of the Kryan division with a fury, spears and swords cutting elves down from behind.

The elves descended into confusion and chaos. They scattered, unsure of where to focus their defense ... or attack. Xander saw the elven division Captain stabbed through the stomach with a spear, his mouth open but making no sound.

Xander kept swinging and blocking. Now that he had more room to move, he twisted and dodged, and the unforged sword seemed to guide him as he swung again and again, taking limbs and cutting through elves. He was calm. He fell into the forms that Caleb had taught him, but more sure of himself than he had ever been in training.

Another ten minutes passed, and then it was over. It was done. Only men remained standing. Blinking, Xander turned and did a quick count. His men were among Pynt's now, but he counted 140 of his own remaining. More than a hundred were dead or injured in his own division. Crushed and trampled, covered in blood.

Pynt approached him, holding a gash on his left arm. "I lost fifty before we got to you," he said.

"Let's check on the wounded and get them somewhere safe," Xander said, and then he frowned at Pynt. Caleb and Iletus had claimed the elven command structure would be at the administration building of Biram. "Then we should press on to the center of the city."

—✝—

Aden turned to Tamya. "You ready?"

They sat fifty mitres from the city, within the trees, their division arrayed behind them. "Of course I'm ready," she said and studied him. She knew he wasn't completely healed from his injuries with the Wraith. "Are you?"

He glanced down at the bloodwolf at her feet. "I'm as ready as he is," Aden said.

Tamya was surprised at the speed of Aden's healing. Hema's injuries were on the mend, but she could tell the wounds from the window pained him a bit. They had been deep cuts. Aden didn't appear to have any ill effects.

"No way I was leaving him at home," she said. "Not for this." Hema spent every waking moment with her. Who could she leave him with even if she wanted to? Didn't matter, though. They were inseparable. And there were elves to kill.

Aden glimpsed up at the sun. "It's time," he said.

Tamya gave her platoon the signal. Up ahead, Kryan militan blocked the narrow road between two larger homes; she could count two hundred of them with spears and shields. The impaled and flayed dead beckoned the humans to come and avenge them. Tamya would oblige them.

Her platoon only took their swords with them, leaving their spears and bows behind with others. She held onto Hema with a rope she had tied around his neck like a leash or collar. The bloodwolf pulled against it with a deep growl, and only his loyalty to her and the leash kept him from sprinting forward and attacking the militan all by himself.

Not for the first time, Tamya wondered at the bloodwolf. For a wild, feral beast, how did he distinguish between friend and foe? He seemed to possess an inherent understanding of whom she wanted to hurt or kill, whom she saw as a threat. Animals possessed ways of sensing things that

248

went beyond her, she knew, and perhaps it was her imagination, but Hema seemed an extension of her own self.

Given those things, it annoyed her that the wolf took to Aden the way he did.

Next to her, Aden raised his hand. The archers pulled back their bows and fired as he gave the signal. The first volley caused the elves to hide behind their shields.

She moved, running downhill to the house on the left, Hema beside her and the platoon behind her. Tamya had both swords out. Three more volleys came from Aden's position, and the elves were pinned down. She passed through the poles that displayed the tortured corpses of men, women, children. The image of her baby's head being dashed against a stone filled her mind, and she screamed within a few paces of the house. Hema roared.

Sprinting, she hit the back door of the house with the right side of her body; the wood splintered and the door fell in off of its hinges. Landing on her feet, she stood with her swords out in a crouch and ready to defend. Hema's hackles rose as she looked around, the house in shadows. No elves here to fight, so she hurried to the next room to the front of the house. Two militan struggled to their feet, leaders of some sort with breastplates and helmets that gleamed even in the dim light of the house.

She released the bloodwolf.

The elf on the right didn't get his shield or sword up in time. Hema leapt upon him and tore his throat out in a snarl.

Tamya parried the gladus of the second elf, and three of the men in her platoon cut him down while she took his hand off at the wrist.

Without a word, she bolted out of the house and into the street. Aden would be attacking the front line soon, and she needed to be at the rear of the enemy position in time. She raced to her right and an elf on a horse turned to face her, a captain with a bright blue plume on his helmet, but she kept running. The horse danced away from her and the bloodwolf, but she closed the distance in the narrow street.

Tamya leapt and struck with both swords at the captain, and he blocked them with his long sword. But the pause gave Hema time, and the bloodwolf sprang at the captain and knocked him from his horse, tearing into him. Tamya's platoon ran by her to the rear of the elven line. They rounded the corner with a shout, and she ran among them after ensuring that Hema had killed the elf. The bloodwolf had done his work. The elf was missing most of his face.

She and her platoon hit the rear of the line moments before Aden and the rest of the division reached the front. The growl of a bloodwolf would cause anyone to flee in terror, much less the sight of one. When the elves spun to see the bloodwolf and fifty armed men coming at them from the rear, some panicked, but most struggled to form a defense. Screams of men and elves pierced the dry air. Dust rose from shuffling and running boots, she saw three men die in a heartbeat, three of her men.

Tamya sliced through the back and side of one elf, and as he cried and fell, she stabbed another through the groin. She saw Hema tear the sword arm off of an elf. As the battle raged around her, she could see – in her mind – a burning stake with her husband writhing and dying upon it. She heard another growl and didn't know if it was her own or the bloodwolf's. Perhaps both.

It was all shouts and screams and blood and death for long minutes. Finally, she stood over a militan and hacked with her swords at his silver breastplate until he was motionless. She felt a hand on her wrist, and she spun to see Aden's sharp nose and big ears filling her vision.

"It's done," Aden said.

Tamya stood straight and scanned around her. Every elf was dead, the narrow street littered with their bodies. Several humans were among the dead Kryan militan, men and elves in bloody embraces.

"Come on," Aden said. "We have to go support Bweth."

The bloodwolf sat back on his haunches and howled.

———+———

The view of Kryan militan seventy mitres away brought back old memories, battles Bweth fought centuries ago. She thought she had left that life behind her. She should have known better. Whether elf or man or dwarf, it was all the same. There would be wars and conflict. And while she had been hidden away in Ketan in the most remote city of the Empire, war and revolution found her there, too. It literally knocked on her shoggin' door.

Bweth gritted her teeth and touched her belly and the life within, feeling the little one kick. This war was different. Caleb was different. For once in her life, she felt as if she fought for something she believed in. Her mind was filled with memories of other wars and battles, killing to further the Empire, for Tanicus, secrets she only wanted to forget.

Caleb was a man she could follow. Bweth stood with him on that wall and fought demics with him. It made her feel proud to be a part of something good and right. Caleb would rather her stay safe with the baby in her stomach, but he didn't understand. To be shown a different way, to know that she battled for freedom instead of power over others, it compelled her to fight.

Hunter laid his hand over hers. Bweth turned and smiled at him. As much as a cause or a great leader like Caleb, she fought for her husband and her child. She had almost lost the man on the wall in the Battle of Ketan, and that moment had finally convinced her of her unlikely love for him. She never thought she would deserve to feel such love. Every moment with him now was a moment of purity that she treasured.

A clear howl carried through the air. A bloodwolf. Hema.

"Shoggit," she said. "They're early."

As she looked into Hunter's eye, he knew her well enough to not ask her to stay back and be safe. They were both outcasts from other families – his from Lior and hers from two Empires, one elven and the other dwarven – but had found a home, a family, with this revolution. That was why she loved him. He knew what not to say. It maddened her sometimes, but the man was in her thoughts more than should be possible.

"Then let's go," Hunter said.

Bweth lifted the spiked mace in her hand and lowered it. The archers behind her knew the signal. They fired. She nodded over to Hunter's platoon, standing behind a wagon with a large log tied to it with a host of ropes. A squad from his platoon began to push the wagon.

Another heartbeat later, fifty arrows caused the militan to duck and cover behind their Kryan shields.

The city was downhill of their position. They crouched in the trees and brush. The elves had seen them, and their reaction was to hunker down and wait for their attack.

Bweth had to peer past the hanging corpses to examine the militan. It appeared to be a whole division with their captain at the rear on a white horse.

Hunter's squad didn't need much effort to get the wagon rolling towards the four hundred elves blocking the main road south into the city. The makeshift ram would gain momentum and decimate the middle of the militan line.

She heard a growl and saw movement at the rear of the elven position. Standing, she could see Aden's division approaching from the rear. The ram would gain blistering speed the seventy mitres down the hill to the city, and it would break through the elven line and run over some of Aden's men behind them.

"Well, break an iron up my arse!" she cursed and ran to follow behind the wagon.

Hunter cursed and jumped up to follow behind her; the sound of his feet crunched among the grass and leaves.

The archers sent another volley into the front of the line. "Stop firing!" she shouted as she ran, her feet pounding now on the road in rhythm with the beating of her heart. Aden's men didn't have shields and would be skewered by the arrows from Bweth's division faster than a militan at this point.

Reaching the back of the rolling wagon, she fastened the mace to her belt and grabbed the hitch at the back of the wagon. Bweth set her feet and did her best to slow the wagon. Hunter was next to her now, both hands at the back of the wagon next to her, also leaning and pulling, his boots digging furrows in the dirt of the road. Hunter's squad was around them, pulling.

The wagon and thick log weighed far too much to be stopped, but their efforts slowed it. At the right speed, it would ram into the line and cause the destruction planned but not trample the unsuspecting humans behind the Kryan line. But tugging on the makeshift ram as they did made it swerve out of alignment.

When she felt the pace was acceptable, Bweth grabbed a panel of the wagon and leapt upon the back of the wagon. With a second jump, she was on top of the log on hands and feet, using the ropes to steady herself. The child within her was kicking like maddy and making her nauseous. The kid was already piffin' her off.

"Left!" she cried. "More to the left!"

Fifty mitres away now, the squad behind the wagon yelled at each other, things she couldn't hear clearly. She stood to her feet in a low crouch and crept her way forward on the log. The ram turned to the left.

"Good! Now straighten the shoggin' thing!" she yelled.

How they did it, she couldn't tell, but the squad was able to adjust their resistance to the back of the wagon so that they would crush the middle of the line. From her vantage point, she could see Aden's men causing chaos at the back of the line. The elven captain screamed at his elves as they were cut down from behind. Some turned, but not enough. They would soon be outnumbered and overrun, and she could see the realization break through on the Captain's face.

Gazing upwards, she saw the remains of an old woman, naked and impaled upon a rough pole. She felt little pity for the Captain.

Thirty mitres away, she turned and shouted over her shoulder. "Let it go!" She could see the rest of her division pouring down the hill towards the elves. They released the ram, and as she faced forward again, she could feel the ram building speed.

Bweth made her way to the front edge of the log and pulled the mace from her belt. She gripped the shield attached to her left forearm and bared her teeth.

Ten mitres away, the ram continuing to build speed, she lifted the spiked mace and twirled it. She spotted Aden almost dead in front of her at the back of the elven position. "Aden!" she screamed.

She watched as he blocked a gladi and severed an arm and spared a glimpse her way. He gawked as he noticed her riding the ram straight towards him.

"Move!" she said.

He didn't need any more convincing, had been moving before her order, in fact, telling his men to make way at the center of the line.

A split second before the ram connected with the center of the Kryan position, she launched herself to the right with a throaty scream. The ram barreled into the elves, bodies either crushed or flying mitres into the air with noise and screams and shouts and the scrape of wood against steel and iron. Bweth hurtled like a missile into the middle of the right side of the Kryan position, her knees carrying two elves to the ground while the mace crushed their skulls.

Her division pursued the ram as it broke through the line, and they cut into the elves. How Hunter made his way next to her, Bweth wasn't clear, but she didn't have time to care. Surrounded by elves, she blocked and parried and struck and kicked at them. With Hunter beside her, they cleared a path through the militan and stood back to back for a moment. Hunter hacked at the elves with his broad, short blade. She made sure to cover his blind side.

She didn't know if she ever loved him more.

With Aden's division from behind and now Bweth's engaged upon the Kryan position, they made short work of the elves. It was over quickly, almost too quick for Bweth to trust, but she and Hunter stood amidst the dead. They checked each other for injuries. Hunter had a gash along his left shoulder. Not deep. She made him sit while she wrapped it to stop the bleeding.

Aden and Tamya approached them, stepping over dead bodies. Tamya had the bloodwolf in a fierce grip at her side, a rope harness around the animal's neck and in her hand. That animal wanted more blood. They weren't done for the day. He would get it.

"What took you so long?" Aden asked.

"Shut the break up," she said, grinning back at him.

———

Lyam led his division along the bank of the lake on the north side of the city. Three platoons jogged behind him. Two more made their way past him to another road into Biram. The water lapped against the bank, and Lyam could hear the noise of battle from the east and the south, echoes of shouting and the clanging of steel.

As a former Ghost of Saten, that ancient forest full of terror and wonder, he made no noise as he moved, and he had trained his division to do the same, taking them into the forest north of the city of Ketan. He heard sounds that made him cringe, but they made it this far without an alarm. He prayed to El they would enter the city without notice.

Lyam was twenty-five years old and had been raised in the forest. The past few months in the city, he felt odd and out of place. And yet the high

253

and imposing walls of Ketan fascinated him. He felt both imprisoned and safe at once behind them.

His earliest memories were of Mother Natali and the Prophet and sermons of El and Yosu and warriors of long ago. For a young boy, the stories were full of myth, legend and heroism, filling him with courage and hope, but he never believed them to be true. Lyam knew about hunting and repelling the raids of the elves into their territory. He became a leader in that world even at a young age, his skills and abilities as natural as the spring rains. But to learn that those old stories might be real, might have really happened, filled him with a fear he could not explain.

When Athelwulf came to tell of how men defeated an army from the Underland and to call men and women to join the city of men in Ketan, he answered. He was chosen as a *Sohan-el*, and his journey to the Stone confirmed all his fears. El was real. Caleb was the embodiment of an ancient prophecy, the *Brendel*, and man would rebel in force against the elves.

Lyam did not consider himself a coward. He would fight. Caleb led them, however wrong the man might be. While Caleb had the pedigree and the history, Lyam could only see the current path leading to death and tragedy.

Caleb's instructions to Lyam had been simple and clear: find a way into the northwestern part of the city along the bank of the lake and support Caleb's main attack from the west by flanking the main force along the road there.

The elves had not placed impaled humans along the bank of the lake. Didn't they think the men would attack along the water or the docks? He could see the piers jutting out into the water, and no elves in sight. But a Kryan legion wouldn't make such a huge blunder, would they? He did not think so; he focused on his surroundings with his forest-trained eyes and ears.

The two platoons ahead of him turned right around a larger house ten mitres from the lake. Lyam breathed deep.

It was too quiet. He held up his hand and knelt. The three platoons behind him dropped to a knee with their weapons at the ready.

The silence was broken with cries and screams of pain around the bend of the next intersection, the clash of swords and shields. His platoons were being attacked. He wanted to rush forward and join the fight and support his platoons, but he knew that such a decision was dangerous. He needed to stick to the plan. Cursing under his breath, he sprung up, jogging and taking the next right into the city past a smaller building made of stone and wood. Arriving at the corner, Lyam didn't see a soul along the narrow lane between buildings. He jogged forward and had to make a decision.

Should he double back to the east and support the hundred men under attack or try to make his way to flank the elves and assist Caleb?

He froze for only a moment. They were his men, and his division would be a bigger help if more of them survived. He led all three of his platoons to the left, and within ten mitres, he could see the rear of the elven position.

Three hundred elves, a full Kryan division, had his fifty men surrounded, fighting for their lives, the elves with spears and swords crushing in on them.

Lyam roared as he charged the elves with his unforged sword out before him like a lance. The hundred and fifty men behind him also ran forward with their own spears and swords raised. Surprised, the elves weren't able to mount a sufficient defense, and Lyam's men cut down more than a hundred within a matter of seconds. The reinforcements gave new courage to the men surrounded by militan, and they made a push against the shields that trapped them. Lyam let his training and the unforged sword lead him as he cut into the elves one or two at a time.

The elven numbers dwindled, but the elven Captain was able to get two of his platoons rotated around to face Lyam. Once they made the adjustment, the battle evened as the militan deployed their shields and gladi in close quarters. Men died all around Lyam, his friends crying out as they lost limbs or were cut down. Blood sprayed to his left and right.

Lyam's unforged sword cut through shields and even swords as he killed elf after elf, but his men were dying, as well. Their cries and groans rang in his ears.

Focused on the fighting before him, Lyam heard a voice from the rear in the middle of the screams and shouts around him, a scream of pain and warning, although he couldn't make out the words. He knew the voice, though, Ytrel, a man from Ketan.

Lyam stabbed an elf through the chest and took the risk to look behind him.

Another force of elves assaulted them from behind.

He couldn't see the size of the force – two, maybe three platoons? – but now his men were the ones flanked and trapped.

Suddenly, there were no lines, no place to defend or attack. Lyam and his men were in a complete melee. It could be a friend or foe at every turn. How many men lost? No time to think. The plan went to complete crit and Lyam battled to stay alive over the next few minutes in a panic.

"Men, fight or die!" shouted Marat, one of his platoon leaders.

In the chaos, men froze and died as gladi found their throats or bellies, other men became consumed by a bloodlust and attacked anything that moved, even their own comrades. Some fought bravely until a random spear or gladus struck them down. Lyam saw all of this as he spun and slashed, stabbed and swiped with his unforged sword, taking limbs and heads. He even cut one militan in half. Blood and death were everywhere;

he could smell crit and piff and vomit as men and elves around him wept and fell.

Some died in an instant. Others took time to die, holding severed limbs or their intestines as they crawled, crying out to El or their mothers in the throes of death. Neither seemed to help the dying.

The numbers on both sides diminished, and within another five minutes, Lyam saw only fifty or more total people, elves and humans, on their feet. He leapt over a pile of three corpses, two men and one elf, eyes open and glassy, mouths slack, faces twisted in terror or pain or both, and he took another elf from behind. He felt a slash at his side, and he twisted to cut a spear in half, the blade of the spear flying away through the air. Lyam took a breath through clenched teeth as he took off the elf's hands at the wrist. The militan screamed in pain, and Lyam silenced his shrill shriek and his pain as he took the elf's head from his body.

Blood poured down his side and over his right leg, but he could not stop. If he stopped, he died. The unforged sword took two more lives before he was finished, blinking blood that was not his own out of his vision, and he saw only men standing.

Three of them. Lyam and two other men, one of them without a left arm, crimson spurting from the wound. He collapsed. The other man, Marat, stood motionless now that the onslaught was over, his breath coming in heaves.

"Great and mighty El," Lyam said, although he wasn't sure the name of El should be spoken here. His whole division gone. Dead or dying around him. As his tears spilled, he cast his gaze around him and held his own bleeding side. Elves and men, all atop one another. It was difficult to see the difference between them among the blood.

Lyam's knees buckled, and he fell to his knees. He dropped the unforged sword among the carnage, covered his face with his right hand, and he wept.

—

Tamya led her platoon up the southern road and into the city, the bloodwolf next to her. She took them off to the right and wound through the houses and other buildings, a tannery on her left, and a road further on would lead them closer in to the center of the city.

Caleb had been certain that the Bladeguard would be in the center of the city, either in the administration center or close to it with some sort of command pavilion. She ducked through two houses, and thirty-five men followed her. One of the men in Favel's division was from Biram, and he showed the division, platoon, and squad leaders the main streets and layouts of the city on a map Caleb had brought. Caleb had made them memorize the thing before they left, which took more time than she had patience for, but now she was glad they had done it.

Tamya led her platoon to the rear of the educational building, and she had two men knock down the door so they could enter through the back. Her knees still pained her from the door she took down earlier in the day.

The center of Biram, the great common field, was on the other side of the educational building. She made her way through rooms, her short swords in her hands, the bloodwolf panting beside her, but they didn't find any elves in the building. Coming into the hall that led to the main doors, she could peer outside through the open doors, like an invitation. She could hear the sound of battle already there. Had others beat her to the battle? She wouldn't put it past Caleb to beat her there and kill all the elves before she got her chance.

She took the invitation and shot out of the door at a run, Hema growling along with her. As she burst into the open, she saw two platoons standing to the side. The elves saw her immediately and rushed to surround her and her platoon.

The elves were in positions as a ring around the center of the city. Beyond the two platoons next to her, she could see Aden and a platoon to her left, fighting through an elven position, and Bweth's division on the main road from the south further on. To her right, another group of men were fighting elves – Xander? Pynt? The elves to the west seemed to be holding their position for now against a large force of men but would soon be overrun. Where the shog was Caleb?

In the middle of the field stood two elves in long robes with long, curved swords in their hands. Bladeguard. And they moved to the south to intercept Bweth and Aden's divisions.

Seeing all of this in a split second, Tamya did not hesitate to join the fight. There were plenty left to kill. She only paused to give orders. Two squads to the right and flank that platoon. She and the other two would take the second platoon. Tamya hurled herself off the steps to land a few paces away from the second platoon, whose lieutenant attempted to get them turned to face her, but not in time.

Her two squads – sixteen people and a bloodwolf – stormed the platoon of fifty with a battle cry that came from deep within them; they fought the elves, outnumbered, with a ferocity that must have made the bloodwolf feel at home. As Caleb instructed, they took out the lieutenant – Tamya set the bloodwolf upon him – and broke the line to take away any advantage of organization. The skirmish spiraled into chaos and individual hand-to-hand fighting.

She spun, dancing in that way that Esai had taught her, cutting and stabbing and kicking at the elves around her. Her men were outnumbered three to one, but they had been trained for exactly this, watching each other's back and taking the elves on one or two at a time. Men fell, but elves fell at a faster pace.

A presence behind her, a hand on her leg, and she twirled to take the hand from a wrist with one of her swords as she stabbed down into the chest with the other. But as her eyes fell on her victim, it was not an elf. It was a man. One of her own men.

"No," she whispered in a hopeless wish as she pulled her blade from his chest. Dervan. Dervan was his name. *A good man from Roseborough*, she thought, although she hadn't taken time to really get to know him. Her men surrounded her, and she heard the bloodwolf snarl as he took down another elf. But she knelt down, dropped her swords and cradled the man. He looked up at her, tears falling down the side of his face.

His mouth moved, and he tried to say something. But only a gasp escaped.

The man had been wounded already, and falling, he probably had reached out for her, his leader, his commander, as he fell. And she killed him. She killed one of her own men as he sought her help.

Tamya saw his eyes become vacant as he died and the last breath left him.

"I'm so sorry," she said, but she failed even in her apology. He didn't hear it. He was already dead.

Glancing up, weeping and sniveling, she saw one of the Bladeguard close in on Aden's division, cutting down men as he went. She wanted to get up and help Aden as her own men finished off both platoons, but she couldn't move.

Bweth's division took down three platoons of elves before they broke into the middle of the city. Of her original 250 men and women, she had just over one hundred left. Blood and gore covered her breastplate and mace, and she knew she would have to mourn the men behind her, only later. But coming into the center of Biram, she could tell they would win this battle. The elves were outnumbered now and on their heels as the divisions of the *Hamon-el* entered the fray on the field.

Two platoons – not full, maybe 80 elves – from the left side blitzed them, led by three legion Captains. Bweth led the rush into them, not the response they expected, but it was effective. The elves went from running to on their heels in a moment. She lost men, but several elves fell in the panic. Crushing one skull, she upended another elf with her shield as she ducked under the swipe of his gladus and then brought down her mace onto his forehead and his skull exploded under her weapon.

She rose to find herself surrounded by the three legion Captains, all of them with large blue plumes decorating their helmets.

Militan were not taught extensive hand-to-hand training. Large numbers working as a unit have advantage in the open field as armies clash, so the individual soldiers of a legion learn how to operate in that mode. Fighting in close quarters or forcing them into a series of quick adjustments took that advantage away, but in most large-scale battles, the legions were almost unstoppable.

Officers, however, were from wealthier families and spent years studying martial arts, especially if their future would include a career in the military. Trained by swordmasters, the officers would be more formidable at hand-to-hand combat. Officers like the three Captains before her.

She blocked one swipe at her from a sword and followed it with her mace, but the elf dodged it. Bweth had to duck a slash from another Captain and staved off a stab from the third with her mace. Cursing, she raised her shield and charged the third Captain, the most recent attacker. He couldn't retract his sword in time, and she hit him full in the abdomen with her shoulder. Grunting, the elf fell on his arse. Her momentum carried her further, and she kneed him the face as she stepped over him. Spinning, she brought down the spikes of her mace onto his neck, killing him instantly. She now faced two Captains as they approached her.

Beyond them, she saw a Bladeguard attack the remnants of her division, killing her men one by one – with a sword she had made for him.

Hunter glanced at her, saw her engaged with the Captains, and after cutting down the militan in front of him, he ran to face the Bladeguard and save the men dying before the swordmaster.

"No!" she screamed. "Hunter! Wait for me!"

But either he did not hear or did not listen. He moved to intercept the Bladeguard.

The Captains coordinated their attack, and she fended off the one to the left with her shield and the one on the right with the mace. She had to finish this quickly, but she could not rush it. A mistake would kill her as sure as the sun was setting to the west where a human division had overrun the elves, pitching the battle more to the human's favor.

Bweth parried the one on the left with the mace, across her chest and spun to meet the other's sword low with the shield. She let the turn continue and kicked out at an elven knee. Hearing it snap and the elf cry, he went down but kept his sword up and stopped the strike of her mace.

Hunter met the Bladeguard now. She saw him take a deep breath and stave off the first attack from the Bladeguard, a simple series of slashes from the swordmaster that were meant to test her husband not to kill. Hunter stepped back and held his sword out in front of him, not taking the bait to attack. Smart man. He might survive if he could keep up his defense. Maybe.

Beating away another sword with her shield, Bweth moved away from the elf with a broken knee to rush the other Captain, attempting to overwhelm his defense, but he was good. Too good. He would not go down so easy, and he instead took one of her strikes and took a quick swipe at her head, which she ducked. Barely. He had the reach and the skill on her. She stepped back to collect herself, breathing heavily, and the other Captain struggled to his feet.

Out of the corner of her eye, she could see Hunter retreating under the assault of the Bladeguard, deflecting the blade with his own, but it was desperation. Hunter was a brawler and a great man with a good heart, but it was like watching a folk musician against a maestro, a genius composer. Her heart sank as the Captain moved between her and her husband.

Crying out in rage, she attacked the elf with the broken knee, circling him and forcing him to move his feet, which he could not, and he tumbled to his good knee again. She batted away the sword with the mace and bashed him in the face with her shield, following that again with the mace, spikes digging deep into his temple and ear.

She spun to face the last Captain bearing down at her, his own face angry but fixed in concentration, his sword a blur as he attacked her. She had to use both the shield and mace to block his attacks.

Looking past the Captain, she saw the Bladeguard patiently, calmly, keep up his attack on Hunter, changing the rhythm of his strikes, and in a sudden moment, he sliced Hunter's blade from his hand and his right arm from his elbow.

He did not cry out, but as he fell forward, Bweth watched, helpless, as the Bladeguard stabbed her husband through the throat.

Tears streamed down her face now, her teeth bared, and she retreated to pass one of the dead Captains, his sword lying next to him. She reached down, picked it up by the hilt and threw it at the remaining Captain with her left hand. He swatted it away easily enough, but the mace followed, hurtling through the air and hitting him in the forehead. He stiffened before falling backwards.

Bweth retrieved her mace from the elf's forehead and raced to kill that Bladeguard. But she couldn't yet because now another platoon of militan attacked her and the men left with her, only fifty now.

Exhausted and empty after a day of battle and watching her husband slayed before her eyes, she wanted to stop, to give up. She dropped to her knees and the mace in her hand thumped upon the ground next to her. Her vision blurred from tears as the battle was joined around her, her stare bound to her dead husband.

Then the child within her kicked again as if to say, *I am here.*

"Alright, wee one," she whispered. She stood and wiped the tears from her face. "I didn't forget about you."

Bweth willed herself forward to confront the elves and add to their dead.

―

The Bladeguard approached from his right as the elves fell before the *Hamon-el*. The second one had fought with Hunter further to the east, and Aden faced the younger elf in a crouch and his unforged sword in a low guard, ready to defend or strike. The Bladeguard closed within ten paces.

He had seen the older Bladeguard slaughter a dozen of Hunter's men before the man confronted him. Aden wanted to keep this one from doing the same level of damage. But that meant facing off against a Bladeguard. He remembered well how Caleb had trouble with Zarek in Biram months before, back at *The Crying Eagle*, and that was Caleb.

Aden stole a glance at Hunter lying dead in his own blood.

This would not be the smartest thing Aden ever did.

But he was trained and given a sword by the Stone, although not in that order. Surely that must count for something. Maybe.

Maybe he should play for time.

"You're Saben," Aden said as the fighting raged behind him.

The Bladeguard halted five paces away, his sword down as he stood straight. His brows rose. "That is correct," he said. "But you have me at a disadvantage. What is your name?"

He hesitated before answering, but what would be the benefit of keeping his name a secret? "Aden."

"Aden," Saben said. "Ah, yes, I have also heard of you."

Crit on a frog. Aden swallowed hard. "Really? That seems unlikely."

"You're the friend of the *Brendel*," Saben said. "The one that helped him break the Prophet out of the Pyts and kill a Demilord, or whatever that creature really was."

"Don't forget killing a Bladeguard."

"Zarek?" Saben shook his head. "A great agent of the Empire, to be sure, but not one of our greatest swordmasters."

"And you are?"

"I've been known to have some skill, yes," Saben said.

"I heard Caleb kicked your arse," Aden said.

Saben raised his sword. "Unfortunate you are not he."

Aden narrowed his eyes at the Bladeguard. "You should surrender."

"To you?"

Scanning pointedly around the center of Biram, Aden said, "The battle is lost. Your Bladeguard training had to have taught you that much. Even if you kill me, you can't kill all of us."

Saben smirked. "Are you sure? Too bad you won't be around to find out."

Then the Bladeguard attacked.

He remembered, for a quick moment, the image of Caleb battling Zarek in *The Crying Eagle*: the speed of the two combatants like a blur, sword and staff moving faster than he thought possible. Saben's attack reminded him of that speed.

Without a thought, he met Saben's sword with his own, and it surprised him. Caleb's training and the unforged sword helped him turn Saben's blade aside time and again, even though he had no time to counterattack. The unforged sword guided his hand into the perfect forms, forms he had been taught but now used at the exact moment needed.

He retreated, backing away from Saben, and at least he could lead the Bladeguard away from the rest of the fighting. It was clear in the middle of the field.

Saben hooked his blade around Aden's with a twist of his wrist and almost wrenched the unforged sword from his hand. Aden rolled his own hand and pulled his blade from Saben's; cursing, Aden leapt back, twirled, and brought his sword around in a low attack, which the elf diverted, but Aden's blade scratched the Bladeguard's shin.

The Bladeguard scowled at him and attacked with a barrage of strikes and cuts, some as feints and others meant for killing. Aden thought it had been fast before. He was wrong. The Bladeguard's assault played like music, short quick stabs followed by a series of long and calculated slashes before picking up the pace to a blinding speed, high then low or reversing the order.

Aden deflected the thrusts enough to stay alive, but he suffered a cut along his right forearm, then another along his thigh, not far from where the Wraith dagger had been imbedded into the muscle. Staggering, Aden tried to counter, but Saben left him no room. If Aden made a mistake, one slip, then he knew it was over. Saben was the better swordself.

Then he did something Caleb told him to never do. Aden swiped out in anger, desperate. But he was so tired. Saben diverted his swipe with ease and countered with a stab to the middle of Aden's chest. Aden could not move his blade fast enough; the stab connected with Aden's sword and only moved it aside. The Bladeguard's sword dug deep into Aden's right shoulder.

The pain caused Aden to stumble; he cried out and fell to his knees, using the sword to steady himself like a cane, to keep upright. His body screamed in agony as he tried to stand again. He could not use his right arm without shooting anguish. Saben lashed out with a foot and kicked Aden in the face, and he fell to his back with a jerk.

He had to get up, *get up, get up and fight. Fight or die.* He tried to will himself, but his muscles wouldn't respond. His vision blurred, but he could see a figure standing over him. And he heard a voice, like it was muffled. *Did the elf have a hand over his mouth?*

"Not bad for a human," Saben said. The figure raised the sword for a killing blow.

And then more movement, a blur of a shadow, even though it was in the middle of the day, and a clang of metal clashing, the dull sound of flesh and cloth connecting, and Saben grunting. Another figure stood over him now, but as a protector. He held a sword in one hand – the blade bright against the sun, not a shadow – and a long staff in the other.

"Enough," he heard Caleb say.

———

He faced Saben as Aden writhed on the ground behind him.

The elf sneered at him. "Caleb," he spat. "So you do have the courage to show your face."

"I was delayed," Caleb said. Lyam's division never came to flank the Kryan position in the west, and the men that attacked that position suffered high casualties to make it to the center of the city. Iletus had brought up another division in support.

As Cyprian strode towards him and Saben, Caleb noticed the battle coming to an end around them. A quick glimpse showed the diminishing numbers of elves and the victory of the *Hamon-el.* As he laid his hand upon the hilt of the unforged sword, the *barabrend,* there was one last thing that needed done now.

Regarding both Bladeguard, Caleb said, "I challenge you to a duel of combat."

Saben and Cyprian shared a frown while standing side by side. Cyprian spoke first. "Interesting. You seek the *conduelae?*"

"I do," Caleb said.

"But as your disciple here pointed out," Saben said, pointing to Aden. "You nearly have the battle won."

Generally, the *conduelae* was not for the winners to seek. The army that was outnumbered or at a severe disadvantage or about to lose would be desperate enough for such a gambit, and one that never worked. For why would the army with the advantage risk it on a simple duel? Pride or show, perhaps, but throughout history, even when the army with the advantage lost the duel, they still wiped out the smaller army. Honor was a fine concept, but few wars were examples of honor, if any.

"I understand your confusion," Caleb said. "But there has been enough death today. I seek to end it now."

Cyprian met Caleb's stare, and Caleb wondered what the elf saw there. He felt that hardness within him. It became his closest friend today, but Caleb felt content and at peace. Cyprian shouted, "Legion, halt!"

Every elf took a step back and ceased their fighting. *Give the militan credit*, Caleb thought. *That was impressive.*

But the men of Ketan were also well trained. Caleb raised the unforged sword a heartbeat later and called, "*Hamon-el*, stand down and hold!"

Armies of men, elves, and dwarves were all notorious for their bloodlust and failure to restrain themselves in the midst of battle and after. They tortured and raped and stole from those they conquered. The only army in history without that reputation? The *Hamon-el* of Yosu. Caleb's army would be the second one of its kind in history.

Every man and woman stood down and fell silent. Except for the bloodwolf, Hema, who howled and growled, hungry for more death and blood.

Caleb didn't turn as he spoke. "Tamya, you will hold that beast or I will kill him myself."

He heard her soft words, and Hema settled to a constant, low growl. That would have to do.

"What would be the terms?" Cyprian asked with a suspicious expression.

Just as when Caleb accepted the duel with Saben years ago, terms of the duel were a tradition. Once the terms were agreed upon, then the parties could decide whether or not to accept the duel.

"If I win," Caleb said. "Those who remain of your army will become our prisoners, and I promise no harm will come to them."

Saben's hard visage never wavered. Was he thinking of the last time Caleb beat him in a duel? Did that cause him fear? Caleb hoped so.

"And if we win?" Cyprian asked.

"Then my instruction to my captains and my *Sohan-el* will be this: allow the Bladeguard to take their elves and return to Taggart."

"Caleb, no." Bweth's voice from his right. Caleb turned and saw her laying in the dirt, grass, and blood, cradling the corpse of her husband. Her face was a visage of anger and hate.

Caleb's heart broke in that moment, for his friend, Hunter, dead, and Bweth who lost her love. But he pushed the grief aside. It was not time for that now. "This is the will of El. You will harm no one unless they do not leave in peace."

And for once, Bweth did not defy him. He saw a touch of fear in her eyes, fear of him. That further broke his heart. A part of him wanted to go to her, hold her, comfort her. But this was war. The killing wasn't done. Not yet.

Saben scoffed at him. "You expect us to believe you will honor these terms? You are a traitor and a savage; you and Galen actively deceived us for years. How can we trust you or these other savages with you to honor these terms?"

"All I can give is my word," Caleb said. "Why would I seek the *conduelae* if I only sought to slaughter your whole army? I could have that now."

"Trusting the word of a savage," Saben muttered to himself.

"And what did you tell the men and women and children of this city before you impaled them?"

"We told them the truth," Cyprian answered. "We told them that the *Brendel* and his revolution would be the death of all men, that his rebellion against the Empire condemned them and the rest of humanity. They cursed you as they died in agony."

Break me, Caleb thought and calmed himself. "Do you accept the duel?"

"I will accept," Cyprian said.

"I was not challenging you," Caleb said.

Cyprian laughed. "We pick our champion," he said. "That is tradition. You know this."

"You misunderstand," Caleb said. "Cyprian and Saben, Bladeguard of the Citadel, I challenge you both."

"Your challenge is to fight us *both*?" Cyprian asked. "At once?"

Holding out the Kingstaff and the unforged sword, Caleb nodded.

It was Saben's moment to chuckle. "You cannot hope to win."

"If it ends this battle without more bloodshed," Caleb said. "Then that is enough."

"I don't understand," Saben said.

"I did not expect you to. Do you accept?"

Cyprian spun his curved sword in his hand with a flourish. "You will regret this, but we accept."

"Good," Caleb said. "Tamya, come help Aden."

Holding onto Hema with one hand, she ambled forward and reached down and grabbed his unhurt shoulder, helping him to his feet. Aden groaned.

Caleb turned to them. "Get him back and sew up that wound," Caleb said.

Aden glared at him. "Crit on a frog, Caleb. I hope you know what you're doing," he said.

"I do," Caleb said.

Aden cursed again as Tamya led him away.

"You know we hurt her before she died," Saben said behind him.

"Saben ..." Cyprian warned.

But the elf continued. "Your precious slave girl, Danelle. You were willing to risk so much for her, and yet you still lost her. We took her from you. We feared Galen – you were his star pupil, his pet project – so we told no one, kept it a secret. But now Galen is captured and probably dead. Soon you will join him. Now is as good a time as any to tell you the truth.

"You took the beating for her, and while you were unconscious and helpless, we took her took her away and raped and killed her. You failed to protect her, just as you will fail to protect the men of Ereland. Legions upon legions will come. Two will replace every elf you kill. You cannot win. What happened here in Biram will happen to all the towns and cities of the land of humans. And they will all curse your name just as Danelle did."

Caleb took a deep breath and clenched his jaw. He closed his eyes and a tear escaped him despite his will to keep it contained. With the memory of the pile of stones over Danelle's body, the old anger, the old hate, rose within him. He could hear the satisfaction and the grin on Saben's face as the elf spoke. He wondered what had to happen to a soul to find joy in another's suffering. However, Caleb had been trained by the same masters. He knew the manipulation Saben attempted. But that did not make the turmoil within him any less.

He leaned against the Kingstaff and lifted the unforged sword to his face and pressed his forehead against the blade. He clung to the peace and calm he felt on Mount Elarus as he approached the Living Stone.

Facing them now, his eyes were open. "You seek to anger me so I will rush in, lose patience, and make mistakes you can exploit." Caleb smiled, but he knew it was not a comforting smile. "Which means you fear me. Knowing you will be two against one, behind all your bragging and bluster, you are afraid of me."

Cyprian bared his teeth. "We are not afraid."

Caleb scoffed. "You lie."

"We speak no lies," Saben said.

Caleb crouched low, spun the Kingstaff and put the unforged sword in a low guard. "Then come and prove it."

The two Bladeguard spaced themselves out before him to attack from different angles, and Caleb stayed motionless as they did. Being the younger, Saben waited for Cyprian to make the first move. The whole center of Biram stood transfixed and silent, hundreds of men and elves. They would all see today the truth of the *Brendel*.

Cyprian came with a high attack from the right, and Saben coordinated low. Caleb shuffled his feet and blocked Cyprian with the unforged sword and Saben with the Kingstaff.

The dance was on.

Most of the time, Caleb held back. The last time he fought without restraint was the Battle of Ketan against the demics on the wall and then the Demilord at the Kulbrim. In the last few months, as he trained the men and women of the *Sohan-el*, he held himself in check. They had all become great warriors, but none could hope to match him. It was not arrogance. Even when in Kohinoor at the Citadel, he held back. Caleb was being personally taught by the greatest swordmaster in the world, some said that ever existed. One of the many things he missed about Galen was when they sparred together. Galen could match him and more. If anything, Galen was the one who had to hold back in those moments.

Caleb had been twenty years old when Galen said, "I will make you the greatest warrior this world has ever known. No one will be able to stop you. No one." Galen taught Caleb things the other students would never know.

For the first time in a long time, Caleb felt free to be the weapon he was created to be. But this was different from the Battle of Ketan or his conflict with the Demilord or even his sparring with Galen. Caleb was trained to be the greatest warrior in the world. And now he possessed the unforged sword of El.

He let himself go. And he could feel the distinction. All his training, every minute detail, was immediately available to him exactly when he needed it. Both staff and blade were blurs in his hand, his mind and heart guided by the unforged sword, that supernatural blade, a synergy that went beyond anything he ever knew before. He was calm, almost detached. Even more amazing, the sword led him in new and creative forms, spontaneous combinations that were genius in the moment. But it was not his genius. He was only a steward.

Blocking every strike, low then high, right and left, fast and calculated or slow and strong, Caleb patiently waited for his moment. He played the game, danced the steps, kept the rhythm, found the notes in the perfect key. He was learning the feel of the sword, almost as if it were the first time. Also, he took the time to learn his opponents.

Each of the Bladeguard possessed his own style, and Caleb found himself fighting at two different speeds and with two separate methods. Saben he had fought before. But that had been years ago. Caleb had learned far more since then. Cyprian was a master, far better than Zarek, maybe one of the best of the Bladeguard. He could see the looks of deep concern on their faces. Were they testing him, too? Probably.

It was time. He felt it within him, like a call. He spun and struck back, forcing Cyprian to parry low and Saben to duck under the staff. Caleb rotated and struck at Saben with the sword and Cyprian with the staff. Cyprian took his sword in two hands to keep ahold of it as the staff hit his blade. Caleb sprung to close the distance and kicked Cyprian in the chest, knocking him back.

Twirling back, Saben was rushing him, and Caleb met the charge by turning Saben's thrust with his sword – feeling a slight gash across his right ribcage, deflected also past the breastplate he had complained about – and bringing the Kingstaff down on Saben's right shoulder. Caleb heard the bones crush under the blow, and Saben went down to his knees with a screech of agony and frustration, dropping his curved blade in the dirt, his right arm hanging limp. Caleb circled the elf and reversed the blade to plunge it into Saben's back and through his heart.

Cyprian had recovered and approached, but Caleb stuck the staff out like a spear. The elder Bladeguard froze with a grimace on his face.

Saben gasped. His countenance was a mask of terror as he grabbed the unforged blade protruding from his chest.

"Oh, Caleb," he said through a moan. "I didn't know."

"Now you do," Caleb answered. He leaned down and whispered into Saben's ear. "Tell me."

"We ..." Saben swallowed. "We never touched her."

"I know," Caleb said. He pressed his foot on Saben's back and pulled the sword from his body. Saben fell facedown and died.

Stepping away from Saben's corpse, he lowered the staff and faced Cyprian.

"Tamya," he called.

She stood straight to his right.

He tossed the Kingstaff the ten mitres to her. It hurtled through the air, and she caught it in her left hand. "Hang on to that for me," Caleb said.

Tamya peered down her arm at the Kingstaff like she had just taken hold of a grider's tail.

He gripped the unforged sword with both hands and held it up before Cyprian. "Last chance," he said. "Surrender."

Cyprian snarled at him and attacked with a series of strikes, alternating high and low with blinding speed, their blades meeting again and again, sparks flying as Caleb parried and moved, ducked and countered.

In that moment, he realized that Cyprian had been holding back as well, perhaps to coordinate his attack with the less-skilled Saben. The Bladeguard had no limitation now, and he assailed Caleb with power, speed, and precision that would have impressed Galen.

But Caleb was no novice, either. He countered and spun, kicking and throwing an elbow that Cyprian ducked. Cyprian turned with a swipe that Caleb couldn't completely dodge, and Cyprian's blade scraped across the breastplate – Caleb thanked Bweth in silence – but found himself with a gash across his shoulder, not deep but it stung like crit.

Taking a deep breath, Caleb pressed the attack high while he struck out with his left foot. Cyprian lifted his knee and absorbed the blow with a thigh. Caleb's left fist struck and connected just under Cyprian's ribs, and he heard the air leave the elf's body. He slashed low as a feint then high with a swipe. Caleb put all of his strength into the attack, and Cyprian brought up his sword to block.

The Bladeguard's sword – one of the greatest elven swords in the world, made by Bweth Ironhorn – shattered upon the impact. Shards of fine steel flew everywhere, and he closed his eyes as he stepped to the left, feeling the sting of small pieces of steel pelting the skin of his face; he brought down his sword and severed Cyprian's hands from his wrists.

Opening his eyes again, Caleb watched Cyprian collapse onto his back. Cyprian's face was cut in a hundred places, and he bled from his eyes. The elf lifted his arms, on instinct it seemed, but his own blood spurted from his wounds onto his face and neck.

Caleb stood over the Bladeguard.

He did not challenge the two Bladeguard to a duel for revenge or power or lust or the need to kill. It was a symbol, a sign. And judgment.

Caleb took the elf's head from his shoulders.

His wounds pained him, but as he checked them over, they were not serious. Scanning the crowd around him, men and elves looked at him with blank and awed faces, silent and frozen. There were no cheers or curses. Just fear and awe.

Rumors would escape this remote city. They always did. His legend would grow, for good or ill.

If that is how it must be, he thought.

He wondered how many more he would have to kill before the Kryan Empire surrendered. *Too many.* His heart sank at the thought.

Chapter 22

The Mines of Kaleti

Fifty men gathered at the gate of the city of Da'ar with Athelwulf, Eshlyn, and Tobiah. Eshlyn and Athelwulf held their unforged swords and a small pack for the journey. Tobiah and the other men of the Beorgai wore their packs and weapons, the *corran*, thick curved blades in a half circle around their fist connected to a bosaur-bone hilt.

The men of the Beorgai were all trained in the weapon from a young age, as well as the bow. Athelwulf remembered well his training in the *corran*, learning from his father. The martial discipline was full of kicks and slashes with the short, rounded blades. They were designed for close combat.

To be considered a man with the Beorgai, a boy must learn those weapons and hunt a mountain panther alone. Athelwulf was fifteen when he climbed the mountain high above the city of Da'ar, setting off alone. He had found the tracks of a panther his first day, hunting the beast until that evening. But the panther hunted him, too, and attacked in the middle of the night. Surrounded by darkness as a boy, Athelwulf slashed and cut at the panther, being bit and cut in return, but he had emerged victorious and cut the head from the panther, staggering back to his home with the trophy in his hand. The next day, he had been declared a man.

Every man who carried the *corran* had a similar story.

Preparing to attack the mines, Athelwulf and the men of the Beorgai all had a short bow slung across their shoulder, as well, and a quiver of arrows at their side.

They would not be riding bosaur to the mines. The paths across the mountains to the mines were too narrow; the bosaur could not travel on those paths. So the small group would have to go by foot.

Shecayah embraced her husband, Tobiah, a tall and athletic man with short-cropped hair and a close beard. Athelwulf stood a few paces away as his little sister spoke tenderly to Tobiah. He promised he would return, and she kissed him.

Athelwulf smiled as Shecayah stepped away from her husband and approached him. "Namir," she said. "You must also come back to me. I am not done getting to know my brother."

He smiled as he gathered her in an embrace. "Yes, sister. I will."

"He is no longer Namir." Athelwulf heard his father's voice from the right. "He goes by a different name than his mother gave him."

Releasing his sister, Athelwulf turned to the elder of the Beorgai. "Father. I am glad to see you before we must leave."

Kiano's eyes were drawn to Athelwulf's sword. The unforged sword. Athelwulf pulled it from the scabbard across his back and extended it to his father.

"Would you care to hold it before we go?"

His father stared at the sword but did not answer.

Athelwulf closed the distance between himself and his father and held out the sword further. "Hold it."

Kiano's hands lifted and took the sword from Athelwulf. He spent a moment staring at the *barabrend*.

"I never thought I would see this day," Kiano whispered. "A day when the *Sohan-el* have returned, when the *Bashawyn* has come to us." He sighed, a grievous sound.

"I climbed a mountain and faced El himself to get that sword," Athelwulf said. "Before that, I spent years repenting to El, and when I laid my hands upon the Stone, El found me worthy." He looked at his father. "When I was young, you told me that El is the god of the heart of all living beings. El judged my heart, Father, and found me worthy."

His father stood motionless, frowning. Was it anger? Sorrow? All of it? Athelwulf hoped love.

"My name may have changed, but I am more your son today than I ever was before I left. I follow the god you taught me."

Kiano inclined his head at the sword.

"They say that the *barabrend* speaks to some," Athelwulf said. "Does it speak to you, father?"

Athelwulf watched as his father glared at him. Kiano handed the sword back to Athelwulf.

"The *Bashawyn* claims that you are a man of honor. A leader," Kiano said.

Eshlyn stood near them now.

"She is kind," Athelwulf said and took the sword by the hilt.

Kiano's eyes narrowed at him. "Then I charge you with the protection of the *Bashawyn* and these men, my men, and the protection of my city."

Athelwulf gave his father a bow. "Father, you have been a strong and able elder to Da'ar. I can think of none better. You have kept them safe. But the time has come when men must choose between safety and freedom. They choose freedom this day. But I will protect them as well as I can. It is my honor as a *Sohan-el.*" He put the sword back in its scabbard and bowed to his father.

"Very well," Kiano said.

"It is time," Eshlyn said, her voice gentle.

"Yes," Athelwulf said. "Farewell."

"Farewell, Athelwulf," Shecayah said, grinning at him.

Kiano said nothing.

Athelwulf walked to where Tobiah and the fifty other men waited. "The mines are a day or more away by foot," Tobiah said. "We may have to camp tonight."

"Then let's get moving," Eshlyn said. "We will follow your lead."

Tobiah began to stride across the long bridge over the deep chasm, and Eshlyn fell into step beside Athelwulf as they traversed the stone overpass.

"Speaking of protecting the *Bashawyn*," Athelwulf said. "We could use the help of your friend, you know."

"I have called him," she said. "He is close, but I do not know how far or if he will come."

"Let's hope so," Athelwulf said. "I have a feeling we will need him."

"The Mahakar makes his own choices and will come when he does," she grumbled at him. "But I agree. I hope he comes soon."

—

The Last Serpent was a large ship, one of the largest Zalman had ever seen.

He had been on several ships in his lifetime, especially when he played for the Landen Eels, and *The Last Serpent* was massive compared to most of them. Some of the Kryan warships had been similar in size.

Aeric's ship was fifty mitres long with three masts down the center of the main deck. A crow's nest sat on top of the foremast. A long iron lance was the bowsprit and other iron spikes decorated the hull of the ship at regular intervals, made to ram and sink other ships, Zalman supposed. The wood of the ship was a dark brown, and Aeric claimed it was built more than three hundred years ago by one of the greatest shipbuilders in history, a man named Gradon at the city-state of Halmano to the north using the strong trees of the forest on that island. *The Last Serpent* had never been defeated in a battle at sea.

Zalman stood against the railing next to Aeric and Carys on the upper deck, overlooking the main deck and the twenty or so men that tightened ropes or did other jobs at the behest of Bade, Aeric's second in command. The waters around them were calm in the afternoon sun.

Turning to Aeric, Carys asked, "So explain to me how this challenge will work."

Aeric leaned over and put his elbows on the railing, staring out to sea. "Ah, yes, the challenge," he said. "All the lords will be there, the kanalor. There are five of us now. There used to be seven, but two of our cities fell to the elves during the war and never recovered."

"Why all of them?" Carys said.

"They will judge the challenge."

"I thought you said there will be a duel."

"Yes, but the duel is only a part of the challenge," Aeric said. "You see, I am the Kanacyn because the other kanalor elect me as such. For me to lose my position, the other four must agree and elect another, or three in this case, since the challenger will obviously vote for herself."

Carys frowned at him. "So you can lose the duel and not lose your position."

"Unless I die in the duel, yes," Aeric said. "But I can also win the duel and lose the position."

"If you die, does the challenger win?"

Aeric shook his head. "The others must still vote. The three remaining kanalor must agree on the challenger or choose another from among them. It could become complicated. Better if neither one of us dies. We will each make our case before the other three and then participate in the duel on the open water."

"What will the weapons be?" Zalman asked.

"We will decide and agree before the duel," Aeric answered.

Carys sniffed, her hair blowing across her face in the strong breeze. "And who is this challenger?"

"A woman named Mikayla," Aeric said. "A worthy opponent."

"Do you think you can win?" Carys questioned.

A couple heartbeats passed before he responded. "I do not know," he said.

Zalman could see her face twisted in thought. "Interesting," she said and stepped away from the railing. "I am going down to the deck. Bade promised to let me see the view from the crow's nest."

Aeric gave her a small bow and smirked at her. "You shall appreciate the view, I'm sure. It is a beautiful day. Almost as beautiful as you."

Carys rolled her eyes but smiled as she descended the stairs to the main deck and then forward through the men working below them.

An anger rose in Zalman when Aeric watched her slyly as she walked away.

Aeric chuckled. "My friend," Aeric said. "That is a fine woman. Intelligent, strong with the heart of a warrior, and fair. A man could ask for nothing more, I would say."

Zalman stood straight and loomed over the Pirate Lord. "You touch her, and I will pull off your arms and beat you to death with them."

Aeric leaned back, and he lifted his hands in surrender. He laughed. "I believe you," he said. "I meant no offense."

Zalman grunted, passed a hand over his bald head, and leaned against the railing again.

Beaming over at him, Aeric said, "Have you told her?"

He squinted back at the man. "Told her what?"

"That you care for her."

Zalman opened his mouth to protest, but nothing came out. He gaped there for a few seconds and then closed his mouth. "It is … complicated."

"Ah, I see," Aeric said. "Often it is. Very. But I will give you some unsolicited advice. Being called a Pirate Lord has its advantages, after all. Pirates often go where they are unwanted."

Facing Aeric again, Zalman saw the man staring off into the sky as if something else filled his vision, perhaps a memory of long ago.

"There are few treasures in the world," Aeric said. "Nothing like love, truly caring for another. You will regret nothing in your life more than letting something like that slip away."

Zalman clenched his teeth. "She hates me," he said.

Aeric shrugged. "She may," he said. "But how will you ever know for sure unless you tell her?" He gave Zalman a pat on the shoulder. "I have work to do and will leave you to think on it." He left the deck, and Zalman was alone.

Carys was far away now, climbing up the rope ladder that led to the top of the foremast where the crow's nest sat. He remembered the first time he met her, how she was so small and yet incredibly strong. And yes, more than beautiful. A part of him wanted to cross the deck and join her at the bow, just to be with her, maybe tell her these things.

But he could not move his feet. First, Caleb's command that he not touch his sister loomed in his memory. But even if Caleb had never said those words, Zalman knew he wasn't man enough for her. There were better men, finer men than he. And last, Zalman's failure to protect her in Landen haunted him; as much as his mind knew it was not his fault, his heart condemned him. He could not get the image and the fear out of his mind.

So he leaned against the railing and watched her.

He couldn't tell her. Not today.

———

After a full day of traveling across the mountains of Kaleti, up narrow paths and through thick forests and around low peaks, Eshlyn and the group with her had to camp that night. Tobiah guessed that they were a few hours away from the mines. There wasn't a clearing large enough for all fifty of their group, so they all found places to rest for the night, whether a small clearing or between roots of large trees. Tobiah climbed a thick trunk and sat in a low branch. Five men volunteered for watches during the night.

Eshlyn slept that night with a clear feeling that the Mahakar was near. What was he waiting for? She didn't sense that he was trying to communicate with her, but he was near. Her sleep was fitful and anxious.

They rose early the next day and made their way to the mines. Winding through the forest, climbing up steep inclines and making their way around difficult terrain, they reached the mines as the sun peeked over the trees to the east.

She smelled the place long before she saw it – an acidic stench mixed with a smoke that billowed into the sky to the west. Grimacing at the smell, they made their way through the brush and neared the mines of Kaleti.

A gigantic, flat shelf had been cut into the mountain and extended out fifty mitres and stopped at a sheer cliff. The ledge was three hundred mitres long, and Eshlyn could see large holes dug down into the ledge, ten or fifteen mitres in diameter, ladders leading down into them from the side. Dark smoke and dust climbed into the air from the massive shafts. She could see four of these gaps in the earth.

And she could feel the sorrow of the Mahakar. Then the anger. He drew closer. Could he see what she saw? Feel her own sadness and anger?

Men and women climbed down into the shafts, all dark-skinned people of Lior, naked or wearing small loin cloths. They were bone-thin with glassy eyes, Sorced eyes. Some working off to the side of the shafts were shackled at hands and feet, breaking rocks or sifting gold out of the dirt. Every one was shaved bald. Elves in simple gray robes with gladi at their side and whips in their hands stood among the slaves. If a man or woman slowed in their work, even for a moment, a whip would snap and strike at them. Most of the slaves had open wounds from small cuts and gashes over their bodies next to scars from previous wounds.

As they were beaten, the slaves had minimum reactions, as if receiving lashes from an elven whip was common.

Beyond the mineshafts, she saw two long, rectangular, wooden buildings.

"The elves live there," Tobiah mumbled to her as he followed her gaze. To the right of those buildings caves were carved into the side of the mountain, two of them, and both with iron bars over them.

Athelwulf's whispered voice in her ear. "One for the women. The other for the men."

Eshlyn drew her sword and heard the movement behind her. She turned to see Athelwulf and the other men dropping their packs in the brush or behind a tree and gathering their weapons. Athelwulf had his bow in hand and an arrow nocked. She dropped her own pack in the brush.

She looked at Ath and kept her own voice low. "What do you suggest?"

"Tobiah and I will create a diversion with most of the men. We will attack the elves and draw their attention to this end of the ledge. Once the guard are engaged, you take ten men around to the left and make your way to those slaves and free the ones in the caves."

Good enough plan, she thought. Athelwulf asked Tobiah for ten men to go with Eshlyn. As they made the arrangements, Eshlyn gripped her sword and thought of the men in the forest she had killed. She swore to them, and to El, to never kill again unless it was necessary. She took deep breaths and prayed to El for his help to keep her wits about her, to act with thought and intention, not to simply react.

Opening her eyes, Athelwulf knelt next to her again. "Are you okay?" he asked.

She nodded.

"Very well," he said. "Then let us begin."

———

Athelwulf reminded the men of the instructions he gave while on the journey: fire arrows only when the slaves are clear; strike hard and fast with the elves – they are guard and most will not be experienced militan. The Empire did not send its best soldiers to guard the slaves at a remote mine in the mountains of Lior. However, even half-trained militan possessed gladi that could kill.

Tobiah was a good man and leader. The other men respected him and listened to him. Athelwulf split their forty men into two squads of twenty, Tobiah leading the other squad. Athelwulf would attack to the left of the first shaft along the cliff, and Tobiah would charge along the right side next to the side of the mountain. Eshlyn would follow with her ten men after they drew out the bulk of the guard. He left it to her to make that decision.

After making sure each man had his assignment, he marked his target and checked the nocked arrow in his bow. Ready. Athelwulf could see fifty guard in various places amidst the slaves from his position to the buildings on the far end. How many were there total? No way to know now, but he assumed less than a third were on shift here, which would place their numbers at close to two hundred.

Seeing the fear and resolution in Tobiah's eyes, Athelwulf emerged from the trees, stopped, drew back the arrow, and fired.

A guard a hundred mitres away, standing alone, found an arrow stuck into the nape of his neck. He gurgled as he died.

Athelwulf advanced, twenty men behind him, and had another arrow drawn before the first hit its target. He fired again, hitting another guard. As Tobiah's group followed, 40 men broke from the trees, experienced hunters with the bow, lobbing arrows at the guard spread out among the slaves. Within a few seconds, Athelwulf saw thirty guard fall to arrows, some with more than one in their flesh.

The other guard reacted, yelling and shouting out for reinforcements along with the screeches and cries of the dying. Athelwulf shouldered his bow and pulled his sword as he sprinted forward and cut down a guard, his sword severing the arm and then slashing through the abdomen. Beorgai raced behind him, but he didn't leave many for them to fight – he killed three more as he neared the first shaft, an enormous hole in the ground that stank of death and waste. Slaves froze on the ladder.

More elves rushed toward them from the buildings at the far end, barracks and perhaps a common building of some sort of storage or both. They stumbled over their own weapons and tightened their belts as they ran in a large group, but Athelwulf counted near eighty elves.

Athelwulf halted a few mitres past the first shaft, the acid of smoke filled his nose as he drew in breath and put the unforged sword in his scabbard. He pulled the bow from his shoulder and began firing into the guards some sixty mitres away.

As other Beorgai reached him and nocked their own arrows, Athelwulf shouted, "Take as many as you can! Fire into the middle of the crowd!" His voice was loud enough to reach Tobiah and his squad who also fired arrows into the elves as they rounded the nearer building.

Getting low on arrows, Athelwulf placed his short bow back across his shoulder and drew the unforged sword. Guard running between the slaves closed in. He fought with two at once, disarming one and severing the other's leg at the knee. As he killed the elf he disarmed, he heard a low bellow off to his right.

He searched the skies in that direction. Was it the Mahakar? The sound wasn't coming from above him, however. Past the second shaft, he could see that another cave was cut into the side of the mountain but not enough to give a view of what made the sound. He had an idea, however, and not one that comforted him.

Searching the elves that came from the far end of the ledge, He watched one break off to the right and sprint in the direction of the growling, nasty, evil sound. A hungry sound.

To his left, Eshlyn led her ten men past him and to the iron-barred cages where some of the slaves remained.

Athelwulf ran past the second shaft, dodging one guard's attack and kicking him into the shaft, and as the elf fell down into the hole, his arms flailed and he hollered, an echo reaching Athelwulf's ears. He had to see for himself what made that noise. The lone elf had almost reached the source of the noise. He carried a large iron key, almost as long as a gladus.

Rounding the second massive shaft and leaping to see over the slaves and men and elves fighting between them, Athelwulf could now see a larger cave, much taller than the ones that held the slaves. The cave was more than twenty mitres tall, and the iron bars over the mouth of the cave were thick. A giant lock held a gate on the makeshift cage. The cave held something, and it was angry.

Athelwulf could see only a shadow beyond those bars, but he put away his sword and readied his bow again. He had to put that elf down. The elf fumbled with the key as he came within ten paces. The battle raging around him, Athelwulf drew and fired. The arrow entered the elf's temple, and he fell, the key tumbling to the ground.

More elves raced behind the one that just died to finish his mission, ten more, and Athelwulf whispered, "El help me." He had five arrows left.

He shot them, taking out the ones in the front, emptying his quiver and killing five of the elves. Athelwulf loped through the fray and neared the men of the Beorgai on purpose. He pulled arrows from their quivers as he passed them and took out one guard after another. Two had the key now, and he took out one, but he was out of arrows and the nearest Beorgai was too far away. The last elf took the key and opened the lock, using all his strength and both hands and eyeing Athelwulf nervously.

The enormous gate was gripped by large claws with three fingers and pushed open. A creature emerged from the cave and into the sun, its black eyes squinted against the light. It was not made for the light or the day, and it seemed sleepy. But it was waking. It stood to its full height of fifteen mitres on short, stubby, thick legs, a short tail with spikes at the end trailing behind it. It had four arms, two on each side, long and muscular arms with three-fingered claws. Stretching its broad shoulders, its body covered with dark orange scales, the creature raised its head, revealing two black horns. It opened its long snout, baring black teeth like daggers and two black tusks thrust from the bottom jaw as it roared.

A Kryan trodall. It was a creature from Chialos, the island south of Lior, and some relation to a crizzard, but it had been trained and bred by elves of war for different purposes. It would kill every human in sight, slave or warrior.

Athelwulf dropped his bow and drew his unforged sword and ran towards the beast.

—+—

Eshlyn passed the first building, ten men pacing behind her. She had also heard the bellow of the creature; she knew it wasn't the Mahakar.

But he was close. He felt almost next to her. She scanned the skies and saw nothing.

She did not turn and look over to the other creature, however. She did not want to be distracted from her own mission.

Passing between the two buildings – the first was a barracks, she could see now, and the second held a large common area with storage at the far end. She ran towards the cages.

Fifty elves stood in her way, their swords drawn.

Shoggit, she thought. She gripped her own sword in her hand and stopped to within five mitres of the guard.

"Note this," one of them said, wearing a breastplate – a leader? "This woman brought some monkeys from the forest with her."

She sneered at him, raised her sword and dropped into a crouch, as Caleb taught her. The image of the two dead men in the forest came to her, and so she calmed herself and refused to let the elves force her into a reaction. She would act.

The other men with her shouted and began to attack. "Stop!" she said.

And they did. She was the *Bashawyn*, after all. As skilled as she might be, or the men around her, it was fifty against eleven. Even minimally trained, the elves had the advantage of numbers. But she came to free those slaves.

"They will come to us," she said. "Watch over one another."

A few men behind her nocked arrows and readied for the battle.

The leader of the elves raised his gladus and called his guard to attack.

Arrows from the Beorgai fired, and a handful of elves dropped, but within a heartbeat her squad was surrounded and fighting for their lives. She raised her sword and parried two gladi before striking down one of the guard and then engaging the other again.

Outnumbered, she heard the cries of Beorgai as they were wouned or killed. She shouted in frustration as she removed the arm of one guard to only have him replaced by two more trying to kill her.

Eshlyn heard the beating of wings and the guttural growl before she saw him. The Mahakar descended upon the elves, paws crushing the guard, then throwing them into the air with his jaws. A dozen elves died within a moment. Some elves screamed in fear and fright, but some turned in desperation to attack, stabbing at the large beast.

The Mahakar needed help.

"Come!" she cried. "Attack now! Help the Mahakar!"

Arrows were loosed, elves fell, and men rushed forward with their *corran* blocking gladi and slicing at necks, arms and thighs, deep gashes that spurted blood. They cut down elf after elf. Eshlyn stalked forward. She blocked the attack of two elves, severed the wrist of one and the ankle of the second. Disarming the second, she hit him in the nose with the hilt of Kenric's sword and the other on the back of the head. Both crumpled, unconscious.

Another guard approached her and slashed at her face. She ducked it and kicked him in the groin. He bent over in pain, his face reddening, and she kneed him between the eyes. The elf collapsed, and she kicked away his sword.

As she turned, the short battle was over. Between the Mahakar and her own ten men, the elves were dead or out of commission within moments. The Mahakar peered at her.

"You do like to make an entrance," she said and stepped up to him. She buried her face into the white fur of his neck. "Thank you," she whispered.

Pulling away from him, she jogged over to the first cage, the one that held men. The slaves within huddled against the back of the cave. Their faces were blank and empty, but they clutched one another in fear. "We are here to free you," she said, but they did not respond.

Clenching her stomach, she brought the unforged sword down upon the lock, and Kenric's blade cut through the iron easily. She sidled over to the other cage, the women also pressed against the back of the cave. Eshlyn sliced through the lock and opened the gate.

She would not have admitted it to anyone, but in her mind, she imagined men and women smiling and ready to be free, people on their knees and thanking her. Of course she would humbly tell them to stand and be free, and they would weep with joy at realizing the dream of freedom from the elves.

But that did not happen. No one moved. With both gates open, not one soul left the cages.

—————

The trodall tore into the humanity before it. It swiped with its arms and killed three slaves with his claws, grabbed a fourth and bit her in half.

The men of the Beorgai froze at the monstrosity that appeared on the ledge of the mines. Athelwulf ran towards the beast and shouted. "Tobiah!"

The man blinked, fear written on his face.

"I'll take the trodall," Athelwulf said. "You lead the men to finish off the guard!"

He didn't slow to make sure Tobiah obeyed, but his brother-in-law turned to shout at the Beorgai around him.

The trodall crushed a slave under his foot, whose arms and legs twitched in a panic as he died. Then it reached out with the two arms on its left side and grabbed one of the Beorgai. The warrior stabbed at the trodall with his *corran*, but the blades bounced off of the orange reptilian skin of the creature. The trodall pulled the screaming man in two.

Athelwulf growled and reached the trodall. He ducked an arm, then rolled under another one, and as he came to his feet, he slashed at the leg of the trodall with all his might. The unforged sword cut into the leg of the monster, and it stumbled. But it attacked again with more arms. Athelwulf leapt back as a fist hit next to him, and the ground shook; he had no time. He sprung and flipped backwards as a claw came at him. He was no circus performer, and he landed on his hands and knees, rolling to his right as another claw dug a mitre trench into the dirt.

Making it to his feet, Athelwulf measured the next strike from one of the trodall's left arms, and he stepped closer to the monster and swung the sword, cutting off one of the trodall's fingers. The creature roared in pain and retreated.

Arrows began to hit the trodall, but they were only an annoyance, bouncing off of the creature's hide or shattering upon impact.

Athelwulf took advantage of the moment and charged the trodall, jumping and stabbing the unforged sword into the abdomen. The sword sunk into the creature's skin, but an arm swung at him in response. Athelwulf curled into a ball as the fist smacked him to the left. He tumbled end over end through the air and hit the dirt as the air left him in a heave. Gasping for breath, he knew he had to get up. Somehow, he had held on to the sword.

His vision was blurred, dizzy, but he saw an orange, muscular arm swing towards him. As Athelwulf stood to his feet without breath, he reacted on instinct, lifting the unforged sword and hacking into the trodall arm. He cut clean through the creature's forearm, and it hung by a thin piece of flesh.

But as he swung, he began to catch his breath and he stumbled, off balance. His left arm extended to the side to right himself, and the long black talon at the end of a trodall claw grabbed his arm and tore it from his shoulder.

Athelwulf howled in pain and shock, and the beast was on top of him, also bellowing in rage and agony. Retreating and barely on his feet, Athelwulf knew the battle was done. In one desperate move, he spun and, with his right hand, hurled the unforged sword at the trodall like a missile. The blade sunk to the hilt into the middle of the trodall's chest.

The trodall staggered, clutching its chest with one of its claws. A hideous and sickening sound escaped his maw. But the trodall reached out with another hand for Athelwulf.

He couldn't move fast enough. He took one final step, but the creature's claw closed in around him, lifted, and began to crush the life from him.

—+—

The men of the Beorgai were trying to coax the men and women from the cages when Eshlyn finally looked over to the east to see the large monster. She stopped in midstep, motionless in horror. The eyes and horns on its head, the black talons on its three-fingered claws, they all reminded her of the demics and the wall of Ketan. But it was far larger than even the Demilord, and its long snout and tail made it more like a lizard.

Athelwulf had been fighting the monster, and they were both wounded. Athelwulf was missing an arm.

That woke her from her fearful daze, and she turned to the Mahakar. Pointing to the creature, she cried out, "Help him, please."

The Mahakar bared his fangs at the monster, spread his wings, and took to the air towards it.

Eshlyn sprinted after him. The tiger flew low and fast. She saw Ath fling his sword and spear the monster. Then he was lifted into the air with a claw.

With a fluttering of large white wings and a snarl, the Mahakar attacked the monster from behind, opening his mouth and biting down upon the neck. The creature bellowed and dropped Athelwulf's limp form to the ground. The Mahakar latched on with his own claws and beat his wings, pulling the creature back. It struck back at the tiger with its own fists and talons, but the Mahakar would not relent as a constant and fierce growl emanated from the tiger.

Reaching the two massive beasts as they fought, Eshlyn took her sword and hacked at one of the demic-like legs, the unforged sword cutting deep into the orange flesh. Amid the noise and roaring and growling, Eshlyn glimpsed up and saw the Mahakar place one paw against the side of the creature's head and the other on its shoulder. Black blood spurted from his mouth as the tiger bit down further, and it began to tear the head from the creature's shoulders.

"*Bashawyn!* Get away!" Tobiah's voice warned her from behind.

The creature shrieked and flailed, and Eshlyn ran back towards Athelwulf. She gawked at how the tiger would not let go, tore at the evil creature with all his might, the wings pounding the air, creating a furious wind that tossed Eshlyn's hair while his fangs sunk deeper and deeper into the scaly flesh of the monster. The two beasts from a fire tale wrestled and struggled for eternal seconds on end, but finally, with one last heaving effort, the Mahakar tore the head from the monster's body, black blood a fountain for a moment, and they both fell forward together. The tiger stood on the creature's back and spread his wings with slight cuts from the trodall talons.

The Mahakar roared.

Eshlyn knelt next to Athelwulf, his body bloody, mangled and broken. She rolled him from his side to his back, but he showed no reaction. His eyes were open but focused on nothing.

"No, no, no," she kept saying, and she cradled his head in her lap. *You can't die. Not now. Not after Esai. No. Please, El. Please. No.*

He spoke no words as his breathing stopped; his mouth went slack, his body still. She held Athelwulf, a *Sohan-el* and good friend, until he died.

And she fell upon his corpse and wept.

CHAPTER 23

THROUGH THE STORM

Aden lay across the bed his division brought for him. They gave him a private room in the education building, an office of some sort, but plenty big for his stay while in Biram.

Lyam ran a stitch through both sides of the gash on Aden's shoulder and pulled the wound closed. Aden winced and clenched his teeth. The salve from the Ghosts of Saten lessened the pain, but it still hurt enough for Aden to bite back a couple curses. He tried to take his mind off of the pain by talking to Lyam.

"I heard you lost a lot of men," Aden said. "How are you doin'?"

Lyam was intent on his work. But Aden could see the sorrow in his face. Lyam paused and shrugged.

As he continued to sew up the wound, Aden gasped at the needle thrust through his skin.

"You heard how Caleb put the elves to work?" Aden asked.

The day after the battle had been a somber one. No celebrations. The dead seemed endless, but they counted the corpses just the same. In the end, only 600 elven militan remained out of an original 4,000, almost an entire legion strong. Almost 500 of that number were in good health and uninjured, captured in the final push at the center of Biram. Caleb set those 500 to work burying the dead. That would take days for them to complete.

They lowered the impaled dead citizens of Biram first, almost 8,000 people. Then they buried them. The elves were still working on that, but next they would bury the dead of the human army, the *Hamon-el*. They lost nearly 1,500 of their own force of 4,000. Another four hundred were injured, like Aden. Two *Sohan-el* had fallen, Pavo and Hekka, good men. All the humans would get an individual grave to the west of the city. Last, the elf prisoners would bury their own in a mass grave to the east of the city.

At the mention of Caleb's name, Lyam's eyes flashed with anger then returned to sorrow.

"Should take a few days, maybe a ninedays," Aden said in a low voice. "Think we could use the rest."

Lyam snorted.

"Caleb not sayin' where we're goin' next, though," Aden said. "But we got time to figure it out."

Lyam pulled the last stitch with a grimace.

Aden squealed. "Crit on a frog!"

"Done," Lyam said, and he left Aden alone without a word.

The door was closed behind Lyam when Aden said, "Hey, thanks!" He sat motionless for a moment and made a note to talk to Caleb about Lyam, worried about his friend.

Aden's chest and shoulder hurt, and he couldn't move his arm without considerable pain. Sitting up, he went over to his pack next to the bed. At the bottom of the pack, his hand gripped a bottle. He retrieved the bottle, and with the afternoon sun shining through the long window, he lifted the glass container to allow the light to search the substance within.

It appeared to be simple, clear water, but it was far from normal water.

When Aden and Caleb had climbed Mount Elarus and pushed through the dark cloud and made it to the Living Stone, a pool of water stretched out before the Stone. Drinking the water completely refreshed and filled him with energy and a deep satisfaction. He had filled his canteen with the water and carried it down the mountain with him. Once in Ketan again, he placed the water into this bottle as a reminder of his time and what El said to him at the Stone.

After his battle with the Wraith in Ketan days ago, he wondered what would happen if he drank the water again. What would it do to his injuries? He had opened the bottle and taken a sip. His wounds healed within an hour. He told no one.

Now here in Biram and injured again, he uncorked the bottle with a wince and took a drink. He felt the pain begin to recede in the next moment. There was more mobility in his arm. The refreshment and contentment also came. He corked the bottle again and placed it in the bottom of his bag.

A sadness rose up in his chest, guilt for keeping this to himself. Others were injured, but what could he do? There was not enough for everyone. At least, that was how he justified it in his mind, as flimsy as the excuse was.

As he sat on the bed again, a knock came at the door.

"Come," he said.

Tamya entered, the bloodwolf at her heels.

Aden smiled at her, but she did not return the gesture. He was used to that.

"I just came to see how you were doing," she said.

"Better," he said.

"Good," she said. "You always did seem to heal quick."

Feeling awkward, he forced a chuckle, but Tamya paced in the room. After the battle, Tamya had also been quiet and brooding. Well, more than normal. She lingered now at the door.

"Hey," he said. "What is it?"

She could not look him in the eye. "I ... I have to tell you something."

He sat up straight. "Okay."

"You know, during the battle, it got kinda crazy," she began.

Aden scoffed. "Yeah."

"Well, I know Caleb warned us, even trained us, but at one point, I turned and ..." She gazed up at him.

He waited, silent.

Tamya swallowed hard. "You know Dervan died during the battle," she said.

His brow furrowed.

"In the battle, we were fighting, and it was crazy, like I said, elves everywhere, and ... well, there's no excuse. I turned and ..." Tamya had a pained grimace on her face. "I killed him. I didn't mean to, but there it is."

"Oh, Tamya," he said and began to stand from the bed, to go to her.

Tamya put out a hand. "No. Stop." She cleared her throat. "I thought you should know. It is your division. I'll put in my resignation as platoon leader later tonight with Caleb. But I thought you should know first."

She spun to go.

His mouth hung open for a moment, then he shook off his daze. "Hey, wait," he said. As she kept going for the door, he said. "Tamya, *wait*."

The bloodwolf stopped and sat on his haunches. Tamya scowled at him. "You're no shoggin' help at all," she muttered. Hema whined at her.

With her back to him, he spoke to her anyway. "It was an accident. I know you didn't mean it. And you're not the only one this happened to. I heard about three others yesterday."

Tamya shook her head. "You don't get it," she said, and she swiveled around to him and pointed at her chest. "I was his leader, not just another soldier or something. And I killed him."

"Not on purpose, though," he said.

"Doesn't matter," she said. "I don't get to be a leader anymore. Not after this. I should have done better, been better."

"Well, I do not accept your resignation," Aden said. "You can shove it up your arse."

"What?" She waved her hands in the air. "Shog you. I'll just go to Caleb now. He'll remove me as a leader."

"No he won't," Aden said, and he did stand now. He took a step towards her. "Because I'm going to go with you and tell him that he can't."

"You think you can tell the breakin' *Brendel* what to do?" she yelled at him.

"To the real," he said. "In this, he'll let me make the decision about my own division."

Her head hung, she put her hands on her hips, and she took deep, heaving breaths.

"Listen," Aden said, his voice softening. "You feel like crit. I get it. I would, too. But it was an honest accident. The very fact that you feel so bad about it proves you need to be a leader. It proves I want you as one of my platoon commanders."

A long minute passed in silence. "Why do you have to be so ... *good*?" she mumbled.

It did not sound like a question she wanted answered. But he did anyway. "You'd rather I be a shogger to everyone? To you?"

The pain in her eyes said, *Yes, sometimes I actually do.*

"I have to go," she said all of a sudden.

He took another step towards her, reached for her. "Tamya, stay," he said. "Please."

This time, her face fell. "Don't do that," she said. "Don't." Her voice sounded tired, exhausted.

"Do what?"

"Look at me like that."

He dropped his hand. "I don't understand."

"Like Berran used to."

Aden blinked slowly and ran a hand through his bushy hair. "I – I ..." he stammered.

"You see the good in everyone. Why? Why do you do that? Berran did that, too. But they killed him anyway, you know."

"I know," he said.

"But you don't. Some people, there's no good in them. There's just hate and bitterness and rage."

He took a step towards her, but she backed away to the door. The bloodwolf regarded them both.

"You think you know but you don't," she said. "Even before Anneton, before Berran and my baby, when I was in Oshra, things happened. Things I can't forget. They haunt me. And killing Dervan? It's just one more thing."

"Then stay and tell me. I want to know it all. I'm not goin' anywhere."

"You think you want to know," she said. "But you don't."

Breathing air in through his nose, he exhaled. "I do. Just start with one thing. You never told me your baby's name. What was your baby's name?"

Her glare of accusation was like a punch in the gut. She opened the door and ran from the room. Hema barked at him and padded after her.

Aden put his hands on his hips in an empty room.

———

A storm gathered to the east, black clouds darkening the sky over the sea far away.

The Last Serpent rendezvoused with four other ships a few kilomitres away from a large island with ruins that Carys could barely see, ruins of white stone. They all dropped anchor and three of the ships sent a rowboat over to *The Last Serpent*. The other kanalor were coming aboard Aeric's ship to witness the challenge.

The last ship drew parallel to *The Last Serpent* in the opposite direction, and a twenty mitre long plank, a mitre and a half wide, was laid between the two ships, which were also tied together by ropes. A man on the deck claimed the name of the ship was *The Titan Song*, Mikayla's vessel.

The first man up the side of *The Last Serpent* with his second in command was of average height but with a large belly. Aeric approached the man and embraced him. "Mana, my friend," Aeric said. "Welcome."

"It is good to see you again," Mana said, his long, thin beard moving on his face as he spoke. He had lighter skin than Aeric, but still a bronze color. "I do not appreciate these circumstances, however."

"I understand," Aeric said. "But tradition holds, no?"

Mana shrugged. "If it must, it must."

Aeric grinned and turned to Carys and Zalman, who stood behind her. "Allow me to introduce our special guests," Aeric said. "This large man is Zalman, a hero of the Battle of Ketan and companion of the *Brendel*."

"The *Brendel*?" Mana said. "Never heard of him."

"A great lord in the north," Aeric said.

"Actually, he ..." Carys began.

But Aeric cut her off. "And this is the *Brendel*'s sister, an emissary of the great city of Ketan. Her name is Carys."

Mana extended a hand to Carys. She placed hers within it, and he smirked at her. "If the flowers in Ketan are half as beautiful, then I wish they were in every room of my palace."

She could hear Zalman grunt behind her. Feeling herself blush, she said, "Thank you. Well met."

"This is Mana of Inoa," Aeric said. "Kanalor and captain of *The Island Maiden*."

"Well met," he said.

Two other men came up on the deck, the younger assisting the elder onto the ship. Aeric approached the elder, a balding man with graying hair, tall and thin. They also embraced, called each other brothers and exchanged their pleasantries. The older man was introduced as Tangi, the Kanalor of Makana and captain of *The Dawnsun*. The older man also made a comment on her beauty, and she blushed again. Were they all trained to compliment women so?

Last, a diminutive man reached the deck, and his face was twisted in anger. "It is a shoggin' hot day for this crit!" he said as his feet hit the deck. "And that storm will be on us sooner than a whale can swallow a breakin' guppy."

Carys saw the small man, brown skin with long straight hair, and she muttered, "A dwarf among the pirates?"

The short man paused and sneered at her. "I'm no dwarf!"

Aeric approached the man. "Loto, it is a common mistake," he said.

Loto put his hands on his hips and spoke to Carys. "I am a man and give me a sword and I'm more man than any on this deck," he said. "You can take that as well as you like."

"I'm sorry," Carys said, hearing Zalman stifle a chuckle behind her. She approached him. "I am Carys, sister to the *Brendel*. I come from Ketan to see the men of the Kanan Eres."

"The *Brendel*? Ketan?" Loto said. "Never heard o' em." He bowed and grinned at her. "I am Loto, Kanalor of the Kahale and captain of the greatest ship in the five seas, *The Godshark*."

Tangi crossed his arms and lifted his chin. "*The Dawnsun* might have something to say about that," the older lord said. "If not *The Last Serpent*, as well."

"Will you shut your stankhold, Lord Tangi?" Loto said. "I haven't even given this fine woman the compliment due her!"

"Brothers, brothers," Aeric said. "We all know the ways, do we not?"

Every lord on the deck said in unison, "We do."

Aeric bowed to them. "As do I. Now please come to the railing of the deck. As you said, Lord Loto, there is a storm coming. Let us get this over with quickly."

Carys peered out to the east again, and the storm was noticeably closer, moving in fast. The breeze stirred her blond hair. The deck beneath her rose and fell.

Loto drew close to her and smiled again. "My pardons, lady. The most beautiful dawns I have ever seen over the Theron Ocean all pale next to you."

She didn't blush this time. "You are too kind," she said. "Well met."

"And you," he said.

They were all led to the railing of the deck. Aeric earlier explained how the three remaining lords would be guests upon the ship of the current Kanacyn. They would observe the duel from the deck of Aeric's ship. Once the duel was done, there would be a meeting of the five lords where they would discuss and vote. Carys thought it a complicated process, for Pirates.

Men and women lined against the railing as Zalman stood next to her and the big gedder loomed over her.

Looking across the long plank spread between the two ships, a woman waited at the far end, her crew observing from *The Titan Song*. She was tall and athletic, thin but strong. Her light chocolate skin was covered in tattoos in patterns that Carys didn't recognize, and her hair was cropped short. There was a hard, bitter set to her eyes. The woman stepped onto the plank, a saber at her waist. Mikayla.

Aeric sighed before stepping up onto the plank. Carys was next to him.

"Can't you wait until the storm has passed?" Carys asked. "Do this another time?"

"Does life wait for storms to pass?" Aeric answered. "As much as we attempt to avoid them, we all must navigate them sooner or later."

"Are you afraid?" Carys said.

"Of what?" Aeric said.

"Of her?"

He shook his head. "No. Not of her. Never. Afraid *for* her? Afraid for us all? Yes."

"Do you know her well? Can you beat her?"

Aeric laughed, but his eyes were sad. "Beat her? Even if I win, I'll never beat her. She has my heart. Know her? Well, I should. She's my wife."

He stepped up onto the plank as Carys watched him, speechless.

The clouds neared. Both ships rocked with the rising waves.

"I am Aeric De'Cal, son of Blane De'Cal, Kanalor of Enakai, captain of *The Last Serpent*, and Kanacyn of the Kananweld. Who comes to challenge me?" His voice carried over the water like a king.

Mikayla set her face against the breeze. "I am Mikayla De'Cal, daughter of Marc Le'San, Kanalor of Halemano and captain of *The Titan Song*. I come to challenge you."

"And what is your challenge?"

"I say before all gathered here that you have become weak in your leadership," Mikayla said. "I call upon the Pirates to raid the lands of men and elves. Our children are hungry, and there are more riches to take from the elves, from the men of Lior and Veradis and resources that would help our people. If I am Pirate Lord, then we will fight the elves and raid the villages."

"Overextending ourselves will bring war with the Empire," Aeric said. "We cannot stand against them. Maybe once, when we were strong, but not now. Not like this."

Mikayla snorted. "We die either way, Aeric. We have a better chance of survival my way."

"No," Aeric said. "I don't think so."

"Then choose your weapon," Mikayla said.

"Don't do this, Kayla," Aeric said. "Please."

"Do you refuse the challenge?" she said across the gap.

Aeric pointed to his right, to the island and the ruins. "That is the ancient city of Evanel," he said. "Isam, a great king and *Sohan-el*, once called it the most beautiful city on earth. He fell in love with her and stayed there the rest of his days. Now it is a memory. We spent our marriage ninedays in those ruins, remember?"

"I do," she said.

"Then don't do this," he said. "Come to my cabin. Let's talk about this."

Mikayla stared at him. "Will you lead us in more raids?"

Aeric spread his hands. "I cannot. Not against other men."

Thunder reverberated across the sky.

"Then choose your weapon," she said.

"Kayla, I ..."

"Choose your weapon!" she shouted.

Aeric took a step further onto the plank. "Very well," he said. He removed his sword and scabbard, and he tossed it to his second, Bade. "I choose no weapon."

Mikayla's brow furrowed. "What are you doing? Pick up the sword. You know we have to do this."

"There is no part of the tradition that says what weapon we must use or if we must. Only that we must choose. And I have chosen."

"Fine, you sodden man," she muttered and removed her own saber, which she threw to a man on the deck of *The Titan Song*. "Then we will fight hand to hand. Happy?"

"No," he said. "Not at all."

"Come, then," Mikayla said, and she walked forward across the narrow wood.

Aeric strode to meet her.

Lightning flashed across the sky above them.

Carys felt the conflict within her as the husband and wife met to decide the leadership of a people. If Mikayla won, Carys wondered if she could convince the Pirates to be more aggressive against the Kryan ships, which would help Caleb and the revolution. But she trusted Aeric. Shoggit, she liked the man, and he seemed like a good leader, cared about his people. She couldn't bring herself to wish his defeat.

The clouds were almost directly overhead now.

Mikayla punched and struck at her husband as they drew close; Aeric raised his arms and blocked each strike. He retreated a step at a time, ducking one fist and lifting a knee to fend off a kick. Mikayla sneered and spun into a backhand. Leaning back, Aeric dodged the blow, but her momentum carried her off balance, and as the ships heaved on the growing violence of the water, she almost careened off the board. Aeric reached out and caught her waist with his hands.

"I have you, my love," he said.

She stepped down on his foot, turning and throwing an open palm towards his face. He yelled in pain and leapt back, her hand glancing off of his cheek.

It began to rain. The drops fell a few at a time, but they were big drops. The rain increased, and soon they were all soaked in the deluge.

And the plank became wet. As Aeric approached Mikayla again, his footing wasn't as sure. More thunder boomed in the dark sky, and the beam between the ships constantly shifted, rose and fell. The ropes between the ships tightened as the distance between them closed then stretched as the storm fell upon them. The ships began to circle together, and Carys felt a nausea rise in her belly.

Mikayla feinted with a punch then kicked Aeric in the gut. He retreated and bent over for a moment, recovering in time to block another kick and weave away from an uppercut. She twirled again, her foot swinging high; Aeric ducked and took another step back, his foot sliding a little on the wet wood. Mikayla attacked with a series of fierce strikes, high and low, kicks and punches, most blocked or absorbed by Aeric's shoulder or hip. They fought five mitres away from *The Last Serpent* now.

As Mikayla struck out again, Aeric reached out and grabbed her hands and twisted them so that she cried out and dropped to her knees. A strong wind blew, rocking both ships, and Mikayla wavered and fell from the plank.

Holding onto her hands, Aeric pitched forward onto the plank, his chest against the wood and his legs hugging the sides. Gasps from around her, Carys saw the woman dangling from her husband's arms. They were both wet, and their grip began to slip. As the ships swayed and undulated, Carys heard the plank begin to creak and groan with the strain, and she saw it start to break at the center.

Mikayla glanced down and then up at her husband with fear.

"Hold on," Aeric shouted amidst the rain and the thunder and lightning. He pulled her towards his ship and then back the other direction. He swung her back and forth for a few moments, and each time she got closer to the ropes that hung down along the hull of *The Last Serpent*. One last time, with a yell of effort, Aeric swung her at the hull and released her. She flew through the air, dropping, but she reached out and grabbed the ropes, crying out but attached to the hull. After a second to collect herself, she climbed up the side of the ship.

The plank cracked and split at the center, and Aeric held fast as his half swept down and smacked against the hull. Aeric hit the side of his own ship, hard, and he bounced off and fell into the savage waves below.

"Aeric!" Mikayla cried, her arms at the railing.

Carys scanned along both ships and waited for someone to help Aeric, anyone, but no one moved. Looking down at the water, she saw an arm rise above the water, then his head bob above for an urgent breath. *Shoggers*, she thought. *Why isn't anyone going in after him?*

She wasn't a great swimmer herself, but Carys was about to jump into the water to help the man when a large figure stepped up on the railing and dove into the water. She whispered his name, both in awe and frustration. *Zalman.*

He hit the water like an arrow, his body straight. When did he take off his shoes? Zalman was under the water for a moment too long, to her mind, at least, but he came up with his arm around Aeric's neck. Aeric thrashed in the water, weakly, but Zalman rose up and punched the Pirate Lord in the face, knocking him into submission. Zalman fought the waves, struggling to get back to the side of the ship, the ship that heaved in the waves.

"Throw him some ropes!" Carys said, and the men on the deck stared at her like she had a horn coming out of her nose. *Shoggers*, she thought, turning to push through the men and women around her. She found a length of rope, prayed to El it would be long enough, and she hurried back to the railing. Lashing one end to the rail, she threw the other down to Zalman, who was at the side of the ship now. Carys prayed again that she had tied the rope tight enough, but it proved secure as Zalman gripped the rope and climbed the hull.

Mikayla cursed and scurried down to where she could help lift Aeric up and over to the deck.

The three other kanalor and the men on the deck drew their weapons as they surrounded Carys and Zalman, a stirring Aeric and panting Mikayla behind them. The pirates had angry, murderous looks.

Carys stood to her feet and drew her own unforged sword before a hundred men. "What the shog is this?" she shouted through the sound of thunder and rain.

Mana spoke above the thundering storm. "It is against the ways for anyone to interfere." The man pointed at Zalman. "He interfered. And the punishment is death."

The pirates on the deck stepped closer.

She lowered into a crouch and raised her sword in a high guard. "But he … *we* didn't know," Carys said.

Zalman stood next to her now, his hands clenched in fists. The storm increased, the deck reeling with violence beneath them.

"Doesn't matter," Loto said. "Those are the ways."

Mikayla pushed her way between Carys and Zalman. "The ways are unclear in regards to strangers and guests," she said. "Stand down."

"The ways still apply," Tangi said. "Even to strangers."

A hand grabbed Carys' shoulder, and she did not turn, but she heard Aeric's voice next to her. "The ways do not apply to the ignorant," he said. "You are not following justice to do so, only tradition and fear."

Loto barked a laugh as the rain ran down his face. "We are not afraid."

"Good," Aeric said, straightening and stepping forward to stand next to Mikayla, the both of them a pace away from a hundred men with daggers, axes, rapiers, and cutlasses. "Then prove your bravery by showing compassion to a man who, ignorant of our ways, reacted to save and rescue, to sacrifice himself for another's life. Surely we owe him our thanks, not our steel. My men will put down their weapons."

Shooting a glance at Zalman, Carys saw him take a deep breath. His eyes were blazing and his muscles rigid.

One by one, the men on the deck sheathed their swords or daggers, or hung their axes back on their belts.

"Very well," Tangi said. "We will not require his life today."

"Thank you," Aeric said, and Carys blew out a breath she didn't know she had been holding. "Now can we get out of the stankin' rain?"

Chapter 24

The Purpose of a Sword

Lyam was drunk. He held a tankard of ale in his right hand as he lumbered through the dark and deserted streets of Biram with Marat. It was late, past midnight, and Marat carried his own flask of some sort of liquor.

The streets of Biram were haunted, at least in Lyam's mind. Caleb forced the elves to take down the dead citizens of the small city and bury them, but the images remained in his thoughts. The ale did little to curb the memories.

They made their way through to the center of the city. Lyam paused in front of the school building. With hundreds of militan now prisoner, the army had to find a place to hold them, and the Imperial buildings at the center of the city were the best option. With the large number of individual rooms and hard locks on the doors, the human army could contain and watch them well enough.

Caleb placed the Kryan officers in the fifteen prison cells at the administration center, separating them from their militan, perhaps for interrogation.

The images swirled in his mind – the citizens of Biram impaled and flayed, his division dead and mutilated around him – and his heart pounded at the despair and rage.

"Breakin' elves," Lyam said.

Lyam took a swig from his tankard and walked across the center field toward the administration building. He heard Marat curse and stumble as he followed. Ascending the marble stairs and pushing open the double doors, he wiped his nostrils with his forearm. Lyam paused at the symbol of the Kryan Empire, the golden eagle, and he hocked mucus into his mouth and spit upon the symbol.

Marat swayed for a moment and took a sip on his flask. *He might be more drunk than me*, Lyam thought. Lyam went down the corridor to the left. Left at another intersection, Marat still following, and they arrived at the prison.

Two men guarded the fifteen cells, all locked and filled with at least one Kyran officer. Three cells held two of them. It took Lyam a moment to count them – eighteen elves in all. Eighteen Kyran officers.

The men were awake but lounged on chairs nearby against the wall. They stood when they saw Lyam stagger through the door. "Lyam," they greeted him. Each man carried a gladus.

Lyam struggled to think of their names. They were both men from Ketan, or maybe from Delaton. He couldn't remember. "Men," he said in greeting and strode up to the cells. Most of the officers were awake, as well, and sat up on their cots at the new arrival.

Lyam stared at the officers. "They give us any information yet?" he asked the guards.

"Caleb asked them questions," one of them said, a young man with a scar on his forehead. "But they don't know nothin' much."

The officers appeared pretty healthy to him. *Maybe they know more than they told Caleb*, he thought. *Might need a little more motivation.*

He drained his tankard and set it on a low table between the guards. "Why don't you boys take a break," he said. "Go for a piff or get some ale." Lyam raised his tankard. "Come back in a few hours."

The men shared a look. "Um … we're not supposed to leave," the other man said. He was middle-aged with a paunch. "Supposed to be here 'til the dawn and we relieved."

"I am relieving you," Lyam answered.

"Sorry," forehead-scar said. "Don't think …"

Lyam spun on them. "Don't you know who I am?" He reached down to touch his sword, the unforged sword he got from the Living Stone, but it wasn't there. He had forgotten it back in his bunk. No matter. "I am a *Sohan-el*, the commander of a division." A dead division. "I outrank you shoggers, and I say you are relieved. Come back in a few hours."

Long heartbeats passed, and Lyam pulled the knife from his belt, a long knife given to him in the Forest of Saten. Paunch-belly sighed, and the two men left the room without a word. Lyam watched them go.

Marat leaned against the wall behind him, confused and silent.

Turning back, Lyam moved closer to the cells. The elves were all awake now. "You gave the orders, didn't you? The orders to flay those people, to impale them and watch them suffer." He took a deep breath through his nose.

None of the officers answered, most staring back with fear in their faces, eyes flashing to the long knife in his hand. A few scowled at him, angry, and Lyam approached the cell of one who regarded him with disgust.

"Did you enjoy it?" Lyam asked the officer. Others cringed and shrank back in their cells. This officer did not. "Did you laugh at their pain, their suffering?"

The officer's nostrils flared.

"Marat," Lyam said. "Give me the keys off the wall."

"Lyam …" Marat mumbled behind him.

"Give me the keys!" Lyam shouted.

Marat gave a start, hesitated, but he obeyed, reaching out to his right and grabbing the keys from the wall. Stepping forward, he handed Lyam the keys. Lyam didn't meet his glare but took the keys. With the long knife in his right hand, he fumbled with the keys and then opened the door.

"Watch the door," he called behind him. Marat retreated and stood near the door to the prison.

The officer sat straight on his cot, facing Lyam, his hands to his side, glowering.

Lyam took a few steps toward the elf until he stood a pace away. "Did you enjoy it?" he asked.

The officer sneered at him.

Lyam couldn't contain the wrath within him any longer. He rushed the elf, dropping the keys to the floor and grabbing the officer in the throat, pushing him against the bars behind the cot. Lyam brought the long knife close to the officer's eye. He heard the rustling of movement in the cells around him.

"Lyam …" Marat's voice soft behind him.

"S'okay," Lyam said. "He doesn't need an eye. But we need him to answer some questions."

"But they said Caleb …"

"Caleb don't know crit," Lyam said. "He lived with the elves, takes an elf around with him as an advisor. He can't do what's necessary. But I can. I lived in the Saten, remember, lost friends to the elves."

Lyam pressed harder on the elf's throat, the knife a few milimitres away. The officer gasped. "Now tell me," he whispered. "Did you enjoy it?"

The officer bared his teeth. "Yes," he said. "I enjoyed every scream, every tear from every man, woman, and child. We killed them like the animals they were."

Yelling, Lyam pulled the knife back to plunge it into the elf's eye.

"Lyam!"

That was not Marat's voice, and the shock froze Lyam in place.

"Lyam!" the voice called his name again, a female voice, and familiar. She was at the door. "Put the knife down."

"Bweth," he said to her. "I'm just …"

"You're shoggin' drunk," she said. "I can smell the breakin' ale from here. And you're stupid. Caleb won't like this, wouldn't allow it."

He lowered the knife, but he turned his head to face her. "I don't care what Caleb thinks, what he'll allow."

"Fine," she said, and she stepped toward him. "Then it be me that won't allow it." He could see her now, sweat and soot covering her body and clothes like she had been at a forge, her red hair matted and pulled back. She hefted the spiked mace in her hand. The two guards were behind her, forehead-scar and paunch-belly.

"They're elves," he said as if that should explain it. "They killed the whole shoggin' town. My whole division."

"Aye," Bweth said. "And me husband, too." She stood a pace away now, the pain and anger in her face mirrored his own. "But if we do this, if *you* do this, then we'll be like them. We'll be no better. Then they win. After all we sacrificed today, they'll win. And that is what I won't allow. My husband won't have died for that." She raised the mace. "So put the shoggin' knife down and go sleep this off."

When he looked into her eyes, he saw the resolve beyond the pain and anger. She would do what she had to do to stop him. Even as drunk as he was, he knew that.

Lyam dropped the knife. It clattered to the ground. "Break you," he said to her. He lurched past her and out of the prison without another word. It took a moment, but as he left the administration building, Marat staggered behind him.

+———

"We need to get back to Da'ar," Tobiah said, standing over her. His voice was quiet and low.

Eshlyn sat next to the body of Athelwulf. The corpse was wrapped in blankets they took from the barracks. Ath's unforged sword rested across the body, Tobiah pulling it from the trodall carcass with some effort. They also had gathered whatever supplies they could for the journey back, for them and the slaves. Or former slaves.

"The slaves, they are still afraid to come with us," Tobiah said. "We will have to force them if they are to come with us."

Forcing men to be free? Not really freedom. But they couldn't leave them here, could they? "Then we will force them. Take them back to Da'ar with you."

"Are you not coming with us?"

She glanced over to her right. The Mahakar lay close, watching her. She could feel his sorrow and willingness to help however she desired. "I will be taking Athelwulf's body back another way."

"I understand," Tobiah said. "What of the elves?"

Eight of the original 250 elven guard lived, and six of those were seriously injured. Twenty-one of their original fifty from the Beorgai had died in the battle, two killed by the trodall, and four more were injured and would have to be carried back to the city. For all technical purposes, it was a major victory. But as with Eshlyn's experience with battles, victories still felt like losses.

"What of them?" Eshlyn asked.

"We should kill them," he said.

"I want no more killing today."

"I understand," Tobiah said. "But if we leave them, they might be able to follow us back to Da'ar and lead a legion to our doorstep. I cannot do that."

"Then lock them in one of the slave cages," she said.

"Isn't that the same as killing them? They will starve or die of thirst in a few days."

She turned back to Athelwulf's body. "Leave them some water, enough for a few days. The Kryans must supply this place somehow. They'll be here soon."

"That is a great risk for our city. Who knows what they heard?" Tobiah said. "Kiano will not like it."

Eshlyn set a hand upon Athelwulf's body. "He may have to get used to things he does not like," she said. "You asked, and I've made my decision. If you wish to kill them, so be it. It will be on your hands, not mine."

Tobiah paused before speaking again. "Yes, *Bashawyn*."

"Thank you," she said. "Now help me get Athelwulf lashed to the Mahakar's back. I'm going to take him back to his father."

—✦—

"And why are *they* here?" Tangi said as the storm raged outside. "This is also against tradition."

Carys didn't think the room was designed to hold so many with Carys and Zalman added to the space. The five kanalor and their seconds all sat around the table. Carys and Zalman sat on either side of Aeric, who would have a nice, puffy black eye where Zalman punched him. Carys shifted in her seat, staring down at Mikayla, who sat at the other end of the table.

"They have information important to our decision," Aeric said. "And it is my ship. And I am the Kanacyn. For now. That is reason enough."

Tangi spoke. "We must first choose the winner of the duel."

Mana sat forward and put an elbow on the table. "Aeric," he said. "She fell from the plank first."

"A technicality," Tangi said. "He saved her from dropping into the ocean."

"Aren't all judgments technicalities?" Loto asked. "I say Mikayla won the duel."

"Fine," Mana said. "Tangi, how do you see it?"

"It is a difficult choice," Tangi admitted. "Aeric could have forced her to submit or concede before saving her, but he did not. Does that give him the right of victory? Was that character or stupidity?"

"There may be no difference," Loto muttered. "He did marry her."

"Possibly," Tangi said. "But I feel it must be considered. He also did not fight her, only defended to protect himself. He was no doubt making a point to us all."

"What point did he make?" Mana asked.

"That the wise choice is to defend and not to attack," Tangi said. "And I believe that point was made in the duel. I decide for Aeric."

Loto raised his hands. "Okay, then," he said. "That is decided. Aeric won the duel. We heard the arguments before the duel. Let's vote on the new Kanacyn."

The ship rocked and rose up and down, the tempest throwing the huge ship with the winds and waves. Carys' stomach protested. She gritted her teeth and gripped the table. Her face got hot. She would not puke, not now.

"If Aeric wins the duel, then it is tradition that he remain as Kanacyn," Tangi said.

"We haven't been holding to tradition very well today," Loto spat. "So keeping with that, I say we need to get more aggressive, take more ships, start raiding villages. I'm with Mikayla."

Aeric turned to the third kanalor. "Mana?"

"You are my brother, Aeric," Mana began. "And I believe you have been a fine Kanacyn, but I agree with Loto. Our children starve. And we are *pirates*. This is what we do. I vote for Mikayla."

Aeric's face fell. "Then it is decided. Mikayla will be the new Kanacyn."

Mikayla had not spoken the whole time, leaning back in her chair with a scowl on her face. She spoke now. "It is not decided."

The heads in the packed room turned towards her. "Two to one, in favor of you," Tangi said. "It is decided."

"I have not given my vote," Mikayla said. "And a tie keeps it with Aeric."

The pirates in the room shared glances and settled on her again. "Since you brought the challenge," Mana said. "We assumed ..."

Mikayla chuckled, but it was a bitter sound. "Don't assume when it comes to a woman," she said. "That is dangerous."

"Then give your vote," Loto said. "Let's get this over with."

"Not yet," Mikayla said. "I want to hear what she has to say."

Aeric's brows furrowed at his wife. "What are you ...?"

"Shut up," she said. "I have the floor now."

"This is highly irregular," Mana said.

Loto groaned in frustration.

"It is my vote," Mikayla said. "And unlike our guests, here, you are not ignorant of the ways. I can take all night if I wish to decide. Aeric brought these strangers to us for a reason, and I'm curious about why they are here and what they would have to say."

Carys looked over at Aeric, and he inclined his head to her, like giving permission.

She stood, and her stomach protested. She swayed.

Zalman peered over at her. "Are you alright?"

She blinked at him slowly. Battling the nausea, she told the room of the Battle of Ketan and the revolution of men, of Caleb the *Brendel*, and the return of the *Sohan-el* to Eres. She drew her unforged sword and explained the reality of the Living Stone. As she spoke, Mikayla sat forward and her eyes became fierce.

"The Empire has responded," Carys concluded, "by further oppressing and killing the men of Ereland. You speak of raiding the lands of Veradis and Lior. I have been to those places, and I tell you they are starving, too. I ask you, I plead with you, do not cause them further suffering."

"Then what can we do?" Tangi asked.

"Join us," she said. "Stand with us against the elves. Join the revolution. Raid the Kryan ships."

"Even if we fight the Empire, the other nations will not trade with us," Loto said. "We cannot stop being what we are."

"The other nations do not trade with you, in part, because they are afraid of the Empire," Carys said. "We fight them on the continent. If you fight them here, on the seas, you will inspire others to stand up to them. Men, dwarves, elves. Maybe you can be merchants once again. Free to trade."

"I am sorry to hear of the suffering in those lands," Mana said. "We will take that into consideration, but open war against the Empire is something else entirely."

"It is a fantasy," Loto said. "You do not know how these other nations will react or even if we can survive against Kryus. This is what we are. This is what we have. We cannot afford the luxury of morals."

A wave of nausea hit her as the ship rocked again. Gritting her teeth, she leaned upon the table. "My parents, my aunt and uncle, they've all given their lives for this revolution. My brother raises an army to stand and fight against the Kryan legions. I have friends risking their lives as we speak to help others and bring them into the revolution, so all men can be free. We have risked everything to be here and speak with you."

Carys slapped the table with the palm of her hand, a wet, sharp sound.

"We believe men are better than the slavery they've been given, better than stealing and causing more suffering of the innocent so their children can eat. El created us to be better than that. You can be better than that. But it will cost you. We are here, paying that price. And we will continue to pay it. We ask you to help us. Be the people you once were. Join the revolution.

"That is why we are here."

The room fell quiet and tense.

Mikayla broke the silence. "I am ready to vote."

Every eye was on her, but hers was on her husband.

"You are an infuriating man," she said to him. "But I vote for you."

"A tie," Mana said.

"A waste of my time," Loto said.

"Aeric remains Kanacyn," Tangi said.

Aeric glowered at Mikayla. "Why?"

"Because you saved me when you could have let me drown," she said. "That is the kind of leader our people need, as much as I stankin' hate to say it."

"I love you," Aeric said, his visage softening.

"I know," she said. "But if what these people say is true, the time is coming when we must change something or die. We may not be able to hide in the south much longer."

"I agree," Aeric said. "But that is a discussion for another time." He shared a knowing smile with Mikayla. "For now, I ask that you all give me some time alone with my wife."

Zalman stood to join Carys, and he had to help her as the people filed out of the room, leaving the husband and wife alone. Loto cursed, Mana grinned, and Tangi sought to continue the conversation with Carys about her brother and the revolution. But as soon as she stood on the wet and slippery poop deck of *The Last Serpent,* she released the contents of her stomach in the rain.

—†—

Zalman busied himself with learning jobs of the ship through the afternoon as the storm passed, talking with the men of the crew. Carys spent most of the rest of the day talking with the different kanalor, first Loto, then Mana, then Tangi, walking about the deck. Did she know he watched her? She stayed within his sight at all times, explaining to many the freedom that El wished for all men. He heard pieces of her conversations, and once or twice saw her looking back at him. Zalman averted his eyes and watched the departing clouds or turned to ask a crewman a random question.

Aeric and Mikayla spent most of the day in the captain's cabin.

Night fell, and he scanned the deck again. Carys stood at the foredeck, alone, facing out to the sea, to the north, the moons reflecting off the ocean at night. Zalman considered returning to below deck with the bulk of the crew or leaving her to her thoughts. Instead, he mustered his courage and plodded up onto the foredeck and stood behind her.

The breeze came from the east and ruffled her shoulder-length blond hair. As he stared at her in that moment, he saw her shoulders twitch, and then again. She made no noise he could hear, but standing close to her now, he saw she was crying.

He cleared his throat. Carys stood straight and took a deep breath, wiping at her nose with the back of her sleeve. After a glistening glance his way, she gazed out onto the ocean again. "Oh, hey," she said, her voice hoarse. "What do you want?"

And he almost left her there. He almost said, "Nothing," and walked away. Almost. He took a step forward and leaned against the railing next to her.

"You are due a compliment," he said. "I owe you several, I think."

Carys squinted up at him. "You're not one of these people."

"I am today," he said.

She sniffed, her face softening.

"You have a heart that is both strong and kind," he began. "You are good. The core of you, it is pure and good. Before I met you and your brother and the others, I didn't know people like you existed. I didn't know they could. Everyone I ever knew – man, elf, or dwarf – they all wanted to take from me, use me like an animal."

Zalman ran a hand over his bald head. "I didn't agree to come on this trip because your brother told me to. I wanted to come because I believed in you, in what you wanted to do, because you are, deep in your soul, a good person."

He winced. "After what happened in Landen ... well, I couldn't take seeing you hurt like that. I wish I could make it all go away. I would fight any battle. But I cannot. Doesn't work that way."

She crossed her arms, her head down.

"I can crush things with my bare hands. Caleb? He could cut down storms if he wanted. But I'm learning this more and more – that isn't strength. Who you are, what you choose to do with those things, makes you strong. Faith, truth, sacrifice, makes you strong. And you taught me that. Carys, you are the strongest person I know."

Carys wept again, and he could hear it. Her chest and shoulders heaved, and sobs escaped her throat.

Zalman wanted to put an arm around her, but he wasn't brave or strong enough. It took all his courage to speak all those words. He had practiced them all day.

"Well," he said. "That was it. I thought I owed you that."

As he began to leave, Carys reached out with her hand and grabbed his wrist, gripping it with surprising strength. He froze. She didn't say a word but buried her face into his chest and wrapped her arms around his waist. Slowly, he took his arms and covered her with them like a blanket, holding her close to him. She cried into his chest. And he let her.

"I'm not strong," she whispered, muffled. "I was so scared. I still am."

"Being scared is no weakness. Just goes to show how brave you really are."

She breathed into his chest. "Thank you," she muttered. "Thank you, you big gedder."

He smiled. For the first time in his life, from his heart, he smiled.

———

The sign for *The Crying Eagle* fell at some point in the last few months, propped up against the outside wall. The inn had been ransacked, combed over by the Cityguard, Caleb supposed.

The floor of the common room was stained with blood. No one had tried to clean it.

Caleb stood in the yard behind *The Crying Eagle* and looked over the mounds of earth, the graves for his Uncle Reyan and Seckon, a young man who'd worked at the inn. The graves had been dug up, again by those searching for evidence in the aftermath of the fight, the corpses stashed in the barn. Caleb made the elves re-dig the graves and replace the bodies. He considered sending the Prophet's body back to Ketan, but he thought this a better place.

The memory of that night haunted him, Zarek the Bladeguard bringing in the Cityguard to capture them, the fight that ensued, and Earon's betrayal. And the Prophet's death.

He drew his sword and held it out before him. A simple sword. No elaborate markings. But it was elegant in its simplicity. A perfect weapon.

The sound of steps in the yard drew his attention, Aden walking up next to him. Aden also surveyed the graves.

"Uncle Reyan loved this place," Caleb said. "He told me that once. He loved Drew and Myrla and the life they built here. He felt at peace here. It is good his resting place is here."

"He was a good man," Aden said.

"He was who he needed to be."

Aden stayed silent, somber.

He will be inflicted with deep wounds, and those scars will follow him all his days.

"I hear what the Bladeguard say. She could be alive."

He knew what the young man meant. Danelle. "Could be," he said. And he tried to contain the hope from growing in his heart, the possibility of seeing her again. A part of him wanted to leave it all, race across to another continent and hunt for her. But she was safer away from him, if she was even alive. Safer away from the sword, from the blades of war.

"I still see her, in my mind," Caleb said. "So beautiful, so strong and good. Too good for me, that's for sure. I loved her, and a part of me thought that maybe, one day, we could be together, live free and in peace. But it was a dream. I was born for other things."

The sword that gives him life will take his life. But what if he survived? What if his destiny wasn't to die at the end of this road? After the revolution was over, could he even dare to wish …

"Caleb," Aden said. "You might want to talk to Lyam. He's having a rough time."

Caleb stared down at the sword again. "Is he."

"Yeah," Aden said. "You know how Lyam lost his whole division. It's eating at him. Bweth said she had to stop him the other night, with the officers in the prison."

He is not a man, but a sword ...

"Do you know what a sword is made for?" Caleb asked.

"Sorry?"

"It is not a shield. A shield is made to protect, not to kill. A sword, it has a point at the end of it. It is made to thrust. For offense, not defense. To kill."

Aden leaned forward. "Did you hear what I said? I think you need to talk to Lyam. He's goin' a little maddy on us."

"I heard you. But did you hear me?"

"I did. But I didn't really understand."

"I'm telling you I know what I'm going to do next." He rolled the unforged sword over in his hand.

Aden ran his hand through his bushy dark hair. "And what is that?"

... and El will wield him as a sword, a blade to cut out the heart of those who slave and oppress.

"I'm going to take this sword and shove it up the Empire's arse," Caleb said. "If they want a war, I'll give it to them."

"Okay. What does that mean?"

"We're going to attack Taggart and take it back from the elves."

Yosu and his Sohan-el stood at the foot of the mountain. The mountain was the stronghold of Bana Sahat and the thousands of evil creatures he bred for death and destruction.

"Come," Yosu said to his warriors. "We will take the mountain."

The Sohan-el were afraid and looked behind them at the small army of elves and dwarves, misfits and drifters. Their number was 153 against thousands.

"Master," Yon said. "We are farmers, herders, nobodies. We cannot win this."

"The day you chose to follow me," Yosu answered. "You were no longer farmers, herders, nobodies. You became the warriors of El.

"And warriors of El do not see with their eyes but with the eye of El. They fight with the power of another world to win freedom for this one. No warrior who goes to battle with the power of El is ever defeated."

Gabryel raised his barabrend. "Then if we fight with the power of El, we will never die?"

"No," Yosu said. "I did not say that."

-   From the Ydu, the 5th scroll, translated into Common Tongue by the Prophet

CHAPTER 25

WHEN A SWORD SPEAKS

The last time Eshlyn rode the Mahakar, she felt free and wild and full of life, as if her soul had been released from a burden as they flew. And like most burdens, she didn't know its weight until it lifted.

This time, while the view was inspiring and full of beauty as they passed over the trees and peaks of the Kaleti, she carried a sorrow within her that the Mahakar could not relieve. She brought the body of her friend and brother to his father.

They circled the city of Da'ar, and people began to gather as they saw Eshlyn and the tiger overhead. The city and its people appeared so small to her, so distant; she felt safer somehow, even high up in the air riding upon the Mahakar, but the weight of Athelwulf's body across her lap brought her mind to her purpose. She guided the animal to the center of the city, and the people ran to greet them.

With a rush of wind from the beating of large white wings, they landed in a clear area left for them by the Beorgai. The Mahakar lay upon the ground, and Eshlyn sighed as she dismounted. The Beorgai approached with caution, a mixture of fear and excitement on their faces. They saw the body, but she knew the Mahakar could cause awe, as well.

Eshlyn called two men over to her. She cut the ropes that held Ath to the Mahakar with her sword as they complied. The two men took the body, wrapped in blankets, from the animal's back, one man gripping Athelwulf's shoulders and the other at his heels.

Shecayah broke through the murmuring crowd first, her stare fixed upon the body. Kiano stepped forward after her, Earon behind him. The three of them approached together. Eshlyn could not read the woman's expression, but the terror and indecision within Shecayah was apparent. Was it her brother? Her husband? Someone else? Either way, death visited the city today.

The men set the body on the ground between them. Answering the question in Shecayah's eyes, Eshlyn said, "I'm sorry. Your brother fell in battle."

Athelwulf's sister clenched her teeth, containing a sob. "Tobiah?"

"He is well," Eshlyn said.

Shecayah knelt next to her brother and began to weep, covering her mouth. Whether she wept at sorrow for her brother or relief that her husband still lived, Eshlyn didn't know, but she thought both.

The agony of grief after Kenric's death continued to visit her at times; however it had lessened, it would never really leave. She both remembered it now and, to some extent, experienced it again. She had become used to the ache deep in her heart. But two fresh wounds added to her grief – first Esai and now Athelwulf. She wouldn't have believed there was room for more, but she found that sorrow expands the heart much as love does.

"All the men fought bravely," Eshlyn said. "We freed the slaves. Tobiah and the others are returning with almost two thousand men and women. They should arrive by the morning and will require food, water, and care. There are some wounded, and the slaves need ... everything."

Kiano stood behind the kneeling Shecayah, and he frowned down at the body. His son. "How did he fall?" His voice was tight, a whisper.

"There was a trodall," Eshlyn said. "It started killing slaves and your men, and Athelwulf stood it down, fought it. He saved many."

Earon stood next to Kiano, now, his face conflicted, pained, gazing down at Athelwulf's body. "He slew a trodall?" Earon muttered.

"Nearly." Eshlyn pulled Ath's sword from beneath the blankets. "He stabbed the creature in the chest before it crushed him. The Mahakar finished it."

Shecayah cleared her throat. "Were there others killed?"

It was clear. Other of the Beorgai. "Yes," Eshlyn said.

"Who were they?" Shacayah asked.

Eshlyn spoke the twenty-one names, and men and women reacted behind her, embraces and sobbing, comforting one another in their grief. Eshlyn knew that this was only the beginning. The world was changing. Others would go off to war soon. Did they know it yet? The anguish within his face was for more than the death of his men or his son. He knew. And he appeared decades older for the knowledge.

She handed Kiano Athelwulf's sword. "He was one of the greatest men I have ever known. He had the heart of a *Sohan-el* even before receiving the sword. I was honored to know him."

Shecayah stood, no longer sobbing, although her cheeks were stained with tears. "Thank you," she said.

Kiano did not peer up from the sword. "We will make preparations to care for those that arrive," he said. He began to depart, taking the sword with him.

"Father?" Shecayah said, and he halted. "What ... what are we going to do with Namir's body?"

"His name was Athelwulf," Kiano said. Eshlyn could barely hear him. "And we will bury him with the other men who died setting those slaves free. With his sacrifice, he is no longer *foredain*. He deserves that, at least."

With that statement, Kiano walked away.

—⊢—

The Cityguard forge in Biram was a basic, stock facility. Three blacksmith shops were spread throughout the city, as well, but she had brought her own mobile forge with her. Bweth took what she needed and created her own custom smithery in the Cityguard forge. She brought her own hammer.

It took most of the day to heat the breastplates down to make them more malleable. A delicate process, but one that also took great strength along with the skill; she now had Hunter's breastplate, and those others of her division that died, ready to begin to work.

They buried him with the rest of the men of the *Hamon-el* that died in the battle. Caleb offered to have Hunter buried at the back of some inn with the Prophet, his uncle, but she declined. Hunter would not have wanted that. Despite his Liorian heritage, he was a man of Ketan, and he would want to be at rest with those men. Even among a thousand graves, Bweth would remember the exact spot.

Bweth began to beat the metal upon the anvil, forming and shaping it. Sparks flew and she soaked with sweat in the heat. She thought of Hunter at every moment, and this only made it feel like he stood next to her, like she was home, however she felt that she would never have a home again. The baby within her belly kicked with each blow of the hammer.

She would always have the babe. And Hunter's secrets along with her own. She clung to that intimate connection with desperation.

That Aden boy tried to talk to her earlier in the day. He had come by her custom workshop here, and he asked her questions. She knew what he tried to do. He was a good boy. But Hunter was a perfect man. He didn't ask those questions. He didn't have to. He knew her well enough.

She hammered at the metal, her mouth in a sneer.

Caleb didn't even try to comfort her. He didn't apologize for her husband's death or the fact that he stepped in and took the lives of those Bladeguard. There was no need for those discussions. She was a skilled warrior, but a Bladeguard would carve her like a duck on Ashinar day. Watching Caleb fight both at once … she never saw anything like that, and she had seen that same man on the wall fighting the demics. But his speed, precision, and cold fury were both frightening and inspiring. While her heart cried for revenge, her mind saw the logic and need of his duel with the two Bladeguard.

So she understood. Caleb possessed his own scars, his own grief, that she knew. She saw the marks on his back, heard the rumors and his recounting of the death of the Prophet. He knew there was no comfort to be had, so he didn't try. Another good man.

It would take her all night and perhaps the next morning to finish the armor she was working on. But the elves were now burying their own dead, and they would be at that for some time still.

The hammer struck the metal again in an eruption of sound and sparks, shaping it to her own form as the baby moved within her.

———

The Last Serpent pulled anchor and left as the other ships broke formation and went their separate ways. Carys stood in the bright and hot afternoon sun at the foredeck with Aeric. He peered out over the waves after *The Titan Song*, Mikayla's ship. It swung slowly northeast.

He noticed her but returned to looking at his wife's boat as it sailed away. "Carys," he said. "You are as beautiful today as the swans of Inoa."

She grinned but did not blush. "Thank you," she said. Zalman's compliment was better.

After a brief time on deck with the crew last night, Aeric and Mikayla disappeared into his cabin once again and didn't appear until noon the next day.

"Did you ask her to stay?" Carys asked.

"No. And she didn't ask me to come with her, either. We each have our duty."

Duty. Responsibility. Those things kept two lovers from spending every waking moment together. It made her sad, all of a sudden. "How did you meet her?" she asked.

"I worked the crew with her on her father's boat, *The Titan Song*. He was a great captain and the Kanalor of Halemano. I was young and full of pride and seeking adventure. Her father always wanted a son and took to me, mentored me, taught me."

"And Mikayla?"

He laughed. "She hated me. At first. Her father had to choose between us for his second. He made the right choice."

"His daughter?"

"Neither one of us," he said. "He chose another man, a good sailor. It forced us to continue to work together, and eventually, well, we fell in love."

"And married," she said.

"Oi," he said. "And married. I was given second here on *The Last Serpent*, after four years, I was made Kanalor of Enakai. She became my second. That was five years ago."

"When did she leave?"

"A year ago," he said. *The Titan Song* grew smaller, sailing toward the horizon, faster now that *The Last Serpent* moved southwest. "Her father was killed."

"Sorry to hear that," Carys said. "By who?"

"They were captured by the *Bird of Prey*, the most famous Kryan warship in the southern waters. The First Lieutenant of the *Bird of Prey* is known as the Seahawk, an infamous and ruthless warrior. They travel with a smaller ship, the *Elan*."

"Not so famous I ever heard of him," Carys muttered.

"Even so, they attacked him at the open sea and took his whole crew captive, sunk his ship, a great old girl, *The Water's Eye*. After torturing him and cutting his hands and feet from his body, they tied him, still alive, to the bowsprit of a Kryan warship where he hung until he died."

"And his daughter became the new kanalor."

"A fine choice," Aeric said. "I can think of no one better."

"She has motivation to fight the elves," Carys said.

"More than most, yes," Aeric said. "But that does not make it wise."

"You said the elves attacked her father. Are their attacks becoming more frequent? More bold?"

He rubbed his chin. "We keep them at bay. For now."

"Tanicus is reacting to the revolution in Ketan," Carys said. "Bringing retribution against all men." She peered up at the Pirate Lord. "Nowhere is safe. Not even here."

"We have never been truly safe. Why does a rebellion in Ketan affect us here?"

"Because you are men outside of his control," she said. "The Empire will not stop with attacks on the borders. They will push further into your waters."

"How do you know this will happen? After years of minor skirmishes, why would the Empire break the peace?"

"Tanicus understands something you do not," Carys said.

Aeric turned to her. "What is that?"

"The Kananweld are not your people."

He frowned, waiting for her to continue.

"All men are your people," she said. "The revolution thousands of kilomitres away is a revolution of men, of their freedom and independence. Freedom anywhere proves it is possible everywhere. Tanicus cannot abide that, so he will punish all men. His weapons are fear and control. That is what he knows. It doesn't matter if you're Pirates or monsters or saints. All men that live apart from his control threaten him. He will attack here, too."

Aeric took a deep breath and gazed out again to sea.

"I've been thinking," Carys said. "I was wrong before."

"Oh?"

"I told you that with El's help, you could go back to the people you once were," she said.

"You no longer believe that?"

"I believe you were right," she said. "You cannot reclaim the past. And that is not what El desires."

"It isn't?"

"No," she said. "You've experienced too much, learned too much, good and bad. You must forge forward, not look behind. You must become something new. Not Pirates, but not the people you once were, either. Something different, maybe greater."

After a moment, Aeric spoke. "You are an amazing woman, Carys. You remind me of Mikayla in so many ways. I do not say that lightly. You've given me much to think about."

She grinned at him. She liked that compliment better than his earlier one. But Zalman's was still the best.

┼

Eshlyn gathered with the elders and the leaders of the Beorgai in Kiano's home the next morning, in the large dining area. Eshlyn sat at one end of the table and Kiano the other. Next to Kiano was Tobiah, returned from the mines with the wounded and 2,000 former slaves, and Shecayah. Also at the table were the nine elders of Da'ar, older men, some even older than Kiano.

Earon leaned back in his chair to Eshlyn's left, his hair clean and his beard trimmed. He didn't really belong at this meeting, but Shecayah wouldn't take her eyes off the man, especially now. Athelwulf had given him over to her charge. She was serious about that responsibility.

Athelwulf's unforged sword lay upon the table before Kiano. Eshlyn could see the Head Elder glance down at the sword.

Shecayah finished giving an update on the former slaves. "They are so afraid, but we have found places for them," she said. "They are from the other tribes of Lior. Some were forced into slavery. Others were sold into it by a family that could no longer feed them."

"We are the Beorgai," Tobiah said. "A tribe made of other tribes, of those who left to be free. This is the place for them."

"Yes," Shecayah said, her gaze upon her husband. "It will take some time, but you are right. They belong here."

"Agreed," one of the elders close to Tobiah said. "They will stay with us. You have done well, Shecayah."

She gave the elder a bow and then addressed her father. "What now?"

Kiano's eyes lowered to the sword, and he touched it.

The sword speaks to some ...

"Kiano," Eshlyn said, her voice soft. "What does the sword say to you?"
Kiano took a deep breath.

"The legend says that the Mahakar was created by El as the soul of Lior, a symbol," Kiano began. "But I do not believe that is true. He came with the first men that settled into our land. By all accounts, he existed before, although the scriptures never mention him. The first we know of him, the Mahakar appeared with the great *Sohan-el* of Lior, Martyn. Oshra was but a fishing village at that time, and the men of Lior spread throughout various places in the forest and the coast. Martyn rode the Mahakar throughout the land, bringing peace and unity, teaching about El and his truth, and protecting the people when they needed him. He was a wanderer with no home of his own."

He scanned the room and his stare settled upon Eshlyn. "But there is a part of Martyn's past that we do not talk about. That is what we do with our heroes and legends. We revere them to the point that we forget their imperfections, and with that, we take away their humanity. And when we do that, we take away what makes them men and women to revere. It is when we surpass our humanity, our imperfections, act bravely in spite of our fears, that we become an example to others.

"Martyn was a violent man when he was young – brash and rebellious. He hurt and killed many in his selfishness as a young man. But then Mychal, the great *Sohan-el* of Yosu, found him. Mychal was old, then, in his waning years, but he defeated Martyn. He did not kill the young man, however. He showed mercy and taught him to live for El. Martyn spent the rest of his life showing the same mercy and justice to others."

"What became of Martyn?" Eshlyn asked.

"An army of evil men invaded Lior when he was an old man," Kiano answered. "He died defeating that army, sending them back from whence they came. Some said the Mahakar died with him, that his life ended with Martyn's. Others said that the Mahakar waited until he was needed again, as a symbol that the men of Lior must rise. Centuries ago, that was the prophecy, that a woman would come with a message for us, riding upon the Mahakar. And you have come."

Kiano sat straight in his chair. "The prophecy was meant to remind us that our safety, our hiding, would be temporary. A time would come when we would join the fight for the truth of El and the freedom of men.

"What does the sword say to me?" Kiano said. "It told me to listen to my son. Not with words. But that is what it said to me. That was the message of El to my heart. My son was right. The world has changed. Revolution has come. It is time to join the *Brendel* and his fight against the Empire."

The men around the table remained silent, but they shared glances, shifting in their seats.

"Father?" Shecayah began. "What are you saying? What do you mean?"

"We will do many things," Kiano said. "First, we will send men and bosaur to assist the *Brendel*'s army. Second, we will be a refuge for those that escape Kryan slavery. Third, we will send envoys down to Oshra to help unite the tribes of Lior. That was never your job. It is ours."

"Who will take the men to join the *Brendel*?" an elder asked.

"I will," Tobiah said, and Shecayah started as he spoke. "I will begin talking with the men today. We will need to leave some to protect the people here."

"We will teach the newcomers how to fight," Kiano said. "And we will protect ourselves. Take all who wish to go."

"When do I leave?" Tobiah asked.

"As soon as you have the men and you are ready," Kiano said.

Tobiah nodded to his father-in-law.

Shecayah leaned forward and her eyes blazed at her husband. "I'm coming with you," she said.

Tobiah sighed. "My love, I ..."

She scowled at him. "I am coming with you."

Eshlyn's head spun. She ran a hand through her hair. "Kiano," she said. "Are you sure? There will be more battles, and many more will die."

"*Bashawyn*," Kiano said. "Why did you come to Lior?"

Eshlyn stammered. "W-what?"

"Why did you come to Lior?" he repeated.

She touched Kenric's unforged sword at her hip. "To help unite the men of Lior against the Kryan Empire and bring them into the revolution."

"And you have done so," Kiano said. "El has been with you. He still is."

Yes, he has, she thought. *El seems to help in ways you don't plan or expect.*

"Very well," Eshlyn said. "I will take your men back with me to join Caleb."

Kiano winced and stood. "I have a favor to ask of the *Bashawyn*," he said.

Her brows rose at him.

The elder of the Beorgai lifted Athelwulf's sword. "I cannot keep this sword," he said. "You must take it for me."

"I already have a sword," she said.

"Not to keep," Kiano said. "You see, when Mochus betrayed and killed Yosu, they buried the Master in the Father Tree."

"I remember the story," Eshlyn said.

"The legend says that after Yosu rose again to defeat the Sahat, to exile them from the world, men would take the swords of the *Sohan-el* that died to the tomb at the Father Tree and leave them there, to honor their service to El and Yosu." Kiano extended the sword across the long table. "I want you to take my son's sword to the empty tomb at the Father Tree. To honor him."

"But ... I don't know where it is."

"The Mahakar will know," Kiano said.

Of course the Mahakar would.

All eyes watched her. "I would love to honor him," Eshlyn said. "But I need to go back with your men, to guide them back through the Saten to Ketan and Caleb's army."

Earon sat forward, his hands set upon the table. "I will take them," he said.

Eshlyn regarded him with skepticism. "You?"

"I know the way. Athelwulf thought I should go back and face Caleb and Carys," he said. "I don't need a sword to tell me to know he was right. Scares the crit out of me, but I have to do it." He pointed over his shoulder. "If you don't trust me, Shecayah here does a great job keeping watch."

Athelwulf's sister bared her teeth at him.

"*Bashawyn*," Kiano said. "Please. I'm asking you. For my son."

She saw that he needed this, needed to know that she would honor his son in this way. It was understandable. Why did it scare her so? Her hand trembled as she stood.

"It will be my honor to take Athelwulf's sword to the tomb of the Father Tree."

CHAPTER 26

THE LAST SERPENT

General Pyram stood at the eastern gate, a large archway in the short wall around Taggart, and Andos, his assistant, hovered nearby.

"We are now officially at war," Andos said, and he didn't sound happy about it. No one who understood war could be.

We've been at war for months now, if not longer, Pyram thought. *We just didn't know it.* He fixed his static frown upon his assistant. The elf usually did not utter the obvious.

As he faced the east again, they watched together as a long column of militan marched in unison towards the Taggart outpost, their shields, spears, and helmets gleaming in the afternoon sunlight. The column extended farther than the General could see. It was a full legion, if not more, complete with a Cavalry at the rear, 500 horses or more, he supposed. One thing he knew, however, based upon his experience in war and the politics of Tanicus: he would not be in command of this legion.

The Wraith had failed, and one scout reported the army of men had decimated the 4,000 militan and held Biram. But that information was thin. The scout barely escaped with his life. He was, in fact, the only one of twenty Pyram sent that had returned. This man, this *Brendel*, whatever he was, knew what the shog he was doing. The Emperor and his Bladeguard had underestimated him. Based on the size of the legion that approached his outpost, they would not underestimate him again. At least, the General hoped not.

Two figures rode fine horses at the front of the column. They drew near, one leading the other's horse. The first rider was a female elf in a long white silk tunic and billowing black silk trousers. Her dark hair was shaved on each side, leaving a strip of hair down the middle, long hair that flowed behind her. Two fine swords hung at her hips, and he saw the tattoo on her forearm. A Bladeguard.

She held the reins of the other horse, and its rider was shrouded in a long gray cloak. Even in the middle of the afternoon, it seemed to drink in the sunlight. It was a shadow on a horse coming toward him, the gray hood hiding the face in darkness. Another Wraith? Three were not enough the last time. Did they think one would be enough?

General Pyram stood with his hands behind his back, his chest out, and he bowed slightly to their new guests. "Welcome, Bladeguard," he said. "I am First General Pyram. This is my assistant, Andos."

"Did you get the communiqué that we were coming?" the Bladguard asked, halting ten paces away.

"We did," Andos said.

Her face was blank. "Are the preparations ready?"

"They are," Andos said. "Did you get our missive in response?"

They had received her message by pigeon a day ago. They responded with what they knew of this *Brendel* and the fate of the Bladeguard and Pyram's army, his soldiers.

"We did," she said. The female didn't dismount; she rode closer to the General and produced her Letter of Regency. "You will want to see this, of course." She did not look at him as she extended the paper towards him. She searched the walls, the gate. He knew that look. She was examining every centimitre of his outpost.

He did not take the parchment from her, and her stare found its way to his frown.

"What are your orders?" Pyram asked.

She replaced the paper in her belt. The Wraith behind her never moved or made a sound.

"I am taking control of the Kryan forces in the west," she said. "You have failed to deal with the rebellion here. The Emperor is displeased."

And there it was. The Emperor and the Bladeguard underestimated the man, made poor decisions by result, and decided it must be the First General's fault. They could blame him for not acting sooner, but if he had acted without strict orders, he ran the risk of being punished for acting beyond his authority. The Empire required orders before action. But Kryus was free to spread blame nonetheless, however it was that they took his army from him, into battle, and failed.

"I am sure he is," Pyram said. "How can I serve?"

"You will bring me any information you have on the *Brendel* and his army," she said. "Then we will take this legion you see behind me and crush him like the vermin he is."

"We have a defensible position here," Pyram said. "And fresh troops. We should wait and monitor his next move."

"And let him gather more strength?" She scoffed. "We will meet him in Biram or on the field. The Emperor wants this over quickly."

The General supposed he did. With every passing day the revolution survived, it gave dreams and hope to other men who might desire the same, and Tanicus' political enemies in the Senate would grow bolder and more vocal. Perhaps they weren't simply underestimating this Caleb.

They were afraid of him.

"What is your name?" the General asked.

"My name is Daelas," the elf said, and she gave him a cold glare. "And this is the Wraith that will take the life from the *Brendel* and cut out the heart of the rebellion."

———

Zalman heard the cries above as he slept in the hold.

It was early morning and a gray light eased through the open trapdoor. Zalman sat up, and a handful of men near him were already on their feet in the dim light and pulling their weapons from next to their cots or hammocks, wherever they slept. The shouting continued up on the deck, and Zalman tugged his boots on, fastened his belt, and hooked his battleaxes on his hips. He didn't bother with a shirt or tunic. The other men climbed the ladder through the trapdoor, and Zalman followed.

The ship bustled with activity, but it wasn't chaos: every man or woman had their job, and they worked it to precision. Zalman stood near the mainmast, trying to get out of the way, and watched as catapults and ballista were drug out of the hold and onto the deck. The crew set the ballista at the edge of the deck against the railing – special spaces in the ship designed for their specific purpose – and the catapults five paces behind them, 20 ballista and 20 catapults on each side of the ship. Bade, Aeric's second-in-command, barked orders to the men and women around him.

Carys approached from the stern, the unforged sword at her side, a quiver of arrows across her back, and a short bow in her hand. She stood next to Zalman and turned around, scanning the ocean in every direction. He followed her gaze and saw only water and mist.

"You see anything?" Carys asked.

He shook his head. While his battle experience was limited, he knew what it was for men to prepare for a fight, however.

Aeric strode from aft towards them, but he spoke past them with a loud and firm voice. "What is it?"

Bade stopped barking his orders. He jumped down from a barrel next to a catapult and jogged to be closer to the Captain. "Crow's nest saw a ship coming our way, possibly another behind it."

Cursing, Aeric adjusted the sword on his own belt. "What direction?"

"From the north," Bade said.

"Is it an Imperial ship?" Aeric asked.

"Looks t'be," Bade responded.

"They've never come in this far south before," Aeric said.

Bade shrugged like it didn't matter now.

"How far away?" Aeric craned his neck to scan the waters to the north.

Leaning back and cupping his hands around his mouth, Bade yelled up the main mast to the crow's nest. "How far?"

A shout came down to them from the man high above them. "Eight leagues, maybe more."

"Oi," Aeric said. "Turn us west, see if they follow."

His second strolled away to obey without another word.

"How far are we from Enakai?" Carys asked him.

The Kanacyn pulled his peerglass from his belt and swiveled his head to the north. "Less than a day," Aeric said.

The Last Serpent began to turn, a slow move, but the sails coordinated with the turn. The wind whipped around them.

Carys tested the string of her bow. "Can we make it before they overtake us?"

"If it is a Kryan warship," Aeric said. "They are too fast. Many also work with a smaller, even faster ship that will run us down and engage us while the larger ship closes in. We'll never make it to port in time for any sort of reinforcements. It is better strategy to attack them. We will face them at sea."

Zalman saw men pile long spears next to the ballista and stones and wooden balls of some kind next to the catapults. They loaded the weapons. He jogged to the railing as the ship adjusted course. He gazed north, trying to see any shapes on the mist. Carys and Aeric joined him.

Carys pointed and leaned over the railing. "There. I see them."

Focusing in the area where she directed, Zalman thought he could see something, but he was impressed with her vision. No wonder she was a dead shot with that bow. In another moment, he could see two spots in the mist, one larger than the other. "They are following," Zalman said.

Aeric looked through his peerglass, and his nostrils flared as he took in a sharp breath. "Oi. They are." The Captain lowered the glass, spun on his heel, and shouted out to Bade. "Reverse course. Ramming speed."

Zalman stared down at the hull and the iron spikes jutting out from the side, and he thought of the large lance at the bow of the ship. Three catapults sat at the foredeck of the ship and were loaded with round, black objects.

The ship wheeled around further, and Zalman saw the shapes in the distance grow closer, the smaller Kryan ship speeding out in front through the fog. The light of the morning brightened as men stood at their stations and waited while others did the work of adjusting lines and sails to give the large ship the best speed and maneuverability.

"Can we sink them by ramming?" Zalman asked.

"The larger warship? No," Aeric said. "But if we're lucky, we can sink the smaller and engage the warship."

"So we will fight hand to hand," Carys said.

"Unless we are lucky," Aeric said. "It is inevitable."

Zalman ran a hand over his bald head. "How many fighting men?"

"No one is allowed on this ship unless they can fight," Aeric said. "Surgeon, cook, carpenter, strikers, doesn't matter. They can all fight."

"How many?" Zalman pressed.

"Thirty-three," Aeric said. "With you? Thirty-five."

"And how many elves will they have?" Carys asked.

Aeric paused a moment before answering. "More than that."

"Give me all the arrows you can spare," she said.

"My crew can shoot, as well," Aeric said.

"Good," Carys said. "But give me all you can. And an extra peerglass, if you have it."

Zalman loomed over the Captain. "Do it," he said.

Aeric gulped. "Very well." He turned to the man next to a ballista near them and gave him the order.

Carys grabbed Zalman's elbow. "Come," she said, and she ran to the foredeck, climbing the stairs and standing just next to the bowsprit, the lance made of iron. As the ships neared them, Zalman got a better look at the Kryan warship. Narrower than *The Last Serpent*, it was just as long, if not longer, and taller, made of dark Liorian wood. The smaller frigate was three or four times as big as *The Happy Lamb*, Chronch's ship, but the Kryan warship and *The Last Serpent* dwarfed it. The frigate would be upon them in minutes.

A man laid a quiver full of arrows next to Carys and placed a bronze peerglass into her hand, and she thanked him as he ran off again. Zalman could count more than fifty arrows in the large quiver.

Aeric stepped up to them, his peerglass against his right eye. "Well mangit all," Aeric said. "That is the *Bird of Prey* and the *Elan*."

Carys nocked an arrow. "What?"

Lowering the peerglass, Aeric sniffed in the wind. "The *Bird of Prey*. That is the Seahawk's ship."

"What the shog are you talking about?" Carys said. "The ship that captured and killed Mikayla's father?"

Aeric faced them. "Yes. And another of Mikayla's captains lost to him last month."

"Shoggers," Carys said.

Aeric said, "Oi," and trotted back to the main deck to prepare for the battle.

More men joined them on the foredeck with bows, quivers and swords or other weapons hanging from their hips. Most were bare-chested like Zalman.

The *Elan* now sailed close, and the men around Zalman nocked an arrow. Carys handed Zalman the peerglass. He gave her an inquisitive stare.

"I can't shoggin' look through the glass and shoot at the same time, you big gedder," she explained. "You have to find me targets. I want officers."

Zalman's brow rose at her. "Yes ma'am."

She frowned while she drew the arrow back. "Shut up. Find me the captain, if you can. But any officer will do."

It took him a moment to adjust his vision to objects suddenly appearing larger, and he had to use slow movements with the peerglass – too fast and it got confusing. Twisting the cylinder focused it; extending it increased the magnification. Bringing the peerglass to bear upon the Elan, he searched the frigate for officers. He counted 20 militan, all with breastplates and shields and gladi ready to board. A sergeant of some sort stood behind them, a short plume on his helmet.

"Sergeant behind the squad on the deck," he muttered. "A blue plume."

"Got it," he heard her say. "Captain?"

He assumed the captain would be further towards the stern, and he scanned the glass in that direction, slow. "Still looking," he said.

There was shouting behind him, preparing to fire the ballista and the catapults. The *Elan* moved to the starboard side, and Carys fired once, the twang of the string sounding in his ear.

"Sergeant down," she said. "Find me that breakin' captain."

Two elves stood next to a large wheel at the stern of the ship, and both had taller blue plumes on their helmets and intricate silver breastplates over longer robes instead of the short tunics.

The spears of the ballista fired at the *Elan* as it sailed past them on the right, most of them missing, but three hit the hull, one punching a nice hole in the side. The pirates around them began firing their own arrows over the *Elan*, a few hitting shields. Most missed their mark. Two arrows wounded militan on the deck of the *Elan*.

On the front line of the militan on the frigate, five militan raised their short bows and fired across the bow. Men on *The Last Serpent* ducked behind cover, but Zalman observed as one pirate received a shaft through his neck, blood spurting as his attempt at a scream became a gurgle. He went down and fell still.

Zalman focused his attention back to the *Elan*. "Got two officers at the stern behind that wheel thing," he said.

"The helm?" Carys asked.

"Yeah, sure," he said.

"Which one is the captain?"

"Don't know," Zalman said. "Take your pick."

"Fine," she said and fired twice. The first took down the elf on the right, through the neck, and the other sailed over the second as he ducked.

Carys cursed under her breath. "Any more?"

The frigate sped by as a few catapults took their shots at it, but nothing hit the smaller vessel.

"No," he said, lowering the peerglass and facing forward now. The *Bird of Prey* was close now, a few hundred mitres away. Flaming missiles began to fire from the *Bird of Prey*, but they fell far short of the bow of *The Last Serpent*. The *Bird of Prey* swung to the east so that it could bring more of its weapons to bear upon *The Last Serpent* before they collided.

"*Elan* coming back around!" Bade shouted from the deck, and the smaller ship raced up alongside *The Last Serpent.*

The pirates in charge of the ballista on the port side were better shots – ten spears shot at the *Elan*, four ripping into the hull. The *Elan* shuddered, and it began to take on water. Five spears hit the deck, and elves dove out of the way as the missiles impaled several of the militan on deck. A few of the militan kept their feet and fired back with their short bows. Two pirates were wounded, one in the shoulder, the other with an arrow into his chest.

Carys ran across to the port side of the foredeck now, an arrow nocked and aiming. Zalman followed and watched her hold motionless for a split second before firing, and the other officer at the helm went down. The *Elan* pitched, the starboard side submerging into the ocean. A few elves leapt from the frigate; others held to the railing as the boat sank.

The crew of *The Last Serpent* cheered.

A ball of flame launched from the *Bird of Prey* and landed three paces away on the foredeck. Men screamed and scattered as two more bounced off the railing and the deck. Three men caught fire, squealing and flailing as the flames began to consume them. The Pirates on the deck responded with skill, throwing water at the burning orbs and dousing their comrades.

Zalman stared forward and saw the *Bird of Prey* within a hundred mitres now. A coordinated volley of arrows rained down upon *The Last Serpent* and men covered their heads with arms and bent behind a mast or whatever was close by to dodge the arrows. Zalman grabbed Carys by the waist and threw her to the deck, hearing her gasp as he covered her with his body next to the railing of the foredeck. One pirate with a bucket of water in his hands got an arrow through his mouth, howling before falling onto a globe of flame. He burned but was already dead by the time he hit the deck.

More balls of flame, more arrows from the *Bird of Prey*. Carys pushed him off of her and jumped to her feet, her bow still in her hand.

"Fire back, you mangers!" Bade's voice from the deck, and the three catapults on the foredeck fired back, as did the archers. Carys ran forward and stood next to the bowsprit again. She fired over and over, so fast it was like a blur. Another volley of arrows from the *Bird of Prey* landed on the deck, and Zalman pulled her down for the moment while to dodge them.

"Will you breakin' stop that!" she said and elbowed him aside so she could have room to keep firing at the *Bird of Prey*.

Zalman noticed that as the Kryan warship turned to meet them, the two ships would collide at full speed but at an angle, less than 20 mitres away. As they turned, the catapults on the port side of *The Last Serpent* flung flaming missiles at the *Bird of Prey*. Ten struck the enemy deck and bounced around; one ball of fire hit the enemy foresail, and the white cloth caught flame.

Ten mitres apart now.

As arrows and balls of flame were fired back and forth between the two massive wooden ships, Zalman put an arm around Carys' waist and hooked the other at the railing to his left. She grunted as he squeezed her. "Hold on!" he said above the din.

She threw her right arm around his neck, burying her face into his bare chest.

The two ships collided with a violent shudder, a deafening noise and a boom of an impact as wood splintered and tore; the clamor from the collision was physical as it passed over them along with the vibrations along the deck. *The Last Serpent* listed to the right, and Zalman felt that his arm was about to be pulled from its socket. But he held on. He thought he heard Carys scream in his ear, but even that was difficult to hear amid the thunderous sound and yelling all around him that seemed to span too much time.

The Last Serpent partially righted itself and slowed, and wood and spikes along the port side dug into the hull of the *Bird of Prey*. Zalman looked up to see hooks and ropes being slung from the Kryan ship over to the railing of their ship, and more than 100 militan waiting to bridge the gap and board *The Last Serpent*.

Carys released him, and he her, and she stood to her feet and was firing at the elves as they attempted to board. Two fell before others realized they needed to hide behind their shields. Five more fell before they realized the shields were too small. The hooks dug into the railing, and Zalman pulled his axes from his belt. He leapt down to the main deck and began to cut the ropes, but there were too many.

The ballista from both ships fired, and at close range, they did severe damage to the wood of the ships or other weapons or the flesh of men or elf. Zalman saw several of the Pirate crew fall, one man nearly cut in half by a large harpoon.

More ropes latched onto the side of the ship, and elves pulled their ships closer, closing the gap. He saw Carys kill three more elves, two of them officers. She jumped down to the main deck to join Zalman, firing the whole way. Zalman spun the axes in his hands and sneered at the militan as they sprung up on their railing and vaulted onto the deck of *The Last Serpent* with a loud battle cry. One last volley of arrows flew from the Bird of Prey, landing among the pirates seconds before the militan attacked. Zalman saw more men fall.

"Keep firing," Zalman said to Carys. "They won't touch you."

She didn't answer with words, but she picked targets and kept shooting arrow after arrow into the militan as they boarded the ship. Within another moment, the whole deck was a sea of chaos, men and elves battling and killing one another. Zalman could see Aeric towards the stern, in the middle of the fray, his sword slicing with furious speed.

Zalman stood behind Carys and protected her right, left, and behind her. A militan approached from the right, and he blocked his sword with one ax and took his shield arm with the other, silencing his scream with a strike through his neck. Zalman spun to the left and batted away the gladi of another militan, kicking out with a leg to catch the elf behind the knee and followed it with the blade of an ax into the ribs. The elf vomited blood as Zalman yanked the weapon from the body, twirling to his right again to battle two more militan that tried to attack from behind. His first strike knocked the shield from one, and he sidestepped a stab to block a swipe from the other.

Men died around him, cut down by the elven gladi among the din of the battle, the clash of metal and bodies slamming into one another. Voices cried out, and the crew of *The Last Serpent* fought with desperation against the overwhelming numbers.

Whirling around, he crouched, cut low, and severed the legs of one militan, both at the knee, and he stood again to hit the other in the face with the flat of a blade, the elf's nose erupting in blood as the jaw broke and moved at an awkward angle. The ax in his other hand followed the strike and was buried into the chest through the breastplate. The legless elf was on his back, screaming, and Zalman crushed his skull against the deck with the flat of an ax.

Next to him, Carys kept firing, picking targets and dropping elf after elf, some only two paces away. She never missed, not that he saw. Without Carys cutting into the militan, the pirates would have been easily overrun, but the battle began to turn. A couple dozen men were dead on the deck, but the pirates started to push back and cause the militan to retreat.

An elf with two swords balanced on the railing to Zalman's right. The elf was no militan. He wore a silver breastplate and fitted plates across his shoulders and thighs. His helmet covered his face and came to a point at his mouth, like a silver beak. He had a curved sword in each hand. The helmet swung to face Zalman and Carys. Dropping to the deck of *The Last Serpent*, the elf slew two of the crew as he approached their position.

The Seahawk. At least, that was what Zalman assumed. The way the elf moved, lithe and fast and confident, it was a safe assumption. The Seahawk launched himself in Carys' direction, both swords spinning, and he slashed another man across the abdomen as he moved, blood and entrails spraying across the deck.

The militan cheered and shouted at the sight of the Seahawk. They rallied and stood firm.

Zalman clenched his teeth and slid to stand between Carys and the approaching warrior, engaging the elf. He blocked one sword as the elf landed and then the other as the strikes kept coming. Zalman knew the Seahawk was too fast, and he retreated, the Seahawk continuing to try and find purchase with those spinning blades. He kicked out at the Seahawk, at his chest, but the elf moved to the side. Zalman's momentum carried him past the elf, and he twirled his axes behind him to block the swords as they sliced at his back. He diverted them, but he felt a gash along his shoulder, a gash that burned.

He blocked two more swipes with his axes as he rotated on a heel, feeling the need to retreat, but he couldn't move far and still protect Carys. The Seahawk leapt to the side to dodge another ax and blocked a second ax strike with both of his swords. Zalman growled in frustration as his vision began to narrow and the cut on his shoulder continued to burn.

Zalman swung an ax at the Seahawk's head. The elf ducked, and Zalman raised his knee, which connected with the face of the helmet, the beak cutting through the leather pants and into the meat of his thigh. The Seahawk's head rocked back, but he was able to get in a stab into Zalman's side. Zalman grunted and brought the other ax around while the elf was dazed; the blade sank deep into the shoulder, through the plate of metal and into the flesh.

The Seahawk cried out, the right arm going limp as Zalman pressed his foot into the chest of the elf to remove his ax. The Seahawk staggered and tried to raise the sword in his left hand. Zalman kicked the sword from his hand and brought both axes together towards the Seahawk's head. The flat side of each blade hit the helmet at once, mangling the silver headpiece and crushing the skull underneath it in a bevy of blood and gore. The corpse dropped to the deck at his feet.

As the Seahawk collapsed to the deck, dead, the remaining militan hesitated, and a few even froze, their faces a mask of horror. Pirates took advantage of the hesitation and struck, attacking in one last desperate push.

Zalman drew a deep breath through his nose, his nostrils flaring, and whirled to face another militan, the gash along his right shoulder beginning to feel as if it were on fire. Blocking a stab of the militan, so slow compared to the Seahawk before, he struck him down.

The wound at his side, which didn't seem that deep before, also burned; the pain grew in intensity to the point that he gritted his teeth and fell to his knees. His vision began to cloud. He was dizzy and weak all of a sudden. Looking down at the wound at his side, black lines like veins grew from the wound.

That is not good, he thought. And then everything went dark.

———

An arrow stuck into the neck of one elf, and with three more arrows held in her right hand, she had already drawn and nocked an arrow as the militan fell. Carys aimed to her left and fired, the shaft sinking into the abdomen of another, even through the breastplate at this distance. The battle had turned, and there weren't many militan left, but she didn't see many men, either.

She had heard the battle between Zalman and the Seahawk behind her, even catching Zalman's brutal victory in her periphery. But when she felt a large weight hit the deck, she pivoted and saw Zalman lying face down and unconscious a pace away.

"Zalman," she whispered and stepped over to him. Laying a hand upon his back, he still breathed, but the wound along his shoulder appeared dangerous and nasty.

Dropping the bow, she drew her sword. Carys crouched over him and rotated in a circle, scanning the battle as it drew to a close on the deck. The last elf was ten mitres away and rushed by three men of *The Last Serpent*; one man stabbed the militan while another bashed him in the jaw with a mace. She lowered her sword as Bade led a handful of men, the remnants of the crew, over to the deck of the *Bird of Prey*.

Kneeling next to Zalman, she saw Aeric limp up toward them. "I don't know what is wrong," Carys said to the Captain as he drew near. "He is wounded, but the wounds aren't that bad. They are strange, though."

Aeric peered down at the corpse below him. "Well, I'll be a skratter," he said. "He killed the Seahawk." He crouched down, wincing at the pain in his leg, a cut along his calf. He picked up one of the Seahawk's swords, carefully, and brought the blade up to his nose, his nostrils flaring as he inhaled. Aeric coughed as he dropped the sword. "Poison blade. Heard rumors."

"Poison?" Carys said. Zalman's breaths came ragged and short. "What can we do?"

"Here? Nothing." Aeric picked up both swords and stood. He threw them over the side into the water. "I don't know if any doctor in Enakai would even know what to do. He's dying."

She heard the shouting and screams of the dying from the *Bird of Prey*.

"No," she said. Had those black veins grown in the last few moments? The blood from the shoulder wound was dark, too dark, and it stank.

No. Not him. Not now. I can't lose him like Uncle Reyan.

A fleeting thought came to her mind through the shock, almost like a voice but more like an impression. Hard to tell what it was, it was so quick. Lifting the unforged sword, she cut across the gash, then into it. Clearer blood poured from the wound, cleaner and not as dark.

"I need water," she said. "Quick."

The Captain staggered to his feet and stumbled in a run to a nearby bucket of water. He brought it to her. She pressed her hands on his back and squeezed as much blood from his body as she could. *I have to get rid of the poison*, she thought.

Taking the bucket from Aeric, she rinsed out the injury on the shoulder. Once. Twice. Once again before she thought it was good enough. Zalman's bronze skin had paled.

"He has a wound at his side," Aeric said.

"Help me get him over," she said, and they rolled Zalman over to his back with some effort. She repeated the process, cutting into the wound and across it and then squeezing as much blood as she could. Rinsing the wound a handful of times, she had Aeric roll him back over. The next few minutes were filled with bleeding and rinsing both wounds as much as she could. They checked a cut on his leg, but it didn't appear poisoned.

After they were done, Zalman was breathing, but it was a ragged breath. His skin was pallid and hot to the touch, slick with sweat.

"You've done all you can," Aeric said. "But some poison made it into his system."

Holding back her sobs, she leaned down and touched her forehead to his feverish one.

"Come on, you big gedder," she whispered. "Don't you breakin' die on me now."

Chapter 27

Waiting to Die

"I'll meet you in Ketan," Eshlyn said to him as they stood next to his horse. Esai's horse. Her stare suggested wrath if he was not there.

As Earon faced her, the morning sun was bright in his eyes over the trees to the east. The breeze cooled the air, not as thick here, high in the mountains, but he would travel down in to the forest today. The heat would return.

The stone bridge stretched out before him over the deep canyon. Earon had a fleeting thought to jump down into that ravine for a quick death. It might be better than whatever Caleb might do to him. The man's eyes continued to haunt him, waking or sleeping. But Athelwulf had been right. He knew. A quick death was easy but would only avoid what was truly right – surrendering to Caleb and Carys' justice. And if that justice was Caleb cutting him down with an unforged sword, then Earon was ready to accept it.

Were there any possibilities for redemption?

Considering Athelwulf's example, how could he deny the possibility? Even though he only knew Athelwulf for a few days, no other man had ever understood him like the great warrior. Earon grieved him like an old friend.

He cleared his throat and ran a hand over his beard. "Ketan," he repeated.

That seemed to mollify her. "Lead them through the Saten but not by Taggart."

Also glancing to the rear, Shecayah sat atop a gray mare, awaiting him, and Tobiah was astride a bosaur ahead of a column of the animals, 150 of them. Further behind the bosaur, 800 men of the Beorgai waited to leave, with their *corran* and short spears.

"I know the way," he said.

With a group so large, Earon would stay as far away from Taggart as possible. He believed a road existed that led into lower Manahem, to the west. They could easily make Ketan from there. That decision was two days or more away, though.

Eshlyn began to leave but paused. She said, "What do you know of the Father Tree?"

The *Abaes*. Her question brought up more memories of his father, painful thoughts. He wanted Sorcos, or a drink, at least.

"I know what the Ydu says about it. Little more."

"What is that?"

He took a deep breath. "It is a sacred and holy place."

"The Tomb of Yosu."

"Yes," Earon said. "Before he lived again."

She was quiet a moment. "What is there? Inside?"

Earon shrugged. "Besides the unforged swords of hundreds of dead *Sohan-el*? No one really knows. Different legends over the millennia but nothing concrete."

"Legends? Tell me."

"Some see a great light or a great darkness. Some say the souls of the First Men speak to you. Others hear silence. Most never speak of their experience."

"Thank you," she said.

"One more thing," Earon muttered.

Eshlyn waited for him to continue.

"My father ... spoke of it," he said. "He said that you must be careful what you bring into that place."

"Why?"

"Because you will leave without it," Earon said. "Whatever goes with you into that holy place, you will be required to leave it."

＋

Bweth stood over Hunter's grave dressed in her armor, a work of art that she wondered if anyone would ever recognize. She doubted it. The only man worthy of understanding the genius she wore lay in the ground at her feet. Holding the mace in her right hand and the shield in her left, she took time to breathe.

There were rows and rows of graves here in the eastern field outside of the city of Biram. So many dead.

"You daft man," Bweth muttered. "O' course you would try to beat a breakin' Bladeguard, and without me, no less, all because people were in shoggin' danger."

She shook her head. Tears ran down her cheeks underneath the helmet.

The man didn't answer. He always did know her thoughts.

"Yea. That is why I loved you. No fear. Showed me that on the wall at Ketan, you did. Did you and your ancestors proud."

A breeze from the south rustled trees and bent what little grass was left between the graves. She chuckled.

Bweth squatted low over the grave.

"You were a king of a man, Hunter," she said. "And I want ye to know I'll see this revolution through to the end. For you."

The babe within her kicked, once.

"Aye," she said, pressing a gauntlented hand to her belly. "And for you."

———

Their swords clashed high then low, Caleb pressing the attack. Aden retreated, barely able to turn the strikes aside. After a few moments, Aden lost his sword, watching as it flew five mitres to the right.

"How is your shoulder?" Caleb asked.

With the morning sun burning down on them, Aden walked over and retrieved his sword. "It's fine."

Caleb spun his blade in his hand. "You heal fast."

Aden didn't answer, lifting his sword to begin again.

"And you're holding back," Caleb said.

"What?"

"I saw it when you fought Saben, and a little with me here," Caleb said. "You're holding back. You could have beaten Saben."

"You're not serious," Aden said, lowering his blade.

"I am. You're one of the most talented swordsmen we have, you and Xander. But you must stop holding back."

"You mean fight out of control?"

"You know I don't mean that. There is a balance you must find, a balance between complete control and complete dedication to the moment, to every move you make. You question yourself as you fight, even if you don't realize it.

"Your questions are good. They lead you to knowledge, but they can hinder you during a fight. Make a decision, and commit to it. Stay in control but commit fully. It is a difficult balance to find, but as we fight more experienced elves, you'll need it to survive."

"You mean to win?"

Caleb scoffed. "No. Survive. No one ever wins a fight."

"That duel with the Bladeguard the other day? Looked like you won that one."

"Then you haven't been paying attention."

Aden ran his left hand through his hair. "So this *balance* you're talkin' 'bout, when did you find it? You remember?"

Caleb gazed away, as if seeing the memory. "Oh, yeah."

"When was it?"

"Well, I wasn't a very good spy," Caleb said with a smirk.

"What does that mean?"

"I was about eighteen years-old, almost nineteen, and Galen took me on a series of missions around Eviland, different types of missions to teach me about different aspects of being a Bladeguard. We didn't really trust each other yet, but he didn't trust anyone else to teach me. So he took me."

"What kind of missions?" Aden asked.

"Espionage, assassination, sabotage, that kind of thing, all part of Tanicus' agenda with the surrounding nations. We traveled under other names, different papers, and I was his servant or slave. As a slave, I could go places that Galen could not, especially in the dwarven kingdoms.

"One particular mission was across the border into Jibryl, the northern part of that nation. A warlord was gathering forces and raiding eastern Kryus and Faltiel. Sending a legion or any official Kryan force could start a war, so we went into the camp to take out the elven warlord.

"But, like I said, I wasn't a very good spy. I'm not … patient enough. We found ourselves in quite a battle. I was able to kill the warlord, but I also roused the camp. Galen and I fought our way out. Watching him, it was like nothing I had ever seen. I wanted to learn how to wield a sword like that.

"Galen was surrounded and far outnumbered, cornered. There was an opportunity for me to run, escape into the night and leave him there, but I didn't. I fought my way to him, and there was a moment, as clear as any memory, when I felt in complete control and fully committed to every slash and move I made. I was in command of myself but immersed in the moment. Tomorrow didn't matter. The next second didn't matter. I stood there and fought side by side with the greatest swordmaster the world has ever known. I wasn't near as good – I don't think I'll ever be that good – but I held my own.

"We made it out of that camp. We survived. And from that time on, it was different. I knew that balance in a battle. And Galen and I became more than master and student. We became friends. For years, before Danelle, he and Iletus were my only friends."

Aden remembered the stories from *The Tales of the Sohan-el* as he listened to Caleb. He wondered if anyone would write down Caleb's story, a man who seemed weak and human at times and then immortal or invincible in others. Would anyone record the tales of this revolution and the lives of those that led and inspired men against the Kryan Empire? People like Eshlyn, Carys, Athelwulf? Perhaps, if any of them survived.

"What was the difference?" Aden asked. "How did you 'let go'?"

"In that moment, I remember accepting death as a part of life," Caleb said. "I knew the reality of my own death, and I didn't worry about it. It didn't factor into my decisions, my commitment. It was … freeing. I wasn't happy or sad or worried. I just was. Death or life, all the same."

Caleb fell silent, and Aden searched the man's crestfallen face. "Does it get easier? Since you found that balance, does it get easier?"

"When I was young and training? It was easy. But after Danelle, after coming to Ereland and being responsible for so many around me, it is ... difficult sometimes. But I know where that place is, and I can find it. Once you do, you can always return to it, for good or ill. But it will save your life one day, and perhaps those around you."

Caleb raised his sword. "So let's go again. And try to find that balance."

Aden crouched into his stance. Caleb rushed him, spinning and attacking him like never before. Their swords clashed again and again, and Aden held a grip on his wits while acting and reacting. He tried to stay in control but fully commit. Beginning to retreat, Aden instead circled and attacked on his own, from the right, forcing Caleb to adjust his own advance. Within another thirty seconds, Aden's sword went flying one more time, and he saw Caleb's blade swiping towards his throat, a killing blow.

The blade stopped centimitres from his neck, and Aden gasped.

Caleb grinned at him. "Much better. Let's go again."

———

She felt the gentle rocking of the ship as she sat next to the bed, Zalman lying there, unconscious. Aeric had given Bade's private cabin to Carys when they came aboard *The Last Serpent*, but now it was for Zalman. His feet hung over the end of the mattress; dressed only in his breeches, his body was covered with sweat, and he stank, a sickly sweet stench. Carys had stitched up the wounds, but the skin around those areas was red and inflamed. Not infected – she checked.

The Last Serpent sailed back to Enakai now. After making sure every elf was dead, Aeric was towing the *Bird of Prey* back to Enakai. They would not waste a great ship like that.

Aeric lost 27 of his own crew in the battle. The remaining eight men all bore wounds to one degree or another. Barring another fight on the way back, they had enough men to sail the large ship. Carys had helped suture a few wounds of those injured, but she sat now at the edge of the bed, her hand on Zalman's arm, watching.

And praying. She knew prayer was important. Carys remembered her mother praying at night, calm and loving prayers of faith, sometimes desperate, although she was too young to know why. Her aunt and uncle both spent time praying as she grew up, and Carys even joined them, especially if Earon did.

Leaving her uncle, the Prophet, and running all those years ago, she didn't pray much on her own. Never saw much of the need. Oh, there were moments during the battle of Ketan that she asked El for help, pleaded to keep Caleb alive, even for just one more day. As guilty as she felt for only praying during a desperate time, it did not stop her from interceding for Zalman now.

She had known men that fell in battle. She had seen death, almost tasted it herself up on that wall. But it was different now, with Zalman. She didn't know why exactly. They had become friends, sure, enduring the last few ninedays together, traveling, fighting side by side. She trusted him, relied on him. He knew what happened in Landen and still thought her strong and capable.

But there was more, and she didn't want to even think it.

The emotions came unbidden, however. Was she falling for him? Just a few months ago he was a criminal in a Kryan prison, and she had hated him. Now her heart fluttered for him like a little schoolgirl? It was maddy, more than maddy.

And why would he love her? He had fame and a million women over his life.

Then she remembered again his compliment to her, how her heart seemed to melt within her. He had given up that fame and eventually those women, she knew. He protected her in a way that both drove her insane and touched her. The man was noble, strong.

And just as she realized it, she was about to lose him.

She heard a noise at the door. Her head turned and saw Aeric and Salto, the ship surgeon, behind her, but after the glance she watched Zalman again. Salto moved to the other side of the bed and leaned over to touch Zal's neck.

Carys knew what the man would find. "He's barely breathing, and his heartbeat is getting faint." Carys drew a labored breath. "He's dying." It hurt her to say it.

"You did what you could," Salto said, a short, stocky man with a moustache that fell to his chest. "You bled what you could out of him. But …"

"But now he's dying slow instead of quick," Carys finished.

Aeric leaned against the door behind her; she heard the wood creak. "You need to eat," he said. "It's been near a day. Please. There's plenty. Take some bread, at least."

"No," she said. "Not until he recovers."

"It may take days, yet," Aeric told her.

"Then it takes what it takes, El willing," she said. "He was wounded, protecting *me*."

"Of course he did," Aeric said. "That is what we do with those we care for."

Frowning, she looked at him.

"Did he not tell you?" Aeric said. "I'm sorry. I thought he did." He cleared his throat. "And do you care for him, as well?"

Shoggers, she thought. Carys turned back to watch Zalman.

"Well, we will be at Enakai within the next few hours," Aeric said. "I can have him moved to my place there. We would not have won that battle without the both of you. I owe you that and more."

"He won't survive moving him, will he?" Carys said to the surgeon.

Salto grimaced.

"Then we will stay here," she said.

"Come then," Aeric said. "I've brought you some food. Eat."

Carys shook her head.

"There's nothing more to do but wait," Aeric said. "Or is El more likely to answer your prayer the more you suffer?"

"I don't think that's how he works," she said. "He does what he will. But I can ask, can't I?"

"Yes, you can," Aeric said. "Is El the kind of god that can bring men back from the dead?"

"He wouldn't be much of a god if he couldn't, would he?"

"I guess not." Aeric gestured to the surgeon. "Let us leave them."

Both men left her there, alone with her friend. At that moment, she felt she was losing the only friend she had in the world.

Carys rested one hand upon her sword and the other upon his stomach, slick with sweat and feverish to the touch.

Speak the words, she heard.

What words? she thought, but she knew.

She leaned over and rested her forehead on his chest. And when she spoke, the words were hers, but another voice seemed to echo her own.

"Live," she whispered. "Zalman, live."

The next morning, Caleb sat on his horse, the fine stallion he'd had for months since traveling across the continent of men. Iletus was next to him, sitting on Cyprian's horse, taken for himself at the end of the Battle of Biram. They faced the men and women of the *Hamon-el* on the eastern road out of Biram.

When they had left Ketan, he remembered smiling, if not eager, faces, some even gawking in awe as they passed him in Ketan. Their number, 4,000 strong, made them feel invincible. Yes, some were veterans of the Battle of Ketan, and they were somber, realizing more than others the danger ahead. Most had marched from the massive walls and gates of Ketan with dreams of heroism and the cause of freedom in their words.

But the *Hamon-el* all knew what war was like now. Demics were evil creatures, unnatural monsters from the Underland. Those men and women were protecting their homes, their children when they fought that battle.

Killing elves was different. They were living, breathing people. The elves died with the same cries and sorrows that men did, their blood the same color as that of men. Men and elves hacked at each other among the horror of the impaled citizens of Biram. War was not for heroes, and the *Hamon-el* understood that now.

Eighty-two men, many of them dealing with injuries, stayed in Biram with the elven prisoners. While the dead had been buried, there was more work to be done in the city, clean up mostly, and the humans would need time to heal and return to full strength before traveling to Ketan. After a few more days, those men would take the prisoners back to Ketan, give news of the battle, and place the militan in the prison in the city.

He wished he could release the militan, but they were now in open war. They would only pick up blades and become a threat again.

Caleb attempted not to think of the irony of practically enslaving elves in his quest to lead humanity to freedom.

In truth, the Battle of Biram was a miracle. A Kryan legion, in a defensible position, waiting on an untested army of men spelled certain death; and yet Caleb's army beat the odds and only lost a third of their own forces while killing over 80 percent of the legion. In stories, the men would have cheered and gone to the next battle feeling even more confident El was on their side. But this was not a fire tale.

Even when you won the battle, even against such odds, death and exhaustion caused more doubt than faith. It was a stronger enemy than any Kryan legion ever could be. Not one man or woman smiled at him as they passed. None looked at him in awe anymore. They had lost their friends, good men and women that had families and wives and children.

And while more than 2,000 men left Biram, those men's faces were haunted by the senseless violence of war.

In those old stories, tales of great armies that won battle after battle, a leader stood before the distraught men under his care, and he gave them a stirring speech, inspired them with the colorful words and phrases soldiers needed to hear.

But when Caleb spoke now to his army, his voice was low. The *Hamon-el* were silent enough that he could hear the faint sound of the wind rustling the leaves of the trees behind him.

"Many died at the battle here. We won a great victory. Many would have said it was an impossible victory. We leave Biram with more weapons and supplies, but we are also armed with the reality that war requires sacrifice, and we have all paid that cost, one way or another.

"We buried our friends, our brothers, but the grief lingers. It will continue to linger. I understand if you are weary and disheartened. I am, as well."

He met the gaze of faces that carried a weight of sorrow, fear, or uncertainty.

"But we fight for something bigger than borders or wealth or conquest. We fight against those that would enslave and oppress. We have tasted freedom. Now we go to battle so that others can be free. Because that is our purpose, we cannot fight like the elves do; we cannot allow our anger and vengeance to guide our actions. We will be held to a higher standard, for we contend for something higher, something greater, and any who cannot abide that standard, I understand. You may leave now."

Caleb found Lyam in the crowd, at the head of his new division, reorganized after the battle. Lyam would not meet his eyes.

"We are at war, at war with the greatest empire in all of Eres. We saw what Kryus did at Biram, and they cause suffering all over the lands of men. Someone must stand against them. I will stand against them. I pray for peace, for a quick end to this war, but until then I will fight and sacrifice so that others may live free. I am honored to stand with any who stand with me."

Looking out over the army, he found the faces of Bweth and Xander and Aden and others. Caleb turned his horse and rode east. He heard Iletus sigh and turn his horse to ride next to him.

Caleb didn't glance behind him, but he heard the shuffling of feet, the clanging of weapons, the snorting of horses, and the creaking of wagon wheels as the *Hamon-el* began the march to attack the Kryan outpost in Taggart.

Break me, Caleb thought.

"What is the greatest weapon in a duel?" Iletus' voice reached him.

Galen's teaching came to him. "Patience."

"Why?" Iletus pressed.

"Because in any duel, the victor is the one that endures until the opponent makes a mistake. Then the victor takes advantage of that mistake and finishes the opponent without prejudice."

"Is going to Taggart an example of patience?"

Caleb grumbled. "I've never been good at patience."

"Yes. Exactly. You rush in and fight when there might be better options." Iletus paused. "Is this the best tactic? Going to the elven stronghold in Taggart?"

"You question me? Now?"

"I am here to help you, to advise you," Iletus said. "The Empire will not underestimate you again. I am simply trying to get you to think of your training."

"I do think of it," Caleb said. "I cannot help thinking of it. Galen was a great teacher, and that is what great teachers do. There are other weapons in a duel, however. They can be effective, as well. Surprise, commitment, passion. A good kick in the crotch. My master taught me all of it."

"Is this one of those weapons?" Iletus asked. "Or do those images of women and children flayed and impaled drive you to vengeance?"

"Oh, they do. I can't deny it, and I won't. But it is more than that. I am being what I was born to be, what I was trained to do."

"I know. I helped train you."

Caleb fixed his eyes on Iletus. "Then you tell me. What have I been trained to be? To do?"

Iletus breathed in through his nose. "You were trained to raise up an army and cut out Tanicus' heart. Galen taught you to be the perfect weapon."

"It was theory then. It is real now, Iletus," Caleb said. "You are a traitor, helping me destroy the armies of your homeland that oppress mine. Do you question it? Is there conflict within you at your choice?"

Iletus lowered his stare for a moment before lifting it again. "No, Caleb. I was there, at the beginning, with Galen as he established and molded the Bladeguard, stood with him as Tanicus built Kryus into an Empire. More than anyone, I know that the Empire is founded on murder and fear and corruption.

"I believed we were mad when Galen and I began to doubt Tanicus and the Empire. But over time, we realized the truth. I argued against Galen's plan to train a human and use him to begin a revolution. For years I opposed it. When he brought you to Kohinoor, it drove a wedge between Galen and me for a time."

Iletus leaned forward, his eyes blazing. "Then I saw how you endured, your commitment, and I knew there was hope. I do not know what the future holds, but there is no conflict. Men must be free and Tanicus removed from power. It must be done for the good of your people and mine." His eyes gleamed, and his face fell. "And maybe for my own soul."

The Bladeguard sat straight again. "Furthermore, I am your friend. I have been, and I always will."

"I know," Caleb said. "Thank you."

He considered the road before them, so peaceful now, the sun bright and the sky clear blue.

Caleb lifted the Kingstaff that lay across his saddle and gripped it until his knuckles went white. "I have to change my answer," he said.

"What is that?" Iletus said.

"You asked me to name the greatest weapon," Caleb said. "I need to change my answer."

Iletus raised an eyebrow at him.

He is not a man but a sword …

"I am."

Chapter 28

The Garden

It was an engine designed to level armies and towns and even cities, made of flesh and bone and blood and steel. After a day of rest and resupply, the legion was ready to move on to Biram, or west to wherever the *Brendel*'s army might be.

General Pyram watched as Daelas sauntered towards him, that Wraith in shadows at her side, completely hidden by the gray cloak. The morning sun warmed a fine spring day, a good day to march to war, killing, and death. Bad weather could be as effective as a wall in slowing an army, although no siege work existed to stop rain or snow or mud. Pyram knew the northern spring. The rains would not come for another month.

Andos stood with him in the field to the west of Taggart, the legion forming up and preparing to move. Pyram loved the sounds of an army, the restless noise of horses breathing and neighing, elves shouting orders or grunting with the effort of loading supplies on wagons, hooves in the dirt, the clanking of steel shields and spears. It all combined in a familiar din that made him feel at home.

As Daelas reached him, he considered her. She was beautiful, her skin like cream, her body slight and strong, but the lone strip of hair gave her a fierce look. He imagined that a night of passion with her would require him to keep the dagger underneath his bracer close. And the one in his boot. She walked more like a warrior than a woman, but her gait combined with the shape of her hips attracted him just the same. His frown did not change, but he smirked inwardly. It might be worth the danger.

"Greetings, Bladeguard," Andos said.

She did not acknowledge him. "General," she said.

Pyram regarded the Bladeguard.

"I have decided that you will join us as we leave today," Daelas said.

"You mean march with you and the legion?" Pyram asked.

"Yes," she said.

He knew Andos glanced his way, but Pyram refused to react. "Are you officially declaring Directive XVII?"

"Do I need to?" she asked. "I have two of your remaining officers willing to sign off on it, if there is need."

Now Pyram did direct his frown to Andos.

"Not I, sir," he said.

"I asked him, but he refused me," Daelas said. "I found others."

"What of the command here?" Pyram asked. "We would leave Taggart without proper command. What if this *Brendel* moves into the forest and around us to attack here?"

"We are leaving this outpost staffed as before, when the first legion left a few ninedays ago," she said. "The only difference is that Andos and your officers will be without their general. I assume you have confidence in Andos to hold this outpost if attacked?"

In truth, he did. Andos was a rare breed in the world – he knew his strength and weakness, what he could do and what he could not. He would delegate and allow others to make decisions according to their expertise. In some ways, he was a better leader than Pyram.

"You are in command of the legion," Pyram said. "What would my task be?"

"You will come as an observer," Daelas said. "Perhaps you will learn what it takes to crush a rebellion."

Pyram clasped his hands before him, restraining himself from showing any signs of anger. He did not like being blamed for the failure of other Bladeguard, especially not by a third one, but it was the way of bureaucracy. His dislike was not due to a need to defend his innocence. He was a soldier at heart and lived to serve Kryus. His hate was due to one truth: more than armies or revolution or dissent, it was bureaucracy that would end up killing the Empire.

The possibility existed, as well, that if they did meet up with the *Brendel*'s army, Pyram might be able to do some good and help secure the victory. Slight possibility. Daelas didn't seem ready to give him much respect, enough to let him lead.

He saw the fear in Andos' eyes. He really should learn not to be so transparent. "Andos and my other officers are well-trained and will do a fine job," Pyram said as he faced Daelas again. He gave her a bow. "I live to serve the Empire."

"Let us hope so," she said. The Bladeguard spun on her heel and traipsed away, the Wraith moving silent along with her, gliding like a spirit.

By the nine gods, Pyram thought. *Maybe it wouldn't be worth the risk after all.*

—✦—

Kiano stood over Athelwulf's grave, north of Da'ar in a clearing reserved for his family. The mountain and great trees with black trunks and leaves of brilliant colors loomed over her as she approached him.

Eshlyn had been standing over too many graves recently. The grief was familiar but no less real. Would it ever hurt less? What would it mean if it did?

"It is time for me to go," she said. Eshlyn carried a pack with extra clothes and food. Tied to the pack was Athelwulf's sword.

The elder did not turn. "Will you return?"

"I don't think so." How could she know for sure? She had been led – or pushed? – on a winding and desperate path ever since that night in Campton, the night her husband died fighting so she and her son could live. Thinking of Javyn now, her heart ached, an emptiness similar to the grief for her friends, Esai and Athelwulf, but deeper, truth be told. She touched the golden marriage bracelet on her arm. "After I go to the Father Tree, I need to see my son."

The elder cleared his throat as he looked down at his own son's grave. "I understand," he said. "And after you see your son?"

"I don't know," she admitted. She wondered about Caleb, Aden, Carys and the others. So much had happened to Eshlyn since she left Ketan. Much could have changed with the others, as well. And she still had to face the Tomb of Life under the Father Tree.

He turned to her now, his face warm to her. "You are the *Bashawyn*. You will always be welcome here. You and your son. We owe you more than we can pay."

Eshlyn glanced down at the grave and stepped closer to Kiano. "You owe me nothing. Friends do not keep debts. Let us part as friends."

Kiano gave her a small bow. "As friends, then."

"Good," she said. She called out to the Mahakar in her mind, with her heart. She knew he was close. He would have stayed in the city, had she asked, but she did not. The Mahakar needed to fly, to soar above the mountains and the trees. While that perspective showed him tragedy, it also caused him joy. She knew the feeling well. However, she had requested he stay near, for she would need him.

She searched the sky to the east, and she saw the flying tiger appear over the trees. He covered the distance to the clearing within a few seconds, the massive wings beating with amazing and almost magical control as he flew over her and landed off to her left. Eshlyn walked over to the Mahakar as he lay prostrate. She reached him and buried her face in his warm, white fur. It smelled so clean and pure, like the forest and the sky all at once. She secured the pack across her back and climbed upon the Mahakar's shoulders.

She swiveled toward Kiano once more, and he watched her. The Mahakar stood, and she forced a smile. Kiano returned the effort. The tiger beneath her reared, lifting his paws, and the wings pounded at the air. They were in the sky in an instant, soaring north over the mountains to the Forest of Saten and the Father Tree.

With the bloodwolf on her heels, Tamya entered the area near Aden's tent and stood in front of the campfire, facing him. Two men sat with Aden, one on either side of him, Vic and Rener, other platoon leaders in Aden's division. The men huddled close to the light of the fire in the dark.

Vic threw down two Tablets, and Aden leaned back and laughed. Rener cursed. "A priest and a general?" Aden said. "No way. You cheat."

Chuckling and grinning, Vic picked up the rest of his Tablets. "Don't hate me 'cause you play like crit," Vic said. "Not my fault."

Rener threw up his hands. "But a full run? That's the third you had tonight."

"Don't talk about runs," Vic said. "I got the crits."

Tamya watched as all three of the men laughed. She crossed her arms and stepped closer. Hema growled.

That got their attention. Aden continued to smirk, but the smiles disappeared from the other two as they noticed her and the bloodwolf.

She narrowed her eyes at Vic and Rener. "Both of you. Leave."

Vic raised a brow at Aden.

"It's okay," Aden said. "We'll pick this up tomorrow night."

Vic and Rener scowled at her as they gathered their things and stood. "See you in the morning," Rener said to Aden.

"Early," Aden agreed. "Caleb wants to get going early tomorrow, try to get past the Acar."

The men nodded at him and left without a word to Tamya, leaving her alone with Aden and his bushy dark hair and those big ears.

"Come on," he said. "Sit."

"I'd rather stand," she said.

He shrugged.

"I went and talked to Caleb," Tamya said.

"Yeah?" Aden said. "What about?"

Her nostrils flared. *Fool man.* He was smug. "You know what about," she mumbled.

"What did he say?"

"You know what he said."

"Me?" Aden squeaked. "How would I know?"

"You talked to him," she said.

"I talk to him a lot, but I don't know what you mean."

It was her turn to growl, and the bloodwolf looked up at her. "I told him that I killed one of my own men during the battle," she said. "And he told me how sorry he was and that it was tragic. But he said that wasn't a reason to quit."

"Well, he's right," Aden said. "It's not."

"You talked to him."

"I promise. I didn't." His voice lowered and deepened, giving him a new authority. Where did he learn that? Caleb? She trusted him, though. He didn't lie. He said stupid things, but he didn't lie.

"He told me same as you, almost word for breakin' word. It wasn't my fault, it was an accident, I should learn from it, crit like that. And when I told him he should get rid of me, send me away, he refused. He said I was free to quit, to leave on my own, but that as for him, he didn't see a reason for me to go."

"Maybe since we both said the same thing, you should realize it's not crit."

"Shog it all, Aden," she said, rounding the fire. "Just send me away. Send me back to Ketan or back to the Ghosts."

"No," he said.

Tamya rubbed her face with both hands and then spread her hands before him. "I don't know if I can go into battle like that again, not leading other men. I don't trust myself. Is that what you want to hear?"

Aden took a deep breath. "You're free to leave anytime. Anyone is. You know that. But no one is sending you away."

His eyes pleaded with her, spoke to her, called to her. She tried to tear away, but she couldn't. His stare caught her and kept her from leaving, from running, even though that was all she wanted to do.

Tamya pulled her arms across her belly. "I don't know what to do," she said. "I don't know what you want from me."

"Tell me his name," Aden said, almost a whisper.

"What?" she breathed.

"Your son," Aden said. "Tell me his name."

She shook her head, finally able to break away from his eyes. The only sound was the wind through the nearby trees and the crackling of the fire and her own breathing. All too loud suddenly.

"Obasi." She bit her lip. "I called him Obasi, after my mother. Her name was Obasa." She wiped a sleeve across her nose. "She sold herself into slavery at twelve years old. While she was the only child, her parents still couldn't afford to feed her, clothe her. So she went to the market and sold herself."

Many in Oshra and Lior chose to sell themselves into deeper slavery. Starving, or watching those you loved wasting away in the crit and death of the Oshran streets, what choice was there? Crime. Or death.

"She was bought by one of the elven officials in Oshra. He was an administrator for the legion commander. He had a large home near the temple complex in the northeastern part of the city. His name was Verlin, and he brought her to his home to serve him, in the kitchens. His house had this beautiful garden."

She looked at Aden. He said nothing. Like a stone, he waited, listening.

"I don't know when he started raping her, but he did. Or is it rape when it is your property?" She swallowed hard. "I don't know, but she had me when she was fourteen years old. That elf was my father. She never told me, but I knew." Tamya pointed at her ears. "And I was raised in that house, knowing what he did to my mother." She remembered, even now, the noises at night, his coming into her mother's room. The smell of him, a dirty kind of clean, emerged with the memory in her mind there in the camp near the fire and the bloodwolf. It nauseated her.

Aden remained silent.

"He started on me when I was ten," she said. "At first, he tried to hide it. Don't know why." She had thought, at times, glad when he visited her, as if she spared her mother somehow. An odd thing to think, but she had been a child. Her mother had been her world.

"When my mother first found out," Tamya continued. "I was twelve, and she was angry ... really angry. She had figured out how to keep from getting pregnant, after me, I guess, and she taught me, you know. That was life for us. But over time, I suppose, it got to her, and she stood up to him. As you can imagine, that did not go over well.

"So I was fourteen, same age as my mother when I was born, when my father, the elf, beat her until she died. I heard her screams and the pounding upon her body with his fists from the other side of the locked door. I couldn't get in to help her."

Aden squinted as he stood to face her, as if what she said brought him pain.

"I tried. I did. I split my knuckles beating on that door, and when he finally opened it, I saw her dead. I attacked him, but I was young, and small, and weak. He beat me, too, but left me alive."

She didn't really want to continue, but she couldn't stop now. How had she gotten so far into it so quickly?

"Verlin had her removed from the house like she was some kind of shoggin' trash, all wrapped up in rags. All I could do was watch, numb and weak and beaten. She was dead. The only person that I cared about. And he had killed her."

Running a hand through his bushy dark hair, Aden took another step towards her.

"Some of the other slaves took me in, tended my wounds. But I saw his eyes, murder in them. I knew he would kill me next.

"He liked to spend time in his garden, and it was beautiful. There were trees and plants from distant lands, immaculately manicured. He went there to work on his books, the budgets and numbers of different things, as if he needed to go there to see something calm and wonderful while he made sure the legions of death had their supplies. Or maybe that's just what I wanted to believe, those naïve times when I needed to believe something good about him.

"That night, the day he killed my mother, before he could come to me, I snuck out of the slaves' quarters. I hurt all over, barely able to walk, but I did. I picked up this cooking knife from the kitchens, had a blade bigger than my hand, and I went out to the garden. He liked to take me there, to … you know.

"He was there, just sitting there, his back to me. Moving as silent as I could, he didn't hear me. Afraid and so angry, I raised the knife and stuck it into his back. It hurt him, and he fell, but it didn't kill him."

Recalling that night, it was like yesterday in her mind. Her father, the elf who killed her mother, screaming in pain and cursing in anger, reaching behind to try to pull the knife from his back as he crawled along the ground where he liked to rape her.

"He carried this jeweled sword around with him everywhere on a golden belt. I took the sword and ran it through his heart as he whimpered and crawled away with a kitchen knife in his back. I killed my father that night in his garden."

Aden moved closer, five paces away.

"I got scared. Did anyone see? Anyone hear?

"I ran from the house, making sure I wasn't seen, and I hid in the city. They searched for me, sent out the Citywatch and militan. But it is a big city, and I wore my hooded cloak to hide the fact I was a half-elf. I found the places of the city where the Citywatch don't go, dark places. Over time, I grew my hair out to hide the ears. I lived on the streets for a while, stealing, prostitution, whatever to survive."

He gazed into the distance, like he remembered similar things. She remembered he grew up on the streets of Asya.

"One night, I saw this man. He was obviously from out of town, and I tried to steal his purse. But he caught me. A young man, but he was strong. I offered to … do things, shog him, you know, for money or food or whatever, just to let me go. He refused.

"Instead, he took me to his inn and fed me. I didn't trust him, but I barely ate as it was. What could it hurt? What could he do to me that I didn't let others do to me for money? But he just gave me food. Of course, it was Berran. He was in the city for a few days. I ate with him every night. And just before he left, he asked me if I wanted to come with him, to leave Oshra and go back with him to Anneton.

"I thought that this man seemed nice enough, and even if he used me for shoggin' or whatever, it had to be a better life than the one I had. So I went with him. But he never touched me, not in any sexual way, at least. I lived with him and helped him on his farm. He talked to me, though, of El and Yosu and his faith. He even told me about the Prophet. I was seventeen when he told me I was free to go. He knew people in Oshra or Botan or Galya or other places where I could start over. Berran even said he would give me money to travel.

"But I didn't want to go. Even if I did, where would I go? So we got married. And I started to forget how critty my life had been before, how bad life could be. When I got pregnant, I believed my life could be good. That is, until I saw Obasi's head bashed against a stone and my husband burned at the stake."

"Tamya," Aden groaned and stepped towards her, his arms open, like he wanted to touch her or hold her.

Retreating, she pushed him away. "Haven't you been listening? I won't forget how critty life can be again. I can't. You say you won't send me away? Then fine. I don't know what I'm going to do, but I quit as one of your platoon leaders. I'll kill elves, but I won't lead men anymore. I won't."

She turned and strode towards the rest of camp. A few mitres away from the fire, she noticed Hema wasn't at her heels. Glancing back, the breakin' wolf was still sitting with Aden. Tamya sneered at the wolf. "Come on."

The wolf whined and looked up at Aden – actually looked up at the idiot man!

Aden scratched the wolf behind the ear. "S'okay, Hema," he said. "Go on."

Tamya left with the bloodwolf at her heels.

—⊢—

Carys awoke with a start in a dark room.

When had she fallen asleep? She remembered wiping sweat from Zalman's body, cooling him as much as she could with wet cloths, forcing him to drink as much water as she could get in him. Between the exhaustion from the battle at sea, the long hours of caring for Zalman, and her own lack of food, Carys grew weary and fatigued. She only laid her head down on Zalman's arm for a moment, she thought. But she had fallen into a deep sleep.

Sitting up now, she saw Zalman was gone. The bed was empty, only rumpled sheets on the mattress.

She cursed and stood, her hand on the unforged sword at her belt. Where was he? Her heart skipped as she had the dreaded thought – Zalman died, she missed it, and they took him from the room.

Carys left the room and scanned the hold, seeing no one. "Aeric?" she called his name. What was the surgeon's name? "Salto? Where is everyone?"

Moving through the hold, she reached the ladder up to the deck. *If they moved him without waking me*, she thought. *I'm going to beat them all within a centimitre of life …*

The sun was bright, and her eyes fluttered against the light as she ascended to the deck. Covering her eyes with her hand, she searched the deck of *The Last Serpent*, the cliff-city of Enakai to her right. When she saw the figure standing at the foredeck, she thought he was a trick of light. But there he was.

"Zalman!" she cried as she raced up the stairs to the foredeck. He turned her way with a tired grin in time to catch her as she threw her arms around him. Zalman took a few steps back to stay upright as he put an arm around her.

"Hey," he said into her ear.

She held him close for a moment, not wanting to let go, but she did. Stepping back and away from him, she frowned at him. She reared back to punch him but restrained herself. He was pale and pasty, and he smelled of sweat and blood. "You didn't wake me, you big gedder."

His grin never wavered. "You were asleep. Really asleep." He cocked that bald head at her. "And snoring. Like a bosaur."

Her frown deepened. "Shut up," she said.

"I thought I'd let you sleep."

"You should be resting," she told him. "You still look like crit."

He rolled his massive shoulders, and even that was weak. He faced the sky. "I needed to see the sun." Facing her again, he said, "But I'm glad you are here."

Her cheeks felt hot. Was this big critball making her blush? What was wrong with her? "I ... I thought you were dead."

"Probably should have been," he said.

"I prayed, and you're here. El ... he healed you."

"Well, then, thank you." His grin melted. "I had a dream. Does El give dreams?"

"I know some have claimed he does, and he did in the scriptures. Uncle Reyan claimed his father saw visions." Her voice lowered. "What did you see?"

"First, I saw a stone with a tree growing from it, like your tattoo and the one the others have, except real, but in a place that was beautiful and calm and peaceful, more than anything I've ever seen. I thought I was in the Everworld, like you and Caleb and Aden talk about."

"You saw the *Ebenelif*," she whispered. "Did you touch it?"

"I waded into the pool before it, and yes, I touched it, but then the dream changed."

"Changed how?"

His brow furrowed, and it would have been a fearsome sight if she didn't know his heart. "I saw a storm coming across an ocean, dark clouds, like it was darkness itself moving towards us."

"From where?"

"From the east," he said. "I think from Kryus." He shook his head. "Maddy, right? Maybe just a dream."

"No," she said and touched his cheek, rotating his head to her. "Not at all. El gave you a vision." She spoke with her stomach clenched, holding back the crying. "He told you that you have the heart of a *Sohan-el*. And break it all, Zalman, you do. Then he showed you a warning. Something worse is coming."

As she peered into those big eyes, she realized she did love him. Not because he was handsome or strong or an amazing warrior. No. She loved him because he had the heart of a *Sohan-el*, a wild and free heart that chose to fight for what was right, even if he didn't always fully understand it. *What a kick in the arse*, she thought.

"Well, if it be a warning," he said. "Then we should go talk to Aeric."

She reached up to hold his face in both hands now. "Yeah," she said. "We do. But maybe later."

He appeared drained and weak, sickly, but she was struck at how handsome he seemed. She had almost lost him, but here he was, now. She would not waste another moment.

Shoggers, she thought, and pulled him down and kissed him.

CHAPTER 29

THE FATHER TREE

The wind whipped by her and her hair stung her cheeks in the furious breeze as the Mahakar soared high above the trees.

After leaving the city Da'ar, Eshlyn had leaned in close and told the animal to take her to the Father Tree, and the tiger adjusted the flight path. The trip over the Kaleti Mountains was cold but majestic, over snow-capped peaks that broke through the clouds and beyond. On the journey to Lior, Eshlyn had traveled past the desert and along the coast, but as they made their way between the cliffs and high places of the Kaleti, she could see passes through the mountains, ancient ways that no one had walked in centuries. But the Mahakar knew them.

Soon they were over the Forest of Saten, above trees more familiar in their dark greens and browns than the Forest of Lior. They continued to make their way northeast, and after another half hour, she found the *Abaes*.

From the sky, she could see it kilometres in the distance. The tree rose 100 mitres above the forest canopy and spread 400 mitres in diameter. For those on the ground or in the forest, the tree would be hidden, surely, but to her it was clear. This was the Father Tree. She gripped the fur at the Mahakar's neck as they descended, and as they grew closer, she could see wooden structures within the thick branches of the Father Tree and the trees around it with bridges and ladders connecting the structures. And coming even closer, people moved along those bridges.

It was a city. In the trees.

An opening appeared in the canopy west of the Father Tree, not quite big enough for the Mahakar, but he swept through it anyway, branches and leaves against her face and brushing past them as they broke through and landed with a jolt.

She gasped and cast her gaze about her, seeing no one at first. She saw the massive trunk of the Father Tree not far away, to her right. Looking up, she saw the small houses in the branches, far above. Then she heard movement, figures in the trees nearby. The memory of Carys firing her bow and never missing came to Eshlyn's mind. "I am Eshlyn from Ketan," she called out. "I am a friend of the Ghosts of Saten. I need to get to the Tomb of Yosu."

A score of men appeared around her, close, arrows nocked in short bows and pointed at the Mahakar. He growled at them, and Eshlyn saw one man shudder. She patted his side to comfort him.

Then another emerged from the brush before them, her step slow but calculated. Eshlyn saw the woman's long white hair. "Mother Natali," Eshlyn said. "Thank El."

Mother Natali carried a walking stick, knotted and twisted, and she leaned upon it. "Put the bows down, boys," she said. "This is Lady Eshlyn."

The men complied, but they continued to ogle the large, white tiger.

"That, my friends," Natali said, "is the Kanalbe."

Eshlyn stroked the animal's fur. "The Mahakar, as introduced to me."

"Yes, that is the Liorian name," Natali said, and then she addressed the animal. "Your legends do not do you justice. It is good to finally meet you."

The Mahakar snorted.

"Mother," Eshlyn said. "I need to go to the Tomb of Yosu."

"And why is that, Lady?" Natali asked, but it was like she already knew.

Eshlyn gestured towards the sword on her pack. "I have Athelwulf's sword."

Natali's face fell. "I was afraid that was his path," she said, her voice quiet. "And you bring it here to honor him?"

"I do," Eshlyn said.

"Then come," Mother Natali said. "The Mahakar will wait for you, won't you?"

The tiger snorted in response as Eshlyn slid from the animal's back.

"Leave the creature be," Natali told the men as Eshlyn approached her. "He is older than these trees. Your weapons will do nothing to him."

When Eshlyn reached her, Mother Natali turned and entered the brush, pushing branches aside with her walking stick. Eshlyn followed.

"Men," Natali muttered. "They rely too much upon tools, weapons, things they can make and fight. There are some things in this world, Lady Eshlyn, that strength and martial skill will never overcome. It takes deeper things like love, faith, hope, to overcome them. Humility. Forgiveness. The great men learn this, however few learn their name or sing of their exploits. To teach those things, that is how we raise great men."

Eshlyn thought of Javyn again, and that ache came to the surface. "I have a son," she said.

"Where is he?" Natali asked.

"Safe in Ketan with my parents."

"War is upon us, Lady Eshlyn," Mother Natali said. "Safety does not exist, not like you mean it."

"I should tell you," Eshlyn said. "There is a small army about to pass through the Saten. They are from the city of Da'ar in the Kaleti Mountains."

"I have heard of it."

"They go to join the *Brendel* in Ketan," Eshlyn said.

"Then we will make sure they find their way safely through the forest," Mother Natali said.

Eshlyn followed Mother Natali through the brush, her eyes flicking upwards. "There's a city in the trees."

"Yes," Natali said. "We call it Jowell, although it was once known as a holy city and by other names. It was built by the Drytweld thousands of years ago. We have improved upon it and repaired it. Many Ghosts live here, and we have kept it secret and safe from the elves. We keep the Tomb of Life safe."

"Because it is sacred?" Eshlyn asked.

"No," Natali answered. "Because it is powerful."

Eshlyn swallowed hard. "What makes it powerful?"

"Truth and knowledge, the most powerful things of all."

As they pressed through the next copse, she saw a clearing before the massive trunk of the *Abaes*. Between two roots of the tree, there was an oval opening, three mitres tall and two across. It was dark, like the blackness was a wall to keep any and all away.

Eshlyn stood before the opening. The Tomb called to her. Or perhaps something within it. Not with an audible voice but it drew her, nonetheless. It stood open. "Can anyone go in?"

"Anyone can try, but few accomplish it," Natali said. "Only the very brave possess the courage to enter. Some say you must be chosen. Others that you make the choice."

"Which is it?"

"Probably both."

"You don't know?"

"I've never gone through that door," Mother Natali said. But she wouldn't say whether it was her fear or a lack of being chosen, and Eshlyn wouldn't ask. "No one has in hundreds of years."

Eshlyn took a deep breath and stepped forward.

"Take only what you need," Mother Natali said.

Removing her pack, she set it down amongst the dead leaves and drew Athelwulf's sword from it. She gripped his sword close to her chest like the fear gripped her heart. What was she so breaking afraid of? She couldn't say, but the terror threatened to overwhelm her.

Mother Natali stood motionless and in silence.

Eshlyn gritted her teeth and forced her feet to move, to plod forward. As she drew closer to the opening of the Tomb, she could feel a presence, even though she saw nothing. She wanted to cry and scream and run all at once. But she didn't. She touched the marriage bracelet on her wrist to muster her courage, and she stepped into the Tomb of Life.

The first thing she noticed was a light, but dim. She stood at the top of a long tunnel that led down into the earth. As the shaft descended, the soil and roots around her became stone. Looking down at her boots, stairs had been cut into the floor of the tunnel, irregular and meandering. The light was down at the bottom of the tunnel.

Turning to face behind her, there was only darkness. Could she pass through it again, to escape? She didn't think so.

It didn't matter, however. Steeling herself, she descended the stairs, careful with each step, the light barely enough to see, and the light grew brighter as she did. After a few minutes, she reached the bottom of the tunnel where a large doorway stood as the entrance to a deep and tall cavern. The cavern was enormous with a ceiling twenty mitres high; a light shone from the end of the chamber. It was a hundred mitres deep, if not more, and spanned another hundred from side to side. But it wasn't the cavern that held her attention and caused her pause.

Swords were driven into the ground of the cavern, blade first, swords of every shape and size, each gleaming and shining in the light from the far end. There were hundreds of them, maybe thousands. A path led through the middle of the field of swords. She began to walk along the path when she noticed a figure at the far end of the cavern. It seemed to be a man. Had he been there before? The light cast from behind him darkened his face. Eshlyn walked towards the man, crossing the vast area between them. There was no sound except for her own boots upon the stone beneath her.

As she neared the man, she could see him more clearly – tall and thick, muscular, he wore a fine crimson tunic over black breeches. A leather belt around his waist held an empty scabbard. His hair was gray and hung to his shoulders. He smiled at her underneath a long gray beard and moustache. The man stepped forward in black leather boots. His eyes were kind. A crown sat upon his head.

The King from her dreams.

"Hello, Lady Eshlyn," he said.

"Uh, hello."

"You have my sword," he said.

Eshlyn extended the sword in her hands to him. "This is Athelwulf's sword."

"I didn't mean that one," the man said, and he pointed at the one at her hip. "That one."

She looked down and then back at him. "Kenric's sword?"

"Your husband was a fine man," he said. "But the sword was never truly his, nor his father's, nor his before him. They were all good men, some more than others, but none of them were a *Sohan-el*. I was."

It took her a moment to put it together, and her brows rose when she did. "King Judai?"

He grinned at her.

"I thought you were dead," she said.

"Oh, to your world, I am," he said.

"Then how are you here?"

"I am very much alive in the Everworld, more alive than you can know," he said. "Yosu sent me to meet you here. I will return after you leave."

"So ... you're a ghost?" she asked.

"No, not a ghost, but I am in a form that you can understand. If I were to come as I am in the Everworld, well ..."

"You're from the Everworld?"

"Yes."

She thought of what little she knew of that place from the scriptures of El, hints and implications more than any real detail. "What is it like?"

"There are no words in this place that could do it justice," Judai said. "The greatest joys here do not compare to the dullest moments there. It is worth any cost."

"Is Kenric there?" Eshlyn asked; she hoped. She thought of Esai and Athelwulf. "My friends?"

He smiled at her. "Yes."

She reached down with one hand to grip Kenric's – Judai's – sword. "You're here for the sword?"

"Among other things."

Eshlyn scanned the cavern. "So what do I do? Just stick these in the ground?"

"Continue to leave a path, but place the swords anywhere you wish."

There was more open area closer to the far end of the cavern, so she walked a few more mitres towards the light. Lifting Athelwulf's sword by the hilt, blade down, she drove it into the stone floor. There was a shower of sparks, and she stepped back. Athelwulf's sword felt at home among the others.

"He was a fine warrior with the heart of El," Judai said. "Now, my sword, if you please."

She pulled the unforged sword from her scabbard and held it up before her. It shone in the light, almost blinding. While her mind knew it was King Judai's sword, her heart believed otherwise. It would always be Kenric's sword to her. Even when she began wearing it and training with it, she thought of it as Kenric's sword. It had become a part of her in some way over the last few months, a connection to the man she loved. But the truth? The sword was not hers.

Taking a few steps to the light, she raised the sword, and with a whispered goodbye, she stabbed the blade into the stone with both hands. More sparks, and she retreated again. She felt lighter somehow.

"Thank you," Judai said. "The transition is near complete."

"The transition?"

"I was the last to brave Elarus and reach the Living Stone. But the *Brendel* has come, the prophecy is being fulfilled, the *Sohan-el* have returned to Eres, and a new age is dawning."

"A new age?"

"The last age of Eres. The world has languished in darkness long enough. The *Brendel* is the match that will set the world afire."

Caleb.

"He is but the beginning," Judai continued, "destroying what has been corrupted so what is right and true can be built again. The *Brendel* carries a great weight, far greater than he knows. He will require the very strength of El and the love of those around him, which in the end are much the same. He will need you before it is done."

"Me?"

"Yes, Eshlyn. You. The end of all things lay upon his shoulders."

"The end?"

"And the beginning, as I said. Every end is but a beginning, and every beginning an end of what came before. The whole world will burn, but it will grow back green again, ready for the glory of the last days."

"I don't understand," she said.

"We rarely do."

She noticed the scabbard on his belt had disappeared. Only the belt remained.

Eshlyn pointed beyond him. "What is in there?"

"That is the Tomb of Life," he said.

"I thought this was the Tomb."

"No. Come with me. I will show you."

She glanced behind her towards the doorway to the tunnel back to the surface.

"You cannot go that way," Judai said.

Eshlyn spun on him. "What?"

"You must go forward, always forward."

King Judai turned and disappeared into the light.

Glancing over her shoulder one last time, Eshlyn walked towards the brightness.

It was another vast cavern, but darker and smaller than the one before. The ceiling was covered with crystal stalactites. They glowed and gave light to the room. A large pond stretched out before her, glimmering silver. At the other end of the pond, there was a stone slab, like a table but lower.

Judai stood next to her. "Follow me." He moved towards the pond, and when he reached it, he strode upon the water. She followed and stopped at the edge of the pond. Searching the room around her, she couldn't see any way around it. Judai paused at the middle of the pond. "Just take the first step." He continued across the silver surface, the liquid rippling with each step.

Wincing, Eshlyn took a step, placing her foot upon the surface of the pool, and it supported her weight. Her knees shook as she walked across the pond. When she arrived at the other side, Judai stood across from the stone slab. It was a rough, gray stone.

"It was cut from Mount Elarus, from the granite at the top of the mountain, before the dark cloud," Judai said. "Yosu's disciples, the first *Sohan-el*, cut this from the mountain and carried it here. And they laid Yosu's body upon it."

"They did all this?"

"Not all this. They dug a tunnel and the cavern, but the pool and the dripstone above us appeared after Yosu lived again. The Everworld touches Eres here."

King Judai reached up and took the crown from his head. He set the crown upon the stone slab.

"That is for you," he said. "My crown passes to you. A queen needs a crown."

She stared down at the crown, a golden crown with rubies and a diamond at its center. It appeared heavy. The light from the dripstone above caused the crown to glisten.

She shifted her feet. Was she a queen? They called her Lady Eshlyn. She was a widow, a mother, a daughter, a sister, a warrior, a leader. *Bashawyn.* She was even a businesswoman. But she never felt she was enough at any of them, much less them all. There was never enough of her.

The crown tempted her. It made sense. Javyn was the direct descendant of the last King of Manahem, the very person standing before her. She was the widow of one heir and mother to another. It was her position to claim.

As a queen, perhaps she could have more control, do more good. It could give her the power to succeed where she felt such a failure. Conflicts and divisions between humanity would be simpler and easier to resolve with that power, with that crown. She could provide so much more for those that were hurting and in need.

Looking at the crown, she felt alone. So alone.

Judai's face was blank. Waiting.

She remembered sailing in the clouds with the Mahakar, her face rippling with the wind, a constant smile upon her face. So dangerous, so alive, so free.

Maybe she was approaching it all wrong.

I wonder if you know who you are, Mother Natali had said.

You have not become Sohan-el *to achieve a position or to rule it over others. You have a purpose ... To fight so others can live. Just as Yosu taught.*

The first *Sohan-el*, the ones trained by Yosu, had not been rulers but servants, men and women without worldly position but armed with the authority of compassion and the truth of El. And that had been enough for them to change Eres for generations. Would it be enough for her?

I will defend the innocent, free the oppressed, and spread light in dark places.

Then the words came to her, unbidden, but they felt right.

"I am Eshlyn, a daughter of El. I am a servant of the Creator, destined to bring freedom to the world of men again. In that, I am more than enough, strong enough to do what I must, but no other role defines me. I am a free daughter of El."

The King's cheek twitched.

"No," she said. "I don't need to be a queen. And I don't need your crown. I already possess all that I require."

She watched as the crown transformed into a golden chain that then faded and disappeared.

A tear rose in the King's eye. "I wish, when I was offered the crown, that I had half of your wisdom, Eshlyn." He smiled at her. "If men learn to serve and not rule one another, there is hope that men will be free again. Thank you."

"You're welcome. Now can you show me the way out?"

"Not yet," he said. "You have one last thing to leave."

"What?" she asked.

But she knew. She lifted her arm and touched the golden bracelet on her arm. Her marriage bracelet.

"No," she whispered. "I understand why I had to leave the swords, but why this? It is mine. You're asking me to leave my very heart."

King Judai said nothing. He didn't have to. She knew that she would not see the way out until she did. Eshlyn removed the bracelet from her wrist.

He said that you must be careful what you bring into that place ... Whatever goes with you into that holy place, you will be required to leave it.

Kenric, the man she loved. She loved him still. Eshlyn clutched the golden bracelet to her chest, and she wept. The tears streamed down her face, and she bent over, her abdomen tightening in anguish. I can't, she thought. El, help me, I cannot let him go.

Her own words came to her. *I am more than enough, strong enough to do what I must ... I am a free daughter of El.*

What choice did she have? She couldn't stay in this place forever, and she wanted to see her son, needed to see him. The world out there awaited her.

Angry, she lay the bracelet down upon the slab. She set her heart, the symbol of the greatest love of her life, down upon the stone. It also faded and disappeared.

A doorway appeared in the wall behind Judai. It had not been there before.

I came with so little, she thought. *And I leave with nothing.*

"No," Judai said. "Not nothing."

"Well, break it all," Eshlyn said. She marched around the stone slab and through the doorway.

Chapter 30

The Acar

The army did not make it past the Acar the next day.

Aden had been through the *Acarleasharam* months before on his journey with Caleb, the Prophet, and Carys as they went to Biram and Ketan. He knew the effect the area could have on people.

The Acar was a dead place. Centuries ago, two *Sohan-el* fought two evil and powerful sorcerers – also called Worldbreakers – and killed them. The result was an explosion of power and death that leveled a town and created a small crater that filled with black liquid over the years, called the Deadwater. The land around the event was black, dark and bleak. No vegetation, no animals, nothing lived there. It stank of crit and acid and rot. And beyond that, the very presence of death oppressed the spirit and soul of any that lived and passed through it.

The *Hamon-el* camped there the next night.

The plan had been to get up early and travel far enough to get through the Acar before they made camp. But two wagons lost a wheel, wagons they picked up from Biram and the Kryan legion, and it took an extra hour to repair them.

It was also Aden's fault. He couldn't find Tamya. He looked all over camp the next morning, and no one had seen her since the night before, her or the bloodwolf. Had she left? Ran off? Was she simply hiding from him? She shared a story from her past the night before, a story she had kept hidden for so long. To Aden, that was a sacred thing, and he loved her all the more for it.

Of course he loved her. She frustrated the crit out of him and that bloodwolf made him nervous, but he knew better now that her cold, angry demeanor was rooted in pain, deep pain he could only begin to understand. He was also beginning to like that bloodwolf.

He could sense her guilt and shame for her past, including the death of Dervan just days before. He wished he could fix it, but he knew he couldn't. It didn't work that way.

But more than that, she had no hope. Remembering her words, even the wrath she sought against the elves, he saw beyond all of it and one truth came to him – she had no hope. And hopelessness killed as sure as a gladus in the heart.

After searching and finding her nowhere in the camp, the army moved on. He longed to see her, but what could he do? They couldn't hold up the whole army any longer. He had a division to lead as they moved to attack the elven outpost of Taggart. A part of him wanted to stay, however, and find her. As the army moved east along the road to Taggart, he prayed to El that she was safe … and that he would see her again.

The *Hamon-el* camped close to the forest and as far away from the Deadwater as they could. Aden stood with Iletus and Caleb on the northern edge of the camp, tents and small fires being set up, men beginning to eat their evening meal. Other than the noise of the preparations, the army was strangely silent. No one spoke or joked or gave orders aloud. People went about their roles in quiet, their heads down.

"It will just be for one night," Caleb muttered, his arms crossed, a frown on his face.

"Of course," he said.

Aden looked over his shoulder at the Deadwater, called the *Mawetamel* in the First Tongue. The western sky was the color of blood as the sun finished setting for the day.

"We wake them early," Caleb said. "And move on."

"We could travel through the night," Iletus said.

"The men need to rest," Caleb said. "I don't want to attack Taggart in another day without a night of sleep."

"You think anyone's gonna get any breakin' sleep?" Aden asked.

Caleb shot him a glare. "It will just be for one night," he repeated.

Aden rolled his eyes and went to check on his men before they bedded down for the night. They were disturbed and uncomfortable, but they would sleep.

But with Tamya on his mind, he was not sure if he would.

He tried reading some of the Fyrwrit, and he even got through one of the *Tales of the Sohan-el*, a story about Stefen, an older *Sohan-el* from the city of Halan – a city Aden had never heard of – that had fought the white apes of the North to save a young girl. But he surrendered to the distracting thoughts in his mind, closed his books, and left his tent.

Aden walked north towards the Deadwater. The stench of the water grew stronger as he neared it, a sharp, strong odor that reminded him of the oil and sewage they threw down the wall at the demics during the Battle of Ketan. The smell overpowered him, and he had to take his undertunic and wrap it around his mouth and nose. It helped a bit, but his stomach protested more than once as he reached the bank of the Deadwater.

It was dark now, the sun below the horizon and the sky a dark gray. The three moons of Eres hung hazy in the sky, like the presence of death permeated the air and clouded the vision.

Aden knelt down at the bank of the black lake. The Prophet told him that the crater from the explosion at the end of the battle between the *Sohan-el* and the Worldbreakers filled with water over time, creating this lake. But even here this close, it did not look like water. It was too thick and sat too still. It fascinated him. What was it? What was it made of?

His face scrunched as far as it could go, he pulled the unforged sword from his belt and stuck the blade into the water. The black liquid bubbled and foamed at the unforged blade. The more he stuck it into the liquid, the more it reacted, like it was trying to move away from the unforged sword. Pulling the sword from the water, he could see no effect on the blade in the moonlight.

He ran a hand through his hair. Again he was struck with how the smell of the liquid was similar to the mixture of oil, tar, crit, and urine they threw down the walls of Ketan to make it slick against the claws of the demics. That ws the same substance that ended up catching fire.

Holding his breath and clenching his stomach against the rumblings of nausea, he removed his undertunic and ripped it in half. Replacing one half around his nose and mouth, just to survive the stench, he wrapped the other half around the end of the unforged sword. He dipped the cloth into the black liquid, soaking it.

Standing, he hiked back to the camp in the gray dark of the night and made his way to his tent. Within his tent, with the cloth soaked in the Deadwater held high in one hand, he rummaged through his pack to retrieve a flint stone with his other hand. He struck it to cause a spark.

And the cloth became engulfed in flame within a second, like a torch. It surprised him how quick it caught fire, and he almost dropped it, holding it out from him as far as he could. He became afraid that his whole tent was about to go up in flame, the fire burned so hot and full. Flicking the sword, he threw the burning cloth to the black ground at his feet – away from anything else in the small tent – and watched it be consumed, the fire dying down within a few moments. Aden could feel the blazing heat from the fire even a pace away. He threw water from his canteen over the remnants of the flame, and he raised a brow at how difficult it was to finish off the last embers. But he was able to extinguish it at last.

Aden considered himself fortunate that he hadn't burned down the whole camp.

He rubbed his chin as he stared at the ground. *The whole camp ...*

It took him hours to fall asleep.

———

The food at the long table was plentiful, piled high upon silver platters. Wine was in goblets, and they ate together that night as friends with Aeric and Bade and a few more of the crew of *The Last Serpent.* Chronch sat next to Zalman.

Carys glanced over at Zalman sitting across from her. His color was better than earlier in the day, but she could tell how weak he was with his sunken cheeks. He caught her looking at him, and he smiled. Her heart beat strong in her chest, and she wanted to climb over the table and kiss him.

What was *wrong* with her?

The conversation was light, and Aeric kept making crude jokes. Carys couldn't decide whether she should be offended at his impropriety or count it a compliment he treated her as one of his crew. She decided on the latter and laughed with the men. The wine was going to her head, so as Bade recounted stories of the crewmembers they lost in the battle with the *Bird of Prey*, she directed the conversation to more serious matters before she started making even worse jokes than the men.

"Aeric," she said, turning to him. "We need to speak again of you joining us in our revolution against Kryus."

The table grew quiet, but as she searched their faces, they were not offended or even surprised.

Aeric set his goblet down upon the table. "You have made your arguments," he said. "We do not need to go over them again."

"But the Empire is now attacking into your waters, close to your homeland. Will you still do nothing?" she asked.

He grinned at her. "Does your brother fight as readily as you? I did not say we would do nothing. Only that we need not go over the arguments again. Bade and I have already discussed how the situation has changed. I cannot ignore it."

"You can't?"

"No," he said. However, his voice was sad. "The Empire is forcing our hand, openly breaking our treaty. The peace is broken. We must begin attacking the Empire."

Zalman bowed at Aeric. "Good."

Carys stammered before speaking. "I … I didn't think it would be that easy."

"Easy?" Aeric said. "I lost most of my crew and must now meet again with the other kanalor. They will look for the profit even though it is now obvious the Empire will not leave us be. As you said, we must be more than pirates, something new, and that frightens most people. But we must, to survive.

"No part of my decision was easy. Men and women will die, and I will throw them into harm's way. We are left with little choice."

"I understand," Carys said.

"We will do other things to keep from violence," Aeric continued, "make peace with the elven lands of Lyr, Jibryl, or even Semadi, to try and put pressure upon Kryus. We do not have their trust, for good reason, and I do not know if we can earn it in time."

"Thank you," Carys said. "We will pray to El for his help and strength, and we will support you however we can."

"I have a feeling we will need all the help we can get." Aeric lifted his goblet and stood. "Carys and Zalman of Ketan, you are people of honor. You know the ways even though you were not raised among us. Your people are our people. Our people are yours. We will join your revolution against the Kryan Empire."

The rest of Aeric's men at the table stood and lifted their goblets. Carys took the cue and joined them, as did Zalman and Chronch.

"To brothers and sisters, together in honor and truth," Carys said, completely making up the phrase on the spot.

It seemed to satisfy the men of Enakai as the whole table took a swig of wine together.

They sat, and a feeling of peace and calm came over Carys, odd in the wake of convincing a group of people to go to war. She met stares with Zalman once more, lingering there too long.

"I have another question for you, Lord Aeric," Carys said.

Aeric turned to her, his face questioning. "Oi?"

She did not take her eyes off of Zalman, however. "Among your people, how do weddings go?"

Zalman coughed, choking on wine.

Aeric sputtered before releasing a guffaw. "It is quite simple. The man and woman stand upon a small boat, holding hands and balancing in the craft while the whole city stands upon the shore and watches them. Then the man and woman each sing a song they wrote to the other, declaring their love and commitment." He beamed at her. "Then the whole city gets roaring drunk."

"I see," Carys said. "And does a priest or someone like that perform the ceremony?"

"If you have need, I will officiate," Aeric said.

"What the shog are you doing?" Zalman growled.

"It is said that the seas will bless the wedding performed by a kanalor," Bade interjected.

Carys stared into Zal's eyes.

"I don't sing," Zalman said. His cheeks were red.

Carys shrugged. "It's only for one song," she said.

"I'm not a man of words," he said.

Carys thought of his compliment to her on the deck of *The Last Serpent* and chuckled. "You can be when you want."

"Zalman," Aeric said. "Don't you love the woman?"

The big man swallowed and his face went blank. He took some time to answer. "More than anything else on El's green Eres."

"Ha!" Aeric cried. "The first line of your song, I think."

Zalman glared at her. "Are you sure about this?"

Carys scowled back. "I shoggin' love you. You think I kiss every bosaur brain that comes along?"

He didn't answer.

"Well, I don't," Carys said. "We are in a war. If I've learned anything over the past few ninedays, we aren't promised the next day, the next minute. I don't want to waste another one. Live or die, I want to be with you."

The man stared at her, his mouth tight.

"Just breakin' marry me, you big gedder," she said.

Zalman chuckled. "Okay," he said. "Since you asked so nicely."

———

Someone shook Aden awake. He snorted once as he sat up and opened his eyes, one hand on his sword. "Whu?"

It was Vic, one of his platoon leaders, and the bare, pale light outside of his tent told Aden that the sunrise was a half hour away. Aden cursed himself for oversleeping, but he had spent much of the night wrestling with his thoughts, thinking of Tamya and the Deadwater. "Sorry, Vic," he said. "Overslept. Are the men ready to go?"

Vic hesitated before speaking. "Something's happening, Aden. You need to come quick."

Aden jumped up and pulled on fresh clothes, his boots, and grabbed his sword as he followed Vic out into the camp. He squinted as he saw men walking to the northern edge of the camp. "Come on," Vic said, and Aden didn't even realize he had stopped.

They jogged together outside of the camp where the army assembled. Almost the whole of the *Hamon-el* gathered to face Caleb, who stood on the back of a wagon, waiting to address them. Others like Aden trickled into the crowd, the last of them.

Aden fastened the sword to his belt as he pushed through the crowd towards Caleb, Vic at his heels. Standing right before the wagon were other *Sohan-el* and division leaders, Xander, Bweth, Iletus, and Lyam among them. The platoon leaders stood behind them and the rest of the army congregated beyond.

Taking his place next to Xander, he spoke under his breath to the young man. "What's goin' on?"

"Dunno," Xander muttered back, leaning down to Aden's ear. "But the scouts Caleb sent out last are back. Somethin's happening."

Aden watched as Caleb scanned the crowd, calm and waiting for the whole of the *Hamon-el* to gather on the black, dead ground with the Deadwater a hundred and fifty mitres away, the stench of the black lake filling their nostrils.

Caleb's chest filled with air, and he lifted a hand to silence the dull roar of the muttering throng. They fell quiet.

"The scouts returned about an hour ago," Caleb said, his voice loud, projecting over the men and women. "They returned with news. A Kryan legion is headed this way along the road from Taggart. It is a full legion, or more, and led by another Bladeguard." Caleb paused. "They will be here by noon."

Talking, muttering, gasps, groans of surprise and fear sounded behind Aden. He exchanged a worried glance with Xander.

A shout from the crowd, one of Bweth's platoon leaders. "What are we going to do?"

Everyone quieted, waiting for Caleb's answer.

"I will meet the legion on this field," he said.

Aden cringed.

"Here? At the *Acar*?" another voice shouted.

Caleb found the man with his eyes. "Yes."

"Wait," Lyam said, taking a step towards Caleb. "You said a full legion? Or more?"

Caleb nodded.

"They have Cavalry?" Lyam pressed.

"They do," Caleb said.

More noise of surprise, murmuring, and Lyam yelled above the din. "We're barely twenty-five hundred strong. A Cavalry alone will decimate our men in an open field!"

"El will help us," Caleb said.

"What?" Lyam threw up his hands. "*That's* your answer? You're going to put us up against a Kryan legion in an open field, outnumbered, where they have an overwhelming advantage, and that's your answer? It is suicide."

Caleb crossed his arms and aimed his steel gray eyes at Lyam. "El helped us overcome, against all odds, at the Battle of Ketan and the Battle of Biram. He will help us here."

"We could move the army into the forest," Iletus said. "Flank them."

"If we move into the forest," Caleb explained. "They will not follow. They know they are at a disadvantage there. Given the reports from the scouts, this is a full legion. They will make their way past us, move on to Biram where some of our brothers still wait, injured and vulnerable, and hundreds of prisoners that would join the legion in a siege of Ketan once they kill the men in Biram."

"We can't do this ..." Lyam said.

"We must," Caleb said. "To protect our brothers in Biram and to save Ketan from a siege."

"But at the Acar?" Xander said. "If we moved into the forest, we could find a place that's ... *not here*."

Caleb met Xander's gaze. "We make our stand here."

In the ensuing silence, Aden could feel the hope bleed from the *Hamon-el*. Lyam said the words the rest were thinking.

"We're all going to die," he said.

Caleb said, "It is possible. But I do not believe so."

"You're maddy," Lyam said. "Out of your breakin' mind."

Xander spoke under his breath. "Lyam …"

"No, Xander," Lyam said, walking further forward, a pace away from Caleb now. "I won't let this crazy shogger lead us into suicide." He looked up at Caleb. "We need to run. We go back to Ketan and join with the rest of the army and we kill them from behind the walls that have never been breached. That is what we are doing."

"I will not run," Caleb said, and even though he did not project his voice, every soul on the black ground of the Acar heard him.

"Of course not," Lyam said. "Why would the great Caleb run from a fight? Will you keep killing while everyone around you dies? Because that is what will happen if we stay here and fight. Everyone will die. Will you take on the rest of the legion all by yourself?"

Caleb did not speak, but his glare carried words that Aden could translate. He would. He absolutely would.

Lyam scoffed and turned to the crowd. "Don't listen to this man, please," he said. "Haven't we done enough critball things in the last few ninedays? Leaving Ketan, attacking a legion at Biram, all of it. It just keeps getting worse. He's just a man with delusions of some breakin' prophecy."

What is Caleb doing? Aden thought. He wasn't saying anything.

"What are you talking about?" Aden said, stepping forward. "You've been to the Stone. You got an unforged sword. You know this isn't some bunch of crit."

"I know some things are real, yes," Lyam said. "I know El is real, but I don't think this man knows what the shog he's doing. I don't even know if he is really the *Brendel*."

Gasps came from the crowd. "What?" Aden exclaimed.

Lyam stepped closer to Aden. "Aden, I think you are the *Brendel*."

Aden lowered his hands. "No, Lyam …"

"Think about it," Lyam said. "You were with him the whole way, breaking the Prophet out of the prison, fighting with him against the bloodwolves and the elves in Biram. You helped him lead the men of Ketan against the Demics and fought against the Demilord. Aden, you went with him all the way to the Living Stone and got an unforged sword! It is just as possible that you're the one to fulfill prophecy as he is."

Aden's heart fell within his chest. "No. The prophecy speaks of his travels to another land, his return, his *scars* …"

"Details and interpretations, all of it," Lyam said. He spun on his heel and faced Caleb again. "You've never even said you're the *Brendel*," Lyam said to him. "Everyone says it about you, like it's true, but you've never even said it. You use it to further your own agenda, but even you won't lie and say you're the *Brendel*, will you?"

Caleb lifted his head at Lyam, but he said nothing.

"Say it now, if you believe it," Lyam said. "Tell everyone now. Make your case. Tell us that you're the *Brendel*."

Caleb said not a word.

After a long moment, the tension and fear and despair in the army around them stronger than the stench of the Deadwater, Lyam slowly faced the crowd again.

"See," he said. "I told you. He won't say it. Because it's not true."

Lyam spun, stepping closer to Caleb, and drew his sword in anger, his unforged sword. He sneered up at Caleb, like a challenge. Aden gaped at Lyam.

But as Lyam advanced with the sword, he strained to keep it upright, and it fell. He had to drag it on the ground as he staggered forward.

"Gets heavy, sometimes," Caleb said.

Lyam growled up at Caleb, struggling with the sword for another few seconds. Then he stood straight and addressed the crowd again. "I'm leaving. I'm going back to Ketan. If the Legion makes it to the city, they'll need our help. Anyone is welcome to come with me."

"Lyam," Aden pleaded. "Don't do this."

"It's done," Lyam said. "I'm not following him into any more suicidal endeavors."

"Suicidal?" Aden said. "But he's right. El has helped us time and again."

"We've been lucky," Lyam said. "That luck is bound to run out soon. Are you coming with me?"

Aden looked up at Caleb. "Why don't you stop him?"

"That would be worse than his leaving," Caleb said. He rubbed his beard, scanned the crowd, and said, "Anyone is free to go."

Crit on a frog, Aden thought. He put one hand on his hip and the other on the hilt of the unforged sword. Lyam was right about one thing. Meeting the Kryan legion on open ground was maddy. But so was standing up to a Demilord and climbing Mount Elarus to go to the Living Stone. He remembered what El told him up on that mountain.

True strength is not your ability but your humility. My strength is enough ... I will always be with you.

A small figure pushed through the crowd. She reached the front, a bloodwolf next to her. *Tamya.* While she would not meet his eyes, the sight of her – at that point of despair in that land of death – gave him a spark of hope.

Yes, meeting the legion on the field was suicide. *Unless ...*

Aden turned to Caleb. "Do you really believe we should make our stand here?"

Caleb nodded again, his eyes firm and calm.

Aden walked forward, climbed aboard the wagon with Caleb and faced the crowd. "It doesn't matter what you believe about who the *Brendel* is," he said. "I stay with Caleb and stand against the legion."

Lyam's shoulders slumped.

Bweth came and stood before the wagon and also faced the crowd. "I'm stayin'."

Xander, Iletus, and all of the other *Sohan-el* joined them, each repeating the commitment to stay with Caleb.

And last, Tamya strode forward, as well, the bloodwolf at her heels.

"Very well," Lyam said. "I'm collecting my things to go back to Ketan. Those who want to live will come with me." He pushed through the crowd and made his way back to the camp.

Standing next to Caleb, up on the wagon, Aden saw men look at each other and begin to leave with Lyam. One after another, men walked away from the crowd. Some left right away, others considered for a few seconds before leaving. They were all good men, people who had fought bravely at the Battle of Ketan or the Battle of Biram, people Aden counted as friends, even Lyam, but over the next ten minutes, Aden watched two thirds of these men leave Caleb's army as they stood at the Acar. It was agony to behold their numbers dwindle, one by one, every individual who left felt like a tragic betrayal to all they had won together, each person who departed from the crowd like a punch in the gruts.

In the end, close to seven hundred were all that remained of the 2,500 who left Biram.

Caleb gazed out over those that remained and lifted his chin, his face full of pain and sorrow. "Thank you," he said. "I am proud to stand with you. Let us do what we can to prepare for the coming battle."

Aden cleared his throat and leaned in to whisper to Caleb. "Um, I think I have an idea ..."

Even through the grief on Caleb's face, the corner of his mouth twitched with the hint of a grin.

CHAPTER 31

THE LAST LESSON

Armies move slowly, Iletus had said, and watching the Kryan legion arrive at the Acar, Xander believed him.

Xander supposed that moving nearly six thousand elves into position – anywhere, really – was a feat, and while it took the legion six hours to set up camp, Xander was impressed. A Vanguard first appeared in the early afternoon, officers and a thousand troops, what Iletus called the skirmishers. They arrayed themselves across the field while the bulk of the legion set up their own camp, complete with a command tent, supply wagons, and battle engines like ballista and smaller catapults. Every militan knew their role, their job, and the most impressive force on Eres covered the eastern side of the Acar by nightfall. Armies may move slowly, but the Kryan legion was the most efficient army in the world.

Iletus, Bweth, and Caleb knew well the tactics of the Kryan military and legion, and had the remaining seven hundred people move the camp closer to the Deadwater, a kilomitre south of that stench, and a half kilomitre north of the hills before the Forest of Saten. The Kryan legions were formidable but predictable. Iletus knew exactly how the elves would position themselves to face the humans on the field. He had drawn it on a map, and Xander watched it happen as predicted.

After moving the camp to the desirable position, the rest of the morning had been a desperate rush to prepare for the inevitable battle. By the time the Vanguard arrived an hour after midday, seven hundred men, women, an elf, and a dwarf were spread out, facing the east, and waiting for the elves.

Bweth Ironhorn stood next to Xander, and she was covered with gleaming armor, sections of steel over her torso, shoulders, arms and legs, complete with a helmet. She did not move any differently, however, the separate pieces both covering her and allowing for freedom of mobility. He towere over her, but looking in her angry eyes, he saw a wrath waiting there that he would not want to test.

He heard a growl behind him, turned and saw Tamya and her bloodwolf among them. Aden, beside him, did not turn, but Xander saw Aden's cheek twitch.

The Kryan legion finished setting their camp three hundred mitres away by nightfall.

"They won't attack until the morning," Iletus said.

Xander stood with Bweth, Aden, Caleb, the other *Sohan-el*, and Iletus in front of the rest of the *Hamon-el*, gazing out over the legion as the sun ducked under the horizon behind them.

"How do you know?" Aden asked.

Bweth snorted. "They are trained to fight after a long march, but they will not force it, not on an army that has been waiting for them."

"They have scouted the area and will dig in for the night," Caleb said. "Soon the militan will assign rotations to sleep and eat while others take watch. We should do the same."

"The battle will begin in the morning," Iletus agreed.

"Rotations in thirds?" Caleb asked.

"That is what I would suggest," Iletus said.

"Xander," Caleb said. "Will you organize the rotations?"

Not taking his eyes off of the sea of elves not half a kilomitre away from them, Xander said he would.

"Good," Caleb said. As Xander began to walk away to address the people behind them, Caleb added, "And Xander?"

"Yeah?" Xander said, pausing.

"Tell everyone that they have another job while it is their shift to keep watch."

"And that is?"

"Pray. Tell them to pray, Xander."

———

Aden took his spell in the rotation and then returned to the camp to rest, by Caleb's orders, but his own thoughts raced through his mind. He was concerned about the battle, about their plan. And Tamya. She disappeared after the morning events, and she had not sought him out. Pushing all of it from his mind, he lay upon the cot in his tent.

When he did sleep, it was in fits, but he did dream.

He was alone on vast white tundra, a tall mountain far in the distance, to the north, he thought. Odd, but he was not cold, even though the wind buffeted him and blew his hair across his face. He stood with clenched fists. The mountain, also white and covered with snow, erupted in flame, the peak exploding in a mushroom cloud and vomiting fire upon the land. It was not lava but flame, a conflagration that rose like a wave and sped towards him.

Aden stood motionless and watched the wave of flame melt the world around him, snow and earth consumed, the ground rumbling in pain, quaking in fear. But Aden did not move. He faced the fire coming for him as he denied the fear rising in his own heart.

He awoke as the wave of flame reached him, his eyes snapping open and sitting up with a gasp. Rubbing his eyes, the night still dark around him and overcome with the stench of the Darkwater, he realized he was not disturbed by the images in the dream as much as the fact that he was alone.

Crit on sleep, then, he thought, and he rose to find Tamya.

He dressed for battle and wandered through the camp. Many of the men were still awake, and he asked a few if they had seen her. It was difficult to hide a half-elf and a bloodwolf in a camp of men, but it took him an hour or more to find someone with any information.

Burt, a man from Xander's division, hacked up a ball of phlegm and spit it to the side, scratching his nose with his meaty hand. "Ya, I seen her," he said. "You wantin' a bit o' shoggin' 'fore the big one tomorrow? I hear we maybe all die, so not a bad idea to get it while you can. But she seem like she wanna be 'lone with that maddy bloodwolf, you know …"

Aden set his hand on his unforged sword and glowered at the man. He didn't know what Burt saw, but the man squirmed in his seat. "Where did you see her?"

"Saw her down near the west side o' camp, just sittin' by herself." He sniffed. "Sir."

Aden strode off to the west, but he had to get information from two more men before finding her outside the camp to the southwest, sitting alone and sharpening one of her swords with a stone. The bloodwolf relaxed next to her, his snout in her lap.

Tamya squirmed when she saw him approaching.

"Been lookin' all over for you," Aden said and stood before her.

"Yeah?" she said.

"Yeah," he said.

"So?" The stone rang against the blade.

"You kinda disappeared." He shifted his weight from one foot to the other. "Thought you run off. I'm … I guess I'm glad to see you still here."

Tamya didn't respond.

"Why are you out here, alone?" Aden asked. "Come back to camp."

She snarled at him. "No one wants me there."

Aden squatted before her. "Not true," he said. "I do."

She flinched, and he recognized the same hopelessness as before.

He took a deep breath. "You know, I've been reading those stories from one of the books that Iletus brought. The *Tales of the Sohan-el*."

Tamya returned to sharpening her blade.

"They did some amazing things, incredible things," Aden continued. "I mean, one story is how this *Sohan-el*, Pater, rode a dragon and took on an army of 500 trodall, killing them all. He was a half-elf, too."

Tamya's mouth tightened.

"I think it's easy to read or hear those stories and not realize they didn't know they was gonna win," Aden said. "I mean, they were people, just like you or me, right? They fought and won against impossible odds, but they had to deal with the same doubts and hopelessness that we all deal with, I think. And once I realized that, I think it's not beating a thousand men or pulling the spine from a trodall that was the greatest victory.

"They had hope when all around them was dark and hopeless. That is a near impossible feat. Hope in the face of despair is the greatest victory."

Aden stood again. "Everyone thinks we're gonna die tomorrow." He clicked his tongue. "Even Caleb thinks his destiny in this whole thing is to die, give his life for this revolution. You know what I think? I think it ain't over yet and they don't know crit about how it'll end. El seen us this far and will see us beyond.

"So I choose to have hope. That's the secret. You gotta choose it. Choose hope."

Tamya spoke to him through clenched teeth. "You're a fool."

"Maybe," Aden said. "But they said that about all those breakin' people in those stories, too."

Sighing, he gazed at her for another moment. Tamya didn't move, looking away from him. "Just think on it," he said. "For me. Good night. See you in the morning."

Aden made his way back to the camp. He thought about going back to his tent, but he knew he wouldn't sleep. Not now.

Instead he went out to the field where two hundred men kept watch. Caleb sat out in front of them, his legs crossed under him. He was a shadow in the haze of the Acar and under the light of the three moons of Eres in the hazy night sky. Aden moved to sit next to him.

Closer now, Aden could see Caleb's eyes were closed. He followed Caleb's example, closing his own eyes and resting his arms on his knees. Time passed, how much Aden didn't know, but he prayed. He fought his thoughts as images and words of Tamya distracted him, but despite the preparations they made, the only way they were getting through the next day was with El's help. So he asked for wisdom and guidance, and in admitting his need for El's help and reaching out to him with his heart, Aden felt peace. Not apart from his concern and fear, but in spite of them.

"Thank you," he heard Caleb say, and Aden opened his eyes and turned to see Caleb still had his closed. A gray light signaled the approaching sunrise to the east.

"For what?" Aden asked.

"Being here with me," Caleb said. "For standing with me this morning. It means a great deal."

"You would have done the same."

"Yes," Caleb said. "But that doesn't make it mean any less."

He frowned at Caleb. "Are you?"

"Am I what?"

"The *Brendel*. You heard what Lyam said, but you didn't answer him when he asked. Are you?"

Caleb was silent for a moment. He opened his eyes and turned to Aden. "What do you think?"

"I know what I breakin' think," Aden said. "I asked you. What do you believe?"

In the growing gray light, Aden saw Caleb grin. "The sun is rising," he said.

Aden shrugged. "Yeah?"

"No matter how dark the night, the sun rises."

"Crit on a frog, Caleb," Aden said. "Do you enjoy not answering my question?"

"I did answer it."

"You did?"

"That is what I believe," Caleb said. "More now than ever, after reaching the Living Stone and surviving that battle at Biram." Caleb finally opened his eyes, taking a deep breath. "Lyam was right about one thing. You've been with me since the beginning at Asya, never giving up, right here with me. I've had few friends in my life, Aden. But you're more than that to me now. You're my brother."

Aden, for a rare moment, was speechless.

"Our time together will end," Caleb said. "Reyan told me you had your own path. Mine will end in my death. It will not matter what I believe, or what I was, but what is true, and whether you believe on your own."

A quiet hung between them until Aden found the words. "But why? Why does your path have to end in your death?"

Caleb lifted his hands, palms up, and gazed at them. "There's blood on my hands. Too much of it, I think. And more will be added today, and in the weeks and months to come, if El helps us and we survive. Those that shed blood pay for it with their own."

"But you could change, right?" Aden said. "You don't have to be like that."

"Sometimes, even if you change, you still have to pay," Caleb muttered. "That's okay. Because I know that there is a life after that end. My father is there, my mother, Reyan, and others. More important, Yosu and El are there. I don't know all that the Everworld is – the Fyrwrit only gives hints of it, probably all it can do – but it is a reward for those willing to give and fight so others can be free. I will see that dawn, too. As dark as it gets, I will see that dawn."

Aden thought again of all those *Sohan-el* in the scripture and the stories, and Caleb was one of them, a man of hope willing to fight despite the odds. He wondered what the end of Caleb's story would be, and he prayed that the man would find peace here in this life even before the next.

The eastern horizon was yellow and orange now.

"Come," Caleb said. "It is time."

———

Caleb watched as three riders and a score of militan trekked across the black ground of the Acar towards the *Hamon-el.*

The sun had risen and the army of humanity was spread out behind him. He hoped the people of the *Hamon-el* had been able to rest. They were going to need it today, he felt as he surveyed the legion, six thousand strong, waiting for the battle to begin. But if they hadn't slept, could he blame them? Neither had he.

The legion held a classic formation – the thousand skirmishers were the front line. They were not veterans or the best soldiers of the army; their role was to engage and distract the enemy while the bulk of the legion adjusted position, flanking and moving forward to crush the opposition.

Behind the skirmishers was the first line of militan in three rectangular formations, phalanxes eight elves deep and a hundred across. The rectangular formation allowed shields to overlap to protect from arrows and any other attacks, advancing like a piece of armor. The third line had two similar phalanxes along the middle gaps of the second line. They would fill in those gaps, or any other that occurred as the battle was enjoined.

At the rear of the legion was a reserve unit, usually made up of the best soldiers, about 500 of the most experienced veterans that would know how to give support if needed. The Cavalry, another five hundred veterans on armored horses, and catapults were with the reserve unit.

The Kryan legion would not use the war engines today, if the elves followed protocol. Those siegeworks were for walls and large armies, not a force of 700 men spread out as they were. The skirmishers alone outnumbered Caleb's army.

As the riders neared, Caleb could see the figures better, and judging by their attire, one was a general, the second a Bladeguard, and the third a Wraith. They walked their horses with the hundred militan, taken from the skirmishers, pacing them in a simple column behind them.

"Shall we?" Iletus asked.

"Aden and Iletus, with me," Caleb said. He turned to Bweth, decked out as she was in that armor – a work of art, to the sure. "You have the army if this is not a peaceful meeting. You know what to do."

"To the sure," Bweth said.

Caleb, Aden, and Iletus advanced on their own feet. He could see they would meet up with the elven Vanguard a hundred mitres away from the *Hamon-el* line and a hundred and fifty from the skirmishers.

The Bladeguard that approached them had a single strip of hair down the middle of her head, dark hair tied back behind her.

"Daelas," Iletus said the name before Caleb could.

Caleb knew Daelas by name and reputation. He had seen her once at the Citadel in Kohinoor, but that was across the room. He had never spoken to her. Or rather, she had never spoken to him, ignoring him. However little his personal experience with her, the stories of her abounded. She was a gifted assassin, proficient in every weapon imaginable, no matter how obscure. He could see the two swords she was known for, one on each hip.

Galen spoke of her only once when Caleb asked about her, and while he praised her abilities, he was not kind about her character.

Her skin is white as milk but her heart is the darkest I've ever known, Galen said. *Not cruel, but cold. No light. No life.* Caleb saw a hint of concern in his master's expression, as if she disturbed him.

And that was all Galen had said of her.

The Wraith was covered in a long gray cloak like the one the Wraith wore in Ketan, the face in shadow. Of his body, only his hands were visible. The General was bald with a scar on his face that made his frown even fiercer.

Daelas did not wear an expression. In another life, she would have been beautiful. Both groups stopped within ten mitres of each other

"So it is true," Daelas said to Iletus. "You are part of Galen's betrayal."

Iletus gave her a bow. "Hello, Daelas," he said. "It has been a few years."

"I was on a special mission in Faltiel," she said. "By order of our Emperor."

"Your Emperor," Iletus said. "He is no longer mine."

"No, he is," she said. "Which we will prove today." She turned her face to Caleb, and he felt her disdain even though only the corners of her mouth turned down. "So this is Caleb, the infamous *Brendel*."

He laid a hand on the hilt of his unforged sword and did not answer.

"I heard about you," Daelas said. "I wanted to kill you years ago. I knew you were dangerous. It was a foolish idea; we all knew it. But Galen would not listen. Now we know why. His plan was to betray the Empire all along. As was yours, I suppose."

Caleb snorted at her.

"I will say this for you," she said, her face twisting into a grimace. "This is the most powerful stench I have ever encountered. Besides that one time in Jennah, to be honest. Fitting, though, that you will meet your end in a place that smells like dead trodall crit."

Caleb faced the General. "I do not believe we have met," he said.

After the General didn't speak, Daelas said, "General Pyram, First General of the outpost at Taggart."

Caleb didn't ask after the Wraith. They lost their identity, and more, when they went through the process to become the Emperor's killers. He did look from Daelas to the General, however. "This is your chance," he said. "Surrender now and we will let you live to return to Kryus."

Daelas chuckled, and the General's frown never changed. "Galen chose a human with some gruts, at least." She scanned the seven hundred behind Caleb before focusing her attention back to him. "You know you have no chance."

"Some would have said it was impossible to reach the Living Stone and get a legendary unforged sword," Caleb said. "That these things didn't even exist. And yet I did. I'm sure you would have said we could not have survived against the three Wraith sent against us. And yet we did. Still more balked that a newly trained army of humans could stand against the elves at Biram, and we prevailed."

Any hint of mirth disappeared from her face. "That was different. I assure you, we have not underestimated you this time. I will not make the same mistakes as General Pyram here, or Cyprian and Saben. A Kryan legion has not lost a battle on an open field in 300 years. I commend you for your victory at Biram, but you cannot win here."

"Forgive me if I listen to different voices than the ones that tell me what I cannot do," Caleb said.

"I promise you," Daelas said. "Whatever happens here, you will lose."

"It is not about winning or losing," Caleb said. "It is about being free. And sometimes freedom is standing up to those that oppress you, regardless of the cost."

"And you are willing to fight for that belief?" Daelas asked.

"Haven't I proven that by now?"

"Very well," she said. "Then I come to make you an offer."

"An offer?"

"Yes," she said. "I challenge you to a *conduelae*."

Caleb scratched his beard. As the one with the tactical advantage, she was offering him the *conduelae* from a place of strength. Six thousand against seven hundred was no contest. Caleb had challenged in Biram to save lives, even the lives of the enemy. He did not believe Daelas had that agenda.

"He fought a *conduelae* with Cyprian and Saben in Biram," Iletus said. "Both at once. And he won. You cannot hope to beat him."

"Who said he would fight me?" she asked. "Although that would be interesting. No, I would claim the Wraith here as my champion."

"He beat a Wraith in Ketan," Iletus argued. "Tanicus sent three against him, and he survived. You believe this one could beat him?"

"You have not asked terms," she said. "Do you not wish to know them?"

"What could you say that I would believe?" Caleb said. "Not after what the elves did in Biram. You cannot wish to keep us alive, and Kryus is not known for wanting to spare the lives of their own militan. Unless you wish to keep my men alive only to torture them, make an example of them."

"Then let that be the terms, then," she said. "If you win, I give my word that we will kill you and every one of your men in battle, giving each as quick of a death as possible. Your rebellion will be crushed, but you will save your men from slow, horrible deaths."

"But I do not believe you will keep to your bargain," Caleb said. "Kryan legions are not known for keeping their terms, win or lose."

"You will take that risk, then," she said.

"What if I lose?" Caleb asked.

Daelas smiled, but it was the coldest smile Caleb had ever seen. "Then Iletus and your men will surrender to us. And we will do with them as we please."

"How can you trust our word?" Caleb said.

"You know this game, Caleb, as does Iletus," Daelas said. "The terms are secondary and always questionable."

She was right. The duel rarely spared the battle. Caleb was the only leader to keep to the terms that he ever knew of, except in ancient stories heralding the honor of the *Sohan-el*. If Caleb won, then once the two armies fought, then his men would be more inspired by their leader's example and fight with more confidence and zeal. Those same men would be discouraged and lose hope if they saw their leader lose such a duel. Disheartened soldiers did not fight well, hence the purpose of the *conduelae*.

"Very well," Caleb said to Daelas when he faced her again. "I accept the challenge."

"Done," Daelas said and then spoke to the Wraith. "Dismount."

Without a sound, the Wraith dismounted.

"Something is not right," Iletus began.

She took the reins of his horse and called one of the militan behind her to come and get the horse. The elf led the horse back to his companions.

"Step forward," Daelas said to the Wraith. And it did.

Almost ten mitres still separated the Wraith from Caleb and his companions.

The way the Wraith moved was familiar.

"Caleb ..." Iletus warned.

"Remove your cloak," Daelas told the Wraith.

And he did.

He heard Iletus gasp before he was able to register what he saw. He blinked at the long blond hair, graying, the strong and lithe elven frame, the mature features. And the white eyes, lifeless eyes.

Galen. His master.

Aden appeared next to him. "What is it?" he asked.

And when Caleb said nothing, staring at his master, a Wraith, Iletus whispered. "That is Galen, the Blademaster of the Citadel."

"Shog it all," Aden muttered under his breath.

Caleb could see the satisfied look on Daelas' face, a sadistic contentment, but his gaze was riveted on Galen. His friend. His mentor. Tanicus had not killed him. He transformed Galen into a Wraith. And now Caleb was supposed to fight him.

"I can't," Caleb said, and he would have been ashamed at the weakness of his own voice if he cared.

Iletus stepped closer to him. "That is not Galen anymore." The elf's voice shook. "I understand that you do not wish to fight him. He was my closest friend for centuries. But he is gone."

"I can't …" It was all he could think or say in that moment.

Iletus licked the corner of his mouth and grimaced. "Caleb, listen. He gave his life to redeem his part in the evil that Tanicus and the Empire has become. He would not want you to shrink away from that now, not for him, and not when he is beyond saving."

Caleb clenched his teeth. "That may be true …"

"I do not know how Tanicus does it," Iletus pressed. "But he steals their soul. They feel no emotion, no pain. They are the walking dead. All he knew of us is gone."

Caleb groaned.

"His skills, however, remain," Iletus said. "If you refuse to fight him, Daelas will release him against the men behind us. Can any of them stand against him?"

"That's just it," Caleb said. "No one can."

"You can," Iletus said.

Caleb's brow furrowed.

"Think about it," Iletus said. "How many people did Galen personally train in his lifetime? One. *You.*"

"He trained others," Caleb said.

"Not like he taught you," Iletus said. "Cyprian, myself, or others did the bulk of the sword training with the new recruits. You got more time with him over sixteen years than anyone else did for centuries. He taught you everything he knew. He made you the greatest weapon. Even greater than himself. And now you have an unforged sword, the greatest weapon in the world. I am sorry. There is no one else who can do this, Caleb. It must be you."

Caleb saw the pain in his friend's eyes but knew the truth of his words. *Break me*, Caleb thought. *El help me. Please.*

He stepped forward three paces. He saw Iletus grab Aden by the scruff of the neck and pull him back. Caleb drew his sword and faced his master.

Daelas sat straight in her saddle. "Kill Caleb. Kill the *Brendel.*"

Without any hesitation, Galen drew his sword, a fine scimitar, and advanced towards Caleb. As he neared, Galen struck high and low with lightning fast slashes.

Caleb slid to his right and turned every one aside, ducking one swipe; Galen moved around him, and he spun to block several more slashes from Galen's blade. Galen lunged into a thrust, and Caleb leaned back while swatting aside the blade and leapt to change the angle. Galen paused and faced him again.

Lifting his sword, the master stepped forward and swung down, then diverted the strike into a diagonal slash upwards. Caleb moved his feet, keeping his balance, and avoided both. Retreating now to his left, he warded off each attack, the strikes coming furious and strong.

It was a familiar feeling, and odd to enjoy the comfort in the memory of hours upon hours sparring with Galen while trying to kill him. The elf wasn't as physically strong, but he knew that strength came not from brute force but precision and efficiency, measured and calculated blows. Caleb was taller and stronger but could not boast being the more precise. Galen might have taught him the forms and the styles and practiced them with Caleb more than any other before him, but Galen had one thing that Caleb could never have – centuries of experience. Learning forms was one thing, but a battle or duel was pure instinct, especially against another skilled opponent. More practice ingrained those forms into the brain, the subconscious, and in that way, elves would always have an advantage.

Galen fought now with little effort but complete focus and superior skill. As a Wraith, he was unencumbered by emotion or fatigue. After a minute of intense battle, his master breathed slow and easy, calm and unaffected.

Caleb almost fell for the feint, able to get his sword up horizontal to stifle the next attack, a stab towards his torso. Galen slashed at his legs, which he blocked, and then slashed at his head. Caleb sprung backwards and leaned away, but Galen's blade cut across his left cheek. Crying out, he stumbled back and parried the three strikes that came after it. He felt his face was wet with blood.

Caleb was not calm and unaffected. Here he was fighting his master and forgetting the first rule of the duel: stay calm. Focused. His heart was gripped with fear, anxious with the shock of seeing Galen as a Wraith. Anxiety, fear, anger, fatigue, they all made one desperate and reckless, a sure way to lose any battle. Whoever's tactic it was, Daelas or Tanicus, leading Caleb to face his master as a Wraith frazzled him. Like he was a shoggin' novice.

Forcing himself to relax, he breathed deep through his nose and out his mouth and deflected Galen's attacks, stepping back and sliding right and left, constantly moving. He focused on the fundamentals, balance and footwork, high and low guards. Galen cut up diagonally again and reversed it into a high horizontal slash. Caleb ducked, his nostrils flaring. But his heartbeat began to slow, even as he exerted himself.

As he turned to stop another high strike, Caleb wasn't fast enough to stop the stab at his gut, but he deflected it enough that Galen's blade stabbed into his side. Galen's blade went deep and then straight through. Caleb leapt away, the blade trailing his blood as it pulled from the wound. Caleb cursed and bent at the waist at the pain.

"Caleb ..." he heard from Iletus from behind him, and he didn't need any more explanation. The reprimand was in the tone, and Caleb knew what Iletus would say. It was what he would tell Aden or Xander or any other student of his.

One cannot survive a duel on defense alone. In fact, it was the aggressor that usually won. Not heedless, but aggressive, on the offensive, not simply dodging or blocking attacks but countering and initiating contact. For it was the one that found the flow of the battle and controlled it that won the day. Reaction leads to death; action leads to victory.

Bleeding from the face and now the side, Caleb knew he would weaken soon. He met Galen's attacks with ones of his own, countering now instead of dodging. He came in close and forced Galen to retreat under his own barrage of cuts and thrusts, high and low, changing up his angles and speed. Ducking another wide slash, Caleb came around to cut across at Galen's chest, which the elf evaded.

When Caleb beat Zarek, it was a fluke. The Bladeguard was overconfident and did not know the strength of the Kingstaff. The surprise caused a hesitation in Zarek that Caleb was able to exploit. In the fight with Saben and Cyprian, it was the supernatural force of the unforged sword that shattered Cyprian's blade. The *barabrend* also gave Caleb the advantage there.

Coming around for another attack, Caleb attempted to lure Galen into a straight meeting of the blades, trying again to break his opponent's sword, but a swordmaster like Galen, even soulless as a Wraith, would not allow it. Galen twisted Caleb's blade down and away and sent his own scimitar towards Caleb's chest. The slash was too fast; Caleb couldn't dodge quick enough, and his master's blade cut across his upper left arm. Caleb stumbled. He ducked into a roll as Galen's blade tried to take his head off. Caleb came up and blocked two more lightning strikes, his left arm useless at his side.

Caleb silently cried out to El again for help.

And that is when the sword spoke to him.

It was not unusual to feel an impression from the sword. General feelings of confirmation or peace were distinct when gripping the hilt of the unforged sword, nothing you could put into words. Outright messages from the blade were rare. When it happened, his mind saw images and interpreted them as words, clear in his mind as if they were his thoughts, although he knew they came from a higher source.

Through the heart.

The message was simple and clear in intent. El was telling Caleb to stab Galen through the heart.

I can't, he thought. There must be a way to beat him without killing him. Even though Iletus said he was no longer Galen, Caleb could not bring himself to take his life. He lost his father and his Uncle Reyan. He would not be the hand that ended the life of his mentor and friend.

And ending Galen's life meant that he would never know what happened to Danelle.

Not that he could win this battle anyway. He wasn't sure, but Galen felt faster, stronger, even more confident than Caleb remembered, if that was possible. Combined with Caleb's wounds and growing weakness, he didn't think he could win.

Through the heart, it came again.

"Caleb ..." Aden's voice this time. "You're holding back."

As he countered a vertical strike with a roundhouse kick that Galen eluded by leaping aside, Caleb first felt disappointment that Aden was right, then pride that the young man was talented enough to see it. Yes, he was holding back because he didn't want to kill Galen. And it was only a matter of time before the Wraith of Galen would kill him instead.

Through the heart.

Caleb peered at the white, lifeless eyes of the Wraith he fought. Nothing remained of his friend, not the core of him, his character, who he was. Killing this Wraith would not be killing Galen.

Galen was already dead.

His heart threatened despair, but he refused it access. He would feel that grief later, all of it. Now it was time to act.

He was a killer, honed as a weapon. Now was not the time to deny it.

Caleb stopped holding back.

A part of him was disturbed to notice the glee he felt when he did, the freedom. The pain of his wounds – to his face, his side, his shoulder – became distant, unimportant. He was one with the moment. Every action and decision calculated to perfection and carried out with ultimate conviction and efficiency. Time seemed to slow; he recognized the supernatural assistance of the unforged sword more than ever. His actions and reactions were beyond instinct, as if he could predict what happened next, split seconds before the action.

He met Galen's sword with his own and countered. Finding the flow of the battle, he knew how to control it now, and he kept his master on his heels. They both moved at impossible speeds, veering and dodging and countering and attacking, the blades blurs in their hands.

Galen's advantage might be in a millennium of experience, but Caleb realized then that it was not the unforged sword that gave him supernatural power – rather, it was the very Creator of the universe that gave the blade in the first place. That was his advantage.

Through the heart, the message kept repeating. Not the voice of the sword but the voice of El.

He was in complete control of himself and the flow of the battle. He could lead it anywhere he wanted it to go.

Along with the insistent message from the voice of El, the sword began to sing, like a familiar hymn of praise that he could not place.

Caleb raised his knee to absorb a kick from Galen, and he met his master's next attack by stifling it, using his body as leverage and knocked the elf off balance with his injured shoulder.

As Galen stumbled and shifted his feet to recover, Caleb struck with the sword and severed Galen's right arm at the wrist.

Galen flailed, blood pouring and splattering in an arc, but he got his feet under him and crouched to face Caleb.

"It is over," Caleb said, but he didn't know why he said it. No one lived in his master to hear him. Galen gazed at the sword on the black ground with those white eyes, still held in the severed hand's grip, and he took a step towards it.

He would never stop, never give up.

Through the heart. Insistent with the sound of a chorus behind it.

Shuffling forward in a rush, Caleb swung his sword low and hacked Galen's left leg off at the knee. Galen fell to the side, inevitable, but Caleb helped him by kicking out at his master's right shoulder. The Wraith twisted as he fell and landed on his back.

Letting out a roar of pain and frustration that echoed through the valley, Caleb lifted the unforged sword and plunged it through Galen's heart, pinning him to the black, dead ground of the Acar. Galen's body shuddered and twitched, his mouth open and gasping for air.

Releasing the sword, Caleb closed his eyes and knelt next to his master's body. It was as if the whole of Eres was silent around him, but the pain hit him full force again, and he gasped and shuddered at the immensity of it. The voice of El was absent. The chorus was silent. He was alone with pain.

After a few seconds, he heard Aden and Iletus walk up behind him.

"Uh …" Aden said. "Caleb?"

"Master …?" Iletus whispered.

Caleb opened his eyes just in time to see the white of Galen's eyes fade, dissolving away to show Galen's clear blue eyes. Caleb inhaled sharply as Galen lifted his head and looked at him.

"Caleb, my boy?"

He leaned over Galen in a heartbeat. "Master!" he cried and grabbed Galen's left hand. Staring down over his body, blood still poured out of it, mixing with Caleb's own. How could a body hold so much blood? And the blade was through his heart. How was he alive? But he could answer his own question easy enough. The unforged sword through his heart both countered the effects of whatever made him a Wraith and was now keeping him alive. But for how long?

"I'm so sorry," Caleb said. "So sorry."

"Sorry?" Galen said. "For what?"

"I couldn't save you," he answered. "I – I couldn't ..."

"But you did save me," Galen said. "I was caught in my own skin, unable to resist their commands. Now I am free of it, of all the suffering. You did well, my boy. Oh, so well. I am ... proud of you."

Caleb was unable to speak. Aden and Iletus moved to stand between him and the enemy, less than five mitres away.

"Now listen." Galen squeezed his hand, his eyes full of desperate pain. "I'm sorry. I did what I thought was best ..."

"Master ..." Caleb growled.

"Danelle didn't run," he said. "I sent her away."

Like a punch in the gut, air left his lungs. "Why?"

"Caleb ..." Galen coughed, blood in the corner of his mouth. "She was pregnant."

Caleb's gut twisted within him, and he moaned, leaning over.

"I ... had to explain it to her. Once I did, she understood ..."

"What did you say?" Caleb growled.

"The other Bladeguard knew about her. I couldn't protect you and her ... and a child. And you would die to protect her." Galen took a short, desperate breath and coughed. "I couldn't let that happen. You had a mission, a purpose. She agreed to go."

Caleb's hair fell into his face as he shook his head. He grabbed the front of Galen's tunic with his other hand. "Where did you send her?"

Tears began to fall from Galen's eyes. "It doesn't matter. She never made it. I failed. I thought it best for everyone. But I failed. They got to her."

"No," was all Caleb could say.

"Forgive me," Galen said. "I thought it was my job to make you the perfect weapon. And what better motivation than revenge?" Galen coughed. "But now I see ... I was wrong. Oh, so wrong. Please forgive me."

His mind was reeling, anger and grief and despair all warring within him for control. *A baby.*

"I *trusted* you," Caleb said.

"I know," Galen said. "I am so sorry ..."

But hadn't Caleb thought a similar thing, just a few days ago? His love for Danelle had been selfish and reckless. She gave him strength and comfort, and he put her life in great danger in return. The Bladeguard of the Citadel had already framed her to hurt him.

And Galen was absolutely correct. He would have given his life to save her and the child, also putting his mission at risk.

A child ...

Would Caleb have ever possessed the strength to send her and the child away? Even for safety? He didn't think so. But now they were both dead.

Caleb sat in the wheezing of his dying master for a long moment. Caleb finally said. "I ... I forgive you."

Galen sobbed again. "Thank you," he said. He reached up with his left hand and stroked Caleb's hair. "I love you, my boy. Like a son, I loved you. You are the one thing I've done right in my life. Thank you."

Caleb's own tears flowed down his face and into his beard, stung at the wound on his cheek.

Galen groaned in pain, gasping for air then finding it with a series of coughs. "You remember my villa in the mountains," he said, his voice tight.

Wiping his eyes with the back of his sleeve, Caleb lifted his head and looked Galen in the eye. "Yes."

"I left it to you," Galen said. "All the old books and papers are there, forgotten wisdom of men and elves and dwarves. It is yours. The letters of law are there to prove it. Promise me you will go there, when this is all over. Find peace."

A part of him desired to see that idyllic villa again; Caleb was surrounded by so much pain, death, and war. He denied himself that dream, rejected it in his heart and mind. He knew he would not live beyond his mission to see the end of Kryan tyranny and remove the elves from the land of men. To hope beyond it was a waste and foolishness. But he could not say all that to his dying master, so he gave what his master wanted.

"I promise," Caleb said. An empty promise.

"Good," Galen grunted. "One last thing."

"Yes?"

"Tanicus ... is a Worldbreaker."

And with that revelation, Galen gripped his hand in anguish, gasping for breath. Pulling his master's hand to his breast, Caleb murmured a prayer and leaned in closer. Galen's eyes went empty and glassy. Caleb stared as his master released his last breath. His body went limp and motionless. Galen, the greatest swordmaster to ever live, died and moved on to the Everworld.

And as two armies watched, Caleb laid his head on his master's chest and wept.

Chapter 32

The Battle of the Acar

Tanicus ... is a Worldbreaker.

The words echoed in General Pyram's mind as he tried to focus on what the Bladeguard was telling him.

Daelas called his name. "Are you listening?"

He nodded at her, although he was in shock. He just witnessed the legendary Galen, made a Wraith, beaten by a human. And the Blademaster of the Citadel revealed that the Emperor was a wizard of an ancient magic, a dangerous magic, so dangerous it was illegal. Illegal. And the revelation came as they stood in the field of the Acar, a monument to the destructive power of Tebelrivyn, that ancient magic.

"I'm listening," he said. Was his frown still intact? He found he no longer cared; although with the overwhelming stench of the Deadwater around him, he had no problem producing a grimace, at least.

"Go back to the command center and prepare the legion to march forward," she said.

"What about you?" he asked.

He saw fear in her eyes. She didn't even try to hide it as she glanced over at the dead Galen and that man.

No wonder the Empire underestimated this Caleb. Who could believe a human capable of such things? But after what he just saw, a display of martial excellence beyond anything he had ever thought possible, he believed that the *Brendel* could take down the Empire. The question, though, was, could he kill a Worldbreaker? And what would remain of the Empire if he did? And did he want an Empire ruled by a Worldbreaker?

"I will lead the skirmishers to engage them here while you prepare the legion to support," Daelas said. "Do not tell anyone what you heard or saw here. Tell them nothing. We will kill every human in that army, understand? Leave none alive."

After the dangerous secret he just heard, he was certain Daelas would make sure he and any other elf within earshot would meet the nine gods soon, as well. But for now, she needed him, and she was sending him away.

He nodded again and pounded his chest in salute. He turned his own mount and rode back across the field, which was damp and muddy as he neared the first phalanxes of the legion.

———

"What the shog do we do now?" Aden asked, his sword in his hand as the General rode back to the east with the rest of the Kryan army.

Iletus also held his sword; his eyes brimmed with tears. The elf didn't answer him.

"Iletus?"

Iletus blinked, a tear traveled down his cheek. "They will attack with the skirmishers first," Iletus said. "And then bring up the rest of the legion to crush us underfoot."

Aden peeked back at Caleb. "So ... we need to go."

Without a word, Caleb wiped his eyes and pulled his sword from Galen's dead body. Galen's body twitched once. Caleb was covered in blood, but he didn't seem to notice his wounds. He sheathed the sword, reached down, and gathered the dead elf in his arms, favoring his own left arm. Standing, he looked past Aden and Iletus to Daelas on her horse mitres away. His gray eyes were cold and merciless. He turned and trudged back to the *Hamon-el*.

Daelas faced them now, and she raised one of her swords. "Skirmishers! To me!"

Iletus and Aden backed away and followed Caleb. Nine hundred militan raced forward with a battle cry.

———

Xander stood with Bweth as they observed Caleb lumbering back with the dead Wraith in his arms. They heard and saw his weeping, although his face was now a scowl of anger. Beyond Caleb, Aden, and Iletus, the Kryan front line was advancing. The elves in that line wore blue tunics and a simple breastplate. They carried gladi and small shields.

Bweth called down the line, "Bows ready!" The command was repeated in both directions as the men lifted their bows and nocked arrows. Xander felt helpless, unable to shoot a bow with one hand. The line of men were spread two paces apart across the field. Bweth turned to Xander now, her armor clattering with every move. "The front line is the skirmishers. They are fodder to throw at us while the legion of trained militan follow. We need to survive this charge."

While their companions were still returning, the skirmishers met up with the Bladeguard and the twenty militan she had with her. They advanced as one at a jog.

The dwarf beside him raised her spiked mace. Lowering it, Bweth cried, "Fire!" The arrows arced over their companions and most fell short or long. A few arrows connected with a charging militan, but only a dozen or so. "Measure better when you fire, you shoggers! Thin that breakin' charge or we dead as crit! Draw!" They drew. "Fire!"

The *Hamon-el* fired again, and more than a hundred fell.

"Better," Bweth said. "Fire!"

Caleb did not speak or regard anyone as he strode past the *Hamon-el* and towards the camp behind them.

Iletus and Aden reached them next. The skirmishers were a hundred mitres behind them.

Xander met Aden's eyes. "What happened?"

"Later," Iletus said. "We ready to organize in our divisions?"

As part of their preparations, Caleb divided the remaining seven hundred into seven divisions of a hundred each.

"We are ready," Bweth said, her voice low.

"But where is Caleb?" Xander asked. "He seemed done. Can we do this without him?"

Aden spun on Xander. "We can and we will. You know the plan. Besides, he'll come back."

"No time ..." Iletus said, the skirmishers seventy mitres away.

"How can you know?" Xander said. "So much blood ..."

Aden turned back to face the elves running toward them. "I saw the look in his eyes."

They fired a total of four times into the skirmishers and reduced the numbers by the time the elves were thirty mitres away, to six or seven hundred. Equal numbers. He could see that female Bladeguard at the rear of the skirmishers on her horse.

"Bows down," Bweth shouted down the line, repeated by others again. "Swords up! Rally to your divisions!" Men sprinted to form up behind their division leader. Within seconds, both Bweth and Xander had a hundred men at their backs.

Fifteen mitres away.

Xander had the fleeting thought that someone needed to give the men a speech, something to inspire them. But there was no time. Bweth lifted her mace, set her shield before her, and ran forward with a battle cry of her own.

"*Hamon-el!*"

Xander raised his unforged sword. All seven hundred men met the skirmishers and shouted.

"*Hamon-el!*"

Caleb swept papers and maps from the long table in the command tent. He laid Galen's bloody and lifeless body upon the table.

He knew the plan. The battle was far from over. Five thousand elven militan were about to descend upon his men, his friends, break it all, his family. But he felt so empty. He couldn't move. Caleb stood there next to his friend, his mentor, his master. How could he leave him?

The Kingstaff stood in the corner of the tent. *To lead with compassion, justice, and strength.*

He tore his gaze away from it. He was seriously wounded, weak, exhausted, overcome with grief and despair. He had killed his own master, who had lied to him. Danelle was dead. And there had been a baby, also gone. It was a crushing weight.

The memory came to him of when he first spoke the vow. It had been to Galen before the master sent him back to the land of men to fulfill his purpose, his mission. If he had known the sacrifice that would be required of him, would he have said the words? Would he have even begun the journey?

It is good we do not know such things, Caleb said. *How could I ever make that choice? Knowing the cost would be so great?*

He was faced with a choice now. Here, in this dead place, he had a choice. To stay here and grieve or join the fight? Join his friends, his people, the ones he led to this very point?

I will defend the innocent, free the oppressed, and spread light to dark places.

"Break me."

Weapons were gathered in the corner, and Caleb drew a knife from the small pile. Taking a canteen of water and a fresh shirt with him, he moved outside of the tent to a fire that still burned low. He shoved the knife deep into the glowing coals. As he waited, he took the canteen and washed his face, ripping the cut and bloody shirt from his own body and wiping blood as he went. He pulled the knife from the coals and placed the searing hot blade on his cheek. Screaming through a clenched jaw, he heard it sizzle and smelled burning flesh.

Mohr, one of the remaining surgeons of the *Hamon-el*, walked up to Caleb and froze. "Caleb. I – don't you want me to see to your wounds?"

"No time," Caleb muttered.

"Great and mighty El," he said. "At least let me help you."

Caleb placed the knife in the coals again, and over the next few minutes, he and Mohr cauterized the wound on his side, both entry and exit, and the cut on his arm. Mohr placed an ointment on the burns and helped him put on the fresh shirt.

Mohr placed a hand on Caleb's chest. "Those are some serious wounds," he said. "You need to rest."

Caleb sneered at him as he pivoted on a heel and walked back into the tent and grabbed the Kingstaff in his left hand, the pain a constant ache in his side and shoulder. He drew the unforged sword, light and ready in his right hand, and he left his master lying there to join the battle on the field of the Acar.

———

She could have run faster without the armor. Break it all, she could have run faster if she wasn't pregnant, the shoggin' kid kicking like a piffed mule within her belly.

Bweth knocked down two elves when she met the skirmisher line, one with her shield and the second with her right shoulder. She bashed into the arm of a third with her mace, hearing the bones crunch, and he screamed in pain. The spikes of her mace silenced him with a blow to the face. Kicking down with her boot on one of the elves she knocked down, her heel on his windpipe, she stepped over to another militan, blocking his gladus with her shield, and she countered with a strike that was met by the militan's shield. Her left fist connected with his nose and she followed the punch with her mace against the side of his neck.

A sword came across her back, deflected by her steel armor. She spun and struck with her shield, coming down on the elf's head with her mace, the skull suddenly sunken and misshapen.

Bweth thought of Hunter, then, and she felt alone. Only two battles with the fool man, and she felt naked on her side, vulnerable. Was that why she built the armor?

Out of the corner of her eye, she could see Iletus fighting to her right, mitres away and leading his own division. He was an artist at work, precise strikes and cuts while evading every attack. Militan after militan fell to his sword.

Far to her left, she saw Aden leading men against the skirmishers. His face was focused, determined. The young man was not angry – she rarely saw him angry, if ever – and he took down a militan with a fast, expert slash after eluding an attack.

Bweth had her own style. Leaping, she gave a vertical strike against a shield, and the militan beneath it went to his knees. Bweth kicked the gladus out of his hand and hit him in the face with her shield. As he reeled, she ended his life with her mace to his forehead.

With another kick from the babe against her ribs, she knew she was not alone. *I know you're there*, she thought.

Humans died to her left, men hardened in the Battle of Biram or Ketan, men who followed the *Brendel* and his cause to their deaths here on this grotesque land. They were cut down by the double blades of a female elf;

those men were run through or cut to pieces as they screamed. Bweth said her own prayers for them as she threw herself into the chaos of the field.

The sound of battle could be deafening at times, a mixture of steel clashing and people screaming in pain or victory or yelling in frustration. And wearing a helmet, as she was, muffled those noises to a dull, constant roar. But even through the noise, she heard the growl of a bloodwolf off to the north.

—+—

Tamya didn't know why she stayed. Months ago, her desire was revenge against the elves, to kill as many as she could. After the last ninedays, since the Battle of Biram, thinking about vengeance only made her feel tired. It had to be something else.

It could be loyalty, she supposed. Caleb and the others had taught her a great deal, how to fight, how to survive. Say what she would about their foolish idealism, but they empowered her, accepted her, even when she brought a breakin' bloodwolf into their city, and no one more so than Aden. They deserved her loyalty, that was true. But loyalty spoke of obligation more than freedom. Caleb and Aden made it clear she was free to go. Why did she stay?

Tamya wasn't sure she liked the answer that came to her mind when she asked that question. In her mind, she saw his face, the beak of a nose and those big ears that stuck out from his bushy dark hair. Every time she tried to do something to push him away or upset him, it only made him more curious. And ignoring him wasn't any better; he would ask her about that, too. He annoyed her more than anything, but she couldn't deny that when she wondered why she stayed, his name came to mind.

But break it all, she did trust Aden. It was ironic that Aden seemed to trust her, believe in her, however she continued to prove that she wasn't good enough. Did she love him? Could she love him? Was she simply lonely? She was confused, for the real.

Now, after firing arrows into the skirmishers – she didn't hit anything – she charged the elves with Hema at her heels.

Both swords were out in a flash, and she sneered while Hema snarled. They entered the fray together; Hema came under a militan's shield and went for his throat. Tamya countered another elf's attack with one of her own and slashed along his abdomen.

As she turned to fight another militan, slicing high while Hema bit at his legs, she realized she felt different during this battle than the one at Biram. At Biram, it was her anger and bitterness that drove her, thinking of her son and Berran and her mother. Here the fury was gone. She did not care whether she lived or died. She accepted the fact that she would probably die and that she deserved to. But she would die here with Aden and Caleb and these foolish men and women of the *Hamon-el*.

So when she turned and saw another female elf with two swords in her hand and a handful of dead men at her feet, she advanced to fight her. She registered the fact that this was a Bladeguard, from her dress and skill, but it did not matter. These were her friends, her brothers, and they were dying. Tamya would give her life to save as many as she could.

Tamya calmly strode towards the Bladeguard. They met eyes, and the Bladeguard smiled, crouching low in a stance to accept Tamya's challenge.

Hema, however, was an animal, a bloodwolf. As restrained as he could be, this was battle. There was blood to be had. The wolf noted Tamya's target and launched himself in the Bladeguard's direction.

"Hema, no!" Tamya cried out, but it was too late. She watched, helpless, as the wolf leapt at the Bladeguard. The female elf slid to the side and stabbed the wolf through the chest with both of her blades. Hema whimpered and howled as he fell to the ground, lying motionless.

Tamya heard a scream, thinking it was her own, and charged the Bladeguard with her swords spinning.

—+—

The battle raged as Caleb joined the fray. Aden, Bweth, and Xander led the *Hamon-el*, even as he had hesitated in his grief. Did that make him a good or bad leader? He didn't have time to decide. His men were fighting for their lives, and many of them died. He sprinted to the fighting, to the right side of the line, the point nearest to him.

The Kingstaff spun like a blur and the unforged sword in his hand flashed as he leapt into a crowd of militan. Within a few heartbeats, the crowd of militan was dead at his feet.

The *Brendel* had joined the battle. And the sword began to sing again.

—+—

Shuffling his feet and sliding over, he avoided the gladus and severed the militan's right arm at the elbow. Aden did not stop moving and brought his sword back around to slice through the elf's neck. Casting his gaze around, the militan numbers were sparse. This part of the battle would be over quickly.

Twenty mitres to the south, he could make out a figure with a sword and a long staff cutting down any who stood in his path. Caleb. He knew he would come back.

He heard the sound of Tamya's cry through the din of the battle, off to the north side of the line. Aden whirled in time to see the bloodwolf launch himself in the air towards Daelas the Bladeguard and die at her hands.

Aden was running through the battle in her direction before he heard Tamya's anguished scream.

They were almost thirty mitres away, with men and elves fighting and dying in between, and he saw Tamya move to engage the Bladeguard. Shaking his head, he cursed as he slid and turned around a militan bearing down on a man with his shield. Aden wove his way through the battle. He knocked an elf down and into the sword of a man as he ran.

Tamya used what Esai taught her well. She kept herself in motion while she struck with both blades, each hand with a mind of its own, slashing high and low or feinting and stifling the Bladeguard attack. For a moment, it was impressive, but Tamya wasn't a match for a Bladeguard.

Aden was still ten paces away.

The Bladeguard slid around to her right, slashing and opening a gash across Tamya's left arm with one blade and disarming Tamya with the other. Tamya leapt back to avoid the stab at her abdomen, and Daelas' blade scraped off Tamya's breastplate at an awkward angle and sliced into her side. Tamya cried out and bent over in pain. The Bladeguard's other sword rose high to deliver a killing blow as she closed in.

Now within two paces, Aden jumped and led with his knees like a human missile at Daelas. The Bladeguard saw him coming towards her but not in time to effectively defend herself; her eyes squinted as her sword arm came down, but Aden's knees rammed Daelas and disrupted the blow. They both went down in a tumble, and Aden was blind while he rolled, somehow able to keep hold of his sword. Covered in the black, dead soil of the Acar, he came to his feet in a crouch and scanned the area.

A blur to his left, and he barely got his sword up in a horizontal block in time to deflect the strike. But he did not satisfy himself with defense alone, countering with a slash at the Bladeguard's midsection, which she evaded with a leap to the side. She landed on the balls of her feet and launched herself back at him with her sword – he noticed now she only held one.

One in the hand of a Bladeguard was enough, he found. Her strikes were blistering, and he had trouble deflecting her attacks, much less countering and attacking. Survival was the goal at this point, and he kept his hands and feet active. Daelas feinted high and attacked low, and she cut him across his thigh. It wasn't deep, but he retreated, deflecting her other slashes as he did. She was a better warrior, and he could see the end of this confrontation coming quickly.

It reminded him of when he faced Saben in Biram, the clear feeling of being inferior. But Caleb had a different take on that duel, telling Aden later that he could have beat Saben, a Bladeguard, and he spoke the secret that Aden noted and repeated during Caleb's fight with Galen.

You're holding back.

Aden's only hope against Daelas was to commit, no hesitation. No question. He gripped the unforged sword with both hands, and forced himself to relax, accepting death was a possibility and refusing to fear it. Immersed in the moment, he let the forms flow through him, led by the unforged sword, and he found he was faster, more confident than ever.

He stopped holding back. There was no time to wonder how he came to that place, only that he was there, knowing the present and resigned to the consequences of each action. Measuring his slashes and strikes, he countered and turned each one of Daelas' attacks into an opportunity to stab or thrust at her. He struck at her legs and then her head.

She was retreating now. He had her on her heels, but he did not take pleasure in it. It simply was. Batting aside her slash at his side, he lifted a leg and kicked her in the knee. The knee buckled, and she cried out. To her credit, even as she stumbled, she slashed around at him, not wildly, but calculated to keep him at bay. He closed within her strike, hitting the inside of her arm with his left elbow and stabbing her through the chest with his sword.

Aden withdrew his sword quickly, blood trailing his blade, and stepped back into a crouch with his sword in a low guard. Daelas gasped for air and faltered, falling back first to her rear, dropping her remaining sword and landing on her back. Clutching her chest, the blood poured past her hands and soaked the front of her tunic; her mouth moved without words and she looked around blindly as if for help.

Aden stepped over her and removed her head from her body with one blow.

Aden jogged over to Tamya, lying on her back, alive but wounded. She reached a hand out towards the bloodwolf, dead in a pool of blood a few paces away from her.

Tamya wept and called out Hema's name in a groan.

He knelt next to her and inspected her wounds. The gash on the arm was deep, as was the one at her side. Both would need attention, soon. He pressed a hand on the wound at her side; it seemed like the one losing the most blood.

"Hema," she said again.

"I know," he said. "Just lie still."

Someone approached, and he peered up to see Xander jogging towards them. He was covered in blood. Looking beyond his friend, he saw only men standing.

"It is over," Xander said. "We are gathering our dead and wounded and falling back to our original position." He pointed to the east.

Swiveling his head in that direction, Aden could see that the phalanxes of the third line of the legion had stepped forward to fill the gaps in the second line and now they were marching as one long formation across the field towards the humans.

The plan. They had to move.

Aden reached down and lifted Tamya in his arms. She embraced him. "Okay. Let's go."

"No," she whispered in his ear. "Hema."

"I've got the wolf," Xander said. "Hurry."

Chapter 33

The Blood on His Hands

Bweth Ironhorn directed people carrying the wounded to the camp where the two remaining surgeons were waiting to help those they could. Several were dead, she could see, but of their original seven hundred, a little more than 400 were standing and ready to fight. The dead were left at the edge of camp while the two dozen injured made it to the surgeons. Bweth watched as Aden carried Tamya back to the camp.

Reforming the line, they spaced themselves out two paces apart, each man with a longbow and a quiver full of arrows at their side.

She stood with Caleb as the men finished organizing the line, and Aden soon joined her at the middle of the line. Gazing out across the field, a couple hundred mitres away, was the marvel of the Kryan legion making its way as a single, unstoppable line across the black dirt of the Acar. It had been more than two centuries since she stood on a battlefield like this and never at the other end of the spears and shields of the Kryan militan. She must admit, it was an impressive and fearful sight. If they didn't have a plan, she would be arguing for running away, however much Caleb hated to run. Or she just might run anyway.

Bweth cringed when looking at Caleb – the left side of his face was burnt and swollen, and blood seeped through two other injuries to dot his shirt, one on his side and the other on his arm. But he stood and faced the Legion. So would she.

She felt nauseous, and she wasn't sure whether it was the Deadwater, the gore of the battle, or her pregnancy. She assumed all three in that moment. Vomit came up into her throat, and she swallowed it down.

Caleb turned to Aden. "You beat the Bladeguard?" he asked. It almost sounded like an accusation.

"El helped me," he said.

Caleb stared back across the field at the four thousand militan marching towards them. "That is the way of it," he said. "How is Tamya?"

"Surgeon patching her up, cleaning out the wound," Aden said. "Deep cuts. We'll see."

"She is strong," Caleb said. "She has survived worse than this."

Aden scoffed. "You have no idea."

"Are you alright?"

"No," Aden said. "Are you?"

It took him a moment to answer, and Bweth didn't think he would until he spoke. "No," Caleb said. "No, I'm not. But this isn't over yet."

"I know," Aden mumbled. "A few hundred against four or five thousand. Are we going to a fight a battle someday where we aren't hopelessly outnumbered?"

Caleb snorted. "I would guess not. We wouldn't need to rely on El if we had all the advantage."

"Great," Aden said. "At least we're used to it."

"El is advantage enough," Caleb said. "Not a bad thing to get used to."

Iletus pointed to the east. "The legion is two hundred mitres away."

"Send the first volleys," Caleb said to Bweth.

She called the order to set arrows and loose. Four arrows flew across the field of the Acar and into the four thousand militan marching at a slow pace towards them. The legion, trained for such a tactic, linked their shields and formed a protective shell around each division. They became like large, armored animals trudging across the field, all in unison. The arrows bounced off of the shields or shattered on impact.

"Another," Caleb said, and she ordered the second. Again, the arrows had no effect other than a minor distraction as they protected themselves.

Which was exactly what they were meant to do.

After one more volley, Aden spoke. "That's it. They're on the ground we soaked."

Caleb breathed in through his nose. "Very well," he said. He met Bweth's eyes, and those gray eyes were cold and intense. "Now, Bweth."

She projected her voice to be heard up and down the line. "Switch to flaming arrows!" she shouted, and the order was repeated. Reaching down into their quivers, each man pulled out an arrow whose tip was covered in cloth, cloth dipped in the Deadwater. Every man of the *Hamon-el* took a flint and steel and lit the end of their arrow, then nocked the flaming missile in their bow.

Yesterday morning, Aden approached them with a plan. After Lyam and the others left, he had gathered Caleb, Bweth, Xander, Iletus, and the other *Sohan-el* together to demonstrate how flammable the Deadwater was. His plan was simple: if they could get the legion on a part of the field covered with the substance, a simple spark would create a deadly fire. Iletus then explained how predictable the legion would be if the *Hamon-el* were already on the field – where they would camp, where they would organize, and how they would attack. They could choose where the legion would be simply by changing the position of their own camp.

So they did.

It had taken four hours and all the buckets and receptacles they could find to soak the ground with water from the dead lake. Bweth had organized the men into smaller groups to work together as Iletus directed them to the area of the field to concentrate on.

Bweth now looked over at Aden. "This gonna work?"

"It should," he said. "They don't seem to suspect anything, since the stench near the Deadwater isn't much better than if you were walking over the crit. Working so far."

"Let's hope it hasn't evaporated or dried out," Xander said. "We'd be shogged for the real."

"It would be a short battle, then," Iletus said.

"We might have to run anyway," Bweth muttered.

"It won't evaporate or dry out," Caleb said. "That substance is … it's not natural. It will work."

"Let's see, then," Iletus said.

Bweth raised her mace. They drew. She lowered her weapon and cried, "Fire," and they loosed the flaming arrows across the field and into the militan. Four hundred arrows like small meteors arced across the sky and fell among the militan and upon the ground around them.

The Deadwater mixed in with the black soil caught fire immediately. And the ground all around the marching militan became a blazing conflagration within seconds – almost a kilomitre across and two hundred mitres deep engulfed in flames.

Cloth and flesh of militan ignited next, and the valley echoed and reverberated with the screams of elves burning to death. The elves rolled on the ground, running wildly in pain, flames consuming them over minutes that seemed like hours. The ordered elven lines collapsed into chaos. Bweth grimaced. She saw Xander kneel down and vomit. That pushed her nausea over the edge, and she also lost her breakfast on the black ground of the Acar.

Bweth could feel the heat from here, more than a hundred mitres away.

Elves began to fall, by the hundreds, flailing and contorting as they died. They cried for mercy, for death, the shrill wails of the militan a constant, terrible roar in her ears. Any regular army would have cheered at the death of their enemy. Not one of the *Hamon-el* did.

Militan fell silent, thrashing then still. Life after life ended as the flames devoured thousands of elves.

"We … we could put them out of their misery," Aden whispered. "With arrows."

"We don't have enough to make any difference," Bweth moaned.

Caleb lifted his hands and stared down at them, silent.

—

General Pyram watched, confused, while the flaming arrows sailed through the air towards his militan.

He had seen the skirmishers decimated, but that was their job. He ordered the single line configuration and observed it form like from his own will, a powerful feeling. The efficiency of the legion swelled him with pride. It was hundreds of mitres away, but he saw through his peerglass Daelas killed by that skinny little boy. Within a matter of a half hour, he had seen a man kill a swordmaster legend and a boy kill a Bladeguard. He almost didn't believe it.

But as impressive as these humans were, they couldn't overcome simple numbers. A few hundred could not stand against four thousand with his best troops and the Cavalry still in reserve. He commanded the militan line to march forward.

The arrows had no effect on his trained militan, on his four thousand soldiers. How could it? It would take engines of war to even make a dent in his phalanxes, and catapults were unreliable in the field, more designed for a siege against a city wall or other such static defenses. Not one elf fell to those arrows.

His brow furrowed at the burning arrows, however. Other armies had used them, of course. It was not a unique tactic but curious to him for some reason. It felt wrong.

When the flaming arrows hit his troops and the ground around them, Pyram watched as the main part of the field caught fire and blazed through his phalanxes and the militan like an enormous angry and hungry spirit reaching out and embracing the legion to engorge itself with his elves. He could have sworn the conflagration was alive. Within minutes, the fire spread and roared over the soldiers in the field. And he watched in horror as the flames consumed over four thousand elves. He saw them writhe and panic in pain and anguish as they burned to death.

His frown did falter, then, as the resounding shrieks and screeches combined to compose a horrifying song of death. General Pyram, five hundred war-hardened veterans, and the Kryan Cavalry watched in disturbed silence.

He realized at that moment why the elves truly underestimated this Caleb. They weren't fighting a man at all. They were fighting a god. Perhaps he could beat a Worldbreaker after all.

The field lay calm, smoldering, finally. The flames still burned, but nothing but flame moved. Blackened bodies of four thousand elves covered the field of the Acar. Officers, militan, all around him were overcome with fear and despair.

The First General composed himself. The Kryan legion hadn't lost a battle in an open field in three centuries. Whether this *Brendel* was a god or no, General Pyram would not allow one under his command to be the first. He found his frown again.

"First Captains!" he shouted into the crackling quiet. "To me!"

Slack jawed, two officers turned in their saddles.

He hated having to repeat himself. Lowering his voice, he projected his voice to its full volume. "First Captains! To me."

This time they responded, dazed but spurred their horses in his direction. The two officers stopped in front of him.

"Listen," he said, his voice low but deep. "This battle is not over. They only have five hundred men, barely trained humans." He didn't want to mention how he saw these "barely trained" humans take down a swordmaster and a Bladeguard. "We have that number alone in our best division." He addressed the Cavalry officer. "Our Cavalry can run them down and lose no one."

"But sir," First Captain Esidor said, and Pyram imagined the elf forced himself not to look at the burning field. Pyram willed himself not to look at it, too. "How?"

"All they have is tricks. They covered the field with some flammable substance," Pyram said. "And the stench of the Deadwater masked the odor. We fell into their trap, and I will admit full responsibility when we face the Emperor's wrath. But I will not be the first legion under Tanicus' reign to lose a battle on an open field. Not to humans."

The two officers nodded. *Keep talking*, Pyram told himself.

"But they cannot use that trick again," Pyram explained. "We will circle around the burning field to the north, making sure we are on dry ground." He pointed at Esidor. "The Cavalry will crush them under hoof while the veterans," he pointed now at the other officer, a Captain Bremus, "suppress the humans with arrows." He lowered his hands to the pommel of his saddle and took a deep breath. "Gentlelves, we can still win this battle."

Steeling themselves, the officers shared a glance. "Yes, sir," they both said in unison.

"Very good," Pyram said. "Captain Bremus, send me a runner before you prepare your division. I have a message to send back to Taggart."

—————

"We might have to run after all," Bweth said to him again as they watched the Kryan reserve division and the Cavalry advance around the burning and smoking field to the north and prepare for an attack.

Lowering the peerglass from his eye, Caleb grunted and leaned against the Kingstaff, more weak than he had been in a long time, his injuries shouting in pain.

Even after all the death they caused this morning, the battle was far from over. They faced slaughter from hundreds of cavalry and veterans.

"We have plenty of arrows," Xander said. "And our longbows have a greater range."

"Hitting elves on the run was difficult enough," Iletus said. "Horses are much faster."

"And the veterans will be effective at covering and protecting with their shields," Bweth said. "We won't be able to take enough of them down before they reach us."

"Our numbers are more similar," Aden said. "We took care of those skirmishers, and they outnumbered us."

"Those reserves are veterans," Bweth said. "Much harder to kill than those skirmishers."

"We could move into the forest," Iletus said. "If we hurry, we could reach the trees and force them to engage us there. That would be equal footing against the veterans and take away the advantage of the Cavalry."

"The Cavalry alone will run us over," Bweth argued. "The veterans will simply mop up whatever stragglers are left."

"What of the injured, the wounded in the camp?" Aden said. "Do we have enough time to strike camp and move the injured?"

"No," Iletus said. "Not to strike the camp."

"We'll make time for the injured," Bweth assured. "But not the camp. We'll have to leave it."

"Whatever we do," Xander said, lifting his chin to the north where the elves were getting into position. "We have to do it fast."

Caleb thought about Galen's body in the camp. He thought about the other dead they would have to leave behind if they ran. Many of the injured may not survive a flight into the woods.

"Get the wounded to safety," Caleb said. "I will stand and fight."

"Caleb," Iletus said. "I understand your anger and grief, believe me. He was my friend, too. But we cannot stay here and fight. That is suicide."

"I didn't say we, Iletus," Caleb said, turning to his old friend. "I said me. This isn't revenge or pride. I will buy you time to get the wounded away."

"And give your life?" Bweth asked him. "Risk it all?"

"For others to live, yes," Caleb said. "If I must. Now go."

"You're really going to go it alone," Xander said. "Against 500 cavalry and another 500 veteran militan?"

"Not alone," Aden said, and when Caleb turned to him, he noticed the glare on the young man's face. "You'll buy more time with two."

"Break me," Caleb said.

"If you're staying, then so am I," Xander said, holding his unforged sword before him. "Make it three."

"Shog a breakin' goat," Bweth said. "It's four."

Iletus glanced over the others. "You are a crazy fool," he said. "I guess we'll see how true that prophecy is. Five."

"They're forming up," Bweth said, and Caleb looked to the north and saw she was correct. The Kryan Cavalry was forming in their lines of attack.

Caleb gestured to Jaff, another *Sohan-el* and a division leader. Jaff was also a former Ghost of Saten. "Take the rest, get the wounded, and make your way to the forest. If they get past us and come after you, then you lead them to fight amongst the trees."

"I could stay," Jaff said, and Caleb believed he would.

"We need your leadership and expertise in the forest," Caleb said. "Now go. Hurry."

Jaff regarded the five warriors standing before him. He bowed to them and hurried off, more than three hundred men following him back to the camp.

Caleb sheathed his sword and grabbed a longbow and a quiver of arrows. The other four followed his lead, except for Xander – he could not handle a bow with one hand. Caleb jogged forward to stand between the Kryan Cavalry and the camp two hundred mitres behind him. Standing a few paces apart, the others did the same. Caleb handed the Kingstaff to Xander, and faced the cavalry with a bow in his hand, his left arm trembling in pain.

He looked to his right and left, and each face was firm with resolve – Aden, Iletus, Bweth, Xander.

Behind him, he could hear the noise of people in the camp, shouting orders, moving materials and people. He didn't know how much time they would need, but he prayed to El they would purchase enough. Wounded, exhausted, it didn't matter. El would help him.

To his left, Iletus handed him a peerglass. "They are ready."

Caleb took the peerglass from the elf and placed it on his eye. The sounds were distant, but he could see the orders being given by the Captain of the Kryan Cavalry. Was that a First General behind him? Yes, the same First General that had been present when Caleb killed his master.

When I killed my master …

Looking through the peerglass, Caleb saw the Captain lift his hand and wave it forward, and 500 armed elves atop trained warhorses charged towards them, hooves pounding the black ground of the Acar.

Clearing his throat, Caleb exhaled through his nose. Breathing deeply caused pain in his side. He tried to remember to take shallow breaths. "Wait until they get within range," he said. "Bweth, we will wait until your signal."

Bweth didn't answer, and he saw her place her hand on her abdomen.

With a last glance at his friends around him, Caleb thought, *if this is my end, so be it.*

But a loud and clear whistle pierced the air, a call of some sort.

Caleb and the four with him all faced south, where the sound originated. There, on the hill beyond the camp and before the Forest of Saten, a figure stood on a horse. It appeared to be a woman. Caleb raised the peerglass again. It was a dark-skinned woman. She wore a long robe of colorful designs. The woman looked his way with bright brown eyes. She lifted her fist to the sky and called out.

"Beorgai!"

Another figure joined her, this one on foot, and it was a man in a green tunic and brown trousers.

"It's a Ghost of Saten," he whispered.

Then the ground began to tremble, faintly at first. Caleb could see trees beyond the woman swaying as if something large pushed through and knocked trees aside. The trembling ground began to shudder, a pounding of feet or hooves upon the land, but by something much bigger than a horse. Much bigger.

"Great and mighty El," Caleb said.

A large beast crested the hill and stopped next to the woman on the horse and the standing Ghost; a dark-skinned man sat atop the creature, twice as tall as the horse and thick through its scaly torso up to the large head protected by a bony frill and a single long horn. The snout was like a long beak.

"Crit on a shoggin' frog," Aden whispered. "Is that …"

"A bosaur," Iletus said.

The ground continued to quake; the rumbling and shaking grew as Caleb saw more of the bosaur join the woman on the hill. The man and woman spoke to one another – Caleb could only hear the voices, not the words – and she pointed to the north, in the direction of the charging elven Cavalry. The man signaled to the others behind him.

"Who are they?" Xander asked. "Where are they from?"

The man's face became determined, and he spurred his bosaur forward and led a line of the beasts over the hill into a charge of their own.

Caleb counted two dozen of the bosaur before he heard Bweth say, "I don't know, but I'd say we need to get outta the breakin' way."

Lowering the peerglass, Caleb scanned and measured the field before them: the elves three hundred mitres and closing to the north, the bosaur-riders two hundred mitres to the south and getting closer. But the bosaur-riders were not aimed at the humans on the field but the charging elven Cavalry, and they would pass fifty mitres or so before them.

"No," Caleb said. "We'll be fine. We stand here."

It took twenty mitres for the bosaur to approach full speed, but Caleb was amazed at how fast the creatures were. As they advanced, the bosaur moved into a formation four abreast, and he counted a hundred of the bosaur galloping across the field to meet the elves.

The woman on the horse, however, rode down the hill and in their direction.

"Look," Aden said. "The elves see it now."

The Captain of the Cavalry slowed and hesitated, looking back at the First General for direction as he faced the hundred massive animals barreling their way. Caleb could not hear what the First General said from his horse at the rear of the column, but he could discern the intent. He ordered them to move forward, to charge and attack the bosaur.

The Captain did what he was trained to do. He followed orders.

With a shout, he lifted his fine scimitar and led the elven Cavalry toward the bosaur. The ground continued to shake as the bosaur bore down upon them, and the thunder of the hooves of five hundred horses combined to make a deafening roar across the dead field of the Acar.

As they neared, the Captain shouted more orders, and the militan Cavalry pulled short bows from their saddles and fired into the bosaur. Arrows arced and fell among the bosaur, but to little effect. Four volleys were launched at the men on the bosaur, but the arrows bounced off of the tough bosaur hide. A handful of men were hit with the arrows, and four fell from their mounts, but the bosaur did not veer off, continuing to move along with the herd.

Searching to the south again, Caleb saw hundreds of other Ghosts of Saten crest the hill, walking, to stand with the woman. Among the Ghosts stood Liorian men with bows and curved blades in their hands. Perhaps three thousand people total.

Caleb's attention was pulled back as the man at the front of the bosaur charge yelled a few words as the two charges neared each other, and the bosaur formation shifted, now ten abreast and ten deep.

Caleb winced as the elven Cavalry crashed into the wall of bosaur, a din of noise sweeping across the field, a combination of shrieking horses and elves, shouting men, and the cries of the dying. Horses and elves were trampled or impaled upon the long, single horns of the bosaur. Screaming bodies and torn limbs flew mitres in the air at the impact, blood flying and spraying as the bosaur crushed and speared the enemy. The massive beasts barely slowed, leaving the mangled and mashed flesh of animal and elf alike in their wake.

Within a few minutes, the bosaur charge slaughtered the elven Cavalry. Caleb could see none left alive.

The Ghosts and the Liorians ran to the field, now, and they followed to support the bosaur, the Ghosts with gladi and the Liorians with those curved blades.

But the bosaur would reach what remained of the Kryan Legion first. The man who led the bosaur reduced speed as he scanned the field and saw the last division a hundred mitres to the north. He shouted another order, and the formation changed again, now fifty abreast. And then he ordered another charge.

Five hundred veteran soldiers, elves that had possibly survived a hundred battles, stared as death bore down upon them.

Caleb could not see the General anymore, down with the Cavalry, and neither could the last captain of the legion. Without any direct order and watching enormous creatures controlled by men barreling towards him, and thousands of Ghosts behind the bosaur, the captain made a choice.

He ran.

The veteran militan scattered, sprinting in several directions at once, overcome by fear. Most ran to the west, the only sensible direction, but many were caught by the dead end of the Deadwater or the burning field to the east where their fellow soldiers had died. Some even tried to run back the way they came, north of the scarred ground and back to their camp.

In the end, it did not matter. The bosaur ran down the majority of the men, crushing and trampling with their hooves, spearing many with their horns; the beasts were too fast. Some bodies and the steel of weapons and shields were hurled into the air.

What the bosaur did not kill, the Ghosts and the Liorians spread out and ran down. The makeshift army shot with bows or worked with companions to kill the veterans. Overwhelming numbers and precision attacks from experienced men and women – Caleb was impressed with the skill of the Liorian men – was too much for even veterans of the mighty Kryan legions.

And that quickly, the Battle of the Acar was over.

As the Ghosts and the Liorians finished off the last of the militan, the woman reached them now, and Caleb lowered the glass from his face. Another horseman, light skinned, crested the hill. He also began to ride towards Caleb.

The woman stopped before Caleb.

"My name is Shecayah," she said. "Of the Beorgai. We have come to join the army of the *Brendel* to fight the elves for the freedom of all men."

"Welcome," Caleb said. "And thank you."

"From the *Bashawyn*'s description," Shecayah said. "You are Caleb, the *Brendel*."

"I am Caleb," he said.

"The *Bashawyn*?" Aden asked.

"I believe you know her as Eshlyn," Shecayah said.

"Eshlyn!" Xander said. "How is she?"

"Last I saw her, she was well," Shecayah said. "She went to the Father Tree to give Namir's unforged sword back to El."

"Namir?" Caleb asked.

Her face fell. "You knew him as Athelwulf," she said. "My brother. He was killed."

Caleb heard Aden sigh and Bweth curse. "I am sorry to hear that," Caleb said.

The other horseman trotted closer.

"What about Esai?" Aden asked. "He was supposed to go with Eshlyn to Lior."

"I believe he also died, but in Oshra," Shecayah said.

Aden covered his eyes. This time Xander swore and kicked over a quiver of arrows.

Caleb moved to speak again to Shecayah, to ask her more of the thousand questions that were on his own mind, when he froze in surprise as he recognized the man riding towards them.

"Earon," he whispered.

Aden lifted his head. "What?"

He was pale, and his hair longer and his face covered in a dark beard, but it was him. Earon, the one that betrayed his own father, Caleb's Uncle Reyan, the Prophet.

Earon, his face pained and afraid, stopped next to Shecayah. He looked away from Caleb.

"Yes," Shecayah said. "Lady Eshlyn gave me the task of bringing this man to you, Caleb." She swallowed hard. "Although I believe he would have come of his own accord."

Caleb's whole body tensed, and he gripped the Kingstaff. Caleb spoke, his voice cold and low in his own ears. "He has much to answer for."

"I understand," she said with a bow. "He is now in your hands. I will tell you, if it makes a difference, he helped us get to you."

"Iletus," Caleb said. Earon still would not look at him. "Take him to the command tent and wait for me there. Don't let him out of your sight."

Iletus walked forward to take the reins of Earon's horse. He led Earon away back to the camp.

A single bosaur-rider came galloping up, halting to address Shecayah. "Tobiah says there are a few elven survivors and asked what the *Brendel* would like to do with them."

"Xander," Caleb said. "Go and see if there are any that we can save or need to take prisoner. There will be others back at the Kryan camp – surgeons and blacksmiths – that we'll need to put under guard, as well. Have the Liorians help you."

Xander turned to address some of the men behind him.

Bweth adjusted the shield on her arm. "I'll go with him," she said, trotting to join Xander.

Caleb met Shecayah's stare. "Come back to camp with us," he said. "We have a lot to discuss."

———+———

General Pyram knelt among five other elves that had survived the devastating bosaur attack.

How he survived, he did not know. He had been thrown from his horse and landed hard on the ground. Rolling, he had seen the creatures run towards him, but not one of their flat feet struck him. His sprained knee was from the fall to the ground. He had reached his feet, dazed, with mounted Liorians aiming short bows at him. The battle was done, and now he sat with five other elves that lived.

Five. Out of the six thousand elves he came with to the field, five survived.

One had both legs crushed, delirious with pain. Two had a broken leg, and two more had both a broken leg and arm. They had all been crying and whimpering to varying degrees, but they had finally quieted down.

A dozen bosaur-riders surrounded Pyram and the five elves in a half-circle, arrows nocked but held low. He was the only one that could be a possible threat, and a dozen arrows would take care of him.

He had witnessed the impossible in so many ways today, but it all came down to one torturous truth: the first legion under Tanicus' reign to be beaten on the field of battle. And he would go down in history as the First General in command of that legion.

The Bladeguard – whether Cyprian, Saben, or Daelas – would not be mentioned in this debacle at all. No, the Emperor would protect his precious Bladeguard and use Pyram as the one to blame. He would probably count Andos and the other officers in Taggart in that number, as well, good elves that had served their Empire honorably. But that wouldn't matter to Tanicus. He would point to their complacency or deficiency and heads would be lifted from shoulders by Bladeguard, the real culprits of the disaster in Manahem.

Tanicus ... is a Worldbreaker.

All of this enraged Pyram, and his frown became a fixed sneer.

A young, tall male with dark features and one arm that ended at the elbow approached with a dwarf in full armor. The young man had a sword at his hip. However young, Pyram remembered the look of the boy that killed Daelas – he shouldn't judge by appearances.

The young man addressed the Liorians on the bosaur. "Hello," he said. "I am Xander, and this is Bweth." He pointed to the dwarf. "We are here to take the prisoners or wounded."

One of the men lifted a hand in a half-wave. "Well met," he said. "I am Tobiah, the leader of the Beorgai here, along with my wife, Shecayah."

"Yea," the dwarf said, a female dwarf. "We saw her earlier."

"Well met," Xander said to Tobiah, and he gestured to Pyram and the other elves near him. "Are these all the survivors?"

"Yes," Tobiah said.

"We'll take these back," Xander said and walked towards Pyram. "Caleb wants to see if we can help any of the injured and take them all prisoner."

Pyram hunched over as Xander came near and put his hands on his thighs. The young man was a few paces away, overconfident and exhausted at the end, relaxing now that he knew the battle was over. Vulnerable.

The young man pointed at ten men. "Come and get the wounded," he said. "Carry them back to the camp. And be careful."

Tobiah pointed at Pyram. "That one can walk on his own," he said. "An officer of some kind, I think."

Xander peered up at the Liorian on the bosaur and came two steps closer. *Just another step or two*, Pyram thought.

"A general," the female dwarf said – Bweth was her name. "Be careful, Xan." She ambled closer, as well. As she moved, Pyram noted the armor, the complexity of it, and he was impressed. She carried a spiked mace in her hand like she knew how to use it.

Kryus was not prepared for this *Brendel* and his army.

Pyram could not stop them here, but he could do what damage he could and make sure he was not taken captive alive to have Imperial secrets tortured out of him. He only hoped that runner escaped and Andos would get his message.

Xander stood over him now. "No one's gonna hurt you," he said. "We'll save any injured we can and see that you're well cared for." He put his solitary hand on his hip. "An officer, to the real? Who are you?"

Pyram turned his frown up at Xander. "I am First General Pyram of the Kryan Army. I led the charge at the Battle of Athata. I survived the Jibrilan Conflict and the War of Liberation and was stationed as the commander at the Taggart Outpost."

The female dwarf in that wonderful armor hurried her steps forward. "Xander ..."

The young man swiveled to address the dwarf.

Pyram took that moment to pull the dagger from underneath the metal bracer on his left forearm, leap to his feet, and swipe the blade across Xander's neck, cutting a gash from ear to ear.

"No!" the dwarf cried and rushed towards him with her mace high above her head.

Xander's eyes bulged in fear and shock, and his one hand reached up to cover the gaping wound across his throat, but the blood was a fountain, showering Pyram as his sneer never changed. The young man fell back, his knees buckling.

The dwarf growled in anger and grief, launching herself at him with her weapons held high. The last thing General Pyram saw was the spiked mace rushing towards his face.

Chapter 34

Going Home

Eshlyn emerged from the Tomb of Yosu under the Father Tree at the same door she entered. While she wore the same clothes, without Kenric's sword and his marriage bracelet, it was as if she were naked. But lighter. Like a burden had been lifted, only a burden she loved with all her heart.

It was morning. Mid-morning by the look of it, although it was difficult to see through the trees. She didn't remember it being morning when she entered the Tomb. And she was starving, her stomach pained with hunger.

Confused, she gazed around her in the light of the day. Mother Natali stood a few mitres away. Eshlyn squinted at the older woman, dressed now in a longer dark blue dress with a white undertunic. Eshlyn's brow furrowed. Wasn't she wearing a different dress just an hour ago?

Beyond Natali, she could see the white fur of the Mahakar through the trees. She could feel his longing, a deep desire to return to his home in the Forest of Lior, which she understood. Her son, Javyn, pulled at her heart.

"Hello, Lady Eshlyn," Mother Natali said.

"Mother," Eshlyn said as she drew near to the woman, the branches swaying high overhead, the noise of the city in the trees filtering down to her. "When did it become morning? I was only in there a couple hours."

"You were in there for almost two days."

"Two days?" Eshlyn cried. Walking down to the Tomb, meeting the ghost – or spirit or soul? She wasn't sure what to call it – of King Judai, leaving both Ath and Kenric's sword, and then relinquishing her marriage bracelet … that had been an hour, two at most. "Impossible."

The old woman's piercing eyes flashed at the door to the Tomb. "That place has been touched," she said. "Touched by the power of El and the Everworld. It does not abide by the rules of this world. It would not be from El and the Everworld if it did. It has been two days."

Two days, she thought. No wonder she was hungry. Eshlyn lifted a hand to her forehead, her breathing becoming shallow, and her mind reeled with questions. Her first thought, honestly, was of her son, two more days away from him. But she did not ask Natali of him. She moved on to other concerns.

Natali handed her a cloth wrapped around some food and bade her to sit near her pack. Eshlyn opened the scrip and saw the deer jerky and flat bread within. She began to eat as Mother Natali also handed her a canteen of water.

"My friends, the army from the Beorgai," she said as she finished the food and between gulps of water. "Did they pass through the forest?"

"Yes," Natali said.

"Good," Eshlyn said, relaxing a bit. She stood and lowered her hand to the sword on her hip ... but it was gone. She grasped her leather belt awkwardly instead. "Then I will meet them in Ketan." She shouldered her pack and began to walk toward the Mahakar.

"They are not in Ketan."

"Wha -?" Eshlyn stumbled and almost fell, but she continued towards the winged tiger, Natali striding along with her. "Then where are they?"

"The *Brendel*'s army engaged a Kryan legion in the valley of the Acar," Mother Natali said. "Since your friends desired to join his army, we sent them there."

Her chest tightened with worry over Caleb, Aden, Tamya, Hunter and Bweth, but most of all, Xander. Her brother. She prayed they were all well, but the last few ninedays had seen the death of her friends, Athelwulf and Esai. It seemed too much to hope.

"Do you know what happened?"

"No," Mother Natali said. "Our scouts have not returned with any news of the battle as yet. But we sent two thousand of our own from the forest to also join the *Brendel*'s army."

"Two thousand?"

"Like I told you before, Lady," Natali murmured. "We are at war. Many of the Ghosts would like to stay hidden here in the forest, but the war will touch us all, I fear, whether we wish it or no. To follow El is to refuse safety in this life. Even in times absent of war, following the ways of El is full of risk – loving those who will not love us in return, forgiving those who may never change, believing in hope when all around us tempts us to despair. Even my Ghosts must learn this.

"I asked for more to join the *Brendel*'s army, and over two thousand answered the call. They may have made it in time to join the battle today."

Eshlyn reached the Mahakar now. He sat back on his haunches, his head pointed to the south, his nose sniffing the air. This close, his longing was sharp. She reached out and touched his fur.

She thought of Javyn, of the emptiness in her heart, gone so long from him, her son, her baby. What had she missed already? It gnawed at her. She needed to see him.

But what happened at the battle? The whole revolution of men was in jeapordy. The Kryan legions were infamous in their cruelty and domination.

The Brendel carries a great weight, far greater than he knows.

She would go to the Acar first.

The tiger growled.

"It is okay," Eshlyn whispered to him. "I understand. One last ride, I promise. Then you can go home."

The Mahakar faced her now. He snorted and lay down to allow her on his back. She climbed upon him and straddled his shoulders, adjusting her pack. She looked up at the city, the Jowell, ancient and extending through the branches of the great trees around her.

"I wish I could have spent more time with you here," Eshlyn said. "And in this great city."

"You are welcome here, always," Mother Natali said. "Should you wish to come back to us."

Eshlyn gave the woman a smile. "Thank you, Mother," she said.

"No, Lady Eshlyn," Mother Natali said, and the old woman bowed low, keeping her eyes on Eshlyn. "For all of your sacrifice and bravery for others, thank you."

Eshlyn returned the bow and gripped the tiger's fur with both hands. The large white wings flapped and pounded the air, and they wove through thick branches, brushing through the canopy to the sky above. The Mahakar hovered for a moment, then veered north to the Acar.

—✝—

Earon waited in the command tent with a dead body on the long wooden table. A dead elf.

The elf was missing his hand at the wrist and leg at the knee. Covered in blood, the elf was still a striking figure with long, graying blond hair.

He had been waiting for mere minutes when Caleb entered the tent, the Kingstaff in his hand and an unforged sword at his hip, the coldest glare on his face, the same gray eyes that haunted Earon, waking or sleeping. There was blood on his shirt from wounds underneath, and the long burn mark on his face was gruesome. Apart from his eyes, Caleb appeared half dead.

Caleb was different than the boy he knew seventeen years ago. That boy was irresponsible, easily distracted, and reckless to a fault. Earon had talked that boy out of numerous risky ideas that could have gotten him killed. For some reason, that boy had listened, and Earon remembered taking pride in being like an older brother to Caleb and Carys. He couldn't deny, even now, a part of him considered Caleb a younger brother he had to protect.

Setting the Kingstaff down in the corner of the command tent, Caleb stood across the table from Earon, bearing down at him with those gray eyes, his hand on his sword.

The reality was far different. This was no boy. A man stood before him, taller, stronger, bearded. Caleb had always been an amazing athlete, quickly picking up skills in games like Sand-bol or Qadi-bol or even silly dares like jumping from the roof of a two-story inn in a Veraden village, but the way he moved now, his body and muscles had been honed and perfected. He moved with unreal confidence and surety, as if every motion was calculated, measured. Even standing across from Earon, Caleb appeared relaxed, and yet Earon could imagine that sword could fly from the scabbard and impale him faster than he could think.

Fast like Zarek had killed his father in Biram.

Beyond Caleb's individual abilities, he had raised up an army. After uniting Ketan to fight a Demilord and the demic horde, Caleb climbed Mount Elarus and received an unforged sword from the Living Stone. He returned to Ketan, trained farmers and ranchers to face the legions of Kryus, and had now won a historic battle in the valley of the Acar.

If he wasn't the *Brendel*, who the shog could be?

The acknowledgement of this reality made Earon feel like the little brother, the one who needed protecting.

They stood in silence for several minutes.

He didn't know what to say, but he had not come all this way to say nothing. So he began to talk. He cleared his throat.

Earon told Caleb how Eshlyn, Athelwulf, and Esai found him in Oshra, how he was drunk and Sorced, so addicted. He kept talking, telling the whole story of Esai's death and how Athelwulf dragged him north and saved his life during the bosaur stampede. He explained how Athelwulf confronted his father, whom he had cursed, and asked for forgiveness, how seeing and hearing the tale of Athelwulf's redemption gave him hope.

"So you see," Earon continued. "Athelwulf saved my life in more than one way. He taught me that I could change. But part of that change was not just kicking a breaking habit." He took a deep breath. "Part of it is coming here and surrendering myself to you, and whatever form of justice you feel is right."

He didn't think it was possible, but Caleb's gaze hardened further.

"I'm so sorry," Earon said. "I was so angry, so full of grief, I believed Zarek's lies. I should have known better, but I betrayed my father." His voice cracked. "I killed him; as sure as Zarek did, I killed him."

The unforged sword left the sheath with a whisper and the tip of the blade was suddenly a centimitre from his chest.

Earon gasped and blinked, the tears waiting in his eyes spilling down onto his cheeks. He spread his hands in capitulation.

"You're right," Earon muttered. "I deserve to die for what I did." He choked back a sob. "I would change it if I could, I swear to you, but over and over, I deserve it."

The sword shook and wavered, and Caleb's arm tensed and flexed, like the blade grew heavy. Caleb grit his teeth and snarled.

"Do it," Earon said. "If you feel it is the right thing, if it will give you peace, if it will satisfy justice, then do it. I deserve it. I understand. I do. Do it."

Earon stared into Caleb's angry visage for what seemed like hours, although it could only have been seconds, face to face with those haunting eyes, confronting the very fear that stole his sleep and drove him to further ale and Sorcos. Looking into those eyes, he accepted his own death as just and true. He waited for Caleb to plunge the unforged blade home.

Instead, Caleb swung the sword away from his chest and dropped it to the ground. He bent at the waist, balling his hands into fists, and roared, a yell filled with immeasurable pain, and Earon knew exactly how he felt.

"Oh, Caleb," Earon murmured. "I'm so sorry."

Caleb opened his fists and lowered his head to study his hands for a long time. He straightened finally and laid a hand on the dead elf between them, turning his glistening eyes to the body.

"I've killed too many people I love today," Caleb said. "I cannot suffer another. You will stay with us in the camp, however. I will put a guard on you. You are a prisoner until I say otherwise."

Earon knew he would not need the guard. "Caleb, I ..."

The flap of the tent opened, and it was Aden, staring at the two of them, back and forth, but his eyes rested on Caleb.

Caleb did not look up from the dead elf. He growled. "What is it?"

Aden swallowed hard. Earon could see the young man had been crying. "Caleb," he stammered. "It's Xander. He ..."

Caleb's head did raise now and spun on Aden. "What happened?"

—+—

The Mahakar soared through the air to the north, sailing a few mitres over the tops of the trees.

As they reached the edge of the Forest of Saten, she began to see the wasteland of the Acar. The sun was straight overhead, around noon, but the sun seemed to dim the closer they came to the Acar.

She had heard stories of the place, even used it as a curse once or twice as a young woman, but the curses did not describe it well enough. It was a whole valley of black dirt and gray dust, maybe a kilomitre or two in diameter. At its center was a small lake of black water, the Deadwater from what she remembered. She could smell the place from the sky as she neared it. If the Tomb had been touched by El and the Everworld, this place had been touched by something far different and evil.

On the eastern side of the Deadwater, a large swath of land was smoldering, and parts were on fire with low flames, small charred shapes within it. Were those bodies? Beyond the burning strip of land, a large camp sat to the east, but it seemed empty. To the west, another camp spread out and bustled with activity. She could see the bosaur and other horses roaming to the south of the camp and a diverse group of people milling about within it. In between, corpses littered the ground, bodies that appeared to be Kryan militan.

If there had been a battle, it was over, and the *Hamon-el* had been the victor.

The Brendel is the match that will set the world afire.

She steered the Mahakar to the west, and they set down fifty mitres from the camp. Eshlyn dismounted from the tiger and buried her face into his soft fur.

"Goodbye," she said into his fur. Would she see him ever again? So many goodbyes, and she didn't have the words.

Stepping away, the Mahakar turned his nose to her and nuzzled her shoulder. His communication was not with words, but the image of him in the sky and returning to her again was clear – call if she ever had need. She chuckled and scratched him underneath his chin.

People were walking towards her from the camp. She recognized Aden and Shecayah.

The Mahakar stood to his full height. She backed a few paces more and watched as the large white wings unfurled. The tiger launched himself into the air, wind beating at her face and kicking up gray dust. She smiled as she watched the tiger soar to the south.

Others from the camp hung back as Aden and Shecayah approached her, their eyes darting from her to the Mahakar as he flew away. She grinned at them as they approached, but her grin faltered when she noticed the deep sorrow on their faces, the tears in Aden's eyes.

She strode forward to meet them. "Well met," she said with a hesitation.

Aden and Shecayah shared a glance, and Aden exhaled, a deep, tragic sound.

Eshlyn steeled herself. "What is it," she said. "Tell me."

Aden ran a hand through his hair. "Ah … it's Xander, Esh. He …"

Eshlyn gasped. "Xander?" Her hand covered her mouth and her vision blurred. "No," she said. "No." *Not after Esai and Athelwulf …*

But looking in their eyes, she knew her denial to be a lie. Shecayah gave her a somber look, drawing close and touching her arm. She didn't know the woman as well, but she could read Aden like he was another brother. He wiped his hand across his face and shuddered.

Xander was dead.

"Take me to him," she said.

"Are we going to get out of this bed today?" Carys asked as she lay against Zalman's chest.

They lay together naked in a spacious bed in one of the suites in an enormous abode high in the cliff city of Enakai. The large open windows let in the breeze from the ocean, and they could see for leagues to the north.

Yesterday had been their wedding, and Carys remained in a bewildering state of joy at the whole event. Aeric had planned the whole occasion, recruiting the participation of the whole city. Food was prepared, ale and wine and liquor brought from hidden stashes, and fine clothes of silk and satin made for the bride and groom. Whoever helped Zalman write his song did an abysmal job, although she couldn't admit to doing much better. They stood in a small boat in the ocean, sang their commitments, and kissed, all while trying to stay balanced in the little dinghy.

The rest of the evening was spent drinking, dancing, and laughing. Her face hurt from smiling so much, her voice hoarse from screams and hollers of mirth.

One of the wealthier citizens of the community had offered a suite in his home, also decked out for the newlyweds, and they accepted. After being shown to the room, they had kissed and touched while cheers and jeers were heard above and below them, such noise and crude songs that even Zalman turned red once or twice. Through chuckles and awkward moments removing clothes while drunk and exhausted from the celebration, they had found their way to a beautiful intimate moment, and she felt so close to him that it hurt.

And then they had found that moment again.

It was early afternoon now.

"Not sure," he said. He waved over at the table across the room covered with fried shellfish, water, wine, and flat bread. "We have food and drink. A beautiful view. Why would we leave?"

She traced the curve of his chest with her finger and chuckled. "I guess we don't have to," she said.

"Do you want to get up?" he asked, staring down at her. "I'm sure Chronch would love help getting the boat ready to sail back."

"No thanks," she said. "I'm fine right here."

He grunted in satisfaction. She could interpret his grunts now ... was that a good or bad thing?

"Are you ready?" she said. "To go back?"

He gave her a questioning look.

"You know, back to Caleb and the revolution?"

"Aren't you?"

Carys thought for a moment. In Ketan, she had been Caleb's little sister and felt stuck in that identity. But she was different now. She was the woman that brought the Pirates to the cause. She was a married woman. *Shoggers* ...

"Yes," she said. "I am."

That seemed to mollify him, but he frowned, deep in thought.

"What?"

"It's nothing, probably," he said.

"Tell me."

"Well, it's just that before we left, Caleb said some things to me."

She rolled her eyes. "I know. You told me. He wanted you to protect me and keep me safe."

"I ... didn't tell you all that he said," Zalman muttered.

"Oh? What did he say?"

"Before we left, he told me that if you got one scratch *or I touched you*, he would kill me."

"He did?" She rose on an elbow.

"He did. And in Landen, you got a scratch from that shogger's blade." He reached up and touched her neck. "And ... uh, I have touched you."

"You have. Quite a lot, actually."

"Yeah."

"Several times."

Sighing, he said, "Yes."

She squinted at him.

"You're right," she said. "Caleb will kill you."

Their eyes met for a moment, and Zalman chuckled. He leaned over and kissed her, wrapping his arms around her and pulling her close.

Breaking the kiss, she smirked at him. "What are you doing?"

"If I'm dead anyway," he said. "It might as well be worth it."

Chapter 35

The Living Water

She lay on a cot alone in her tent, although the tent had been moved closer to the center of the camp, arranged by either Aden or Caleb, she was sure. Aden, more than likely. Her gaze flashed over to the thick bundle in the corner: Hema, dead, lay wrapped in a blanket.

The surgeon, a man by the name of Mohr and trained by the elven physicians in Ketan before the Battle of Ketan, checked the stitches along her side and her arm. He cleaned both wounds again with clean water, and she choked back sobs and cries at the intense pain.

"They are both red and inflamed," he said. "You need to keep them as clean as you can. Clean them yourself, if you can. I'm worried about infection."

Tamya didn't look at him or speak to him, her face to the wall of the tent. Tears continued to stream down her cheeks, thinking of Hema, her bloodwolf. Dead.

"Probably this place," Mohr mumbled under his breath as he stood, but she heard. And she didn't need further explanation as to what place he referred. The Acar. It smelled of death and crit, even more so now that dead elves littered the field.

The Battle of the Acar had been a success, the whole legion destroyed on the field. The surgeon gave her snippets of information when he checked on her.

"Be well," the surgeon said, rubbing a thumb over his thin black mustache. He said that every time he left, as he did now with a frustrated huff.

And she was alone again, which she thought she wanted, but her solitude intensified the thoughts of Hema. When she closed her eyes, she saw him leaping through the air, attacking that Bladeguard, and his death replayed in her mind over and over, those blades stabbing through him. She remembered his whimpers and cries as the blood poured out of him.

The flap of her tent opened again, and she knew who it was before she opened her eyes.

Aden moved silently through the opening of her tent and sat on the edge of the cot. Even in the shadows of the tent, out of the afternoon sun, she could see his eyes were red from crying. He held a bottle of something in his hand.

"Talked to the physician," Aden said. "He said he was worried about you, about infection."

He laid a hand on her arm, and oddly enough, it comforted her and made her want to tell him to move it.

"Xander is dead," he said. "And Athelwulf. And Esai. Both while they were gone."

Tamya groaned, tears falling down her face. Athelwulf took her in and helped her keep the bloodwolf. Esai had been a friend, teaching her how to fight with two swords. She had spent almost as much time with Esai as with Aden. And Xander, a good friend, a good man, a great swordsman.

And Hema was now gone. It felt so empty without him here. She felt so alone.

She saw her own anguish mirrored on Aden's face.

"The battle was over," he said. "We won. Xander was offering help to the wounded, the prisoners. We were going to take good care of them, but one attacked him. In a split second, like that, he was dead. A waste."

She moved her right hand so she could hold his. He gripped hers.

He stared off. "So much death. This place, it is a curse. You can feel it in the air."

And he was right. She could. She wanted to tell him she was right after all – life is a tragedy. Hope is foolishness. But she couldn't bear to hurt him anymore. She could feel his grief. She shared it.

"Anyway," he said, lifting the bottle in his hand. "After talking to the surgeon, I can't lose you today, too. I won't."

"Aden," she said. "What is that?"

He examined the clear liquid of the bottle.

"This is water from the pool next to the Living Stone," he said.

She raised her brows at him.

"When you drink it, it heals you," he said. "I call it the Living Water. I saved some from when Caleb and I went, months ago. It refreshed us up on the top of that mountain and helped me heal quickly after the Battle of Biram. And the Wraith." He extended it to her. "Here. Drink it."

"Aden, no," she said. "There has to be others that need it more than me. I don't deserve it."

"No one deserves it, Tamya. No one."

"But why me?" she whispered.

"You know why."

Tamya bit her lip, refusing to speak.

"I love you," he said. "And it doesn't matter if you don't feel the same; I love you."

"You don't want me," she said. "I'm broken."

"You're not as broken as you think," he said. "Merely wounded. And wounds can heal. Some wounds are deeper and more painful than others, and deep enough to kill, but they can be healed."

"No," she said. "Too broken."

"Nothing is ever too broken to heal," he said. "Not for El. I have something here that can heal your wounds, or heal them faster, at least, and you refuse it. Just like you refuse the one thing that could heal those wounds from your past, those beautiful, tragic wounds."

"What is that?" she asked.

"Love," he said. "The love of El, the love of friends around you. My love. But you push it away, to protect yourself. But it doesn't. It just lets those wounds fester. Just like that Deadwater sits there and festers."

Aden exhaled in exhasperation. "And who are you to tell me what I can want? You're strong and brave and clever. And beautiful. El save me, you're beautiful." Aden nodded. "You're right, there are other injured people who could use it. It is selfish of me to give it to you. But I lost one friend today, and found out that two more have died. So many dead. I can't lose you. Not if I can help it. Maybe I get to be selfish today. Either way, I'm choosing it. So drink it."

She looked at him and shook her head.

"Please," he said. "I'm begging you."

Tamya realized, if she were stronger, she would throw it back into his face, tell him what a fool he was for choosing to hope. Hadn't he learned yet? After so many dead or gone? But she couldn't do it. Not to him. Maybe, she thought, she needed him to have hope. His hope was a part of him, and so she couldn't deny him now.

Taking a deep but shuddering breath, Tamya said, "Okay."

Aden smiled and pressed the bottle to her lips. "A few sips is all it will take, I think," he said.

So she did. She drank two swallows, and he pulled it back from her. The water was rich and sweet, clean and pure and bold. Instantly refreshed, she gasped at the relief. The pain began to subside and become a dull ache instead of the deep, burning torment. Her body relaxed.

Peering up at him again, she saw him beam at her. He put the cap back on the bottle. "Look," he said. "A little of the Living Water left."

Tamya sat up, still holding his hand.

Aden cleared his throat. "I wish I could share this with everyone, but ..." He trailed off, his eyes distant and staring beyond her. "Share the Living Water with everyone." He turned back to her and clutched the bottle of healing water to his chest. "I have an idea."

Propping herself on her elbows, Tamya frowned at him. "You gonna tell me what it is?"

"Nothing is ever too broken to heal," is all he would say.

He released her hand and stood up, moving towards the tent flap, his face full of resolve.

Tamya swung her legs over the end of the cot. "Aden."

Pausing at the entrance, he looked back at her.

"Take me with you," she said.

He took her measure and then reached out for her. "Can you walk?"

Tamya stood, stepped towards him, and took his hand.

+—

With the afternoon sun warm and hanging in the western sky, Aden hiked through the camp. He wanted to run, but Tamya followed him, holding tight to his hand. She seemed better already, the Living Water doing its work deep within her, healing her festering wounds.

The Living Water.

He wove through the tents and the people, and some asked him questions as they noticed him. He saw Eshlyn standing by a tent, talking with Bweth and Caleb, the tent where Xander lay dead.

"Aden," she called. "Where are you going? She's supposed to be resting."

He ignored her, pressing forward.

It couldn't work, could it? he thought. *But what if it does?*

Eshlyn moved from the tent, and she followed him, as did Bweth and Caleb, both calling his name, as well.

As they followed him, others in the camp joined them. He broke from the camp, people shouting to one another and him as he marched north. Tamya paced him, her hand in his. With the other hand, he clutched the bottle of Living Water to his chest.

It was close to a kilomitre from the camp to the Deadwater, and he clenched his teeth to keep from retching as he came near. He didn't bother with a cloth to cover his mouth and nose this time. He reached the Deadwater, unable to take a deep breath because of the stench.

A few seconds passed as he watched the thick, black Deadwater before him. It was eerie and unnatural in its stillness. He stepped at the very edge, the toes of his boots centimitres away from the horrid substance. He had been so excited there in the camp. What kept him from it now? What made him afraid?

This place, he thought. *It is death, and it resists me. It resists the life in my hand.*

During his hesitation, a crowd gathered behind him, muttering or moaning about the stench. Tamya did not speak as she stepped up next to him, but she looked him in the eyes. And it gave him courage, somehow.

He took the cap off of the bottle.

"Aden," he heard Caleb whisper from his left. He saw Caleb standing with Eshlyn and Bweth. "Is that ...?"

Aden grimaced in guilt. They had been at the Living Stone together. An understanding passed between them. This was how he had been healing so

424

fast, and he kept it to himself. But even as the understanding passed, so did the forgiveness in Caleb's expression, and Aden did not know how much he had needed that forgiveness until it was given.

Caleb glanced from the bottle to the Deadwater.

"Do it," Caleb said.

To his left, Tamya clutched his hand even tighter, and he saw something in her gaze that quickened his heart. Hope. Her eyes were soft and pleaded with him. "Do it," she said.

Aden faced the Deadwater now, and clenching his teeth against the putrid odor, he extended his arm over the water and poured what was left – only a few drops – of the Living Water into the Deadwater of the Acar.

The air was heavy and still, and the crowd silent. He couldn't even hear a breath.

At first, nothing happened, barely a ripple where the clear, pure water hit the dark liquid, and his heart sank. *Nothing?*

But then the black liquid began to bubble a mitre away. The churning of the dark substance increased, like it boiled, and the roiling moved towards the center of the lake. At the center, the Deadwater foamed and exploded in a great upheaval, spouting eight or ten mitres high. The water growled and thundered.

People gasped around him, crying out in surprise and fear, and Aden leaned back and covered his face with his forearm, and as he lowered it to look at the Deadwater again, it began to fade from black to a gray. The entire lake bubbled, and unnatural waves heaved from the shore to the center, causing fountains of liquid to shoot high in the air and crashing again. The Deadwater transfigured to a lighter gray.

The crowd grew behind him. He could hear more people muttering and whispering in awe, but most were quiet. A current rose within the lake, a circular flow like a giant was mixing the Deadwater with an invisible spoon. The current increased its intensity, and Aden took a step back, recoiling from the spray. The whole lake churned into a funnel that lifted mitres above them. Wind whipped around them; it stung Aden's face, and he wanted to turn away from the violence of the transformation. But he couldn't.

Was the water even more clear? Was it even gray anymore? He couldn't tell for sure.

People around him fell to their knees, cowering from the wind and the power on display. He heard someone scream, but it was faint among the other noise of the wind and the bellowing water.

And within an instant, the wind stopped and the water fell with a crash, liquid splashing up around them, droplets hitting the crowd like rain. Aden could taste the water, sweet on his tongue.

The lake before him was now clear, and as it grew still, he could see down to the depths of the rocky, brown bottom.

The stench had dissipated leaving the air crisp and clean. Aden scanned around him, and the haze of the day had dispersed, and the sun seemed brighter.

There at the Acar, Aden took a deep, satisfying breath of clean, brisk air. He smiled and laughed.

"Great and mighty El," he heard Eshlyn say to his left. People wept for joy behind him.

Aden knelt down next to the clean water, his knees falling into the lake. Tamya joined him there. He released Tamya's hand and plunged his cupped hands into the lake, bringing the water to his mouth and drinking it. It refreshed and energized him, not quite like the water at the Living Stone, but it was good and clean, like a cold drink on a sweltering day. He let out a breath.

Tamya was on her knees next to him, drinking as well. Then Caleb, Bweth, Eshlyn and others knelt at the clear lake and did the same.

We can't call it the Deadwater anymore, Aden thought. *Or this valley the Acar. It is no longer a curse. We'll have to think of a new name.*

Tamya's face was full of awe. And hope. Good El, he saw hope there. She smiled at him. "Nothing is too broken to heal," she said, and she beamed at him.

And between the healing of the Deadwater and the hope he saw in her eyes, Aden considered the latter to be more miraculous.

———+———

That evening, Caleb stood along with the 400 of the *Hamon-el*. Behind them 1,000 of the Beorgai and 2,000 Ghosts of Saten also gathered. Next to him stood Eshlyn, Iletus, Aden, Bweth, and the other *Sohan-el* who remained after Lyam left and took two thirds of their army with him back to Ketan. Several of the *Hamon-el* held torches to light the way since it was two hours after nightfall.

Ten mitres away, the Lake of Living Water rested calm and serene, reflecting the moonlight like crystal.

In between the gathering of people and the Living Water, a long row of graves had been dug, over 300, the casualties of the Battle of the Acar, the men that fell that day.

They placed Galen in one of those graves, and Xander, even Hema the bloodwolf was buried here on the banks of the Living Water.

It was the way of battle and people that after a long and bloody day of violence, after hundreds and thousands died, one more death could launch an army into despair. Xander's death had burdened the camp with great sorrow. He was a leader to many, a *Sohan-el*, and a friend to all. Caleb glanced over at Eshlyn. *And a brother to others.* His murder came as a shock, a waste. To fall in battle was understandable, but to be attacked by a prisoner or the injured you were trying to help after the battle was clearly won, that tested the mind of people.

Thank great and mighty El for Aden, Caleb thought.

The healing of the Acar gave the people hope again, the people of the *Hamon-el*, at least. And along with the new additions to the army, the Beorgai and the Ghosts of the Saten, a bright sense of confidence and expectation was the mood. Drinking the water, while it did not seem to heal, refreshed and revitalized everyone who tried it. The injured began to heal a little faster, and infections in wounds cleared.

They needed to grieve the lost, however, so they gathered at the banks of the Living Water to bury their dead and remember their friends in life. Not only the ones that died in the battle today, but the news of Athelwulf and Esai's death was raw to many who considered them brothers and friends.

So much blood. So many dead. And so much more ahead of them.

Caleb, Aden, and Eshlyn all spoke over the graves and before the army. A hymn of El was sung by the group, echoing across the valley. People came up to Eshlyn and Caleb and spoke words of consolation, embracing them or shaking their hands, milling about to comfort one another.

He saw Earon, flanked by the two men he put in charge of the man, approach Eshlyn and tell her how sorry he was to hear about her brother. Caleb did not look at him.

While he did nothing but dream of killing his cousin for months, when it came down to it, he could not. He was weary of revenge. The freedom of El could not be won with revenge and bitterness. He had to lead by a different way, and so he spared Earon's life. For now.

One by one, people left the gathering, saying final goodbyes to friends. Aden and Tamya lingered at Hema's grave before walking back to camp. Iletus stood at Galen's grave with Caleb for a long time, his arms crossed, his face tight. Eventually, he followed the others to the south.

All who remained were Caleb and Eshlyn, alone.

He stood next to her, a pace away. Before them were Xander and Galen's graves.

"He was a dumb kid," Eshlyn said as she stared down at Xander's grave. "In Delaton, you know. I thought he would always be a dumb kid."

Caleb nodded.

"You know, there was this one time, he and Joob tied a torch to a horse's tail. Joob's horse, of course. And they let it go just to see what the poor thing would do. It ran through town and set old man Lenard's radishes on fire. Took them all night to catch the horse and contain the flames. Xan got close to the horse, walked up behind it, but that noble animal farted, and it ignited from the torch and burned off Xan's eyebrows." She barked a laugh. "Da was so breakin' mad. The whole town was furious."

Her brief smile. "Never thought he'd become one of the greatest men I'd ever know. I was so proud of him." Her voice lowered and thinned. "I never told him ..."

"Yeah, you did," Caleb said. "And he knew."

She ground her teeth, clenching her fists. "I want to kill them all. For Ken, for Xander."

"I know."

Her fiery gaze caught him. "Is that why you're here? Why you do it? To kill them all?"

Is it? Sometimes I wonder. Is all this revolution talk just an excuse for revenge? His mother, father, Reyan, Danelle. "I hope not."

"How do you do it? How do you keep going in the face of so much tragedy?"

He hesitated. "I don't know. Not just one thing. Faith that it's right, that it's worth it, that the people gone believed it's worth it. And that maybe I'm the only one who can finish it."

Eshlyn sniffed, and they stood in silence for a few minutes.

"I have his sword," he said, his voice soft. "Back in my tent. I'll make sure you get it."

Eshlyn breathed in deeply. "I don't need it," she said. "Give it to someone else. Or we can take it to the Father Tree."

He had heard her brief story about how she traveled to the Father Tree and went to the Tomb of Life with Athelwulf's sword. She also left Kenric's sword there. Eshlyn didn't share any details of the Tomb of Life itself.

"Okay."

She glanced over at him. "You look like crit."

While the Living Water and the surgeon had helped clean and dress his wounds better, he felt weak and the pain was sharp. He willed himself not to wince and stand straight.

Hovering over Galen's grave, he thought of Danelle and the unborn child.

"I *feel* like crit," he said.

"I see Earon is still alive," she said.

"For now," he said.

"What are you going to do with him?"

"I don't know," he said. "It will come to me when it is time. Or maybe Carys will kill him when she comes back." He scratched his chin. "If she ever comes back."

"If she does, will you send her away again?" she asked.

"No," he said. "Not again. Although I feel I should remind you that I did not really send her away the last time."

Eshlyn smirked at him, the light of the moonlight reflecting off of the Living Water exposing her features. "True," she said. "But you did send me away."

He paused before speaking. "Yes. I did."

"Are you going to send me away again?"

"No," he said. Something had happened to Eshlyn while she was away. She had returned more confident, more assured. She possessed an inner strength. She shone with it. It made her more beautiful, if that were possible. "I don't think I can."

He could also see the grief within her, building and ready to burst to the surface, but she held it back.

He did the same thing.

"Are you done?" he asked.

Her lip quivered. Eshlyn regarded him with wet eyes. "Done what?"

Caleb reached over and grabbed her hand. "Done being strong for the day. I know I am."

Eshlyn's whole body broke with a sob, and she pulled him close into an embrace, throwing her arms around his neck and burying her face there. And he let her weep.

No words needed to be spoken. They mourned their friends that were gone, those that sacrificed for others, people they would feel empty without for the rest of their lives. They were both exhausted at the long roads that brought them to this time, tragedies and victories and simple survival. And for a moment, only a moment, they shed the burden and responsibility of leadership and allowed themselves to be wounded, to hurt, to be vulnerable. To be human.

Caleb didn't know how long they stood there, clutching and leaning into one another, but soon her sobs quieted. He began to pull away, and they untangled themselves, their faces centimitres apart. He felt close to her, and he did not want to let her go. Her hair smelled like the wind and the forest. She gazed into his eyes, and those deep eyes spoke her own desire. Eshlyn reached up and touched the wound on his cheek, gentle like a caress.

He wanted to kiss her, just lean in that short distance, so near, to feel that comfort, and he could see she wanted it, as well.

Then he thought of Danelle. Yes, he loved her more than he could say, but in the end, it was selfish as she gave him strength and comfort and he gave her pain, sorrow, and death in return.

Eshlyn had lost her husband, friends in the Battle of Ketan, companions along her journey to Lior and back, and now her brother. If he kissed her, if he did that, what would be the end of that story for her? He would die at the end of this revolution, possibly sooner, and that would only bring her greater grief. It would add to her immense sorrow.

He is not a man but a sword …

It was dangerous to let her that close to him. Danelle taught him that lesson. He would not do that to Eshlyn. He cared for her too much.

Caleb forced a sad smile, and he reached up and wiped the tears from her cheeks. Holding her head gently with both hands, he kissed her forehead. He released her, turned, and walked away back to his tent alone.

CHAPTER 36

TAGGART

The next morning, Eshlyn entered the command tent, a large tent taken from the legion the *Hamon-el* encountered in Biram. A long table rested in the middle of the tent, although not as large as the one in Ketan. The sun was bright outside, so the sides of the tent had been folded up to let more of the light and breeze in. The table was covered with maps, taken from both the legion in Biram and the one they encountered here at the Acar. They were fine maps made with thick paper covered with colors and symbols.

The Acar continued to change. The ground changed from black to brown, and she had even seen grass this morning, small shoots here and there. Life had come to the Acar.

Familiar faces sat around the table already: Shecayah and Tobiah from the Beorgai, Aden, Bweth, Iletus, and Caleb. Another man, Jaff – a *Sohan-el* and a former Ghost of the Saten - also sat with them as their representative. Jaff was a good man, but Eshlyn felt the sharp pain within her at Xander's absence.

Caleb stood as she entered, smiling at her, stretching the ugly scar across his cheek. As attracted as she was to the man – and after last night, how could she deny it? – he confused her. Eshlyn was not a young schoolgirl; she knew when a man wanted her, desired her. Caleb's gray eyes, so cold and hard most days, had been so soft and warm as they embraced near the Living Water. Had it all been wishful thinking on her part? No, she had not imagined it. But why had he walked away? Eshlyn had no answers.

The end of all things lay upon his shoulders.

And she could see it, the weight there, the weight he bore with such strength. She forced a grin back at him and sat at an empty folding wooden chair.

Caleb sat again.

"We have a few things to discuss," Caleb said. "First, I would like to send a messenger back to Ketan and ask for Lyam and others to return and join us again."

Eshlyn did not know all the details, but Aden had told her of how Lyam left and took a majority of the army with him, accusing Caleb of many things.

"What?" Aden said. "After what he did?"

Jaff, a middle aged man with dark, balding hair, shook his head. "But he was wrong. The things he said to you, Caleb, the things he did, were inexcusable."

Bweth snarled. "In a real army, we would have hung him for desertion."

"Perhaps it is good we are not a real army, then," Caleb said. "While he was wrong, he was not ... completely wrong."

Murmurs came from the group.

"Caleb," Eshlyn said, frowning at him. "Explain."

Caleb sighed. "Yes. His accusations were unfounded and divisive, but I bear a portion of the blame."

"How?" Iletus asked.

"After Biram, after the horrors we saw there, my combat with Saben and Cyprian, this revolution became ... personal to me."

"That is understandable," Bweth whispered.

"No," Caleb said. "On this whole campaign, the Empire has made it personal, made it about fighting me, not mankind. They've attempted to manipulate me, and while we beat the legion at Biram and the Acar, they were successful in making it personal."

"But you are a threat to them," Iletus said. "Your name is being cursed and hailed in the streets of cities all over the Empire. Of course they would focus on you."

"Their strategy is sound," Caleb said. "But this revolution is not about me. It is about *us*. And I lost sight of that. I should have made sure that everyone with me, those that have made so many sacrifices to stand with me, share the vision. I cannot expect men who do not share the vision to share the risk, no matter how right I am. True unity comes from that shared vision.

"And so while Lyam was wrong to react as he did and must shoulder the blame for that, the frustration and fear he felt were valid. So I must admit some of the blame. In doing so, I believe it is right to allow any of those who left to return, if they desire." Caleb scanned the group. "What do you think?"

"I think Lyam should be flogged," Bweth said. "But I won't kill him if you invite him back."

"It is kind of you," Iletus said to Caleb. "But dangerous to bring in someone who has been so divisive in the past."

"You are a wise and good leader," Shecayah said. "Forgiveness and mercy are strength."

"Humanity will not be free if we allow the divisions to begin so soon," Caleb added. "Within the very beginnings of our revolution? It will not survive long and we will only become the people we were when Tanicus swept mankind under his authority."

"You say Lyam shoulders some of his own blame," Jaff said. "He must realize his own wrong before there can be unity, right? Otherwise leaving and division will always be an option."

"Anyone is free to leave at any time," Caleb said.

"I agree with Jaff," Aden said. "Lyam is my friend, but in order for us to fight together, he must understand that he cannot react like that. He is a leader, a *Sohan-el* with an unforged sword. More must be expected from him."

"Send a messenger to him," Eshlyn said. "If he desires to join us again, bring him here, before this council, and discuss these very things. You cannot know his response, but then unity and reconciliation are more possible if you make the attempt."

"Agreed," Aden said, and the rest also gave their consent.

"Good," Caleb said. "Thank you." He turned to Eshlyn. "When you return to Ketan, I ask that you speak with him about this and send him back."

He will need you before it is all done.

Eshlyn sat forward in her chair. "I'm not going back to Ketan. Not yet."

The people at the table shared shocked glances.

"But I thought you would want to go back to be with your son, your family," Caleb said.

"I do," she said. "Which is why when we send for Lyam, we will also have Javyn brought back with them."

"You're bringing the boy here?" Caleb asked. "Into a war zone?"

War is upon us, Lady Eshlyn. Safety does not exist, not like you mean it.

"Can you honestly say that it is safer in Ketan than here?" Eshlyn asked. "Or that anywhere is safe? I am needed here and would rather have him with me."

The group was silent for a moment. Caleb was pensive.

"I will help you care for the boy," Shecayah said.

"I'd be glad to have ya," Bweth said. "Who else's gonna help me when this babe kicks his or her way out of me? Caleb will put a sword in the wee one's hand and Aden will talk the kid to death. I say welcome."

"Hey ..." Aden groaned.

Iletus smirked at her. "With the diverse army we have with us now, we will need your leadership, Lady Eshlyn. If you want the boy here, then bring him. I will put the boy on my back and protect him myself. No one will touch him."

"What do you say?" she asked Caleb.

He peered at her, a curious expression. "Lady Eshlyn," he said. "Welcome to the *Hamon-el*."

———

Earon sat on a cot in a small tent. Two men stood outside his tent at all times, a rotation of guards to watch him. This was a prison as much as the Pyts in Asya, and while Caleb did not kill him, he may have done the next best thing to punish Earon. He left him alone with his thoughts.

The flap to the tent opened, and a young man stood there at the opening. Earon remembered him from that night in Biram, months ago, the night his father died. Aden was his name.

"May I come in?" Aden said. He carried a cup of water and a leather bag.

Earon surveyed his prison. "Do I have a choice?"

"We always have a choice," he said. "We just may not like the ones we have." He grinned at him. "May I?"

Earon shrugged, and Aden moved into the small tent and sat next to him on the cot, a leather bag across his shoulder. Earon eyed the cup.

"A cup of water for a dying man?" Earon said.

"I don't know if you heard," Aden said. "But the Deadwater has been healed."

"I heard you did it," Earon said.

"Could be," Aden said. "Not important, really. What is important is that while the whole camp is enjoying the refreshment of the Living Water, no one has brought you any. So I brought this. For you." He extended the cup to Earon.

Earon looked over at the young man. "Why?"

Aden lowered the cup to his lap. "Why did you help me back in Biram?"

"I ... excuse me?"

"You know, that night in Biram ... well, you remember that night."

Earon spoke low. "I remember."

"When it all went to crit, that Cityguard had me dead, and you helped me. You threw a chair at him, distracted him, and helped me. Why?"

He recalled that night. Not a day went by that he didn't think of it, replay it in his mind, feel the pain and regret anew. Drunk or Sorced, he remembered. That night in Biram, it had all happened so fast. His mind had spun with the reality of his own betrayal, his father's death, and the ensuing violence. Throwing a chair at the Cityguard was a gut reaction, a decision he couldn't explain. There was no reason.

"I don't know," he said. And it was true. He didn't. "I just did."

"Hm," Aden said. "Okay. Well, I figure I owe you my life, so here, have a cup of the Living Water." He lifted the cup to Earon again.

Earon stared at him.

"Okay, I know it's not a fair trade," Aden said, "my life for a cup of water. But it's a start, at least. Crit on a frog, man, just take it."

Earon reached out and took the cup of water. "What is in the bag?"

"Ah, yeah," Aden said. "Almost forgot." He pulled out two books, one larger volume and another smaller one, out of the leather bag. "Brought these for you. Thought you might want to borrow them."

Earon took the books, and opening one, saw that they were the testimony and the scriptures of El. The Ydu and Fyrwrit.

"They are Xander's copies," Aden said. "I have your father's originals, if you're wondering. These were copied by Drew, you know, the innkeeper in Biram. They should do."

Earon didn't know what to say, but he said, "Thank you."

"Great," Aden said and flashed him another smile. "You can get that back to me later. We'll be seeing each other a lot, I think."

"You know what Caleb's planning to do with me?" Earon asked.

Aden clicked his tongue. "Not a clue," he said. "Probably put you in a cell in Taggart once we get there, but honestly, I don't think Caleb even knows. So how could I?"

The young man rose and began to stride out of the tent. He pushed back the flap and paused at the opening.

"You know," Aden said. "I was hiding out and stuck in Asya when this crazy man came and asked me to bust this other crazy old man out of the Pyts. It all changed from there."

Earon cocked his head at him.

"Funny thing about choices," Aden continued. "Sometimes there are choices you don't even know you have. See you."

And then Aden left Earon alone with his thoughts again. But along with his thoughts, he had a cup of water and the words of El.

—

Andos stood at the wall of Taggart with two of his officers, men that technically outranked him, but they deferred to him. Being General Pyram's right hand for more than a century, he could not blame them, although he did not feel qualified to make any real decisions.

It was unfortunate, then, that he was faced with one that could determine life or death for six hundred elves.

The wall of Taggart was not imposing. It was three mitres tall, only a half-mitre thick and made of stone. A stone platform behind the wall circled the city and provided a way to peer over the top and defend. The remaining contingent of elves in Taggart was stationed at periodic places around the wall, although more were here at the western side of the city. They could hold for a time – how long Andos could not say – but a day at least. In the end, however, the army he saw would overcome them. There was no doubt of that. No reinforcements would arrive in time. The legions in Asya were a ninedays away.

Andos looked to the west again. The first sight was a hundred large creatures spread out in a line, and Liorian men sat atop them. Those alone could decimate the wall he stood behind. In front of the bosaur were thousands of men, some light skinned and dressed in forest greens and brown leathers, others dark-skinned and in long, colorful tunics gathered at the belt. Out beyond the bosaur, he could see the tops of catapults, Kryan catapults aimed at the city of Taggart.

A man with shoulder-length brown hair and carrying a staff dismounted from his horse, adjusted the belt that held his sword. A dark-haired woman stepped down from a wagon and joined him, and they moved towards the gate.

"We can't surrender," one of the officers, Captain Clofus, said. "These are barbaric men from Manahem, Lior, and that gods-cursed forest. They'll kill and skin us for sure."

Andos gripped a letter in his hand. "And who was it that flayed and impaled the men of Biram?" he asked. "If they did that to us, it was we who taught them."

The other officer – Captain Tranas – glared at him. "These are animals," he said. "You know that to be true. We cannot trust them. All we can hope to do is send another pigeon to Asya and delay them as much as we can."

"That does not sound like much hope," Andos said. Viewing the bosaur and siege engines again – the ballista were in their possession, as well, he assumed – he recalculated his earlier estimate. "They will raze this city in a matter of hours."

The man walking towards them wore a simple white shirt, brown leather breeches and leather boots. The sleeves of his shirt were rolled back, and Andos brought his peerglass up to his eye, adjusted his position, and looked at the man's forearm. Seeing the tattoo, he cursed.

The woman was striking, dressed in divided skirts and a white blouse. She wore no weapons.

Andos didn't need to read the letter in his hand again. It had arrived two days ago via messenger. He knew Pyram's handwriting better than his own, and he had memorized the contents of the letter.

Legion defeated on the field. You have command if I do not return. Be wise. Tanicus is a Worldbreaker. – P.

"If we surrender," Captain Clofus said. "They will kill us and we will have given them a defensible position that the Imperial reinforcements will have to fight."

The man and woman stopped twenty mitres from the wall of Taggart, with a hundred elven shortbows trained on them. The man raised a hand

and made a gesture. A large wagon pulled by two horses emerged from the army of men and also rode forward. A young man sat in the driving bench of the wagon. There appeared to be people in the back of the wagon. Were those elves?

"We should fight now," Tranas agreed. "Make them burn this outpost down, taking away any advantage they might have in the future. Our deaths will mean something then."

"Give the order to kill those two," Clofus muttered and pointed at the man and woman. "Let's get on with this."

Considering the face of the man standing before them in his peerglass, Andos had the feeling that giving the order to fire on those humans would be a monumental mistake.

Andos lowered the peerglass from his face. "I am going out to meet them," he said.

Both officers cursed at him, beginning to argue with him.

Andos lifted a hand, and they fell silent. He wished he possessed that frown, General Pyram's stoic frown that could alone demand obedience, but he did not. However, he knew Clofus and Tranas well enough to know that neither wanted to make a decision. Because in a bureaucracy like the Kryan Empire, it was the one that made the decision that would suffer the blame and the torture.

Tanicus is a Worldbreaker.

No one else had read the message. He did not allow it, and they did not ask.

"I will go and meet with them," Andos said. "And discover what their terms will be. If anything happens to me," he reached into the pouch on his belt and tossed a silver moon to one of the officers, "flip a coin between the two of you for the command of Taggart."

He stepped down from the platform behind the wall and approached the gate, closed with a platoon of militan hovering behind it. "Let me through," Andos told them.

The elves glanced at each other, but no one was willing to challenge the order, so they opened the gate, lifting the long wooden bar and pushing one of the wooden doors outward a mitre to allow Andos to leave.

Andos did not wear a weapon, only his blue tunic and breastplate. He carried the parchment in his hand with him.

The wagon reached the man and stopped when Andos was twelve paces away. He closed the distance and halted five paces away from the man and woman and the wagon behind them. Andos could see now that there were more than two dozen elves in the back of the wagon. A threat? A demonstration? Would the man slaughter these militan to prove his resolve?

"My name is Andos," he said. "First Captain and secretary to First General Pyram of the Taggart Outpost."

"I am Caleb," the man said, and Andos noticed now the fresh wound across his cheek. His eyes were cold and gray, and yet there was fierceness to them that Andos had never seen in a human. Even if the man had not just won a battle against a Kryan legion, Andos would have believed he was the most dangerous man in Eres from those eyes alone.

Caleb pointed at the woman. "This is Lady Eshlyn." Inclining his head to the wagon behind him. "And that is Aden. Well met."

The young man, Aden, hopped down from the wagon and stood next to the woman. He laid a hand on his sword and his kind face showed no fear. He also had a tattoo on his forearm.

The woman, Eshlyn, shifted her weight and emanated a strength and authority greater than any officer he had ever met in the Kryan Legions.

Andos had spent his whole life around men and women trained to live in submission to him, and he had been taught – and believed without any evidence to the contrary – that elves were superior beings in every way to the other races. These who stood before him were counter to everything he had ever known, and if they were any indication of the revolution of men, then Andos knew Tanicus was right to be afraid.

Eshlyn waved a hand at the wagon. "These are all that lived from the Battle of Acar," she said. "There was a fifth injured elf, but our surgeons could not save him. I am sorry. We release them back to you."

"I – wha – excuse me?" Andos stammered.

"These are all the prisoners we were able to take at the end of the battle," Aden said. "And we are returning them to you."

"You … treated the prisoners and are returning them?" Andos asked.

"Yes," Caleb said.

Andos kept his jaw from dropping. "What news of General Pyram?"

Caleb's eyes narrowed. "All others perished."

Andos addressed the elves in the back of the wagon, projecting his voice. "Does he speak true?"

"Yes, sir," one of the elves said. "He does."

"First Captain Andos," Caleb said. "We are here to accept your surrender. You will leave Taggart and its resources to us."

"We also ask that any humans in your service that wish to remain be allowed to do so without harm," Eshlyn said. "They will be well taken care of."

"In exchange," Caleb added. "We will let you leave if you retreat with your militan back to Asya."

Andos lifted a brow at the elves in the wagon … and the large army behind them. "You will simply let us leave? Alive?"

"Yes," Caleb said. "But if you choose to try and hold Taggart against us or harm the humans in your care," he gripped the staff in his hand tighter, "we will kill you all."

"You are that *Brendel* they speak of, correct?" Andos asked.

"You have an hour to give an answer." Caleb turned to leave and the other two prepared to follow him.

"No, wait," Andos said, and he unfolded the parchment in his hand. All three paused. "General Pyram sent me this message. It says … well, it claims that the Emperor is a Worldbreaker, a Great Wizard of the *Tebelrivyn*."

Caleb faced him again. "Yes?"

"Is it true?" he asked, keeping his voice low.

"An elf I have trusted with my very life gave me that information," Caleb said. "It is true."

Andos found the constant frown then. "How am I to believe, if we surrender, that you will allow us to live and walk away? You'll only have to fight us another day."

"Believe me?" Caleb said. "I will let you go because I do not wish to shed any blood today. If you choose to fight us now, or return after we have been merciful and let you live, or harm any humans on your way back to Asya, then that will be your choice, not mine, and you will suffer the consequences. When you are surrounded by dead elves, you will remember with your final breath that I gave you the chance to escape the Blades of War."

Standing before the only army that had defeated a Kryan legion on the field in three hundred years, Andos believed him. He folded the parchment and placed it back into his belt.

"Very well," Andos said. "We surrender. Taggart is yours."

Epilogue

Emperor Tanicus, the High Evilord

Olympus, the High Nican, the High Priest of the nine gods of Ashinar and First Minister of the Senate, stood before the large, golden doors to the throne room.

He had been summoned by the Emperor.

Olympus was short, even for an elf, and thin with close-cropped dark hair. He wore a long golden robe, the hood pushed away from his head.

He eyed the two Sunguard that stood sentry at the entrance. They nodded to him and opened the doors.

Olympus waited until the doors swung wide, and then he entered the throne room.

Emperor Tanicus, the High Evilord of the Kryan Empire, sat on his throne and looked down from the dais. Four Sunguard were in the room, one on either side of the throne and two inside the door. An elf was already kneeling before the Emperor – High General Felix, the First Minister of Defense, he could tell by the golden armor the elf wore and the long, ridiculous plume on his golden helmet.

Olympus knelt next to Felix. The Sunguard shut the doors behind him.

"Rise," he heard the Emperor say, and so the two elves did.

"Our Empire is at a crucible, gentlelves," the Emperor continued. "Rebellion and enemies surround us, but that is as it should be. Greatness always creates enemies."

"Yes, my lord," Olympus heard Felix say with conviction.

The reports from around the Empire were not encouraging. Faltiel and Vahalal were allied on their western border, the first time in centuries an elven and dwarven kingdom agreed on anything.

And a revolution rose in the land of men.

While everyone had heard of Ketan declaring itself free, now other cities were also fighting back against the Empire. Oshra burned and its citizens united. The Pike was dead, and the Kryan legions were leaving that city. Landen was united now under the Southern Dygolor, and the militan were surrounded in the northern part of the city. Asya was a morass of violence and rioting. Thousands were dead.

The latest report was the most chilling – a Kryan Legion had been defeated on the field, and the western outpost of Taggart was now in the hands of this *Brendel* character and his army.

The Kryan Empire was not at a crucible, it was besieged on every side.

"First Minister Olympus," Tanicus said. "How goes the Senate?"

Traditionally, Kryus was a theocracy, but that tradition had waned in the centuries leading to the Emperor's rise to power, what the history books now called the Kryan Ascendency. A holdover of that ancient tradition, the High Nican was also the First Minister of the Senate.

"They are anxious, my Lord," Olympus said. The truth was they were in a panic, but he wasn't going to say that here. "The opposition grows to your policies as more news of the rebellion in Ereland circulates. There are ... rumors of a more serious move within the Senate."

"I do not care for rumors," Tanicus said. "Have you investigated these rumors?"

"Yes, my Lord," Olympus answered. "I have Moonguard assigned. They have nothing concrete so far."

The Emperor spoke through clenched teeth. "I will also assign Bladeguard to the investigation. I cannot abide opposition. Not now."

Olympus glanced over at Felix, who didn't flinch. If Bladeguard got involved, then those investigations would result in assassinations – the deaths of Senators and their families.

"I am suspending all activity of the Senate until further notice," Tanicus said. "Olympus, you will be the authority while I am gone."

"*Gone*, my Lord?" Olympus asked as he shuffled his feet.

"Yes, High Nican," Tanicus said. "I will lead the fight against this rebellion myself. I leave in two ninedays. The gods will help you."

It was unfortunate that Olympus didn't believe in the gods. With a rebellion in Ereland and a coup waiting in the Senate, they could use some divine intervention.

The Emperor paused. "General, I will require five legions ready to travel with my fleet."

"In two ninedays?" Felix asked. He bowed. "My Lord, I live to serve, but we do not possess five legions to spare."

Even the elves on the street knew that, as much as the Kryan Ministry of Information tried to spin the current circumstances. No reinforcements existed, much less 30,000 militan.

"I did not ask for excuses, General. Five legions. Two ninedays. Draft more, call up veterans, conscript among the prisons. Do what you must. We will bring the full might of the Legion against this revolution. I want trodall, vualta, and the Deathguard."

Felix took a breath. "The Deathguard have not been used in battle for two hundred years," he said. Olympus had heard accounts of the destruction they caused and how difficult they were to control.

"The time has come the world sees them again. And get me Julius," the Emperor said.

The legendary Bladeguard? Olympus thought.

"No one has seen the elf in a century," Felix said. "He has retired."

"Then find him," the Emperor said. "We deal with zealots. I need a zealot to battle them."

"Yes, my Lord."

Tanicus seemed to tower over them as he stood.

"General, do you know the greatest danger to the peace of Eres?"

The General furrowed his brow. "My Lord?"

"Chaos," Tanicus answered for him. "Chaos brings conflict, death, starvation, and puts an end to progress. High Nican, what does Ashinar instruct is the solution to chaos?"

The High Nican paused as he attempted to ascertain the answer the Emperor sought. Olympus was not the trodall-headed minister of the military – he was the High Priest. He should know. After perusing the ancient scrolls of Ashinar in his mind, he believed he found it.

"Order, my Lord," Olympus said with a bow.

"Yes," Tanicus said. "Order, control, power. These humans do not understand the folly of their rebellion. I hold back the tide of chaos that threatens to sweep Eres into the greatest darkness it has ever known. Without me, we are all lost."

Olympus offered a curt nod.

"To combat the chaos that threatens, all of Eres must be united against it," the Emperor said. "And I shall give them that unity. We will achieve it through power and control. Any who oppose our purpose must be crushed for the good of all."

Tanicus met the gazes of both elves before him.

"We are at the crossroads of history. We cannot allow this foe to bring any more chaos. We find the man at the heart of this rebellion. If we cut out the heart, the rebellion will die. As I did with King Judai, I must go and lead the armies of Kryus against this *Brendel*."

Olympus stiffened as Felix remained silent.

"We hold back chaos, the great destroyer, with our power and control," the Emperor said. "For the good of the world, gentlelves, we cannot fail. We must not fail."

"Yes, my Lord," both elves responded.

Acknowledgements:

I heard once that a writer or artist should always attempt to challenge him/herself with each project, to labor to make the next book or painting or song even better than the one before. I also heard one of my favorite authors say, about his revision and writing, "I just try to make it awesome."

The Blades of War is an attempt to "make it better" and "make it awesome." Those are somewhat subjective terms, so I hope you appreciate that it is as awesome as I endeavored to make it.

As usual, nothing happens in a vacuum or without a great deal of help -

To the Beta readers, especially Gina Deaton, thanks for your input and sacrifice of time to get through the rough first draft and make great suggestions.

To Jermiah Briggs, as always, you blow me away with great artwork that fits the theme and tone of the book.

To my two amazing proofreaders, Shane Ardell and Gregg Mooney, you helped make it a better book.

To my wife – there are a countless number of books for authors on how to write a novel, but there should be a book on how to love a moody and obsessive artist that is never completely satisfied with anything he creates ... and you should write it. I love you.

Saving the most important for last once again, to my El, my Yosu, and my unforged sword, I would go headfirst into any battle as long as You were with me.

About the Author:

M.B. Mooney has traveled extensively and writes novels, short stories, and songs. He lives in Lawrenceville, GA, with his wife, Rebecca, and three children – Micah, Elisha, and Hosanna.

If you would like to see more of his work, check out his website at www.mbmooney.com.

Also like him on Facebook – www.facebook.com/MooneyMB and Twitter @MBMooney1